SONS and DAUGHTERS

SONS and DAUGHTERS

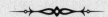

Chaim Grade

Translated from the Yiddish by Rose Waldman
Introduction by Adam Kirsch

ALFRED A. KNOPF
New York
2025

A BORZOI BOOK
FIRST HARDCOVER EDITION
PUBLISHED BY ALFRED A. KNOPF 2025

Published by Alfred A. Knopf, a division of Penguin Random House LLC,
1745 Broadway, New York, NY 10019.
Previously serialized in the Yiddish language.
Copyright © by The Estate of Chaim Grade.

Knopf, Borzoi Books, and the colophon are registered trademarks
of Penguin Random House LLC.

Library of Congress Cataloging-in-Publication Data
Names: Grade, Chaim, 1910–1982, author. | Waldman, Rose, translator. |
Kirsch, Adam, [date] writer of introduction.
Title: Sons and daughters : a novel / Chaim Grade ; translated from the
Yiddish by Rose Waldman ; introduction by Adam Kirsch.
Other titles: Beys harov. English
Description: New York : Alfred A. Knopf, 2025. |
"This is a Borzoi Book published by Alfred A. Knopf."
Identifiers: LCCN 2024017235 | ISBN 9780394536460 (hardcover) |
ISBN 9780593318140 (ebook)
Subjects: LCGFT: Novels.
Classification: LCC PJ5129.G68 B4913 2025 | DDC [FIC]—dc23
LC record available at https://lccn.loc.gov/2024017235

penguinrandomhouse.com | aaknopf.com

Printed in the United States of America
10 9 8 7 6 5 4 3 2 1

The authorized representative in the EU for product safety and compliance is
Penguin Random House Ireland, Morrison Chambers, 32 Nassau Street,
Dublin D02 YH68, Ireland, https://eu-contact.penguin.ie.

Contents

Introduction

Adam Kirsch

Sons and Daughters is quite probably the last great Yiddish novel.
Chaim Grade wrote it from the mid-1960s through the mid-1970s;
it appeared in serial form in two New York–based Yiddish newspapers: first in the *Tog-Morgn Zhurnal* (Day-Morning Journal) and then
in the *Forverts* (Forward). Even at the time, the audience for Yiddish
fiction was disappearing: "It is lonely to have to publish a thousand
copies of your own book, and if you sell five hundred of them, you
are a best seller," Grade told an interviewer in 1978. Today, those
readers are all but gone, along with the writers who addressed them.

It's not that no one speaks the language anymore. Yiddish, the
mother tongue of Ashkenazi Jews in Europe for a thousand years,
is still spoken by about 150,000 ultra-Orthodox Jews in America,
Europe, and Israel. (In 1939, before the Holocaust and the passing of the American Jewish immigrant generation, there were about
eleven million Yiddish speakers worldwide.) But, with some recent
exceptions, these traditionalist Jews would not dream of using the
language for literary fiction, which is a fundamentally modern and
secular genre.

The sharp opposition between Yiddish literature and Jewish tradition is, in fact, one of the major themes of *Sons and Daughters*. Near
the end of the story, which is set in Poland in the early 1930s, Grade
introduces a character clearly based on himself as a young man—

Khlavneh, a Yiddish poet from Vilna. When he visits the family of his future bride, Bluma Rivtcha, in Morehdalye, the village where most of the novel takes place, Khlavneh finds that his literary calling earns him two kinds of hostility.

His prospective father-in-law, Sholem Shachne Katzenellenbogen, is a rabbi who holds fast to traditional Jewish piety; for him a Yiddish poet means a freethinker, a secular Jew who has cast off Torah law. Bluma Rivtcha's brother Naftali Hertz is another such modern Jew, who actually moved to Switzerland and married a Christian woman. Yet he, too, despises Khlavneh, not for being a writer but for having the bad taste to write in Yiddish "jargon." "A jargon boy is a common person, an ignoramus, a boor," Naftali Hertz thinks, furious at the idea of being related to one.

Inevitably, language lies at the heart of *Sons and Daughters*, a novel about a family struggling with the meaning of Jewishness in the twentieth century. The younger members of the Katzenellenbogen clan are certain that the way of life led by their forefathers is no longer viable. In the highly nationalistic climate of interwar Poland, the Jews' traditional survival strategies—avoiding politics, accepting blows without retaliation—have stopped working. Gangs of Poles boycott Morehdalye's Jewish merchants, standing in front of their shops to prevent Christians from entering. The familiar poverty, whose textures Grade evokes on every page, threatens to turn into outright ruin.

Meanwhile, the Jews of Morehdalye are being touched by the same modern ideas and influences as the rest of the world. Bluma Rivtcha, who seems destined for an arranged marriage to a rabbi in the book's first section, yearns for a career of her own. Her older sister, Tilza, who married the man her father picked out for her, now regrets it and dreams of romantic love. Young men who in earlier generations would have become rabbis now hope to become professors or revolutionaries.

Grade shows that each of these possible Jewish futures speaks a different language. Naftali Hertz, the oldest Katzenellenbogen brother, ran away from his yeshiva to study at a secular university in Switzerland; he now speaks German, the language of high culture. Refael'ke, the youngest brother, plans to be a Zionist pioneer in the land of Israel, where he will speak a modern Hebrew. The budding revolutionary Marcus Luria throws his lot in with the Soviet Union, where Russian is the language of the future. And Shabse-Shepsel—the book's most frightening character, a demonic clown who would fit in perfectly with Dostoevsky's Karamazovs—tries to establish a new life in America, where English reigns.

Amid all these competing tongues, Khlavneh's—and Grade's—loyalty to Yiddish also represents a particular vision of the Jewish future. Yiddish writers of his generation—Grade was born in 1910—staked their work on the belief that the unique culture of Eastern European Jewry could, and deserved to, endure. It need not abolish itself in favor of any future. At the same time, it need not be enthralled to the past, whose decrepitude seems to have infected Morehdalye's very plants: "Alongside the path, willow trees drooped, their thick leafy tops sagging, barely stirring in the breeze, mumbling, as if in a trance, that they'd gotten lost somehow. How they yearned to be growing along the shore of a wide, happy river where cold, fresh water flowed."

The alienation of children from the values and traditions of their parents is a central subject of modern Yiddish literature—most famously in Sholem Aleichem's stories about the dairyman Tevye and his daughters. But a better reference point for understanding *Sons and Daughters* is Ivan Turgenev's classic Russian novel *Fathers and Sons*. That book, about a middle-aged landowner whose son returns from college infected with the ideology of nihilism, was published in 1862, a century before Grade wrote his Jewish variation on the theme.

Indeed, *Sons and Daughters* could be considered triply belated. The struggles over religious belief and parental authority that preoccupy the young Katzenellenbogens in the 1930s would already have seemed passé to their Russian or French contemporaries. (Marcus Luria is obsessed with the amoral philosophy of Friedrich Nietzsche, but Naftali Hertz scornfully points out that he's behind the times: German intellectuals had worked Nietzsche out of their systems before World War I.) Grade, in turn, was writing about the 1930s from the perspective of the 1960s; and today's reader is encountering the story more than half a century later. That long delay in publication, which has given *Sons and Daughters* a quasi-mythical status among scholars of Yiddish literature, is owed in part to the fact that Grade died before he was able to turn the serialized narrative into what he'd intended to be a two-volume novel. The plotlines that remain unresolved at the conclusion of *Sons and Daughters* would most certainly have been given a more satisfying denouement in the second volume; as it is, the book stops without quite ending. After Grade's death in April 1982, his literary estate was controlled by his widow, Inna Hecker Grade, who resisted scholars' and translators' attempts to work on his papers. It was only after her death in May 2010 that Grade's manuscripts—including typeset Yiddish galley proofs of a novel that was clearly based on the serialized chapters in the *Tog-Morgn Zhurnal* and the *Forverts*, and which Grade referred to in the 1978 interview as *Sons and Daughters*—became accessible. Thus this book, which has been under contract with Alfred A. Knopf since 1983, could finally appear in an excellent translation by Rose Waldman.

Today, of course, the problems of Jewish identity and destiny take very different forms than they did in the 1930s. This pathos of distance helps to give *Sons and Daughters* a meditative quality. A patient writer, Grade lavishes description on trees and snow, beards and furniture; he is a connoisseur of light, whether it's the glittering of sun on leaves and branches or the red glare of the electric lamp left on for Shabbat.

Equally distinctive is Grade's tenderness toward religious tradition, which has few parallels in twentieth-century Jewish literature. Most of Grade's fiction deals in one way or another with rabbis; at one stage, his title for this novel was *The Rabbi's House*. The comparison sounds odd, but one might say that Grade was to the Lithuanian rabbinic establishment what Anthony Trollope was to the Church of England—a keen observer of the pride, envy, and careerism that kept clergymen hungering for advancement.

Yet he was never cynical about these all-too-human rabbis. In *Sons and Daughters*, the revolt of the younger generation against Judaism drives the plot, but Grade doesn't forfeit his sympathy with the old men who are trying to keep Judaism alive. This is especially clear in the contrast between Marcus Luria and his father, the ascetic sage Zalia Ziskind. The son is a mere pawn of trendy ideologies, while the father is a true tzaddik—a man so conscious of the suffering of human beings, and even of animals, that he can think of nothing else.

The young Grade surely never expected that rabbis and study

houses would become his great subject. He was once a yeshiva student himself, but in his early twenties he rebelled against religion: as Khlavneh says, "I left the synagogue and went to the Jews in the street." What made Grade return to the synagogue—in his fiction, if not in life—was the Holocaust, which virtually annihilated the religious culture in which he had grown up. The rebel against Jewish tradition was now almost the only one left to become its elegist— the "gravestone carver of my vanished world," as he wrote in a 1970 letter.

The Holocaust lies outside the scope of *Sons and Daughters*, which never directly alludes to the fate in store for all of its characters. But it is the novel's inescapable background, as it was the central fact of the author's life. Grade was born and raised in Vilna, a major Jewish center that was known as the Jerusalem of Lithuania. When the Nazis invaded the Soviet Union in June 1941, there were some seventy thousand Jews in Vilna; by the end of the war only a few hundred were still alive. Most of the dead were shot and buried in mass graves in Ponary, a forest outside the city. Among them were Grade's first wife, Frumme-Liebe, and his mother, Vella.

Grade survived by fleeing east to the Soviet Union, where he spent the war as a refugee in Central Asia. In his memoir *My Mother's Sabbath Days*, he writes about returning to Vilna in 1945 and finding everyone he knew gone, the synagogues in ruins, the door to his childhood home covered in thick spiderwebs. By 1948 he had made his way to New York with Inna, his second wife. Only then did he begin to write the fiction for which he is best known today. (Before the war he had been celebrated as a poet, and he continued to write poetry to the end of his life, but little of it has been translated into English.)

Though he lived in America for thirty-four years, Grade never entered American literary life the way his great rival Isaac Bashevis Singer managed to do. Partly that is because Singer spoke English and Grade didn't, making him a less effective advocate for his work. But it has more to do with their different ways of conceiving their task as Yiddish writers after the Holocaust. For Singer, the Holocaust confirmed what had always been his basic intuition about the modern world—that it is demonic and grotesque. His lurid fables of sexual obsession and metaphysical bewilderment reflected modernity in ways American readers could intuitively grasp, even if they knew little or nothing about Judaism as a religion.

Grade, by contrast, felt responsible for preserving the memory of the Jewish tradition in which he had been raised. This was the austere, intellectually demanding faith of the Lithuanian misnagdim, the "opponents" of Hasidism, and especially of the musar school, which taught the believer to scrutinize his own conscience ruthlessly. Grade's portrait of this faith can be quite subversive in its own way: just look at Tsemach Atlas, the protagonist of his long novel *The Yeshiva*, a rabbi whose religious strictness increases as his actual belief drains away. But Grade also wanted to show the beauty of this Judaism: its humility and moral delicacy, its hatred of cruelty, its ability to reach the sublime in the midst of material poverty and wretchedness.

In *Sons and Daughters*, traditional Judaism appears to be on the road to extinction, besieged on every side by the forces of modernity. The greatest irony for twenty-first-century readers is that, today, ultra-Orthodox Judaism is not just alive but thriving. In Israel and America, tens of thousands of Jewish men spend their lives studying the same texts, saying the same prayers, even wearing the same kinds of clothing as Sholem Shachne and Zalia Ziskind. Instead, what disappeared was Yiddish, along with the secular, Eastern European Jewish future in which Chaim Grade and so many others placed their hopes. We can be thankful that it survives, in all its human complexity and passion, in the pages of this book.

Cast of Characters

Meir Moshe Baruchovitz: Husband of Sirka Baruchovitz

Sirka Baruchovitz: Sister-in-law of Zalia Ziskind Luria; younger sister of Zisse'le Luria; aunt of Marcus Luria

Chavtche Epstein: Youngest daughter of Eli-Leizer and Elka'le Epstein

Draizel (Halberstadt) Epstein: Long-suffering wife of Shabse-Shepsel Epstein

Eli-Leizer Epstein: Father-in-law of Sholem Shachne Katzenellenbogen; rabbi of Zembin

Elka'le Epstein: First wife of Eli-Leizer Epstein, and mother of his six children

Manya Epstein: Wife of Refael Leima Epstein

Refael Leima Epstein: Older son of Eli-Leizer and Elka'le Epstein; dayan of Zembin

Sarah Raizel Epstein: Third daughter of Eli-Leizer and Elka'le Epstein

Shabse-Shepsel Epstein: Younger, devious son of Eli-Leizer and Elka'le Epstein

Tamara Epstein: Second wife of Eli-Leizer Epstein

Vigasia Epstein: Third wife of Eli-Leizer Epstein

Gnendel Ginsburg: Mother of Tzesneh Ginsburg

Shmulik'l Ginsburg: Father of Tzesneh Ginsburg

Tzesneh Ginsburg: Friend of Bluma Rivtcha Katzenellenbogen, with designs on Zindel Kadish

Nosson-Nota Goldstein: Government-sponsored rabiner of Zembin

Tzalia ("Tzalia the Lip") Gutmacher: Proprietor of Tzalia Gutmacher's Ready-Made Garments in Bialystok; Bentzion Katzenellenbogen's boss

Menashe Halberstadt: Father of Draizel Epstein

Beinush Kadish: Son of Tzakok Kadish; father of Zindel Kadish

Shterke (Teitelbaum) Kadish: Wife of Beinush Kadish; mother of Zindel Kadish

Tzadok Kadish: Father of Beinush Kadish; grandfather of Zindel Kadish; dayan of Morehdalye

Zindel Kadish: Son of Beinush and Shterke Kadish; grandson of Tzadok Kadish; former unofficial beau of Bluma Rivtcha Katzenellenbogen

Baila'ke Kahane: Daughter of Yaakov Asher and Tilza Kahane

Heshe'le Kahane: Son of Yaakov Asher and Tilza Kahane

Tilza (Katzenellenbogen) Kahane: Elder daughter of Sholem Shachne and Henna'le Katzenellenbogen; wife of Yaakov Asher Kahane

Yaakov Asher Kahane: Son-in-law of Sholem Shachne and Henna'le Katzenellenbogen; husband of Tilza Kahane; rabbi of Lecheve and rosh yeshiva

Annelyse (Müller) Katzenellenbogen: Non-Jewish wife of Naftali Hertz Katzenellenbogen

Avraham Alter Katzenellenbogen: Older brother of Sholem Shachne Katzenellenbogen; rabbi of Bialystok

Bentzion Katzenellenbogen: Second son of Sholem Shachne and Henna'le Katzenellenbogen

Bluma Rivtcha Katzenellenbogen: Younger daughter of Sholem Shachne and Henna'le Katzenellenbogen

Henna'le (Epstein) Katzenellenbogen: Wife of Sholem Shachne Katzenellenbogen; eldest daughter of Eli-Leizer and Elka'le Epstein

Karl Katzenellenbogen: Non-Jewish son of Naftali Hertz and Annelyse Katzenellenbogen

Naftali Hertz Katzenellenbogen: Eldest son of Sholem Shachne and Henna'le Katzenellenbogen

Refael'ke Katzenellenbogen: Youngest son of Sholem Shachne and Henna'le Katzenellenbogen

Sholem Shachne Katzenellenbogen: Rabbi of Morehdalye; son of Refael Katzenellenbogen, former rabbi of Morehdalye; husband of

Henna'le Katzenellenbogen; son-in-law of Eli-Leizer Epstein, rabbi of Zembin

Marcus ("Mottel") Luria: Son of Zalia Ziskind and Zisse'le Luria

Zalia Ziskind ("Zelme'le") Luria: Former rabbi of Visoki-Dvor and rosh yeshiva; Sholem Shachne Katzenellenbogen's rabbinic assistant

Zisse'le Luria: Wife of Zalia Ziskind Luria; mother of Marcus Luria

Banet Michelson: Husband of Kona Michelson; son-in-law of Eli-Leizer and Elka'le Epstein

Bania Michelson: Younger daughter of Kona and Banet Michelson

Kona (Epstein) Michelson: Second daughter of Eli-Leizer and Elka'le Epstein; wife of Banet Michelson

Tubya Michelson: Elder daughter of Kona and Banet Michelson

Aida Noifeld: Older daughter of Emanuel and Chana Rochel Noifeld, Reform Jews who befriended Naftali Hertz Katzenellenbogen in Switzerland

Janet Noifeld: Younger daughter of Emanuel and Chana Rochel Noifeld

Leopold Silberstein: Fiancé of Chavtche Epstein

Khlavneh Yeshurin: Fiancé of Bluma Rivtcha Katzenellenbogen

Part 1

A S THEY TOOK a stroll—Bluma Rivtcha, the rabbi's daughter, and Zindel Kadish, her prospective fiancé—the eyes of the townspeople followed them indulgently, lovingly. Everyone knew how much suffering the rabbi's other children had caused him, and so they wished him joy from his younger daughter, at least. Zindel's grandfather, the elderly dayan, was also entitled to some joy from his grandson. Some years ago, Zindel's parents had moved overseas to Canada, where they'd divorced and seemed to have forgotten about bringing Zindel across to join them. He remained at his grandfather's home, the one consolation of the man's old age.

Zindel was a young man of twenty-three, with dark brown eyes and a head of black hair. He boasted a wide forehead and the straight nose of a sensible person, a dimpled chin like that of a pampered only son, cherry-colored lips, and a sweet smile. Even in the heat of summer he wore a proper suit, complete with vest, shirt, and tie, and a wide-brimmed hat tilted at an angle. He walked ramrod straight with raised shoulders, always looking directly ahead, as if he never—not for a moment—forgot that he was of marriageable age, the dayan's grandson, and a student of Warsaw's Tachkemoni, a yeshiva and university combined. As they strolled, he kept throwing sidelong glances at the fair, rose-colored profile of his bride-to-be, her coal-black hair swinging over her left temple.

Bluma Rivtcha was not very pleased about having to wear long-sleeved blouses, long skirts, and stockings every time she went out. Not that her father said anything, but when she put on something immodest, his face clouded with pain. And, of course, she didn't want to cause him distress. The one thing she was still allowed to keep free was her hair, no scarf containing it until she got married. She squinted up at the sun and waited for a breeze to blow through her uncovered tresses.

The Morehdalye residents knew that every afternoon the rabbi studied Talmud and Jewish law with the dayan's grandson. But over the last few days their schedule had been disrupted: the rabbi's son-in-law had come to visit. This change gave the prospective son-in-law more time to take strolls with his bride.

The couple walked to the edge of town, down the path that led to the Narev River, until the curious onlookers could no longer see them. With the couple out of sight, the inhabitants pulled their heads back from the windows. The rabbi's house sank once again into gloominess despite the dazzling summer's day outside, with everything glinting like brass.

THE RABBI'S HOME WAS the first house you saw when you entered Morehdalye, and the last one you saw when you left. A long wooden structure, it stood at the corner of the synagogue street with windows on all sides, looking out on the row of houses with balconies, the beis medrash on the hill, and the dirt road winding through Morehdalye toward Zembin and Lomzhe. Some of the bedroom windows provided a view of the yard and garden opposite the dilapidated stable, chicken coops, and dried-out, broken-down well. The low shingled roof of the rabbi's house was overgrown with greenish-yellow moss, and it sunk lower each year. Bushes and tall grass went untrimmed. Alongside the path, willow trees drooped, their thick leafy tops sagging, barely stirring in the breeze, mumbling, as if in a trance, that they'd gotten lost somehow. How they yearned to be growing along the shore of a wide, happy river where cold, fresh water flowed.

On the windowsill of the rabbi's beis din chambers stood a copper menorah ornamented with two small lions. It remained in this very same spot all through winter, all through summer. Some of the shutters were perpetually closed; the rabbi and his wife rarely looked out those windows. When you walked up the steps of the long, narrow veranda, the floor planks creaked and sighed "Time for some home improvement." And when the front door was opened, its hinges squeaked, as if in reply to the planks, "It's falling apart outside because it's falling apart inside."

In the drowsy silence a dry August heat glowed. The brief shadows lay motionless. Dazzled by its own brightness, the sun peered out fiery-peeled, hovering mid-sky, as if it couldn't figure out where to go from there. On the other side of the bridge, a dust cloud floated from a peasant's wagon plowing through deep white sand. A student's weary voice wafted out of the open windows of the beis medrash on the hill and zigzagged through the empty daytime synagogue street.

The plaster was peeling on the bluish-white outer walls of the rabbi's house; inside, in the cold hall, it was dim. Pale green and yellow-spotted plants sported bizarre shapes, as if they were beings from another world with prickly heads and round hands—half plant, half creature. The tall gray mirror, the round table on heavy curved legs, the armchairs with sunken seats, and the shadow of the sukkah room's winged roof—all were mired in outdated rigidity. Speckles of light trembled through the trees at the window, becoming lost in the folds of faded materials like rays of sun in stagnant water.

With his elbow pressed against the wall, the Morehdalye rabbi, Sholem Shachne Katzenellenbogen, stood at one side of one of the windows, his son-in-law, Yaakov Asher Kahane, at the other. Yaakov Asher was the rabbi of Lecheve and also the head of its yeshiva. The father-in-law was tall, thin, with narrow shoulders. His gray beard rose past his cheekbones but barely grew below his chin. Through his large round glasses peered sharp eyes, veiled by an aged sadness that had set in years ago, like gray spiderwebs hanging from the branches of an evergreen.

The rabbi was almost sixty-five, and his son-in-law nearly forty. Shorter than his father-in-law, Yaakov Asher was broad-shouldered, corpulent, with a strong, brick-like forehead, fat lips, and a red beard. Yellow sun spots dotted his face and his stubby fingers. His lapels were dirty; the jacket itself was tight beneath his arms and across his stomach. He kept twisting his face as he spoke—his collar and tie were tight—and stubble from his beard pricked his sweaty neck. Anyone with a bit of perceptiveness could instantly discern that this rosh yeshiva was a zealous man, one who toiled in the study of Torah. Like his father-in-law, the son-in-law gave off a sense of sadness. In his eyes, sorrow smoldered.

Yaakov Asher stuck a finger of his right hand into his beard and sighed. "Well, she certainly *tries* to conform. She tries to be friendly with the townswomen and my students. But you can't fool the world, and Tilza can fool *herself* even less; she's not that sort of person. So it's no good. The yeshiva's growing, may no evil eye harm it. Our family has a respectable livelihood, thank God. But your daughter doesn't want to be a rebbetzin. Or, more precisely, it's not so much that she doesn't want it, but she *can't*. She's not cut out for it."

Sholem Shachne was annoyed. He felt that his daughter's husband was reproaching him. Still, Yaakov Asher was considered one of the Torah greats, so despite his annoyance, his father-in-law addressed him with respect.

"I warned you before the wedding that Tilza doesn't want to lead a rebbetzin's life. But you answered me, '*My soul desires her,*' and that you hope it'll be different after the wedding. Well, who's at fault, then?"

Yaakov Asher's face flamed as red as his beard. His father-in-law seemed to be hinting that he was at fault, that a man was supposed to be able to change his wife, as it is written, "*And he shall rule over her.*" He replied, "I thought it would be different once she became a mother and felt the town's respect." He spread his arms wide.

"I hope my daughter isn't doing anything to shame God," the rabbi said, and his son-in-law, wincing, replied, "Heaven forbid! But she's unhappy, and everyone in Lecheve knows it, sees it. And that's not good. Not good."

So that his son-in-law wouldn't notice his agitation, and in order to calm himself somewhat, Sholem Shachne strolled around the hall. He stopped in front of two large photographs framing both sides of the window that looked out onto the synagogue street. Gazing out at him from one photograph was his wife's father, Eli-Leizer HaLevi Epstein, the elderly rabbi of Zembin. The Zembiner, who ruled his rabbinical court with a firm hand, who didn't wear an overcoat with a slit in the back but an old-fashioned black coat, wide and long, the sort favored by pious Jewish men. Never, not once in his entire life, had he worn a soft-collared shirt or a tie. His tallis katan was buttoned up to his neck. For as long as the town of Zembin could remember, he'd worn a stiff black hat during the week and a mid-height top hat on Shabbos and holidays. A soft fedora with a crease in the center was too modern for him, a sign of indulgence. His chest was covered with a wide, thick white beard, like that of a grandfather, and his eyes, too, had a grandfather's soft expression. Only his raised eyebrows, clipped whiskers, and short, wide, stubborn nose revealed his obstinacy; they announced that he was a man who would not make concessions.

As if to escape his father-in-law's perpetual rebuke that he was too lenient with his congregants, Sholem Shachne moved over to the other portrait, the one of his late parents. In the picture, his father, the former Morehdalye rabbi, Refael Katzenellenbogen, sat in a deep chair with an ornamental backrest. He held a holy book in his hands, pressed against his knees. A smile flickered in his heavy-lidded eyes. His wife stood behind him, one hand on the tall backrest; with the other, she pressed a Korben Mincha prayer book to her heart. Sholem Shachne and his older brother, Avraham Alter, both in short pants and little caps, stood in the front, near their parents.

Sholem Shachne now stood between his son-in-law and the portrait of his parents, as if he were the present speaking to both the past and the future.

"When my oldest son was chafing against who knows what, he used to tell me, 'You see, Father, how Grandfather looks in this picture? His half-closed eyes? That's exactly how Grandfather went through life, that's the way you go through life, the way you want *me* to go through life—half-blind.' But what did he achieve, my eldest with his open eyes?" Sholem Shachne turned to face his son-in-law directly. "He toiled for so long in Switzerland, roamed around there until he sweated himself out a title, doctor of philosophy. But in the end, what does he do? Sits in a library and produces texts for students."

The son-in-law didn't reply. He knew all too well that his brother-in-law, the doctor of philosophy, was a cad. He'd fooled his father, his rosh yeshiva, and his friends. He'd told them all he was traveling to a yeshiva and then fled to study secular subjects. Abroad, he'd gotten married and now had a grown son. For years and years he hadn't visited his father. The cad!

It was so quiet in the cold hall that it seemed you could hear the plants growing in their pots. The main road outside the window, the one leading to Zembin and Lomzhe, gleamed in the sunlight, vacant for miles. Only the shadow of the sukkah room's winged roof stirred, growing longer and longer until it reached Sholem Shachne's feet. Again he spoke, his tone filled with the melancholy and resentment festering in his bones. Each word he uttered hovered in the void of the cold hall, frozen as an echo in a vaulted stone cellar.

"All right," he finally said. "I can understand that my oldest, Naftali Hertz, abandoned the Torah because of a dream. He wanted to study secular subjects and change the world. But which great goal in life did my Bentzion have? During the day he's a salesman in a Bialystok shop, and in the evening he takes business courses. And because he started late—he did spend time studying Torah in the beis medrash—he's now a twenty-six-year-old who's still just a student learning to become a businessman. And once he finishes, he'll probably become a manager of a little factory—*if* he's lucky and finds a position. A lovely accomplishment for a Katzenellenbogen! But try telling that to Bluma Rivtcha, and right away she snaps that Bentzion doesn't want to conquer a world. Bentzion wants—she says—to be an independent person who earns his own money. You understand?" Sholem Shachne asked his son-in-law, but then realized he was actually talking to himself.

The rabbi walked back to the window. He and his son-in-law faced each other silently, tugging at their beards. Sholem Shachne was also worried about his youngest son, nearly twenty years old, whom he'd sent to the Lecheve Yeshiva, where he'd hoped his son-in-law would keep an eye on him. But if day after day Refael saw that his sister Tilza was unhappy with her life there, Yaakov Asher's presence was more likely to make things worse than better. "When I daven, I beg God that at least from Refael'ke I should be spared the grief I've suffered from his older brothers. What do you think—is he following a righteous path? I mean, can you tell if he's trying to emulate his older brothers?" Sholem Shachne asked, his eyes wide and sharp behind his glasses.

The son-in-law spread his arms wide again and shrugged. "What do I know?" he said. Refael'ke, he explained, lived with him and ate at his house. He was careful to provide Refael'ke with the best yeshiva boys as friends, and he was also studying privately with him. What more could he do?

Sholem Shachne knew his children well. He knew they weren't talkative by nature unless they really trusted the other person. Refael'ke's not trusting his brother-in-law was a bad sign. Further, it vexed him that his son-in-law responded to everything with "What do I know?" Did this mean Yaakov Asher really did know but didn't want to tell?

"His mother wanted his sister to keep an eye on him," Sholem Shachne said, "to make sure he slept on a clean bed. She wanted you to make sure he was studying. That's why we sent him. Refael himself didn't want to travel to a yeshiva. He doesn't enjoy eating at strangers' homes. But who knows if it's his sister who's corrupting him?"

And once again, his son-in-law said, "What do I know? You know your son and daughter better than I do."

This was the third day of Yaakov Asher's stay in Morehdalye. Supposedly, he had come for a little vacation. After all, the weary students also went on vacation in the summer, and even those who stayed did more strolling around town than studying. So the rosh yeshiva was entitled to a bit of travel, too. His in-laws wondered aloud why he hadn't brought along his wife and child, their daughter and grandson. Averting his face, he'd replied that Tilza hadn't wanted to come, and then added his standard "What do I know?"

At mealtimes, he sat at the table despondently, like a stranger. You could tell he felt pained at having married into a family where the children were abandoning Judaism.

Earlier, before their discussion in the cold hall, his father-in-law had asked Yaakov Asher to spend a little time studying with Zindel Kadish, so he could probe his character, feel out the kind of young man he was. As a rosh yeshiva, Yaakov Asher knew how to converse with young men to discern their level of devoutness. Yaakov Asher had acquiesced and had spoken with Zindel Kadish. Now, his father-in-law asked, "So what can you tell me about the dayan's grandson? Do you think he's a match for my daughter? Is he worthy of being my successor?"

"Well, as for his scholarliness, there's no point discussing it," the son-in-law replied. "He's a poor scholar, this Tachkemoni student, and you know it. You study with him. But as for everyday matters, the lad didn't want to talk to me. I saw that he'd formed some opinions, but he refused to share them with me. And that's no good. That's no good at all."

"You trust no one! I don't understand how you can lead a yeshiva for young men when you don't trust a soul!" Sholem Shachne cried, exasperated, and swiveled away from the window.

"Unfortunately, I've been too trusting in the past," Yaakov Asher replied, equally exasperated. His regret over his belief that his wife would change for the better after marriage choked him.

Father-in-law and son-in-law realized they could no longer have a calm discussion. And to fight—that they certainly didn't want to do. Arms clasped behind them, they ambled out of the cold hall into the kitchen, where the rebbetzin was setting the table for lunch.

B LUMA RIVTCHA AND ZINDEL were already on the bridge, pausing at the railing to peer into the Narev. Along the length of the
shore, little whitewashed houses, trees, and bushes were reflected in
the water. Three long-nosed sailboats, painted yellow, red, and blue,
and a wide rowboat tied to the shore rocked and splashed. Somewhere on the shoreline were washerwomen. Because the shore was
curved and twisted, they couldn't be seen, but you could hear the
noise they made as they wrung out their laundry. The water in the
center of the river had a bluish cast, and the opposite shore, sandy
and bare, stretched alongside the river like a golden wave. A sweet
freshness wafted up from the Narev, but also a deep, cold melancholy, as if the waves were weary from their ceaseless swelling.

Bluma Rivtcha was telling Zindel about her father feeling demor-
alized and bitter because none of her brothers had wanted to remain
in their town.

"There's no future for the youth in this town," Zindel said. "That's
why your brothers didn't want to stay here. And why I don't want to
be the rabbi."

"So why are you studying in Warsaw's Tachkemoni and learning Talmud with my father?" Bluma Rivtcha bent over the railing,
watching the water as it frothed and bubbled. "Do you not want to
be a rabbi at all, or do you want to be a rabbi in another town, but
not Morehdalye?"

"I want to be a rabbi in America, or even in Australia. Anywhere,
as long as it isn't in Poland." Zindel turned away from the water to
the sandy path along the shore, which snaked up a hill and climbed
higher and farther, until the sky descended upon it and swallowed
it up.

"I'm guessing you're not serious." Bluma Rivtcha turned to face him. "I'm sure you don't mean to fool your grandfather, my parents, and the entire town. They all see you as the future rabbi here."

"I don't plan to fool anyone. Everyone will know it when the time comes. But so far, you're the only one I've told. I'm sure you'd also be happier living abroad in a big city than here in a small town."

"If I'm going to be a rabbi's wife, I'd rather be in a small town than in a foreign city." Bluma Rivtcha looked around. "Let's walk along the higher shore on the other side."

Although they'd known each other since childhood, Bluma Rivtcha had never told Zindel she liked him, and he, too, had behaved primly toward her. They couldn't forget that in the minds of her father, his grandfather, and all of Morehdalye, hoping to reap some nachas and joy from their rabbinic children, they were considered an almost-certain match. That's why Zindel immediately regretted confiding his dream to Bluma Rivtcha. Beneath the high, clear sky, in the surrounding vastness, it seemed to him that the echo of his words had already reached the town. When they returned from their stroll, he worried, everyone would already know about this conversation. And it was all for naught: The only reason he'd confided in her was that he'd been so certain Bluma Rivtcha would be pleased.

"Why do you say you'd rather be a rabbi's wife in a small town than in some city abroad?" he asked as they went up to the other side of the river.

"I don't know." Bluma Rivtcha walked more rapidly, as if she were racing against the setting sun. "Actually, I do know why. To be a rabbi's wife in Morehdalye is to live as one with the townswomen. It's hard, but at least you're among your own. But in foreign surroundings I wouldn't be able to do it. For the women there and for their husbands, I'd be the rabbi's wife and nothing else. What would connect me to them?"

They passed a field of greenish-white cabbage wrapped in large leaves. Bluma Rivtcha was so irritated by what Zindel had confided that her hands flitted about restlessly. She tore a flower off a stem at the side of the road, then a little leaf, which she rubbed between her fingers. "Your grandfather would be heartbroken, too, if you became a rabbi in a country where the rabbis and the people are of a different sort than us. Do you have any idea how my father looks at a beardless American rabbi?"

"Your father would agree to this sooner than to another option," Zindel replied, his dark eyes smiling as sweetly as when he'd spot his bride-to-be passing the window of the beis medrash during his study sessions with the rabbi. At that moment, Bluma Rivtcha felt repulsed by him. She understood what he was trying to say: Her father was so afraid she might abandon religion altogether that he'd rather she become the wife of a rabbi overseas whose congregants were beard-less Jews.

The setting sun grew larger, then sank into distant plains. Clouds with charred purple edges floated by. In the water a pale gold rib-bon of light sparkled, drawing one's heart toward distant lands. Bluma Rivtcha kept walking along the high shore, and she fancied that her forward motion was delighting the large yellow sunflowers, the fields of barley on bearded stalks, the meadow of clover. In the space where the fields ended and the dark forest began, thin birch trees with silver barks glistened. On their branches, countless dainty leaves glittered in the waning light, trembling and winking at her from the distance. "You've got worries? Go on!" The town on the other side of the Narev, with its white church steeple on the hill, winked at her, too. But with each step she took, it seemed to Bluma Rivtcha that the farther away she walked, the sadder the town she was leaving behind became. The svelte poplars on the church hill grew darker, resembling tall nuns dressed in black, mutely frozen at their evening prayers.

It was already nightfall when Bluma Rivtcha and Zindel returned from their stroll, the sky seeded with green stars. Zindel went to his grandfather, and Bluma Rivtcha remained standing in front of her father's house, beneath the drooping willow branches. She had lis-tened to their murmuring since childhood. They'd whisper secrets from the hidden plant world and advise her on how to behave among people. Now, too, they rumbled with suggestions. Her leafy friends were even squabbling among themselves. From one tree she heard, "For heaven's sake, her father mustn't find out that Zindel wants to become a rabbi in a foreign land and wants her to join him. Should her father find out, he'd again start searching for a match for her from among the overly pious yeshiva boys." Another tree, rumbling even louder, insisted on the precise opposite: "She must definitely tell her father! This way, he'd no longer be able to keep her here; he'd have to let her travel out of town to learn a skill."

Truth be told, Bluma Rivtcha had never been crazy about Zindel's saccharine smile. But she kept telling herself that nothing had been promised, that they weren't getting married yet, and in the meantime, she was curious to discover what kind of person Zindel had turned out to be after studying in Warsaw's Tachkemoni. Today, she'd learned he was nowhere near as pious as she'd believed. He didn't seem to mind that he was fooling an entire town. Even to her, he wasn't being entirely truthful. Because he wanted to become a rabbi, he considered a rabbi's daughter a suitable match for him. But he evidently liked her even less than she liked him. Her two older brothers had abandoned the town and Judaism entirely. But Zindel never skipped prayers—not for a single day. During the three weeks preceding Tisha B'Av, he didn't cut his beard or bathe in the Narev, just as Jewish law dictated. Even today, while they strolled in the fields, he hadn't forgotten to say the Mincha prayers. His fantasies reached no further than becoming a rabbi in some small synagogue abroad.

"If you *are* choosing a yeshiva boy, it might as well be a serious Torah scholar. Much better choice," a willow swaying above her head seemed to say.

"Yes, if you come right down to it, he's just a dull fellow." Bluma Rivtcha chuckled to herself, and then went inside her home.

Last summer, Zindel Kadish had come to the rabbi's house and told him that because of his secular studies at Warsaw's Tachkemoni, he'd fallen behind in his study of Talmud and Jewish law. So Sholem Shachne offered to study with him every day. His intention was merely to draw a young man closer to Torah. That Zindel was trying to attract his younger daughter, the rabbi hadn't noticed.

This knowledge did not, however, escape the rebbetzin, Henna'le. And when Zindel went back to Warsaw after the High Holidays, she told her husband that though the young man was studying for the sake of knowledge, he was also trying to charm them because he liked their daughter. Sholem Shachne didn't want to hear it. True, Zindel was a refined, educated young man, but he was not a scholar, and who knew if he was even truly devout, considering that he was a student at Tachkemoni. Bluma Rivtcha would surely be able to get a bridegroom who was a distinguished scholar and feared the Lord, just as her sister, Tilza, had.

Throughout the winter, the rabbi searched for a potential husband for his daughter. The best boys in the yeshivas of Mir, Radin, and Kletsk were interested in the match. First, they were enticed by the bride's pedigree: Sholem Shachne had a reputation as a discerning, albeit strict, Torah scholar. The bride's grandfather was the old Zembin rabbi, and her brother-in-law was the Lecheve rosh yeshiva. The dowry would be the rabbinic seat in Morehdalye, a prestigious community, and the bride herself was very gifted—although it was said that she was unsure about whether or not she wanted to marry a Torah scholar. But precisely because the bride was ambivalent, the yeshiva boys were even more attracted to her. Each young Torah scholar desired to impress her. Bluma Rivtcha, however, found fault with them all.

One boy, an absentminded genius, came for a Shabbos. But Bluma Rivtcha decided he looked encumbered by his brand-new clothes; he was the sort of genius who was meant to look disheveled. At first, Bluma Rivtcha was dazzled by his clever responses. He provoked and confused her with his mockery of worldly progressives. But even before Shabbos had ended, her interest in him faded. Her father took her aside. "Well?" he asked.

She told him that the boy with the brand-new clothes had an old, soiled head. "He claims that people shouldn't study foreign languages, shouldn't read books, not even newspapers. All the wisdom of the world, he claims, can be found in the Talmud."

Sholem Shachne brought her another boy, someone who was mature, smart, and well-read. But Bluma Rivtcha was repulsed by his fat neck and sunken cheeks, and because he added three or four teaspoons of sugar to his tea. He pared an apple for a quarter of an hour and scrutinized each segment individually, deciding whether it was worth putting into his mouth. It was obvious he was lazy and shallow, the sort of person who didn't need a wife, but a maid.

A third boy, with thick lips and cold eyes, created a sensation in Morehdalye when he gave a talk in the beis medrash. Sholem Shachne praised him: besides being a good speaker, he was also a tremendous scholar.

"Maybe," Bluma Rivtcha responded, "but he's also a born businessman." He'd managed to extract from her how much of a salary her father received and whether he had any side sources of income. "Surely, he's already met a dozen girls. Well, let him look further."

"But you don't want a quiet Torah student who's removed from anything worldly and sits in a little corner studying," Sholem Shachne chided her.

"No," she replied. She didn't want to marry a man to her father's taste and then be miserable, like her sister, Tilza, was with her husband.

ALL THROUGH THE NIGHT, the rabbi's sighs were audible. In response, his wife, Henna'le, went on a tirade. If he had only been a bit more flexible with his two older sons, they would never have left him and gone so far away. But at least his sons didn't want to hurt him. A son-in-law, on the other hand, wouldn't care that much about causing grief to his in-laws. Certainly, Bluma Rivtcha had a stronger character than Tilza. Still, she could fall under a husband's influence, and who knows who that husband would be? Much better if her own father acted as the shadchan between her and the dayan's grandson.

For Sholem Shachne, the thought that the chair on which he and his father had sat and made judgments on intricate Jewish law would soon be occupied by this poor excuse of a scholar was difficult to swallow. It was with a heavy heart that he made his way to Zindel's grandfather, the dayan, Tzadok Kadish. On his part, the dayan also had reservations. Four decades ago, Tzadok's father had been the rabbi of Morehdalye. When he died, the townspeople selected the town's shopkeeper, Refael Katzenellenbogen, to take his place, instead of Tzadok, the heir apparent. Refael was a great scholar and fervently self-sacrificing. And the former rabbi's rightful heir, Tzadok Kadish, was forced to agree to be merely the town's dayan. Refael had been the rabbi for twenty years; then his younger son, Sholem Shachne, inherited the role. And once again, Tzadok had to satisfy himself with being the town's dayan.

Besides this rivalry, Tzadok also disagreed with the Katzenellenbogens on another matter. Unlike the Katzenellenbogens, Tzadok was in favor of studying both Torah and secular knowledge, which was why he'd sent Zindel to study at Tachkemoni. But ever since Zindel's parents had gone to Canada and gotten divorced, the dayan had begun to feel his decrepit old age. And so he now allowed himself to be persuaded by the rabbi, his rival of so many years.

"Neither of us was successful, Reb Tzadok," Sholem Shachne

said. "I didn't succeed in preventing the younger generation from dragging big-city filth into Morehdalye. Even with my own children I was unsuccessful! And you were unsuccessful in making compromises. The youth no longer need your rabbinical dispensations for their enlightenment; they do everything they want without them. So perhaps the affection between your grandson and my daughter is divinely ordained. Common sense dictates that since your grandson is both educated and a Torah scholar, he'll have a positive influence on my Bluma Rivtcha. I'll provide him with food and board for life, and his dowry will be my rabbinic dynasty—when the time will come. The townspeople won't be against it; they want to give pleasure to us both. And they, too, now want a more educated rabbi. Are you against the idea?"

"Against it? I praise and thank God for His kindness." The dayan smiled sadly, all his wrinkles showing on a face almost entirely covered by his beard and peyes. "But you'll have to prod Zindel to study more. He's quite behind in Talmud and Jewish law." The rabbis regarded each other bleakly, the same thought running through both their heads: *May our successor not shame us, not in this world or in the world to come.*

The next summer, when Zindel came home for vacation, Sholem Shachne—already regarding him as his daughter's fiancé—began to teach him how to rule on matters of Jewish law.

→ 3 ←

ARLY ON THE MORNING after their conversation in the cold
hall, as they set out to the beis medrash for prayers, Yaakov
Asher told his father-in-law that he was getting ready to leave for
home. Sholem Shachne understood that these words were the preamble to what was really bothering his son-in-law—or, rather, to
whatever had brought him to Morehdalye in the first place.

After prayers, once the other congregants had dispersed, the
rabbi imagined that the curtain covering the Torah scrolls in the
aron kodesh, the table on the bimah, the bookcases holding the holy
books, and the lecterns were all waiting along with him to hear what
Yaakov Asher was about to say. A tall white yahrzeit candle, stuck
to the amud, burned dimly with a kind of flaming sigh, as if it was
embarrassed to be burning in the middle of a bright day in a beis
medrash flooded with sunlight. Yaakov Asher finally walked up to
his father-in-law. As he opened his mouth to speak, Sholem Shachne
imagined that the rays of sun had also become frightened, and so
they paused, suspended, outside the windows.

"Yesterday, you told me that I trust no one. You wondered how I
could lead a yeshiva if I can't trust anyone. The truth is that nowadays you shouldn't trust anyone. But as it happens, in the case of my
students, I trust that they're definitely pious boys. Because in this
day and age, you can't force anyone to attend yeshiva. Whoever isn't
up to sitting and studying won't come to a yeshiva at all or will leave
right away. That's why I don't have much faith in the dayan's grandson. There's a long way to go from studying in Warsaw's Tachkemoni
and taking a few lessons with you in the summer to actually becoming a rabbi. A very long way."

Yaakov Asher paced back and forth in front of the eastern bench
where his father-in-law was standing. Perspiration dotted his face,

and he kept wrinkling his forehead, as if struggling over a difficult lesson. The rabbi, tall and thin, was wedged into the eastern corner, near the aron kodesh. He had a feeling he was about to hear some bad news. His son-in-law paused in front of him, wedging him farther into the corner.

"I just said I trust my students because no one forces them to sit and study. But if it happens that a student *is* forced, then that's not good. I'm bringing this up because of your Refael'ke. I surrounded him with friends—the best students of Torah! But he has befriended different types of boys outside the yeshiva. That's the reason I came to Morehdalye. I want to let you know that I'm relieving myself of any responsibility toward Refael. I know I've been here for a few days already, but I just didn't have the heart to tell you earlier."

In that first moment, the rabbi sighed with relief. The truth was, he'd already suspected for some time that his youngest son was up to no good. But when his son-in-law had begun to speak, the rabbi thought he was going to say he wanted to divorce Tilza. And so, the relief. But after a minute, once the fright over the fate of his daughter's marriage faded, he began to feel the pain of this piece of news. A shudder went through him. From the dim flame of the yahrzeit candle, he imagined he saw a barefoot Jew stepping out, so tall that he reached the rafters. The Jew drew closer to him, passed through him as if he were a gate, and vanished into the eastern wall.

"And with whom is Refael'ke friends outside the yeshiva?" the rabbi asked.

"What do I know?" Yaakov Asher said, as was his wont.

But his father-in-law looked at him with such a piercing, pleading look, Yaakov Asher immediately recanted. "Actually, I do know who he meets up with, who he's friends with. He gets together with the chalutzim in town. You know, those young men who want to be pioneers in Palestine. Refael has told Tilza quite a few times that he wants to become a chalutz and move to a kibbutz in the land of Israel."

"And how does my daughter answer him?"

"Tilza doesn't encourage him. But she tells him he's an adult and has to decide on his own what he needs to do." This reply was followed by a long, gloomy silence, which declared—wordlessly—that Tilza herself regretted not having made her own decisions on the direction her life should take.

"So what should I do with him?" Sholem Shachne had no strength to stand anymore, and he collapsed onto a bench. "Should I send him to another yeshiva, to Radin or Kletsk?"

"He won't go there willingly, and to force him certainly won't work. Besides, how can we be sure he won't find the same sort of friends in Radin or Kletsk? You have to keep him here in Morehdalye, near you, and watch over him," Yaakov Asher murmured into his beard. Father-in-law and son-in-law again plunged into heavy silence. The yahrzeit candle continued to burn in mournful semidarkness. But the sun's rays came back in through the windows, dancing over the benches and lecterns, skipping off the chandeliers onto the table at the bimah, and from there hopping over to the sparkling copper washstand at the entrance to the beis medrash.

AT LUNCH IN THE RABBI'S HOUSE, an oppressive mood clouded everyone's faces. Henna'le served cold borscht lightened with egg. But her hands trembled as she carried the heavy plates. On one hand, she always stood up for her children; on the other hand, she didn't want them acting against their father's wishes. Henna'le remembered well Sholem Shachne's hot-bloodedness in his younger days. He used to tell people the truth right to their faces. But since his children had grown up and had begun to rebel against him, he'd learned to keep quiet and keep his feelings to himself. The fact that he was now speaking with such open bitterness at the table made it clear how deeply troubled he was.

"It is me the prophet laments when he cries out, '*My enemies are the people in my own home.*'" The rabbi ignored his borscht and instead chewed on a crust of bread dipped in salt. "My greatest enemies are my own family. I send my youngest son to Lecheve, and my older daughter encourages him to do whatever he desires. Should I send him to the yeshiva in Bialystok and ask my brother, the Bialystoker pedagogue, to keep an eye on his nephew? But my son Bentzion is there! A shopkeeper by day, takes business courses at night, and his greatest dream is to become a manager in a factory. What will his younger brother learn from *him*? The only choice is to bring Refael'ke home and keep him near me. But then who can assure me his sister Bluma Rivtcha won't corrupt him?"

The rebbetzin was standing at the table, doling out portions of cold chicken. "What makes you think Bluma Rivtcha will corrupt him? With luck, she'll soon be engaged to an educated student— Zindel, the dayan's grandson." Henna'le forced a laugh, so as not to inflame her husband any further.

But with tears in her eyes Bluma Rivtcha cried out to her parents, "Instead of worrying about *me* ruining Refael'ke, make sure Zindel doesn't!"

"What kind of nonsense is that!" the confused Henna'le fumed at her daughter.

Sholem Shachne spit out the bread and glanced anxiously at his son-in-law, who just that morning in the beis medrash had candidly told him he didn't trust Zindel.

"What are you saying?" he asked his daughter. But Bluma Rivtcha, not wanting to cause her father any more anguish, remained silent.

"The trouble with today's youth is that they conceal their impurity inside purity." Yaakov Asher swayed over his plate of cold chicken like a biblical priest over a sacrifice at the altar. "If a young man wants to live decadently, he won't come out and say it. No, he'll claim he's drawn to the idea of becoming a chalutz so he can build the land of Israel and save Jews. Another one desires even more decadence, so he claims he wants to save the entire world. A third wishes to become rich, so he quotes from *Ethics of the Fathers:* 'Man shall despise the professional rabbinate and not make Torah his livelihood.' And a fourth simply has all kinds of fantasies and expresses them in grand sayings: 'A person must follow his heart.'"

Bluma Rivtcha turned red and felt her ears burning. She could not understand how her sister could live with a man who had such stale opinions. Not to mention his stubby, stained fingers, red beard, and sweaty face. Who cared that he had a keen head for studies! True, he was able to deliver sharp arguments on subtle points of Jewish law, but the younger generation was completely uninterested. By nature not very talkative, Bluma Rivtcha now replied rashly, her voice high-pitched to mask her shyness.

"Refael'ke isn't friends with chalutzim because he's out for a good time. It's a different world out there, and people have different ideas. That's why young people don't listen to rabbis and rosh yeshivas anymore. Because these pious leaders keep rehashing the old clichés—that everything new stems only from lust and debauchery."

Pleased with her response, Bluma Rivtcha felt her face flush with happiness. Her brother-in-law, however, turned away from her. He'd traveled here to inform his father-in-law that he was losing a son, and now he was being mocked? Rebbetzin Henna'le stood between her son-in-law and daughter as between two fires. Not knowing what to do, she resorted to an old, trusted tactic: she smiled like a deaf old woman who can't hear a word of what's being said. But just as his son-in-law had done, the rabbi turned his narrow, rigid shoulders away from Bluma Rivtcha. At that moment someone entered the rabbi's chambers and Henna'le suddenly regained her hearing.

"That's probably Zindel, come to take his lesson," she murmured to her husband. And indeed, just then Zindel Kadish stepped into the dining room. The rabbi bit back his anger and soon everyone in the household was staring into their plates—as if the only thing of interest in the rabbi's house were food.

A S AN UNMARRIED GIRL, Tilza had been a moody bundle of emotion, constantly gazing out the windows of her father's house with big, black, dreamy eyes. Behind her shoulders dangled a pair of long, thick, chestnut-colored braids. Tilza was plump and olive-skinned, with a high bosom, wide, sensuous lips, and thick eyebrows. Because of her perpetual daydreaming and moodiness— though she didn't really know what was gnawing at her—Tilza some- how failed to notice she had developed a voluptuous, womanly body, which young men ogled hungrily. She paid no attention to status and had friends from simple homes. When she spoke, it was from the heart, usually with her pale, chubby hands clasping her bosom. Some townspeople claimed Tilza wasn't very sharp; others felt she was too soft and sincere. Her parents thought she was simply a dreamer. Even in her sleep, she dreamed of flying birds.

Tilza enjoyed strolling down flat, bare stretches of road, her long braids flapping behind her. The decaying shed in her family's back- yard pained her. "Why does it bother you? We don't even have any animals," her mother wondered. But merely looking at decrepitude made Tilza sad. Even wood that had been sliced from tree barks and was lying in a pile in the yard, the slats still releasing a fresh woodsy fragrance, made her ache. The pile brought to mind the big trees that had been recently chopped down, falling to the ground with a hushed sigh. If she saw a baby carriage with rusty wheels atop a pile of trash, she averted her head. She couldn't bear seeing an object that had formerly brought everyone joy now wallowing in the trash. The worst were the days before the holidays, when women would come to their home with slaughtered chickens to ask the rabbi about their kosher status, and her father would stick his soiled fingers into each chicken's craw. On the day before Yom Kippur, when all of Morehdalye performed the kapparos ritual, Tilza's face twisted with revulsion, and she felt like crying. Why did the day before the holiday have to be so common, and why on the eve of this holiest day did there have to be such shrieks from creatures about to be slaughtered?

Tilza borrowed thick novels from friends but never finished reading them, not even halfway. It was enough for her to skim a few pages and then go back to daydreaming. According to her father, all novels were taboo, immoral. But Henna'le persuaded him to allow Tilza to read novels and to be friends with anyone she chose. As long as they presented no danger and Tilza was obeying her parents and not lying, she should be allowed her daydreams. And, indeed, until one day, her father let her be.

Ezra Morgenstern, the Hebrew teacher in the talmud torah, had come to Morehdalye from a town somewhere in Volyn. While he taught the children, he wore a yarmulke. But when he socialized with the town's youth, he wore no hat and his hair hung down to his nose, as he made fun of diaspora Jews and their political factions.

One day, Tilza went for a walk with Ezra along the outskirts of Morehdalye. Ezra stretched out on the grass and Tilza stood beside him, her chestnut braids swinging in front of her like the falling leaves on a tree. Ezra was an admirer of the chalutzim and his ridicule of their opponents distressed her, even though there was no one around to hear him.

At one point, Ezra sat up and spoke more softly, pointing to the bridge above the Narev River. "Do you see? The Morehdalye youth stand on the bridge and see a wide river, blue sky, vast fields. But in the midst of all this abundance, our youth are trapped like prisoners. I understand why you hold the Narev so dear. You've bathed in it, and there at the shore the waves wash over the tombstones in the Jewish cemetery. So many engraved stones of grandfathers and grandmothers, great-grandfathers and great-grandmothers! But let a young gentile throw a stone at a young healthy Jew, and a piece of his heart shatters. It's not the gentile or stone that scares him, but the fact that he knows he's in a land of enemies, and the old graves won't help him. Neither these graves—the stone witnesses to the many years the Jewish community has been here—nor the lineage of the Morehdalye Jewish community recorded on parchment protect the Jew when a gentile hurls a stone at him."

Agitated, Tilza plaited and unplaited the edges of her dark braids. She sat down on the ground next to Ezra. In a conspiratorial tone, she said, "I've heard some people say that the land of Israel is also filled with stones, graves, and ruins."

Physically Ezra Morgenstern looked like a mere boy next to Tilza, but in intelligence he was way ahead of her. He didn't dare hug her or kiss her full, voluptuous lips; she was liable to take offense and burst into tears. Instead, he picked up one of Tilza's braids, placing it in the palm of one hand as if to weigh it, and with his other hand stroked her hair.

"It's true," he said, "that the land of Israel is full of stones, graves, and ruins; full of hot sand, thorns, swamps, and salty water; full of the sort of heat that peels your skin, and malaria that turns your face yellow and burns your bones. But when the chalutz sees ruins, he yearns to rebuild them. When he sees swamps, he longs to dry them out. And when an enemy lies in wait around some corner, the chalutz feels that at least he'll be buried under the stones of his own home. He protects himself in a different way than when he's accosted in a foreign land. And the nights in the desert are inky black, the stars as big as your eyes peeking through your braids."

Ezra stretched out on his back again, hands clasped behind his neck, and began to hum a Hebrew tune, "How Beautiful Are the Nights in Canaan." Tilza stared at the Narev's high shoreline and at the Jewish cemetery, where tombstones overgrown with moss lay tightly squeezed one on top of the other. She gazed at the green meadows speckled with white and yellow flowers, at the town with its little houses that looked like sheep huddling together against a gust of rain, at the horizon dipping below her father's house—it seemed such a loss to leave it all behind. She imagined telling her parents that she wanted to leave their old house with its low rotting ceiling, their yard with its dilapidated shed—that she wanted to leave it all to go to the land of Israel.

But before she could talk to her parents, her father spoke to her. People had informed him that she had been strolling about with the Hebrew teacher outside of town.

"Not only will you never again exchange another word with this degenerate, but I'll hound him out of the talmud torah, too. His words poison the young men in town. He tells them to travel to the land of Israel and live on a kibbutz where people don't put on tefillin, don't observe Shabbos or kosher or the laws of family purity—they don't believe in God at all. So long as I'm rabbi, this heretic will *not* be a teacher here." Sholem Shachne fumed and frothed. Back then, he was still very sure of himself. He had many pious townspeople on his side, so he fought against every transgressor.

On one hand, Tilza ached when her father was ridiculed by the freethinkers. But on the other, she cried for nights on end in sympathy with the teacher whom her father and the other devout townspeople had harassed until he left his job and Morehdalye as well.

After this incident, Sholem Shachne brought Yaakov Asher Kahane to Morehdalye to meet Tilza. Since Yaakov Asher didn't have a beard at the time, the yellow-flecked skin on his face and hands and his thick red hair were even more conspicuous. But his blue-green eyes, which emanated kindness and respect for every person, warmed Tilza.

Yaakov Asher was immediately enchanted by Tilza's dreamy, mournful eyes and her long braids. What touched him even more were her words, which were somewhat childish but openhearted. At their very first meeting, she told him she had always longed to live a life of beauty. "Where can more beauty be found than in Torah?" he replied. "What can be prettier than a woman lighting Shabbos candles or Jews walking and singing on Sukkos, holding their lulavim?"

Rebbetzin Henna'le was unmoved by her husband's awe over the young man's brilliance and Torah scholarship; she could tell that her daughter wasn't enthusiastic about him. Nevertheless, the rebbetzin agreed that Yaakov Asher was a mature man and a suitable match for their daughter. Tilza needed a man who would also be a father figure.

Only later did her father realize that although Tilza had agreed to marry Yaakov Asher, she had hardly changed at all. After the wedding she cut off her braids and covered her hair with a scarf. She became a rebbetzin and the mother of a little boy. But she still looked around her in the midday brightness with dreamy, nocturnal eyes.

When her father came to visit her in Lecheve, he couldn't believe his ears. That the wife of a rosh yeshiva could have such complaints about her husband's students! *Why do the boys have such long peyes and tzitzis? Why do they walk around in rumpled clothes and have such dirty hands and filthy nails? The married yeshiva men pray and study, but these*

young men rock and shout in the most bizarre way. On Purim, the entire
town of Lecheve gathers to stare and laugh at the yeshiva boys acting like
idiots, singing and dancing wildly. Lecheve is a muddy hick town, and the
men and women look so shabby. Why does everyone have to know when the
women's mikveh is being heated and which women are immersing for their
husbands that night? They're all so shamelessly pious.

"Is that so?" Sholem Shachne stared at his daughter, astonished.
"But you know that the yeshiva boys are poor. Where they live, the
water practically freezes in the buckets. So they dress poorly and
don't bathe, so what? Here I was thinking you're unhappy because
the students steal from people in the street or fall down drunk in the
gutter. I thought you were unhappy because your husband is rough
with you. Or because he's stingy, or a bad father to your child."

"Yaakov Asher is very attached to our child and is nice to me,"
said Tilza, smiling sadly as she searched for the words that would
make her father understand. Her husband cared about her, yes, but
he didn't know how to be tender—just as he knew the proper chant
for Talmud study but didn't seem to know how to sing. "What I'm
lacking from Yaakov Asher is the Song of Songs," Tilza finally said,
her cheeks burning like wine-red leaves.

"A Jew sings Song of Songs to God, not to a woman," Sholem
Shachne admonished his daughter. "Your husband is at fault. He's
spoiling you by not demanding that you tend to his students, like
the wives of other roshei yeshiva." Then he informed Tilza that
in the summer Refael'ke would be joining Yaakov Asher's yeshiva.
Her youngest brother was also creating problems: he didn't want to
attend a yeshiva where he would have to eat at strangers' tables. So,
by all means, why not have Tilza hold him to her standards, make
sure he's washed and his clothes are clean, that he doesn't rock and
sway over the Talmud, doesn't scream during prayers. He can even
have trimmed peyes; it makes no difference, as long as he's studying
the Talmud.

EVEN AS A CHILD, Refael'ke had been able to sit at his father's table
for hours on end, listening to what everyone was saying without inter-
jecting a word. He grew up and became tall and strong like a tree,
with wide shoulders and muscular arms. His forehead was smooth

and high, pale and refined, framed by curly hair, and the corners of his mouth were rounded like a child's. He was nearsighted, so he wore big glasses just like his father. His eyes, calm and wise, peered questioningly through them out at the world. At times, one could detect in his expression a smile of mild, good-natured cynicism, one you would expect only from a much older boy.

Sholem Shachne thought his youngest son had been born with exceptional character traits, the sort other people couldn't attain even with much effort. Some people had a temper, others were arrogant by nature, and still others were naturally frivolous—vices Refael'ke didn't have. He was forced to exert himself for one thing only: to advance in his studies.

Apart from Sholem Shachne's grief that Refael'ke now seemed to be following a downward path, he couldn't forgive himself for having failed to realize that Tilza hadn't forgotten Ezra, the ostracized talmud torah teacher who had incited Morehdalye's young men to become chalutzim. So that when her brother confided to his silly sister that he, too, wanted to become a chalutz, she apparently recalled her Song of Songs, her passion for that Hebrew-speaking freethinker, and advised Refael to do as his heart desired.

AT THE BEGINNING of the month of Elul, Sholem Shachne traveled to Lecheve to bring Refael'ke home, only to discover that his daughter wasn't speaking to her husband. Tilza was furious at Yaakov Asher for traveling to Morehdalye to warn her father that Refael'ke was straying from the proper path.

Sholem Shachne wanted to pour all his accumulated bitterness out onto his daughter. But his son-in-law pleaded with him not to speak unkindly to Tilza, or whatever peace their marriage still held would be destroyed. So Sholem Shachne focused on his son, demanding that Refael'ke explain why he wouldn't study. Refael'ke replied that he was lacking for nothing in Lecheve and that his sister Tilza wasn't at fault. He himself had been curious to know what the chalutzim did and thought. If, however, his father wished, he would return home with him to Morehdalye.

⇀ 5 ↼

ZINDEL KADISH DID NOT return to Warsaw's Tachkemoni for the new semester. His grandfather insisted on his staying in Morehdalye, and Sholem Shachne viewed this as a miracle, his salvation. First, Refael'ke would now have a study partner. Second, Bluma Rivtcha would have an opportunity to become more attached to her groom-to-be. And third, it was essential that Zindel study more Talmud and Jewish law. He'd had more than enough of secular education!

So every day the rabbi gave a lesson to Zindel and Refael'ke, and afterward he'd watch through the window of his study as they either went back to the beis medrash for more study or set out on a walk to the outskirts of town. Their Talmuds would remain on the table, and the rabbi would stare at them, wondering, *Will my son who is planning to become a chalutz ruin my future son-in-law? Will my educated future son-in-law persuade my son to go abroad to university?*

From a window in the kitchen, a little head sporting a big sheitel was also watching. Rebbetzin Henna'le very much wanted the two young men to become brothers-in-law. But Zindel and her daughter were still distant. When Zindel came to their house to study, Bluma Rivtcha made small talk with him for a few minutes and then either went to her room or left to go into town to meet her friends. When the rabbi asked Henna'le, "Well? Am I allowed to know what's happening between your daughter and her intended?" Henna'le didn't know what to answer. She laughed to herself. To think that she'd lived to see this! Sholem Shachne *wanted* their daughter to spend time with a boy!

ZINDEL AND REFAEL'KE STROLLED along the outskirts of town. Above their heads gray clouds appeared to be racing the boys to some destination—although, of course, the clouds didn't know what they hoped to reach. The autumn fields stretched out, naked and prickly. From behind fences, fruit trees boasting hard green pears and rose-colored apples bent over onto the road. Out of a weed-filled nook on the Narev came the cries of wild ducks, and somewhere a stork's wide wings were flapping—it was testing itself before setting out on a distant journey. Soon, it would soar. In the town and on the roads surrounding it, the trees were still covered in dark green foliage; only one tree, on the church hill, was already wearing a flaming red crown. A wind ripped a cluster of leaves off its branches and scattered them like sparks. The svelte poplars around the church appeared even taller. Their long blue shadows crawled downhill, right to the shore of the stormy Narev.

Refael'ke's long pauses between words could exhaust a person. On this stroll, too, he was mostly silent while Zindel, who was older, kept blustering. "Tell me why your sister thinks it's all right for you to become a chalutz, for your brother Bentzion to take business courses, for your wayward brother abroad to muddle around with his philosophy books, but if I want to become a modern rabbi, not an old-fashioned one like your father, she either laughs or is furious with me. Make me see the sense of it."

"Bluma Rivtcha doesn't like a person who dwells in the middle of the road," the unruffled Refael'ke eventually replied, "and *you* want to stay there for the sake of a good career."

"That's not true!" Zindel took a stride forward, as if to prove he wasn't one to stop in the middle of a road. He was studying Talmud and legal texts, he insisted, and wanted to be an ordained rabbi because he *did* believe in eating kosher, in putting on tefillin, and in observing Shabbos. But laws aside, Jews did live their lives clinging to some bizarre customs. They feared not only God but also sooth-sayers, and they were convinced of the validity of superstitions to a degree that made sense only for idol-worshippers. Zindel neither believed in these strange practices nor did he want to pretend that he did. That was why he didn't want to be a rabbi in Poland. "Here an educated rabbi must always be on the defensive, always answering to accusations that he's a freethinker. But abroad, even an Orthodox rabbi has to be educated." Why must he be a rabbi in a small-town wooden synagogue with a flat roof shaped like a peasant's hat, instead of a spiritual leader of a Jewish community that has a brick synagogue with a stately marble staircase and large, magnificent windows? Also, he hated the idea of giving a sermon in the singsong style of an itinerant preacher. Instead of weaving convoluted explanations for Midrashic legends or recounting foolish stories from women's books of moral instruction, it would be so much more beautiful to speak in a cultured language—such as English or German—to quote verses from the Bible or from great poets, and to be dressed in a long black frock coat with a white collar. In that world, a rabbi was a respected personage, even by Christians. While in Poland and Lithuania, Jewish spiritual leaders were laughed at—even by Jews. "That is, if they aren't devout," Zindel concluded, and stopped abruptly, watching Refael'ke with suspicion. "I see you're laughing at me, too, just like your sister. In your family the children take after your fanatical grandfather, the Zembin rabbi. But he's a right-wing religious fanatic and you are left-wing religious fanatics—fanatics about freethinking. You don't know a middle road."

"A hand is either right or left. Have you ever seen a middle hand?" Refael'ke smiled, his dimples showing.

"But the head is in the middle," Zindel retorted.

Refael'ke liked this answer. He turned his gentle eyes toward Zindel and asked him in a whisper whether his grandfather knew of his plans. The corners of Zindel's mouth trembled.

"That's the reason my grandfather isn't letting me start the new term at Tachkemoni—because I confided in him regarding what I intend to do. Yes, my grandfather is enlightened, but he also takes a dim view of modern rabbis."

For a long while, Refael'ke wiped his glasses and rubbed the side of his nose, as he always did when forced to say something he didn't want to say. "I promise you I won't tell my father about this, but *you* must tell him. You know, of course, that my father is expecting you to marry my sister and eventually become the rabbi of Morehdalye."

Despite the mildness with which Refael uttered his comment, Zindel shuddered. He replied indignantly, "If your sister would agree to come with me, I'd tell your parents. But as long as she disagrees and keeps her distance from me, I have no obligation to tell them."

Zindel was incapable of living without secrets, so he concealed a tidbit even from his bride-to-be and her brother. Since he had to remain in Morehdalye for now because of his grandfather's decree, he had also begun studying English with a teacher. He didn't feel obligated to reveal this fact to the rabbi's family.

TZESNEH GINSBURG HAD BEEN studying foreign languages at the University of Warsaw. But when riots broke out against Jewish students, she cut her studies short and came home to Morehdalye.

In town, the girls from well-to-do homes flocked around her, and when she went on walks with friends, the group would erupt with laughter at her jokes. Tzesneh was thin, with a pale, gaunt face, big blue eyes that were cold and smart, and thin lips that featured a perpetual sneer and a mean smile. She seemed to be trying to conceal herself within her entourage as she made wisecracks about every young single man in the town.

"Tzesneh knows she isn't pretty," people would say about her, "and that's why she makes such stinging remarks about boys." Indeed, it appeared as if, given the choice, Tzesneh would choose to remain an old maid.

Bluma Rivtcha was also one of Tzesneh's friends, and Tzesneh would sometimes come by the rabbi's house. Sholem Shachne didn't like it. Fräulein Ginsburg gave off a whiff of big-city jocularity and debauchery, of the carelessly destructive capriciousness of an only child. Certainly, one couldn't learn modesty from her. But the rabbi had already become accustomed to refraining from giving his daughter his opinion about whom she should befriend.

Back in the middle of the summer, Bluma Rivtcha had introduced Tzesneh to Zindel Kadish and afterward asked her what she thought of him.

"He's a pretty one, but effeminate, with the face of a doll," Tzesneh replied coldly, scornfully.

"He just appears that way. His personality is not soft at all." Bluma Rivtcha flushed with resentment at Tzesneh's finding fault with Zindel as well.

Oftentimes, when a group of the town's girls were going for a stroll and Zindel Kadish walked by, always well-dressed and with a sweet smile on his lush lips, the girls would feel the heat rising to their faces and would lower their eyes. Only after he passed by would the Morehdalye maidens turn back to gaze for a long time at the handsome young man.

Tzesneh Ginsburg would also stare at him with moist eyes, her thin lips twitching with lust. But she was offended that he held himself aloof from her and so she poked fun at him, scoffing that he walked around like someone who does the earth a favor by stepping on it. "He considers himself so noble," she said, "that it's beneath him to share a bed . . . with himself!"

The girls all laughed, and in the meantime something else occurred to Tzesneh. "You can tell he's a dimwit just by looking at his sweet little-girl face."

With this statement, however, her friends disagreed. "Not true! Zindel is refined and educated. Not for nothing did Bluma Rivtcha choose him as her bridegroom."

Tzesneh shrugged her narrow shoulders. "I don't think I've ever seen an engaged couple act so distant," she said casually. "Those two hardly take even a stroll together."

And so Fräulein Ginsburg was quite surprised when one evening in late August, Zindel showed up at her door and asked to become her student. Since he wasn't returning to the rabbinical seminary in Warsaw, he wanted to take lessons in English from her three times a week. How much would it cost him?

Though she was used to always having a sarcastic remark on the tip of her tongue, Tzesneh's mouth now became as dry as the whalebone in her corset. Her pale face flushed, and her eyes lit up. She smiled, revealing two rows of dazzling, lustful teeth, ready to bite into Zindel's dimpled chin as if into a juicy apple. But just a moment later, she was speaking with the cool superiority of a teacher. She'd be pleased, she told him, to take him on as a student in English. They would discuss payment later. If he wished, they could even work out a trade; he could pay her by giving her Hebrew lessons.

Bluma Rivtcha found out about this from friends. "Why didn't you tell me you were learning English from Tzesneh Ginsburg?" she asked Zindel, laughing, when he came to their house for his lesson with the rabbi.

Furious at being stuck in a small town where nothing could be kept secret, Zindel replied angrily, "What's there to tell? Aside from Fräulein Ginsburg, who else is there in Morehdalye who can teach

English?" He gave her a meaningful look, trying to convey that of course he had to learn English. The place to which he intended to travel, the place to which Bluma Rivtcha did not want to accompany him, required a knowledge of English.

"Did Zindel tell you about this?" Bluma Rivtcha interrogated her brother later.

"No, he didn't," Refael'ke replied, serene as always, not understanding why his sister's face was so inflamed.

The rabbi's daughter remembered only too well the many times Tzesneh had supposedly mocked Zindel's effeminate appearance. Yet it seemed that it was precisely his softness and those hazy eyes that had attracted her—she, the mannish university student.

"Mameh, Mameh, Zindel is studying English with Tzesneh Ginsburg!" Bluma Rivtcha ran into the kitchen and blurted out this piece of news. But Henna'le couldn't understand why her daughter was laughing with so much rancor that her eyes filled with tears.

6

Tzesneh's father, Shmulik'l Ginsburg, dealt in watches and wedding rings, selling jewelry in the homes of wealthy Poles. A small, bouncy man with restless eyes, he moved about his home with the clever, sardonic little smile of a distant relative who knows more than he tells. When his wife and daughter fought, he never injected a word. And when the bickering between the two women grew worse, Shmulik'l would twist himself up on the couch, his little hand at his head, and fall asleep.

Tzesneh's mother, Gnendel, was in a constant state of agitation over her daughter, fretting that Tzesneh would be living at home till her braids turned gray. Whenever people came to visit, they were subjected to Gnendel's singing the praises of her brilliant daughter—her education, her success with boys. Even when the town girls came by and sat around the house poring over the photo albums Tzesneh had brought with her from Warsaw, Gnendel kept interfering.

"Oh, this is Professor Zovodsky, who wanted to convert to Judaism if only Tzesneh would marry him."

"Not true." Tzesneh raised a pair of hate-filled eyes at her mother. "Professor Zovodsky is certainly a friend of the Jews; that's why I accepted his autographed picture. But he never proposed to me and never wanted to convert for me. He has a wife and children!"

"Oh, I made a mistake. I confused him with Professor Julius Vilenchik. He's the one who wanted to convert for you," Gnendel replied coldly. "This same Vilenchik also told you that you learned more English in a year and a half than others learn in five years."

"Professor Vilenchik converted to Christianity. How could he have wanted to convert to Judaism for me?" Tzesneh jumped up, enraged.

"But for your sake he wanted to become a Jew again. What an exasperating daughter! She doesn't want anyone to know that she has a good head and that men like her," her mother sighed to the girls, who hadn't raised their heads from the photo albums, as if they'd heard nothing.

Unlike her tall, skinny daughter, Gnendel had plenty of flesh and fat squeezed into her tight brassiere and corset. Her stockings, skirt, and blouse were so stretched they looked like they were about to tear. She walked as if on springs, banging the floor with her high-heeled slippers, constantly digging her short, nimble hands into her wide, pudgy hips. As soon as the town girls left, mother and daughter would start bickering.

"No one believes a word you say," Tzesneh hissed in fury. "My friends repeat it to their families, to acquaintances on the street, and everyone chokes with laughter."

"Just because you laugh at everyone, you think everyone has your nature." Gnendel rolled her big eyes up to the hair piled high on her head.

Tzesneh bit her thin lips. "The girls are convinced that all those professors you mentioned were lovers who later rejected me."

"Better that than they should say that no men are interested in you. Silly girl! Do you have a better friend than your mother?"

BUT EVER SINCE the dayan's grandson, Zindel Kadish, had begun frequenting their home, Gnendel was feverish with hope. Perhaps her daughter had finally met her match—and royalty, no less! While Zindel and Tzesneh sat in her closed room for his lesson, Gnendel paced the other rooms on tiptoes so as not to disturb the "children." If she heard someone stepping onto their porch, she ran outside to warn him not to speak too loudly when he entered the house. She carefully moved the chairs around the table so they would not make any noise. She dusted the picture frames on the wall and repolished the samovar and the doorknobs so that everything sparkled as if it were brand-new and very expensive. On the table lay an embroidered tablecloth on which a porcelain kettle was steaming with freshly brewed tea. Glittering glass teacups vied with a gleaming silver sugar bowl. On a large tray sat a big, round lemon torte. Gnendel repowdered her face, piled the hair on her head even higher, and eavesdropped. Behind the closed door, the lesson dragged on. First the dayan's grandson had enunciated English words out loud. Then Tzesneh practiced some words in Hebrew. Eventually, the couple just chatted, quietly and comfortably.

Into the house came Gnendel's husband. Seeing refreshments on the table, Shmulik'l happily rubbed his hands together and meekly asked if he could have some tea and cake. But his toweringly coiffed wife turned toward him a pair of such voracious eyes that he crumpled up like a little rabbit.

"Go to the synagogue and loiter around near the dayan. Let him see that you attend services." She gestured with her head toward the room where the couple was sitting. "Go, I tell you!" she growled even more heatedly at her husband, and he shuffled out of the house without a word, with the slumped shoulders of a bent little man who's accustomed to being bossed around.

The tutor and her student sat in the small room at a table, which had been moved to the window facing an old, thick linden tree in the yard. Zindel didn't take his eyes off the English textbook, and Tzesneh didn't take her eyes off his rounded jaw and the delicate corners of his mouth. She felt a smile tugging at her lips; her pale, bony face glowed. His shoulders, she felt, were those of a strong and manly man, but the shape of his head and the way his hair curled were like a boy's. Zindel had already told her he was twenty-three. She'd considered then that, although she was only four years older, in experience she was way ahead of him. He was a ripe piece of fruit, with sweet sauce poured over delicious flesh but still untouched. At the thought that she could be the first woman to receive pleasure from him, Tzesneh felt a sense of euphoria pulsing behind her forehead, the veins in her temples throbbing. Her breath quickened and shudders ran through her, as though she had taken a long swig of vodka in one gulp. She hated her mother even more than usual, as Gnendel, ready with her matchmaking schemes, crouched like a spider on the other side of the door. Tzesneh imagined that the pictures on the wall, the two stuffed bookcases, the cupboard in the corner—they were all staring at them in silent astonishment and anticipation. *Will a wedding come of this?* they wondered. But Tzesneh refused to think that far ahead. She kept smiling provocatively, eagerly, a bit ashamed of herself that she couldn't tear her eyes away from Zindel's white neck beneath those stiff pink ears, where his curly black hair, thick and gleaming, came to an end.

As soon as they finished their English lesson, Fräulein Ginsburg put a book with large, bold Hebrew letters on the table. She turned to a page that had a graph for grammar: singular male, singular female, plural male, plural female. "Now you'll teach me Hebrew. I know a little," she said.

"One lesson right after another?" Zindel wondered. "You're not exhausted?" Tzesneh said no, she wasn't tired at all. But barely had they studied ten minutes before Tzesneh folded her long hands across the nape of her neck, twisted, stretched, and yawned several times.

"*Przepraszam!*" she excused herself in Polish, covering her mouth with her hand. Then, Tzesneh abruptly asked Zindel why he wanted to learn English. People were saying he was preparing to marry the rabbi's daughter and eventually become the rabbi of Morehdalye. Knowing just Polish would be more than enough if that were the case.

Annoyed as he always was at people wanting to know everything about him, Zindel replied—half resentfully, half charmingly—that the rabbi's daughter didn't yet want him. Tzesneh cackled straight into his face and told him she didn't believe him. Of course Bluma Rivtcha wanted to marry him, but maybe she just didn't want to travel to the ends of the earth with him and abandon her parents. Bluma Rivtcha was modern, but she was still a rabbi's daughter.

For a while Zindel sat there, astonished. "So she spoke to you? She told you?" he eventually mumbled, with as much distress as if the public had found out about a crime he had committed.

Tzesneh could barely contain her laughter. She moved from her chair to the sofa. "Bluma Rivtcha is a private person and she would never reveal such things. But when you said you wanted to learn how to read and speak English, I figured out the reason on my own. Obviously, you want to travel somewhere where English is the mother tongue . . . Aren't you uncomfortable sitting on that hard chair? Come and sit here on the sofa. You're not so religious that you're afraid to sit near a woman, are you?"

Zindel moved to the sofa, and for a long time they sat and talked. Tzesneh imagined all the blouses and jackets in her armoire listening along to everything the young man was saying. But the more he spoke, the cooler her hot, thin bones became. In his words she recognized a mixture of practical calculation and the ineptitude of a man who devotes all his time to sacred studies.

"I'm not in favor of a Reform synagogue with an organ and a women's choir; that's too much," Zindel said. "But one must admit it's much nicer when all the congregants sit in their places, rise from their seats simultaneously, and sing as one, as opposed to how it's done in our synagogues and Hasidic shtiebels, where everyone is at a different place in the service. We sway, we squash together, we shriek, and we run around like crazy people." Zindel glanced at his listener to judge the impression his words had made. Tzesneh looked out the window at the yard and the linden tree in the early autumn dusk. Her expression became serious for a moment, as if she were standing on a ship that was moving farther and farther away from a familiar shore. Zindel was a tasty morsel, she thought once again, but first he had to be made into a man. Her eyes, always moist and catlike, in the manner of spiteful people, were now, in the darkness, glowing with cunning and satisfaction.

"You must go back to Warsaw and complete your studies at the rabbinical seminary. For your career, it's important that you have the title of an educated rabbi. I'll probably also go back to Warsaw for the winter."

The two of them went from the dark little room into the great room, the light from all the lamps blinding them.

"The tea has already become cold. Sit down, children," Tzesneh's mother sang out, her left hand stuck to her hip and her right hand raised in the air, like a mother of the bride dancing toward the bride and the groom when they return from the chuppah. Seeing her mother dolled up in a long dress with a scarf tossed over her shoulder, Tzesneh's eyes glittered with wrath. As for Zindel, already intoxicated by the intimate turn his conversation with the fräulein had taken, and by her clever suggestions and hot breath, the refreshments arranged on the table and the mother's warm greeting served only to confuse him more. He sat down at the place Gnendel had indicated and watched as her short nimble fingers sliced the torte. The Morehdalye rebbetzin had never made such a festive occasion of his presence, despite considering him all but their daughter's fiancé.

"With my Tzesneh you'll learn more English in two months than in two years of Warsaw schools. Did you know, in Warsaw they wanted to make her professor!"

"Mother!" Tzesneh burst out, then bit her lip. To her annoyance, in front of Zindel she couldn't expose the lie.

Gnendel glanced at her daughter with a loving smile. "What's the matter, my child?" and continued talking to their guest: "Your grandfather, the dayan, doesn't know us well. My husband isn't the sort of person who hogs the spotlight, and our only daughter would never go around flaunting that she has more sense in the soles of her feet than most have in their heads."

Tzesneh's many attempts to interrupt her—"Mother, please!"—were all in vain.

Each time, Gnendel responded with the same loving smile, "What's the matter, my child?" and went on praising Tzesneh to the young man. Meanwhile, without realizing what she was doing, she filled all the glasses on the table with a strained dark red tea and sliced the entire torte into a deck of cards, as if their guest was meant to eat and drink it all.

7

B ESIDES HAVING A TASTE for handsome young men, Tzesneh
Ginsburg also enjoyed strangers' secrets. And a secret hovered
over Zindel Kadish. A riddle: Why had Zindel's parents gone to
Canada, gotten divorced there, and abandoned him to his grandfather? When Tzesneh asked him if his parents ever sent letters,
he looked uneasy and mumbled something incomprehensible. But
with the sharp, sinister eyes of a thieving cat, she treaded noiselessly,
extracting bits of information from the townspeople about the old
dayan, his son, and his former daughter-in-law.

The dayan, she was told, had a stomach disorder and had to eat
stale challah dunked in warm milk. He was a "tidy woman," losing
no crumbs in his long beard. His frock coat, shirt, and even his boots
were always clean. Pinned to the buttons on his vest, a pocket watch
dangled on a silver chain. In his bookcase, not a single volume lay
askew; on the stove, not a dirty dish in sight. Tzadok had become a
widower when he was still middle-aged and he'd never remarried. A
few times a week, a woman came to clean his home, and she claimed
she had almost nothing to do there. Even the bed he slept on looked
practically untouched, as if he had no body at all.

This was the sterile, cold-white cleanliness in which his son Beinush was raised—Beinush who, it seemed, was born tired and surly.
In town they barely noticed him growing up, so detached was he all
through childhood and adolescence. Later, he left to study in another
city and came back knowing Russian, Polish, and especially Hebrew.
No one, it was said, had a better grasp of Hebrew grammar. But
he wanted nothing to do with the youth studying modern Hebrew,
the ones preparing to emigrate to the land of Israel. Visitors to the
dayan's home would mention how Beinush always sat in the same
corner, silent, with a sulking, disgusted expression, as if he were sit-

ting in an empty railway station in the middle of the night and could hardly wait for a train to spirit him away.

In the Morehdalye talmud torah, his classmates were terrified of him. If another boy wronged him in some way, Beinush would dig into the boy's muscular flesh with such sharp nails, would glare at him with such ferocious, glittering eyes, that the victim was too stunned to even scream. The other boys disliked Beinush and poked fun at his persnickety manners. During lessons in class, he wore a large black silk yarmulke, which was constantly falling off his long, narrow head. He had to keep holding it in place with his hand, but he refused to wear a different one.

"With Beinush Kadish you can't win": those around him mocked his obstinacy, and no one doubted that he'd end up an old bachelor. Little could they have imagined that Shterke Teitelbaum would fall in love with him and marry him.

Shterke was a baker's daughter and the director of finances at the talmud torah where the orphans of Morehdalye and its environs learned, ate, and slept. Next to Beinush, Shterke looked like a strong, many-branched maple beside the thin, crooked root of a skimpy bush. Shterke had masculine shoulders, overlarge eyes, lips, and teeth, too-wide cheeks, and a thick neck. When she spoke, it sounded like a thunderous trumpet. Only her eyes twinkled with maternal goodness. Her large, warm hands seemed to have been created for cooking and cleaning, for caressing and calming. Friends asked her bluntly why she was attaching herself to such a bitter, dry soul. Was it because he was educated? Shterke laughed, marveling at them. "Don't you see that he's also handsome? And the reason he's so bitter is because he's been motherless since he was a child."

The Morehdalye girls of marriageable age had kept their distance from the dayan's son, so they hadn't noticed Beinush's deep, dark eyes and silky eyebrows, his well-wrought nose, precisely formed lips, and beautifully carved hands. But Shterke Teitelbaum—perhaps because of her masculinity—noticed, and because of her goodness she assumed she'd be able to transform him into a mellower person by clasping him to her breast as she did with the other orphans in the talmud torah.

Right after the wedding, Beinush Kadish and his wife left for Bialystok. He worried that if he stayed, Shterke would invite her family and friends to his home, where they'd make themselves much too comfortable.

But news soon reached Morehdalye of the couple's glum situation. Although Beinush had attained an excellent position as a teacher in a Yavneh school, and they'd found a nice apartment, Beinush still looked irritable, his brow perpetually furrowed, as if he'd misplaced an expensive object. He invited no one to his home, visited no one else, and demanded that his wife do the same.

A woman by the name of Mariasha Blum came back from Bialystok saying she'd visited her friend Shterke. With her own ears she'd heard Beinush Kadish harassing Shterke for having invited a friend over—two weeks earlier!—who wore her hair cropped and had stubbed her cigarette out in a tea tray filled with water. Though half a month had passed, Beinush shouted, he still felt like puking every time he recalled the cigarette filter smeared with the red tint of that visitor's swinish lips. "But if a woman allows herself to be called Shterke," he yelled, "it's no wonder she has a friend with no better taste than to crop her hair and dip a cigarette in a tea tray." Mariasha Blum said that the louder he shrieked, the harder his wife laughed, most likely out of embarrassment that her friend from town was there to hear this. "But you knew my name was Shterke before you married me," she laughed. And he replied that earlier he hadn't given much thought to what it meant that a woman should allow herself to be called Shterke all her life.*

Beinush Kadish never came to visit Morehdalye because of his loathing for the townspeople, and his wife never came because she was ashamed. Her relatives, too, upon returning from a visit to her in Bialystok, had no desire to speak about it. But when, after visiting Bialystok, the dayan Reb Tzadok was asked how the children were doing, he wrinkled his face up and said, "Good, very good." No one believed him. People in Morehdalye felt that beneath his big scraggly beard, the old dayan was just as evil as his son. But then the Morehdalyians found out that Shterke had become a mother. So perhaps the dayan hadn't fooled them. His son and daughter-in-law, it appeared, were living as husband and wife.

* The Yiddish word *shter* means "to spoil; to hinder." *Shterke* is a diminutive form of *Shterne*, which means "star." But in this case, it seems Beinush considers *Shterke* to mean "a woman who spoils things."

This same Mariasha Blum was burning to uncover the truth. So half a year later she traveled again to Bialystok, and came back wringing her hands. "Dearies, I really shouldn't say." But she did say, telling them what Shterke had told her: on his free days, she noticed, her husband left home with little sacks of kernels and bags filled with pieces of bread. She wasn't going to ask him what it was all about. If he didn't tell her on his own, she knew she could never pry it out of him. But one time, she followed him and watched as he sat down on a bench in the city park and fed the birds. Shterke was touched. The thought flashed in her mind that all of Beinush's peculiarities would vanish in smoke if, instead of feeding birds, he had a child to love. But as soon as their little infant came squealing into this world, the father squealed, too. He cried that he'd never felt lonesome when he'd been on his own, that all he'd desired his entire life was silence. Now it was worse than death for him. This time Shterke didn't laugh. She squealed, too, and even louder than her husband. He knew she was pregnant, she yelled. So why had he sat silent and let her have the child? He couldn't have imagined, he said, what his life would be like with a screamer in the house. According to Mariasha Blum, Shterke sobbed her heart out, beating her chest. "It's my own fault. It's not in my nature to get divorced. It's not!"

Even when Zindel began attending school and grew into a relatively quiet boy, his father went on screaming about the lack of peace in his home. The hatred between Beinush and the students in the Bialystok Yavneh school increased, becoming even greater than the former hatred between him and the Hebrew teachers in the Morehdalye talmud torah. Added to that, he began to fear that war would break out again. That the Bolsheviks, who held that all were equal and should intermingle, would again invade Poland. Beinush decided to leave Europe for Canada. On that side of the ocean, at least, it was quiet, and the vulgar and the educated didn't mix. He would leave Zindel with his grandfather in Morehdalye, meanwhile. Shterke, however, would accompany him. Beinush got his way. Shterke went along with the plan and left her little Zindel at his grandfather's.

Although Shterke had cried to her friends that divorce was against her nature, the truth was, she didn't know herself well enough. From the moment she settled in Canada with her husband, her world felt bare and desolate without her son, and she turned her husband's life into the same hell he'd made of hers in Bialystok. In a letter to Mariasha Blum, Shterke referred to Beinush not by his name but as "the epileptic," though he'd never actually suffered from epilepsy. "The epileptic," she wrote to her friend, "demanded that I accompany him here, because he's accustomed to me caring for him. He promised that as soon as we settled in, we'd send for our only son. But now he says that Zindel should stay with his grandfather a while. So I'm leaving him. Even if 'the epileptic' convulses and shakes like a madman, you can be sure that this time I'm leaving, especially knowing he'll be even more terrified to live in a strange country on his own. And, with God's help, as soon as I get myself organized, I'll bring my little boy here."

One-half of the plan Shterke carried out successfully. She divorced her husband. But the second half she could not achieve. No matter how much she pleaded in letters to her father-in-law, begging that he send her little son, her life's sole consolation, the old man replied that he, too, had no other consolation left but this one grandchild. Besides, such a young boy would be defiled the instant he set foot in the Americas. In Poland, meanwhile, Zindel would behave like others in town and learn both Torah and secular knowledge.

So year after year went by, and Shterke, who'd never remarried, continued writing letters to her former father-in-law and her growing son. Zindel replied with caution and trepidation, as if he weren't sure the one writing him was truly his mother. Zindel's grandfather, on the other hand, replied in a friendly, peaceable tone (with what seemed to Shterke a snide undercurrent), saying that Zindel had grown into a beautiful young man. He was studying in a Warsaw yeshiva that was also a university. Shterke in Canada and her relatives in Morehdalye were certain that the mad old dayan with the sickly stomach was taking revenge on his former daughter-in-law at the bidding of his son. In Morehdalye they discovered that Beinush Kadish had left his job as a teacher in Canada, finding it too chaotic to be involved with the students. He'd always had a good head and a certain diligence, so he studied English conscientiously and took courses to become a pharmacist. Now he was working in a pharmacy, filling and dispensing prescriptions.

Hearing this story, Tzesneh Ginsburg laughed heartily, displaying her cold, dazzling teeth. She pictured Beinush Kadish the pharmacist—standing between shelves of beakers and glass pots, stir-ring and weighing remedies, handing them with jittery fingers to his customers. And all the while uttering barely a word, his sour face never flashing a smile.

Whom did Zindel take after, his father or his mother, Tzesneh wondered, her chin becoming even bonier as she smirked. She counted on using Zindel's secret, the history of his divorced parents, to poke and prod him.

At the next lesson, Tzesneh again observed him obliquely, specu-lating that he'd inherited the pretty lines on his face from his father and his broad, strong body from his mother. But from what she'd seen, Zindel was neither as pathologically crazy as his father nor as good-hearted as his mother.

After Tzesneh's English lesson with Zindel, she stretched and yawned and explained that this time she wasn't in the mood for a Hebrew lesson. Just as before, she persuaded him to sit beside her on the couch. But instead of looking at Tzesneh, Zindel had become entranced by a picture on the wall—of two inky-brown horses in a sea-green meadow. The mare was standing and the foal was lying down.

"Every time I look at the colt, I feel like kissing his moist nostrils and raised ears. Just look at his sweet muzzle!" Tzesneh said, inch-ing closer to Zindel. But he continued to sit stiffly, now riveted by another picture: dressed in long, old-fashioned pleated dresses, hold-ing parasols over their wide-brimmed hats with colorful, fluttering ribbons, two women stood on a yellow sand dune observing the blue ocean. Zindel turned his head away from the painting and looked out the window, to the yard, where the linden tree teemed with golden autumn leaves. In the room it had begun to darken. Tzesneh's catlike eyes glittered more brightly.

"So how do you say in English 'I like you'?" she asked, and as he slowly enunciated the three words in English she tossed her arm around his neck. "You pronounce it exactly right. You must have already said it a few times in Polish or Yiddish to Bluma Rivtcha," Tzesneh teased.

"Not true," he replied calmly. "Bluma Rivtcha and I aren't all that interested in each other."

Tzesneh, too, wasn't all that interested in Bluma Rivtcha at the moment. All at once, Zindel felt a pair of damp, puckered lips on his mouth. A narrow, supple body, with taut breasts like hard goose-berries, pressed against his chest and forced his back to the sofa, lips still stuck to his mouth. Zindel couldn't catch his breath. He pushed her off.

"Are you not attracted to me, or do you not want to touch a woman because you're preparing to become a rabbi?" She gave a hoarse little laugh, and her hot breath scorched his face.

"What do you mean?" he answered, affecting innocence, and sat up slowly, still confused by her lustful lunge.

"Explain to me the difference between Orthodox and Progressive rabbis," she said, as if she were really curious, as if she hadn't intended to play around with him and therefore wasn't shaken by his rejection.

Zindel spoke enthusiastically, almost as if he'd been waiting to be asked. Meanwhile, Tzesneh ran her fingers through her tousled, chestnut hair. Shivers of unfulfilled desire coursed through her body. She was glad the darkness had dimmed the room, masking her fever-ish face. *Only with me is he such a cold fish*, she thought. *Just look at how passionately he talks about the clashes between rabbinical dynasties!* She interrupted him with a wicked little laugh. "I get it. The old-fashioned rabbi from here prefers long beards and wild, coiling peyes that have never seen a comb, while you hold with the modern Ortho-dox rabbis with their well-groomed beards and trimmed peyes. Am I right?"

"You're talking exactly like Bluma Rivtcha, and with even more derision." Annoyed, Zindel began to sulk.

"Bluma Rivtcha? I hadn't realized she was that sensible," Tzesneh prodded him again, hurt by his indifference. Then she threw both arms around his neck, as if to test whether he really wasn't afraid of women, like the other yeshiva boys. This time, Zindel didn't push her away. Surprised and elated, Tzesneh felt his fingers running down her spine to her hips, where he began stroking the cheeks of her skinny bottom. *Soon he'll be lying supine at my feet*, she thought, and wanted to show him how clever she was.

"Do you want to learn English and travel abroad so you can be an enlightened rabbi," Tzesneh exhaled into his ear with her hot breath, "or do you want to go to Canada to reunite your parents?"

Gnendel had always said it was this she-devil in Tzesneh, driving her to flaunt her cleverness, that frightened the desire out of boys. Tzesneh instantly felt Zindel's hands slipping from her body. He turned mute, not even bothering to utter his innocent "What do you mean?" Tzesneh tried to say something, to laugh, to kiss him. But he remained unflinchingly silent. So she switched on the electric lamp, and its pale reddish glow blinded them both.

"What's so terrible about what I said that has you offended?" she asked, astonished.

"How would you know if I'm thinking about going to Canada to make peace between my parents?" he asked. "And why should anyone go poking their nose into another person's life, anyway? How does anyone know what happened between my parents?" He became increasingly agitated. "You see? Bluma Rivtcha never speaks about these things with me."

If she didn't find him so attractive, she would have opened the door right then and told him to leave, or else stuck her long tongue out at him and laughed right in his face. Just look at how anxious he is, this yeshiva boy, thinking people shouldn't remember his parents' divorce. Must take after his father, the epileptic, the Hebrew teacher, and after his grandfather, the dayan, the pious stickler. A family of religious fanatics who turn everything into a secret. On the other hand, she had to admit, there was a certain boyish charm to his secretiveness. Well, for the time being, she wouldn't worry over what would come of all this. For the time being, what she wanted was to enjoy life and make her Morehdalye friends burst with envy. So she patted Zindel's forehead with her narrow hand and pacified him: starting today, she would no longer ask him anything or want to know anything he himself didn't tell her.

8

THE RABBI WONDERED WHY his daughter had stopped going out with friends. She slunk around the house and shuffled from room to room, grumbling under her breath. When she spotted Zindel through the window coming to his lesson, Bluma Rivtcha would lock herself in her room until he left. "Did they have an argument?" Sholem Shachne asked his wife. But Henna'le had no answer. And she didn't feel like asking her daughter either.

One day as they were getting ready to eat, at the precise moment the rabbi was reciting the blessing over the bread, Bluma Rivtcha, her face flushed, came into the room and burst out, "Father, it's time you knew the truth. Zindel Kadish wants to travel abroad and become a modern rabbi."

Other than a crust of bread dipped in salt—so that his blessing was not in vain—Sholem Shachne could eat nothing more for lunch. Henna'le's hands trembled. Only Refael'ke remained sitting serenely, defending Zindel. What crime was Zindel committing, after all? He wasn't planning to flee and convert to Christianity. All he wanted was to marry Bluma Rivtcha and become a rabbi in a Jewish community abroad.

Bluma Rivtcha glanced at her brother and said furiously, "Yes, Zindel *did* mumble something about me joining him, but he didn't mean it. He wanted to know if I liked the plan, but what he was really saying was that he's found a source of greater happiness in his life than me."

Sholem Shachne paced the dining room. Choked by agitation, he muttered to himself, "A pious boy, a scholar, is too old-fashioned for Bluma Rivtcha. So I agree to an educated boy, not much of a Torah scholar, but at least someone sincere, a devout Jew. And Zindel isn't even a devout Jew. Heretics and libertines do less harm to Jewishness than these rabbis out deceiving the world with their two-bit Judaism.

"And you"—Sholem Shachne turned to his son, incensed—"you knew about his plans and didn't tell me?"

But Refael, keeping his cool, claimed he hadn't said anything because he didn't want to cause his father pain. Plus, Zindel wasn't actually going anywhere yet; it was merely a dream for the future. And Zindel had no intention of turning Reform. He wanted to get his rabbinical certification so he could rule on Jewish law. So why did he have to be a rabbi in Poland specifically? Why couldn't he be one in America?

"I won't give him rabbinical certification, I don't trust him anymore, and I won't entrust my daughter to him!" The rabbi paced back and forth with increasing feverishness.

"He's not taking me yet, and I'm not going yet." Bluma Rivtcha laughed with flaming cheeks.

"I don't even want to give him lessons in Talmud and Yoreh De'ah anymore," Sholem Shachne cried.

Bluma Rivtcha leaped up. Anger turned her cross-eyed, her pupils meeting at the tip of her nose. She stamped her feet, crying that if her father won't study with Zindel, people will say she's jealous of Tzesneh Ginsburg.

Sholem Shachne shrugged. He had no understanding of such womanish sophistry. But then his rebbetzin entered the scene. He was being a tempestuous little boy, she argued. No wonder all his sons had scurried away from him as fast as they could. Before anything else, he should have a talk with the dayan. Zindel's grandfather still held some sway over his grandson.

But Zindel had already won permission from his grandfather to return to Warsaw's Tachkemoni. He'd argued that without a diploma from the rabbinical seminary, he couldn't become a government-recognized rabbi even in Poland. And if he could successfully make it to Canada, he'd become a devout rabbi there and bring his grandfather over. All of them—Zindel, his father, and his grandfather—could live together. Here in Morehdalye, however, the rabbi's Bluma Rivtcha was still ambivalent about becoming engaged to him. As if he were damaged goods!

So when Sholem Shachne initiated the conversation with the

dayan in the beis medrash, Tzadok smiled, revealing all the wrinkles and folds of his hairy face, and said, "Looking at the facts, I don't get why you don't want your daughter and son-in-law to live in a country where Jews aren't harassed. In Morehdalye, Zindel would be a rabbi earning a pittance, slandered by his congregants, who'd claim that a student of Tachkemoni was neither scholarly enough on one hand or devout enough on the other. In Morehdalye, after all, the custom has always been to wrest the rabbinical inheritance from those who were rightfully owed the position according to Jewish law."

As meticulous and circumspect as the dayan was with his clothing and appearance, so too was he with his words. But those who knew him intimately knew that the more benevolent Tzadok's smile looked, the greater the fury it masked. Nevertheless, his face gave nothing away. Sholem Shachne's face, on the other hand, could be read like an open book, revealing all he felt inside. When Tzadok had crooked his finger, hinting at the time when his claim to his father's rabbinical seat had been stolen from him by the Katzenellenbogens, Sholem Shachne responded from his heart, gesturing with both hands:

"How can you say you don't understand why the young couple shouldn't settle in America? In America a rabbi has no say over his Shabbos-desecrating congregants. In America your average laymen are leaders and shammoshim of the synagogue! Zindel may well become a rabbi in a temple where men and women sit together, where people pray in watered-down prayer books." The longer Sholem Shachne spoke, the more hotheaded he became and the larger his eyes grew behind his big round spectacles.

Conversely, Tzadok's eyes grew steadily smaller, sinking more deeply into his bristly face. He tugged so long at a hair in his mass of beard that he finally succeeded in plucking a response from it. "In the beginning I, too, was worried about Zindel being corrupted there. But he's assured me that he'll be a rabbi in a synagogue for people like us, and I believe him. We're discussing all this based only on Jewish law; it's no sin to want to travel. And the fact is, he hasn't gone anywhere yet. Besides, my grandson tells me your daughter isn't even sure she wants to be his wife. At any rate, after Sukkos, with God's help, Zindel will go back to Tachkemoni, and if the match is divinely ordained, it will stand."

. . .

SHOLEM SHACHNE UNDERSTOOD, in the end—and he didn't hide this knowledge from his daughter: the dayan and his grandson wished for the marriage arrangement to hang in the air for the time being.

When Zindel's grandfather told him about his conversation with the rabbi, Zindel stopped coming to the rabbi's home for his lesson, to avoid being eyed as an imposter. And Bluma Rivtcha no longer waited for him. She gazed out the window aimlessly, watching the trees near the house ablaze in wine-red colors. As long as the trees were leafy, one couldn't see into the house from the street, and the house felt protected. But when the leaves fell, she knew, she'd no longer be able to stand at the window looking out. Rumors would spread that she was pining after the dayan's grandson.

At times, Bluma Rivtcha strolled with Refael'ke on the footpaths among the mowed fields, walking up to the bridge above the Narev. Brother and sister gazed out over the railing at the water, inhaling the raw smell of rot. Leaden waves rolled with the begrudging groan of weary travelers, chased from their resting spot and told to move on. No, she wasn't in love with Zindel, Bluma Rivtcha told herself, and he was even less in love with her. He considered marriage in the same practical terms as he did a diploma from Gymnasium or rabbinical certification. All the girls in town, Bluma Rivtcha knew, were gossiping that Tzesneh Ginsburg had snatched the handsome, educated boy away from her. Well, let them gossip.

But when Zindel Kadish stepped into the rabbi's house after Sukkos to bid them farewell, Bluma Rivtcha addressed him cheerfully and asked if he'd be able to catch up on the courses he'd missed.

"And you won't come to Warsaw in the winter?" he asked her, not knowing where to look.

"Me? What would I do in Warsaw?" Bluma Rivtcha laughed the way an adult would at a child asking them to join in a little dance.

The rabbi pressed Zindel's hand for a long while and said to him sincerely, "Go in health and peace, and don't forget the Torah we learned."

Rebbetzin Henna'le, too, had resolved not to remind the dayan's grandson of his promises, and merely wished him that his grandfather would derive much joy from him. Refael'ke escorted Zindel out, and Bluma Rivtcha burst into ebullient laughter, saying to her dumbfounded father and mother, "I will certainly not be traveling to Warsaw, but Zindel's English teacher, Tzesneh, will go back to university in Warsaw this winter—you can be sure of that."

9

O N THE WILLOW TREES outside the rabbi's house sagged the last sodden clusters of withered leaves, just as they had the year before and the year before that. Bluma Rivtcha waited for the first snowfall, hoping it would brighten her mood and ease her heavy heart. But the gray, murky autumn with its oppressive clouds refused to end.

On one such muggy, leaf-dropping day, Bluma Rivtcha discovered that her prediction about Tzesneh Ginsburg had materialized even earlier than she'd expected. Although Tzesneh had told everyone during the summer that she wasn't returning to university in Warsaw, because of persecution by antisemitic students, she did, in fact, go back after Zindel Kadish left for Tachkemoni.

"Everyone's going somewhere to study, trying to achieve something; I'm the only one not allowed, because education *contaminates* you. All I can do is be a wife, a Jewish woman, a rebbetzin. But I want to go off and learn a skill, too—though of course it's too late for me anymore to be educated the way Tzesneh Ginsburg is," the rabbi's daughter cried all through the house, so that her father, mother, and brother would hear her. But no one there responded. They felt that Bluma Rivtcha wasn't truly ready yet to carry out her plan of learning a profession. She herself was questioning whether it wasn't too late to begin. In her father's heart, hope ignited anew: Now that she saw how little the integrity of an educated person like Zindel Kadish was worth, might she not agree to a match with a sincerely pious boy, a Torah scholar? God could still provide.

The naked branches accrued a layer in frosty dew. The sky gradually changed its complexion from watery blue to silver-gray. The air filled with light snowflakes that fell to the ground with a flutter, a twitch. But Bluma Rivtcha's hope that a snowfall would lighten her heart had been in vain. And the good news that her sister, Tilza, was pregnant didn't bring her comfort either. This news had reached the family in a letter addressed to the rabbi from his son-in-law, Yaakov Asher. The letter began as usual: first the phrase "With God's help"; then a verse from the weekly Torah portion; and then an honorific to his father-in-law, the eminent Talmudic scholar. These were followed by his presentation of the good news, in which he managed to insinuate, between one rabbinical stylistic flourish and another, that his dear wife was not too pleased with the situation.

"Why should she be unhappy?" the rabbi asked his wife.

Henna'le removed the folded sheet of paper from her husband's hands and fiddled with it for a while, touching its words as if to elicit their secret. Finally, she replied, "Maybe Tilza is afraid of a difficult birth? She had difficulties the first time around."

She's unhappy about her pregnancy because she doesn't like her husband—the thought flashed through Bluma Rivtcha's mind. And to avoid shouting it aloud to her father, she ran to her room.

A week later came another letter from the son-in-law, and this time, without any rabbinical flourishes, he explained that Tilza was leaving their little boy with him while she traveled to her parents in Morehdalye. Outside, the wind and snow swirled, and the air must have been whirling around the rabbi, too, for he looked at his wife with a confused, incredulous expression. Henna'le rushed to calm him.

"All right, so our daughter is feeling a bit nostalgic for home. Nothing wrong with that, is there? Yaakov Asher will stay with his child for a little while. That's no calamity."

Tilza, big yellow stains beneath her eyes, arrived on the first day of Chanukah, wearing a long, frumpy dress and a thick knitted jacket. Her mother greeted her with concern, her younger sister with curiosity, and her father with suspicion. Tilza hugged Refael'ke and began to sob, "I've been even lonelier since you left Lecheve."

Her father turned glummer, but didn't speak.

"You've been feeling homesick for your mother's Chanukah latkes?" Rebbetzin Henna'le joked, with a fake little laugh to smooth things over. But her little laugh seemed to grow frightened of itself, and, like a scrawny chicken, it retreated into a nook of the large shadowy kitchen.

All year long, the copper menorah adorned with lions sat on the windowsill of the rabbi's beis din chambers, waiting patiently for Chanukah evenings, when it could beam out over the dark, wintry landscape. But the sole red flame could not melt the ice on the eaves or light the public square, the synagogue street. Sholem Shachne hummed the Chanukah melody morosely under his breath, "Maoz Tzur . . . O Mighty stronghold of my salvation." His two daughters, the short rebbetzin, and his youngest son stood a bit apart from him. All around them, shadows huddled thickly. Only on the ceiling was there a bright, trembling disk—the reflection of the first Chanukah flame. Even this holiday, the rabbi thought—the holiday of the miraculous cruet of olive oil—could not unite him with his children, not even for a quarter of an hour. Each one of them was occupied with whatever they hadn't attained or whatever they still hoped to attain in their lives.

After supper, Sholem Shachne and Refael'ke retired to the beis din chambers to study the Talmud, while the three women remained seated at the dining room table. Tilza's wistful glances wandered the room, pausing on the cupboard filled with glass dishes, the mirror on the wall, the table with the Shabbos candelabrum. Everything hung or rested in the same corners as always. All at once, she burst out, "I don't want to have another child! It's still early on; I'm going to do something about it. That's why I came here."

"Tilza! Don't bring those words to your lips in front of your father!" Her mother wrung her hands and pinched the folds of skin on her face.

"I won't tell Father, and I didn't openly tell my husband either. But he understands that I don't want to have another child with him."

"If someone dislikes their husband that much, they don't have to live with him," Bluma Rivtcha blurted, impetuous, belligerent.

Henna'le jumped up and waved her hands about as if extinguishing a fire. Tilza turned to her sister and said she didn't hate her husband. No, she was full of guilt because he was doing everything he could to make her happy. But still, she couldn't live his sort of life.

"Just now, when you're pregnant with your second child, you decide to remember your girlish fantasies?" With dry fingers, Henna'le thumped the edge of the table.

Tilza closed her eyes and let out a heavy sigh. Yes, just now she was suffering more than before. As long as she had only one child, she still dreamed that some change would occur in her life, though she didn't know which form that change would take and who would bring it about. But the moment she became pregnant again, a sense of powerlessness and disbelief washed over her. She could already see herself sinking deeper in the Lecheve swamps. Her scarf dipping lower over her eyes, and Yaakov Asher's beard and peyes growing longer, thicker, wilder.

The more Tilza spoke, the more Bluma Rivtcha's mouth twitched with barely contained wrath. Her older sister had always been so immersed in her fantasies that she'd never noticed life around her, or what was happening to herself. Tilza had never thought that a woman should have a profession and be financially independent. The princess had simply waited for a prince to carry her off to a magical palace. Well, then! Her red-bearded Jew had finally arrived, whisked her to Lecheve, and turned her into a rebbetzin.

10

SHOLEM SHACHNE WAS STILL FRETTING, probing Tilza's motives for coming to Morehdalye, when the fifth day of Chanukah brought him a new aggravation. His older brother, Avraham Alter, the moreh hora'ah in Bialystok, informed him in a letter: "Your son Bentzion avoids my home. All I know is that he works in a factory during the day and is taking business courses in the evenings. But he never steps into my home, so I can't answer your question about how he's getting on. My suggestion is that you come here and find out for yourself."

That evening as he lit the olive oil wicks in the menorah, the rabbi watched the five entwining little flames melt the ice on the windows. *Just think*, the rabbi reflected, *tomorrow, the eaves will once again be covered in white frost. And it's the same with me. I struggle, I struggle like Job, till I finally reach some sort of understanding of why God punished me with so much grief in raising my children. But as soon as the perpetual anguish in my heart begins to thaw, a new frost, a new affliction, appears.*

"What do you think?" Sholem Shachne asked his wife. "Has Bentzion already joined the Leftist unions?"

"Absolutely not!" she replied at once. "Bentzion's just the opposite of our other children. He was never interested in saving the world. Still, as a father, you should go down there and find out what's happening with him."

"Now I should leave home, when Tilza has to be sent back to Lecheve?"

But the rebbetzin assured him he had nothing to worry about with his older daughter. She would soon miss her little son and go back on her own, without their having to argue about it. And, in time, she'd give birth to her second child.

"Shameless woman! She ran here to cause her husband even more grief!" the rabbi huffed in a rage. And the rebbetzin barely—just barely—managed to restrain him from going in to Tilza and stamping his feet at her, or worse, driving her out into the frost.

Then Sholem Shachne had a long consultation with the ringlets of his gray beard. He tweaked them and tweaked them and finally let Henna'le know that he wouldn't be going straight to his son in Bialystok. Just like all other rabbis, he had promised to travel to a few towns twice a year to collect funds for the yeshivas, and this year he'd yet to go anywhere. So he planned on making a small detour on the way to Bialystok, to stop at Ostroleka and appeal to the Jews there for funds. Besides, there was something he wanted to discuss with the Ostroleka rabbi.

The rebbetzin gave her husband a look of surprise, mixed with a hint of alarm. She knew he'd once had his eye on the Ostroleka rabbi's son as a match for Bluma Rivtcha. Now that it was pretty much over between Bluma Rivtcha and Zindel, Sholem Shachne was probably thinking of giving this match another try. But the young man in question was so fervently pious that Bluma Rivtcha would never in her life agree. Her father, however, was incapable of grasping this; in his own way, he was as much of a fantasizer as his daughter Tilza. All of this ran through Henna'le's mind, but she didn't utter a word. She just clapped her hands like a chicken would its wings: "In such bitter cold," she cried, "you're going to slog from station to station till Ostroleka?"

"Torah scholars shouldn't have to starve because of bad weather," the rabbi replied despondently, and the rebbetzin understood: In Morehdalye, he was ashamed to preach that the world existed in the merit of those who studied Torah. Were he to say such a thing, his congregants might not go so far as to interrupt his sermon, but many would think to themselves: *If Torah scholars are the pillars of the world, then why did your own sons abandon their studies?* So here in town he remained silent. But in Ostroleka, where no one knew of the drama in his home, he could say whatever he thought and felt.

With his fur coat and shtreimel on, ready to leave, the rabbi went to bid farewell to his youngest son in an empty room. Under his left arm he held his bulging tallis bag, and his right hand he placed on Refael's shoulder. "You're the youngest. But at times you show more thoughtfulness than your older brothers and sisters. See to it while I'm away that—heaven forbid—things don't fall apart here."

Refael'ke stared up for a while at his father with a mute gaze and a wise, gentle smile before he responded, "You once told me there are times when the best solution is to hand the keys over to the thief, so that he'll be embarrassed to steal. I'm not such an honest thief, yet I can't bring myself to 'steal' another's knowledge. So I'm telling you outright: I can't be, nor do I wish to be, the guard."

Sholem Shachne placed his tallis bag on the table and began to unbutton his fur coat. "I get it! You haven't given up your desire to become a chalutz! I'm not going, I'm not going, I have no more strength for all of you. Oy, God Almighty!"

Refael'ke placed the tallis bag beneath his own arm, escorted his father out, and replied serenely, "Father, you can go. No need to worry that something will happen before you get back. Nothing will happen. Even when something changes in Morehdalye, it changes very gradually."

Maybe it's all my fault, the rabbi thought when already en route. After all, he knew his children weren't out to break his heart; on the contrary, none of them had become an apostate out of spite. So he had no choice but to admit that he simply hadn't been successful, that he'd failed to instill in them the sense and strength to rebuff the trends of the times. But how, then, had the Ostroleka rabbi succeeded in influencing *his* children to follow a righteous path?

The Ostroleka rabbi, Yom Tov Lipa Kaplan, was more famous in the rabbinical world for his poverty than for his Torah scholarship. He didn't even own a threadbare fur coat and a ragged shtreimel— clothes that even a poor Torah scholar gets once in his life, for his wedding. At gatherings among the rabbis, he showed up dressed like a peasant Jew, in a tall stiff hat with a brim. The weekly salary he received from his little town wasn't enough to cover even three days of the week for him and his large family. Nevertheless, there was no chance of his acquiring a position in a larger community, since he was neither a friendly person, nor a good speaker, nor did he have a reputation as a great scholar. There was a distance, a sense of reserve between him and the residents of his little town. Although his name was Yom Tov, meaning "holiday," no festive spirit ever showed on his face. A tall, slim man, dour and cold, he smelled of the dust of

crumbling texts in a vacant synagogue. Stubbornness and distrust—
the kind one associates with long-haired meditators in dark, mossy
woods—wafted from him.

He had a houseful of children, and they all grew up to be as fervently pious as their father. Because he couldn't afford a dowry, he was
unable to attract sons-in-law who were good students of the Torah;
consequently, his older daughters didn't marry exemplary yeshiva
boys, and after the wedding these men became either insignificant
religious functionaries in town or shopkeepers in the surrounding
area. His sons Yom Tov Lipa sent to separate yeshivas, fearing they'd
be too comfortable together, that they'd act too casual and brotherly
or fight with each other, instead of immersing themselves in Torah.

The oldest son went to study in Mir. Sholem Shachne had traveled
there to choose a bridegroom for his younger daughter, and though
a hive of exceptional scholars had swarmed around him, it was precisely this quiet son of the Ostroleka rabbi who'd caught his eye.
By outward appearances, the boy was unremarkable—scrawny, with
a gaunt face and gray eyes. But his smile beamed kindness, intelligence, refinement. His high forehead shone with erudition and common sense. As Sholem Shachne spoke to him of Torah and Talmud,
he observed the Ostroleka boy's hands. They exuded nobility—the
hands an angel kept beneath its wings. In his heart, Sholem Shachne
pined for such a son-in-law. He could not understand why this boy
hadn't been snatched up yet. Heavens! What had happened to Jewish
girls! Could they no longer discern the qualities of such an outstand-
ing boy? But neither could he, at that point, think of presenting such
a man to Bluma Rivtcha. No way would she have then considered an
accomplished Torah scholar. But now, however, after being burned by
Zindel Kadish, she would know how to appreciate this Ostroleka boy.

From the train station to town, Sholem Shachne had to ride
another six kilometers by wagon. He was the lone passenger in a
wide upholstered sleigh, which sliced through the woods along a
winding trail. The snowy trees, with their outstretched branch-hands
and crystalline fingers, looked to him like a congregation of Jews
from the great beyond, reciting an eternal hymn to God's oneness. A
calm descended on Sholem Shachne. His heart quivered with hope,
as the midday sun had earlier quivered like gold on the snow-coated
branches. He himself couldn't understand where this certainty rose

from, the certainty that, should Yom Tov Lipa consent to the marriage match, Bluma Rivtcha, too, would agree this time. The question was how to win the Ostroleker's trust. Since his own children
obeyed him, he'd look askance at someone whose children didn't.

"And how's your rabbi, Reb Yom Tov Lipa, doing?" Sholem
Shachne said to the Jewish coachman's back.

"What should he be doing? He's marrying off his oldest son." The
coachman swiveled around toward the passenger. "Rabbis almost
never wander into our hick town, so as soon as I saw you and you
asked me to take you to our rabbi, I figured you must be the bride's
father. Am I right?"

When his passenger gave no reply, the coachman turned back
toward his horses. He was wearing a sheepskin coat and a tall fur
cap that sunk down to his eyes, and had a sprawling black beard and
large, coal-black eyes. For a moment, the rabbi imagined the coachman was a masked bandit, leading him to his gang of robbers in the
woods. He should grab his tallis bag, crawl furtively under the sleigh,
and flee into the depths of the forest, draping his tallis over his head
so that the robbers would think he was a tree and pass him by. Sholem
Shachne wiped the beads of sweat from his forehead. His fright, he
realized, was mere hysteria, brought on by his great disappointment
that the Ostroleka rabbi's son was already engaged.

Flanked by trees, they rode along the border of a wide valley
between wooded mountains. Beneath them, squat houses huddled
together, half-buried in snow, as if terrified by the endless, dazzling
vastness, the high blue sky, and the bright golden sun—all peering
down as if astonished and delighted by that little settlement amid
a desert of snow. The panorama of this wide-open terrain freed
something in the rabbi, too, easing the tightness in his chest for a
while. He sighed, relief and lightness coursing through him, and
began to reproach himself: How many complaints he had against
God, for punishing him with troublesome children! But didn't God
have even more complaints against him? He'd done nothing for the
sake of Judaism in his community! And even now, traveling for once
on behalf of his yeshivas, he had a match for his daughter in mind!
Well then, he'd gotten the punishment he deserved even before he
reached Ostroleka.

11

O N AN EMPTY TABLE stood a tall, weighty copper candelabrum, engraved with ornamental flowers and buttons—the
sole object of beauty in that barren room. A wall clock gazed out
with a deadened yellowed face, its pendulum swinging—at the fierce,
monotonous pace of a dutiful soldier marching alone: One-two!
One-two! There was no rug on the floor, no curtain over the windows, not even a sofa with a plush cover to absorb the clock's fierce
clanging. Instead of chairs, long rough-hewn planks lined both sides
of the table. The glass panes were missing in the bookcase doors. On
the spot of earth near the brown brick oven lay a stack of wood with
pieces of bark for lighting a fire. The Ostroleka rabbi was known to
keep his distance from the villagers, and in much the same way, his
little home stood at quite a remove from the other huddled houses.
No matter how hard the family tried, their oven would not retain
heat, and the rabbi possessed that same coldness and aloofness, looking more like a common village Jew. He sat on a chair at the head of
the table, one hand on his forehead, the other on a closed Talmud, as
if to keep his unexpected guest from knowing which tractate he was
studying.

The guest, in his rabbinical shtreimel and fur coat, had been sitting at the table for some time and still didn't know how to start
the conversation. Like the Ostroleka Yom Tov Lipa, the Morehdalye Sholem Shachne wasn't the sort with a knack for making small
talk, or spouting rabbinical aphorisms, or even steering a conversation toward the Torah in order to show off his learnedness. But
the silence was lingering too long, and left with no choice, Sholem
Shachne began to speak. "Ostroleka Rabbi, I hear you're due a mazel
tov; your eldest son is engaged. Who's the father of the bride?"

"A rabbi," Yom Tov Lipa replied, with little enthusiasm. "The Korniker rabbi, Reb Nissen Pinnes."

"The Korniker rabbi? Reb Nissen Pinnes?" Sholem Shachne creased his forehead, turning his skin into a map of dots and lines for towns and rivers. "I must admit, I've never heard of this community or this rabbi." He said this without arrogance or disdain, but with, perhaps, a bit too much astonishment.

A peeved smile flickered on Yom Tov Lipa's lean and angular face, and he replied in a deep grumble. "My mechuten is not known as a legendary Torah scholar or community activist. For me and my son, the most important thing is that he's devout and his children obey him. That's why my son has waited so long. He wanted a bride from a suitable family."

In these words, Sholem Shachne heard what he'd already guessed at earlier: Yom Tov Lipa would never have allowed his child to marry into Sholem Shachne's family. Both rabbis sat quietly for a while, listening to the stillness of the snow-covered valley outside, shrouded in the foggy breath of the surrounding wooded mountains. The clock's pendulum persisted with its stern, monotonous clang. Finally, Sholem Shachne spoke again: "Ostroleka rabbi, by regulation of the gatherings in Vilna and Grodno, I've come here to collect funds for the Vaad HaYeshivos."

"No purpose in collecting money in Ostroleka. The people who can afford it and want to give have already sent their money," Yom Tov Lipa replied. Annoyed, Sholem Shachne tugged at his beard.

"So you're telling me I've traveled in vain," he said gloomily, then quickly reversed course. "Actually, perhaps I haven't. If you'll settle a question I've been wrestling with, then my trip won't have been for naught. I'm sure you know—as do all the rabbis in our area—that my children don't wish to follow in my footsteps. God knows, I've done all I can to set them on the right path, no less than you did. So why were you successful when I wasn't?"

"How should I know what's happening in another's home?" Yom Tov Lipa said, seeming to address his two mute friends on the table: the black linen-covered Talmud and the copper candelabrum. "But since you're asking me, here's what I think: Perhaps your children saw too much luxury, too many worldly pleasures, in your home, so now they desire more?"

For a moment, Sholem Shachne just sat there, bewildered. "How many worldly pleasures have I indulged in," he said resentfully, "that my children should take me as a model and go looking, as you claim, for even more?"

But the Ostroleka rabbi was unmoved by his guest's anger. He sat up stiffly, speaking toward the bookcase in the corner of the room. "The children of rabbis hear from their fathers that this world is a gateway to another world, that life is like the shadow of a bird flitting by, and that only those who've prepared on the eve of Shabbos will have food for the eternal Shabbos in the world to come. But after these fathers have finished uttering all these wise and sincere words from the Sages, the children observe how these very same fathers literally kill themselves to have Shabbos and holiday indulgences— drinks, rich soups, fish and meats, tzimmes, kugel, and taygelach; sweet pastries, fruits and compotes of all kinds. The children see how their fathers, the rabbis, squabble with their towns for a raise in wages. They sew themselves fur coats, clothing of silk and satin. In the summers, they go on vacation, where they graze like cows. When it comes time to marry off their children, they speak of tremendous dowries and throw weddings fit for barons. As for Jewish law, they're fine, of course, no problem there. After all, they eat only the most strictly kosher meat and drink only the most strictly kosher wine. When they sew new clothing, they're careful to avoid shatnez. But the children are more forthright than their fathers, so they question: If the soul is what's most important, does it really need so much rich kosher meat? And if we wear clothes that, even without mixing wool and linen, are nonetheless beautiful clothes, won't that lead to pride? And to push to become a rabbi in a larger city, with greater pay and greater honor, to be prepared to fight with opponents over this—is that permitted? When children see this, they say, 'Well, if we're permitted kosher worldly pleasures, why should we not be permitted non-kosher worldly pleasures?'"

Yom Tov Lipa's sorrowful face lit up with his loathing of these well-to-do religious functionaries, and his voice boomed and echoed like the felling of trees in a distant forest. "Even this habit of rabbis, traveling around to yeshivas in search of a distinguished scholar to take as a groom for their daughter, it reeks of arrogance and loathsome pleasure-seeking. And if the rabbi can't find the appropriate scholar, he lets his daughter linger, or else he stops caring whether she marries someone who's not observant. I didn't have dowries for any such exceptional scholars. The young men I found for my daughters are by no means earth-shattering intellects, but they're sincere, and they're devout. Now, my oldest son—you know, of course, he's one of the brightest boys in Mir and could have become the son-in-law of a big-city rabbi. But he looked not for a family that could pride itself on its scholarliness, or its pedigree, or its wealth—but for a family with no division between parents and children; a family in a quiet settlement, where he'll be able to sit tranquilly and study. I hope his younger brothers studying in Kletsk and Radin will follow his example."

"And how do you get along with your congregants?" Sholem Shachne asked, no longer able to resist taking his own shot at the Ostroleka preacher—who held sway over his children, yes, but could not say the same for his worshippers.

But the provincial-looking rabbi replied, with utter confidence, that while he didn't fight with his congregation members, they knew well what he thought of them. "The Jews here assume that by fasting on Yom Kippur they atone for a year's worth of feasting and guzzling."

"But your answer doesn't account for everything." Sholem Shachne rubbed his hands together. They were cold, but his heart felt even colder. "I know Jews who fast every Monday and Thursday, make do with a crust of bread between fasts, and even these Jews have children who sometimes stray." He sat silently, head tilted, and thought to himself: *On a cold day like this, the Ostroleka rabbi doesn't think to offer his guest a glass of hot tea.* Still, he did not regret his trip to this godforsaken village. He now knew something he hadn't before. Bluma Rivtcha wouldn't be a suitable match for this rabbi's son even if he weren't engaged. "Ostroleka Rabbi, I can't travel back today. I'm exhausted from the trip. Besides, I heard that the nearest train stops at your station only after midnight. Which means I'd have to ride to the station through dark woods. Is there an inn in your town?"

"There is not. You'll have to sleep here." The rabbi stood, his head nearly touching the ceiling. He stepped toward the corner with his bookcase and rapped his fist several times on the wall. The knocks echoed as in a wasteland. "I'm calling my rebbetzin from the room where you'll sleep. It's warmer there. You can use your fur coat as a quilt," Reb Yom Tov said, and retook his seat. He propped his hands behind his head and sank back into silence, his eyes wandering to the tall copper candelabrum. He looked like a man meditating in the woods, immersed in a mute and mystical prayer.

Into the room came the rebbetzin—an elderly woman, heavy as if swollen, with a wrinkled, anguished face. But her eyes shone with goodness, and with the joy of one who's survived a serious illness, grateful to God for the chance to see the light of another day. The rebbetzin wore a heavy sheitel, a long black dress, and a gray wool knitted sweater. Her arms dangled weakly; her shoulders arched backward as if she were unable to straighten her spine. But she gazed upon her husband with such a pair of eyes, as if she knew her life were owed to him and his prayers. And he, in return, stared back at her with love and affection. His voice changed markedly; he spoke in a soft and gentle tone. "Be so kind, Faiga, have the children bring in something warm. The Morehdalye rabbi will stay with us tonight."

"The food is ready," the woman half groaned, panting as she spoke. She was evidently suffering from rheumatic pains, as well as asthma. "The guest will have to forgive us that we don't serve with the kind of abundance as other places."

Sholem Shachne understood that his fur coat and shtreimel made him appear wealthy. So he replied, "Not at all! Here in the Ostroleka rabbi's house, I feel just like I'm at an inn." Uncharacteristically, Sholem Shachne launched into a conversation with the poor, sickly woman in an attempt to lift her spirits. "I heard you're due a mazel tov, your older son is engaged. You and the Ostroleka rabbi should say a prayer of thanks each day for the miracle that all your children—may no evil eye harm them—have remained loyal to the Torah."

"We're simple people," the woman rushed to answer, as if she really were afraid of an evil eye. "My father and my father-in-law, may he rest in peace, were workers, not rabbis. So we thank and praise God that we've been given sons and sons-in-law who are Torah scholars."

The rebbetzin left the room, and eventually—without waiting for a prompt from the Ostroleka rabbi—Sholem Shachne removed his coat. Then he continued to sit there in silence at the table, as if in a contest for who could refrain from speaking the longest. Meanwhile, he pondered, immersed in his thoughts: *Could that be it, that because this family descended from workers their children are not yet weary of their lineage, so they've clung to the Torah—while my children, with generations and generations of scholarly ancestors, have already had their fill?*

12

T HE OSTROLEKA RABBI'S two younger daughters, aged fourteen and seventeen, came into the room. Both wore big, clunky
shoes, thick white knit stockings, and long, flaring black dresses. The
youngest, her blond braids tied with pink ribbons, stared cheerfully
at the guest, with a touch of curiosity. The older one, slender, hair
parted down the middle, braids knotted on the nape of her neck,
looked at her father with an expression of complete earnestness. In
their hands were trays with two bowls of broth and plates of steaming
hot potatoes. Each plate bore a wooden spoon, and beside them were
slices of black bread. The girls placed the dishes on the table and the
younger one gave the guest a little chuckle, revealing all her teeth.
"Mother cooked meat today, too, we'll bring it in soon. You can wash
up for the meal in the kitchen, but the water is cold as ice." And she
balled her hands into small fists, as if trembling from cold.

"After the meal we'll bring a pitcher of tea," the older sister said
to her father, in a grave tone. The younger sister skipped out of the
room, trailed by the flutter of pink ribbons and blond braids. Her
older sister followed, head down—though she, too, as if against her
will, bobbed charmingly on her pair of tall legs, like a gangly bird
hopping round a lawn at the end of summer.

These were not glum girls, Sholem Shachne noted, despite living
in poverty in a backwoods town. His own girls, the moment they were
old enough, were griping about Morehdalye's narrowness, complaining they found it suffocating. "Where do your daughters study?"
Sholem Shachne asked. "Is there a girls' cheder in the village?"

"Why would I trust my daughters to a Hebrew teacher, a stranger?
How can I be sure he won't teach them to write from a book of sample
letters?" The Ostroleka rabbi raised a pair of pointy eyebrows at his
guest. "I myself taught my girls how to read Hebrew from a prayer

book. As for writing, they learned to write letters from their mother's Yiddish book of prayers . . . Well, let's go and wash for supper."

Whether because he was extremely exhausted from the trip, or rattled from having spent the day with this eccentric rabbi, the memory of this encounter would remain with him. For a long while after, Sholem Shachne would think back to this little shul in the godforsaken village of Ostroleka, and the night he'd spent at the home of this unrefined "holy man."

During evening prayers at the Ostroleka shul, Sholem Shachne sat behind a large oak lectern and observed the scene. Long and narrow, the shul was packed with cupboards, benches, tables, and lecterns, but all were warped and misshapen, lopsided and twisted. The pulpit, engraved with a pair of priestly hands raised in ritual fashion, bowed and strained downward, as if to bury itself as deeply into the earth as possible, to stir the prayers up from below. A little Jew, with a coat draped over his shoulders in lieu of a tallis, was reciting the evening prayer, his chin raised haughtily, as if yearning to ascend, to touch his head to heaven. The bimah, accessible by a few crooked wooden steps, looked as if it were suspended over a chasm, a sea of black shadows. Above the platform hung an oil lamp, dangling beneath the white enamel ceiling. Its paltry red glow fell upon a Jew with a pitch-black beard. He stood, unmoving, at the bimah. In the denseness of all this wood and darkness, a few distinct features of congregants stood out: a pair of metal spectacles resting on a pointy nose; a face sagging above a white beard; a hand draped over the back of a bench. It felt to Sholem Shachne that he'd been here in this godforsaken settlement for untold ages. The Jews in this synagogue all looked to him like ascetics, men who meditated in the surrounding woods and emerged only for prayers, to join a minyan, after which they'd just as quickly slip back into the woods, each one living in a little hutch beneath a leafy tree.

In the house, the Ostroleka rabbi's daughters tended to the woodstove; the heat came through a wall in the room designated as the guest's bedroom. Normally, the Ostroleka rabbi would use this room to study and then sleep there on a low, worn sofa with a black-lacquered wooden frame. Unlike the bare dining room, this room contained more objects and furniture, and of a finer quality, including a small square glass cupboard with ritual objects on its shelves, a Chanukah menorah, an esrog box, a besamim tower with a little flag, a black shofar. In the other corner of the room was an old, dark brown dresser with round iron knobs. On the chest stood a large copper alms box with two handles at its sides. Three pictures, embroidered on fabric with faded gold and silver threads, hung on the wall. One work of embroidery depicted the Western Wall; the other two, holy tombstones in the holy land. The daughters, it seemed, had embroidered these pictures and hung them in their father's room as a reminder for everyone to toss a little money into the alms box on the dresser, to be sent to the land of Israel.

As the day passed, the Ostroleka rabbi mellowed some toward his guest, though he still spoke in surly tones. Sholem Shachne fretted that the rabbi, having given away his room and bed, would have no place to sleep. But the rabbi grumbled that he need not worry. "I have a custom of mishmar, dedicating two entire nights a week to Talmud study. So tonight, I'll study near the woodstove in the dining room, and early tomorrow I'll lie down in the bedroom where my rebbetzin and the girls sleep." Yom Tov Lipa left the room and quickly reappeared with a jug of water, a basin, and a two-handled pitcher for the ritual handwashing. All of these items he placed on the bench, so that the Morehdalye rabbi would be able to wash his hands in the morning. Then he went out again and came back with a chamber pot. Sholem Shachne was aggravated, grumbling that the rabbi had no obligation to do so much for him, not at all. "Go to sleep!" the village rabbi muttered. He disapproved of all this rabbinical stooping and bowing and thanking. From the table he grabbed the copper candelabrum—filled with candles half the size of yahrzeit tapers that could last through a night of studying—and shuffled off to the other room, leaving the door slightly ajar so that his guest could see enough in the dark to get undressed.

It was warm in the room, and the blanket sufficed; Sholem Shachne didn't have to use his fur coat as an additional quilt. As soon as he closed his eyes, he fell into a half sleep. He saw himself in the tiny Ostroleka synagogue, sitting there, forgotten by the rest of the world. He'd quit his rabbinical position in Morehdalye, abandoned his family, his collection of books—he'd even left behind the Babylonian Talmud he'd studied his whole life. Now all he did was sit in the Ostroleka synagogue reciting Tehillim. But even as he envisioned this, Sholem Shachne knew it wasn't true. He was merely amusing himself. Neither sleeping nor dreaming, he mused on the grief his children had brought him. No matter how much pain he derived from his two daughters and two younger sons, at least he had the fatherly pleasure of seeing them. That wasn't the case with Naftali Hertz, residing in Switzerland—the source of Sholem Shachne's greatest heartache. Naftali Hertz, the doctor of philosophy who worked in a library in Switzerland, who had a wife and son. But the family knew this only from letters Naftali Hertz sent them once in a blue moon. He had never invited his parents or siblings to come see him, and he hadn't visited his family in years.

Sholem Shachne felt a sob welling up in his throat, but a chill spread over his neck, and the sweet psalm he longed to utter would not come out. "*I shall dwell in the house of the Lord . . .*" he began. "*In the house of the Lord . . . forever, Oy, . . . in the house of the Lord forever.*" The words tangled up in his throat and he could not expel them. Suddenly, he saw the Ostroleka rabbi approaching, with the heavy candelabrum in his hand, the candles in them burning like a bandit's murderous eyes. In the darkness, the Ostroleka rabbi's face was concealed. But the flames glowed blood-red, inching steadily closer, threatening to ignite the sack of straw beneath him, to burn him alive on account of his wayward children. "What could I have done that I did not do? Do I deserve to be burned alive?" Sholem Shachne whimpered, and he jerked up in a cold sweat.

Above him stood the Ostroleka rabbi, clutching the candelabrum, shaking him awake. "What's the matter? I heard you crying in your sleep from the other room," Yom Tov Lipa muttered crossly, as if reminding his guest that peaceful sleep is reserved for the truly righteous.

"I don't know what's the matter with me. Maybe I'm not well," Sholem Shachne groaned, and sat up, sweaty, panting. "I see there's a lectern here. Perhaps you could study in this room?" he pleaded. "I'm not going to fall back asleep anyway."

Yom Tov Lipa left the room and soon came back with a thick Gemara. He sat down to study, his tall, broad shoulders concealing the lectern and Gemara from view. From where he lay, Sholem Shachne saw only a yellow strip of light on the Ostroleka rabbi's wrinkled cheek, a speck of shadow on his nose, and one large eye with a steady pupil. *Isn't it a pain for him to stand up the whole time, with that copper candelabrum in his hand?* Sholem Shachne wondered, and again pleaded with the irritable rabbi, "Recite some commentary on one of the biblical texts, Reb Yom Tov Lipa, to ease my heart. We've discussed this and that, but we haven't discussed Torah."

"I don't believe in spouting novel interpretations of the Torah." The Ostroleka rabbi thumped the Gemara on the lectern. "Rather than concentrate on the important issues—that our children should have basic knowledge of Tanach, that our children should not abandon Judaism—today's rabbis spend their time boasting and publishing subtle disputations on the Torah. Pleasure-seekers! Yes, authoring books that shake up the world is also a form of pleasure-seeking!"

With his bare fingers, as if immune to fire, the Ostroleka rabbi straightened a candle's wick, continuing to sway above the glowing Gemara, muttering his complaints against religious leaders: "Judging by the way rabbis speak to their congregations, you'd think they had a clear view of the world to come, as if the World of Truth was right there before them, easy as stepping across a threshold from one room to the next. But just let that rabbi give a cough, and away he scurries to the gentile professor in the big city for advice. And he'll even claim he's doing it for the sake of God. 'It's a mitzvah to guard one's health,' he'll say. So the rabbi runs to the professors and his rabbinate is left in shambles. Soon enough, the children emulate their fathers, and they, too, coddle themselves. Half-naked boys and girls cavorting with each other, and they call themselves descendants of Judah the Maccabee! Well, who's to blame for the debauchery of all these supposed Maccabees? The rabbis! For all of it, the rabbis alone are to blame!" the Ostroleka rabbi concluded. He then turned silent and bent back over his Gemara, as if he'd completely forgotten about the guest on the bed behind him.

Yom Tov Lipa is healthy as a tree in the woods, and his children obey him, so he has no understanding of another's illness in body or soul, Sholem Shachne sighed to himself, still crestfallen that the vision of himself living in a corner of the Ostroleka synagogue, reciting Tehillim, had been merely a dream. Would that he were a simple Jew from this poor village! He'd be spared the suffering of an older daughter fleeing her pious husband and running back to her parents' home; and a younger daughter longing to flee her parents' home and run to a freethinking husband. Not long ago, he was traveling to Lecheve to save his youngest son, now he was headed to Bialystok to check in on his middle son, while his oldest son in Switzerland was beyond all reach. He wanted nothing to do with his parents, and who knew, maybe nothing to do with the God of Israel at all.

13

A SIGN HUNG OVER a large shop on Lipowa Street in Bialystok: Tzalia Gutmacher's Ready-Made Garments. "Tzalia the
Lip"—that's what Bialystokers called the store's owner, whose thick
lower lip hung down like a padlock. He had a withered, wrinkled,
amiable face, punctured by shrewd, cynical eyes. Lodged in one
corner of his mouth, without fail, was a cigar, and the other corner
seemed fixed in the smile of a man who, unless he plays cards every
day or downs a shot of liquor or has a witty friend to entertain him,
is bored to death. Tzalia Gutmacher sold off-the-rack clothing in
cheap fabrics, sewn by third-rate tailors. His clientele consisted of
villagers, craftsmen, poor merchants, and a few well-off Jews who
liked to haggle. When a coat in Tzalia Gutmacher's shop cost a hundred zlotys, the customer knew to offer fifty. And when the customer
left the shop with his purchase, all wrapped up, he'd kick himself for
not having offered even less.

The salesmen—all beardless men with heavy guts from guzzling
whiskey and scarfing down goose sausage—wandered the large stockroom with pretentiously elevated shoulders, peering about with
cold, knowing eyes. No matter how many people filled the shop,
the salesmen dragged their feet, to let their customers know that, in
this establishment, there was no rush to make a sale. They also made
sure to yawn every so often, broadcasting to all that they'd been out
partying the night before. With their local customers, they spoke in
Polish and Belarusian; with Jews, they used Germanisms to avoid any
confusion; and among themselves, they sprinkled in the occasional
Hebrew word. The skill lay in understanding how to handle each
individual client.

If, say, a customer wasn't sure what kind of suit he wanted, the
shopkeeper would have to employ his powers of perception. To a

middle-class young man with a sweaty forehead and thinning hair, you might hand a double-breasted jacket with wide shoulder pads. And if there is no such jacket in his size, you grab him a jacket two sizes smaller, yanking and pulling in such an artful way that the armpits don't feel too tight and the sleeves don't look too short. A dandy should always be persuaded to take a single-breasted jacket, wide as a sack but with narrow lapels. Stout men like jackets and pants that are long in the sleeves and legs, just as tall, lanky men like suits to fit them short. There's a certain type of customer who becomes attached to the first suit he tries on but still wants to consider a few more and bug the salesman a little longer. This client must be shown suits of ever-declining quality. Another type isn't satisfied until the fifth suit, and then ends up buying the tenth. With this sort, you start with the worst and gradually bring out better and better suits. You must know just how much time to give customers to gaze at themselves in the mirror and get used to the cut and color, but also the precise moment to go back—that moment right before the suit loses its charm and starts to feel ugly. If the customer complains that the fabric is coarse cheviot wool, the salesman needn't say a word; it's enough to smile in a gentle, offended way and rub the fabric between two fingers, until the customer sees for himself that it's the finest worsted wool, even softer than cashmere. The most prized art of all is the ability to assess, in a single glance, what kind of sale a particular customer must be "blessed with," and how many times to let him walk out of the store in the haggling process.

Tzalia Gutmacher's salesmen knew these fundamentals well, and they proved their effectiveness on the customers. As always, the proprietor stood in the middle of the large room, pretending to be engrossed in a discussion with a manufacturer, laughing heartily at one joke or another. In the meantime, though, he'd be swiveling in every direction—and with the wink of an eye, the arch of an eyebrow, or the cigar between his fat lips, rolled from one corner of his mouth to the other, he reigned over the room, signaling to his salesmen which customer to approach first.

Bentzion Katzenellenbogen hated his prestigious ancestry more than anything. Short, with pointy elbows and a pale, narrow face, he was adamant about making his own luck. If he could, he'd have traveled to the other end of the world, where no one knew of his rabbinic roots, just like his older brother, Naftali Hertz, had—escaped from yeshiva and fled abroad. This was why Bentzion never asked his parents for the money to take business courses—he wanted to support himself. But ten people applied to every job, and without a recommendation you couldn't get anywhere. So he was forced to lean on his father's brother, Avraham Alter Katzenellenbogen, the Bialystok moreh hora'ah and a partner in several businesses. Avraham Alter had directed him from one merchant to the next, but they'd all turned him down. Finally, his uncle sent him with a letter to the clothes merchant, Gutmacher. This time the young man lucked out.

"I have no shortage of salesmen." Tzalia the Lip's eyes roved over this young man with the face of a soused herring. "But since your uncle is the moreh hora'ah and your father is a rabbi, we'll find something for you to do. But be a good fellow, not a slacker."

The other salesmen welcomed the young rabbinical scholar into their clique. Wanting to make an adult of him, they gossiped about women and encouraged him to drink. But Bentzion had no interest in their vulgar chatter and no taste for liquor. They also failed to turn him into a good salesman, which earned him the nickname "Barefoot."

"Barefoot," they mocked, "you think wool is like the Talmud, like you have to study it in depth: *Curly goats from the mountains are superior to domestic ones. There's genuine alpaca from camel-goats and there's alpaca made from rags. Double-sided wool from a sheep's forelegs is the best. On the right and left sides of the stomach, the wool is of lesser quality; around the neck, even worse.* Heavens, who cares about all that? The main thing is to know how to 'dress' the customer. Get it, Barefoot?"

The Morehdalye rabbi's son could not and did not want to learn the dirty tricks of baiting a customer. If it were up to him, he wouldn't be working for a place where the customers haggled like they were at a fish market and the salesmen were all cheaters, turning their customers into fodder for entertainment. No matter how many times the salesmen tried befriending him, he resisted. He peered through his glasses down at his toes, tugged the hairs on his narrow chin, and remained stubbornly silent. Eventually, the others came to despise him and provoked the store owner: "Get rid of him, he's good for nothing, that Barefoot."

But the owner felt a peculiar pleasure in having a devout rabbinical scholar among his grimy lot. He told his workers, "Cool off, he's not causing me any loss," and to the rabbi's son he said, "True, you're no good at selling, but you're a good advertisement. Let the world know that a rabbi's son, the Bialystoker moreh hora'ah's nephew, works for me."

Instead of rejoicing that his pedigree had saved him from being fired, Bentzion only grew more irritated. He was convinced that his ancestry brought him more trouble than gain. Because the salesmen knew he came from a rabbinical home, they regarded him as a religious fanatic and pounced on him at every opportunity. Lately, they'd taken to bossing him around and calling him the "Machine," because of his speed—jetting from one end of the shop to the other, pulling the pieces he wanted from hundreds of hangers in the blink of an eye.

It was a wintry market day, and Gutmacher's shop was teeming with customers. Wooden racks, bearing row upon row of clothes, covered three walls of the spacious shop. At mirrors mounted on walls, pillars, and doors, customers stood admiring themselves in their potential purchases. A young man, trying on a raincoat with exposed stitching and epaulettes, paced back and forth in front of a mirror. Another held a pale gray gabardine with a long belt and slit pockets in one hand, and a brown coat with appliquéd pockets, wide lapels, and a high collar in the other, struggling to decide between the two. A craftsman stood hunched over a table rifling through a tall stack of folded trousers. A little baron with prickly blond whiskers stepped out of the fitting room wearing a pair of jodhpurs over his boots. But rather than study his own reflection in the mirror, his eyes wandered to a dandy with a chin like tangled roots. The dandy ambled about in a sports jacket, striped knickers, and long stockings tucked into step-in shoes. A Jew with the tarred beard of a blacksmith stood in one corner, stuffed into a heavy padded coat. Another Jew with a protruding stomach and a vest pocket filled with sharpened pencils was also trying on a new overcoat, with much groaning and straining. The salesmen slid from one client to the next, and the "Machine," Bentzion Katzenellenbogen, ran to and fro with outfits on hangers. In the center of the hall stood Tzalia Gutmacher, casting glances in every direction, ensuring that the customers were well served. At the cash register stood Madame Gutmacher—tall, with a round face, coiffed hair, a low-cut dress, and the muscular arms of a strong woman who lifts barbells in a circus.

Suddenly, all eyes turned in one direction. Conversation among the salesmen and customers came to a halt. Mrs. Gutmacher lifted her bare, bulky arms from the register. Her astonished husband removed the cigar from his mouth. Right across from him, in the center of the hall, stood a rabbi in a shtreimel and a skunk fur coat with a beaver collar. He wore gold-rimmed glasses. With his overgrown gray sideburns, he looked like an aging dictator.

"My son Bentzion Katzenellenbogen works here," he announced.

Tzalia Gutmacher and his crew hadn't expected their slight, rabbinical colleague to have a father with such a commanding and stately appearance. So it surprised Gutmacher when Bentzion simply stood there with his eyes lowered, as if wanting to bury himself from humiliation. And the rabbi, too, tugged crossly at his beard and spoke to his son in a curt tone. "How are you, Bentzion?"

"Okay. And how's Mother doing?"

"Well, thank God," the rabbi replied dryly, and looked around him at the hundreds of suits on hangers, at the buyers and sellers.

"Herr Gutmacher is my boss," Bentzion muttered, suddenly remembering he needed to say something.

"Yes, I'd already figured that out—that you're the boss." Sholem Shachne offered his hand to Gutmacher and sharpened his eyes. "I see you have no shortage of goods or customers, thank God. I hope your clothes are not tainted by shatnez."

For a moment, the boss was speechless. He shoved the cigar back into his mouth, pulled it out again, then glanced at the rabbi's son, waiting for him to respond. "Devout Jews looking to avoid shatnez don't come shopping here," Bentzion murmured.

His father lunged as if to smack him or shout: "So what are *you* doing in here, then?" The owner, too, glared at his employee with anger and ridicule: *What a Barefoot! He studied the Gemara and still doesn't know how to answer his rabbi father!*

"God dwells in one's heart, not in stiff fabric and linings. If a person wears clothes mixing linen and wool, can God not sleep at night?" Tzalia laughed cheerfully. "Just ask your son, and he'll tell you how well we treat him."

"God is everywhere, including in the clothes a Jew wears." From beneath the rabbi's whiskers, a sharp smile unfurled. "If you can manage without my son for the afternoon, I'd like to ask you to excuse him. I traveled here expressly to see him."

Tzalia Gutmacher was happy to rid himself of this visitor who'd waltzed in and started grilling him about kosher clothing and scrutinizing his clientele. "If a father, especially the rabbi of a city, comes to visit his son who works for me, who am I to get in the way of that," the owner said loudly, making sure his Jewish customers would hear.

14

SILENTLY, Sholem Shachne and Bentzion stepped out into the frigid air. The snow-banked streets were teeming with people in sopping boots and muddied coats. Passersby shoved their way forward. At stores and warehouses, large carts idled, their drivers shouting and unloading cargo. A man with tired, red eyes emerged from a pub, leaving the door ajar. From inside, plumes of smoke billowed into the street; from outside, dirty snow whipped into the tavern on a gust of wind. Sholem Shachne stood there, enveloped in the cloud of smoke, listening to the laughter, the drunken words and curses emanating from the pub, until someone slammed the door shut from inside. The rabbi walked on through the sloping streets, twisting uphill and downhill. His galoshes sank in the trampled, yellowing snow. Before his eyes, signboards jutted out at him, long and narrow, round and three-cornered, as if torn from above their shops and soaring through the winds. In Sholem Shachne's memory, the pure snow of Ostroleka still gleamed; he could hardly believe that, just twenty-four hours ago, he'd been in that bright, clean village. Both here in the slushy and chaotic Bialystok and there in that little village it was the middle of the month of Teves. But above the village hung a spiritual silence, hovering beneath a high blue sky, and when the sun shone, the ice glimmered like diamonds. True, the Ostroleka rabbi's home was bare and plain. He earned a pittance for wages, and his children wore rags. But despite his poverty and spiritual seclusion, he took more pleasure in this world than anyone.

Sholem Shachne turned to his son in a huff. "Why so quiet? And you're walking like you're headed off to slaughter! You haven't even asked about your brothers and sisters. Where are we headed? I've seen where you work, in that Godless shop. Now I want to see where you live. Take me there."

Bentzion folded into himself. His small, pale face turned as wrinkled as an old man's. He *did* want to ask more about how his mother was doing, his younger brother and sister, too, but his father's visit to the shop had frayed his nerves. The other salesmen would only mock him even more now. They'd laugh at him for being a staid rabbinical scholar, with no knack for handling customers, just like his father— a man who walks into a shop he knows nothing about and the first thing he asks is do they sell shatnez! "And you don't even look like your father," they'll tell him. "He's a tall and handsome man, and you're just dull little Barefoot." Where he lived, no one yet knew his father was a rabbi. Now, they, too, would find out.

"I live far from here, on the other side of the park, almost on the outskirts of town," Bentzion sputtered, his voice trembling.

"If I can make it all the way from Morehdalye, I can make it to where you live, no matter the distance. Who are your landlords? You've never told us whose home you're living in," his father said, with an accusative stare.

"Who would you have them be? They're Jews. But they're not your sort of people," his son said with somewhat uncharacteristic reluctance, and he squirmed like a hedgehog beneath its spines. His father glared at him with even more mistrust.

To shorten the walk, they cut through the city garden. The silent old trees with their twisted, chandelier-like branches and the pristine snow again reminded Sholem Shachne of Ostroleka and its rabbi. The devotion with which his family looked upon him! The joy they'd felt at obeying their father! Sholem Shachne turned to his son and said, "Why are you so terrified? Do you live with communists? Is that why you don't want me to visit you?"

Bentzion burst into nervous laughter. "I happen to live with a mortal enemy of communism." He grew quiet again, anxious and irritable that he was being forced to show his father where he lived.

They exited the city park and halted before a three-story house with a stately entrance, its balconies and windows hung with drapes, in a peaceful neighborhood that was home to city officials. They ascended to the second floor and stopped at a door with a small metal sign: "Joseph Mirsky, Master's Degree."

"Your landlord is a Jew?" Sholem Shachne asked.

"Yes, yes, a Jew," Bentzion replied impatiently, and tugged at the bell, which emitted a short, harsh clang.

The door was opened by an older, dark-eyed woman with mussy gray hair, her chin sprouting small white whiskers. Tucked into the folds of her face were the worry and gloom of an ailing woman who derives no joy from her life or her children. From behind his father's shoulders, Bentzion muttered in Polish, "This is my father." The woman, surprised, held Sholem Shachne's gaze for a long while. The rabbi stepped into the hallway and removed his galoshes.

Soon, another woman came in, younger than the first, swollen bags beneath her eyes. It was immediately apparent that she was the older woman's daughter. Her hair, parted down the middle, sparkled black atop her head but was graying at the temples. Long earrings dangled from her ears to the middle of her drooping cheeks. Like her mother, she, too, looked anxious and unhappy with life.

"This rabbi is our lodger's father," the older woman told the younger in Russian. Shocked, the daughter stood there speechless. Until finally she cried, "Please come in!" Then she hollered to her husband within, "Joseph, Joseph, our lodger's father has come to visit."

Lamps were on inside the house; a wine-red luster bathed the clean, well-furnished rooms. Silver and porcelain dishes glinted from glass-door cupboards, golden spines from bookcases with polished panes. Sholem Shachne followed behind his son, his gaze halting on a large portrait in the dining room. Peering out from a thick black frame was a man with hair as long as a woman's, short whiskers, and round protruding eyes. He wore a steel breastplate, cut like a waist-coat, one hand resting on the hilt of a sword. The rabbi glanced around the room. He noticed the younger woman standing at the other side of the table, still eyeing him with curiosity. Beside her, wearing a sweater with no jacket, stood a short man with hunched shoulders and a pointy balding head. He stared piercingly at the guest, and didn't bother to remove his hands from his trouser pockets, as if to show the rabbi his disdain. Sholem Shachne remembered a bit of Russian from his past, so he said loudly, "*Dobri Vetcher.*" But the landlord responded with only a nod of his head, twisting his face into a contemptuous smile.

Bentzion led his father into his room. It was long and narrow, like a hallway, with an iron-framed bed, a little table, two chairs, and an old chest of drawers laden with textbooks. From the ceiling beam hung a small, simple electric lamp, the kind used in bathhouses, which cast a dingy glow, like unclean water, upon the peeling walls. Exhausted from a long day of slogging around, Sholem Shachne had no strength left to take off his fur coat. He gestured to his son for help and then plopped down in a chair. The dark winter night was already glimmering through the window. The rabbi glanced about the room, his gaze landing on his son's clothes rack in the corner, draped in a sheet.

"A handsome, spacious home," Sholem Shachne said, "but your room was probably the storage space at one time." Sholem Shachne then asked his son about the picture of the general in armor that hung on the wall. "I've seen that face before. Is he a relative of the family?"

"A relative of Joseph Mirsky?" Bentzion tittered. "It's the Russian tsar, Peter the Great!"

"Right, right, indeed it's him, the great-grandfather of the Russian kaisers. I still remember him from the pictures during Nikolai's era. The same murderous eyes. So why is he hanging in your landlord's house? Is he a Russian, this Joseph Mirsky? You told me he's a Jew."

The rabbi's son again began to chuckle quietly, so comedic was his landlord's history. He spoke in a whisper, so that he wouldn't be heard in the other rooms, and gestured with his small hands, as he did when he studied the Gemara. "Joseph Mirsky is a Russian Jew. But he claims that his parents had already distanced themselves from Judaism. He escaped the Bolsheviks, planning to travel to Paris like the other monarchists. But he didn't have the right connections. The other tsar-supporters, the generals and noblemen, didn't bother with him because he wasn't in their league; he didn't have their rank or status. So he stayed in Bialystok, wallowing about, till he got a position in the Russian division of the local Archive. Since he's educated, holds a master's degree, and is an enemy of the Bolsheviks, the Polish trust him. In Bialystok he met a mother and daughter, they, too, Russian intellectuals, and the daughter married him. His wife and mother-in-law brought a fortune into the marriage, everything in this house is theirs, but all day and night they fight with him; his wife beats him. He plays cards and boozes with the other Russian immigrants. So when he comes home drunk after a game of cards, his wife beats him. The mother and daughter also speak Yiddish, but he speaks only Russian. If someone makes an error in Russian grammar or language, he grimaces like he has indigestion, as if someone poked him with pins. At least once a month, his wife threatens divorce. He then lugs the tsar off the wall and prepares to pack him up. It's the only object in the house that's his. He brought him along from Russia and claims that this Piotr Wielki is the greatest person in the world."

"The great-grandfather of pogrom-nik and idiot Nikolai is the greatest man in the world?!" The rabbi shrugged. "I once read somewhere about the actions of this Piotr Wielki and I remember thinking then that he's a bigger tyrant than Herod the Great. I know that this kaiser accomplished great things for the Russians. Well, Herod also accomplished great things. He rebuilt the Jewish Temple and gave the Jews food from his granaries during the famine years. But can you imagine a Jew like us hanging a picture of the tyrant Herod in his home?" Sholem Shachne wrinkled his forehead as when pondering a Talmudic nuance. Suddenly, he gaped at his son in alarm. "Since your landlord isn't a native Russian—you can tell just by looking at him that he's not Russian by birth—he must be a convert!"

"A convert? He doesn't go to church. I haven't seen a cross in this house, and neither he nor his wife has ever mentioned that they're baptized," Bentzion murmured, somewhat frightened.

Sholem Shachne knit his brow, adjusted the glasses on his nose, and whispered, "A Jew who converts doesn't do it because he believes in Jesus. He does it because it's advantageous. A convert like that, someone who converted to the Greek Orthodox Church, wouldn't say a word about it in Poland. Because a man who changes his faith for the sake of career is respected nowhere. Still, it pleases him—this fugitive convert—to remind himself that the great Russian kaiser, sporting his suit of armor, clutching a sword, is his kaiser, too. Surely, he's been holding out hope that Nikolai's escaped princes and officers will become titleholders in Russia again, that they'll make him a dignitary among them."

Bentzion chewed on his nails and remained silent. It was true that Joseph Mirsky was always repeating that one day the old Russia would return. When his wife and mother-in-law fought with him, they yelled that he was a man without character, a sellout. His wife and mother-in-law considered themselves Jewish, but he snickered at bearded Jews and sneered at the way they swayed while davening. He even mocked irreligious Jews and claimed they were constantly trying to cheat other people. Bentzion had always felt that his father, a "Gemara Jew," was prone to inventing fantasies in his head. But this time it seemed like his theory might be correct.

As if he'd heard his son's thoughts, Sholem Shachne said, "From what you told me, it seems fair to assume his father had already turned the coin. At any rate, if he's not an actual convert, he's in that category. Did you see the way he looked at me, with such anger and disdain? And you're staying in the home of this antisemite! You'd rather live in a storage room, as long as it's not among your own kind, as long as it's not your uncle's. You don't even make time to visit him. Avraham Alter wrote to me. And today, when I went to see him, he reminded me several times—with distress!—that you avoid his home."

"Because his home is completely devoid of spirituality. Even though Uncle is a rabbi, everything about that place is businesslike," Bentzion cried despondently.

Even in his agitation, Sholem Shachne did not forget that hitting an adult son was out of line; he managed to restrain himself from leaping up and giving his boy a smack. He hadn't skimped on smacks when the children were young, but since they'd grown up and stopped obeying him, he was always second-guessing himself: Were they disobeying him because he'd slapped them too frequently, or because he hadn't slapped them enough? The rabbi groaned like a sick man with no strength left to battle his disease.

"You work in a shop that sells shatnez to the town Jews, even though Jewish law prohibits it. I'm sure there's some violation of the Shabbos going on in that shop, too. You live in a house that belongs to a convert or semi-convert. But with your uncle the moreh hora'ah, you won't step foot in his home because it lacks spirituality. Very interesting. Your brothers and sisters are rebels just like you, but at least they're not hypocrites or liars."

"I'm not a hypocrite. Or a liar." Bentzion's frail body trembled, and he struggled with all his might not to burst into tears. "Since I don't want to become a rabbi, I don't want to exploit the privilege of being a rabbi's son. But my uncle and his sons exploit the Torah for business. All they talk about in that house is money—money, money, and more money. Even my boss, Tzalia Gutmacher, speaks less of money and profits than Uncle and his family."

Sholem Shachne felt his heart twisting with empathy for his son. *My children's sincerity is their misfortune*, he thought. *Because of their integrity, they're unwilling to accept compromise, and when they're forced to, it makes them ill.* "You have to get yourself out of here," Sholem Shachne said.

"You're right, this isn't the place for me," Bentzion replied, defeated. It was true, he wanted to live among strangers, people unaware of his privileged background, but not with a landlord who looked at his father with such hate and derision.

15

AVRAHAM ALTER KATZENELLENBOGEN's beard hung stiffly from his chin to his waist, as if it were made of porcelain like a seder plate. He was close to seventy, but still active. He had huge, backward-slanting ears and eyes as large as eggs. His gaze bounced around restlessly, and his forehead was perpetually creased in thought, as he brooded over his various business problems. There was his partnership in a factory that exported prayer shawls, on which he placed his stamp assuring buyers that the tzitzis had been woven for the sake of heaven, not profit; there was the courtyard he owned a share in, which was constantly garnering complaints from neighbors; and then there were complaints from the other Bialystok moreh hora'ahs, claiming he was encroaching on their territory.

When he wasn't hearing lawsuits in the rabbinical court, he was sitting at home with his sons and sons-in-law, deliberating over business opportunities. His adversaries claimed he was adept at rigging things in his own favor, so that, for example, he *alone* was responsible for all kosher inspections of delicatessens. But he justified his maneuvers, claiming he had a lot of expenses, which compelled him to be aggressively ambitious. One day God would help him and he'd be able to involve himself only in the rabbinate.

Avraham Alter barely had time to daven, yet he found the time to acquire every new book published in Hebrew. He was preparing for the day when he'd finally be able to extricate himself from his business ventures and focus solely on studying Torah texts and worshipping God. In the meantime, he made some book transactions of his own. For one, he bought a large Vilna Talmud, meaning he no longer needed the medium-sized Zhitomer Talmud or the small Berlin Talmud. He figured he might as well sell them. His sons and sons-in-law also had their own shelves of books, and occasionally a scuffle would break out among them. One brother-in-law would claim that the other took his copy of the *Shulchan Aruch*. The other yelled exactly the opposite—that the copy had been stolen from him! Finally, Avraham Alter would have to intervene. "I may have sold your copy of the *Shulchan Aruch*. Or maybe I bartered it? You can take my copy. If you don't like it, take a set of Midrash or Mishnayos. Take whatever you want."

The father and his married children lived in a large house with several wings, each with many rooms, and each room with doors that led from one to the next. The family never used the rooms for their designated purposes—instead, they drifted anywhere, employing them arbitrarily. In the rabbi's chambers, they'd sit down to eat; in the bedroom, they'd conspire over business matters; and in the dining room, they'd daven hastily before the time for praying had passed. People were always stepping in and out of the house as if it were an inn on market day.

And so it was today. Waiting in one corner of Avraham Alter's chambers was a blond-bearded bookseller, pipe clenched between his yellow teeth. And in a corner of the courtyard stood Avraham Alter's partner, a lanky innkeeper with a high elastic collar and a drawn face, wrinkled like the fruit from last year's Sukkos. While they waited, Avraham Alter sat behind closed doors, convening with two young men who'd come to propose a partnership in a small cotton and quilting factory. Avraham Alter spoke rapidly; the young men, cheeks full as wheat buns, had to cough several times before they could get a word in, like cantors preparing to sing a new tune. Barely had these potential business partners left when in waltzed a bride and groom, along with ten relatives, to erect a chuppah. The entire chuppah ceremony took all of a few minutes—the bride circling the groom, the swaying, the groom uttering the words to consecrate the marriage— and already they were shouting "Mazel tov!" Someone handed out snifters of liquor and everyone fought over a piece of black cake. The groom, something of a Torah scholar, was pained by the unsuitable haste. He pushed his way over to Avraham Alter's son, enraged: What was he—a chicken to be slaughtered, one-two-three?!

But Avraham Alter's son blew a puff of expensive tobacco into the groom's face and yelled back, "According to halacha, the length of time a chuppah takes makes no difference."

Avraham Alter's oldest son wore a wide-brimmed hat, slanted down over the nape of his neck. His scholarly forehead perspired, his cheeks glowed clear and oily. He rolled his fat stomach forward and grinned directly into everyone's face, with the confident and cynical smile of a distinguished Torah scholar who also had a head for practical matters. Nobody could ask and answer as many difficult Rambams as he, just as no one could outsmart him in business dealings. Everyone knew he was highly accomplished in everything he did.

His brother-in-law, the oldest son-in-law of Avraham Alter, was highly accomplished, too. He had long, dark blond peyes, worn curled up behind his ears. And on his face, not a trace of a hair. He was spectacularly handsome, with a rounded jaw, a straight, rigid nose, and deep brown eyes. He wore a semi-rabbinic coat of the best Bielitz material, longer than a jacket, shorter than an overcoat. He moved around the rooms the same way he talked—very quietly. Instead of replying to others, he'd merely grimace with his finely carved teeth. But though he wasn't a talker, he boasted a reputation as a world-class orator. It was also said that he studied Talmud for nights on end, composing extraordinary, innovative commentaries on biblical texts. But all this didn't stop him from being his father-in-law's first counsel on matters of business. Still, if one examined his smooth, cold facial expression, it wasn't hard to discern that he'd been a licentious teenage boy, and that even today, in the dark alleyways of big cities, where no one knew who he was, he still sought out prohibited pleasures.

By chance, Avraham Alter's younger son-in-law had a round black beard. He was a tall, gangly man with stooped shoulders, bony hands, a long nose, and thick, perpetually chapped lips. In his brand-new overcoat, he looked dressed up even on weekdays. He, too, wanted to be involved in the family business dealings, but no one minded his advice. So he walked around resentfully, bitter that his father-in-law never solicited his opinion and that the world was unaware of his own late father's brilliance. His father, he believed, had been a greater Talmudic master than the Rogatchover genius and a deeper thinker than Rabbi Chaim of Brisk.

From time to time, Avraham Alter's two daughters came in to join the men. They were slender young women of medium height, wearing berets pulled down over one ear, masculine-looking suits with slit pockets, white blouses with boyish piping, and low-heeled slippers. These young, tight-lipped rebbetzins smoked when they were alone with their husbands, making sure their parents and strangers knew nothing of it. With their figures, it was impossible to tell whether they'd already had children and how many. Nobody called them wanton because they were prudent and had good sense. They were the sort of girls who, when still unmarried, tended to fall for play-boys and, among intellectuals, preferred the poets. And the sort who, later, with no great objection, would settle down with safe husbands, in accordance with their parents' wishes.

Both sisters entered the main rooms only when they had some-thing to tell their husbands; they paid no mind to the others around them. Their mother, on the other hand, lobbed smiles in all direc-tions whenever she made an appearance, exchanging a few words with everyone. She wore a sheitel like a hairdo and a long, slim dress. And she paced from cupboard to cupboard, shuffling the glassware around, like the mother of the bride just before or after a wedding. Her long, stiff neck and oversized head made her look like a floor lamp topped with a shade.

The Bialystoker moreh hora'ah and the Morehdalye rabbi sat together at the table. "You're staying here for Shabbos?" the older brother asked. Sholem Shachne shook his head no. "Well, what did your Bentzion tell you? Why won't he enter my home?" Avraham Alter asked. But just at that moment his older son-in-law summoned him over to discuss a business matter, and Sholem Shachne was relieved to be spared from lying—or worse, telling the truth: that his son felt his uncle's house was devoid of spirituality.

Avraham Alter's younger son-in-law took a seat at the table and said, "My father, may his memory be a blessing—," but just then he saw his father-in-law returning. Instantly he rose and walked away. Avraham Alter sat down again, determined not to let himself be dragged away again. He continued where he'd left off. "If your Bentzion would come to my home, at least then you'd know for sure he puts on tefillin every day. Thank God, *my* children behave like Jews." He twisted a curly hair of his long, wide beard around two of his fingers.

"Indeed, how did you pull it off?" Sholem Shachne asked, peering through his glasses at his brother with weary eyes, like hazy lamps on a bare, dark street. "I believe I've always refrained from worldly pleasures more than you have."

"Indeed, that's why!" Avraham Alter cried, and shifted his skull-cap from his nape to the top of his head. "Because you refrained from enjoying this world, kept your children from enjoying what this world has to offer, now they don't want to obey you. But I wasn't as strict with my children, so they didn't go seeking pleasures outside the home. And if it so happened that they did go looking somewhere they shouldn't, I ignored it, feigned obliviousness. Children should never think the door is closed to them. Sure enough, they all came back."

Involuntarily, Sholem Shachne began to laugh, recalling his talk with the Ostroleka rabbi. The Ostroleker had preached precisely the opposite: that his children didn't obey him because they'd seen him indulging too much in worldly pleasures. Avraham Alter was just about to say something more when his son came back in, bent down close, and whispered, "Father, you must come in again for a bit. People are waiting." Avraham Alter jumped up in a huff. Could he have no peace!

But Sholem Shachne was even happier than before to be interrupted. Now he didn't have to say, "Bentzion doesn't visit you because this is more the home of a businessman than a rabbi. And even if your children do observe the laws of Shabbos and keep kosher, who knows with how much integrity they observe the laws of buying and selling."

16

O N THE WAY BACK home from Bialystok, Sholem Shachne
stopped off at Lecheve to see his son-in-law. Guilt over having given his daughter as a wife to such a brilliant scholar plagued
him—a wife who, out of pure capriciousness, up and left him with
their child while she dashed off to her parents. Though perhaps she'd
already come home to her husband?

It was before noon on a Friday when the rabbi disembarked at the
Lecheve train station, in a snowstorm so severe he couldn't see three
paces ahead. But Sholem Shachne knew his way well to the nearby
town, and he set off on foot. His shtreimel, collar, and beard instantly
gained a film of snow. The wind roared in his ears; frost burned his
forehead. The suitcase he carried grew as heavy as a sack of stones.
Time and again he paused, switched the case from hand to hand,
and plodded onward. Even with his knitted wool gloves, his fingers
went numb. One moment he imagined the town was just up ahead,
its homes close enough to touch. The next, it seemed he wasn't in
Lecheve at all, that he'd gotten off at the wrong station. A dizziness
overcame him. He couldn't say what was happening. Did he have
a fever? It was easy enough to catch pneumonia, trudging around
like this, and who knows? He might be greeting his dead ancestors
any minute now. And well, maybe the time was right? After all, he
couldn't expect to draw any more joy from his children. And at least
if he were to die now, Bentzion and Refael would still recite Kaddish; any later, who's to say how far they'll have strayed? Their older
brother, evidently, had already severed his roots entirely.

Just then a sleigh came barreling at him, the coachman reining in
his horse just in time. The coachman leaned out, saw a man on foot
in a shtreimel and fur coat. "What's a Jew doing traipsing about in a
snowstorm like this?" he shouted, honking his horn.

"Is this Lecheve?" the pedestrian shouted back.

The coachman gaped at this lost soul, who resembled a rabbi and spoke as if in a daze. "Do you not know where you are? Of course this is Lecheve! What did you think it was, Warsaw? Who're you looking for?"

Once he explained to the coachman that Lecheve's rabbi and rosh yeshiva was his son-in-law, the coachman invited him up into his sleigh and drove him to the home of Yaakov Asher, where he, too, stepped inside.

Yaakov Asher's eyes bulged out at the sight of his father-in-law. "In this weather?! Why didn't you warn me you were coming?"

But before his father-in-law could respond, the coachman chimed in, "The rabbi was walking in the complete opposite direction of town. He might have been wandering a day and a night had I not been coming home from the village for Shabbos."

Yaakov Asher grew more alarmed. For his father-in-law to have shown up unannounced, and in such weather, he must be bearing bad news. "How's my wife, Tilza?"

"She's well. In good health," Sholem Shachne replied, peeved with himself for not having considered how much this unexpected visit might frighten his son-in-law. "I went to see my brother and son in Bialystok, so I stopped off here for Shabbos on the way back."

Once the coachman had taken his leave, Sholem Shachne expected his son-in-law to start pouring his embittered heart out over the grief his wife had caused him. Sholem Shachne would then be forced to admit, "You're right! You could have taken a wife from a family much more pious than mine and enjoyed your life." But in fact, Yaakov Asher didn't utter a single word against his wife. He didn't have to, so acutely obvious was his sorrow and humiliation at her leaving. Besides shame, it seemed, he was ridden by fear that the people of Lecheve would discover his pregnant wife had run off to her parents because she didn't want to have another child with him.

His son-in-law's refusal to cast any blame only increased Sholem Shachne's suffering; he was ready to rend his garment as if mourning over the dead. He recalled the story in the Talmud of a scholar who'd prayed for his own daughter's death because her beauty caused pain to others. Sholem Shachne's rage smoldered so fiercely inside him that it melted the ice in his bones. Earlier, he'd been afraid he'd collapse from pneumonia, convulse from fever and chills. But when he saw the quiet catastrophe at his son-in-law's home, he told himself he must remain healthy and find a solution.

Yaakov Asher washed his face and changed into a fresh suit for Shabbos. He put on a clean shirt with a soft collar and no tie. With his fingers he combed through his rumpled beard, as if to purge it of any weekday worries, but he could not wipe the sorrow from his eyes. A sense of defeat enveloped him; even his clothes looked disparaged. Sholem Shachne watched as his son-in-law covered his eyes and said the blessing over the Shabbos candles, as if, God forbid, he were a widower. Afterward, he busied himself with his Heshe'le, a four-year-old, red-haired boy, sad just like his father. He changed the boy's clothes in honor of Shabbos, tied the shoelaces of his little shoes, and said to him, "Heshe'le, do you recognize Grandfather? He brings you regards from Mommy." Heshe'le looked at his grandfather and was silent. He understood what bringing a siddur meant, he understood that his father's heavy, yellow-freckled hands were not his mother's warm white ones. But how one brought regards from his mother he did not yet understand. His father placed a cap, instead of the yarmulke he wore in the house, on Heshe'le's head, and took him to the neighbor's house across the street, so that his father and grandfather could go daven.

Outside, the blizzard had calmed. The fine gold flames of the Shabbos candles winked from homes half-buried in snow. And it seemed to Sholem Shachne, as he walked with his son-in-law, that these flames were taunting him: In each Jewish home, an honorable woman awaited her husband's return from davening. But not *his* daughter, who'd left her husband and child behind.

By the time the two rabbis entered the beis medrash, the young men sitting and studying had already heard from the coachman that the rosh yeshiva's father-in-law was in town and the story of how he'd gotten lost. The students and their rosh yeshiva prayed in one room, the townspeople in another. Pacing around the students' room were twenty or so young bachelors, their short black beards flecked with blond. Their faces radiated youth, their eyes sparkled with scholarly shrewdness and vivacity. Yaakov Asher, too, did his best to look lively, but he couldn't help casting surreptitious, fear-filled glances over at his father-in-law, worried that his students might ask themselves: If

Rebbetzin Tilza went to visit her parents, how is it that her father is here in Lecheve?

After Maariv, the young men jostled their way toward the guest to wish him a good Shabbos and ask whether he'd be giving them a Torah talk. The Morehdalye rabbi replied that he planned on staying in Lecheve for a week, so he hoped he'd have that chance. Once again, Yaakov Asher glanced at his father-in-law, alarmed. A full week! But Sholem Shachne's expression was impenetrable, a warning against anyone who dared try to dissuade him.

At dinner, Yaakov Asher held Heshe'le on his knees and pleaded with him to eat. His voice and hands shook, as if he were embarrassed even before his child that his mother had left them. Afterward, he went to put Heshe'le to bed in the other room and Sholem Shachne remained alone at the table, gazing at his daughter's candlesticks in thought: *My Henna'le always excused Tilza, saying she's a dreamer. But if she truly had a powerful imagination, she'd be able to envision the pain she was causing her husband. Could she be so ungenerous that despite understanding the depth of her husband's suffering, she still didn't care? Apparently, her fantasies revolved only around herself and her delusions, not the other people in her life, not even her own husband.*

The same neighbor who watched over Heshe'le while Yaakov Asher went to daven also cooked for him. To ensure that Yaakov Asher wouldn't have to divide his portion of fish and meat with his unexpected guest, the pious neighbor brought over some of her own food. But when she came back later to retrieve their plates, she saw that both men had eaten very little. The same thing happened the next day, at the cholent meal, where father- and son-in-law discussed the Torah, the yeshiva students, Heshe'le, but never brought up the subject of Tilza. Then, they both turned silent, and each knew what the other was thinking.

Saturday evening, Heshe'le stood on a chair between his father and his grandfather and helped hold the braided Havdalah candle. Sholem Shachne held the wine-filled goblet in his palm and hummed a sweetly melancholy niggun. The men sniffed the besamim cloves and examined their nails beneath the Havdalah flame as they recited the blessing, *Blessed be Him who created the lights of fire.* Darkness enveloped the room, dappled by the trembling red glow of the Havdalah candle. With eyes like a pious old man's, Heshe'le stared at his tall, gray-bearded grandfather and his red-bearded father. High on the walls, thick shadows, like emissaries from another world, looked down upon the two men and the little boy. And much later, when Heshe'le was fast asleep, a murky silence lingered in the corners of the room.

The first to bring up Tilza was her father, who started in as if they'd been discussing her all through Shabbos. "It's just not plausible that she wouldn't have told you what she needs from you. A daughter who's already a mother herself doesn't tell her parents all that's going on between her and her husband. But a husband should know what his wife requires of him."

Rather than respond with anger, or spread his hands and give his usual "What do I know?" as he'd done repeatedly on his recent visit, Yaakov Asher looked down glumly at the floor, as if at his feet lay a heavy package he'd been forced to drop, its weight beyond his strength. After a long silence, he murmured: "You and my mother-in-law have said many times that Tilza doesn't know what she wants. She's to be pitied. It's true she brings me suffering, great suffering, but she herself suffers, too."

Once again, Sholem Shachne marveled at the even temper of his son-in-law, who continued to excuse his wife. But he himself did not want to excuse her. He ranted with the full force of the fury he'd choked down all Shabbos: "Tilza doesn't really know what she wants, so her suffering holds no weight with me. She's spoiled, and you spoil her even more. Tilza sees you falling all over yourself to please her, so she thinks she's in the right. Every single day, and in every way possible, it is your duty to remind my daughter that she's a mother and a wife, that you're the Lecheve rabbi and rosh yeshiva, that you have no patience for her madness. But I see I can't count on you, so I'll have to do it myself. It's a decision I made well before Shabbos, as soon as I arrived here and saw your situation. You'll travel to Morehdalye, and on my behalf, you'll tell my family that I won't be returning home until Tilza comes back to Lecheve."

"She'll say I put you up to this," Yaakov Asher groaned, panting.

"I wish my Tilza believed you had such strength! But unfortunately, she knows you're spineless when it comes to her, forgive me, and she'll realize you're merely carrying out my orders. Tell my family that if they won't persuade Tilza to return, I'll never come back home. I don't want to look at such a daughter! I'd rather drag myself from town to town and die among strangers."

All of his brewing resentment disgorged, Sholem Shachne wiped the froth from his mouth and began speaking with a bit more composure, though still with firmness. "Tomorrow you'll depart for Morehdalye. I'll remain here to run the yeshiva in your place and look after Heshe'le. No need to take him along to Morehdalye! Why should a mother like Tilza have the pleasure of seeing her child? She certainly won't want to come back if we send Heshe'le along."

Yaakov Asher listened and squirmed as if under a whip, but he remained silent. How humiliating it would be, how emasculating, for his father-in-law to learn that he was afraid of even speaking to his wife.

17

A THICK SNOW FELL STEADILY. Tilza gazed out the window, imagining her parents' house somewhere high above earth, surrounded by wind and clouds. Her imaginary world had no contours, no recognizable forms or faces, and this notion brought her pleasure. As before her marriage, she again enjoyed pining and suffering—for no reason, just because. Around her drifted her mother, sister, and youngest brother, all waiting for her to rejoin her husband. Her inability to make them understand heightened Tilza's suffering, and she felt at odds with herself. She and her sister Bluma Rivtcha agreed on nothing, and Refael was still too young to understand her grieving heart. Her girlhood friends had all married and become ordinary women. Tilza wasn't drawn to them, and because she'd become a rebbetzin they didn't visit her either. But there was one former friend who showed up.

Liza Hirschhorn, a lanky woman with kind, bright eyes and a soothing voice but a pockmarked face, was uninterested in reading books, nor did she dream of life in a big city. What she'd wanted, instead, was to get married as early as possible and raise a houseful of children. But this kind of talk frightened young men, who preferred to spend some time as a couple first. Her craggy face and taciturn demeanor didn't help attract potential fiancés either. When all her cheerful friends were already raising children, she was still unmarried. The townswomen all thought her incapable of wooing a man. No suitable shidduch materialized. Until, somehow, she'd found herself a husband.

Monia Mintz, a supplier of wood and food products for the Polish army, hated chaos more than anything. Which was why he'd chosen to remain a bachelor and live in Morehdalye, despite having business in Lomzhe, Zembin, and Bialystok: in a small town, life was more peaceful. For the same reason, he lived in high style, dropped into the beis medrash on occasion, and gave often to charity. If people didn't regard him as a miser or freethinker, they'd leave him in peace. But as he grew older, and suffered his first long bout of sickness, he looked around him and realized he needed more people in his orbit.

He first began to pay Liza Hirschhorn regular visits; then he sent a shadchan. Liza was over thirty by then, and he was twenty-five years her senior. It was said that he presented Liza with a stipulation: they were not to have any children. Some townswomen agreed it was better to have a husband like him than no husband at all. Others felt the opposite: better to remain an old spinster than to take on such a stubborn mule.

When she visited Tilza, Liza's voice was soft and warm, just as always. Her eyes shone sadly and maternally, like a woman who loves hosting loads of family—sisters and sisters-in-law, nieces and nephews. Sitting in Tilza's room, Liza asked so many times about her little son in Lecheve that Tilza could bear it no more and revealed she was pregnant again. Liza was so overjoyed at the news the tears sprayed from her eyes.

"I'm so happy for you, Tilza. I know your husband is a gracious man and holds a significant place among scholarly Jews. Once you give birth, I'll come visit to see your children. My Monia will certainly allow me that. Every time I visit old friends, Monia reminds me not to forget to buy gifts for their children. It's only he himself who has no patience for children, though I'll never understand how one can lack the patience for sweet little boys and adorable girls." Liza laughed, her eyes still gleaming with tears.

The visit rattled Tilza to the bone. In the evening, she sat with her mother in the dark beis din room and repeated her conversation with Liza. Her mother listened and nodded her head with concern. "Now, do you see? Your friend would give everything for the joy of having a child."

Anxious already that Sholem Shachne had not yet returned and that she hadn't heard from him or their son-in-law, Henna'le found this an opportune moment to rebuke her daughter. But she spoke in a low voice, so that Bluma Rivtcha, lolling around in her room, would not overhear. "You know what I can tell you, Tilza? It's true you're spoiled, as Father claims. You know your husband will put up with anything you do, so you do whatever you want. If you'd have been married to Liza's husband, Monia Mintz, you'd never dare sail off and leave him with a child on his hands, because you'd know that Monia would never let you come back home."

Noises drifted in from Bluma Rivtcha's nook. It sounded as if she were singing under her breath, in an angry, tuneless key. For days now, she'd been sitting in her room reading books, sewing, embroidering, or having long conversations with her brother Refael'ke. With Tilza, however, she could not see eye to eye. Bluma Rivtcha had told her sister point-blank: just as she'd never had the courage to defy her father, she now lacked the courage to leave a husband she didn't love.

Henna'le's eyes darted around the beis din room as if its shadows could eavesdrop, and then leaned her head toward Bluma Rivtcha's room. "Ever since Tzesneh Ginsburg left for Warsaw to be with Zindel—at least, that's the rumor—your sister's been avoiding her friends. All day she lounges around the house. Can you imagine your Yaakov Asher capable of such a thing, two-timing and humiliating his fiancée the way this dandy—the scholarly Zindel!—has? Everyone already considered him Bluma Rivtcha's fiancé and the future Morehdalye rabbi!"

"Bluma Rivtcha claims—and rightfully so—just like you and Father, that I'm a dreamer and she's the practical, sober one. Well, Zindel is even more practical than her, and he chose a bride who's more useful to him," Tilza said, her coal-black eyes flashing angrily. But her anger quickly abated, and she cried to her mother, "I know Yaakov Asher loves me and he's a dedicated father. But he loves me in his pious way, the same way he washes his hands before he eats bread. He's never teased me or laughed with me like other young couples do. I'm so lonely in Lecheve. But I can't be seen with women who don't live a pious life. I'm the town rebbetzin! Never mind attending one of the evening discussions organized by the town's youth. That's out of the question! So I ask Yaakov Asher to sit with me at home. But he groans and carries on about how busy he is. After all, he's the rosh yeshiva and rabbi. He rations his time the way a poor man rations his bread, making it suffice for all his children. I always dreamed of a different sort of life."

"So you dreamed! So what?!" Her mother, incensed, slapped her hands against her apron. "And if you'd have married someone who wasn't a scholar, wouldn't he have to attend to his business matters? So your husband's no chatterbox and he's measured with his time. Would you rather Yaakov Asher take his beard off when he's home with you and turn into a loafer? A frivolous lover? Bluma Rivtcha's right. Even though you cut your braids off many years ago, you're still wearing them in that head of yours. Your father and I have spent a life together and loved each other without such fantasies."

"That's exactly the problem! You and Father swooned over each other even though you had an arranged marriage, and now you can't understand why your daughter can't do the same." Tilza sighed, and Henna'le, caught off guard, blinked her eyes as she always did when she didn't know how to respond, pretending to be deaf.

But her mother and sister were right. It was true—in her imagination, Tilza still wore her long braids. She had not yet forgotten her Hebrew teacher, Ezra Morgenstern, who'd spoken so eloquently about Eretz Yisroel and weighed her heavy braids in his palm. After she'd gotten married, she realized how greedy and sweaty a man became as he drew near a woman, and ever since, she'd enjoyed recalling Morgenstern with his thick hair and dark-skinned face, his fiery eyes and full lips. Whenever he led discussions, you could tell he was a seething kettle, but he was always polite with her, hands at his sides. If she'd have known then what she knew today about men, she would have made the first move, drawn close to him, solicited hugs and kisses. If her father had not chased him from Morehdalye and they'd married, how different her life would be. These days, her father was powerless against the new breed of Morehdalye chalutzim. He couldn't even keep Refael'ke from contemplating a move to Israel, where he planned to work on a kibbutz.

This past autumn, the Morehdalye chalutzim had hired themselves out to timber merchants to chop down trees. They lugged cords of firewood through deep mud to the yards of the well-to-do. The chalutzim's fathers, wealthy men themselves, discussed this in the beis medrash, praising their children for acting on their words. To live in the land of Israel, their children asserted, you first had to experience suffering.

Refael'ke listened to these discussions and watched with envy as the chalutzim walked about hauling sacks on their shoulders. Nevertheless, he kept his distance, not wanting to cause his father any grief. With the arrival of winter, though, the young men were out of work. Instead, they gathered at the town's library, exchanged books, and held discussions in the evenings.

On one such evening, Tilza wrapped a white wool shawl around her head and asked Refael'ke to accompany her to a library gathering. A shaft of light beamed from a nearby lamp, piercing Refael'ke's glasses. He took them off, rubbed his nearsighted eyes, and deliberated over the right thing to do. If he'd been avoiding the chalutzim all this time to keep from hurting his father, he couldn't go to the library now, either, while his father was away, since eventually he'd find out. In the end, Refael'ke said, "I don't want to go," and Tilza understood his reasons.

"And may *I* go?"

"You can go. Father won't worry about you running off to Israel at this point." Refael smiled and put his glasses back on. "It's dark and slippery outside, so I'll walk with you there. Just ask someone to walk you back home."

The library building consisted of one large square room, with a stage for plays and lectures. On the rough wooden shelves that lined the room's perimeter lay sparse rows of tattered books, more paperbacks than hardbound. A long electric light, hanging from the low ceiling, shone dimly through the clouds of cigarette smoke. The crowd was composed of young unmarried men in hats, short coats, and tall boots. Up on the stage, seated behind a table, was the chairman, a middle-aged man with a large bald spot, drooping cheeks, and a beard shaped like a trowel. Though he was silent, it was easy to tell by his wide mouth and thick lips that he had a powerful voice. Near him stood the speaker, a tall young man, unmarried, wearing a blue turtleneck sweater. He had a long face and protruding eyes, but his hair was thick and handsome, full of curls that coiled and crimped at his temples. On the table, midway between the chairman and the speaker, stood a pitcher full of lemonade and an empty glass. The audience gazed tensely at the lemonade from their benches, as if parched or perhaps bothered by the one, same question: Why had the pitcher been placed there on the table if no one was drinking from it?

As Tilza stepped inside and took a seat on the last empty bench, the audience turned their gazes from the stage. For a moment they stared at her, until they were bored and swiveled their heads back around. Either they hadn't recognized her as the rabbi's older daughter, or they had and it made no impression.

The man onstage spoke in a passionate, combative tone about committees, certificates, and white paper. He derided a British minister. He reserved even more anger for a certain sort of Zionist who was trying to split up the chalutzim movement. He went on about resolutions and divisions for so long that Tilza's head began to ache. The chiseled faces of the young men, too, listening drearily in silence, looked worried and blank. The room's stingy electric light grew even dimmer in the dense cigarette smoke, the plumes whirling upward as if the smokers were trying to escape their own confined and gloomy thoughts. The speaker, incidentally, concluded on a confident note, declaring that, despite all Zionist enemies from without and within, the fifth wave of immigration would not be blocked. But no one applauded or cheered.

The next speaker was a soldier in uniform, though his jacket was missing buttons and he had no military belt—a dark, slim, sharp-eyed young man. His speech was even blander than the last: "Compared to many other small towns in Lithuania, Polesia, and Volin, Morehdalye is backward. Up until now, it's been impossible to find a single Jewish farm in the entire area that trusts chalutzim to work alongside non-Jewish farmhands. And the community shows no support for the chalutzim movement, despite us having our own city councilman here . . ." And with that the speaker glared accusingly at the trowel-bearded chairman. The soldier then turned back to the crowd and explained that next summer there'd be a work opportunity for chalutzim with a certain landowner. This farmer planted cabbage, carrots, onions, turnips, and potatoes, and was now planning to grow tobacco. The only problem, however, was that the apartment he reserved for trainees was far too cramped, forcing them to sleep three to a bed. This farmer also neglected to provide any flour for baking bread, never mind butter, cheese, eggs, or milk. All he'd permit was sour milk and potatoes twice a day. And even if a chalutz managed to acquire his own products for baking and cooking, there weren't enough women comrades to manage the kitchen. The trainees would also need farm equipment, but the treasury was empty . . .

Back in Lecheve, Refael'ke had already told Tilza about how hard the road was for chalutzim, both before and after the move to Israel. So Tilza listened to the speakers with downcast eyes, regretting that she'd come. No longer would she be able to daydream of that summer evening in the meadow with Ezra. Her thoughts were interrupted by the shout of someone in the crowd: "The pious zealots of this town and the rabbi are at fault! If not for them, Morehdalye would have had an agricultural training team long ago!" Tilza didn't even raise her head to see who was shouting. She remained immersed in her thoughts of Ezra, and it occurred to her that she hadn't really gotten to know him very well. If her father had let them go out a little longer, who knows, maybe she'd have lost her interest anyway. Quietly, Tilza shuffled out of the room to the dark outdoors. She had no desire to speak with anyone there, nor to ask anyone to walk her home.

So when Tilza's husband arrived in Morehdalye, he didn't have to put up a fight. She was ready to come home. As a result, Yaakov Asher told the family that Sholem Shachne had remained in Lecheve only to watch over Heshe'le and lecture the students. But alone with his wife, Yaakov Asher revealed the truth: as long as she stayed in Morehdalye, he refused to return. "I didn't want to tell it to your family, because I didn't want your mother and siblings to fight with you. I don't want to force you to come back. But tell me, what complaints do you have against me?" He spread his hands out and his voice broke.

Tilza looked carefully at her husband's hands, with their stubby yellow-freckled fingers, at his red beard that grew down over his neck, his protruding forehead, always crinkled and sweaty from toiling over the Torah or worrying about the yeshiva, and she asked herself: "Indeed, what is it I have against him? So I don't like that he keeps gaining weight and his jacket keeps getting tighter? Why not focus on his good qualities? He's well-mannered, smart, kind, educated, and a renowned rosh yeshiva. He has such kind eyes that, with a mere glance, all your limbs grow warmer. Who am I to cause him such suffering?"

Tilza listened silently as her husband spoke to her in the same manner her father once did. "You're a fine woman, and you were raised in a devout Jewish town with a long history. How is it you've come to lust after the glitz of material objects? I love my students deeply for their sharp minds, their piety, sincerity, and kindness, for their willingness to travel to a foreign town just to grow in their study of Torah. But all you see in my students is their unattractive clothes and unworldly behavior. You know, there are moments when I've thought of standing in the middle of the market and crying out: 'Who is like our nation of Israel, one nation on earth?' Where in the world can you find such honorable Jews as the Jews of Lecheve? They take food from their own mouths to feed our students, and their greatest hope is to find a scholar for a son-in-law. They practically cut their own fingers off to pay me a rabbi's wage, and even add a little more for being the rosh yeshiva. But all you see is poverty and miserable lives, disheveled women and dispirited men. Filth and barbarians— that's all you see in everyone and everything. The Lecheve men and women feel it. They know how you act toward them, but they ignore it on my account. Even my students, young boys, are aware of all I'm forced to swallow for you.

"Your father says I'm at fault, that I've spoiled you. And he's right! If you weren't pregnant, I'd give you the option—there's such a thing as divorce in Judaism, after all," Yaakov Asher said, and his voice, like his hands, shook with great aggravation. To say such words to his own wife!

But her reply, which she, too, uttered with an aching heart and burning eyes, was unexpected. "I don't want to divorce you either. I'll go home with you. But don't walk around here sighing and broken-hearted. I don't want Bluma Rivtcha to think I don't love you and am only going home because I have no other choice."

"Why do you care what Bluma Rivtcha thinks?" Her husband, face covered in sweat, eyed her with a weary smile.

"I just don't want it!" Tilza stamped her foot and flung her head back, as if she still had long girlish braids to toss.

18

T HE DAY AFTER PURIM, Henna'le's two younger sisters, Sarah Raizel and Chavtche, spinsters both, arrived unexpectedly from Warsaw. On their way to visit their father in Zembin, they stopped for a day in Morehdalye.

Chavtche, youngest child of the elderly Zembiner rabbi, was short and agile. She had restless blue eyes, which always seemed to be laughing at anyone who thought they could outwit her. In the family, they claimed this was the very reason Chavtche remained unmarried: men were afraid of a woman with too much intelligence. But Chavtche was unconcerned. Even without a husband, she wasn't gloomy. Friends came to her for advice, and she traveled often, visiting this or that relative.

Abandoning her father's home and his devoutly religious standards had also come easier to her than to her sisters. The others had had to tear themselves away, but Chavtche had flitted off easily and joyfully. Chavtche believed nothing was worth sacrificing oneself for—not even convictions such as the denying of God's existence, or of equal rights for all people. Let everyone do whatever they wished; it wasn't her concern.

Indeed, she had no concerns. Chavtche lived off the earnings of her older sister, Sarah Raizel, who managed a paper shop and was better at business than her bosses. The customers and other employees trusted her more than the store owners. Sarah Raizel had a round face, white as flour, a puffed-up bosom, and a large, heavy body perched on spindly legs that carried her lightly and swiftly around the stockroom. Her long, nimble hands would open the credit books— and lo, she'd land on the precise page of her customer's account. With her pencil she'd point to the spot on the overstuffed shelves where the items they were looking for lay. Every transaction was filed in her head like the items in her handbag, like the underwear in the drawers of her dresser. But as soon as she left the store and went home to Chavtche, she lost all her skillful efficiency and became suddenly powerless.

The sisters lived together. Sarah Raizel dressed carelessly, in wide dresses made of cheap fabrics. It seemed as if she were trying to look dumpy, so that Chavtche, in comparison, would look sharper in her tight-fitting clothes and her round, stylish hats, pacing lightly in low-heeled shoes. Chavtche did her best to look even shorter and slighter than she was, as if in her diminutiveness lay the secret of her power over Sarah Raizel, the latter earning the money for the former to spend. The family incited Sarah Raizel: "Why are you letting yourself be exploited? Live your own life. And what'll happen if Chavtche gets married?" But it was perhaps Sarah Raizel's fear of Chavtche getting married that made her give her all her earnings in the first place.

Chavtche riffled through Sarah Raizel's handbag and asked, "Are you out of money? When are you getting your wages? I have to pick up my winter coat before we travel to Gita-Gittel in Czyżew."

Whenever Chavtche demanded it, Sarah Raizel put everything aside and went traveling with her, no matter how much her bosses begged her not to abandon the shop. This time, too, Sarah Raizel joined her. She even carried her younger sister's suitcases. Chavtche knew she wasn't a welcome guest at the home of her brother-in-law, the Morehdalye rabbi. Well, what did she care? That was the least of her worries! Hands folded beneath her short cardigan, she paced around the guest room and told the family, "Back in Warsaw, I received a letter from a Zembin friend. She writes, 'I'm sure you'll come to the dedication ceremony for the newly renovated talmud torah, which your father fixed up using the lottery money he won.' And that's how I found out about Father's windfall! And that he'd fixed up the talmud torah at his own expense! And now they were celebrating. Well, even if he didn't invite me, I'm going with Sarah Raizel to the dedication ceremony." Their older sister, Kona, and her husband (the wooden noodle, Banet Michelson) were traveling directly from Warsaw, Chavtche explained, and she insisted that Henna'le and her husband must come, too, even if they weren't invited.

"Actually, Father did invite us," said Henna'le, oldest of the four sisters, "but we haven't yet decided if we're going."

"Father invited you and your husband because his wife isn't scared of you. You can't see her for who she is," Chavtche said without skipping a beat, giving Henna'le and her husband a sly look. "It was Vigasia's idea—Vigasia! What a name!—that Father should use his lottery winnings to rebuild the talmud torah and leave the rest for her and her sons. I heard she has three sons, provincial fools, watchmakers. Father may well have cast us all out of his will already and put Vigasia and her sons in our place. We don't even know how much money Father won. He claims that after all the deducted taxes and percentages, he's left with no more than two thousand zlotys, but others say he made out with more than five thousand, and some that it might even be more than ten thousand. So we all have to go to Zembin. Let him see he has his own biological children, not just stepsons. What do you say, Sarah Raizel?"

Her older sister nodded her head. She didn't dare think differently.

"And what do you say, Henna?" Chavtche turned to her oldest sister. "From you, at least, Father has nachas. You think if Mother were still alive we wouldn't all be invited to such an occasion?"

Henna'le didn't think Chavtche the brightest, but she didn't want to bicker. So she looked to her husband, waiting for him to respond. Sholem Shachne, though, had always felt the Warsaw aunts were a bad influence on his children. "Your father didn't invite you because you don't live by his values," Sholem Shachne said meanly.

"That's what I'm saying!" Chavtche flashed her blue eyes at her brother-in-law—the rabbi with the aristocratic beard. Hands still folded beneath her short cotton cardigan, she again paced in measured steps across the guest room in her brown suede, low-heeled shoes. While she paced, she glanced obliquely into the mirror on the wall to check whether her clothes fit precisely—her white blouse with a black collar, her brown skirt of heavy knitted wool speckled with black polka dots. "That's just what I'm saying! Father knows his daughters aren't the most devout, and this Vigasia has him convinced that *her* sons are saints. This way, she'll get him to leave her sons our inheritance. And you?" Chavtche spun around to Bluma Rivtcha. "Grandfather loved you as a child. Are you going?"

"I'm not going, and I don't care if Grandfather doesn't leave me anything. I want to earn my money on my own." Bluma Rivtcha's cheeks glowed rosily in annoyance, and her long, narrow eyes grew narrower.

"When you become a millionaire from your earnings, don't forget to invite your aunt over," Chavtche interrupted her niece, and then started in on her nephew. "And you, Refael'ke, will you come?"

"Grandfather didn't invite me either," Refael'ke answered calmly, casting his usual smile.

"Fine. So don't come!" Chavtche cried. And she fled Morehdalye as swiftly as she'd come, Sarah Raizel dashing behind her, panting, like a low-flying fat white goose, neck outstretched, heavy wings batting.

For a long while, Henna'le continued to turn the matter over in her head. Should she go or not? Finally, she made up her mind to go. She'd see her elderly father and take a look at the woman he married, see whether she was indeed as sly a woman as Chavtche made her out to be.

Sholem Shachne never had any doubt. Of course he wasn't allowed to refuse his father-in-law's invitation to the dedication ceremony! It pained him only that Bluma Rivtcha and Refael'ke weren't interested in seeing their grandfather on his special occasion.

Brother and sister stayed home. They gazed out the window and saw that, from the suburban fields to the horizon, the ground was covered in high mounds of snow. But here and there rose a solitary tree, already stretching its naked branches higher upward, a few of its twigs trembling, like a blind person feeling the way forward with outstretched hands.

"Soon we'll be able to remove the double glass in the window and get rid of the yellowed cotton between the panes," Bluma Rivtcha said.

"It's too early. We might still get a frost. Don't do anything without Mother," Refael'ke, the mature one, replied.

Until she was seventeen, Bluma Rivtcha had traveled frequently to see her grandfather in Zembin, staying for weeks or months. Her grandfather, wrapped in his tallis, had looked to her like an old apple tree, not too tall or girthy. She missed her grandfather and remembered the fragrance of his washed beard on Fridays after he returned from the mikveh. She also missed her Zembin friends. But it was precisely because of them that she didn't go to the dedication ceremony. Each of her Zembin friends had attained something: they'd learned a skill or found a job in a shop or married a young man they cared for. Bluma Rivtcha alone had attained nothing.

"No matter what Father and Mother say, I'm going to travel to Warsaw and find work in a shop, or go to nursing school in Vilna. I don't know yet where I'll go to or what I'll do, but there's no way I'm staying in this town. I don't want to be a loafer like Aunt Chavtche, living her entire life on someone else's money. I don't want to be like Tilza either, who married a man she didn't like and still doesn't, but is trapped, because Father demanded it, because she never learned to stand on her own two feet. I don't want to be like her. You hear me? I don't want it!"

"I hear," Refael'ke answered softly, and remained silent for such a long time that his sister ended up joining him in his silence. Both stood looking out the window, their eyes wandering to the mountain. There, in front of the white church, was the town's marketplace. Because of the distance from the rabbi's house to the marketplace, all you could see were spots of wagons and street stalls, horses, and a swarm of people. In the gray sheen of daylight, the peasant women's headscarves gleamed. Colorful kerchiefs winked in the distance, like cowberries peeking out of the snow. The young boy and girl in the rabbi's house turned their gazes from the church market to the few blocks directly across from them, surrounding the synagogue courtyard.

Bluma Rivtcha had always wondered why the crooked, patchwork houses had so many windows stuffed with rags and so many entries boarded up. It was almost as if the town's Jews didn't want their homes to have too many ways in and out. They seemed to prefer the coziness of crawling inside through one low door, like tiny woodland creatures who, frightened of big open spaces, crawl their way through dense thickets. Lately, her father, too, Bluma Rivtcha realized, seemed to want to shut himself in little rooms, away from his befuddled children and the cold outer hall. His living quarters had become too big for him. Even when he studied in his library during the day, he drew the curtains closed against the light. It was more pleasant to study in a dark, candlelit room, he claimed.

All at once, Bluma Rivtcha and Refael'ke heard the distant but unmistakable echo of hammers clanging on anvils. The smithy wasn't visible from the rabbi's house, but they had no doubt: the clanging was coming from the smithy down at the river's shore, behind the commotion of the parking lot, the squat houses, the warehouses and stables. The hammer's steady blows rang out cheerfully and echoed assertively, as if the metallic racket were an announcement that the ice on the Narev had already cracked, that the floes were drifting, the pale blue sky had risen higher, and the world was wide open, already breathing the early spring air.

19

T HE MOREHDALYE RABBI HAS finally realized he can't persuade the world of his views, so he's trying to at least persuade his children. His father-in-law, on the other hand, the Zembin rabbi, no longer demands anything of his children but continues waging his lifelong war with the city and the rest of the world." So went the gossip among the town's businessmen and religious functionaries.

The difference between the two was just as evident from their homes. Unlike the Morehdalye rabbi's roof, its shingles overgrown with weeds, drooping ever lower like a gray cloud, the Zembin rabbi's was fire red, as if to broadcast to all: Here lives a zealous Jew! The window shutters and courtyard gate gleamed, wearing a fresh coat of dark green paint. The chimney above and the walls inside had just been painted, too, in a white bright enough to blind. Not a single step on the stairway needed repair, no door creaked from rust, and the glass veranda wasn't missing a single pane. No one who passed it on the way to the Zembin marketplace, amid the row of opulent two- and three-story brick houses, could miss the rabbi's flaming-red abode. It seemed to brag: "Look at the new wing that's just been added, see how I'm made of wood but strong as iron, as iron-strong as the opinions of my owner, the town's rabbi, Eli-Leizer HaLevi Epstein." If, however, one were to ask the Zembin rabbi himself, he'd reply without fail that it was on account of the children that he was forced to fix and paint and expand the house so often. If it were up to him, the world would still be living in limestone structures, and people would still be traveling by oxen, not rushing around in trains and planes—straight to purgatory.

The year 5690,* when Eli-Leizer turned eighty, was also the sixty-

* 1929/1930.

year anniversary of his marriage to the former Zembin rabbi's daughter, and exactly fifty years from when he'd taken over the rabbinate after his father-in-law's death. For fifty years he'd been steadily engaged in battle with enlightened homeowners and plain old insubordinates who refused to obey their rabbi. Kaisers fell, the world war ended, a strengthened Polish government arose, but the Zembin rabbi went on waging his wars. He feuded with enemies old and new: the young generation and their political parties.

His rebbetzin, Elka'le, three years his junior, looked to be twenty years younger because of her short stature, narrow shoulders, and brisk movements. She had been seventeen years old at her wedding and had provided her husband with ten children. But she'd miscarried twice, because she couldn't sit still even during pregnancy. Two others had died in infancy. So Elka'le was left with four daughters and two sons. She'd given birth to her oldest daughter, Henna'le, a year into the marriage, and her youngest daughter, Chavtche, had been born twenty-four years later. Elka'le was forty-one by that time, Henna'le twenty-four and the mother of a two-year-old boy. In the family they giggled over this newborn aunt, who was two years younger than her nephew, and the people of Zembin marveled at their rebbetzin, who looked no older than her eldest daughter.

Unlike her husband, the rebbetzin got along with everyone. Elka'le never uttered a harsh word to any of the women in town and never chided girls whose dresses were too short. She didn't poke her nose into community affairs at all, and never even entered the beis din room during a hearing or meeting. She never missed a davening or the reciting of her techinos, yet she always acted without arrogance. Her conversations with other women revolved around nachas from the children and, more often than not, food. Elka'le would visit neighbors to taste their sweet and sour fish and stuffed cabbage. She prepared raspberries for tea for wintertime, when one was prone to catch a cold or a cough. And she invited these same neighbors to her home, to get their opinions on her food. Her poppy-seed hamantaschen, chremslach, and dairy pastries were famous in Zembin. During the years when the rabbi was still earning his livelihood selling salt, candles, and yeast, the rebbetzin served the townswomen like a poor shop owner who can't thank her customers enough for stopping in. Later, when the rabbi received a salary from the town's Jewish community, the rebbetzin would thank the treasurer who brought their money as if he were doing it out of charity. Whenever a woman came to her with the complaint "Your husband's causing my husband such grief," Elka'le didn't excuse herself by saying it was not her place to get involved; she simply sat there speechless for so long and so gloomily that the sharp-tongued woman would grow ashamed and join the rebbetzin in her silence. People said Eli-Leizer loved his Elka'le from the depths of his soul. Even he, the aggressive fighter, seemed to appreciate his wife's agreeable nature.

Looking at the rabbi, you could tell he was on in years. He struggled to bend over; his arms and legs were feeble. He'd doze off suddenly in the middle of reciting a page of the Gemara to the town's householders. More than once, he'd been confined to his bed and a doctor had to be summoned. Only when confronting freethinkers and libertines did he recapture his youthful roar—a lion's roar—as if the fighting were restorative. But looking at the thin, vivacious rebbetzin, you could never tell she was a woman of seventy-seven. She still bustled about, busily cooking and baking, going to the neighbors to taste their dishes, inviting them over to see how her flattened dough had risen. And it was amid just such bustling—in the year 5690—that she stepped into a neighbor's home with a full plate of pickled beet brine and collapsed. Elka'le died with a loving smile on her face, as if joyful to be arriving in Paradise just in time for the seder, bearing her mitzvah of beet brine, pure as an eye, tasting of the legendary wine reserved for the righteous in Paradise.

Zembin looked like a tree struck by lightning, charred and shriveled. But the first one to emerge from the dark turmoil and remind everyone that it was the eve of Passover turned out to be the widower himself, the Zembin rabbi. He ordered his beadles to pin up notices from the beis din all over the neighborhood, listing the products suspected of being chametz that one should avoid on Passover. And because of the holiday, Eli-Leizer wasn't required by Jewish law to sit shiva. So he put on his satin kaftan and his top hat and, as he did every year at this time, drove to the Polish regiment on the outskirts of town to persuade the commander to allow his Jewish soldiers to have their seder. "A man of steel and iron," the town's men muttered to each other.

A short while later, he again had the chance to show his grit. To the surprise of everyone, even his own children, the old rabbi got married to a distant cousin—on Lag B'Omer, just one month after Passover. A brouhaha erupted anew in the city, but this time it was a mix of laughter and fury. Eli-Leizer's adversaries cried delightedly, triumphantly: "Haven't we always said the rabbi lacks a Jewish heart? Sixty years he lives with a woman, the only creature in the world who hasn't fought with him. Then this tragedy strikes, and he can't even stay a widower until after Lag B'Omer."

Those close to the rabbi came to his defense: "He's an old, sickly man, he's not allowed to be alone by Jewish law. So in order to bring a woman into his home to care for him without violating the laws of yichud, he married her."

"That's exactly what we're saying!" Eli-Leizer's opponents replied. "This is precisely the problem! The Zembin rabbi lives by Jewish law, and he wants to force the entire world to live by Jewish law—yet without a shred of mercy."

But when the townspeople got a good look at the new rebbetzin, everyone, even the rabbi's opponents, were struck by an awed, solemn silence, as when opening a treasure of silk and velvet squares lined with red plush, filled with estate jewelry.

Rebbetzin Tamara, thirty years younger than the rabbi, gave off a faint, delicate glow, luminous in her widowhood and pedigree. Tall and slender, draped in folds of clothes, she resembled a large bird with feeble wings who'd just emerged from a leafy hideout, stumbling about on tall legs over autumn's mowed and prickly fields. Tamara had a weary face, a half-extinguished smile, and such sadness in her eyes it seemed she'd come from a world where the sun neither shone nor set. She had the aura of having descended from a great family lineage that was petering out, a glorious background in decline. Still, you could tell that she was willing to embrace her new environment. Gradually, Zembin began to believe that this woman of such rare refinement would soften the stubborn old rabbi. With her at his side, he'd likely be embarrassed to slam his fists on the table during meetings in the beis din room and threaten to place people under cherem. So enamored did the townspeople become of the new rebbetzin that they began to speak ill of her predecessor.

"It's said that even a rabbi's *maid* can make rulings on Jewish law, but Rebbetzin Elka'le, may she rest in peace, daughter to a rabbi, wife to a rabbi for sixty years, remained a simple Jewish lady. *Too* simple. She didn't even *attempt* to change her husband's coarse behavior. But his current rebbetzin, may she live long, is a true Queen Esther and will bring him under her sway."

But Zembin was destined to suffer yet another unimaginable horror. On the morning of the Shabbos following the holiday of Sukkos, Tamara stood among the women in their section of the beis medrash, looking like a tall, svelte poplar amid squat, rumpled shrubs. Suddenly, she collapsed into the hands of the surrounding women, her siddur dropping from her long, pale fingers. She gave a deep sigh, and in the blink of an eye she was dead.

The people of Zembin were terrified, afraid even to attend her funeral. Gusts of wind tore at the rooftops and shutters. That year, the trees shed their leaves earlier than usual, thrashing about with severed branches, producing otherworldly shrieks. Women stood in cliques in the courtyards, whispering in fright, as if the Angel of Death were flapping its large black wings before them: "During her lifetime, Rebbetzin Elka'le was a tenderhearted person, but in the World of Truth she became furious that another woman had taken her place, so she dragged the new rebbetzin to her."

All winter long, the old rabbi struggled without a woman in the house. But after Purim he again remarried, this time to an elderly widow with a somewhat bizarre name: Vigasia. Nearing seventy, she was nevertheless vigorous, stocky, a head taller than the rabbi, with little hairs on her chin and a thick, loud voice. She spoke crudely and dressed like a poor woman in long black shopworn dresses, more like rags than clothing. But her black eyes shone with intelligence and with the quick, penetrating glare of a keen observer. Vigasia didn't feel threatened by the superstitious resentment of Eli-Leizer's first rebbetzin, nor by the untimely end of his second. And she had no patience for the pretense of not getting involved in community affairs. She *did* get involved and even boasted about it. During din Torahs, Vigasia sat in the beis din room on a tall stool and knitted. If she felt the litigant was lying or being too abusive, she cut him off. "Now don't shout, sir! This isn't a marketplace!" She watched over the rabbi, making sure he got sufficient food and rest. And she protected his dignity, too. Because Vigasia didn't hail from rabbis, she encouraged and emboldened her husband to command the respect he was due, and to exhibit an appearance befitting his position as rabbi of Zembin.

20

ELI-LEIZER FINALLY RECKONED with the fact that his tirades against Shabbos desecrators weren't getting him anywhere. So one Friday evening he sauntered into a barbershop, climbed up onto a tall stool, and sat himself down. On the other stools, the clients all turned their startled, soapy faces toward him. The dumbfounded barbers, too, clutching razors in their hands, stopped in their tracks. The barbershop owner walked over to the rabbi and, with extreme tact, asked him what he wanted.

"What do I want? I want to cut and shave my beard in honor of Shabbos, that's what I want. Why look so surprised? Fifty-plus years of being Zembin's rabbi is more than enough for me. I'm ready to be a sinful Jew, just like you."

As the story was later told, the Jewish customers, their half-shaved faces covered in lather, scattered and fled the barbershop like little boys stealing apples from an orchard who suddenly spot a guard running over with a stick.

A week later, Eli-Leizer walked into another barber's shop. Here, the owner argued with Eli-Leizer: "In the winter, Fridays are so short that no matter how much my clients and barbers hurry, they can't get done before it's time to light the candles."

Eli-Leizer let him finish and then burst into laughter. "Some tale! You see, the old fool and ignoramus I am, I was under the impression that Jewish laws against Shabbos desecration were made for short winter Fridays, too, not just for long summer ones. From now on, anytime someone consults me on a question of Jewish law, I'll send them over to you for a final ruling, you shameful Jew."

From that afternoon on, the barbers scrambled to finish their clients' cuts and shaves on Fridays, as if it were the eve of Yom Kippur before the Kol Nidrei prayer.

One winter Shabbos morning, before going to daven, Eli-Leizer peered out the window, surveying the freshly fallen snow on the roofs of the houses across from his. Icicles dangled from the eaves, sunbeams reflected in them like golden flames in crystal chandeliers. The sky shone pure blue, as on a summer's day. Snow lay in tall heaps on the doorsteps, as if to block out everyday worries during the Shabbos rest. Through his window, the rabbi saw a man step off his stoop with a tallis bag tucked under his arm. The Jew paused for a moment, his face turned up at the distant sun, probably waiting for its rays to coil their way into his beard and ears, the way a grandfather awaits the pleasure of his grandchild's little fingers tickling and pinching his nose and whiskers. Eli-Leizer murmured verses of Tehillim to himself, absorbed in his thoughts. *The men rest easy here in my city,* he thought. *They don't worry about whether they're allowed to carry their tallis on Shabbos, because they know I badger the shammes every Friday, making sure he checks that the eruv is intact, no tears anywhere. A Jew, a believer, knows in his gut—even without a calendar—when the seventh day of the week has arrived. All you have to do is look at the sun. In its shine you instinctively feel the sanctity of the holy Shabbos.*

Suddenly, the rabbi creased his forehead and raised his eyebrows, straining his sight. Despite his old age, his vision was sharp. Still, he refused to believe what he was seeing: a Jew, bundled in a heavy coat and holding a parcel in his hand, rushing through the marketplace to catch the bus headed to Bialystok, at the station near the firemen's barn. Soon came another Jew—tall and broad, in a big winter hat and a fur-collared coat with a wide belt round the middle. Beneath his arm he carried a bulging briefcase as if it were a tallis bag (may the comparison of the sacred and profane be forgiven!), and strolled serenely, head raised, as if desecrating Shabbos were an honor. Then arrived a boy and girl. Their arms were locked, and in their free hand each carried a small suitcase. More than that, Eli-Leizer refused to see.

The congregants of his beis medrash greeted him with some surprise: ordinarily he was the first to arrive, but today he was late. Instead of making the usual gesture to indicate that the service should begin, the rabbi slammed a fist down on the lectern. "In the name of God, I decree upon every observant Jew here to follow me to the bus station." His intimates, as well as the regular householders, shucked off their talleisim and followed him.

Near the steps of the idling bus stood a long line of people—peasants from the surrounding villages, Christians from the city, and Jews. Eli-Leizer spared no word for the Jewish passengers. He merely instructed his followers to form a circle around the entire bus and link hands in a chain, as when they danced around the bimah on Simchas Torah. The rabbi positioned himself directly in front of the engine. Passersby stopped to stare, curious to see what would happen. The Poles in line muttered angrily among themselves. But the Jewish passengers stood there silently, heads lowered—ashamed to raise their eyes, and yet reluctant to leave.

The driver, a hulking gentile, walked over to the rabbi and addressed him in a friendly tone. He would have to call the police, he explained, and they'd haul the rabbi away in cuffs for disturbing the peace and causing the bus company to lose money. The rabbi spoke fluent Russian, and knew Polish, too. After all, he was constantly dealing with town officials, and he'd lived his entire life across from the market where Jews and gentiles did business. So he answered the driver in a mishmash of languages. "Call the police, do what you want, you can even run me over with the bus. As long as Jewish passengers board this bus on our sacred day of rest, I will not budge."

The Poles' muttering turned to shouts. "No problem for us if the zhids don't ride today!" "Go to Palestine! Go to Madagascar! You can institute your regime there!"

The Jewish passengers began to inch away, one after the other, and the Poles pressed forward through the bus's two open doors, laughing at the zhids, pleased that they'd now have a roomier ride.

Eventually, the bus company got wise and opened a station on the city's outskirts. Any Zembin Jews who wanted to ride on Shabbos were forced to trek along the Bialystok highway in order to catch the bus. Although some Jews persisted, the pious of Zembin consoled themselves that at least there was no overt Shabbos desecration anymore, nothing out in plain sight. The rabbi's followers congratulated him on his victory, wished him mazel tov, and quipped, "Rabbi, if you were able to pull the Shabbos desecrators by their hair and chase them from the bus station, you'll be able to pull us businessmen out of gehinnom in the afterworld."

But instead of feeling pleased, the old rabbi sighed. "But how do we pull the crowd out of the cinema now?" he griped. "The three Jewish owners of this abomination claim they leased the hall on Saturdays because there isn't enough of a crowd otherwise. People go to this circus only on Friday night and Saturday. What can be done?"

"These lowlifes shouldn't be allowed into the theater on Shabbos in the first place. This way you'd spare yourself the job of pulling them out," Rebbetzin Vigasia offered.

Eli-Leizer declared a cherem on the Jewish owners of the cinema and on any Jew who went there on Shabbos. The owners, unintimidated, went ahead and opened the hall on Friday night. The entrance lamps were lit, the cashier stood in his booth, ready to sell tickets, but the crowd never came. The regular cinemagoers had discussed the issue: "It's true," they said, "the rabbi is too tempestuous, but still, how can we enjoy these sinful pictures with a cherem weighing on our heads?"

The fuming cinema owners, along with a hired gang of hoodlums, besieged the rabbi's home and shouted through the windows:

"You old fanatic! You're not leaving your home until you lift the injunction and let people into the cinema!"

"You've buried two rebbetzins already. Why not bury the third, who's inciting you to steal our livelihood?"

"For fifty years you've been wringing double wages out of Zembin's people, so that you can travel to the spas. You've become a rich man, but we've stayed poor."

"Don't we have enough problems and worries all week long—now you're taking the pleasure of Shabbos away from us, too? Go to the land of Israel and take your troublesome rebbetzin with you. That's what other rabbis do in their old age. Go, go away and let us live in this world!"

From the rabbi's house came no response. A woman stopped by to ask the rabbi a question on Jewish law; a young man wanted to discuss a Torah passage; two businessmen came wanting a din Torah; community members sought guidance on community affairs—the hostile barricaders chased them all away with whoops and raised fists, ready to confront anyone. Some distance away stood a group of curious onlookers, conversing among themselves. There was nothing new, they said, about the rabbi waging battle with the masses—with the householders and even the religious functionaries—but for his opponents to block him from leaving his house, well, that was unheard of! What would happen when he wanted to go to the beis medrash for afternoon and evening prayers? They stayed to watch.

But when Eli-Leizer appeared on his veranda, ready to elbow his way through the barricaders to go to the beis medrash, come what may—let them heckle or even beat him!—not one of the gang laid a hand on him. Instead, they surrounded him so that he was pushed back into his house, bellowing that neither he nor his rebbetzin would be leaving until he removed the injunction and let Jews come to the theater.

The barricaders left late at night and returned at dawn, so that the rabbi wouldn't be able to sneak out in time to make the early minyan. But no one tried to leave or enter the rabbi's home. The gang lurked by the windows. Not a shadow of a person inside. They tried the door. Locked. Only later did they discover that, in the deep of the winter night, the rabbi and rebbetzin had snuck away to the talmud torah. The townspeople snickered at the duped theater owners. "For half a century, here in Zembin, it's been a known fact that you can never get your way with the rabbi. And you thought you'd succeed?"

But the huffing cinema owners replied, "Never mind, his new rebbetzin, and he, too, will get tired of their exile in the talmud torah. They'll try to come back home. And when they do, we won't let them back in until the old fanatic surrenders."

Eli-Leizer's followers, too, begged him to let it go this time around. "These hoodlums won't yield. Who knows how long the rabbi and rebbetzin will be in limbo in the talmud torah, sleeping on sacks of straw?"

Indeed, Eli-Leizer told his followers, they were right: Some of the rooms in the talmud torah could not be used at all, they were in such disrepair. What's more, the orphans, who already slept a few to a bed, were now in even tighter conditions, with a room sacrificed for the rabbi and his wife. As a result, the two decided to retreat to the old age home. "What do you think, people? Will the managers of the old age home agree to add two more beds? Heaven forbid, I'm not demanding a separate room. I'll live together with the men, and Vigasia is willing to room with the other women. Either I'm the rabbi of Zembin and the people obey me, or I'm no more privileged than any poor man and a spot in the old age home befits me."

All of Zembin began repeating the rabbi's words to each other. The hoodlums' hearts turned heavy, and they grumbled to the cinema owners: "That's it for us. We're done with this business. It's not worth it, just for free entrance to the cinema for us and our wives, to cause the old rabbi to catch pneumonia in the drafty talmud torah and die. The world will condemn us, they'll blame us."

Besides the scholars and pious business owners, a few coachmen, fruit vendors, and butchers also sided with the rabbi. These stout Jews gathered round the rabbi's house and yelled at the three cinema owners who still stood guarding the house, albeit without their cronies. "Bastards! When the rabbi tells us our ox isn't kosher, we don't say a word! If he tells a businessman to pay a penalty, he pays up like a good little boy. But you're somehow privileged? All you'll do is alienate your customers, who'll stop coming to see your foul pictures even on Saturday night when Shabbos is over. Step aside before we start cracking heads!"

The rabbi came back home, triumphant, and the rebbetzin's stock rose greatly, too. The townspeople said to one another, "If Elka'le had agreed to suffer these hardships with her husband, well, that would be understandable. She had a whole life together with him, a family, their children. But Vigasia's only just married him and has proved herself willing to endure all these troubles. She even encouraged him not to back down. A true 'woman of valor.'"

The rabbi's followers once again came in to wish him mazel tov, this time for his victory over the Shabbos desecrators. But he greeted them with burning cheeks, banged his fist on the table as was his way, and roared, "Woe and alas to religious Jews who shy from battles. Everyone keeps telling me I won't change the world. But if all these supposedly pious Zembin Jews were truly ready to sacrifice themselves for the Creator and his Torah, they'd announce a cherem on the Tarbus schools, on its teachers, activists, and all the parents who send their children there. During my few days in the talmud torah, the melamdim told me dreadful things about the Tarbus teachers. One of the teachers told his students that the Prophets would have been opposed to the Gemara and the *Shulchan Aruch*, just as they had been opposed to the bringing of sacrifices in the Jewish Temple. 'There will come a time,' he said—this teacher, this rabble-rouser!— 'when Jews will go back to studying only the Bible and do away with all those nuances and interpretations on the Gemara.' Another freethinking teacher mocked the part of our liturgy where we say, 'Our eyes should live to see Your return to Zion, with mercy.' 'These fanatics,' this teacher jeered, 'think all their trembling during davening will shake out a Messiah who'll drive them on rubber-wheeled wagons to the land of Israel.' And yet a third blasphemer told the schoolboys that anyone who speaks Hebrew and moves to the land of Israel is ten times the Jew than someone who observes mitzvahs but doesn't move to the land of Israel."

Eli-Leizer sobbed, and Vigasia sobbed along with him. The rabbi wiped his eyes and told his followers, "It's hopeless. If a general has no courageous soldiers, he cannot lead a war. Which is why I won't announce a cherem on the Tarbus schools. I have no one to back me up. But there's one thing I refuse to budge on. Any Jew who sends his child to these Hebrew libertines won't be called up to read the Torah in my beis medrash and won't be allowed to lead the services, even on his parents' yahrzeit."

21

THAT SAME WINTER, the rabbi had Zembin stewing again. On Asara B'Teves, ironically a somber day of fasting, he received the happy news that he'd won a fortune on a lottery ticket. Just as unanticipated problems befell this old man, so did this unanticipated windfall drop upon him now. Exactly how much he'd won nobody knew, but they all tried to guess what he'd do with the money. Those mathematically inclined predicted he'd divide the money among his heirs. Others thought he and his rebbetzin would emigrate to the land of Israel and live out their lives in peace. But the intellectuals scoffed at all such notions, claiming, "The rabbi is too old and too stingy by now to make any changes in his life. He'll put his winnings into a savings account and earn interest on it." But a few days later, they all found out that the rabbi and his rebbetzin were donating the money to renovate the talmud torah.

Eli-Leizer's followers, who'd lately been feeling ambivalent about his ceaseless bickering, once again raised their heads high in praise, insisting he'd never waged a battle for his own honor or benefit. On the contrary, he'd take the shirt off his back for a religious Jew. No wonder he was concerned for the orphans in the talmud torah. His followers even quoted him as saying he was ashamed that, as rabbi of this city, he'd been unaware of the orphans' living conditions. Nothing short of Divine will had orchestrated his need to flee home and take refuge in the talmud torah, so that he and his rebbetzin, in their old bones, could feel the frigidity of that ramshackle building where little children froze and yet continued to study and learn.

The men of the community asked the rabbi why he didn't use his windfall to publish a sefer—one on aggadah, allegorical innovations on the Talmud, and one on Jewish law—as befit a scholar of his age and caliber. Eli-Leizer's answer was that enabling young Jewish boys to study the five books of Chumash and Rashi's commentary took precedence over his own publications. "Who will study these scholarly texts if Jewish children grow up to be ignoramuses? Besides, I bought the lottery ticket in my wife's name, too, so she has a share in the winnings. And it's she who's insisting that the money should be spent on renovating the talmud torah."

Indeed, Vigasia had advised the rabbi, "You keep griping that your children and grandchildren aren't following your path. The orphans studying Torah are your grandchildren. See to it that they don't live in a dump."

About their rabbi, the people of Zembin liked to say that because he was always on the lookout for sins in others, he'd been punished—with the exception of his eldest daughter, who was married to a rabbi—with irreligious children. Years ago, Eli-Leizer had consoled himself with Henna'le's grandchildren. They'd traveled often to Zembin when they were young. The old man would caress the little ones with trembling hands, sobbing, kissing, and blessing them. During davening in beis medrash, he'd sit beside them, shrouding them playfully under his tallis, hugging them. And during their visits Eli-Leizer forgot all about his current skirmishes with the community; instead, he sat and studied with his grandchildren, teasing and cracking jokes to keep them from getting bored. To teach them modesty, he regaled the two girls, Tilza and Bluma Rivtcha, with tales of pious women from the past, who wore tall headdresses and were always clutching siddurim. At Tilza's wedding, not even the bride's and groom's parents danced, sang, and cried with as much abandon as her grandfather. Meanwhile, Rebbetzin Elka'le, who was still alive at the time, had spent more time in the kitchen than in the hall among the wedding guests, as if she were a hired waiter. And when, laden with plates, she circulated among the guests, an abrupt little laugh would burst from her every so often, as if she alone recognized that her granddaughter would not be happily married to this man, the future Lecheve rosh yeshiva.

Far rarer were visits from his Warsaw daughter's children. But on the few occasions they did come, their grandfather showered them, too, with gifts, all the while crying bitterly over their enrollment in Polish schools, as one might if a pearl necklace had come undone and the pearls had scattered in the mud. He pleaded with God to set his

Warsaw grandchildren back on the proper path, and called on their misguided parents to repent. But instead of becoming more devout, the Morehdalye grandchildren grew only more enlightened, visiting their grandfather less and less often. In fact, ever since Eli-Leizer had remarried, his children and grandchildren hadn't come to Zembin at all.

His daughters, who were already angry with their father for marrying their distant cousin Tamara six weeks after their mother's death, became even more irate when he married again that same year—this time to a crass and unfamiliar woman. Vigasia had been ready to welcome her husband's children and grandchildren affectionately, devotedly. But when time passed, and she saw that no one from her husband's pedigreed family had deigned to show their face, she said, in her typical manner, "Oh well, that's too bad. But so be it." Her old husband, though, missed his grandchildren, and was ashamed for the community to see that his family had abandoned him. "As long as my children still visited," he groaned to Vigasia, "I held out hope that I could influence them to change. What's left to hope for now? Even my oldest—the only successful one of the bunch—my son-in-law, Sholem Shachne, never comes to visit anymore." Which is why Vigasia's suggestion had seemed to him so fitting: they would fix up the talmud torah and simultaneously become enriched by a host of new grandchildren—the many little boys studying Torah there.

The orphanage had once been the home of a rich man. He'd died without heirs and bequeathed his property to the Zembin orphanage. Over the years, the one-story brick building, with its many rooms and windows, had fallen into disrepair, but the community didn't have the funds for an extensive renovation. Now, with the rabbi's winnings, the ovens that held no heat and emitted carbon monoxide were rebuilt. Walls and ceilings were re-plastered, double windows installed, broken steps and wobbling doors made new again. In the kitchen, new tables were needed; in the bedrooms, new beds; in the classrooms, new benches. Since all the repairs were being done inside the building, they were able to work through the winter. While one room was being repaired, the children and their melamed simply moved to another.

The expected completion date for the renovation was originally to be the fifteenth day of Shevat, on the Chamisha Asar B'Shevat holiday—New Year's for the trees—when it was customary to hand out carob pods to the children in the talmud torah. But the work stretched on for another three weeks. Finally, a week into the month of Adar, the crew began their cleanup, clearing the rooms of strewn scraps of bricks, crooked cast-iron hinges, wood shavings, tin and iron fragments.

The rabbi's shul leaders asked, "Don't you want an engraved plaque at the talmud torah's entrance, honoring you and your rebbetzin for funding the renovation?"

But Eli-Leizer replied, laughing, "My rebbetzin and I have no interest in a plaque engraved with our names. It'd be just as well if everyone forgot I did the repairs. They can forget right away! Even up in heaven they can forget!"

"And a dedication ceremony for the new building? Would you allow that?" the leaders asked.

The rabbi thought for a while. Finally, he replied that yes, a day after Shushan Purim, he would host a dedication ceremony for the building. Later, he confided in Vigasia that he'd agreed to this because he wanted an excuse to invite his eldest daughter and her husband from Morehdalye.

"What about your son from Bialystok and your Warsaw daughters? Will you invite them, too?" Vigasia asked.

"I don't believe I will," Eli-Leizer answered slowly, as if he were uttering his somber thoughts aloud. "My children are angry at me for remarrying, so if I invite them and they refuse to come I'll be heartbroken. And if they do come, I'll be heartbroken anyway, because of their way of life. Better to not invite them."

"But if you invite my sons, they'll come. And you won't be disgraced by them. True, my sons are simple craftsmen, clockmakers, but they're pious," Vigasia boomed in her robust voice. She thought to herself: *Though the orphans studying Torah are like grandchildren, my "old one" would nevertheless really want his biological grandchildren to come.*

22

AT THE HEAD of the long table in the beis din room sat Eli-Leizer, forehead wrinkled, gazing at the aron kodesh across from him. Even in a room filled with guests, he homed in on the Torah scroll, mentally isolating himself with it. On both sides of the table sat the rabbi's followers. They nibbled on pieces of cake, sipped liquor, and wished each other "L'chaim!" Some swung their heads, drummed their fingers, and hummed *Vetahar Libeinu, And purify our hearts so that we may serve You in truth* . . .

Because Zembin was a border city, between towns of Lithuanians and Poles, Eli-Leizer's followers were a mix of Hasidim and Misnagdim. The group of Misnagdim was made up of businessmen, craftsmen, and scholars. The businessmen had long, clean beards and wore soft fedoras, short jackets, and polished boots. The craftsmen's hands looked worked to the bone, their fingers callused and bent like scraggy roots, backs stooped from sitting at the workbench all day and bending over sacred texts half the night. The middle-aged scholars were the most esteemed among the Misnagdim. They sported stiff hats and frayed overcoats, round beards that looked like shapely Passover matzohs. They had delicate fingers that moved as if in sleep, sullen faces, weak teeth, and throats that caught cold easily. When they coughed, the dry sound echoed through the beis medrash. On Shabbos Hagadol, when Eli-Leizer delivered his pilpul—expounding on the topic of chametz discovered during or just after Pesach—the scholars, elbows resting on their lecterns, adopted various methods of listening. One stared up at the chandelier, as if to indicate that the rabbi's novel interpretation was baseless, mere fluff. Another ran his fingers through his beard, first to the right, then to the left, to indicate that the pilpul was two times nothing: nothing plus nothing. And the third curled his peyes clockwise, then counterclockwise, as if to say that he could just as easily twist and braid the rabbi's words. When it came to scholarliness, the people of Zembin had little respect for their rabbi.

The Hasidic zealots in Eli-Leizer's group were hot-blooded, with luxurious, overgrown whiskers and flushed faces, like the fiery lion that lay on the altar in the Jewish Temple. They wore Polish hats, long coats, trousers tucked into boots. The young ones, though, adhered to the newer fashion of elegant boots with soft, wrinkled bootlegs beneath their long pants. Yet neither young nor old tucked their tallis katan and tzitzis into their pants. No, only a Litvak Misnagid did that.

At the marketplace, in their shops, the Hasidim stood, caps pushed up on foreheads wrinkled with worry, fretting: How will I make enough for Shabbos provisions? Where can I snag an interest-free loan so that I don't default on a promissory note? But in the shtiebel, during davening, they strode about, huffing, fat fingers tucked in their gartel. Occasionally, a freethinker would drop in among these zealots, some sort of noodle with a long, dull face; but instead of debating him, the Hasidim would laugh in his face and sometimes end up smacking him. "Sheigetz! I'll tear you apart! Rip out your very root!"

Now, at the dedication ceremony, the most important men at the rabbi's table were the melamdim of the talmud torah. They were well aware that most parents—even the pious ones—preferred the new, young, clean-shaven teachers who were teaching at other schools. The only person still defending the old-fashioned cheder was the rabbi, may he live long! But he wasn't going to live forever. "And then, who will stick up for us?" the melamdim asked each other mutely, with frightened, watery eyes, their shoulders stooped. "Who will make sure we won't lose our jobs?" The dedication ceremony of the talmud torah was therefore, first and foremost, a special occasion for them. Indeed, they shared in the joy, swayed with it. Still, they couldn't shake the gloom that clung to their sparse, hoary beards like spiderwebs on autumn bushes.

The talmud torah's supervisor, however—a man with a wide, gray beard, black whiskers, and cunning eyes—appeared to be a happy man. Hardly had he finished one cigarette when he started lighting up the next, while his eyes, head, and shoulders swiveled restlessly to and fro, incapable of staying still for a single second. Deep in his heart, it bothered him that he wasn't a supervisor of some estates in Warsaw, or else a wheat merchant, or, at the very least, the community treasurer, rather than the supervisor and alms collector of the talmud torah. But he wore a face that said the world had been good to him. He always had a wisecrack at the ready and was a friend of every Agudah member among the rabbi's supporters. Still, when he'd meet with a member of the Mizrachi group, he'd murmur into the man's ear, "The truth is, I've been opposed to fighting my whole life. And honestly, I *support* the land of Israel. But does it hurt anyone if an orphan knows how to pray?" The Mizrachi would agree that it hurt no one, and he'd donate some money to the talmud torah.

At the head of the table, Eli-Leizer, wearing his velvet yarmulke, was engaged in conversation with his oldest son-in-law, the Moreh-dalye rabbi, who looked excited and warmed by the devout crowd around him. But Eli-Leizer's younger son-in-law—Banet Michelson, the freethinking shipping clerk from Warsaw—sat among the Jews at the table as if on hot coals. He couldn't bear his wife's family, thought each of them pigheaded and stubborn as a mule. He also despised their ugly habit of squinting their eyes. In fact, he even felt hatred for his own two daughters, Tubya and Bania, when they flirted with boys by squinting. Banet Michelson was a squinter himself. His daughters laughed at him for this, but he argued that he'd caught the habit from his wife's family, just as one might catch a skin rash. Banet also couldn't forgive his wife for being corpulent and of average height (she took after her father), while he, her husband, was tall and slim, with thin prickly hair on his sour-faced cheeks.

The only time Banet was in a good mood was when he played chess and his opponent lost. This reception at his father-in-law's house, with its swarming, excitable crowd, was especially vexing. He glared at everyone, grumbling, "Just look! Two glasses they drink, and already they're making wild gestures. Why are they feeling so good, these asses? Do they even know lashon kodesh? Does a single one of them know how to pronounce the liturgy correctly, where to accent the words? Even the rabbis don't know Hebrew grammar. And who in this crowd has ever in his life read a poem by Friedrich Schiller? They've never even heard the name! And have they heard of Nachman Krochmal, these cows?"

The talmud torah supervisor went on chain-smoking. The cigarette glowed red between his whiskers and beard, like a small flame in a dark, dense forest. To ingratiate himself with the rabbi's younger son-in-law, the freethinker from Warsaw, he whispered in his ear that he, too, was a fan of Hebrew, and that everyone should learn Polish. What could you lose by studying the language of your country?

But Banet Michelson despised flattery, and to him this big-bearded Jew resembled the "hypocrite eagle" title character of Abraham Mapu's book. "Ever looked into *Moreh Nebukhe Ha-Zman*?" Banet Michelson asked him. That was Nachman Krochmal's book on religious philosophy, *Guide for the Perplexed of Our Time*.

"Of course! The *Moreh Nevuchim* by Maimonides!" The talmud torah supervisor winked cunningly, as if he and Banet were conspiring in the same sin.

The Warsaw shipping clerk jerked up from the table, mute and pale, deeply offended. This person didn't know that *Moreh Nevuchim* and *Moreh Nebukhe Ha-Zman* were two different texts by two different authors! Banet refused to converse with such an ignoramus! Not only was this supervisor no freethinker, he wasn't the least bit devout either. And yet he held a position among the devout, like a thief on the board of a charity organization.

Banet no longer wanted to sit back down at the table. He paced round the beis din room until he bumped into a squat, round Jew, short-necked, with a large balding head covered by a scrap of yarmulke. This Jew's weathered cheeks were as naked as his balding head. Who could say, Banet mused in frustration, whether this Jew was one of those people who tried to "trick God" by removing their beards with an ointment instead of a razor, or if he was a hermaphrodite whose beard simply didn't grow? Or perhaps an illness had caused his hair to fall out? Most likely he was a scoundrel who got drunk at strangers' parties. "Do you play chess?" The Warsaw shipping clerk glared down at the little Jew the way a tall, thin, crooked-beaked bird of prey would look down at a happy, white-bellied grasshopper.

"Chess? Oh, you mean that board game with wooden kaisers and soldiers? No, I don't play."

A communist in a yarmulke! Banet thought, and turned from the man in disgust. His eyes alighted on another Zembin resident, communing ecstatically with God, humming "ay, ay, ay" to himself. *Just look at him glazing over! This narrow-minded fanatic is convinced he has ruach hakodesh, imbued with a Divine prophetic spirit.* Banet giggled to himself. He felt a bad taste in his mouth, a dryness in his throat. His skinny, bony fingers cramped with an intense craving to move figures around on a chessboard.

"Do you play chess?" He was feeling dizzy, so he hadn't realized he was asking this question of his sister-in-law Chavtche.

Chavtche had just barely escaped the women's table, where Rebbetzin Vigasia was lording over everyone. She was in an irritable mood and replied angrily to her brother-in-law, "You know I don't play chess, so why're you asking?"

Indeed, Banet would not have asked had he realized he was talking to his sister-in-law. It was she, this spendthrift girl, who'd stirred up this porridge in the first place, who'd made them all come to Zembin. "If you don't have the brains for chess, how will you figure out if your father's leaving you an inheritance?" her brother-in-law mocked her.

"And you who know how to play chess—are *you* so wise? If my sister Sarah Raizel didn't ship her boss's goods through your office, you'd still be sitting around penniless, my dear shipping clerk," Chavtche mocked him in return, and left him standing there, numb.

The rebbetzin presiding over the table in the guest room, and the rabbi over the one in the beis din room, kept throwing anxious glances toward the doors and windows. It would soon be time to go to the beis medrash for afternoon and evening prayers, and from there to the talmud torah for dinner. But Vigasia's three sons hadn't yet arrived. Then, at the precise moment the rabbi stood from his seat, the three Bolekhev clockmakers appeared, like the three angels at Abraham the Patriarch's house.

They were middle-aged men with grayish beards, each spaced a few years apart. All three wore metal-framed spectacles, black Jewish hats, long gray overcoats, and heavy boots. But they trod so softly into the rabbi's home, it seemed they were wearing boots made of chamois. For a while they stood there silently, arms hooked around one another, as if someone from outside had pushed them into this noisy room. Slowly, they sidled toward their mother. They didn't offer her their hands, but whispered something that those around her couldn't hear, as if in the middle of the Shimoneh Esrei when it is forbidden to interrupt the prayer with talk. Vigasia abruptly silenced her clanging voice, got up from the table, eyes beaming, and quietly told the women around her that the three guests were her sons. The rabbi's daughters and the townswomen were in shock. None of them had expected the loud, brassy rebbetzin to have such refined sons, their faces as saintly as lamed-vovniks'.

23

JUST AS HAPPY as Eli-Leizer felt at the sight of his oldest daughter from Morehdalye, so disconcerted did he feel upon the sight of his unexpected guests—his daughters from Warsaw. But he quickly regained his composure, made the appropriate sounds and gestures to welcome his children, and asked them how they were doing. There, he'd done his part. His daughters were astonished. Their father looked younger and stronger, his shoulders had straightened, he wore a clean kaftan and a laundered tallis katan. "You can clearly see his wife is taking care of him," the three older daughters agreed happily. Only Chavtche, the youngest and smartest, noticed that their father had addressed them with lowered eyes, a sign he was hiding something. In a triumphant tone, she told her sisters, "Well, didn't I predict this? This market woman, Vigasia, has got our father in her claws!"

The townspeople were invited to dinner at the talmud torah, where the festivities for the public would transpire. In the meantime, the rabbi's close circle and visiting family members spent their time in the rabbi's house. Seated at the head of the guest room table was Rebbetzin Vigasia, wearing a dark red velvet dress that appeared to have come from the wardrobe of her first marriage. But over this festive dress she wore an ordinary gray jacket, as if she were begrudging herself this joyous occasion. The only thing she was visibly enjoying was the heavy Shabbos sheitel she wore on her head.

Down the length of both sides of the table sat her husband's daughters. Like the rabbi, Vigasia had become disconcerted at first sight of them. But she, too, soon regained her booming voice, her calm demeanor, her clever, sober expression. The refreshments on the table were still Purim-inspired: hamantaschen filled with poppy seed, and other baked goods made with oil and eggs, honey and sugar, or filled with nuts and grated apple. There were also women's drinks on the table: sweet, thick mead; wine made of raisins; and a light red alcohol-inflected drink made from preserved currants. Platefuls of pears and apples were on display, too, next to which were placed small silver-handled paring knives.

The Morehdalye rebbetzin was not yet sixty, ten years younger than her father's wife. But her withered face and kind, grandmotherly eyes made her look much older, and she made use of this in her own way. She'd shake her narrow head in her little round hat, thus sparing herself the need to chitchat. Near her sat her sister Sarah Raizel with her swelling bosom. Her large, pale blue eyes hung on Chavtche's every move, trying to figure out what she was thinking. Indeed, in that moment Chavtche's brain was working hard: Had Father already handed over his will to Vigasia and her sons? But she didn't want anyone to notice how anxious she was, so she swiveled her head happily in all directions, like a bird sipping from a shallow puddle.

Kona, the second sister, was entirely different. Unlike Chavtche, she didn't attempt to conceal her worry and sadness. Kona had not yet forgotten all those fights she'd had with her father in her unmarried days, before she'd managed to escape out into the world. Back then, with all of Zembin trembling in fear of him, her father couldn't imagine that his own child might not yield to him. He wanted to marry Kona off to a rabbi, just like her older sister, Henna'le. But Kona got her way in the end and married an enlightened boy. Although many years had passed, Kona still couldn't forget those squabbles with her father. And her husband, the enlightened Warsaw shipping clerk Banet Michelson, was an even moodier person than she: he seemed to always be in a state of discontent. But as if to spite the two of them, their daughters, Tubya and Bania, had grown up to be pliable as cats, happy and eager. Kona was vexed that her daughters were such gigglers and chatterboxes, with no deep interests. She also fretted over the unmarried state of her two younger sisters, Sarah Raizel and Chavtche, and at the way Chavtche manipulated Sarah Raizel, and at the way Sarah Raizel let herself be manipulated. Kona was forty-six and still bore rosy cheeks and thick chestnut hair. With the broad, warm hands of an efficient woman, she prepared meals and clean laundry for her husband and children, did all the shopping, and tidied all the rooms in her house. She did all this quickly, without undue fuss. But once she was done with this work, she'd remain sitting with her hands in her lap, sighing. This was how she behaved at home in Warsaw, and this was how she behaved here, now, at her father's dedication ceremony in Zembin. Kona fretted: Why was her older, well-adjusted brother, Refael Leima, abroad in America? Why had her younger, wilder brother, Shabse-Shepsel, not come from Bialystok for this occasion? And why had she and her husband come? But now that she and her husband *had* come, she was vexed that Tubya and Bania hadn't wanted to. The longer she looked at her father's wife, the more hurt she felt for her dead mother; although when her mother had been alive, she'd felt exasperated at her state of perpetual contentment. Even a well-cooked pot of borscht made her mother happy.

Vigasia kept reminding her husband's daughters to enjoy the refreshments on the table. Henna'le pecked like a bird at a sliver of cake, took a sip from her goblet of wine. Kona didn't taste a thing; food wasn't on her mind. Sarah Raizel stared with peculiar curiosity at a large apple, as if a turtle would soon stick its head out from beneath its skin and relate a thousand-year-old history. The only one relishing the moment was Chavtche. She'd already drunk a goblet of mead and was now filling up on the pale red, less-alcoholic drink made of preserved currants. With her small fingers, she kept chipping off piece after piece of the hardened hamantaschen, eating them with gusto. Now she was cracking Turkish nuts with tongs and tossing them into her mouth. A maid, hired for the special occasion, stepped into the guest room, and Vigasia asked her to take the seltzer water and glasses back inside. Chavtche became indignant. "My mother did everything herself to the point of collapse!" she felt like crying out.

Chavtche knew she should control herself, but she couldn't resist showing her sister that she could outsmart Vigasia, the shrewd interloper. So she said to her, "I heard you used to live with your sons in Bolekhev. Are they merchants?"

"Craftsmen. My three sons, may they be healthy, are watchmakers. Thank God, they earn enough to make a living, and require no luxuries," Vigasia said, to reassure her husband's youngest that nobody had designs on her inheritance.

"How can a small town like Bolekhev provide for three watchmakers?" Chavtche asked in the Gemara tune her father used.

But Vigasia replied entirely tunelessly, in a voice that sounded like it could have come from beneath a man's whiskers, "The same God who provides for a worm under a stone can provide for three devout Jewish craftsmen. Barons and plenty of peasants live near Bolekhev. They come to my sons to fix their old watches and buy new ones."

"Well, rebuilding the talmud torah must have cost a small fortune," Chavtche said, smoothing out the black bow on her white blouse.

"Whatever costs money is worth money." Vigasia, too, set to smoothing something out: the sheitel on her head. "We didn't rebuild the talmud torah," she continued. "We wouldn't have enough money for that. We only fixed what was most necessary. Now the orphans will be able to study, eat, and sleep in warm, bright rooms."

Chavtche looked around the guest room, with its faded reddish wallpaper and its wrinkled, yellowed curtains. In one corner stood a large, old-fashioned clock in a narrow cupboard—its wood cracked, its black varnish worn away. The table, when you leaned on it too heavily, creaked like an old man. The chairs wobbled. "This house could also use a change of furniture and a renovation," Chavtche needled her father's wife, insinuating that she wasn't a good homemaker.

But Vigasia replied, her loud voice as calm as before, "At our age, we have no interest in luxury and decoration anymore. Both the rabbi and I feel that whatever money we can save, we should donate to charity."

Henna'le listened to the discussion, ears pricked, and hid her smile. She clearly enjoyed the way her father's wife was twirling clever Chavtche around her little finger. The perpetually fretting Kona, too, wasn't bothered that her younger, shallow, breezy sister had come up against someone stronger than she. Even Sarah Raizel looked at Chavtche with an expression of mute complaint in her pale blue eyes: *Why did you hatch this trip to Zembin?* Sarah Raizel's bosses at the paper warehouse had been furious that she was abandoning the shop to travel with her sister. But Chavtche herself was convinced—now even more than before—that coming here had been imperative, that things were even worse than she'd thought. If Vigasia could persuade their father to leave her sons an inheritance, his sense of justice would compel him to leave some money to his biological children, too. But if Vigasia was persuading him—as she claimed—to give it all away to charity, he'd leave them nothing!

Chavtche became even more suspicious and peeved by Vigasia's lack of attention toward her and her sisters, as if the rabbi's children were already regarded as strangers in their own mother's home.

The townswomen who came into the house were adorned in hats and scarves, as when they went to shul on holidays. Some wore long coats with large buttons and some wore fur stoles. They carried handbags lined with silver and colorful earrings that waggled when they bowed and raised their heads to Vigasia.

"Good morning to you, Rebbetzin."

"Mazel tov to you, Rebbetzin."

"May you and the rabbi both live till one hundred and twenty, Rebbetzin."

Vigasia responded with barely a nod, as if she'd been accustomed to nothing less. And when she did reply with a word or two, her voice rang out as if the ring holding keys to every room and cupboard in the house had joined in on the clanging. *She sits on our mother's chair like a queen on a throne*, Chavtche thought. But to prevent this cunning stranger from noticing how distressed she was, Chavtche gave an affected laugh, *ha ha, heh heh*, like an old woman without a tooth in her mouth.

Although Purim had already passed, it was still winter outside. Frostily and indifferently, the day peered through the window—like eternity, which never gets older or younger. The crowd in the rabbi's house kept getting bigger, the mood more buoyant and festive. No one mentioned it in so many words, but in the minds of all the guests was a sense of anticipation—for the moment they'd all set out, with song and dance, to the dedication ceremony and gala dinner at the talmud torah.

24

MIDNIGHT SHADOWS FILLED the room. The chandelier above the table cast a rosy, speckled glow over the faces in the narrow rectangle. On one side sat Vigasia's three sons, the Morehdalye rabbi across from them. The Zembin rabbi sat at the head of the table, and his rebbetzin crouched behind him, wanting no one to see the joy on her face, the nachas her sons were giving her, or the pain she felt as she recalled the days of her young widowhood, left alone with five children. One little son and her only daughter had been taken from her. Which made her work even harder to support the remaining three, at first when they went to cheder, and later to yeshiva. To keep their mother from working too hard for them, each son left yeshiva at seventeen to learn the respectful and refined craft of watchmaking. But whenever they had a free moment, they studied, poring over the holy texts.

And in the order they'd left, one by one, they got married—to Bolekhev girls from devout families. Even as unmarried boys, Vigasia's sons had always been tight-lipped, moving about with eyes lowered. And with each passing year, they grew quieter, allowing others to speak and rarely inserting a word. Vigasia hid behind her husband, so that people wouldn't see her wiping tears from her eyes.

Her mind was a beehive, swarming and buzzing with thoughts of the dedication ceremony. The hubbub and joy had lasted well into the night. The festivities opened with the rabbi's speech to the orphans, instructing them to be pious Jews. Then, everyone drank, wished each other "L'chaim," and commenced to eat the dinner that had been prepared by hired cooks under Vigasia's watch. She was still feeling dizzy now from the throng of guests with their flushed faces and straggly beards.

The first course was pan-seared carp, salted, peppered, and flavored with chopped garlic and onions. The guests—from all different social ranks—couldn't stop praising it. Later, the waiters brought in a hot meat stew and cold ox tongue, well cooked in greens and then recooked in wine, garnished with sliced kosher mushrooms. Everyone licked their fingers, savoring the delicious foods, and smacked their lips in awe at the rebbetzin's achievement. Gradually, they ate their way toward the cold, thick, sticky-sweet compote and boiling glasses of tea. The rabbi's daughters, too, enjoyed the meal, and all complimented Vigasia—all except Chavtche, who still considered her a usurper.

"Well, so be it. I won't let it distress me," Vigasia told herself, and yet, she felt distressed. Her husband's daughters were asleep in their childhood rooms now. The only one from her husband's family still at the table was the Morehdalye rabbi. He was listening to the old-est of the three watchmakers explain how, when the old Bolekhev rabbi died, the town had been too poor to hire a new one. So they'd prevailed upon him to accept the duties of the rabbinate. He now adjudicated on questions of Jewish law but took no wages. Instead, he continued to earn a livelihood repairing watches.

Sholem Shachne stared back at him with large, quiet, bespectacled eyes, biding his time. Finally, he asked, "You're a native Bolekhever, you live there, and yet you take no money from them. How is it, then, that the townspeople respect you enough to abide by your deci-sions on law?"

"But that's exactly why I don't charge them! I don't want to be sad-dled with the yoke of their respect," the watchmaker replied, smiling beneath his pious whiskers. "But yes, they abide by my decisions. Otherwise, I'd step down immediately."

"And how are the youth of Bolekhev?" Sholem Shachne continued.

"Oh, I wish it for both our cities," the old Zembin rabbi inter-jected, and proceeded to tell his son-in-law about Bolekhev. "The town still consists of all wooden houses with straw roofs. It's far from a railroad, so newspapers don't reach it quickly and can't spread the stench of enlightenment. The Jews there are paupers; they eke out a livelihood, and mostly from chopping trees in the woods or fishing in the surrounding lakes. And there's almost never a fair in Bolekhev; the merchants have to slog from village to village. None of the stores sell fashionable city clothes, so the Jewish girls don't wear short dresses. And the town knows absolutely nothing of secular schools;

all the boys study in a cheder. Bolekhev, thank God, still conducts itself in the old, traditional manner."

As Sholem Shachne continued to observe the three silent brothers opposite him, he began to notice, despite their overall similarity, differences in their faces and expressions. The oldest, the unpaid rabbi, had a smooth forehead, a wide jaw, and mild eyes. You could tell he had a calm demeanor. When people came to him with questions on Jewish law, he probably deliberated for a long while before deciding in favor of kosher. The middle one had a longer, narrower beard, a drawn face, small, beatific eyes, and prominent ears, pricked as if to hear what the grasses in the field were whispering. The third, the youngest, had a ruddy face. He was constantly creasing his forehead, and his eyes, beneath raised brows, stared into the distance, absorbed in thoughts of the Divine.

Though Sholem Shachne wasn't garrulous by nature, he now had an urge to talk. "If you live in such a poor community that you have to earn a living fixing watches," he said, "there must be little time left for studying Torah, isn't that true?"

The three brothers were silent for a very long time, as if the question had come from the other shore of the river and was taking a while to reach them. Eventually, the youngest brother replied, "In the winter, Bolekhev becomes so shut in by snow that even the local peasants don't come to fix their watches. So you sit in your workshop or at home or in the beis medrash, and you study."

The youngest brother turned silent; then, the middle brother—the one with the drawn face and a Kabbalist's long, narrow beard—said, "The doors in our town are low. To get inside, you have to stoop. And it's quiet in our town, so quiet that we literally feel God's breath upon us, and we can see with our naked eyes how He looks after His creations."

For Sholem Shachne, a rational man among people but a dreamer in his own mind, a mental image began to take shape: three squat houses on three corners of Bolekhev. Each of the watchmakers sitting in his home, bent over dials and springs and wheels that rotated in a quiet tick-tock, reminding them that time does not stand still. Most people, engrossed and embroiled in the chaos of the material world, don't take notice of life passing by. But the three brothers were constant recipients of this message—from the clocks ticking on the walls behind them, from the minuscule mechanisms of the watches into which they peered through their loupes. Every so often a peasant from the village would step in, or a baron from an estate, or a Jew from town. They'd want to repair or buy a watch. But once they left, the craftsmen would turn back to their workbenches, tools in hand, and listen to the pendulum's steady reminder that time was fleeting and man was an evanescent being that slipped from earth like the shadow of a passing bird. In this way, the three watchmakers lived the life of a lamed-vovnik, linked in thought with other hidden ones like them. Because the truth was that every person lived a double life. One for the world: with wife and children, at work, and in the beis medrash. And one in secret, with and for himself only. But even in this hidden, secret life, a person was linked in thought to others like him. If he was a sinner, there was doubtless another person somewhere sinning with him. And if he was a saint, he certainly wasn't alone: his peers were scattered all over the world. No one else realized that they were masked. Only they themselves recognized each other, by a particular expression in the eyes, and by their silences. As a certain saint had once said, "A fine state of affairs it would be, if we were only what the world sees!"

The Morehdalye rabbi looked around. He fancied that his thoughts were making the room's midnight shadows even thicker. *Who can I really blame*, he thought to himself, *that my children have deserted me? They've simply inherited my overactive imagination!* The only difference being that his was an old-fashioned dream and their heads were filled with fantasies of a more modern strain.

The others, too, sat idly around the table, becoming ever more entangled in the web of silence. The noisy event of a few hours earlier slowly sank to the nether regions of their brains, as when the sun sets beneath a mountain and the green-gold light slips from its peaks, making the mountain appear suddenly dark and sinister. A deathly pale moon hung suspended in the window. Beneath a wide metal plate, the light from the electric chandelier dangling over the table trembled on their faces in a feverish, red-speckled glow. Eventually, even the stern, cerebral Zembin rabbi was seized by an unexpected thought: How was it that his Vigasia, a woman of seventy, had more black than gray hair beneath her sheitel, while her sons, not yet fifty, were already entirely gray?

At the precise moment he had this thought, his son-in-law, Sholem Shachne, spoke up: "If a person lives in a quiet neighborhood, far from country roads and their constant pedestrian traffic, he is able to think of higher matters."

"That's exactly what I always say," Eli-Leizer replied, pushing his yarmulke around, as if to drive away the naughty thought of his wife's hair color beneath her sheitel. He began to speak of the Zembin of sixty years ago. It had been a quiet, pious town then, and the rabbi's house was its jewel. But a decade later when he became the rabbi after the death of his father-in-law, Zembin was beginning to grow. And from that time, a demon took hold of the town. The wooden houses around the marketplace were demolished, replaced by stone houses of up to two or three stories high, like the towers of Babel, with balconies even. Trees once surrounded the marketplace, swaying as if in prayer. But people felled them and put up telegraph poles that buzzed through the night, a metallic noise that seemed to proclaim the world's lawlessness, its anarchy. Everyone could do whatever they wanted. Summertime, boys and girls strolled about until after midnight, chattering, singing, bursting into unchaste laughter, disturbing his sleep. He was the rabbinical authority, after all, the protector of the community, and he was forced to look on as his city was destroyed. To everyone else, Zembin was growing, becoming a metropolis, supposedly less susceptible to fires than in the past, since stone and limestone buildings didn't burn as quickly and thoroughly as those of wood. But in the rabbi's eyes, Zembin was aflame all day and night, in the hellish fire of enlightenment.

"Zembin is burning in a hell of sin and indulgence, God protect us!" the old Zembin rabbi said. From behind his stooped shoulders, the head of his rebbetzin kept poking out, an odd look of surprise on her beaming face. Though Vigasia was known to listen to her husband's spiels, groaning along with him, agreeing to everything he said, this time she wasn't paying him any mind. Instead, she gazed at her sons and thought about their father, a man who was both a Torah scholar and a merchant. At the age of thirty-four he'd suddenly collapsed and left this world. So when she looked at her sons—may they live long and be healthy!—she imagined how their father would have looked had he lived to their age, his curly, pitch-black beard turned gray or white.

T HEY WENT TO BED at two in the morning. Eli-Leizer, unlike his Morehdalye son-in-law, wasn't the type to pick at his scabs, but tonight he couldn't close an eye. His thoughts gnawed at him. Why, indeed, hadn't he been rewarded with such children as Vigasia had? Her husband, it seemed from her description, had been a sincere, devout man, and something of a scholar, yes, but not particularly distinguished. Nor had he sacrificed himself unduly for the sake of Torah study. He hadn't accomplished much, in general, because he'd died young. Maybe because his children had such scant memories of him, yet had heard such wonderful things from their mother— maybe this was the reason they'd been so careful to emulate his ways. *If I had died young,* Eli-Leizer thought, *perhaps my children, too, would honor my memory.*

The old rabbi was glad when it turned light outside. At last, he could get out of bed, recite a chapter of Tehillim, and put an end to thinking such thoughts. The joy of the dedication ceremony had already faded; now he wanted his guests to leave so he could get back to his routine duties. The ones he really wanted gone were his daughters, but the first to leave were Vigasia's three sons—as if in fear that, without them, the clocks of Bolekhev would all stop and no one would know when it was time to recite the Shema. In truth, Eli-Leizer's daughters, too, would have left immediately, but Chavtche had insisted they stay to have a serious discussion with their father. At the last minute, though, Henna'le regretted it. She told her sister that she was heading into the city for a bit, openly admitting that she didn't want to be there when Chavtche fought with her father over their inheritance.

Vigasia retreated to the bedroom, leaving the beis din room or the guest room for her husband to talk things over with his children.

Chavtche, meanwhile, had determined that the conversation should, in fact, occur in what had been their mother's bedroom, before being usurped by this stranger. "Come," she commanded, and her father and sisters followed. Impetuously, she thrust the bedroom door open, alarming Vigasia, who was already seated on a tall chair, mending her husband's tallis katan. The two older sisters stepped back, and their father gave Chavtche an irritated glance.

But Vigasia stood up at once. "Come in, come in! It'll be much homier in here," she said, and immediately left the bedroom, torn tallis katan in hand.

Piled high with linen, the pair of beds looked like two old tired doves on a snowy day, hunkered down under feathery wings. The tablecloth on the table, the pillows in their pillowcases atop the wobbly, high-backed armchairs, and the floral curtains on the window were shabby, wrinkled, and faded, yet meticulously mended and laundered. It was clear that Vigasia was not one to spend extra money on new fabrics, wallpaper, or furniture. She was being stingy with their father's money, Chavtche thought, so that more would be left to her sons. Out of habit, Chavtche folded her soft, nimble hands on the lining of her short beige jacket and began pacing the room in small steps, looking down at her square-toed, low-heeled shoes. Sarah Raizel, her sister with the swollen figure of a waterlogged cucumber, a closely shorn head, and a thick white neck, hid away in the corner in a wide green dress, dreading the discussion with her father. Kona, the eldest of the three, and already dressed in a dark gray travel suit and hat, sat at the edge of her chair, staring mutely down at her warm, white hands and stumpy legs. In addition to the pity she felt for her father, brothers, and sisters, Kona now pitied her father's wife, too, who didn't know how to stay out of her stepdaughters' way.

Chavtche opened the argument by telling her father that, without furnished apartments or the money to take a suitable husband and open a laboratory or shop for him, she and Sarah Raizel could never get married. He took care of everyone's needs: orphans, yeshiva boys, businessmen who'd lost their fortunes, poor people of all stripes. When would he start providing for the welfare of his own children?

"You're provided for, you're provided for," Eli-Leizer murmured, his back to the window, head lowered.

But Chavtche insisted on knowing what exactly they'd been provided for—this world or the next? Had he left money for his children in his will, or did he plan on helping them with the lottery money while he was still alive?

"You're provided for, you're provided for," the old man murmured again. For a moment he was silent; then he raised a pair of cold, wondering eyes at his daughter. "On second thought, why am I any more obliged to provide for you and your sisters than for other Jewish children?"

Ruddy fever-spots bloomed on Chavtche's cheeks. Her blue eyes flashed. Beneath her coiffed strawberry-blond hair, her forehead blazed in anger, as if stained by a blood-red birthmark. With anger, for her, often came laughter, and so it did now: *ha ha, heh heh*. She shifted from one foot to the other, as if dancing. "You must be more concerned about us because we're your children."

Her father grimaced. "Is that so? And I, old fool that I am, thought that one's children come before others only if they follow a righteous path. But if they don't, then God-fearing strangers, especially talmud torah orphans, come before them."

Throughout the exchange, the two older sisters kept silent behind guilty faces. Now, their father glanced at them, turning slowly to the window that faced out on the courtyard. The snow was still piled high. A warehouse roof peeked out from it, as did the naked, outstretched branches of a tree. A dull gleam had filtered downward from the glassy sky, and it lay unmoving, as if frozen to the hardened snow. Though Eli-Leizer wasn't prone to fanciful thinking, he'd always had the odd sense that his home looked out onto two worlds. On one side, the windows of the beis din room faced the noisy market and surrounding stores. There, the peace and sanctity of Shabbos came only once a week. And even then, the Shabbos wasn't entirely sanctified or peaceful: it too had been desecrated by freethinkers. So on the whole, that side of the house represented the everyday bustle of life. But on the other side, the windows of his bedroom and library faced the quiet backyard. There, his house was linked to an entirely different world, akin to the world to come, the World of Truth where public space didn't exist at all; instead, each person had his own peaceful realm, had earned his own partition. Chavtche was still speaking into her father's bristly ears, but he was no longer listening. He continued to gaze out at the snow-filled yard as upon a crystal palace of pure Shabbos peace, in a universe at the end of days. In that universe, this deluded world was forgotten—this world of lies, where children came to visit their father only because they imagined he'd won a jackpot.

When the Warsaw guests finally left, Rebbetzin Vigasia asked her husband, "Is your Morehdalye son-in-law always this despondent? Go and have a talk with him alone before he leaves. Something's troubling him."

Eli-Leizer sadly nodded his head. "Something's troubling both of us." And he ventured out in search of his son-in-law.

Soon, they were both sitting at the table in the beis din room. The sun's golden light played on the ark's curtain, on the leather spines of the rabbi's books, and on the faces of the two scholars. The father-in-law, over eighty, said to his sixty-five-year-old son-in-law, "I understand that my Warsaw grandchildren didn't come—I understand that. It wasn't me who chose Banet Michelson, that freethinker, as a son-in-law. Who knows if he even puts on tefillin every morning or keeps Shabbos? Of course his daughters aren't interested in their grandfather. But why didn't you bring along Bluma Rivtcha and your youngest son? Why is Refael'ke at home? Why didn't he go back to the Lecheve Yeshiva?"

"Bluma Rivtcha wasn't in the mood, and neither was Refael'ke. Bluma Rivtcha and the dayan Reb Tzadok's grandson, whom we thought of as her fiancé, parted ways. He wants to go abroad and become a modern rabbi, not our kind. And I was forced to bring Refael'ke back from Lecheve last summer because he'd become friends with chalutzim there."

For a short while, Eli-Leizer remained speechless. He realized that in heaven, too, there was a faction siding against him. He raised his eyes to the ceiling and mumbled, "Creator of the universe, are you punishing me for my sins, or are you making me suffer out of your love for me?" But then he stopped sighing and scolded his son-in-law, "You should have told Refael'ke that you'd rather he become a woodcutter than belong to that gang defiling our holy land with their behavior. You should have told him that the hunchback Mendelssohn and the 'Berlintchkes' started down that slippery slope by studying Tanach with a newfangled commentary and by davening in a modern Hebrew. From there they moved on to studying German and philosophy, and by the end they'd converted to Christianity. That's what you should have told him."

"I've told him more than enough. That's exactly the problem with him. He listens calmly to what other people say but remains convinced of his own opinion. He doesn't want to cause me pain, though, so he continues to study a little in the beis medrash," Sholem Shachne said in a strangled voice, his eyes glazed over.

"And Bentzion?" the old man asked in a muffled tone, as if his son-in-law's quiet sadness were contagious.

"I went to visit him in Bialystok. He works in a shop there and is taking business courses. He's adamant about shucking off his privileged rabbinical pedigree," Sholem Shachne said resentfully.

"And from your eldest—you're still hearing just as little?" the old man asked.

"Oh, I hear nothing from him." Sholem Shachne smiled into his whiskers, the smile like a wan stripe in a spider's web.

The old rabbi stood. He looked like the gnarled trunk of a bulky apple tree in bloom. He motioned with his hand as if in need of a prop to lean on. "You're already a grandfather," he said, "and I, thank God, a great-grandfather. But in truth, neither one of us has children."

"I'm so ashamed before my congregants to have such children, I'm ready to leave everything behind and flee to the other end of the world," Sholem Shachne said.

"And I'm not ashamed at all!" the old man cried, his voice regaining strength. "I did everything possible to set my children on the right path, and if I didn't succeed, it's not my fault. These corrupting Jews have wrecked my family, and that's why I war against them so stubbornly."

In the windows of the homes and shops around the marketplace, the sunset was already burning cold and slow like frozen raw meat. The old rabbi's knees felt stiff from standing. He sat down slowly, eyeing the long oak table with the bleak gaze of a teacher whose students have all abandoned him. Shirt unbuttoned, he scratched his chest, his armpits, his neck beneath his beard. He huffed and groaned, raised himself up, sat back down, and pointed a finger at his son-in-law. "You're a greater scholar than I am, and that's something I've always been proud of. Not only that, but you've always been a fiery pillar of zealotry, like the pillar of fire that lit the way for the Jews in the desert! But lately, you've lost that; you're not the same anymore. If I were a resident of Morehdalye, I'd demand that they fire you from your position. A rabbi who openly admits that he no longer wants to, or cannot, wage war against the people trying to undermine Judaism, such a rabbi should not be allowed to head a community. Why are you laughing? You should be crying, not laughing."

"Am I laughing? I didn't realize I was laughing," Sholem Shachne said, looking around as if in search of a tittering imp, hiding in the folds of his clothes or beneath the table. "My son-in-law, the Lecheve rabbi, resents me for giving him my Tilza as a wife. Tilza still hasn't made peace with being a rebbetzin. So perhaps I should be scolding you in turn, Father-in-Law, for giving me your not very pious daughter as a wife? No matter what my children do, their mother looks for reasons to excuse them. Everything they do, your daughter justifies."

The old rabbi gaped at his son-in-law, speechless. All at once, the low clouds outside turned the room dark. The golden glow of the twilight sun that had played on the ark curtain and on the spines of the holy books was suddenly snuffed out. Only on Sholem Shachne Katzenellenbogen's spectacles did a few flecks glimmer, like tears.

Part 2

1

R EFAEL LEIMA, the Zembin rabbi's oldest son, looked like his
father: average height, broad-shouldered, and a big round face
like a clock with Hebrew letters as numbers. In personality, however,
Refael Leima and his father were opposites. Refael Leima had been
a quiet, serene child, and remained so as a teenager in the Slobodka
Yeshiva, his face imbued with gentleness, his lips turned up in a permanent smile. Only when he came home for the holidays and heard
of all his father's bickering did his smile fade. In the beis medrash,
when people informed him of his father's latest battles, he teetered
forward, like an old bookcase shoved from its corner, bidding farewell
to the world, as if it knew that one more push and it would collapse.

Refael Leima married late and became a rabbi in the small town
of Dalhinev, a place surrounded by fields, grasslands, and swamps.
In this remote community, among its anxious, overworked Jews with
bent shoulders and veiny hands, Refael Leima took refuge from his
father and his beis din, from the endless clamor of prohibitions and
admonitions to those who dared break with tradition. But the echoes
of Eli-Leizer's battles reached his son even in this secluded outskirt.
His hands would tremble as he read his father's letters, in which the
rabbi insisted—taking heaven and earth as his witnesses!—that all his
battles were fought for the sake of God, and for the sake of God only.

Over the years, Refael Leima's family grew, but his salary did not.
During the war between the German kaiser and the Russian tsar, the
impoverished village became even poorer. And when the occupied
cities and towns in Lithuania and Belarus found themselves under
German rule, like flood zones under cold, muddy water, the rabbi
and his family were left even hungrier than the other Dalhinev families. They had no garden from which to dig up potatoes for the winter, or goats to provide a glass of milk for the children. Although

Refael Leima never complained of his situation, his father found out and wrote him a letter. "No one in Zembin," he wrote, "would think the slightest bit wrong of me if I installed you here as a dayan and my assistant. Mother misses you, and the Zembin townspeople think the world of you. Would you rather languish in a remote, inhospitable place with your wife and children so long as you're not with your father, because you'd rather take it easy than fight for mitzvahs?" And to conclude the letter, Eli-Leizer ordered him, by the decree of "Honor your father," to come back home.

Refael Leima's wife, Manya, was as mild-mannered and quiet as he. When they conversed, they exchanged smiles like newlyweds. In fact, they could hardly hear each other because they were too busy gazing into each other's eyes. Perhaps Refael Leima and Manya shared such love because neither had been young when they'd gotten married. Even during the war years, Manya never raised her voice to Refael Leima, never complained or became bitter that their children were forced to go to sleep hungry. But on this wintry night, as Refael stood beneath a dangling oil lamp in a frigid room with his father's letter in his hand, Manya spoke to him in a harsher tone than usual. She had already asked him whether the situation in Zembin was better than in other cities or towns, and he'd replied that it was. Many wealthy barons lived in the villages surrounding Zembin, and they brought their products into the city. And the Zembin Jews had learned how to hoodwink or bribe the Germans, who looked the other way when Jews smuggled in goods. "Well then, why don't you want us to settle in Zembin? Do you think I won't get along with your mother?" Manya burst out, tears in her voice.

"Of course, you and my mother will get along well. The question is whether my father and I will," Refael Leima replied.

But because Manya had become upset, there was no need for the topic to be broached again. Refael Leima arrived at his father's house in Zembin. The war between the nations had already ended, but between the town rabbi and his enemies, war was still raging. Despite that, the rabbi's enemies held nothing against his son, who became their new dayan. It was Refael's bad luck, however, that a war of a completely different nature soon erupted.

In the way Eli-Leizer Epstein presided over the old beis medrash, the non-Orthodox rabbi Nosson-Nota Goldstein—or the "Rabiner," as he was called—presided over the new beis medrash. In time, the Rabiner's supporters began to prod him. Why shouldn't he, too, have the honor of performing marriage ceremonies or holding a baby during his bris? Why did he allow himself to be treated like a second-class religious functionary, satisfied with the measly tasks of handing out birth certificates and keeping accounts of funerals and weddings? Besides the many languages he spoke, the Rabiner was also renowned as a scholar and an observant Jew. In addition, he had a stately appearance—tall, with good carriage, and a beard like a waterfall.

Eventually, Nosson-Nota was persuaded by his faction and approached the community leadership, demanding the right to perform marriage ceremonies and the honorary role, on occasion, of holding a baby at his bris. Upon hearing the Rabiner's demands, Eli-Leizer responded with unbridled ferocity, as if he were answering gentiles who'd just decreed that Jews must convert to Christianity and he, Eli-Leizer, was ready to martyr himself for the sake of God and Torah. "If you agree to this demand," he cried to the community leadership, "our future generations will rue your decision. Why should young students of Torah push themselves in their studies when the official state rabbi—just because he can jabber in grammatical Polish—is afforded the same honors as the community rabbi? This cannot be! I'm willing to step aside and let any underling, any beadle's assistant, perform marriage ceremonies or sit on Elijah's chair at a bris—anyone except the Rabiner! And those who side with the Rabiner will meet an end like the rebel Korach and his crowd."

Rabbi Goldstein, hearing that Rabbi Epstein had likened him and his faction to Korach and his crowd, began to create problems for anyone who didn't invite him to their ceremonies. Fathers of newly circumcised infant boys, who needed the Rabiner to enter their baby's birth in the birth certificate ledger, were made to bring along their mohel and two witnesses to confirm that the child had indeed been circumcised; only then would the Rabiner bestow the favor of making the birth official. For any couple whose marriage ceremony had been performed by the community rabbi, the Rabiner forced them to redo it, or else he'd refuse to enter their marriage in the ledgers. Some tried to outsmart them and invite both rabbis, but to no avail: both refused to attend.

Finally, someone came up with an idea. A bright-eyed man with a wheaten beard—a resident whose neshama yeseira glowed all through the week—approached the Rabiner. Dejectedly, he said, "Because I daven in the new beis medrash and you're my rabbi, you should be the one to perform my son's marriage ceremony. But the bride's father davens in the old beis medrash, and he says he won't come to his daughter's chuppah if Rabbi Epstein isn't the marriage officiant. So I had the idea to ask Refael Leima, the dayan, to do it. And the bride's father agreed. I imagine that Eli-Leizer won't be against his son officiating, and you, Rabbi, I hope, won't oppose it either. After all, you hold nothing against Refael Leima. People even claim you're old friends."

"Not just friends—*good* friends, from back in the day in the Slobodka Yeshiva, before I traveled to Berlin to study in a rabbinical school," the Rabiner replied happily. He was pleased at this compromise. It had been beneath his dignity to give in to Eli-Leizer, especially because he had to save face in front of his faction. But he also recognized that spoiling people's occasions was gaining him many enemies. So, this man's idea was perfect. And when Refael Leima was asked, he agreed, provided his father was fine with it.

"Agreed," mumbled Eli-Leizer, his forehead crinkling.

Soon enough, however, more and more people began asking Refael Leima to do the honors at their occasions, and his father changed his tune. "Is this why I brought you here?" he yelled at Refael Leima. "If all this was about my own honor, then yes, it would be appropriate that they give the honor to my son, for a man isn't jealous of his own son. But my point was that a state rabbi is not the equal of a community rabbi! Now that you go in place of me *and* Rabbi Goldstein, you substitute for *both* of us, which means you're tacitly giving your stamp of approval to the idea that he and I are equal. Is this the meaning of 'Honor your father'? Is this what 'Honor the Torah' means to you?"

After that, Refael Leima stopped accepting these invitations. But secretly, he snuck in through a side door of the Rabiner's home and begged him to avoid any conflicts. The Rabiner promised to swallow his pride as much as he could. He was pleased that Refael Leima, a childhood friend from his days in Slobodka, was able to win him over more than his father could.

In the dark entry hall of his apartment, Refael Leima spoke to his wife in a whisper. He didn't want their children to overhear how resentfully he spoke of their grandfather. "Now do you see why I didn't want to move here? My father is convinced that everything he does is for the sake of heaven. And that's the crux of the problem! A person fights more relentlessly for God's sake than for his own honor. But I can't bear it anymore. Where can I escape to?"

Manya felt a shudder in her bones, chilled by the loneliness and sorrow coursing through her. She knew that the rabbi's other children would be of no help to their brother, because they, too, clashed with their father. So she went to have a talk with her mother-in-law, who involved herself only with housekeeping. As Manya spoke with her, she sensed pain in Elka'le's words; clearly, despite not getting involved, she suffered a great deal over her husband's behavior. "Your husband takes after his grandfather, my father, the former Zembin rabbi. He was a kind, smart man who got along with everyone. A fact your father-in-law's always throwing in my face, claiming that it was just such indulgence that corrupted the people of Zembin. So how do you expect me to make him act differently toward your husband than he does toward everyone else?"

Refael Leima took on the look of a cowering person. Terrified of his father's ire, he was constantly squeezing himself into shadowed corners. His kind, elegant smile vanished from his face. It was as if the ugliest weather of each season traveled with him. Clouds floated in his eyes; autumn's damp seeped into his bones; the dreariness of dark winter days settled in at the corners of his mouth. Only when he and Manya spoke furtively in the hallway of their room did he still crack a smile. In the corridor's dimness, Manya couldn't see his face, but she could feel the smile in his warm voice. At any rate, the secret between husband and wife eventually came out. He and his family, Refael Leima informed his father, were moving to America.

Instead of the furious outburst Refael Leima had been expecting ("What would drive you to move to a treyf country?!"), his father said, "Go in peace! Ever since I brought you here, I've realized more and more that you're not suited to take over my rabbinate. You're a compromiser by nature. We here are still pushing the wagon of Judaism uphill, but you have no desire to help uphold this laden wagon.

In America, on the other hand, the wagon has already rolled down the hill and tumbled over. Maybe there you'll help turn it right side up again."

Zembin was roiled by the news. The rabbi's enemies claimed his son was fleeing from him. The rabbi's supporters argued the opposite: Zembin was to blame because they'd let the dayan live in need. As they said their goodbyes in the rabbi's home, Rebbetzin Elka'le still refused to believe that her Refael Leima was moving away. She stood there speechless, merely gazing at them all—her son, her daughter-in-law, and the grandchildren who were already as tall as her.

The rabbi, however, was unperturbed. "So your son is moving to an irreligious country," he shouted at Elka'le. "There's no need to be distressed. As sure as he and I are on bad terms, that's how sure I am that he won't cut off his beard in America. And that he won't become a rabbi in a shul where men and women sit together. I'm certain of it."

2

S HABSE-SHEPSEL, Refael Leima's much younger brother, was away at yeshiva when Refael Leima and his family were living in Zembin. With the same intensity that Refael suffered over his father's constant fighting, Shabse-Shepsel was ready to fight anyone who opposed his father in any way. He believed him to be one of the generation's greats, exceptionally brilliant, pious, and studious, and he battled anyone who said otherwise. But the more Shabse-Shepsel acted the part of a zealot and loyal son, the less his father trusted him. When he'd offer a biblical interpretation, his father would listen with distrust. Shabse-Shepsel's shrewdness, he felt, was either illusory or deceptive, and he suspected him of repeating others' interpretations as his own. With Elka'le, he shared his opinion of their son. "Children are usually stubborn, but your Refael Leima always gave in easily, even as a child. He always wanted to get along with everyone and is actually *too* settled in his ways. But Shabse-Shepsel isn't settled at all. He's a mess and he messes up others."

Elka'le listened and remained silent, her face bearing the guilt of a docile servant girl whose master has reproached her for burning his food.

Seeing his father dismiss him with a wave of his hand—"Pay no mind to what the dunderhead says!"—only made Shabse-Shepsel grow even more excitable, and fight even harder for his father's honor.

"Father, may he live long, is one of a kind, his zealotry unparalleled in our generation. He's our generation's Elijah the Prophet!" Shabse-Shepsel proclaimed, falling into a mystical trance, eyes squeezed shut and palms pressed into fists as when saying the Shema. But when Eli-Leizer got word of this, he couldn't help but feel his son was mocking him.

Just as certainly as Eli-Leizer's rivals believed him to be incapable of empathy, so surely did the Zembin Torah scholars feel his care for them. When the young men of Zembin left for yeshivas in another town, Eli-Leizer would escort them to the city's border, give them food for the trip, a little pocket money, and warm letters to take to their rosh yeshivas, asking them to dote on the Zembin boys. When these young students returned to Zembin for holidays, they'd spend more time in the rabbi's home than in their own. Eli-Leizer would daven with the students in his beis din room on those days. And after prayers he'd serve them refreshments: wine and liquor, fruit and cake. With pride and joy, the old man would clap his hands and call out, "Children, let us dance!" And as he danced, he would shed tears of happiness, exclaiming, "You boys are Torah scrolls! Living, breathing holy Torah scrolls!"

Unlike most boys, Shabse-Shepsel didn't stay put in the same yeshiva for years; instead, he spent every semester in a different community. Neither did he remain standing at his lectern in the house of study, but he paced around, hands in his pockets, arguing with other students. "Why are you glued to your spot?" he'd sneer, laughing at the other students and the rosh yeshivas with their heavy beards. Only on holidays at his father's home did he act like the other Zembin students, dancing and singing along with them. But though his father rejoiced with the others, he would not be pleased with his son, even avoiding eye contact. He considered this son a buffoon, an impersonator, and a bit of a madman. You never knew what tricks he had up his sleeve; in fact, minutes before he performed them, he himself probably didn't know what he was up to. In a constant state of anticipation, Eli-Leizer waited and waited for his son to leap out at him with something. Indeed, he waited so long that it happened.

Now in his thirties, Shabse-Shepsel was still unmarried. His older brother, Refael Leima, had married late, because he was sluggish and a bit clumsy by nature, not to mention constantly disparaged and treated like a dog by his father. Shabse-Shepsel, though, was the reverse: aggressively ambitious, tremendously resourceful, crafty and quick—like the man in the Gemara who could shoot a bird in flight. Shabse-Shepsel possessed a mental list of countless names and addresses of potential brides, just as he knew pages and pages of Gemara by heart. But because he had so many young women to choose from, he turned his nose up at the whole lot. "She's not the one!" he repeated. His old father, too, was reluctant to suggest a shidduch for him, fearing that Shabse-Shepsel wouldn't hold up his end of the promise.

But then came a year and a half when Shabse-Shepsel, traveling among different yeshivas, never came home, not even for the holidays. Until suddenly he showed up in Zembin, married, a wife at his side! She was short, but with a large head, thick, teased chestnut-colored hair over a protruding forehead. Her face was angular, and she had a sharp upper jaw; a small, wide nose; a mouth filled with healthy, dazzlingly white teeth; and the big, inky, hostile eyes of an attic cat. On the day Shabse-Shepsel brought his wife into his father's house, she was wearing an old-fashioned, dark blue velvet dress with sleeves down to her wrists, pearls running from the bosom up to a high collar, and a bustling train trailing behind her like a peacock's tail. Her feathered hat looked even more outdated—a ship with a mast. Shabse-Shepsel, too, strode in ceremoniously, wearing a suit jacket with a slit in the back and rounded coattails to his knees, and a low top hat on his head. By then, none of the sisters were living in Zembin anymore; his parents were on their own. When Shabse-Shepsel introduced his spouse, Rebbetzin Elka'le lost her power of speech, and the rabbi, too, was silent for a long while.

"What's your name?" Eli-Leizer finally turned to his daughter-in-law, watching her through narrowed eyes.

"Her name's Draizel," his son replied defiantly.

"Draizel? Is that spelled with or without a *yud* between the *zayin* and the *lamed*?" the rabbi asked in a mocking tone, as if a couple had come to him for a divorce and he needed the precise spelling for the paperwork.

But Elka'le couldn't keep her resentment in check anymore. She burst into tears. "Why," she asked, "did you begrudge us the joy of escorting you to your chuppah?"

"You hear that?! If I'd have waited for my family to make it to my wedding, I tell you, somebody would have snatched my bride out from under me!" Shabse-Shepsel cried happily, and smiled adoringly at his wife. "Isn't it true, Draizel'e, that you'd have been snatched up?" But Draizel was silent as a deaf-mute. Her coal-black eyes glowed antagonistically, as if to signal that she'd heard and seen everything.

Shabse-Shepsel told them all about his wife's background, explaining that she was the heiress to a substantial fortune. But even as his son rejoiced over his wife and his own good fortune, Eli-Leizer noticed the ridicule in his voice and the mockery in his eyes.

As if Shabse-Shepsel's surprise marriage wasn't enough to throw the town into uproar, he and his wife then chose to stay at an inn instead of at his parents' home. The Zembin residents who'd known him since he was a boy still believed, despite his lack of maturity, that he could one day become the rabbi of a large city. After all, you could practically see his mind thrumming with activity. So when he arrived at the beis medrash for davening, people wished him "mazel tov" and asked whether he was seeking a rabbinate position. Between his wife's dowry and his own natural talents, he could aim for the largest city.

Do I have what it takes to be a rabbi?, he wondered. He knew his father considered him contrarian and hotheaded, with the kind of topsy-turvy mind that could easily declare something treyf as kosher and vice versa. "No, no!" he said. "I'm not a dayan of my father's caliber, nor do I have my father's zeal for scolding non-observant Jews, nor could I ever rip my enemies apart like herrings the way my father does—may he live long! No, I shouldn't be allowed to be a rabbi. Nor do I want to be."

"Well, your older brother, Refael Leima, held a rabbi's position in a small town and was a dayan here before he left for America, and he's a completely different person from your father," the townspeople argued.

"Ha! Do you hear yourselves? That's why Refael Leima left for America! He realized he couldn't see eye to eye with Father," Shabse-Shepsel cried, laughing at the men's stupidity. He twisted his head this way and that, drawing it inward to his narrow shoulders, extending it outward. His facial expressions kept changing: now he was choking back laughter; now he was flaming with rage. While he spoke, he threw his slender hands around and twirled his fingers, as if in them lay the entire Torah and all the wisdom of the material world. The creasing of his forehead, the twitching of his shoulders, the waving of his hands—all exuded his sense of himself as a genius, a man who picks up new knowledge through one ear and absorbs entire subjects from one word. No need for him to write anything down; he remembered it all by heart. But he would not become a rabbi, no chance. He was going into business! And Shabse-Shepsel and his little wife floated away as unexpectedly as they'd come. Though his parents never said as much to anyone, whispers circulated among those close to the rabbi that Shabse-Shepsel hadn't even bothered to bid his parents farewell.

The next time Shabse-Shepsel came to Zembin was for his mother's funeral. Because she'd died on the eve of Passover and the holiday released them from the requirement of sitting shiva, he returned home to his wife immediately after the funeral. And he hadn't shown his face in Zembin since then—not during his father's short-lived marriage to his second wife, Tamara, and not since his marriage to his third wife, Vigasia.

3

THE PEOPLE OF GRODNO despised Menashe Halberstadt, a rich widower and owner of a dinnerware shop, for his miserliness. It was said he counted his money by oil lamp, to save on electricity, and as soon as he'd finished counting, he extinguished the lamp and calculated his earnings in his head, to save on oil! The town still remembered his wife as a young woman, her face perpetually flushed, her lips luscious, looking as if she spent her days in front of an oven with veal simmering and a sweet browned babka rising. But over the years, loyalty to her husband had bent her toward her husband, in appearance and behavior. Her constant anxiety about spending even a groschen more than necessary had aged her prematurely. When her neighbors were getting rid of their old clothes, she'd volunteer to take them, supposedly to use as rags and potholders but really to revamp and add to her wardrobe. Their shared stinginess drew husband and wife closer together, and the day she died she was still in love with him—with his appearance, his cleverness, his knowledge. Menashe was well versed in Kabbalah, which only added to the Grodno people's hatred of him. Indeed, the only thing Menashe wasn't stingy about was recounting the Gemara passages he'd studied. Those he had no problem sharing! He had a melodious voice and enjoyed leading the davening. But people joked that whenever he was offered the honor of reading from the Torah, which implied a donation, he grumbled that he'd rather finish davening in his own seat. And when they'd see him take out the small, shabby leather pouch he used as a wallet—worthy of a pauper!—they grimaced in disgust. But those same grimacing faces froze whenever he extracted hundred-dollar banknotes in foreign currency from this pouch. His home was full of old, threadbare armchairs, springs missing from the seats. And the rumor was he'd held on to all these sagging rocking chairs because he'd sewn sacks of money into them.

Each evening, his only daughter, Draizel, sat on the sunken, faded red floral-print couch and gazed at her father in his armchair. Menashe regaled his daughter with tales of century-old dinnerware companies and workshops, of painted dishes and polished glasses. He quoted wise adages from Jewish texts, Draizel regarding him with a respect that bordered on fear, as if she weren't quite sure he was her father.

Menashe looked completely unlike his daughter. He was a tall, broad man with small, gray penetrating eyes, a sturdy nose, and a triangular face—its angularity emphasized by his beardlessness. His daughter, on the other hand, looked to be in a perpetual state of tension and alarm: short, with large, distrustful eyes, ready to spring like a cat at any moment. But beneath her locks of hair, her ears were long like her father's, and she kept these ears pricked so as not to miss a word of his brilliance.

Menashe's bearing, when he spoke to his daughter, was that of a teacher giving a lesson to a student. He never sat without his suit jacket, or in an unbuttoned shirt, or in slippers, but was dressed in a dark gray jacket with white trim, an elastic removable collar with a buttoned black bow tie, a velvet vest with a pocket-watch chain looped through two buttonholes, and a pair of shiny black boots. The wealthy widower polished his boots himself, using wax and a little rag. And he washed and starched his own elastic collar, and tightened up the buttons of his jacket. His dinnerware shop, too, he ran on his own. All his daughter, the house-sitter, had to do was cook supper and listen to him.

But though Draizel was in thrall to her father and rarely interacted with people, she still managed to hear the derisive comments people made about him. Comments like "He can't live because he's afraid to spend a groschen, and he can't die because he's afraid to leave so much money behind." In fact, her father himself told her about the insults he suffered in the beis medrash. Despite his good voice, and even on a Shabbos when he had yahrzeit for one of his parents, the congregation refused to let him lead the services. On Simchas Torah, when everyone was called up to do a reading, he was left for last. If he shared his interpretation of a Gemara passage, people either walked away or insulted him to his face: "How unseemly for a scholar like you to be such a miser." Out of politeness, Draizel never asked her father why he was so stingy. But though she loved him, and therefore loved the possessions that were dear to him, she grew to hate the money that brought him so much shame.

During the war years, some of the older dinnerware companies in other countries stopped manufacturing new sets of dishes. Some factories in Bremen and Mehrin, in fact, didn't resume work even after the war. When Menashe realized this, he packed the rarer, more expensive dishes in his inventory into crates and hid them, expecting future price hikes. He could barely allow himself to sell even the cheap stock he had in the shop. Although customers paid whatever he asked, his hands would tremble as he counted out the dozen plates for them. Soon, customers stopped coming in. "He groans like a man on his deathbed when he sells you his wares," they complained. "May he and his dishes both crack!"

Menashe wasn't bothered by this. He slowly sold the cheap glassware and placed the fine porcelain in the dark rooms of his house. Then, he closed his store and went to make deals on the stock exchange, where he'd done trades with foreign currency in the past. At the end of the war, when kingdoms fell and powers kept changing— Russians, Germans, Bolsheviks, Poles!—no trader beat Menashe in his ability to predict the next day's exchange rates. Evenings, he sat in his deep chair across from his daughter, smiling wisely. He regaled Draizel with accounts of rash speculators who'd lost money at the exchange that day, while he himself had made a fortune again. "If the price of gold drops today, it can go up tomorrow. But paper money— marks, kerenskis, ducats, zlotys—has to be exchanged for dollars at just the right moment. A smart person doesn't keep all his money in one business. That's why in the Gemara there's . . ."

Just as Menashe Halberstadt knew when and where to buy and sell on the exchange, so, too, did he know when and where to die. Well into his seventies, he went to sleep one night and never woke up. "A lucky man! That a miser should have such an easy death!" someone said, without fear that the corpse would come back to strangle him.

"Pity that my wish didn't come true. I'd wished for him to outlive his money," said another. "Can you imagine what he'd look like if he used up all his money and was left without a groschen?"

But a third person laughed at them both. "He was smarter than the two of you. He was a Torah scholar with absolute faith that he'd soon be resurrected and find his entire fortune with his daughter—untouched, not a single groschen missing. By all accounts, the heiress has the same personality as her dear father."

The Grodno Jews assumed that the community would demand a high burial fee and that the dead man's daughter would refuse to pay it. In turn, the chevra kadisha would refuse to do right by the stingy dead man, and there'd be all kinds of uproar. But Grodno was in for a shock: Draizel paid the amount demanded for an honorable cemetery spot. Her manner and behavior drew a large crowd to the funeral, where—when the soil was poured onto the grave—everyone watched as she cried bitterly over her loneliness in the world.

During the days of shiva, a minyan davened at the dead man's house each day. The curious worshippers tried to sneak a peek into the side rooms where the expensive hand-painted dinnerware lay hidden, but Draizel kept those rooms locked. In the salon where they davened, there were wobbly rockers with shabby seats; a bookcase with holy books strewn about haphazardly; footstools covered in oilcloth, made floppy by their lack of stuffing; all kinds of useless little tables and, above all, stacks and stacks of old newspapers. As other people told it, Menashe Halberstadt collected old newspapers and eventually sold them by weight to rag collectors. It appeared his daughter hadn't yet had the heart to throw them out.

After the shiva, Draizel hired a porush—one of those recluses who devote their lives to holiness and the study of sacred books—to recite Kaddish for her father each day for the next year, and she shut herself in the high, cold, dark rooms of her house. The gossip around town was that Draizel had inherited a fortune. But they spoke of this without envy and with a sense of disquiet, as if they foresaw the rich heiress alone in the dark, cold rooms being transformed into a bizarre four-legged creature.

When she finally ventured out, the neighbors watched as Fräulein Halberstadt passed by in a full-skirted dress and lace-up boots. Because of her shortness, this getup made her look comical, especially because short, tight dresses and pumps were in fashion at the time. Draizel went from store to store, buying a trousseau fit for a bride. She spent a fortune on tablecloths and linen, on silk underwear and clothes. Day after day she walked out of the finest stores with packages beneath her arms, and the people of Grodno understood that Fräulein Halberstadt was preparing to live very differently from her father. But they couldn't understand why she went on wearing those lace-up boots, like an old, slovenly woman who must wade through puddles and ponds.

Rumors that Fräulein Halberstadt wasn't tightfisted, that she never haggled while shopping for her trousseau, attracted the kind of young men who were looking to marry for practical reasons. *So she's no beauty, so what! As long as she doesn't have her father's personality, she's someone you can get along with.* Each potential suitor already fancied himself the owner of her pots, filled with gold coins. (People claimed she had sacks of dollars sewn into her rickety footstools.) Draizel quietly assented to the shadchans' propositions to meet with these "owners," and stayed just as quiet when they stood before her in her guest room. The young men did the talking, and the bride-to-be watched. She watched them in silence until it became clear to her that they were after her money, and it became clear to them that this ugly witch with money wouldn't have them. Her rejection of these young men only intensified the rumors that she was exceedingly wealthy.

Around that same time, Shabse-Shepsel Epstein had departed the yeshiva in Radin in the middle of the winter semester and set out to either Kamenitz or Mir. Or perhaps to Kletzk—he himself wasn't sure which yeshiva he'd study in until Passover, the end of the semester. Meanwhile, he remained stuck in Grodno, and since he was there anyway, he began asking around about potential shidduchim. The Torah students weren't sure if Shabse-Shepsel was as knowledgeable about Talmud and Jewish law as he claimed to be, but they agreed he was definitely more knowledgeable than any of the potential rabbinical or well-to-do prospects in Lithuania. Despite his vast knowledge, he'd never heard of the girl named Draizel Halberstadt until a shadchan mentioned her. "If you can figure out how to please this capricious fräulein," the shadchan said, "you'll no doubt strike it rich. Money is no object to her. She's the exact opposite of her father: he would have taken a bullet before parting with a groschen, but Draizel spends freely."

Shabse-Shepsel felt a rush of heat in his bones, a scorching as from fever. He needed her money like a hole in the head! But he'd show the world that this rich heiress would go mad for him. And when he saw the woman in question, he seethed even more: such a tiny thing, the size of a fig, a hag with a short, wide nose—would she dare say no to him?!

The room darkened, but Draizel sat still as if welded to her chair. She wore a black velvet blouse with a white detachable collar, a skirt, and those lace-up boots of hers. Outside, a bluish snow fell; a muted light seeped in through the window. The ratty objects in the room hung in tangled gray shadows. The lamp emitted a yellowish light, its pale glow on Draizel's forehead like a stain. Her wide-open, questioning eyes shone in mysterious anticipation. She looked like a sorceress who'd met a sorcerer and now wanted to discover which of the two knew more magic.

All evening, Shabse-Shepsel spoke about his family, whose pedigree went back all the way to Spain. The wealthiest and most respectable family in all of Spain had been the Benvenistes. They were part of the royal court, with many "grandees" among them. "A grandee," Shabse-Shepsel explained, "was a type of prince who wore a wide, round hat adorned with ostrich feathers, tall boots, short pants, and a sword at his side. Yet despite their noble stock, when it was decreed that all Jews must convert to Christianity or leave Spain, the Benvenistes abandoned their property and possessions and set out upon the world. Part of the family settled in Turkey and in the land of the Greeks. There, they had children and grandchildren who to this day go by the name of Benveniste. They're Sephardic. But another part of those Golei-Sfard—as the exiled Spanish Jews are called in Hebrew—wandered and wandered until they arrived at a town in Germany, where they settled and called themselves Epstein. Which means that the Ashkenazi Epsteins are just as princely as their cousins, the Sephardic Benvenistes. And I am Don Shabse-Shepsel Epstein!" he proclaimed, left hand on his hip, where the grandees used to hold their swords, and right hand up in the air, as if he were greeting a crowd at a parade.

"But you're not from the princely family of King David," Draizel said, sneering at the young man who boasted of his pedigree. "Father told me there are Jews who can trace their lineage all the way back to King David."

"And just because they tell you so, you believe them? A bastard, too, can say he descends from King David; go and prove otherwise!" Shabse-Shepsel burst into laughter, and the sound echoed toward the high ceiling of the dark, dusty guest room. He felt a hatred at that moment for this bride-to-be, in her modest little white collar. What a stinker! But he'd show her! Did she think she could challenge him? Well, he'd show her. He'd break her, destroy her! He was perceptive enough to realize that his snide tone was precisely what was getting to her. He said, "Even the Gemara speaks of Jews who are descended from gentiles who'd raped Jewish women! Yes, you heard right. Descended from idol-worshippers in Babel to the Russian Cossacks, the pogrom'kes! These men violated Jewish women and thus bastards were born. But the Epsteins and their cousins, the Benvenistes, descend from age-old, one hundred percent Jews. There's a Jewish Prophet by the name of Obadiah, and he left us with only one chapter. Because of that, these few words of his are like gold. And in his chapter there's a verse, '*Vegalos yisroel asher b'Sfard,*' meaning that Jews have been settled in Spain from the time of the Temple's destruction—and those are the very Jews from whom the Epsteins are descended. One hundred percent Jewish!"

"I know some Epsteins in Grodno and some in Bialystok, and they're certainly no princes," Draizel retorted stubbornly. "And I never heard about any of this from my father, either."

"Your father, may he rest in peace, didn't know a thing about it, because you're Halberstadts, not Epsteins," the suitor cried, throwing his hands up and springing from his chair. "But *I* did hear this from my father, may he live long, and I know how to differentiate between an authentic Epstein and an imposter. The authentic Epsteins, cousins of the Benvenistes, all descend from the tribe of Levi, like Moses and the High Priest Aaron, but the imposters have nothing to do with the tribe of Levi. That's why my father signs his name 'Eli-Leizer Ha*Levi* Epstein.' My father has been rabbi of Zembin for more than fifty years, and the world trembles in the face of his Torah scholarship, his brilliance, his piety and pedigree."

The more bizarrely her suitor spoke, the more Draizel shrank into her armchair, staring up at him with fearful eyes. She saw that this suitor, like the others, wanted to impress her, but he had no designs on her money. Not only was he not making a fuss over her, he was yelling in her face. She would be happier with him than she'd been when living with her father. True, her father used to speak intelligently, very intelligently, though not exactly with the calmness and steadiness of a light autumn rain on a tin roof. There had been times when she wanted to rush outside, mouth wide open, and inhale the snow, the wind, even the smoke from the chimneys, so constricted and stifled did she feel in those stale rooms with her father. But she knew the hatred everyone felt for him, and as the only one with the patience to listen to his words, she couldn't bear to interrupt or upset him. With this young man, however, their exchange was cheerier and lively. He was as worldly as her father, and no less of a scholar. Draizel said, "Families descending from such aristocracy as yours should have their own doctor, a personal physician."

Shabse-Shepsel stared at the fräulein with wondering eyes, as if she'd woken him from sleep and he was seeing, in the flesh, the beautiful princess he'd envisioned in his dream. "It hadn't dawned on me that I should have a personal physician." He smiled crookedly. All the lines in his face twitched, as if he could barely control himself from bursting into either tears or laughter. But he did neither, and merely shuffled out with a stiff, raised head, hurling a few words over his shoulder. "Go to sleep," he said. "Tomorrow evening, I'll come again."

During their engagement, Draizel confessed that she wanted to have an enormous wedding celebration and invite his entire rabbinical family. Shabse-Shepsel shuddered from head to toe. No way! An Ashkenazi Epstein from the Sephardic Benveniste family wasn't allowed to marry a Halberstadt. If his father should find out, there was no way in the world he'd ever allow the marriage to take place! They would go and see his parents only after they were already married.

And so Shabse-Shepsel did.

4

THRILLED TO HAVE SHOCKED his parents by marrying without
their knowledge, Shabse-Shepsel, after returning to Grodno
with his wife, took up where his father-in-law, Menashe Halberstadt,
had left off: trading on the exchange. But times had changed. The
city was no longer jumping from one government to the next; the
border between Russia and Poland had solidified. Swapping curren-
cies was no longer as profitable an endeavor. Though Shabse-Shepsel
still managed to lose money in speculations anyway.

Draizel realized her husband was a schemer. In an attempt to
straighten him out, she shared an analogy: a good tailor measures
fabric ten times before he cuts it, but a bad one slashes the fabric
without a second thought, ruining the clothes.

"You must have heard that brilliant tidbit from your father, may
he rest in peace." Shabse-Shepsel laughed. Nevertheless, he agreed
with his wife that he wasn't doing well at the exchange. It was deathly
boring there, he claimed. Just a few traders ambling around, buzzing
like flies trapped in a jar.

With currency trading in the dumps, Shabse-Shepsel decided to
start a business in a healthier field, where no swindling was involved.
From the villagers at the old market he bought sunflower seeds, dried
plums, honey (along with the honey residue for making mead), wax
for candles, and threads. He then turned around and sold these items
to people in the city. In addition, he leased a small outdoor space on
Lacemakers Street. The space stood between two buildings, secured
by an iron gate. There, he set himself up to sell two kinds of products: carved gravestones and farm tools, such as threshing machines,
steel scythes, reaping knives, pickaxes, and spades.

Shabse-Shepsel would often abandon his business in the old market and stand all day at his place on Lacemakers Street, until eventu-

ally a baron showed up, seeking a slab of stone for a grave, perhaps, or else a peasant seeking a tool for his work in the fields. Shabse-Shepsel sold his wares on the thinnest of margins, sometimes even taking a loss. If the baron returned later complaining that the stone had crumbled while he was carving the epitaph, or if the peasant claimed that his tools were falling apart, Shabse-Shepsel would shrug his skinny shoulders and say with a smile, "What are you worried about? Take another stone! Take another tool!" But when he sold his provisions in the old market to Jewish customers, he spoke to them impatiently, arrogantly, mockingly: "So how much are you willing to pay without haggling? How much?" Meanwhile, he went about extending credit to everyone.

When retailers or female customers asked him, "Don't you write down the amounts people owe you?" he replied haughtily, "I remember all of Talmud and Jewish law by heart; do you think I won't remember a few groschens?" Very quickly he found himself with no money and no goods to sell, and right away he began talking to his wife about starting a new business.

"You're squandering the money my father worked his entire life to amass," Draizel sobbed.

"There's a verse for situations like this," Shabse-Shepsel said, laughing like the demon Ashmedai. "The evil man prepares so that the saintly man can spend."

"My father's the evil one? You bought stones and irons and handed them out to gentiles. You're kinder to gentiles than to your wife." Draizel sobbed even louder.

"Price shouldn't be a factor when it comes to preventing the desecration of God's name. And what can be of greater shame to God than when a Christian says that a Jew swindled him?" Shabse-Shepsel yelled at his wife, feigning anger, as if he were talking to a little girl. "There's a story in the Gemara about the tanna Rabbi Shimon, the son of Shetach, whose students bought a donkey from a gentile. The tanna found a diamond hanging on the donkey's neck and returned it to the former owner. When his students asked him why he'd returned the diamond, he replied, 'What, you think Shimon is a pilferer? To hear a non-Jew laud the Jewish God is more important to Shimon, son of Shetach, than all the world's treasures.' But what does a woman understand? And who else would have told you a story like this? Your father, the miser and ignoramus? Well, may he have a blessed afterlife!" Shabse-Shepsel again cackled like Ashmedai.

Draizel swallowed her tears, trembling with hurt. But his devil-ish laughter and the confident way he quoted from holy texts had a greater impact on her than her father's calm and insightful quips. "Fine," she told him. "If I approve of your new business, I'll give you money." But she had conditions. He would have to stop insulting her father and explain to her what had made him think of renting a place to sell both gravestones and farm tools. Never in her life had she seen or heard of anyone selling these two products in one shop.

"What? You think Don Shabse-Shepsel Benveniste is some small-time merchant on Lacemaker Street in Grodno? I'm an original! I think of things no one else does!" he said proudly. But this time he actually had a plan that would please her. He wanted to go back to studying the Gemara day and night.

"If you do that, you can eventually become rabbi in your father's place," Draizel said, pleased.

Shabse-Shepsel sprang up as if his jacket had caught fire. "You want to become the rebbetzin of Zembin? To take my mother's place? Never! Never in your life! And I don't want to take my father's rabbinical seat either, never in my life! I want to study Torah for its own sake and make some money from business on the side. Get it?"

Shabse-Shepsel decided he'd invest in a business with a resourceful partner and split the profits. Which led him into a business venture with Aryeh Leib Halperin, a young man from a family of rabbis—the only one of them, in fact, to become a businessman instead of a rabbi.

Aryeh Leib had opened a textile factory in Bialystok, where he employed both religious Jews and Poles to work the electric looms. Like other cloth manufacturers, Halperin competed on a global scale: he opened fabric warehouses in Chorbin and in Shanghai, where he sold coats, wool quilts, and tablecloths. But he lacked the capital for so much material. Meanwhile, he had to pay his non-Jewish employ-ees for Saturdays and Jewish holidays, even when his factory was shuttered. Before he could fully establish himself, he was forced to close his shops. And it was right around that time that he found him-self in Grodno and became acquainted with Shabse-Shepsel, whose own businesses had recently failed.

On Lacemaker Street, two pale brown buildings framed Shabse-

Shepsel's open space, each with three rows of windows and an entrance flanked by two trees. The chestnut trees were already frozen, leafless, asleep for the winter. Only a few twigs and branches still stood out, sharply, against the deep blue background, lit by the mild glow of a late autumn noon. No one walked up or down the entryway steps, no curtain stirred, and not a soul peeked out from the windows. Only two men could be seen, standing between the buildings, in that gated space where a few knives and rakes still lay. One of the two was the owner of those tools, Shabse-Shepsel Epstein. Skinny as his walking stick, he wore a rumpled cap and a short jacket, whose coattails—even in this calm weather—swung as if blown by a wind. The other man, Aryeh Leib Halperin, the son of "greats," was a tall, broad Jew with full cheeks and an overgrown pitch-black beard that glimmered with a bluish reflection. He wore a stiff black hat, a shirt and tie, and the long kaftan favored by religious Jews. Were it not for his heavy stick, which was forbidden to be carried on Shabbos, one might have imagined—judging by his appearance, attire, and manner of speaking—that every day was Shabbos for him. Fresh-faced and bright-eyed, he looked no older than thirty-five. But his broad figure and deep voice made him appear old enough to have married children. He gripped his heavy stick with his left hand, and with his right he caressed his round beard, humming in a velvety-soft voice.

"Rabbis' sons like me and you," Aryeh Leib told Shabse-Shepsel, "understand each other well. On one hand, we know how much a person must toil in the study of Torah to be a genuine scholar; on the other, we know the bitter reality of a community rabbi's life. Which is why we must go into business. But we must choose the sort of business that's connected to Judaism and close to our hearts. When I went into the textiles field, what I should have done was set up looms for talleisim, not for fabrics to make coats. But now, I have a much better business in mind—for Jewish ritual objects, in fact." Aryeh Leib transferred his stick to his right hand and, with his left, lifted his beard, humming into it as if it were a flute. "I'm going to print a Talmud with the earliest commentators in the margins, the Tosefeth and Alfasi at the end, and the annotations of later commentators at the very back."

"But such a Talmud has already been printed in Vilna!" Shabse-

Shepsel cried out, surprised. "The Ram Widow and Brothers Publishers printed it."

"But we're also going to add the Yerushalmi at the end of every tractate, and so far, no one has published the Babylonian and Yerushalmi Talmud together." Aryeh Leib again switched his stick from hand to hand and purred through his beard that publications of Tanach generally did a great injustice to the Aramaic Yerushalmi. Mostly, only fragments and tidbits from the Yerushalmi are included, and in the tiniest print. "So what we have to do is publish a Tanach according to the Amsterdam Kehillas Moshe's model, with all the annotations and commentary. A 'twenty-four-volume Bible' like this must be printed on parchment paper with gilded binding, covered in green or black linen, with silver corners and brackets. And because this 'twenty-four' will cost a fortune, it will become the standard Talmud that Jews buy as wedding gifts for their sons and sons-in-law."

"And what will it say on the title page?" Shabse-Shepsel asked, unable to control his curiosity. "Who are the publishers?"

"Well, it'll say 'Printed and published by partners Halperin and Epstein,'" Halperin replied serenely.

But Shabse-Shepsel became incensed, foam gathering on his lips. "Epstein must be listed first. The whole world knows that my father, the Zembin rabbi—may he live long—is this generation's luminary. So the title page must say, 'Printed and published by partners Epstein and Halperin.'"

Already tired from passing his stick from hand to hand, and from shifting his heavy feet, Halperin decided not to press the issue. He mumbled into his round beard that they'd find a way to agree on the wording of the title page. In the meantime, the question was how much money Shabse-Shepsel was able to invest. To start, he'd have to put in at least five thousand zlotys. Later, of course, he'd have to add more than double that amount. Did he have that much money?

Shabse-Shepsel shrugged his shoulders: he didn't know how much he had. He may well have ten times that much. But the cash was hidden in the iron safe, and his wife, the shrew, held the key. The money had been her father's, the miser's. At the bank, too, her signature was needed. "You already have my consent," Shabse-Shepsel said. "Now you have to get my wife's." And a day later, he brought his partner to his home.

To impress his guest, Shabse-Shepsel told his wife to host him in a room usually closed off to strangers. Even there the space was tight, full of dust, the odor of wormy wood lurking beneath cloths. But on one wall stood a hulking, red wood credenza, and behind its thick glass were painted plates, platters, saucers, goblets, and pitchers. And the dishes displayed in that red wood armoire hinted at the greater treasure of glassware, porcelain, and sterling dishes presumably locked away in the other room—like a night sky seeded with twinkling stars that hint at distant and unseen celestial bodies.

But Aryeh Leib Halperin clearly didn't know much about these things. He sat with pious lowered eyes and blew with his fat lips as if into a saucer of hot tea. Across him sat Draizel, observing him. She did not like his handsomeness, his broad and fleshy figure. Instead of speaking in a thick, masculine voice, he cooed like a turtledove, touching his whiskers and round beard as if they were pasted onto his face.

Halperin's attempt to portray his great knowledge of the publishing industry, despite having started in textiles, was evident. Clearly, he implied, he could be relied upon. He began by telling them that the Widow and Brothers Ram of the world-renowned Vilna publishing house hailed from Grodno. No small thing, Grodno! Brilliant men had been publishing books with the local Polish royal press long before Vilna had been dubbed the Jerusalem of Lithuania. Which was why it was important that the crown be returned to Grodno. This meant that though the actual printing press would be in Bialystok, the firm listed on the books would be "Grodno Publishers." Then their guest launched into a discussion of materials. Years ago, they'd made the pages of books out of rags, he explained, so what you got was a coarse, threaded paper with a watermark woven into it. "Indeed, those old sheets of paper used to keep for a century, while the paper nowadays, made of burnished pulp, turns to dust in just a few decades." But Halperin's diligent efforts to charm Draizel with his knowledge were in vain. A clever little smile played on her lips, saying wordlessly, "No, you're not going to distract me. Me, you will not fool."

Her husband's sudden cry sent a shiver through her. "Do you hear what's being said to you? Our family name will be on the title page of every book: Published by *Epstein* and Halperin. Don't you get it?"

Shabse-Shepsel cried, furious at the smile that skipped across Draizel's lips like a little mouse.

"Of course your wife hears what's being said to her. She gets it," the guest calmed the man of the house.

Though he'd just stood up for her and calmed her husband's yelling, Draizel found Halperin and his smooth tongue more repulsive with each passing minute. She felt a pulse beating in her temple. All this chatter about different kinds of fonts—four-cornered, Rashi-style, feminine "wooden," narrow and wide, fat and thin, angled right, angled left, rounded and elongated—was giving her a headache. While he talked, Halperin kept lifting himself to adjust the flaps of his jacket, and Draizel was pleased that the ratty chair's threadbare springs were poking him in his big behind. Already, his glib talk about the founders of various types and typefaces was swirling around in her mind, and she saw red, yellow, and green letters jumping about in front of her as if on electric cables.

Her husband, puffed with pride, kept shouting the same refrain at one-minute intervals, making her quiver each time. "You hear what's being said to you? In the expanded Talmud we'll publish, we'll include all my father's commentary. And here's how his name will appear on the title page: Mystical Vision of the Prophet Elijah by the genius, Rabbi 'Eli-jah' Leizer HaLevi Epstein. Father, may he live long, is a greater genius than the Maharam and even than the Maharam Schiff. Our Talmud will be the only one to include Father's commentaries. Right, Aryeh Leib?" Shabse-Shepsel stretched his hands out to his partner, who set a pair of glazed eyes on him, as if to ask, "Your father has a treatise on the Talmud, and that simple accomplishment merits him the title 'Vision of Elijah'? Who are you ridiculing here, me or your father?" But though Aryeh Leib would have liked to pose this question, he knew to remain silent.

Shabse-Shepsel understood what power his yelling and banging held over his wife, so he carried on until she finally gave him her signature for the bank. She also gave him a sheaf of bills from her father's strongbox. And it was with vengeful glee that Draizel handed over the money, knowing that he would now have to answer to her, not the other way around. But Shabse-Shepsel, too, handed the bundle of bills to his partner with an impish glee. "Here, take the noodles!" he cried.

Aryeh Leib took the capital and immediately set off for Bialystok, where he intended to establish the printing press. The two had agreed that Epstein would receive only thirty-five percent of the profits, because he wouldn't be involved in any of the publishing operations. Instead, he'd remain in Grodno to study.

Winter had just begun; Shabse-Shepsel had barely dipped his toes into the intricate questions of the Talmud and already his wife was nagging him. Before this printing business, when Shabse-Shepsel was out working, Draizel had sat home like a werewolf. But since her husband had become the house-sitter, she'd started going out around Grodno, coming home with fresh gossip. "Your partner—the fatso with his rosy little cheeks and shiny black beard—everyone in Grodno seems to know him. They say he sits around with his family in Bialystok, completely relaxed, doesn't dip his hand into cold water, and puts food on the table with other people's money."

Absorbed in the complexities of the Talmud, Shabse-Shepsel gaped at his wife with astonished eyes, the way Jews leaving shul might gape at a coachman driving into the center of town smack in the middle of Shabbos. Eventually, though, Shabse-Shepsel descended to earth from his heavenly spheres and asked his wife how she knew such a thing. The desire to spit in her husband's face and shout that he was the devil in disguise sapped the moisture from Draizel's lips. But because she knew how much pleasure her yelling and crying gave him, she kept her composure. Placidly, she replied that in every town along the train line between Grodno and Bialystok people knew that Aryeh Leib Halperin was a glutton, a drunkard, and a lazy liar. And his wife was no different—a shallow woman who'd birthed a brood of freeloaders. Once upon a time Halperin had smooth-talked people into giving him money for his textile business, all of which he'd squandered. Then he'd devoured the funds for a tea company. And now he was burning through every cent he'd wrested out of people for his fictitious printing press.

"He took money from other people, too, for the publishing venture?" Shabse-Shepsel asked amusedly, as serenely as if they were discussing the business speculations of a distant relative. "Is that so? Is that so?" He smacked his lips and gazed about the room with pious eyes, as when he'd rise on tiptoes to kiss a mezuzah on a door frame.

Another day, his gossipette had a new story waiting for him when he arrived home from the beis medrash. "People say your partner and his father, the rabbi, are at each other's throats. His father keeps scolding him for guzzling down strangers' possessions and destroying the good reputation of the family. And the son retorts, 'Better to guzzle others' possessions than let wife and children starve, the way you did.' See? See how your smooth-talking partner runs his mouth even to his own father?"

Rather than cast an expression of confusion or defeat or mock innocence, as was his style, Shabse-Shepsel jumped up, tugging at his whiskers joyfully. "That's the sort of man he is? Who refuses to be intimidated? Who answers his father, the saintly little Rabbi Oizer'l, like that? Never in my life did I give cheek to my own father like that! But this one does. Oh, that's good! Very good!" Shabse-Shepsel chirped, and threw his hands and feet about, terrifying his wife, who thought he'd either lost his mind or been stricken with epilepsy.

Each day the snowstorms grew in force and Draizel's opinion of her husband's partner diminished. "The young Torah scholars are badgering Halperin, demanding he return at least a portion of what he swindled out of them for his printing press. Go to Bialystok and salvage whatever money you can before that deadbeat burns it all."

But Shabse-Shepsel kept putting it off, despite the mere hundred kilometers, and only three train stops, between Grodno and Bialystok. First, he was afraid to set out in such frosty weather. Then, he caught a cold (though he had no fever). He kept coughing dryly and touching his cool forehead. Yet a third time, when his wife pressured him to go, he groaned, *My soul thirsts for Torah. I don't want to waste time I can use for studying.* So passed an entire winter. Draizel ceased her talk about usurpers, but her dark eyes still pierced her husband accusingly. Only after Purim, when the frost let up, did Shabse-Shepsel finally pull himself together and leave for Bialystok.

Rather than just a day or two, he lingered an entire week, returning with the pious, transcendent expression of one who's gone to pray at the tomb of a saint and made a vow to fast.

"Did you get our money back from the deadbeat?" Draizel asked breathlessly.

"Heaven forbid!" Her husband shuddered, as if she'd asked if he'd bowed to an idol. "I made inquiries in Bialystok about my partner's situation and was told he was again penniless. Well, I won't humiliate a person who can't pay. As is written in the Torah, 'Do not be a creditor.' "

"And where were you all week?" Draizel asked with a fake smile, to show he could no longer surprise her.

"From Bialystok I went to Zembin, and there I bought a house with a storefront, from a Jew who's moving to Grajewo to live near his children. I'd like us to settle in Zembin. But I made a pact with the seller, Itzel Zimmerman, that my purchase must be kept secret from the entire town, especially from my father, until we actually move."

"Why isn't your father allowed to know?" Draizel asked.

"If he finds out, he'll buy the house and the entire estate from Itzel Zimmerman himself rather than have me settle in Zembin. Understand?" Shabse-Shepsel said, with triumphant, vengeful fire in his eyes.

This truly caught Draizel by surprise, and she didn't hide it. She flew into a rage. "You despise me. You married me to squander my father's money," she cried, no longer concealing her hatred.

He burst into laughter. Pointing his finger at her, he said, "But that's why you married me, to spend your father's money. Look! Just look at her! Such pretentiousness! That big-eyed gaze of yours! When my business was failing, you could barely keep from dancing for joy. You think I didn't notice? You wanted me to keep losing. You wanted people to see I'm a failure."

"True," Draizel replied, sobbing. "All Father's money brought me was unhappiness. When Father was alive, I was ashamed to go out in the world because everyone hated him for his stinginess. And when he died, men wanted to marry me only for my inheritance. I grew to hate those men *and* my inheritance. But you—you exploiter!—you're worse than all of them. You married me just to show you could do it. You're squandering my money, and worse, you ridicule me to boot."

Draizel wept long and bitterly. Until, finally, Shabse-Shepsel had had his fill of her tears. A part of him felt a little worried; another part pitied her. He began to calm her. "Oh, silly you, in Zembin you'll be the rabbi's daughter-in-law. Everyone will treat you with respect and want to be in your good graces. The money we lost shouldn't feel like a loss to you, because you want your husband to love you for yourself, not for your money, right?" And Shabse-Shepsel laid out his plan—how they'd open a large shop in Zembin where they'd sell the glassware and porcelain that had been stowed in crates ever since her father shut down his store. The ragged furniture and the rest of the junk in the house weren't worth bringing along. "To move the crates of dinnerware, though, we'll have to put in a lot of work and money."

"But I went to your Zembin right after our wedding, and there are no connoisseurs there; no one who'd appreciate such exquisite dinnerware," Draizel murmured, downcast. She shivered, as if she'd been shoved into the cold in only a blouse.

"There'll be *some* connoisseurs," Shabse-Shepsel huffed. "And once the Zembin boors see our porcelain treasures, they'll go reaching into their nest eggs. The rich city women and villagers will be drooling for a set of plates from Epstein's. But we'll have to pay a fortune for the house. I used everything I had on me as a deposit."

Hunched into her blouse, Draizel sat silently, head lowered, dejected. After her father's death, during the days and weeks she'd sat home alone, she had now and then taken out the polished dishes and gazed proudly at her reflection in them. Her trousseau, too, had brought her pride and happiness. Now, though, both the expensive dinnerware and her entire trousseau lay untouched, and nothing any longer brought her joy.

5

S HABSE-SHEPSEL TRAVELED to Zembin at the beginning of the month of Nissan. His father heard news of his arrival from others; his son did not stop by. Shabse-Shepsel's house stood among the circle surrounding the marketplace, close enough to his father's home that if the old man squinted, he could see his son lugging furniture through the door and movers hauling crates into the store.

Only after he'd finished unpacking the store's stock and displaying the samples in his house did Shabse-Shepsel appear at his father's door, just as he'd done long before, when his mother was alive and he'd come to introduce his wife after their wedding.

This time he arrived at noon and without his wife. When he stepped inside, he blinked a few times as if blinded by sunlight, despite it being a dreary day. Dressed in a short suit jacket but no coat, as though it were midsummer already, his wrinkled hat high on his sweaty forehead, Shabse-Shepsel kept swirling a stick in his hand. Although he had never seen Vigasia, he refused to spare her a glance and acted as if he barely noticed his father. He paced back and forth in the beis din room, paused for a beat at the shelves of holy texts, and then resumed his pacing again.

"Why would you move to Zembin so suddenly, without even letting me know?" his father asked.

"Why shouldn't I try my luck in my native city? And why should I have to tell you beforehand?" The rabbi's son avoided using the less respectful "du" form of address, but neither did he use the respectful third-person "Father."

With some astonishment, Vigasia observed that her husband lost all his forcefulness when he spoke with his son.

"And why did you come without your wife?" he asked his son, smiling glumly.

"How does this concern my wife?" his son replied impatiently, continuing to act as if his father's wife were not in the room. He paused again near the shelves of books. "I have to check something important in the *Aruch Hashulchan*, but where is it? I don't see it in its usual spot." He turned his head and placed his walking stick beneath his arm.

"Sholem Shachne borrowed my *Aruch Hashulchan* when he was here for the dedication ceremony," his father replied. "What do you need it for? Are you studying at all?"

"Of course! I study always and everywhere! Even when I'm riding the train or standing in a store or walking around the market, I study Talmud and halacha by heart!" Shabse-Shepsel cried, then hurried to the door. "I must be going. I have no time."

Eli-Leizer stood rooted to his spot, helpless and awkward, the way his older son, Refael Leima, used to stand when Eli-Leizer roared at him for his lack of zeal. Now the old man was silent, as downtrodden in his silence as his son used to be, and neither did the smart rebbetzin Vigasia utter a word.

Shabse-Shepsel became a congregant in the new beis medrash, the fortress of his father's enemies. Worse, a fresh new battle had just flared up against his father. The cantor of the new beis medrash, Zisel Yedvabnik, a hefty Jew with a curly gray beard, doubled as Zembin's shochet. He was a graduate of the cantorial school in Tshenstekhev, could read music, and even composed his own tunes. When he led the services on Shabbos and holidays, he wore a jacket with velvet lapels and a top hat. He'd scoured Zembin for boys with good singing voices and had formed a choir to accompany him. Men who davened in other shuls, hearing word of his beautiful performances, began rushing through their own davening to hurry over to the new beis medrash. His Shabbos and holiday singing brought a charge to his congregants' spirits that lasted through the week, the way a cloud aglow with the sun's rosy hue goes on shining once the sun has passed.

The old rabbi watched Zembin as it became ever more swept up in the cantorial craze. He sighed. "A city of Jews degrades the Shabbos and holiday davening to go and hear this idiot yodeling? Men and women stand squeezed together in the shul's courtyard chattering and joking, stirring up sinful thoughts. Willingly or not, they end up desecrating the Shabbos. Already the freethinkers are arguing that if the community subsidizes the cost of the choirs and choirboys, it should also help sponsor a theater. If Zisel Yedvabnik were a God-fearing man, he'd at least melt their hardened hearts with his singing, inspire them to atone for their sins. But he's a libertine who merely performs tricks with his throat. And his listeners savor it like a succulent dish. Besides, how could such a man be a shochet, and immerse himself in all its relevant laws, when he's constantly consumed with the tuning of his larynx and the singing of notes, his choirboys at attention like birds on a wire?"

Nevertheless, the rabbi refrained from waging war against the cantorial fad. He didn't want people to accuse him of looking for a pretext to harass his enemies, the congregants in the new beis medrash. Among them were the Rabiner, the rabbi's longtime adversary, and Jews of various social standing who were devotees of Dr. Theodor Herzl. Eli-Leizer didn't want to get into it with any of them—not with the Rabiner and the Zionists, and even less with the common masses who'd whine that he was spoiling their Shabbos and holiday. *Forget it, forget it, I must be silent*, Eli-Leizer sighed. But eventually he realized that his silence was making things worse. Instead of Jews preparing for Passover with trepidation, terrified lest they violate the prohibition of chametz, they were joyfully anticipating the cantor's "improvised compositions." On Shabbos Hagadol, only a sparse audience attended the rabbi's oration. But on Passover in the new beis medrash, when Zisel Yedvabnik yodeled and trilled during davening, they were practically clinging to the walls.

Eli-Leizer issued a pronouncement prohibiting the consumption of any meats slaughtered by Zisel, because—Eli-Leizer claimed—Zisel's hands shook while performing his task. This was the season when the sky was turning bluer and clearer with each passing day, but had it suddenly started snowing, it would not have brought such astonishment to Zembin as did this pronouncement against Zisel's meats. A few butchers and shochets revealed that, after Passover, the rabbi had visited the slaughterhouse several times, observing things as he used to when he was younger. It was true, the rabbi and Zisel weren't on very affable terms. And everyone was aware of the rabbi's feelings about this new preference for singing over praying. Still, no one had expected him to announce an injunction against the cantor.

On the first day of Iyar, feeling wounded and bitter, Zisel refused to lead Shabbos services. And the ba'al tefilah who replaced him couldn't be heard. The beis medrash fumed. Zisel shuffled from person to person, sobbing dry-eyed that the rabbi had slaughtered him without a knife. Wearing no coat or top hat, Zisel stretched his long hands out of his too-short jacket sleeves to show everyone they didn't shake. Whether his hands trembled when an ox lay tied up in front of him, the crowd couldn't ascertain, but everyone agreed that the cantor-slaughterer did have heavy, clumsy hands. They also took note of his bluish cheeks, red-tipped nose, and rather bedraggled but clean beard. Instead of speaking with confidence, he babbled, looking utterly pitiful, as if the rabbi's injunction had also eradicated his composure and power of speech. Despite this, the entire beis medrash was on his side. They were indignant: *Why had the ancient fanatic banned our slaughterer and cantor?* Leading the group was the Rabiner, Nosson-Nota Goldstein, more incensed than everyone that the rabbi hadn't consulted him. The crowd's wrath swelled, rocking them like a wall of waves. The frenzy, the seething and rumbling, needed an outlet, and it found one in Shabse-Shepsel, the rabbi's son, who was all alone in a corner.

His tallis over his head, Shabse-Shepsel stood at his lectern, studying from a large Gemara. He examined the text, then reviewed and recited it by heart, tossing his head up and down like a bird flinging its beak in a puddle. The Zembin people knew that Shabse-Shepsel was no older than thirty-six or thirty-seven, but he was so gaunt, wrinkled, and jaundiced that it seemed he'd already lived an entire life. Only his eyes still twinkled—pale blue, sharp, audacious, but also terrified. In each toss of his head, in each exclamation that seemed to emanate from a deep cellar—"Huh? What?"—lay the uneasiness of an animal that sleeps with its ears pricked for predators. The congregants came over, encircling him, while the Rabiner with his cascading beard complained, "As you probably know, your brother Refael Leima and I studied together in Slobodka before I left to study in Berlin. We remained friends, even after your father took Refael Leima from his little town and moved him to this one, to be the dayan here. For your brother's sake and for the sake of peace, I relinquished my own honor many times for your father, and I quietly helped your brother leave for America. I'd like to be friends with you, too. And perhaps you can explain why your father banned Zisel Yedvabnik's slaughtering all of a sudden, with no rhyme or reason!"

The rabbi's son emerged from his reverie, mumbling and shaking, the way a devout Jew shakes water off his body as he leaves the mikveh. He replied impetuously, "Whatever Father's rivals may say about him, they'd all admit that Father, may he live long, is a man of integrity. He wouldn't ban a slaughterer without legitimate grounds. It's true that the shochet's hands didn't used to shake, but now they do. And one of the signs that the cantor-shochet isn't trustworthy is the situation with his choir. Yedvabnik—and I'll tell it to him right to his face!—dresses his choirboys to the nines: in sharp-cornered yarmulkes with fringes and skinny, pale blue silk talleisim round their necks, as is the fashion in German temples. To emulate the Jews who pray in German temples is no better than emulating gentiles, as the Torah commands us: 'Do not follow their ways.' We're forbidden to emulate gentiles, even their clothes. Father knows what he's doing."

Zisel Yedvabnik stood dumbfounded. The congregants, too, were stunned into speechlessness. When they regained their composure, they all started hollering at once, and the Rabiner outyelled all of them. "For yarmulkes with fringes, you ban a slaughterer? Even if fringed yarmulkes and blue talleisim fall in the category of emulating gentiles, the cantor doesn't deserve a punishment like this! Was he caught desecrating the Shabbos? Committing adultery with a gentile woman? I've never heard such a thing in my life!"

"Who cares about what *you* never heard?" Shabse-Shepsel grimaced at the Rabiner. "In fact, if a shochet is accused of bedding a prostitute, there's one rabbinical opinion that says his slaughter is still kosher. It falls under the yutzru tukfu exemption, for when a sinful inclination is too strong to withstand. And at least he didn't cause others to eat treyf. On the other hand, a shochet who commits a sin that doesn't stem from great temptation, let alone when the sin entails more heresy than temptation—a shochet like that surely wouldn't be concerned about Jews eating non-kosher. And your shochet, Reb Zisel Yedvabnik—I'll tell it to him straight to his face!—has his choir wearing fringed yarmulkes, the way they do in Reform temples, where they're Jews only in name. Such a shochet would have no qualms claiming that he'd performed a kosher slaughter, even if he hadn't severed most of the animal's trachea and esophagus. That's the reason my father doesn't trust his slaughtering. Father knows what he's talking about!"

Shabse-Shepsel intoned all this with his eyes squeezed tightly shut, and with such exaggerated devoutness you could have sworn he really meant it. This enraged the rabbi's enemies even more, and they repeated it with a sense of triumph to the rabbi's confidants. And the confidants went to the rabbi, pleading that he lift the ban on the cantor-shochet or else the entire community—the entire world!—would soon turn against him.

When Eli-Leizer got word of how Shabse-Shepsel had supposedly defended him, he stamped his feet and shouted, "Lies! Pure lies! Everything my mixed-up son says is a complete lie! It's true that I think the cantor is corrupting the community with his singing. Instead of people davening with fervor and devoting their free time to studying Torah, they wait around for hours to hear the cantor's trilling, they schmooze in the middle of davening, and then they offer their critiques on his voice. Besides, I don't feel it's our place to toss out old customs and start up new ones. Despite all this, I would never ban Yedvabnik's slaughtering because of the fringes on his choirboys' yarmulkes. I was displeased with his behavior, so I went to the slaughterhouse to see how he slaughters, and I noticed that his hands shake. That's why I banned him. Not for any other reason, heaven forbid. Go out in town and tell everyone I've been slandered. This is libel."

People repeated his father's words to Shabse-Shepsel. He raised his palms to the sides of his head, dangling them like an ass's ears. "Of course, Father, may he live long, is right that I'm mixed-up and don't know what I'm talking about. If Father says he banned the cantor-shochet for his shaky hands and not for the fringed yarmulkes, I revoke my opinion, I drag it through the mud, destroy it completely like chametz on Passover. I take back every word!" And Shabse-Shepsel bobbed about with such blazing eyes that he seemed ready, should his father give him a wink, to jump in a fire.

Zembin split in two—one side claiming that the rabbi had simply meant to protect the town from eating non-kosher, the other claiming that the rabbi's dislike of the cantor had made him seek out a fault. But everyone knew the rabbi would never revoke his decision.

So the worshippers in the new beis medrash, led by their Rabiner, wised up and decided on a plan: As of that day, Zisel Yedvabnik would lead the services along with his choir and receive double wages. Zembin would come to hear him even earlier in the day than before, and the rabbi, the fanatic, would realize he'd accomplished nothing.

6

J UST AS THE ZEMBIN RABBI'S PASSOVER had been spoiled by
his mixed-up son, the Morehdalye rabbi's, too, was spoiled by his
children.

With each passing day, Bluma Rivtcha became more agitated. She
attributed it to her eagerness for spring's arrival, with its fresh greenery and bright countryside. Once the snow melted and the sun dried
the damp country roads, she and Refael'ke could set out across the
plowed fields. They'd laugh together, chitchat, inhale the sharp fragrance of spiky rosebuds and unfurled white blooms. On the bridge
overlooking the Narev they'd pause to look down. The odor of raw
water, rotted foliage, and stirred sludge would waft up from the river.
They'd rent one of the fishing boats tied to the shore and set out,
upstream and downstream. Refael'ke would row and she would gaze
out into the distance. The water would undulate beneath her, and the
wind would muss up her hair. Oh, how she loved it when a breeze
blew her hair over her face! How did that song go?—"Listen! Not
much longer and spring is here!"

In preparation for Passover, Bluma Rivtcha helped her mother
scour pots and air out the clothes, linen, and holy books. But when
her mother spoke, she didn't hear. Bluma Rivtcha simmered in secret
anticipation of Zindel Kadish and Tzesneh Ginsburg's Passover
return, when they'd presumably announce their engagement. That
Tzesneh had swiped her fiancé, and that her gullible and devious
fiancé had allowed himself to be swiped, did not bother her in the
least—or so she went on broadcasting to anyone who'd listen. And
yet, despite her declaration, she kept sneaking glances out the window, to see if the couple might be walking toward the synagogue.

But the only one returning from Warsaw would be Tzesneh.
Henna'le brought this piece of news home from the marketplace,

and she looked to her husband, the Gemara-brain, to explain to her how the dayan, Tzadok Kadish, would hold a seder without his grandson. A flushed Bluma Rivtcha cried out, "I'll bet Zindel didn't come because he and Tzesneh split up."

Her parents, and even Refael'ke, stared at her, dumbfounded by her bizarre fantasy. But the next morning, Sholem Shachne returned from davening uncharacteristically agitated and reported that Bluma Rivtcha had been right. Shmulik'l Ginsburg had seized him in the beis medrash. "Rabbi! Give me advice." His wife had driven him out of the house, demanding that he do everything in his power to make the dayan's grandson take their daughter back.

Sholem Shachne had barely gotten the words out when Bluma Rivtcha interrupted, "And surely you told him you couldn't help, because Zindel hadn't acted any kinder to your daughter."

"Right. That's what I told him," Sholem Shachne replied innocently, nodding his head.

"How ugly this all is!" Bluma Rivtcha shouted, and ran to her room to cry it out, tearing a handkerchief with her teeth in fury.

Tzesneh's mother released all her pent-up fury at the failed engagement on her husband. She loathed her Shmulik'l as it was, with his stumpy legs and his moist little eyes and his tiny hands that he rubbed together with the joy of a beggar in front of free food. And yet, Gnendel begrudged him, he'd snagged a woman like her as a wife—two heads taller and with large black eyes, a tower of hair on her head, a high bosom, broad hips. He'd not only gotten her pregnant but also gotten her to raise a daughter who spit insolently in her mother's face. He, her little husband, had attained all that, but in daily life he was a schemer, not a conqueror; a haggler, not an earner; a peddler, not a merchant. For any need, he could recommend the best worker. But he himself couldn't tie a cat's tail. He once opened a little soda company and had to close it because he couldn't squeeze the metal handle. And could he hammer a nail into a wall? His wife had to do it for him! Despite this, he, not she, was the breadwinner. He sold pieces of jewelry to the wives of Polish officials and to rich Jewish women. When Shmulik'l sat at the table, absorbed by his jewelry cases, his spindly fingers resembled the legs of a spider. She couldn't bear to look at him. If it were up to Gnendel, she would have divorced him long ago, swept him from her life like autumn's cobwebs. But she didn't want her only daughter to be raised without a father or with a stepfather.

And yet, ever since Zindel Kadish had begun learning English from Tzesneh the summer before, and when they had both gone to Warsaw for the winter, Gnendel had dared to hope that her luck, too, would turn. All her life Morehdalye had looked down on her for being stuck with her grasshopper of a husband. But now Morehdalye would change its tune; they'd be standing on their heads. Zindel, the dayan's grandson, had rejected the rabbi's daughter and chosen Gnendel's daughter instead! And soon enough the Morehdalyens would have even more to say; their eyes would pop with envy. Gnendel had plans she didn't even share with her daughter. But now all these plans vanished like a bend around a river, turned to naught, and the Morehdalyens would have something to snicker at to boot.

Head drawn into his shoulders, Shmulik'l Ginsburg kept to the corners of the room, to avoid getting caught in the thick flames of his warring wife and daughter. Tzesneh yelled, "Do you think, Mother, that I don't realize why you're mad that the yeshiva boy and I split up? You imagined that I'll go with him to America, take you along, and leave Father here. I know you!" She bit her thin lips with her sharp teeth. Her bony chin and cheekbones jutted out; the skin on her face shone ruddy and sweaty.

Gnendel felt a rush of hatred for her daughter. She despised her character and her physical ugliness the way she'd always despised her husband and his hopping around like a flea. "Zindel realized what a shrew you are, so he got rid of you before it was too late."

"He got rid of me because his grandfather wrote that he'd never ever agree to his grandson becoming your son-in-law. Your pedigree was beneath him." Tzesneh's face wrinkled, folding into an evil smile, filled with malicious pleasure at being able to hurt her mother. "His grandfather also warned him not to come home for Passover so as not to associate with our kind. Well, what do you have to say now?"

Gnendel suddenly realized how rash she'd been, prodding her husband to cause a stir and crow around town about how the dayan's grandson had duped their daughter. She quickly changed her tune. During chol hamoed Pesach, she stood amid a group of women in the marketplace, feet steeped in mud, hands on her hips, laughing loudly. "So, you want to know about the dayan's grandson? Well, my Tzesneh told him that crying like a little boy won't help. She didn't like him and didn't want to marry him. And that was that. He was so ashamed that Tzesneh had rejected him he didn't come home for Passover. Well, you tell me. Isn't that the behavior of a little schoolboy?"

But Tzesneh didn't make fun of Zindel to her friends at all. Quite differently from her mother, she spoke about him with heartache and empathy. "In today's day and age, that a young man should be so scared of what strangers will say or think!" She gave her friends an example. "Say, we were walking on a street in Warsaw. Pandemonium all around, shoving and pushing. People, horses, wagons, automobiles, jumbling and moving together like icebergs swirling in the eddies of the Narev. And amid this tremendous clamor, if I laughed a bit loudly, Zindel would hunker into himself and groan, 'Please, it's not becoming to behave like this.' But you know where he was the biggest wimp of all? The most like a yeshiva boy? When the talk turned to his parents. He's planning to go to Canada and become a modern rabbi there. But if you ask him about his divorced parents who live there, his face turns colors and he's thrown completely off-balance. You'd think his father had converted to Christianity! Or his mother had run off with a soldier! What's so embarrassing about parents being divorced?" Tzesneh asked with a sadness in her voice, yet unable to contain her laughter at Zindel's comical behavior. "Perhaps he'd make a fine husband for the rabbi's Bluma Rivtcha. But for me, no. I have different ideals."

Everyone in town knew that once Zindel and Tzesneh had left for Warsaw, Bluma Rivtcha had begun avoiding her friends. She didn't want to suffer through their silences or any talk about her ex-fiancé. But now the Morehdalye girls felt that Bluma Rivtcha had emerged triumphant. So they set off to visit her during chol hamoed, full of secrets, ready to whisper and gossip through the night. Now that Zindel had been burned by Tzesneh, certainly he'd be thrilled if Bluma Rivtcha took him back.

But Bluma Rivtcha reacted coldly, in strained silence, and her old friends understood she'd moved on. They began to besmirch Zindel, saying he had the face of a little doll, that he was fussy and persnickety like an old bachelor bookkeeper. Besides, he wasn't very smart. People said his father, Beinush, wasn't smart either; in fact, he was a crackpot. Come to think of it, why *had* Zindel's parents divorced? Zindel never spoke about it. "If he's that ashamed," her friends said, "there must be a reason, right?"

"Why should Zindel have to tell strangers about his family? And why would strangers even want to know?" Bluma Rivtcha looked down at her fingers instead of at the girls sitting next to her on the sofa. Quickly, the girls backtracked, claiming it was Tzesneh who was slandering Zindel, not they. "Tzesneh is a snake," they said. But Bluma Rivtcha didn't want to speak badly about Tzesneh either, and she continued to stare at her fingers until the girls got up and left.

Then, Refael'ke came into the dining room, taking the gossipers' place on the sofa. "Father and Mother are still very distressed that Bentzion didn't come home for Passover," Refael said quietly.

"Well, good for Bentzion! He wants nothing to do with these provincials. They seep into your bones, meddle in your every move and thought," Bluma Rivtcha burst out, and then launched into her usual grumbling about how Bentzion had managed to abscond—albeit with some delay—and once he was done with his business courses in Bialystok, he'd be able to support himself, while for her there was hardly anything left to accomplish. She was already twenty-four and she hadn't even gotten started. Her youth was slipping away, her time wasted on fights with her father, who wanted to force her to marry just like he did with Tilza. "You," she warned Refael'ke, "are already twenty. If you putter around too long, you'll regret it. Only Naftali Hertz started early enough. He was just eighteen when he fled yeshiva and went abroad to study. In fact, even while he was still in yeshiva, he was already educating himself and preparing for the university exams in Switzerland." Bluma Rivtcha turned silent for a while, brooding, staring at her mother's candelabrum, which had remained on the table since the seder. She began to speak again, but in a furtive voice, as if wary of their mother's candelabrum. "I have no memories of Naftali Hertz since he's gone abroad. The last I remember of him was after the war, exactly ten years ago, when he came for Tilza's wedding. I was fourteen; you were ten. He never visits, rarely writes a letter. He never sent us a picture of his wife and child. Do you think he doesn't want to visit because she's irreligious? But he's not religious either and Father's forgiven him. So why is he so secretive about his family? He's like Zindel Kadish, keeping the secret of his divorced parents."

"I don't know," Refael'ke answered slowly, and thought for a while. "It could be that Naftali Hertz's marriage is bad, and he doesn't want people to know about it, just the way Zindel doesn't want people to know his parents divorced. Besides being embarrassed, he probably doesn't want anyone prodding into his life, just like you and Bentzion don't want anyone prodding into yours. And who says Father forgave him for fleeing yeshiva and getting married without a word? It's true that Father and Mother wait for his letters, but Father hasn't forgiven him, and Naftali Hertz must feel it," Refael'ke concluded.

But instead of clearing the matter up, his lengthy answer somehow muddled things even more, and Bluma Rivtcha became yet more suspicious and curious about Naftali Hertz's motives. She and Refael'ke gave each other a look, tacitly agreeing to end the discussion. They were relieved when their father stepped into the dining room.

Sholem Shachne—perhaps for the first time—felt guilty about his daughter. If he hadn't tried to get the dayan's grandson as a son-in-law, the Tzesneh story would never have happened and Bluma Rivtcha wouldn't have become the talk of the town. As for Bluma Rivtcha, besides her other disappointments, she was upset that the beautiful spring mornings had yet to arrive. Morehdalye was still drenched in the muck of newly melted snow. Women hustled about town, preparing for the second half of Passover. Charcoal fumes and the odor of oily Passover foods wafted from homes. And like the earth below, the clouds above, too, appeared unclean. They hovered in one spot, stagnant, drooping like filthy curtains.

"As soon as Passover ends, I'm going to Vilna," Bluma Rivtcha told her father. "I'll go to the school for nursing. Becoming a nurse doesn't take as long as other professions." She gazed through the window at the buttery sunset with such wide eyes it seemed she wasn't sure the sun would shine tomorrow.

"I understand, I understand," the rabbi said, nodding as sadly as a tree in autumn that becomes more leafless with each day. "Well, and what are *you* planning to do?" he asked his son. "Are you staying in Morehdalye for the summer?"

"If you're not against it, Father, I'll go visit Grandfather in Zembin."

"Grandfather?" the rabbi asked, surprised. But immediately he discerned that his son was requesting this only because he didn't want to upset his parents: what he would really have liked to do was join a kibbutz of chalutzim. "By all means, by all means!" Sholem Shachne said quickly, and began to speak at a clip. "I'll be very pleased if you go to Zembin and sit and study there. Or at least if you'll study more there than here. Lately, you've just been moseying around. I understand; Morehdalye is a small town and you've become bored. But in Zembin, all the boys who've gone off to yeshivas in other cities come home for summer vacation, and they all stop by to visit Grandfather. So you'll have people to spend time with and study with. But befriend the students of Torah only, not the chalutzim. In general, the larger the city the greater the test of character, because there are so many more temptations that can lure in a young man. Your uncle Shabse-Shepsel just moved from Bialystok to Zembin, and he's at odds with Grandfather, and the rest of the world for that matter. So you'll have to behave carefully around your uncle. I already told you how hurt Grandfather was that you and Bluma Rivtcha didn't come to the dedication ceremony for the talmud torah. Still, he'll be so happy if you come now. His rebbetzin, Vigasia, will treat you well. She looks severe, but she's really a smart, kind woman, and she supports your grandfather in all his battles against the freethinkers. But at any rate, don't get involved in that; you must sit and study."

Generally laconic by nature, Sholem Shachne couldn't stop talking now. His words came in a rush, in ever-thicker waves, like a man who, before a fast, gobbles down his food and speeds through the after-meal prayer. Sholem Shachne realized he'd one day end up entirely alone with his wife, and the thought of it distressed him. Already he was nostalgic for the month of Elul—already! In the middle of Passover!—when the mild, sunny days passed in deep spiritual contemplation and with a sweet, pure sorrow. The nights became quieter then, and a deep silence hovered over everything like a cold pond. Here and there, amidst the greenery of the trees, a bundle of reddish leaves might flare up, heralding the arrival of autumn. A Shimoneh Esrei–type murmuring buzzed in Sholem Shachne's memory, like the shadows of flames playing on a wall. Sholem Shachne knew he was mixing up the order of things, but he couldn't help himself. He was already yearning for Yom Kippur, when he could stand with his tallis over his head all day and sob his heart out over the disaster his family had become.

Abruptly, unwillingly, he began to laugh. This had been happening to him more and more often lately. Only when his son and daughter gaped at him, astonished, did he cease, staring back at them with the bewildered look of a man who's been woken from sleep mid-scream.

The rabbi was laughing because he'd remembered something his rebbetzin had told him. The other day, Tilza had complained that because her parents had always loved each other so much, and only had eyes for each other, they never noticed what was going on with their children. Tilza had never been very smart. Bluma Rivtcha was smarter than her older sister and was now on the verge of discarding her Judaism. Refael'ke would emulate her—surely he would, sooner or later—though for now he was still making trips to see his grandfather. So it seemed Henna'le and he would remain alone. That they'd stare into each other's eyes for days on end, weeks on end, months on end. And all that staring had better not bring them to loathe each other. His Henna'le had a blessed nature. When she wanted not to see or hear something, she squinted her eyes innocently and shook her head like a deaf-mute. Perhaps he, too, would learn how to go about the world as a deaf-mute. As the Gemara said: "The work of a person in this world is to make himself deaf."

7

LAG B'OMER HAD ALREADY come and gone by the time Refael'ke arrived in Zembin. The trees were in full bloom, white and rose-colored. The homes and shops that circled the market looked luminous, tinted in white, green, brown, and red, as if rinsed and prepared for a holiday of sunshine that would last through the summer. The market spilled over with so much light you had to squint or shade your eyes with your hands to find what you were looking for. Refael'ke gazed with interest at the sellers and their products in the street stalls, the peasant women in their colorful scarves, and the sophisticated women in their finery. They all moved slowly and spoke in modulated voices, as if the deep blue sky had spun a dream around them in the middle of the bright day. Refael'ke admired it all, yet at the same time could not help thinking about his parents, now a family of two, alone in the empty rooms of their old house. Right after Passover, Bluma Rivtcha had left for nursing school in Vilna, but he, feeling sorry for his parents, had kept postponing his trip day after day. Finally, his father himself had begun to prod him. "If you're planning to go, go. Stop wasting time."

Now in Zembin, Refael'ke's eyes wandered over the marketplace as he asked himself, "Am I going to spend my time here studying?" Then, he hurried off the cart that had brought him from the train.

His grandfather was expecting him. Eli-Leizer's daughter and son-in-law had sent letters that their youngest was coming to Zembin. Still, he gaped, amazed, at the young man standing in his beis din room, surrounded by luggage. How tall Refael'ke had grown! His grandfather couldn't believe it. But what a bad time it was for the boy to have come. *My problems and heartaches grow every day*, he thought. *Even if the boy were willing, I don't have the presence of mind to teach him proper behavior.* But he managed to croak, "Sholem aleichem! How's your father doing? And your mother?" With each word, the ice that had formed around his heart began to crack. *I should be happy to have such a guest*, he realized, especially because another person could now join the minyan he'd established in his home after falling ill.

Eli-Leizer placed his right hand on Refael'ke's high shoulder, and with his left hand caressed the boy's cheeks, fuzzy with dark blond hair. "This is my grandson, Refael'ke; my Henna'le's youngest son," he told Vigasia, and hiccupped. He wiped his eyes with a handkerchief and coughed, annoyed at himself for jabbering like a woman. But tears ran from his eyes, ever thicker and faster, brought on by the pain Shabse-Shepsel had caused him since settling in Zembin. But the tears flowed for another reason, too: the latest chillul Hashem in town, God's name desecrated yet again.

A few days before, on Lag B'Omer, a Tarbus schoolteacher had taken a stroll in the woods with his students. As the boys sat in a semicircle on the grass, the teacher told them about the Jews' revolt against the Romans in the times of Bar Kokhba. He told them about the great tanna, Rabbi Akiva, who instructed the Jews to take up swords. "Not like today's religious functionaries, like the Zembin rabbi, for instance—an old, senile dotard who expects Jews to sit with folded hands here in exile until the Messiah comes and redeems us. Those fanatics, they have the perfect remedy when there are pogroms against Jews: to nail mezuzahs to our doors! Never mind that mezuzahs have yet to protect a single Jew from a pogrom. In fact, quite the opposite! The mezuzahs *attracted* the pogromites, showed them where Jews lived so they could slaughter them. That's why we go into the woods on Lag B'Omer. To commemorate and remember the times when Jewish heroes fought with bows and arrows, with spears, even with bare hands, against their oppressors."

One of the students repeated this to his father, and the father immediately went to the rabbi's house, arriving just when the daily minyan was meeting. He beat his chest in regret, bemoaning his refusal to heed the rabbi's admonitions, when he'd long ago warned that sending one's son to the Tarbus school was akin to sacrificing that son to idolatry. The rabbi's minyan glared at the man with hostility. They had no strength left for a new fight. But to everyone's shock, the rabbi—the old zealot—replied that he had no intention of starting a war with the Tarbus school. "Three times a day I say in my prayers, 'My soul shall be humble as earth toward others.' Should I now become upset that some little teacher, a maskil, called me a senile dotard?" The rabbi's close circle couldn't believe their ears. They left the house delighted that there wouldn't be yet another battle to fight.

Once Eli-Leizer was alone with Vigasia, he admitted that ever since Shabse-Shepsel had moved to Zembin he was afraid to do anything that might incite the freethinkers against him, lest his mixed-up son jump in and cause an even greater chillul Hashem.

In those days, Shabse-Shepsel was preoccupied with setting up his dinnerware shop. The walls, ceiling, and doors still smelled of fresh paint. On the shelves lay rows of glassware, some sparkling with a bluish-white hue, others gleaming with the cold gray of steel. Plates, trays, saucers, and coffee cups stood in tall stacks on other shelves. Shabse-Shepsel and Draizel hadn't yet unpacked the more expensive sets, but they'd purchased additional inventory—a cheaper line—from a Bialystok wholesaler: small pot-bellied decanters with narrow necks, deep glass bowls, teacups in various shapes, and glasses for gas lamps. Shabse-Shepsel was preparing to do big business. But as soon as he got word of the Tarbus schoolteacher's slander, everything about the shop faded from his mind. "Some libertine calls my father, the genius Rabbi Eli-Leizer Epstein, a senile dotard before a city full of Jews, and they remain silent?! My father, may he live long, is called stubborn and cruel by an abomination of a man, and no one shreds this abomination to pieces like a herring? Small wonder, then, that people sit silent when this rebel, this rabble-rouser, makes blasphemous suggestions like ripping our mezuzahs off our doors and trampling them because they don't protect Jews from pogroms. Soon he'll be telling us to remove our Torah scrolls from the aron kodesh and trample those, too!" Shabse-Shepsel seethed, foam on his lips, as if his seething might convince him that, yes, this is precisely what the teacher had said. "We must declare a cherem against him, while we blow the shofar next to black candles. In the past, Father himself would have done this all on his own. But now that Father is elderly and knows his congregation is a herd of oxen, he's unwilling to declare a cherem or persecute the freethinker on his own. It's up to the religious Jews. They must go to the rabbi and plead bitterly: 'Help! Save the city!'"

The townspeople shrugged their shoulders. "Why should we believe that the teacher is a blasphemer on the basis of what some little boy says?" some argued. Others claimed that declaring a cherem would turn the entire world against the rabbi. And then there were people who told Shabse-Shepsel right to his face that he was making it up; the teacher had never said those things.

"He certainly did say those things!" Shabse-Shepsel stamped his feet and balled his hands into fists. Unruffled, the men edged away from him, this son whose zealotry surpassed his father's.

But people on the streets—the irreligious more quickly than the religious—believed that the teacher had indeed called for mezuzahs to be torn from doors and trampled. "For such words, we have to burn the very place where he stood!" the masses cried. "And is this why we're being ripped off in taxes? For maintaining such a treyf school?" The Tarbus schoolteachers and activists began to worry. Frightened and furious, they summoned Shabse-Shepsel for litigation at his own father's beis din.

"I'll come. Of course, I'll come!" he cried out joyfully, as if this were the very reason he'd settled in Zembin.

Refael'ke was already in Zembin when the two factions met at the rabbi's home. He stood in a corner, looking on. Shabse-Shepsel, who hadn't set foot in his father's house since his rushed visit on arriving in town, now bustled about and acted completely at home, as if he'd been there the day before. His old father became nonplussed and spoke to him in an overly friendly tone. "Don't you recognize Sholem Shachne's youngest? He's your nephew, Refael'ke."

Shabse-Shepsel gave the young man a hasty glance. "Ah, that's you?" he said coldly, not adding another word.

The crowd who'd gathered for the hearing didn't recognize their rabbi. Their great fighter of these last fifty years, instead of roaring like a lion, as he used to, now sat silently at the head of the table, head lowered. This time it was the two factions who were foaming at the mouth. One man yelled that cherems could no longer be called in this day and age. Another shouted that there was no need for a cherem: a prohibition against the Tarbus school, just like the one on meat brought in from the outside, would suffice. "A prohibition against the school my children go to?" screamed a third. "No way! There'll be bloodshed!"

Shabse-Shepsel shouted louder than everyone, pointing his finger at the teacher. "A cherem isn't enough for him. We must uproot him completely! God's name is inscribed on the furled parchment inside each mezuzah: *shin-dalet-yud*, an acronym for *Shomer dalsos Israel*. God protects the Jewish doorways. And here comes this shameful, impious Jew saying the mezuzahs haven't protected us against pogroms. Saying we must rip them off our doors and trample them."

"It's not true. I never said that," the teacher croaked. The teacher was a tall, skinny man with a thin face. On this warm, early summer day, he wore a thick, fraying winter coat, with sleeves too short for his long arms. He clutched his bent-up coat collar with one hand, and with the other the wide brim of his rumpled hat, as if he were in a snowstorm in the middle of a field. Instead of a shirt and tie, he wore a red knitted wool shawl around his neck and shivered as if gripped with malarial fever. It was obvious to the crowd that he was ill. Evidently, he'd crawled out of bed and pulled some clothes over his gaunt body just to come here and expunge the slander, both from himself and from the school where he taught. He had the refined and somewhat anxious appearance of a yeshiva boy who's no longer very religious, but who isn't yet a rebellious or serious freethinker. "It's true," he said, "that when I spoke to the boys on Lag B'Omer, I told them that the diaspora Jews rely on miracles and mezuzahs that haven't protected them from pogroms. But I didn't tell them to rip the mezuzahs off and trample them. In fact, I shudder at the suggestion."

"But he's not repeating what he said about my father," Shabse-Shepsel cried mockingly to the crowd. "He's not telling you that he called the Zembin rabbi a dense, ignorant mule, comparing him to a dry, bitter root stuck in the earth. He's not telling you that he called Father, may he live long, a religious fanatic and a monster who has no understanding of people, not even of his own children. He's not sharing his view that, because the Zembin rabbi has not succeeded in keeping his daughters and grandchildren pious, he shouldn't be allowed to censure others. This, he's not telling you, the scoundrel!"

"I never said any of that," the teacher defended himself, glancing around at the others, as if asking whether the rabbi's son was sane. "A few groups of students heard my words, and they know the truth.

And how could I have even said any of this? I haven't been in Zembin long and know absolutely nothing about the rabbi's children. I did say one inappropriate thing. But it was aimed at the rabbi's school of thought, not at the rabbi himself."

"Tell us what you said!" Shabse-Shepsel yelled in a piercing voice, a voice that was clearly not drawn from his depths; he yelled without fury, merely from his throat, like in a theater or when a teacher yells at children. "Tell us what you said about Father, may he live long. Tell us this minute!"

"I said he's a senile dotard," the teacher murmured, and looked reluctantly at the rabbi's son, whose weak chin and sparse beard quivered in monstrous delight. "But whatever I said, I said in my own name. The other teachers didn't know I'd be giving a speech to the boys, and later they in fact lodged a complaint."

"They know how to play you!" Shabse-Shepsel laughed. "Your non-believer friends sent you here to the rabbi to take all the blame, so that parents won't take their children out of your heretical classes. Well, it won't help you. We'll hound you out of town, and as for your school—we'll smoke it out like an epidemic."

"I'm not leaving town, nor will you succeed in closing our school," the teacher replied, faintly but with composure.

"Then Father will announce a cherem, along with every biblical curse and calamity, on the Tarbus teachers and the parents who send their children to that impure school!" Shabse-Shepsel shrieked.

But the crowd said nothing in response, their faces shadowed even in the middle of this bright day, like tired old men warming themselves at an oven on a winter night. Throughout the exchange the aging rabbi sat there silently, and his broken spirit seemed to infect the townspeople. At first his silence had confused them, then it saddened them, and finally it scared them. Workers in tall cloth hats, Talmudists in hard black caps, old men who were as afraid of removing a single hair of their milky-white beards as of removing a single stone from a tzaddik's grave, and even the enlightened ones, with their trimmed beards, who sided with the teacher—all stood around the Zembin rabbi, crushed by his despondence. It appeared as if Shabse-Shepsel were ranting against and humiliating *him*, not the modern Hebrew teacher. Only one person, a boorish market trader, could not fathom why everyone had suddenly been struck dumb. Using both hands, he parted the crowd and trumpeted in the teacher's direction: "I'll teach him a lesson—that freethinker!—for saying we should trample on our mezuzahs!"

A tall young man rose up against the tradesman, emerging from a corner where he'd been listening quietly all along. "The rabbi hasn't asked you to assault the teacher," Refael'ke said serenely, his usually twinkling eyes now burning dryly.

"It's the rabbi's grandson, the rabbi's grandson." The comment passed from person to person among the crowd.

The market trader overheard them. Though his appetite for smacking someone around had been whetted, he perceived strength in the tall young man's serene composure and edged away from him and the crowd. Refael'ke assured the teacher he needn't be afraid. But the teacher had already sensed that the threat was over. He mumbled something about his health, that he had to get home and lie down, and took his leave.

Only then did Eli-Leizer raise his head from the table. He re-proached his son in a low voice, as if unsure of his own words. "I have never refrained from waging battle against those who openly desecrate Shabbos or from announcing a cherem against a butcher suspected of selling non-kosher meat. I have stood up against every transgressor and even against a powerful, influential figure who'd been stealing from Jews. But from everything we've heard here, it's clear that this teacher never suggested ripping off mezuzahs and trampling them. What was his sin? He prattled. Well, for prattling you don't place a person under cherem."

Eli-Leizer sensed the people's astonishment; they were unused to this mild tone. Raising his voice, he spoke more severely to his son. "In general, you shouldn't be getting mixed up in my business. You know quite well that a rabbi isn't allowed to make judgments in another rabbi's city. Especially since I'm so many years older than you, never mind that I'm your father."

Here was Shabse-Shepsel's chance to demonstrate his great re-spect for his father in front of the entire community. He replied in a sort of coded language, the language of hidden holy men, address-ing his father in the third person, as was the custom of refined, rab-binical children. "I'm not making judgments for Father, may he live long, nor interfering with his rabbinate at all. I was simply sticking up for the Torah's honor, and I remembered Father's hallowed words, 'The Torah is our witness that the war between the Jews and Amalek, may his name be erased, will continue in each generation until the Messiah's coming. Not only gentiles are Amalekites; the irreligious Jews who've thrown off the yoke of Torah and mitzvahs, they, too, fall in the category of Amalekites'—this is what Father said. *Praised be God for his kindnesses.* As long as Jews have carried the yoke of Honor for Heaven, they've waged war with the Amalekites among the gentiles. But since Jews have thrown off the yoke of Torah, it has been decreed that instead of warring with the Amalekites among the gentile nations we must battle the Amalekites multiplying among the Jews themselves. And there's absolutely no difference whether we're talking about the Jewish communists in Russia, or the clean-shaven pharmacists who've transformed the beis medrash into a temple, or the Zionists in Zembin—all who are against the true believers are Amalekites, and it's a mitzvah to hate them, to persecute them, to uproot them. This is what Father, may he live long, has always said. And it's impossible to imagine a worse Jewish Amalek than this Hebrew teacher who poisons young Torah-learning children with heresy. He must be placed under cherem, annihilated, driven out of town in a trash wagon!"

Sweat dripped from Shabse-Shepsel's sparse beard. His pleading eyes seemed to beseech his father: Do not deny the Torah of Moses that you've taught to others all your life. At the same time, his shrill tone rang with the ridicule and triumph of one who delights in his enemy's defeat. Once again, the townspeople, who'd heard him speak this way in the past, didn't know whether he meant what he said or was being a comedian, a joker, a spiteful, rebellious son. Perhaps he was of two minds, and both respected and hated his father? Whatever the case, everyone knew that this time Shabse-Shepsel was telling the truth. It was true that in all his life the rabbi had never compromised. And it appeared that even the rabbi himself hadn't forgotten that, because while Shabse-Shepsel was speaking, his father listened with a half-frightened, half-amazed expression, as if demons were passing through him, or as when one screams into the vastness and hears his own sinister echoes.

The Jews began shuffling out of the rabbi's home, and Shabse-

Shepsel hastily shoved his way in behind them to avoid remaining alone with his father. Eli-Leizer snapped out of his trance and called after his son, "You imbecile! Rabbis don't have the same authority they once did. Nowadays, you sometimes have to feign deafness or blindness to avoid sparking a riot against the Torah. And you're certainly not doing this for the sake of heaven; you just want to embarrass and humiliate me."

"My actions are all for the sake of God, just as Father's were in all of his battles," Shabse-Shepsel said from the other side of the door. "The Torah hasn't changed and will never change. It cannot be that a later generation is permitted what a previous generation wasn't. And if, indeed, the Torah does change, then why has Father demanded that we, his children, follow the exact same path he did?"

Eli-Leizer remained sitting at the beis din table, silent, and the emptied-out room seemed to agree with his silence. "Come sit next to me," he murmured to Refael'ke, not raising his eyes, as if ashamed of his grandson. Vigasia, meanwhile, sat in a deep, high-backed chair, knitting a green wool sweater for her old husband that she'd been working on since early summer. Throughout the previous exchange, she'd kept hidden from view, but now she moved out into the open, the large skein of wool in her lap and the long needles between her dry, nimble fingers. The rebbetzin clicked her needles and watched the rabbi place his hand on his grandchild's shoulder and hug him close. Refael'ke inhaled the odor of his grandfather's beard, an odor of old, wrinkled flesh, sweat, and tears.

Eli-Leizer both reproached his grandson and tacitly begged him to side with his grandfather. "Of course, I waged war against the freethinkers all my life, but to compare freethinking Jews to the progeny of Amalek—that I don't believe I've ever done. And if I did do it, I didn't intend it as literal truth, the way my son with his crazy head is interpreting it. Oh, what a son I have! And well, will I have any more nachas from my grandchildren? Look at you, Refael'ke. You're the son of the Morehdalye rabbi, brother-in-law of the Lecheve rosh yeshiva—and your friends are the gang at Herzl's cheder?" The old man groaned, as he did on Yom Kippur while reciting the pieces of liturgical poetry that other worshippers skipped over. "I'm in my eighties now and I still don't understand the Zionists. It's one or the other! If you don't believe in God and the Torah, what do you need the land of Israel for? Aren't there enough countries in this world? Let them go and settle somewhere else. What right do irreligious Jews have to demand a piece of the land flowing with milk and honey? God gave it to the Jews on the condition that they follow the Torah and its commandments. A new fad—a Jewish country! Nowhere in the holy texts does it imply that Jews must establish a country before the Messiah comes. In fact, many of our sages explicitly forbade it. And not only are the freethinkers contaminating our holy land by settling there, they're also trying to use their heretical ideologies to ruin Jewish cities and towns throughout the diaspora."

"Eli-Leizer, you must lie down and rest. And you, Refael'ke, go to the beis medrash to study for a few hours," Vigasia interrupted them, taking a break in her knitting to show that she was waiting for Refael'ke to leave. And Refael'ke, as quietly as he'd sat and listened to his grandfather, rose from the table and slipped out of the house. Eli-Leizer stayed put, hunched over, breathing audibly through his nostrils into his beard. He mumbled sleepily, like an elm in a field when a breeze passes through its tangled, leafy branches: "On one hand, my mixed-up son is as devoted to me as a gentile to his idol; on the other, he embarrasses me by mimicking my every move. Do you know why Shabse-Shepsel hates me so much?"

"How would I know?" Vigasia twisted her needles to pick up a dropped stitch. "You probably didn't give him enough attention when he was a boy, or you hit him too much."

"I did just the opposite. I gave him too much attention and I hit him too little," the old man grumbled.

Vigasia thought about her three sons, who had grown into fine Jews, thank God, despite her being a young widow and never lifting a hand to them. Lost in her reverie, she didn't realize she'd shifted her body and the skein of wool had fallen from her lap. Swiftly, she stamped her foot over the ball of yarn as it rolled away, and she bent to retrieve it. She grew dizzy, gasping, but eventually, very slowly, regained herself and sat back up. After that, though, it was as if her old age had fallen away, and when she spoke, her voice rang with masculine strength and wisdom. "You say your son is *your* enemy? I'm afraid he's his own enemy."

"His own enemy?" Eli-Leizer repeated, trying to shake off his tiredness. But the impromptu nap had made his eyelashes, nose, and ears sticky. He sank into the thickness of his white hair, and unwelcome memories of fights and cherems unraveled in his mind. And as if in fear of his own recollections, he fell asleep with his head on the hard table.

8

W ITH HIS QUIET EYES and fresh, rosy face, Refael'ke imbued
his grandfather's house with the tranquility of a summer
morning in the village. When Vigasia spoke to him, her robust, masculine voice spilled over with motherly tenderness. "Refael'ke, you
haven't put a thing in your stomach today. Go wash up to eat." Vigasia wished that her sons had given her such a grandchild. A young
man of silk and velvet! A replica of his father in height, appearance,
and refined behavior. But he wasn't going to be a rabbi like his father,
that was clear. He didn't even hide the fact that he was drawn to the
chalutzim. She said to him, "It's unbecoming for you, a rabbi's son,
to consider yourself an equal of young men who don't abide by the
Torah."

He smiled and replied that he considered himself to be in league
with those young men who *did* observe the Torah's teachings.

And he spoke to his grandfather in much the same manner. It was
midday, and both were stooping over their Gemaras at the long oak
table in the beis din room. From outside came the echoes of the
noisy marketplace, but the sunrays dancing on the shelves of holy
books distanced and muted those workday sounds. Eli-Leizer spent
a bit of his time studying, but mainly he conversed, trying to guide
his grandson toward a righteous path. Now it was his grandson's turn
to reply, and the grandfather listened, his nose and rumpled beard
thrust into the Gemara, as if he were trying to verify whether the
Sages agreed with Refael.

"I can like my home in Morehdalye and still want to settle abroad,"
Refael said. "Why must I hate the cities and towns of the diaspora
just because I love the land of Israel?"

"What kind of comparison is that?" His grandfather swiped at his
beard in anger. "Anyone who tries to beat the redeemer to it and

declare the land of Israel as our own Jewish country doesn't believe in the Messiah's coming."

"There'll still be plenty for the Messiah to take care of," Refael'ke said, smiling so cleverly and lovingly as if he were the grandfather calming his excitable grandchild.

The old man listened and marveled. He sensed that beneath Refael'ke's serene, clever manner of speaking, he was as stringently pious and logical as his father, though his piety ran in a different direction. Eli-Leizer didn't understand what was happening to him. Alas, how much had he endured in his life for insisting on his own viewpoint! And now here came a boy and easily pushed him—the old sentinel!—off his seat in his tower. Something about Refael'ke tempered the forcefulness and harshness with which he'd always responded to the world. Still, Eli-Leizer knew that if Shabse-Shepsel had not settled in Zembin—bringing him untold humiliation with the mimicking of his piety and his zealotry—he would not have been so docile.

"You know what I'll tell you?" Eli-Leizer said to his rebbetzin that night, while, with much huffing and sighing, he pulled his tallis katan over his head, after which he sat down at the edge of his bed in only his long underwear and yarmulke. "You know what I'll tell you, Vigasia? My son-in-law, the Morehdalyer, gets more nachas from his youngest son who's not devout at all than I get from my son who's supposedly more devout than me."

For a long while, Eli-Leizer couldn't fall asleep. He tossed and groaned in his bed, a vision of Refael Leima before his eyes. Though Refael Leima was far off in America, lately he was more and more often on Eli-Leizer's mind. Now, in the darkness of the night, he saw an image of his son as clearly as if it were midday. Refael Leima stood awkwardly in the middle of the room, a flat yarmulke on his large, round head, and a bashful smile on his broad face. It was the smile of a person who knows he's a failure—exactly the look he used to give when his father scolded him for not offering support in his battles against the freethinkers. He'd gaze at his father with kind, sad eyes, thick lips slightly parted, as if his reply was stuck to a corner of his mouth. He would smile with a face like the full yellow moon hovering outside the window. *And where is his beard? In America, even the rabbis don't have beards,* Eli-Leizer asked and answered himself. It was impossible not to feel that God was giving him his just deserts—*midah keneged midah,* measure for measure.

Even Shabse-Shepsel held Refael'ke in high esteem. After their initial unfriendly meeting in the rabbi's house, Shabse-Shepsel warmed to him and enjoyed talking with him more than with his own wife at home, the neighbors in the street, or the townspeople in the beis medrash.

Shabse-Shepsel had painted his house, located in the loop around the marketplace, in a striking fashion: yellow walls and a green roof. Inside, the dinnerware shop had an expensive look: blue walls, a white ceiling, and samples of dishes displayed on clean glass. A fresh coolness, an airiness, filled the entire store. Shabse-Shepsel flitted around the shelves laden with dinnerware. The atmosphere felt festively immaculate, but also somewhat famished, as on the day Passover is to start, when eating chametz is already prohibited but matzoh is not yet allowed until the seder. With his skinny body and nimble movements, Shabse-Shepsel looked as if he were created for a glassware and porcelain shop, where one had to be both dexterous and cautious not to break anything. Even the warm May morning seemed cleanly washed, transparent as glass. Refael'ke stood around in the shop and watched his uncle conduct business.

A pregnant woman with a long, freckled nose walked in, her high stomach brazenly pulling her dress up to her garters. Her gaze, too, was audacious and haughty, eyeing the slim young man with a certain provocativeness, as if taking pleasure in his shock and self-consciousness. The woman asked to be shown tea glasses and fretted over the decision. First she wanted wide, deep, thick glasses; then she demanded taller and narrower ones made of thinner glass and with carved "eyes." In the end, she regretted that choice and said she'd rather buy a half-dozen cups because both tea and coffee could be drunk in cups. At last, she settled on six white cups with a red hen design and asked what they cost.

"My store is pricey. A cup is one and a half zlotys, and six cups are nine zlotys, not a penny less. But you can get six cups for three zlotys right there." Shabse-Shepsel pointed through the open door to a different shop. He made a face, as if warning the woman that if she pestered him for one minute more, he'd toss her out like a rag. His arrogance made the right impression. The woman became intimidated and immediately left.

"Uncle, why are your items more expensive?" Refael'ke asked. "And why did you tell the woman to go to another store?"

"A ragamuffin like her has to be taught to understand the difference between Epstein's dinnerware shop and some dinky store by a little Zembin shopkeeper who sells glass and clay dishes," Shabse-Shepsel warbled, his head raised superciliously above his thin, craned neck and his arms at his sides, as if demonstrating how a soldier must stand in front of his superior. "From now on, this slob will know that in my shop you can't grope our items or haggle over prices. Other people will learn this from her, and soon people will be salivating to shop here, precisely because it's more expensive. Get it? That's human nature."

He spoke, as was his wont, loudly, scorn and triumph in his voice, as if he were laughing at one person while reviving another. But at the same time, he kept twisting his head anxiously and touching his sparse beard, as if uncertain whether he'd remembered to say what he was supposed to.

"Which tractate in the Gemara are you studying now? If you tell me one of your interpretations, I'll disprove it. What's the matter? Not a fan of spouting your own interpretations? I guess you're like your father; he's not a fan of long, subtle interpretations either. He can delve into a single page of the Gemara for a year or forever. Once, for a short time, we were study partners, and while your father was still plugging away on page seven, I was on page twenty-seven. Well anyway, are you pleased you swapped Morehdalye for Zembin? It's alive here! My father is still fighting the freethinkers, and if his age tires him out, I prod him, prop him up. But Morehdalye is a cemetery. Your father is terrified of inciting even the slightest controversy, lest the others reply 'And are your children any better?'" Shabse-Shepsel laughed.

A true zealot doesn't ridicule others this much, Refael'ke thought. He said, "I wanted to ask you, Uncle, why you're more fanatic, I mean, more extremist, than Grandfather. You're waging battles in his name, battles he doesn't want to fight—for example, the one with the Tarbus schoolteacher. Why do you do it?"

A wan, pathetic smile quivered on Shabse-Shepsel's face, and he replied in a conspiratorial tone, somewhat out of context, "Ever since I was young, Father's treated me like a dog." But instantly, you could tell that he regretted confiding in someone this young and naïve. In a flash, he wiped away his dejected expression and huffed, "Why am I more extremist than Father, you ask? Father, may he live long, is old, and occasionally forgets where he is in this world. So I remind him of his past behavior and I deal with things the way he would have if he had his former strength. I, after all, am not yet burned out, thank God."

Into the shop stepped Meir'l Grosfatter, a Jew who sold eyeglasses. Besides being an optician, he was also the Torah reader in the new beis medrash, the one where Shabse-Shepsel davened. It was said that, just as precise as Meir'l was in fitting glasses, and just as vigilant as he was about not omitting a single musical flourish or accent when chanting the Torah, so vigilant and precise was he in remembering whom he owed money to and who owed him. Even his appearance hinted at his "mine is mine, and yours is yours" attitude. He had a neat little beard, clean nails, and clear eyes—a dove at the river. He had come into the shop now to buy a dozen glasses, a gift for his daughter who'd recently married.

Pleased, an invigorated Shabse-Shepsel skipped around the customer and started showing him all kinds of wine and liquor glasses: tall, deep goblets; squat ones with protruding bellies; others round and triangular, smooth and engraved with rays, arrows, or stars all the way to their stems. The more glasses the shopkeeper showed, the more uneasy the customer became. He kept asking nervously, "How much might this cost me?"

But Shabse-Shepsel put him at ease. "Don't worry, Reb Meir'l, don't worry. A man who's the Torah reader in the new beis medrash is a man I trust. I'll sell them cheaply to you and you can pay in installments. I can do this because these products are still from my father-in-law's inventory. He bought these glasses years ago for a third of what they cost now. And how about a dozen plates? Don't you need that? I have real porcelain! Tap it with your fingers and you'll hear it tinkle like a piano. You see those gold-rimmed plates, with little green branches between the pink and red roses in the center? You'll still need a set of jugs along with these, and a pair of sugar bowls and teakettles to make tea."

Meir Grosfatter squirmed, pleaded, and protested that friends and relatives had already bought his daughter more than enough dishes. She'd just gotten married, after all, and didn't need that much yet. Besides, he didn't have enough money for a tea service like this—not today, not tomorrow, not ever! But Shabse-Shepsel squirmed and pleaded even more, protested even louder that Meir should live as many good years as the number of tea sets Shabse-Shepsel still had at home. These products had been bought very cheaply before the war by his late father-in-law, the miser. So it would be a joy, an honor, and an advertisement for Shabse-Shepsel if these dishes graced the home of Meir's only daughter. Meir could pay whenever he was able and however much he was able. And even if he never had the money, Shabse-Shepsel would forgive the debt entirely. He'd forget about this bit of glassware and crockery . . . He'd already forgotten! Shabse-Shepsel spoke as if gripped by a fever; his hands trembled. The way he begged made it seem as if he stood to lose both this world and the next if he couldn't convince this man to take the dishes. Feebly, the customer continued to ward him off, stuttering in astonishment, mumbling in confusion, until finally he gave in. At which point Shabse-Shepsel turned unexpectedly toward Refael'ke and, under his breath, so that the customer wouldn't hear, he said, "Heaven and earth may be destroyed, but the Gemara's claim, 'Whoever wants to lose money should deal with glassware,' will endure forever." An impish mockery burned in his eyes, and his facial features nearly burst apart from suppressed laughter.

9

T HE MOMENT REFAEL'KE set foot in Shabse-Shepsel's home, his aunt Draizel bloomed. The wrinkles above her high, pointy jaw smoothed over. Her big black eyes, always full of distrust, lit up with the curiosity of a woman busy wondering, though somewhat self-consciously, whether she should look upon this young man as a mere boy or an adult. Her husband and his father, she felt, even though they didn't get along, hated her equally. Vigasia wasn't fond of her either. Only Refael'ke didn't dislike her. In her mind's eye, she saw her husband and father-in-law as two birds of prey with twisted beaks, always ready to devour. Refael'ke, on the other hand, she saw as a serene and colorful bird from a distant, tropical land. Draizel spoke with him warmly and affectionately, as an aunt to a nephew, but her cheeks reddened and her voice turned chirpy. "Refael'ke, come and visit us. The house isn't properly cleaned up yet; we moved in not long ago. But I'll show you pretty samples of my father's dinner sets. We don't keep those in the shop."

By the looks of the objects and furniture scattered around the house, one would think that its inhabitants were moving *out*. Only the freshly painted walls attested that they were moving *in*. Draizel and her husband had been living in this house—the shop downstairs, the apartment upstairs—since just before Passover, and now it was almost Shavuos. Two months, and still no curtains hung on the windows. The sun's dazzling brilliance beamed right in, making the half-bare rooms look even barer. At a long table in the dining room sat a half-dozen chairs, their backs turned to each other like feuding family members. In the bedroom, the two iron beds, messily strewn with linen, had been pushed against opposite walls, as if husband and wife wanted to be as far from each other as possible. While Draizel showed Refael'ke around the house, she again apologized that things weren't yet in order, and led him into the guest room.

There, the curtains were already up, and they filled the room with a jittering light and with shadows. Here lay the broken pieces of furniture, the antiques Draizel had brought along from her father's house. In one corner was a trunk with four carved lion's paws for legs. On the wall, above a chest of drawers with gilded handles, hung a half-sized mirror framed in bronze. In the middle of the room: a few old chairs and two low, shiny black tables, their thin legs overlaid with mold. One entire wall was blocked by a large, burgundy wood credenza, the top half of its doors inlaid with thick panes of glass. Behind those doors, the shelves were crammed with dinnerware. From one corner, Draizel pulled out an item wrapped in cotton stuffing and a piece of linen, and unfolded it to reveal a wine decanter. The decanter glowed blue and rose, like the reflection of budding branches in a lake.

"See this, Refael'ke? This flask was made in a factory in Bremen, modeled after glassware made in Venice, an old Italian city. The lower half is wide and protruding, the upper half is long and narrow. The handles are semicircles, and the neck has a head-shaped stopper. Look here and you'll notice that the flask resembles a woman in a wide ballgown with a slim, cinched waist, her hands on her hips as if she's dancing toward someone."

Draizel removed the trunk's arched lid, overlaid with leather and trimmed with metal corners, and sorted through the metal dishes that lay inside. She took out a brass jug with a narrow neck. It had a cap on top, its slim, twisted handle looked like an ear, and the jug's spout on the other side, like a stork's beak. "This is a Russian jug, made for mead or some other drink. Can you see how beautifully it's crafted? Do you have an eye for such things?"

"No, I don't. I don't get why this jug is any prettier than another," Refael'ke said.

"How is it possible that you don't have an eye for such attractive curves?" Draizel laughed, secretly pleased and charmed. With her hot, dry fingers, she caressed the cold brass tenderly, as if it were a warm, living creature. "Father loved pretty dinnerware and taught me to love and appreciate it. He felt more at home among antique artwork than with the neighbors." Draizel moved as if in a dream, and her voice, too, became softer, more mysterious. "Now I'm going to show you something even more beautiful."

She opened the upper glass doors of the cupboard and pulled out a wide, flat plate that bore a drawing of gold stalks and white field-flowers against a dark blue background. Draizel turned back to the cupboard, gazing at the plates with such enchantment in her eyes, as though a world of secrets were reflected in these dishes. Then she took out an even wider dish that had a cream-colored background, colorful butterflies along the rim, and pale brown hills with tall foliage painted on the dish's lid. Amid the foliage sat two Chinese sages wearing red clothing and holding red silk parasols over their heads. Not far off was a little white house with a red pagoda-style roof. Another Chinese sage peered out of a window. He had a round, sleepy face, like a full moon, and a mustache that ended in two thin points.

Refael'ke was more amazed at his aunt's state of rapture than at the remarkable illustrations. She puttered around in the armoire again and took out a porcelain tray, its two handles twisted into the shape of a two-headed green snake. At the bottom of the tray, blue fish poked their heads out of water and musicians sat playing fiddles and flutes at the edge of a green meadow. Couples danced. The women were dressed in pale gold hoopskirts; the men, the marquises, in long white socks and jodhpurs. Draizel scrutinized all of it with eyes that suggested she was beholding the vanished Garden of Eden of her youth. She searched the left side of the tray for the initials of the manufacturer, drumming on the porcelain with her short fingers.

"Not even a tuning fork makes such beautiful tones. Do you hear, Refael'ke, how deeply and gracefully the echo reverberates? No? You don't hear or understand? How can that be?" she wondered aloud again, and explained that when she was still a child her father had taught her how to tell a porcelain's age and quality by drumming on it. "Quality porcelain chimes with a mysterious depth, as if someone were speaking to us from another world. When my father was younger, he dealt with hundred-year-old dinnerware companies in Germany, in Bremen and Mehren. He sold the products to wealthy customers, great connoisseurs. He also bought and sold Limoges porcelain, from France. If a dish was outrageously expensive, he'd keep it for himself. Now and then, a true connoisseur would show up, but Father refused to sell, no matter how much they offered. My father had a reputation as a stingy man. It's true, when it came to charity, clothing, and even food, he was stingy—but not when buying antiques. He used to say that no currency is as strong as antique glassware and porcelain, which, ironically, can so easily be broken."

Refael'ke watched as his aunt opened the bottom doors of the armoire and removed a large water pitcher. It was made of dark brown clay, with a black design on one side, a tall neck, and an ear-shaped handle. His aunt caressed the pitcher tenderly while staring at her young nephew, as if hoping her gaze would convey just how passionately she might caress his fresh cheeks covered in soft blond hair. Refael'ke felt, rather than understood, the hint. He blushed and stood up. Draizel placed the pitcher on her shoulder and took his hand. "Once upon a time," she said, "women would walk like this with their pitchers to the well, and they'd find their bridegrooms there. I read that in some warm countries it's still the custom, same as in biblical times. Just look!" Draizel measured herself against Refael'ke. "Even with the pitcher on my shoulder I'm still not taller than you. Your parents and sisters must love you very much."

Barely had she managed to remove the pitcher from her shoulder—forget about hiding it!—when her husband strode into the room. He glanced at them and burst into laughter. "I figured she'd wheedle you into coming in here, so she could brag about her antiques." Shabse-Shepsel grimaced as if he were nauseous enough to vomit. He pinched his beard and scratched his skinny, sweaty neck, but seemed not to know where to put the rest of himself: his hands, his body, his flesh and life. He was clearly annoyed by the quiet midday and the sluggish, empty market, with no prospects for fighting or shouting. But then his wife sat down on a chair, lips puckered with resentment, shoulders high like a porcupine raising its quills in defense, and Shabse-Shepsel's face became enlivened, rejuvenated; his eyes lit up with a blue glow. "You see that trunk with four paws, Refael'ke? I had to lug this turtle here from Grodno, because my 'rag collector' here claims it's extremely rare. And this cupboard, this half-wood, half-glass clunker—you see it? This one I had to lug here because my connoisseur-ess says it's made of premium wood, the same that was used for Noah's Ark, and you can't find such ornate carvings on anything in the entire world. Now take a look at these moldy chairs. Draizel is mad over this chair because its backrest isn't four-cornered or triangular but rounded like the wheel of a loom. What joy! Its back is round! And that chair—the one over there with the thread-bare seat and shabby armrests—my rebbetzin says that if you look at its short, crooked legs you can tell it once belonged to a kaiser, and it's worth a fortune. Well, does your aunt know what she's talking about? A chair isn't more important than a person, is it? When a person stands crooked and lame, he's a cripple. Believe me, not even a mother trembles for her child the way my wife trembled when these old wrecks were moved here." Shabse-Shepsel pointed at the mirror above the chest of drawers and glanced at his wife to see what impression his words had made.

But Draizel, to deny him the pleasure of watching her squirm, remained silent, her sealed lips curled into a deliberate little smile, as if to say, "Why should I be the one to lose control? You take this one."

But Shabse-Shepsel didn't allow himself to lose his temper either. He continued speaking with a sweet, loving smile. "You're a smart one, Refael'ke. Your silence shows that you're smart. So help me understand, what kind of a person was he, this father-in-law of mine? When I scooped up his daughter, bargain that she was, he wasn't alive anymore. But I've heard plenty about him and his miserliness— the things they say defy belief. He used to go to the market himself to buy food: fish scraps, wilted vegetables, rotten fruits, foul-smelling eggs. People said he was willing to stand at the butcher for hours, outwaiting all the women, just for the chance to get a piece of liver or jellied calves' feet for pennies. He wore hats stained with grease, jackets with missing buttons, pants that were coming apart. But if he saw a rare copper or brass dish somewhere, or a porcelain plate with a design—his stinginess vanished. On these tchotchkes he never scrimped. If he had an attractive home and at least invited guests to see these dishes, I'd understand. But not even a dog came by to visit. He lived in a cold, dilapidated house, full of garbage and dust, piles of old newspapers he was too stingy to throw out. But still, he spent a fortune on dishes and bought broken chairs from feudal estates. Now you tell me, Refael'ke, was not my father-in-law a little screwed up?

Like an idol-worshipper! But just ask his Draizel'e and she'll tell you that her father had the carriage and the good taste of a baron, and how heartbreaking for her to have gotten stuck with me."

Draizel's eyes widened, grew darker and deeper. Her lower lip turned dry, her smile twitched and trembled like a streetlamp's halo in a dark room. She coughed and rasped several times, clearly deciding whether to reply or not—and did not reply. Refael'ke stayed silent, unaware that he'd raised his shoulders in shock at his uncle's shaming of his late father-in-law and goading of his wife.

Shabse-Shepsel was delighted, and he continued to provoke his wife. "Not for nothing do they say that an apple doesn't fall far from its tree. Menashe Halberstadt's only daughter, too, is in love with plates that have drawings of little people, and with metal dishes that have copper snake heads and wild animal legs. She's an even bigger idol-worshipper than her late father, and even crazier. You're laughing, Refael'ke? Right. How can you not laugh?"

"I'm not laughing," Refael'ke answered somberly, and cast a nervous glance at his aunt. For her part, she stared back at him with trepidation, worried that he was, indeed, laughing at her.

"You sly fox! Your mouth isn't laughing but your eyes are. I can see the laughter in your expression." The uncle jabbed his finger at his nephew and chuckled, as if to tickle Refael'ke into laughter. Refael'ke felt his face burning with anger and embarrassment, and he stood up as if to leave. But then he noticed his aunt's face and discerned the fear in it. She was scared to stay alone with her husband, afraid he would tyrannize her even more. Refael'ke sat back down and faked a smile, as if it were all a jolly joke.

"Uncle, who did you leave in charge of the store?"

"No one," Shabse-Shepsel said, and wiped his perspiring forehead, as if his mind were stewing with thoughts like water simmering in a pot. "I should stand in the store selling cheap glassware to women while Draizel'e gazes at her reflection in her treasures? Let *her* stand in the store and let the flies sit on her like on a butcher's block. For all I care, let the entire stock be robbed."

"Since I have nothing else left of him, I must gaze at my reflection in my father's dinner sets," Draizel eventually said to Refael'ke. But she spoke mildly and shrewdly, like a "woman of valor" who is learned in the language of women's books of moral instruction. "I'd gladly change places with him in the store so that he can go to shul to daven and study. But how can I stand in the store if he makes fun of me in front of strangers there, too? And if I answer even a single word, he yells, 'Why're you acting as if you're equal to me?'"

"Exactly. Why *are* you acting like we're equal? I hail from the Benvenistes! Our families bred ministers who led the kaisers from Spain and Greece by the nose. The sultans of Turkey too—the Benvenistes led them by the nose. And that woman who shook up the world, Doña Grazia Benveniste, she, too, comes from our family. Old history books claim she had enough money to buy entire countries, and she did in fact buy half the land of Israel. Kings stood at her door for a loan like beggars. But if she happened to be having a conversation with Sephardic Torah scholars at that moment, she let the kings wait. These were great scholars, great rabbis. You know the ones I mean? They wear clothes that reach the ground and smoke pipes that are almost as long. Well, how do you match up, Draizel'e? Do you have a grandmother like that?" Shabse-Shepsel cried, and it was impossible to tell whom he was mocking, his wife or Grandma Doña Grazia Benveniste.

"What do your tales of bygone Spanish nobles matter? There's certainly no evidence of their nobility in you," Draizel replied with feigned serenity, to prove that she could goad him too. "In the beginning, after we were married, I was impressed by your pedigree. But since we've moved here to Zembin, your native city, I see the locals don't have much to say about your Spanish cousins—the Benvenistes, as you call them. And the Epstein pedigree *certainly* doesn't impress anyone. Name a city or town, there's another Epstein."

The banter seemed to give Shabse-Shepsel great pleasure, so much so that he was practically scratching himself beneath his armpits. "And the rabbi of Frankfurt a hundred years ago, the genius Reb Nosson HaLevi Epstein—who was he, my grandfather or yours? And the rabbi of Brisk, Reb Avraham HaLevi Epstein; and the Koenigsburg rabbi and Kabbalist, author of the book *HaPardes*, Reb Aryeh Leib HaLevi Epstein—whose grandfathers were they, mine or yours? Pshh! Maybe you compare the Zembin rabbi, the greatest rabbi of our generation, my father Eli-Leizer HaLevi Epstein— maybe you compare him to your father, the Grodno stock trader and usurer, Menashe Halberstadt? You rotten thing, you have the gall?"

Refael'ke sprang up and barely managed to step between the two of them. Draizel threw herself upon her husband with jagged nails and shrieked in a voice not her own, "Yes, I have the gall. I'm a person, too. You squander my fortune, humiliate me, and then have the nerve to denigrate my father. I'll scratch your eyes out."

The nephew stood between husband and wife like a tree stump between two animals with raised paws and bared teeth. Enraged, Refael'ke glared at his uncle, debating whether to give him a kick of such force it'd send him flying out of the room. But he couldn't do it. Instead, he placed his long arms around his aunt and held her, trying to calm her down.

Draizel felt Refael'ke's velvety-soft face against her own, and the touch sent a sweetness coursing through her. But it also turned her weak. She felt faint. The young embarrassed aunt clung to the young unmarried man's broad chest and sobbed softly, regretfully. Rattled by her sobbing, Refael'ke pressed Draizel to him even more forcefully, and she cried with even more self-pity.

"What did I say? I didn't say anything," Shabse-Shepsel said with a forced laugh. But with his terrified eyes and pale face, he looked like someone who'd just sobered up after being drunk, or someone recovering from a fit of craziness to see the disaster caused by his wild romp. "I didn't do anything, didn't mean anything," he stammered, and again forced himself to laugh.

"Go down to the store," Refael'ke told him, and Shabse-Shepsel instantly vanished without a word, like a shadow. But Refael'ke had to remain in the room for a long while, his aunt still clinging to him, sobbing and trembling. Finally, she regained her composure and he was able to leave.

10

T HE CHERRY TREES WERE blooming in the Zembin orchards. Around the marketplace and roads, lean birches with silver bark were turning leafier and denser, emitting a softer green glow that fizzled with blossoms. The pungent fragrance of flowering trees and tall bushes assailed the nostrils, potent enough to cause a headache. At the lake's shore, young people cut reeds to spread around their houses in honor of the Shavuos holiday. Little boys carved whistles out of water reeds. The voices of children, fresh and happy, echoed far and wide, floating beneath the clear, pensive skies. Each day, the distant lands seemed to lie in wait for welcome guests, for clouds, but instead, the guests that arrived were rains. Afterward, the earth gave off a steamy bath of milky-white fog. When the fog evaporated, stretches of leafy foliage lay revealed, the sun twinkling upon its millions of diamond water droplets. The air was tepid and clean, like the breath of a well-nourished infant in its cradle. Once again, the elderly Zembin rabbi was unable to sleep at night. Just beneath his window, young men and women laughed, whispered in each other's ears, kissed each other shamelessly. Other elderly Zembin Jews were sleeping badly, too, the starry skies winking secretly to them through their windows, telling them their time was coming sooner rather than later. Who knew how many more holidays they were destined to celebrate? They must thank and praise God that they'd lived to see another Shavuos.

On the day before the holiday, news spread around Zembin that Shabse-Shepsel would be making a dedication ceremony for his new house on Motzei Shavuos and inviting all the town's important people. The rabbi got word of it from his followers, and though he didn't mind so much that his son wasn't a regular guest at his home, he was nevertheless mortified to have heard this piece of news from strangers. "What does he mean by this?" Eli-Leizer asked Vigasia.

"You should know better than me what your son means by this,"
Vigasia replied, stressing the *your*. "You're always saying he imitates
you like a crooked mirror. You held a dedication ceremony for the
talmud torah. Now he's holding a dedication ceremony for his new
home."

"Well, he didn't come here for my occasion, so I'm not obligated
to go to his," the old man mumbled, and turned silent, filled with
resentment for his wife. He and Vigasia had a harmonious relationship. She was no less pious than he was, and like him, she believed in
being frugal with household expenses so that more would remain for
charity. At times it even seemed to him as if they'd lived together all
their lives. Only when it came to the children did he feel she was a
stranger, a woman he'd taken on in his old age. She was always weighing them against each other—My children! Your children!—and her
tone was both prideful and accusatory, as if it were her achievement
that her children had followed their father's righteous path and his
failure that his children hadn't.

EVER SINCE Shabse-Shepsel had conceived of the housewarming
plan, his good mood drove him to repeatedly buff his nails and hum
to himself. Initially, Draizel had refused to hear of the ceremony at
all. Was she really about to face the women in front of whom Shabse-
Shepsel was always mocking her in the dinnerware shop?

But Shabse-Shepsel denied it. "There's not a grain of truth to your
accusation. I never poke fun of you to the women. In fact, the Zembin
ladies keep wondering why you don't show your face, so I'm forced
to make up different excuses. But once the ladies see your dinnerware
sets, they'll be fawning all over you. It'll be good for business. All of
Zembin will come here to buy dishes. Ay, Draizel'e, Draizel'e, you
still don't realize who your true friend is." Shabse-Shepsel shook his
head like a loyal father and flattered his wife with smooth talk. She
needn't worry, he insisted. He wasn't about to spend money on the
Zembin gluttons and work Draizel to the bone cooking, baking, and
preparing a dinner for them. Besides, if people were occupied with
food, they wouldn't look at the dinnerware. They'd have the guests
for Motzei Shavuos over for cake and coffee only, some whiskey for
the men and sweet liquor for the women. That way everyone would

look at the coffee cups and goblets. Ay, how they'd look! Draizel must display her prettiest dishes in the cupboard and on the tables. All of Zembin would be buzzing that the home of the rabbi's daughter-in-law is a museum!

"And will your father and his rebbetzin come?" Draizel asked. "If they don't come, I'll have to bury myself in shame nine cubits in the earth together with all my dinnerware."

"Well, you know how to get things done," Shabse-Shepsel said, laughing, and then sighed deeply, making a pious face. "You know my father and I aren't on good terms. But if you'll ask him, he'll come. You, he won't turn down."

After the scene between his uncle and aunt, where Shabse-Shepsel had denigrated Draizel's dead father, Refael'ke had come home seething and found the old couple at the table finishing their dairy meal. Refael'ke related what he'd seen, concluding that his grandfather must force Shabse-Shepsel to grant his wife a divorce. She was suffering untold pain. Eli-Leizer's mustache was still moist from the meal, and some dairy farfel noodles stuck to his beard. But instead of wiping them off he yelled at his grandson, "In theory, you're making sense, but the reality is you're a mere boy. If I try to separate the demon from his wife for both their sakes, he'll refuse out of spite, just like he married her for spite." The grandfather finally wiped his mustache and beard with a handkerchief and began to murmur the after-meal prayer. More than anyone else, he was annoyed with himself for not having the guts to reprimand his grandson, off wasting time with that crooked uncle of his instead of spending the day studying the Gemara. He even lacked the guts to instruct his grandson that a young man of marriageable age, a man of twenty, should already be wearing a fedora, not a cap, and shouldn't be wearing a shirt open at the neck as the modern, wanton boys were wearing.

Vigasia was just then finishing up her glass of tea and interjected herself in the conversation, as was her habit. "Anyone with eyes can see that Shabse-Shepsel is miserable if a day passes without a fight. He's his own worst enemy. And as far as his little wife goes, I'm not all that certain she'd accept a divorce from him. It seems to me she loves him, and I'd say she loves her problems, too. The more she suffers from him, the harder she'll clamp him in her pincers."

The evening before Shavuos, Draizel came to the rabbi and began arguing with him. "It's the nature of a father to forgive his child. And with me, you've never had any dispute. So I hope you and the rebbetzin won't humiliate us and that you'll attend our special occasion."

Eli-Leizer and Vigasia were speechless, their faces taut. Refael'ke, too, gaped at Draizel, astonished, and on his face glowed a quiet smile, the way a corner of sky begins to brighten a summer morning. Draizel understood that her nephew was surprised. *What, did she have the brain of a cat? To forget so quickly how her husband had tortured her?* And from the looks of the rabbi and rebbetzin, you could tell they, too, were shocked. She blushed to her skull and tried to explain herself. "The rich women in town are curious to see our dinnerware sets, and Shabse-Shepsel says it's a good advertisement for our store. I have things that even you, Refael'ke, didn't see when you visited us. I hope you'll come to our housewarming, too."

"We're all going to come," Vigasia determined, and invited her husband's daughter-in-law to stay for the Shalosh Seudos meal. But Draizel thanked her and kindly declined—her husband was waiting for her. She floated out of the room like a butterfly, or like a bee rushing home on a summer's night, pollen on its legs and wings.

"Whoever's pretty is pretty, but I am smart." Vigasia smacked her sneering lips and gave Refael'ke a triumphant look. "Well, who was right? You think she'll accept a divorce from him? Sure! She loves him and loves her problems. Besides, she believes him when he says he's a treasure. The more he treats her like mud, the more she believes." Vigasia was quiet for a while, despondent, and then said with a sigh, "Not to go to the housewarming would be the smarter and healthier choice. But if we don't go, people will say I'm alienating you from your children." Then she told her husband and his grandchild to quickly wash up for the meal.

When she returned from the kitchen, however, with two bowls of cold borscht, she found her husband still standing there, stooped, his grandson beside him like a young, lean pine beside a short, thick shrub full of prickly burs. So Vigasia remained standing there, too, the bowls of borscht in her outstretched hands. And because she didn't know why she was standing there like a block of clay, she flew into a rage at Refael'ke. "What are you dilly-dallying for? Maybe you can explain to me why your aunt wears a long coat with big buttons, and a hat with an ostrich feather? A connoisseur of antiques like her should have sense enough to know that her appearance elicits laughter."

But on Motzei Shavuos, as she greeted her guests, Draizel's attire drew no laughter at all. She wore a dark brown dress with pleats down the side and, out of all her antique jewelry, only a single gold brooch with a green stone. She'd teased her hair high, and a sheer green silk scarf fluttered over it like a summer's breeze. The other women her age wore their hair and dresses shorter. They sat in hats that looked like narrow pots and stretched their legs forward in tightly pulled stockings, even with the Zembin rabbi—champion of modesty!—sitting in the same room. At the wealthy older women's table, one could admire styles that were in fashion before the war: combination outfits, with matching dresses and coats; long jackets with side buttons; loose waists and fitted waists; sharp-cornered lapels and rounded ones. Wide bows adorned some of the women's necks, while others had necklaces resting on the blouses they wore underneath their jackets. And they still wore old-fashioned, wide-brimmed hats, trimmed with flowers, ribbons, or upright ostrich feathers. Among these dames were a few hags in faded red or yellow silk, their dresses down to the floor, wide as a bell on the bottom and with a train, as if they were queens.

Vigasia was the only one among the women's crowd in a long black dress buttoned up to the neck, without a single piece of jewelry. The Shabbos sheitel on her head sat firmly, pressed down to her ears, as firmly as the manner in which she sat on her chair. Hands folded over her flat chest, her stomach pushed forward a bit, she looked like an overworked cook who'd plopped down for a few minutes' rest. Still, she exuded power and intelligence, and her glimmering black eyes openly mocked the flighty women with their weakness for fashion.

Age, status, and style of clothing made no difference: every single woman oohed and aahed over Draizel's antiques. The men, too, were astounded, and many expected a scene from their wives when they got home, out of envy of the rabbi's daughter-in-law.

"And what's this?" A woman pointed to a porcelain container adorned with the image of a broody hen hatching eggs.

"This is a teakettle. You make only tea in it, nothing else," Draizel said, smiling graciously.

"And this one?" another woman asked, pointing at a silver dish with a lid that resembled a soldier's spiked helmet.

"That's a sugar bowl, that's all." Draizel smiled again and flitted around her wares like a mother around her talented children, feeling both joyful and anxious, lest someone compromise them with an evil eye.

While the older women fiddled with a tea set on a smaller table, Vigasia eyed a clock on top of a dresser. On a wide, dark wood plinth stood four marble pillars topped by a marble roof, and atop the roof was a large white clockface with gold hands. Two four-legged animals flanked the clock, and an eagle with outspread wings clasped its rim. At her sons', the Bolekhev clockmakers, Vigasia had seen barons bring the most bizarre clocks in for repair. But she had never seen such a wasteful extravagance of a clock. If Draizel was as enthralled by these things as her father was, there had to be something off about her. But Vigasia couldn't grant herself the freedom to shrug and cry out, "May my enemies be this crazy!"

In his stiff black hat, his soft white heart beating beneath his bushy beard, the old Zembin rabbi strained to look happy and schmooze amiably with the men around him at the table. He made little Torah quips, joked and teased his grandson Refael'ke on his left, acted lovingly toward his son sitting on his right. Shabse-Shepsel's face wasn't scornful this evening. When the guests arrived, he greeted them calmly and in a friendly manner, dressed in his Shabbos jacket, a wide-brimmed hat, and a necktie pinned to his shirtfront. But as the crowd became enraptured by the dishes, his happiness vanished. Instead of beaming with pride, his face creased in aggravation; and the more time passed, the more his face clouded over, until he could bear it no longer. Seated at the head table, he launched into a speech, using the language of Koheleth:

"Our world is vanity of vanities. My wife thinks Zembin is the city of Shushan and she's Queen Vashti. She dreams of extravagant balls and of dishes and gadgets, like those mentioned in Megillas Esther. But I'm not as dumb as King Ahasuerus. I don't support such vanity." Shabse-Shepsel laughed. His old father glanced at Refael tensely, as if to ask him, "So why did this mess of a person invite everyone to a housewarming?" Refael'ke, too, looked suspiciously at his uncle, worried he was about to create a scene.

Draizel brought in some Shavuos refreshments on a big silver tray—cheese buns and coffee—and the people were duly impressed.

It wasn't that they hadn't seen a richer selection of refreshments in other places, they had—but never on such serving pieces. The cups, trays, and milk pitchers, made of delicate porcelain, sparkled. Their gold rims and handles gleamed. Inside and outside, the dishes shimmered with gardens of all kinds of painted flowers, through which golden peacocks strolled. The respectable townspeople at the rabbi's table acted as if they hadn't noticed the beautiful designs on the dishes: they sipped, nibbled, and, with heavy hearts, conversed with the rabbi. But unlike the men, their old wives acted unabashedly enamored with the dishes, not even pretending to hide their envy. The younger women, sugared buns between their fresh lips and dazzling teeth, stood around Draizel and examined the pieces in the credenza.

Draizel had heeded her husband's suggestion and substituted the dishes she'd originally placed in the cupboard with the antiques still wrapped up in the crates. Now these antiques glittered in a rainbow of colors and shapes from behind the glass: two dark blue glass pitchers with milky-white specks; a low, wide bowl, flaming red on the outside, emerald green on the inside; a decanter adorned with blue enamel dots and a lion crest. Draizel explained to the women that this lion was the coat of arms of a noble Polish family, and the women pressed to know the name of the Polish baron and where he was from. Besides porcelain dishes painted with flowers, animals, or people, an assortment of ceramic figurines peeked out of the cupboard: a white rabbit with big, bulging eyes and pointy ears; a pouting turkey with a blue head, red chest, fuzzy gray belly, and a fan of colored feathers behind it.

Awed, the young women turned speechless. They sighed and murmured wordlessly, until one of them with yellow freckles on her full cheeks said loudly, "All these things are just souvenirs you have to be careful not to break. You can't eat or drink from them."

"You hear that, Draizel?" From the men's table, Shabse-Shepsel jumped up with a cry of joy, like a fountain gushing forth. But in hardly a blink he switched from a triumphant to a lamenting tone: "This is exactly what I always claim! True, dishes are a necessary thing. You even have to make the Shehecheyanu blessing on new dishes. But my Draizel has filled every corner of the room with these tchotchkes, and she plays with them like a child with dolls."

The freckled woman jerked like a wild goat and burst into laughter. But since no one laughed along with her, she quickly turned quiet, a look of guilt on her face. To smooth over Shabse-Shepsel's outburst, the women began to chatter, the men acted as if they were deaf and mute, and the old rabbi lowered his head as if he'd dozed off. Only Draizel didn't pretend she hadn't heard her husband's words. She remained standing with lowered arms and stared at him with an odd sense of wonder.

"You should bring some drinks to the table," Vigasia said, trying to cheer her up with a good-natured rebuke.

"I'm going right away," Draizel replied in a barely audible voice, and left the parlor.

Using the large silver tray she'd brought the coffee cups in on earlier, she now brought an array of glass tumblers: round and polished, on straight and twisted legs, tall and narrow, low and wide. Together, they looked like an extended family of sisters and cousins—ballet dancers in sheer dresses. Once filled with red wine, clear liquor, and honey-golden cognac, the tumblers would transform into a garden of newly budding tulips and roses. The guests were dazzled by the wealth of glass. But Draizel had yet to place the loaded tray on the table when a bitter Shabse-Shepsel cried out: "Just look at this bon vivant! How many times have I told her that whoever drinks too much wine in this world won't get to drink from the wine reserved for the righteous in Paradise! A glass of wine here means one less glass of wine there. But as much as I tell her, it makes no difference; Draizel'e wants to have both worlds. When I was a little boy, I heard a story from Father, may he live long, about the students of the tanna Rabbi Shimon, who were jealous of a very rich man. Rabbi Shimon led his students out to a valley. There, he chanted an incantation, and immediately the valley filled up with gold coins. The rabbi told his students, 'Take as many gold coins as you want, but know that this will eat into your share of Paradise.' Well, do you think any of them so much as touched a gold coin? But Draizel'e doesn't want to learn her lesson. Why are you all standing there speechless? Tell her, tell her what is written in our holy books. That the life of a person is like a shadow of a bird flying past. And, Father, you, too, should rebuke your daughter-in-law. Tell her she won't take her treasures of glassware and porcelain along with her in her grave."

The guest room turned so silent that not a single clink was lost when the heavy tray fell from Draizel's hands and the glasses shattered on the floor. In the chaos that followed—women shrieking, men bumbling—only Draizel remained calm. Deathly pale, unmoving, she looked over at her husband, her eyes questioning whether what she'd just done was what he had wanted. In the first moments, Shabse-Shepsel's lips twisted into a little smile. But almost instantly his lips and chin began to convulse, his arms and legs shook, the air turned dark before him, and he fell back dizzily into his chair.

"Water! Water! He's fainting!" someone yelled.

But Vigasia waved her hands to quiet the racket. "Shh, shh. People like him—when they collapse, they recover quickly. All he needs is to cause enough problems in this world to himself and others. Then he'll be fine. Time to go home!" she shouted to her husband.

The old rabbi stood. Before he and Vigasia left, he looked around the room a few times, as if gazing into a mirror for the first time in his life to see whether there was any resemblance between him and his son.

Later, Draizel excused herself. She explained that when her husband began maligning her, she became so befuddled she couldn't feel her fingers releasing the tray of glasses. But some of the guests insisted she'd dropped the tray deliberately. Others busied themselves analyzing Shabse-Shepsel's motives: Had he arranged the housewarming intending all along to end it with a scandal, or did this mayhem come about unexpectedly? And was his fainting real or fake? People repeated Vigasia's quip: "If someone feels a need to portray himself as a crazy person," she remarked, "he's definitely a crazy person."

11

E VEN THE SHARP VIGASIA couldn't get a handle on Refael'ke: He wasn't friends with other young Torah students, nor with the hatless, freethinking boys. And he didn't go out strolling with girls either. So what was he thinking?

It was true: Gemara no longer held Refael'ke's interest. But he didn't want to hang around with chalutzim or girls because he didn't want to upset his grandfather and father. Besides, he was ashamed of his feelings for girls. Though he knew it was a foolish notion, he still couldn't shake the idea that, were he to single out a girl—take a stroll with her and stroke her cheek, perhaps—he would then be duty-bound to marry her. He knew his father would eventually realize he had to accept fate and allow Refael to become a chalutz. Then he'd be able to show openly all that he now kept in check. In the meantime, he was enjoying life within his grandfather's confines, observing the world from this angle. Everything seemed new and interesting to him; at times, even comical.

Refael'ke and Vigasia stood near a window in the beis din room, and at the other window stood Eli-Leizer and Zushe, the mashgiach of the talmud torah—a Jew sporting a wide gray beard, black whiskers, and cunning, mocking eyes. All of them stared from the open windows, observing the scene outside. Along the edge of the market, buildings glittered in the sunshine: the firemen's shed; two-story stone buildings with shops on the lower floors and apartments above; sprawling, one-story houses surrounded by little gardens where acacia and jasmine were blooming. Long rows of booths lined the marketplace, but today they were closed, without stock, without buyers and sellers. Today was Sunday. Still, the sun-flooded marketplace teemed with a large, festive crowd: a Bundist youth gathering had come to Zembin.

Besides young men from the surrounding towns, older, respectable guests had traveled from larger cities: Lomzhe, Grodno, and
Bialystok. Dressed in blue shirts and red ties, the youth group
marched through the streets for a while and then made their way to
the marketplace. There, a stage was prepared with a wooden table
and loudspeakers. The group marched round and round the marketplace, their mops of hair swinging, holding unfurled red flags
and banners on sticks: "Long live the Tzukunft Bund youth's comradeship!" "Proletariats of all countries, unite!" "Down with the
chauvinism of all other nations!"

The group had no orchestra, but sang without pause nonetheless. Ahead of the faction marching on foot, dozens of young men
rode on bicycles adorned with flowers. At the side of the marchers
strode the Bund's own militia, stout boys in military hats, jackets with
stitched pockets, and straps crisscrossing over their chests. On their
arms they wore red bands. They had sticks in their hands, and steel
bayonets lay in their sheaths. Were the Polish hooligans to launch
a knife attack, the Bundist militia was ready. Polish policemen were
stationed throughout the marketplace, and all around it the people of
Zembin swirled and pushed: men and women, old and young, Jews
and Christians.

"If you look closely, you'll notice the crowd isn't all that big," the
Zembin rabbi said to Zushe. "This group just knows how to position
themselves and march in such a way it looks like a lot of people. It's
like what Jacob did when he sent Esau a gift of a flock of sheep. He
spaced them far apart so that it looked like there were more of them."
Zushe stood quietly, smoking continuously. The rabbi wanted to yell,
"Is everything a joke to you?" but lately, he'd been feeling so downtrodden he didn't dare antagonize even his own sexton. "Zushe, you
know everyone. Whose children are they, these boys?"

"Do I know them?" Zushe laughed, inhaling cigarette smoke. "Do
you, Rabbi, remember the former novices in the Children's Bund?
Well, those bastards grew up, got married, and brought new bastards into this world. Now those new bastards lead today's Children's
Bund. Take Mendel Merkin for example, the son of Shmuel Duda,
the tinsmith. When he was young, he belonged to the Children's
Bund; today, he's the Bund councilman in our community, and his
son leads the current Children's Bund."

"Shmuel Duda was a devout craftsman. It upset him deeply that his son had become a Bundist. I knew this 'gem' of our community was always lashing out against everything sacred, but that he himself has a son who's a leader, or rather, *mis*leader—that I did not know," the rabbi said, half sighing, half mocking. "And whose children are the other Bundists? I'm their shepherd, in a way, so I must take account of my sheep. Woe is me!"

"Some are from other places, and some from here. They hail from the back alleys around the bathhouse. It's hereditary, like poverty," Zushe joked, and the old rabbi smiled against his will.

"So, it's like a doctrine that passes from generation to generation, as the verse says: 'And the words that I put in your mouth shall not abandon your children and children's children from now till forever.' I wish the children from respectable families would follow their devout parents' paths the way these children do," the rabbi said, and Vigasia, as if she were her husband's echo, cried, "May rabbinical children be so loyal to the Torah!"

It was easy to see how much Refael'ke was enjoying the group in the marketplace. His face glowed and his eyes were bright. He liked their songs and their laughter, their blue shirts and red berets and unkempt hair. He liked the movement of so many young legs in knickers and high wool socks. Ecstatically, he stared at the muscular boys, who strained to either hold themselves upright or stretched forward in front of the poles holding the red flags. Who truly cared about the Bundist slogans written on the canvases! As long as they were striding! As long as they were marching! As long as they were demonstrating that they weren't afraid of the Poles who thought Jews were too big for their breeches. Refael'ke watched the marchers as they formed a human chain around the grandstand and stood there, their heads clustered together beneath the flags. Surrounded by Bundist activists, a speaker strode up onstage—a tall, bony man with a head of gray hair and a gray pointy beard.

"That's him, the chief bumpkin among these potato heads," Zushe said. "That's our community councilman, the Bundist Mendel Merkin, father of the little goy who's leading today's parade."

Like his stature, the speaker's voice was reedy, piercing, and sharp. He spoke of how during the tsar's day the Small Bund had fought the Cossacks' whips, fought their own backward parents, fought influential people and religious functionaries and the owners of factories and workshops—a life-and-death battle for people to work twelve, instead of thirteen, hours a day, for wages to be higher, for master craftsmen to respect those beneath them, and for sidewalks to be built alongside the roads to the factory so that children wouldn't drown in mud on their way to work in the early morning. "We of the Small Bund, my friends, men and women, we fought a three-pronged fight—as Jews, as workers, and as young workers who are exploited even more than older ones."

Mendel Merkin spoke with such ardor it seemed he had only recently escaped the tsarist prison. But Zushe wasn't impressed and blew smoke through his nostrils. "Psheh! Mendel, the tinsmith's son. He f-f-fought hard enough till he succeeded in f-f-fighting his comrades for a well-paid position."

The rabbi was extremely displeased to see the mashgiach of the talmud torah acting envious of a Bundist's position. But he remained quiet and merely shook his head, like a half-wilted willow forced to stand even in its sleep. "The tinsmith's son may boast about how much he achieved in ruining Judaism and scaring business owners. But against the kaiser, all they accomplished was to bring pogroms against Jews," Eli-Leizer said, sighing, and moved his hairy ear closer to the window to better hear the second speaker.

Before the revolution in 1905, Comrade Kamashenmakher had worn a black felt hat, a white collar with a big black bow, and the round, soft black beard of a folk-teacher and agitator. When he was exiled to Siberia, he wore a Russian shirt beneath his peacoat, tall boots, a Russian fur cap, and coiled whiskers. Now, his head was a large, smooth ball, and there was no sign of hair on his face either. He used the flowery language of an orator, the type who served as a cheerleader at Russian political meetings, and had the hard, angular chin of a Party secretary, along with a fist like a hammer. He was the leader of the trade unions in Bialystok, driving fear into the Jewish factory owners when he came to strike a deal with them for higher wages. Comrade Kamashenmakher had come to the gathering in Zembin to speak in the name of the trade unions. The previous speaker had focused on the past; Comrade Kamashenmakher spoke of the Tzukunft Bund's future battles.

"The Tzukunft Youth Bund still has a struggle ahead. We must fight for our workers' right to a doctor when they're sick or injured on the job. We must fight to abolish the new slavery of Guild law, which enslaves the apprentice to his associate craftsman and the associate to the master craftsman. In Poland, the Tzukunft Youth Bund must continue its fight against a government of aristocrats and generals—the prison wall from outside—and against the dark leadership of yarmulkes and shtreimels—the ghetto wall from inside. We must also be on the alert against both the antisemitic hooligans who shout '*Zhidzhi du Palestini!*' and against the Zionist panic-inciters who darkly predict that Jews have no future in Poland. But you, you here believe in a future for Jews in a free, democratic socialist party, the PPS!* Down with the politics of the Poles on the Polish streets! Down with the terrified emigration politics on the Jewish streets! Long live the universal proletariat of the Second International comradeship!"

Loud applause echoed from the marketplace, and in the rabbi's house, Refael'ke, too, laughed loudly, cheerfully. The notion that Polish workers were better friends to Jewish workers than the chalutzim seemed bizarre to him. But Vigasia wasn't inclined to laugh. Though she hadn't understood everything the screamer had screamed, she knew that the words spewing from his mouth were impure. *May his mouth twist up*, she thought. "And I have to stand here and listen to this? Tfu!" she spat, and left the beis din room, slamming the door against a husband she'd lost respect for because he himself had lost his courage. Not only had his "lion's roar" left him, but so had his entire power of speech! He stood there wordless, mouth agape, beard dangling, eyes glazed over: Was he hearing correctly? Was the Bundist comparing rabbis to antisemites?

"The religious functionaries have always been and continue to be the boot-polishers of noblemen and the slaves of bloodsuckers," Comrade Kamashenmakher shouted into the loudspeaker. "The rabbis have always tried proving, with biblical verses, that wealth and poverty come from God; but we Bundists, the grandchildren of Prophets, fighters for social justice . . ."

"What did he say? We Bundists, grandchildren of Prophets—is that what he said?" a stunned Eli-Leizer asked Zushe.

"Yes, that's exactly what he said. We Bundists, the grandchildren

* Polska Partia Socjalistyczna, the Polish Socialist Party.

of Prophets. In fact, they have great-grandchildren, too—the tiniest worms of the Children's Bund. They're called 'Skifists,'" Zushe said with a yawn, so bored he didn't even light a new cigarette.

"*Woe to the ears that heard these words!* Jews, we're not permitted to hear such words!" The rabbi threw his hands up on his head and shuffled to the door.

Pleased that the rabbi was leaving, Zushe followed him and cried into his ear, "If the little Bundist and his gang were really grandchildren of the Prophets, the rabbi would rather renounce the Prophets themselves. Right, Rabbi?"

"True, true. I'd rather renounce the Prophets, God forbid," the rabbi agreed, and trudged out of the room, escorted by Zushe. But Refael'ke remained at the window and continued to watch.

People applauded this second speaker even more than they had the first. Then, two young men shouted something into the loudspeaker. But the crowd on the streets was already dispersing. The row of policemen lining the market also thinned out, and Refael'ke thought that the festivities had ended. But suddenly he heard loud applause and an announcement: "The athletes of Morgenstern! The Worker-Athletes!" and onto the market square marched more than thirty half-naked adolescent boys in white shirts and short black pants. They remained standing in groups of four, in eight rows. A moment later, they nimbly rearranged themselves in four rows of eight. Then they split off into two long rows, facing each other, and started doing gymnastics. They bent and twisted in every direction, sat down and quickly jumped up again. They kicked their left feet out and stretched their right arms; then switched left feet for right and stretched their left arms. In no time, the crowd at the marketplace ballooned. They laughed, clapped their hands, and kept shouting, "Bravo, Futurists! Long live the Worker-Athletes of Morgenstern!" Mentally, Refael'ke rocked along with the boys' rhythmic movements and watched them, agog. From the window they looked like a group of white sailboats fluttering, bobbing up and down on swelling green waves beneath a blue sky. Refael'ke couldn't tear his eyes away from the young bodies flowing from one form to another, like waves and clouds. At the same time, he wondered why each party had to have its own sports association. Why couldn't Bundists and chalutzim unite?

A few days later, Refael was alone in the beis din room, and through the window he watched the Zembin Maccabee soccer players practicing. It was a weekday evening, the village wagons had already driven away, the dealers had closed their booths; only the wind still riffled through the straw left lying between the stalls. Zembin's residents were happy to ignore the soccer practice by the marketplace. Only a pair of small boys lingered, chasing after the ball when it flew too far. But the team members were absorbed in their game. Each kick of the ball echoed in the vastness. There it flew, off to the side, and a cluster of boys ran after it, trying to keep it out of their goal. Then it flew back and another cluster went running. They looked to Refael'ke like a group of birds before migrating to warmer countries: now in a triangular formation, now in one long outstretched row, now in the opposite corner, rising through the sky. Again they formed a triangle and fluttered off, quivering, twinkling.

The next morning, when his grandfather's followers met in the beis din room for davening, Refael'ke overheard that the Polish team Sokol had challenged the Maccabees to a match. The parents of the Maccabees, and even people with less to lose, had begged the boys not to go, because if the Jewish team were to win, the hooligans would kill them. The gentiles were still furious at themselves for not having started a fight at the Bund gathering. The rabbi chimed in, too, saying that the fathers of the soccer players had complained to him. "Rabbi, it's not good," they'd cried. "Every time our sons win against the Sokols, the Sokols beat up our children without mercy. Our boys come home bruised and battered, but still, they refuse to stand down."

"My answer to the fathers," the rabbi said, "was that I'm not surprised. 'Up in heaven,' I said, 'they noticed you had no qualms about your sons playing ball on Shabbos, desecrating the Shabbos, so God sent you a problem that *does* bother you.'" The rabbi's followers nodded their heads. Refael'ke, as was his manner, listened and was silent, but his soft eyes turned hard and shiny like glass.

That evening, he waited until the Maccabees had finished their daytime work and came to the vacant marketplace to practice. Refael'ke stepped into their circle, as if he were one of them, and quietly, but firmly, said they must play against the Sokols. "And if the Sokols raise their fists, just hit them back. The more Jews at the match, the better. I'll come, too."

The Maccabee soccer players had no concern about the political leanings of their team members. As long as you weren't lazy, as
long as you were a good defender or goalkeeper—that's all they cared
about. The team was composed of the sons of middle-class families:
their fathers were men about town, market dealers and craftsmen.
On weekdays, this group didn't daven at all. And on Shabbos and
holidays, though they went to the beis medrash, they stood outside
socializing for most of the davening. They joked around, crossed
their legs in shiny boots, spit from between their teeth. They thought
not of political parties but of Jewish honor, and they were prepared
to bleed for it. So they were pleased at the rabbi's grandson's advice,
and they did indeed go to play the Polish Sokols.

Though the Maccabees won, three to two, no scuffle broke out.
The Jewish team had brought with them strong young men and a
large crowd of onlookers, forcing the Sokol players and their fans to
restrain themselves. On the way back from the arena, once the Maccabees reached the edge of town, a little boy ran ahead of the team,
holding the ball. Behind him, in two rows, walked the winners, the
Maccabee players, and behind them, the entire Jewish crowd, the
rabbi's grandson among them. Though he kept to the sidelines,
everyone was aware that he'd gone to the soccer field. The townspeople were proud of the team's win, and they gazed at the rabbi's
refined grandson, his tall, broad shoulders.

"Does he belong to the Poalei Tzion or the Tzeirei Tzion?" one
man asked.

"Neither. He's from Morehdalye," another replied.

"Well, wherever he's from, he's a fan of the chalutzim and will
move to the land of Israel," a third cut in.

That evening, all of Zembin was talking about the Maccabees' win
and the fact that the rabbi's grandson had persuaded the team to
compete with the Poles. The rabbi's followers brought this piece of
news to him when they came to daven, and then rushed out the door
before Refael'ke had returned.

"You come off as such a quiet one, but still waters run deep," Vigasia greeted him, arms crossed over her sagging breasts. She refused
to say any more and waited for her husband to give his precious
grandson the real dressing-down he deserved.

But Eli-Leizer, eyes bulging with alarm, fixed Refael'ke in a stare, trying to gauge whether he'd caught some of his uncle Shabse-Shepsel's insanity. Finally, the rabbi sat down, groaned, and rebuked his grandson in a pleading tone. "How can you take up with the good-for-nothing Maccabees? Calling themselves Maccabees is a desecration of God's name. As if Judah Maccabee were on the team. The youth today think the Hasmoneans were a family of strong fighters. But what you don't realize—or maybe don't want to realize—is that the Chanukah miracle lies in the pure and holy cruet oil that burned for eight consecutive days in the Holy Temple, though it should have been barely enough for a single day. I've heard that the trick in this ball game is to use only your feet and head, not your hands. What connection could that have to Judah Maccabee?" The rabbi then got to his point. "Maybe these louts would have thought things through this time and decided not to play against the gentiles—but you had to go and egg them on! Couldn't you choose better friends than these Shabbos desecrators, these ball players?"

"Today is Sunday. The players didn't desecrate Shabbos," Refael'ke replied, and added, "So far, avoiding retaliation hasn't kept the hooligans from attacking us Jews."

"You know what I'll tell you, Refael'ke?" Vigasia shot her husband a daring glance, peeved that instead of thundering at his grandson the rabbi was pleading for mercy. "You know what I'll tell you? Go back to Morehdalye in good health and there you can behave however you want. Let your parents be the ones to worry."

Whether because Eli-Leizer was looking for a scapegoat upon whom to spill his bitterness or because he no longer was willing to swallow Vigasia's dwindling respect for him, he sprang from his chair and shouted, "Why are you chasing a child of mine out of my house? I'm still alive, you know, and I'm the boss here!"

Vigasia gaped at him. So the old man had the strength to yell at his wife after all. Against Zembin's wanton youth, he'd become weak as a rag. Same toward his half-insane son, Shabse-Shepsel, and his foolish grandson. But the wise Vigasia knew how to stay quiet and dodge an argument. "You don't want me to get involved, fine, I won't," she said, and stomped out of the room.

The rabbi sat back down. Sighing, he thought that if his Elka'le were still alive it would never have dawned on her to suggest such a thing—to send a grandchild away just because the boy had done something foolish. Vigasia, after all, wasn't the biological mother or grandmother; she wanted him to behave toward his children the way the Levi zealots had behaved in the desert: to show no mercy, even for their own family members, when those family members had worshipped the golden calf. *But these days, how does one call up such strength from within?* he thought, and croaked to his grandson, "See what you did! A fight between me and my rebbetzin. That's what you did!"

Refael'ke was silent. He looked at Eli-Leizer guiltily, as if promising that from now on he'd be careful not to disturb the peace of his grandfather's old age.

12

IN THE WOODS around Zembin, gentile women in white scarves stooped over in the grass, tearing off edible green shoots. Gentile boys picked blackberries from the bushes alongside the paths. The berries had just ripened: sweet, fuzzy green gooseberries; juicy wine-red currants; strawberries like potbellied dwarves in red fezzes. Now, the cherries were having their turn: black and shiny or with cream-white complexions. And more good news—the first bluish plums had appeared. Along the length of the village fences, low fruit trees on thick crooked roots bowed over the roads. With every breeze they rustled their message to the passersby: in no time at all, their apples and pears would be ready. But in the vegetable gardens, everything had already ripened. On display in the market were fresh carrots that looked and tasted as sweet as red gelatin. Long green leeks were whistled between teeth. In baskets and on the ground lay piles of white radishes in grooved, hard brown shells, along with thin, misshapen cucumbers and young potatoes with rosy skin. The peasant women removed the linen coverings from the woven baskets to show customers their freshly beaten butter and sour cream, hard salty cheeses, jugs of curdled milk, and translucent eggs, each yolk like a shining sun. And the villagers' faces shone, too, tanned and freckled. Only the faces of the Jewish shopkeepers and market dealers looked cloudy and wrinkled.

The Polish students had arrived home on vacation from the universities of Vilna, Warsaw, and Krakow, and again established bojówkas, their own political paramilitary squads, to bar the city and village Poles from buying from Jews. The Jewish shopkeepers then lowered their prices even more. The Christians again wanted to buy from the Jews, because they were selling their products dirt-cheap and were also extending credit, but the guards of the "Patriots," as the bojówkas were called, shouted at them: "*Swoj do swego!* Stick to your own kind!" They berated the Christian shoppers: "Traitors of Poland! Slaves to the Jews!" And they hurled themselves upon the "traitors" and beat them.

So the Poles, even the villagers, kept away from the Jewish stores. The faces of the shopkeepers in their shops and the craftsmen in their workshops grew ever more haggard, their eyes turning ever glassier—like those big, old, crooked-beaked birds who poke their drenched heads from wet autumn shrubbery to gaze dejectedly at the vast, bare expanses beneath the sorry sky. Despite this, the merchants, market dealers, and craftsmen did not want to seek government assistance. They arranged a meeting, hatched a plan, and the elderly rabbi wrote a letter to their Zembin compatriots in America.

For many years, the rabbi had believed that moving to America was akin to renouncing Judaism, heaven forbid. But his opinion had evolved, especially since his son Refael Leima had moved there. So the style in which Eli-Leizer wrote to his Zembin compatriots in New York was very different from the way he'd spoken about the back-alley youths when they'd left Zembin for America. The rabbi wrote the letter on long yellow sheets in a fussy, ornamental script, all angles and frills. As he laid out his entreaty in writing, he sighed deeply, reliving the problems of his impoverished congregation:

"You children of Zembin in New York must certainly remember Reb Shmuel Tabaka, from the liquor store on Bialystok Street—a Jew who studies a chapter of the Mishna every day and gives generously to charity. The Poles have opened two liquor stores on the same block as his, and the gentiles frequent those. The government places a tariff on liquor, so Shmuel Tabaka can't lower his prices even if he wanted. And there aren't enough Jewish drunks in Zembin, thank God, for him to make a living. So his shelves are packed with flasks of wine. The wines sparkle, but his face is dark as night. You children of Zembin certainly remember the three sons of Simcha Zelig, the leather merchant—the three brothers who own the shoe store across from the market. It should be known, my Zembin children, that the antisemites have forbidden the villagers from buying men's boots and women's shoes from Simcha Zelig's sons, for so long now that they're left 'naked and in want of everything'—destitute. And an even worse fate has befallen Bluma Roza, Isser Tzalke's widow, and her daughters, who sell undergarments on Broad Street. Amalek's descendants, may they be eradicated, knew that men don't walk into an underwear store, so there would be no one to resist them—they broke into the shop and stole Bluma Roza's stock. Worse, they're making the widow and her daughters go to trial for cursing and insulting the Polish government.

"And these three businesses," the rabbi continued in his letter, "I mention merely as examples, to give you a sense of what life is like for all the shop owners around the market, all the street stall dealers and the craftsmen who display their handiwork. It's as it is written in the Gemara, '*Im barzim nuflu shalheves, mah yaasu eizovu kir.*' And what this translates to, dear children of Zembin, is: 'If fire has beset the great cedar trees, what can the little grasses on the walls say?' In other words, if the great have fallen, imagine what can happen to the small!" Eli-Leizer went on quoting wise adages from the Sages before coming to the point of his letter. "In Zembin there are now two sorts of people in need: blatant paupers, who already take support openly from anyone and everyone—may God have mercy on them! And the well-to-do who've lost their money and would rather kill themselves than take charity from others, such as the store owners I mentioned by name earlier in this letter. We therefore held a town meeting, where it was decided that we should open a gemilas chesed fund from which businessmen and craftsmen can borrow money without interest. An announcement was posted throughout the city, stating that the first donors to the fund must be the Zembin Jews themselves. And to me, their rabbi, the community entrusted the duty of writing to our Zembin compatriots in America to ask for help, so that our holy community will not, God forbid, die in this silent war. Although the gentiles do on occasion attack the Jews and beat us, the goal of these antisemites is specifically to suffocate us in a 'silent' war. Help us, and God will help you in all your endeavors," the rabbi concluded, and humbly signed, "So speaks the lowly Eli-Leizer HaLevi Epstein, resident of the holy community of Zembin."

As he signed the letter, and as he folded the sheets with trembling hands, the rabbi shook his head sadly. According to what he'd heard, American Jews were closing their shops on only one Shabbos each year—the Shabbos of all Shabbosim, Yom Kippur. He would very much have liked to add to the letter, "Children, if you do not keep your store closed on Shabbos, you may bring upon yourself a Shabbos of all Shabbosim all year round. You'll have no business, so you'll really rest." But would they listen to him? It would merely undermine his own efforts; they'd send no money at all. In fact, the ex-Zembiners might even tattle on him to the Zembin community leadership for rebuking them.

Besides this letter, Eli-Leizer wanted to write another to Refael Leima in Chicago, to tell him about the suffering Shabse-Shepsel was causing. Initially he'd shared this plan with no one, not even Vigasia. But after the housewarming episode that led Draizel to drop the tray full of glasses, Eli-Leizer no longer disguised his intentions. To his wife and Refael'ke, he said, "I'm going to write to my oldest son in America, and I'm going to tell him that if my health and honor are important to him, he must bring this brother of his who's short-ening my life over to America. He'd also be saving Shabse-Shepsel from the insane asylum or prison. With Shabse-Shepsel, anything could happen."

Eli-Leizer remembered quite well how he used to harass Refael Leima for not being enough of a zealot. Now he was forced to write him bemoaning Shabse-Shepsel's excessive zealotry. The old rabbi sighed. He shook his head with even more sadness than when he'd written to the Zembin compatriots. It was he who'd driven Refael Leima to leave for America. Because of his father's constant reproach-ing and bickering, Refael Leima had left for a country where he'd been forced to struggle so mightily, at first as a melamed in New York, until finally he landed the position of rosh yeshiva in Chicago. Was it right to demand that he take on the burden of his screwy brother, too?

To make up for old criticisms, Eli-Leizer piled on lavish words of praise for Refael Leima, as if addressing one of the leaders of the generation: "Dear Rabbi and Genius, lauded everywhere, corner-stone of our nation, Sage, Master, keen mind who uproots mountains and grinds them to dust with his hypotheses, new growth from the old orchards on Mount Lebanon—that is he, my son, my oldest son, Reb Refael Leima. May his light shine in America, where he holds the crown of a rosh yeshiva, as it shone when he was rabbi in the holy community of Dalhinovke, may God protect him, and as it shone when he was the extraordinary dayan in the righteous community of Zembin, may God protect him."

But when it came to the actual body of the letter, Eli-Leizer forgot his Hebrew and his rabbinical embellishments, and instead wrote in simple Yiddish about the humiliations he'd suffered from Shabse-Shepsel.

In the meantime, weeks passed without Shabse-Shepsel paying a visit to his father. Refael'ke, too, avoided seeing Shabse-Shepsel, at the request of his grandfather. "As soon as he spots anyone in the family, his mind starts whirring with ideas of what tricks to play on them in order to infuriate me," Eli-Leizer said.

His rebbetzin agreed. "True as gold," she said. "If we hadn't gone to his housewarming, maybe he would never have goaded his wife into smashing the tumblers."

But Shabse-Shepsel wouldn't allow himself to be alienated. One day, in Tammuz, he popped in at his father's house unexpectedly, his face looking jaundiced, his lips sagging. The hairs of his sparse beard had grown sparser, and his fragile teeth had inched farther apart. His forehead was sweaty, and the Tammuz heat burned hellishly in his pale blue eyes. Though a month had passed since the broken-glass incident, he spoke about it as if it had occurred the night before. It made no difference to him, he claimed, whether the tray of tumblers had fallen out of Draizel's hands, as she insisted, or if Draizel had thrown them down deliberately, out of anger at her husband's insults. If the former, she was incompetent; if the latter, she was spiteful. She wanted him to snap; well, she would snap first! He'd give her a divorce. Let her go back to Grodno—or to the other side of the Sambatyon River where the red Jews were—together with her bags and baggage, glassware, and worm-eaten furniture. He'd be a free man again. And then he'd be able to honor his father properly. "The first thing I'm going to do is publish Father's two books on Jewish law and Talmudic allegories. I'll distribute them all over the world."

If Shabse-Shepsel had hoped to see his father turn frantic with fury, he achieved his goal. Eli-Leizer stamped his feet. His hands shook and froth bubbled at the corners of his mouth. "Rebellious son! You want to honor your father? Leave Zembin, so that I don't have to see you ever again!"

"Don't get so angry. You'll have a stroke, heaven forbid," Vigasia shouted at her husband, becoming angry herself in the process. Then she yelled at Shabse-Shepsel, "I persuaded the rabbi to go to your housewarming because I didn't want people to say I was pushing a father and son apart. But in my heart I knew you'd cause a scandal. From the moment I set eyes on you, I knew you were your own worst enemy, and that wife of yours enjoys having problems. She got herself tangled up with you like a bat in a net of hair. Yes, I'm sure she'll accept your divorce just like hair grows on my palm. You don't even truly plan to divorce her; you just want to give her a fright. Get away from here. Go, before I chase you out with my broom."

Shabse-Shepsel left his father's house, smiling coolly beneath his stringy mustache; and with the same cool smile, he told Draizel that his father had instructed him to divorce her. Rather than reply, Draizel set out immediately to her father-in-law's house. Dressed in a long, flared dress and in shoes with hard leather tips, she banged her heels on the cobblestones and shook the air with her sharp, pointed elbows, muttering to herself along the way, shifting the scarf around her head, charging forward without pause as if preparing to wreak havoc in the rabbi's home. But when she stepped inside, she immediately burst into sobs. "Isn't it enough that your son wasted away my fortune?" she cried. "Now you want him to divorce me?"

The rabbi insisted that he never told his son to divorce her, but Draizel bawled with the pleasure of someone who'd been longing for a good cry. "Is this how the Torah advises one to treat an orphan?" she howled.

And Vigasia yelled back, "Silly you! Crybaby! If he wants to give you a divorce, grab it. He's liable to abandon you and let you languish as an agunah."

"So I'll be an agunah," Draizel sobbed, enjoying the cry even more. "I will never take another man as a husband."

Although he had not yet received a reply to his first letter, Eli-Leizer drafted a new letter to his son in America. But this time he opened with the community's problems, the situation of the Zembin Jews. With his son, he didn't have to be careful as he'd been with the New York compatriots. He wrote bluntly that if the Zembin storekeepers had closed their doors early on Friday over the past years, if they'd closed up shop in time for candle-lighting, they wouldn't be standing there now with their doors open all week and no customers walking in. "I should be lucky," Eli-Leizer wrote, "to have as many good advocates up in heaven as the number of times Jewish tavern-keepers have served treyf to their Jewish customers. Even my injunctions did nothing to help. And now things have turned rotten. On market day, the villagers eat and drink in the newly opened Polish taverns and never set foot in the Jewish ones. Well, do our Jewish brothers understand that we alone—our own sins—brought this about?

"On a positive note, however, I want to tell you about the self-sacrifice of the Jews here. The antisemites realized that their team of fighters couldn't completely prevent people from buying from Jews. After all, the villagers know that Jews sell cheaper and extend credit, while in the Polish stores they rip you off and customers have to pay in cash. So, to keep Poles from finding their way into Jewish shops, the antisemites got smart and convinced the authorities to change the market day from Tuesday to Saturday. Refael Leima, my son, I was struck by such terror you'd think I'd seen the Angel of Death with an outstretched knife, heaven forbid," he wrote. "All these years I've waged war with Jewish breadwinners because of their desecration of Shabbos, and I've lost. They continued working and selling till late Friday night, when Shabbos had already begun. So of course, now that their children's bread depends on it, they would all start working on Shabbos. But never underestimate a Jewish soul! Especially at a time when the entire Jewish public is involved. No wholesaler, no retail store, no street stall dealer, no craftsman, no tavern owner and no innkeeper—not one opened his business on Shabbos! Even those who had quietly been conducting business on Shabbos now kept their shops closed. The villagers came to the fair and saw it was like Yom Kippur for the Jews. Everything was closed. This happened one week, then another, until the peasants threw themselves upon their bojówka leaders, kicking and shouting that they don't want market day on the Jews' *Sabbota*. And so, the magistrate was forced to switch market day back to Tuesday. Perhaps in the past, truth be told, I was a bit too strict with my congregation," Eli-Leizer confessed in his letter to Refael Leima, "so you must do everything you can to get our Zembin compatriots in Chicago, like our Zembin compatriots in New York, to contribute to the gemilas chesed fund, so that we can support the townspeople who've become poor but won't accept charity."

Once he'd finished writing about the community's troubles, Eli-Leizer turned again to the grief Shabse-Shepsel was causing him and to his son's latest plot to divorce his wife. Eli-Leizer begged Refael Leima to work as hard as he could to bring Shabse-Shepsel and his wife over to America. "You may very well ask," he wrote, "'If he causes *you* problems in Zembin, won't he do the same for me in America?' But the answer is that all his hatred is directed at me alone, not at you or any of his sisters." Eli-Leizer concluded his letter, and this time placed his own round stamp beneath his signature. He then asked Refael'ke to address the envelope.

"All this big to-do, for nothing." The old rabbi gave a wave of his hand. "Refael Leima has never been very good at getting things done. How will he get papers if there's a quota? And can I assume that Shabse-Shepsel will want to move? Go, Refael'ke, mail the letter, and on your way back pay a visit to your screwy uncle and try to find out if he's bored yet of living here in Zembin. After all, the gangs don't let the peasants shop at his store, either. So if he does want to leave but doesn't have the money, tell him that money won't be an issue."

Already Shabse-Shepsel had a reputation in town as someone who's not always all there. Either he'd demand two or three times what a set of glasses cost elsewhere, or he'd give away expensive dishes practically for free. Once, a man bought dishes from him at the price he'd asked for, and a day later Shabse-Shepsel was telling everyone that he'd been cheated. Jewish customers no longer wanted to deal with him; and he, for his part, preferred dealing with non-Jews, as he'd done in Grodno when he'd sold field tools. Shabse-Shepsel began to sell cheap glassware to the villagers from around Zembin. But since the students who'd come home on vacation had formed their bojówkas, his store had become even emptier than the others, because he wasn't from Zembin and had never built a Christian clientele. Now, on this Tuesday market day, he stood in his empty shop and schmoozed with his nephew, as relaxed as if it were chol hamoed.

"Why don't I visit Father, you ask? Because Father hates me. That's why I don't visit. You weren't there, so you didn't see how Father stamped his feet when I told him I wanted to publish his two scholarly books. I wanted the world to know it had a genius in Zembin. And I planned to add my own thoughts to Father's interpretations, so that the world would know who I am, too. Father realized this. That's why he flew into a rage. He doesn't want us to be published together, like Rabbi Akiva Eiger and his son Reb Shlomo Eiger, and like the Chassam Sofer and his son, the Ksav Sofer."

Like everyone else, his nephew no longer trusted Shabse-Shepsel. He said impatiently, "Forgive me, Uncle, you're talking nonsense. Or you're joking. Grandfather doesn't want you busying yourself publishing his books because he doesn't believe you mean it seriously." And looking Shabse-Shepsel right in the eye, Refael'ke added, "Pity on your wife; leaving you would be her salvation."

"By all means, convince Draizel to accept a divorce from me," Shabse-Shepsel said, laughing crassly and cruelly. But his laugh quickly morphed into a jagged smile. "Father thinks I moved to Zembin to bring him suffering. The truth is, I moved here because, with none of the other children home anymore, I thought Father would finally notice me. As a boy, as a young man, when I came home from yeshiva for the holidays, Father never even looked at me. Well, he noticed that I was around the house, but he didn't pay me any attention. He didn't think very highly of me. He didn't think very highly of Mother either. Just some woman—that's what she was to him! He loved her, but he didn't have a high opinion of her. Me, he didn't even love. You understand?"

"No, Uncle, I don't."

"Well, it's the kind of thing you wouldn't understand," Shabse-Shepsel said under his breath, staring at his nephew with a friendly but strained expression. "You're absorbed now by the blending of Torah and Haskalah, the diaspora and the land of Israel, Yiddish and holy Hebrew. How does one interfere with the other, you ask. So your head can't handle anything that relates to 'feelings,' anything that's not from the 'world of the mind.' Plus, you never experienced this in your father's house. Your father, too, is upset that his children won't follow his path. But he's never told you you're no more important to him than a stranger's children, just because you won't behave like him. My father said that! And it's true, he always had a higher opinion of other Torah scholars in Zembin than of me. And he showed it openly in front of everyone. Do you get it now?"

"I still don't understand. Your father paid you no attention as a boy, so you've moved to Zembin hoping he'll pay attention to you now that you're older?" Refael'ke smiled, his eyes and full lips twinkling. Lying wasn't in his nature, but he didn't think saying the complete truth was a smart idea at this moment either. So he fudged a bit. "Grandfather is preparing to write to Uncle Refael Leima, to ask that he bring you to America. Would you go?"

"You hear that?! Father is preparing to write Refael Leima, but I already wrote him!" Shabse-Shepsel called out triumphantly. But then he glanced at his nephew from the side of his quick, cunning eyes. "Tell me the truth, Refael'ke. Is Father preparing to write Refael Leima or has he written already?"

"Yes, he already wrote," Refael'ke admitted, "and I mailed the letter today. But Grandfather isn't sure Refael Leima will be able to get papers, because of the quota. So I'm to let you know that if you want to leave Zembin and don't have the money, he'll help."

"I get it. Father wants to be rid of me." A peal of laughter burst from Shabse-Shepsel's mouth, but tears burned in his eyes.

"The bojówkas don't let the villagers shop in any of the stores, including yours. Why stay here?" Refael'ke asked.

"What do I care about those village peasants?" Shabse-Shepsel drawled, pointing at himself with a skinny finger. "Selling common glassware to the common masses doesn't make me any money. I do it simply to move things around. I make money from selling expensive dinnerware sets, the kind of sets that only *I* sell, not the Polish stores. No one can beat me in that respect!"

"Uncle, stop with your dinner sets! No one in Zembin is asking for them. They don't earn enough to buy them, and they don't have the head for such things. Anyway, Draizel says you already took almost all the sets out of her cupboards and sold them for pennies. And just a few minutes ago you told me you wrote Refael Leima, even before Grandfather did."

"I wrote him, but not about bringing me to America. I knew that Father would whine to him about me, so I sent him *my* point of view. Refael Leima will understand me. In his heart he'll know I'm right. I also wrote to my sisters in Warsaw—your aunts Kona, Sarah Raizel, and Chavtche. They, too, will take my side. I didn't write your mother, because she's the oldest and her marriage was arranged. She didn't suffer from Father the way I did, and the way the younger children did, so she won't understand me. You won't understand me either, because you're naïve and you're still just a kid," Shabse-Shepsel said, laughing again. The words flew from his mouth like sparks, and he paced back and forth across the customer-less store, as if across an empty schoolyard. Then, abruptly, he stopped in front of his nephew. "But what? Even though Refael Leima understands me, even though deep in his heart he sides with me and not with Father, he'll still want to fulfill the commandment of 'Honor your father.' He'll send me and Draizel the papers, provided he can get them. Of that I'm certain. But I'm not sure yet if I'll go. And if I *do* go, it will be with great fanfare; it will ring across the world!" Shabse-Shepsel snapped his fingers, and new desires burned in his restless eyes.

Suddenly, a racket in the market. A large group of people careening and shouting. Both uncle and nephew instantly understood that a scuffle had broken out between the Jewish dealers and the Polish bojówkas. Refael'ke ran out, and Shabse-Shepsel followed behind, leaving his dinnerware shop open and abandoned.

13

THE MARKET WASN'T YET up and running, but already wagons stretched down the roads that led into town. Barefoot peasant women, in colorful dresses and floral headscarves, ambled along the paths. They carried shoes in their hands, laced together and thrown over their shoulders. Only when they neared the city did they look for a rock where they could sit and slip their shoes on. They held baskets of eggs, butter, and cheese. Some held live chickens under their arms or in woven baskets. Among them all, one woman walked empty-handed. Wearing a long black dress and dusty, high-laced shoes, hatless, her gray hair in braids, she approached the market with five daughters trailing behind her. The younger girls walked in front, the older ones behind them, all wearing shoes like their mother's and with dark braids—the younger daughters' thin and fine, the older ones' thick and long. They looked, this peasant woman and her daughters, as if they'd just come from the funeral of her husband, the children's father—as if they were homeless now, headed to the market in search of a shop owner to employ them all. Behind them, a young gentile boy was prodding a brown cow with a white spot on its nose. And behind the young boy, a tall peasant led a horse by its bridle. The peasant walked slowly, head lowered; and his horse, too, followed slowly, its long neck hanging toward the ground, as if both already knew, and were pained by the knowledge, that they'd soon have to part. Behind them were more wagons, rolling through the deep, hot sand, more peasant women and their children, sauntering in clouds of dust. The villagers inched forward until they reached the city, crossing themselves as they passed the white church.

Steadily, the marketplace filled with people and animals. The dealers' voices mixed with the neighing of horses, the mooing of cows, the bleating of calves. Peasants stood on wagons filled with their goods, sacks bulging with fresh potatoes, carrots, radishes, green onions, dill, and parsley. A Jewish fruit vendor with a full black beard, thick mustache over fleshy lips, and eyes like big blue plums, stood on a wagon with a scale in his hand, weighing paper bags of cherries or apricots for his customers, who had plucked these shiny fruits from wooden crates. The Jewish fabric sellers crammed their stands with fabric for coats and suits, and striped and floral linens for petticoats, dresses, and aprons. The used-clothes dealers, brisk and irritable, hung the ready-made clothing in their opened stores, and placed piles of pants on the tables. The city bakers, their faces ashen from kneading troughs of dough through the night, unfolded drop-leaf tables in their stalls and weighed them down with long, thin breads and plump white challahs. From another direction came a late arrival: two Jewish dealers, their wagons overstuffed with white furniture and wooden dishes, tables and stools, large bowls and spoons, basins, sieves, and brooms, hearth brooms and brushes. Amid the thicket of buyers and sellers sat a blind Christian beggar, singing church prayers, a bowl of coins by his feet. An invalid with tousled hair stood stiffly on a crutch and played harmonica. The sun, in the high blue sky, grew ever more dazzling. And in the dry air, the odor of horse dung, stale straw, and grass was pungent.

Suddenly, there was a jostling and clamor in the shoe and hat sellers' corner. A newly arrived group of young gentiles, part of a bojówka, started harassing the peasants trying on boots and hats at Jewish stalls. To prevent Poles from making a purchase, these sentinels berated each villager individually. "You're a Pole, are you? A Catholic? A Jewish sympathizer—that's what you are! Why not buy from your own?"

A few peasants were silent; others mumbled something in response and slowly stepped away. The Jewish sellers scolded and cursed the young men who'd chased their customers off. But they responded with cries of "Nashi i vashi!" "Ours and yours!" Everyone could sense a fight brewing. From all directions, curious people pushed and jostled their way over. Refael'ke and his uncle shoved their way forward, too, Refael'ke cutting a swath through the thick crowd with his pointy elbows. As soon as he understood what was happening, two things became immediately clear. First, if he were to get involved in the fighting, he'd frighten his grandfather and cause him grief. Second, he was definitely getting involved.

Behind him ran his uncle Shabse-Shepsel, looking rapturous, as if he were the tanna Rabbi Akiva, who could barely contain himself waiting for the moment to give his life for God. As the two of them cut through the crowd, they saw a small, gaunt Jew wearing no jacket, just a vest and rolled-up shirtsleeves. He stood by his stall, which was filled with hats, waving his small fists and screaming as loudly as his voice would allow at a Pole in a student's cap. The young academic looked like the pampered son of a wealthy, aristocratic family, with rosy white cheeks like big apples, blood-red lips, and blue eyes with fresh veins at their corners, as if the sun of his life had just risen there. He stared at the little Jew the way one might at a bizarre fish in an aquarium. Mouth glimmering with bright, even teeth, he laughed at the *zhid*'s comical gestures. Nearby stood the man who'd bought a hat, a tall, skinny peasant, blue-black as a prickly conifer, listening nonchalantly, coolly chewing on a green cucumber as they fought over him. At a stall a bit farther down stood a shoemaker, a beardless, hatless Jew in a felt apron, holding the shiny black bootleg of a boot. With his penetrating eyes, awash in anger and despair, he stared at the bojówka guards and shouted that they were worse than the Russian pogromites. At least the Russians had killed in a single blow, while these men wanted to slowly starve the Jews to death.

"What do you mean, slowly? We, too, want you gone in a flash. We just don't want to touch your impure bodies with our hands," a pockmarked gentile replied.

"Rest assured, if you won't leave Poland, we'll do with you what the Russian soldiers did, and what our own army did when they took over the government and shot you like dogs," said another man with fat red cheeks and a long, straw-like mustache.

A third man, with crow's feet and crossed eyes, tried to pull the boots off the shoemaker's arm. "Why are you flapping that boot like a horse's tail? Give it here!" he shouted, but the Jew shoved him away with all his strength. At the same time, the handsome student grabbed the Jewish haberdasher's beard, trying to make him scream and shake harder.

Refael'ke saw that a few Jewish dealers—tall, broad men—had

pushed forward, so that they were now the first row of onlookers. But they stood unmoving, staring darkly and silently. "Jews, why are you silent? Aren't you ashamed that they're spitting in your face? Give them what they deserve!" Refael'ke cried. Then he flung his long arm out over someone's head and, with the full breadth of his palm, smacked the student in his face. The bojówka guards swooped down on Refael'ke. Instantly, he received a deafening blow on his ear. In his nose, he felt a sticky flow, and his lips turned wet with gushing blood. It was a miracle his glasses hadn't fallen from his nose. He took them off and stuffed them in a jacket pocket. The pain of the blow made his head split. His strong neck swelled in outrage, and he pitched his large arms forward, prepared to grab the attacker. But nearsighted without his glasses, he couldn't see who had assaulted him.

"Who's this big shot?" one dealer asked another.

"Our rabbi's grandson," the other replied nervously.

"Is that so? Well, let's not abandon him," a third man said, and all three moved toward the bojówka fighters who were blocking the handsome student.

"Save my nephew! Save the rabbi's grandson!" Shabse-Shepsel clamored, raising his hands to protect Refael'ke. Seeing the bearded Jew defending the young man, the Poles lashed out at him and knocked him to the ground. In the meantime, other market dealers showed up and started in on the gentiles, kneeing them in their stomachs, taking boots to their groins, fists to their ears, foreheads to their piggish mugs. They whispered to each other, "No knives, play it clean, don't leave any marks."

Dizzy from the unexpected blows, the gentiles groped in the air as if searching for sticks, nails, knives; and the market dealers responded by giving those hands hard, dry smacks. The bojówka youths roared and cursed. "Jewish sons of bitches!" they yelled, and weakly kicked Shabse-Shepsel, who was already lying on the ground.

Now it was Refael'ke who jumped to Shabse-Shepsel's defense. "Jews," he cried, "save the rabbi's son! They're trampling him!" But no one heard. By now, the thirst for murder was rising among the Jewish dealers, too. But as was always the case, the moment the Polish fighters started getting beaten up, policemen swarmed into the crowd with nightsticks, led by a chief holding a revolver. Only then did the Jewish dealers stop fighting and help the rabbi's grandson lift his bloodied uncle.

Afterward, Zembin had much to chatter about. Besides the fight with the bojówka-niks and the business with the police, there was also the matter of Shabse-Shepsel and his father. Immediately after a half-dead Shabse-Shepsel was lifted from the ground, when people still thought he couldn't hear or see a thing, he croaked, "Don't take me to my house, take me to my father's house." People assumed he didn't want to scare his wife, although it would be odd, then, that he had no problem scaring his old father. But when Shabse-Shepsel and his nephew were brought into the rabbi's house, the old rabbi and his rebbetzin, wringing their hands, threw themselves upon their tall, healthy grandson. Granted, the young man was also a little battered, but nothing compared to the bloodied Shabse-Shepsel, gasping for breath. As he was laid onto the sofa, his hands and legs shuddered. He lay with his head turned to the side, eyes glazed, his gray beard jutting out, sticky and bloodied. His teeth rattled from cold, and his lips were parched from heat.

Vigasia brought in two towels that she'd soaked in cold water and wrung dry. She handed one to Refael'ke and placed the second one on Shabse-Shepsel's forehead. "Should we call a doctor?" she asked Shabse-Shepsel. He murmured no. "And should we go inform your wife?" Vigasia cried loudly, as if he were already almost dead. In her voice, as in her entire demeanor, there was not a speck of tenderness.

Shabse-Shepsel's body convulsed. "No, no, don't tell my wife. Certainly not. She'll come here and make such a racket my head will crack. I want to lie here and rest in my father's house, on the same couch I used to lie on as a boy."

Later, people said that the old rabbi, just like his wife, wasn't as scared and shaken up as would be expected. He watched his battered son lying on the sofa from a distance, as if afraid of getting any closer. One visitor informed the rabbi of what had happened in the market and concluded by telling him his grandson was a hero. The rabbi sighed quietly. "Why is he a hero? For starting a fight?" Then he spoke even more quietly, so that his son wouldn't hear him. "Was Refael'ke really in such danger that Shabse-Shepsel had to save him?"

The man found the rabbi's question so strange that he didn't know how to respond. Afterward, he discussed it with others, shrugging his shoulders. "Never in my life could I have imagined such mistrust, such cruelty, even, from a father toward a loving son!"

It was true, Eli-Leizer did suspect his son of having let himself be beat up and brought to his father's house. He thought Shabse-Shepsel was trying to take revenge on him in some way. Even the naïve Refael'ke took the towel off his bruised nose and stared, astonished, at his uncle's skinny face, trembling and shining with an odd sort of joy and secret rapture. Refael'ke hadn't forgotten what his uncle had told him not long before they'd run out to the market: that he'd moved to Zembin so that his father, who'd never looked his way, would finally take notice of him.

14

E VERY YEAR, on the Shabbos preceding the twentieth day of
 Tammuz—the anniversary of Dr. Herzl's death—a memorial
service was held in the new beis medrash. On that Shabbos, even
Jews who regularly davened elsewhere came to the Zionist-leaning
beis medrash. And each year, early that Shabbos morning, the old
rabbi could be found standing near the ark in his beis din room, tallis
over his shoulders, murmuring the words in his thick siddur at his
oaken lectern.

And so it was this year. Soon, his followers—those who were part
of his regular minyan—would arrive, and together they'd daven.
Refael'ke crept into the room. He was heading to the Herzl memorial, he informed his grandfather, at the new beis medrash, since they
didn't need a tenth person to complete the minyan here, anyway. On
Shabbos, enough people came to daven. His grandfather pulled his
tallis over his head. With eyes buried deep in his siddur, he muttered
the words louder. Refael'ke knew his grandfather hadn't yet forgiven
him for instigating the fight with the bojówka at the marketplace, and
if he went to the memorial, his grandfather's grudge would intensify.
He paused at the doorway, fresh-faced, his strong neck protruding
from his buttoned white shirt like a pale young pine stretching from
the woods, out over the road. His grandfather continued to ignore
him, babbling angrily to himself, as if arguing with God over why he
couldn't have nachas from his children and grandchildren. Seeing
this, Refael'ke quietly opened the door and went out.

Like a dark cloud, the marketplace fight with the bojówka still
hung over Zembin. The mood in the beis medrash was mournful, tearful, like before the Yizkor prayer on holidays. The elderly
Chovevei Zion members with milky-white beards and eyes glazed
with a gentle sorrow, the middle-aged Mizrachi men with trimmed

beards, the young, beardless men (who did not, of course, shave with a razor, in keeping with Jewish law)—all davened quietly to themselves or chanted in a low, melodious tone. A portrait of the first Zionist leader, with his clever black eyes and dark beard, hung on the wall before everyone's eyes. Even the youngest didn't slip outside to prattle during the Torah reading, as they did on a regular Shabbos, so as not to cheapen Herzl's memory. The maftir was given to the Rabiner Nosson-Nota Goldstein, an ardent Zionist whose cascading beard hung even lower than Dr. Herzl's. When the rabbi finished reading from the Prophets, the mood in the beis medrash grew even more polite. People paid respectful heed, waiting to hear what the rabbi would say about the dignitary, Dr. Herzl, in his speech before the memorial service, which the cantor in the eight-sided yarmulke would conduct.

After so many years of fighting between the rabbi and the Rabiner, the rabbi remained the most eminent personage in town. Only during the welcome reception in the marketplace for the province's governor, where the Rabiner gave a speech in Polish, and on the Shabbos of Herzl's yahrzeit, where the Rabiner gave a speech in Yiddish, did the Rabiner rise in prominence. Now, Nosson-Nota recalled something he'd heard from the townspeople: In 1904, on the day Dr. Herzl died, the Zembin rabbi had ordered every beis medrash in town to close, to ensure that no one would eulogize the dead man. But people broke down the door of the new beis medrash and *did* eulogize the great leader. Times had changed; now, Eli-Leizer Epstein wouldn't dare do such a thing. But every once in a while, people recalled what he'd done, and the Rabiner now hinted at that frightful story in his speech:

"From the haftorah, everyone knows about Prophet Elijah's killing of the four hundred false prophets. But when Elijah fled to the desert behind Mount Horeb and cried to God, '*Kanoi kenaisi!* I have been angry on God's behalf,' he was answered from heaven that God was not in the wind, nor in the earthquake, nor in fire, but rather in *kol demama daku*, a still, teary voice. But here, in the present day, the rabbi's zealots have not learned the lesson from the story of Elijah. They insulted Dr. Herzl after his death, just as they mocked and slandered him during his lifetime. Like Moses, raised in the pharaoh's palace in Egypt, who was rebuffed by his Jewish brothers when he came to free them from bondage, so did Dr. Herzl come from a rich, happy world to free his brothers from exile, but was rebuffed by the fundamentalists, the fanatics. That's why his heart burst. And like Moses, he wasn't privileged to lead his nation of Israel into the land of their forefathers."

"A chillul Hashem! A desecration of God's name! To compare Dr. Herzl with our leader, Moses, is a chillul Hashem the likes of which has never been heard!" Shabse-Shepsel jumped up from his corner and flapped his long, thin arms.

The clear, summery Shabbos morning slipped into the beis medrash through the windows and seemed to join the crowd in their amazement. First of all, they marveled that Shabse-Shepsel, who'd been beaten nearly to death just that past Tuesday, had already recovered so fully that he was able not only to make it to the Shabbos davening but to leap up like that and start shouting wildly. They then wondered about another thing. Because Shabse-Shepsel had chosen to daven regularly in the Zionist beis medrash, a place his father never set foot in, it was presumed he was a Zionist. So what had suddenly flipped over in his brain? His unexpected outburst and chutzpah rendered the crowd speechless, and Shabse-Shepsel took advantage of their silence. He ran up onto the bimah, tallis fluttering at his sides, and pointed his finger at the Rabiner, still rooted to his spot, mouth caught open in the middle of his speech.

"Your Dr. Herzl didn't believe in the Creator of the universe, nor in the Torah, nor in the coming of the Messiah. When the Turks refused to leave the land of Israel, Herzl was just fine with the idea that we Jews accept a piece of land somewhere in Africa! And if you, the state-appointed rabbi, compare the atheist Dr. Herzl with Moses, then you're just as much an atheist and a sin-inciter as him! Father was right to persecute you! If Father weren't so old and weak, he'd be standing where I'm standing now and saying what I'm saying. But since Father can't do it, I will! I won't allow a memorial service for a man whose impiety brought shame to the Jewish people."

His words held the worshippers in their grip. They were even more astonished and frightened. To them, it seemed, they were watching Satan in a tallis, standing on the bimah and blaspheming. Before the crowd could regain their bearings, Refael'ke sprang to the bimah, and in the tense silence they could hear his words clearly, his furious tone: "If you don't step down immediately, I'm going to kick you off. Yes, we're allowed to compare Dr. Herzl to the Prophets, because he was a prophet, too, the first prophet since Malachai. Grandfather will be devastated by your behavior, because your intentions aren't pure." Refael'ke moved toward his uncle threateningly, ready to push him off. But Shabse-Shepsel didn't fight back, nor did he utter a word. He backed his way off the bimah, flashing the same twisted smile he always flashed when he invoked the name of his father to cause a scandal.

Stepping down off the bimah steps, Shabse-Shepsel descended into a seething crowd, who pushed against him like a stream of water between ice floes. From every direction, they cursed and berated him.

"You Jewish rat!"

"For such words, your mouth should be sealed shut!"

"Pity that the gentiles in the market didn't pummel and bloody you more!"

"You think just because you have a beard, you're wise? A billy goat has a beard, too!"

"What, we can't touch him because he's the rabbi's son? Sons like him—may they be sown abundantly but reaped sparsely."

"I hear it's hell on earth for your wife, too. Well, why doesn't she bury you? Better Jews than you lie in the earth!"

Shabse-Shepsel kept silent and turned ever paler, but the crooked smile didn't leave his ashen lips.

"Look, he even sneers at us!" someone called out, hands stretching toward him, ready to rip him apart. Refael'ke had to protect his uncle from the crowd. He tried to appease some of the men with his words; others, he had to fend off with his elbows. Eventually, he managed to usher Shabse-Shepsel outside to safety.

Zembin was of two minds. In the minority were those who believed the rabbi was innocent. Why blame the father, after all, if his son is deranged, an evil apostate, a bad apple, a demon? But the majority held a different view: True, the old fanatic was no longer ordering synagogues to be closed on Herzl's yahrzeit, because he knew he wouldn't be obeyed. But had he not railed against Dr. Herzl all these years, had he not said all sorts of horrible things about our own Rabiner, his half-wit son would have never jumped up the way he did.

All the complaints and grievances against the old rabbi that had been festering for years now swam to the surface, causing an uproar. "You can see how much hatred the rabbi and his son have toward Zionist Jews!" people cried. "In times like these, when they're burning the very earth we step on, when they're shouting from every direction in Poland: '*Zhidzhi, du Palestini,* Jews, go to Palestine!'—at such a time the rabbi and his son call Dr. Herzl an atheist and bar us from memorializing him! Such a rabbi should be dragged out of town on a trash wagon, should he not? And we should break his son's bones, should we not?"

Shabse-Shepsel could no longer open his dinnerware shop. He was warned that they'd throw bricks through his window and turn his glassware into a pile of shards. "Well, so I won't open the store," he said, shrugging his narrow shoulders, his face like ferns in autumn, turning ever paler and yellower. Later, his nephew Refael'ke came over and told him that a letter had finally arrived from Refael Leima in America. He would be sending papers for Shabse-Shepsel very soon.

"Is that so? Refael Leima didn't reply to *me* yet, and already he's replied to Father?" Shabse-Shepsel said, giving his beard a tug, his face glistening like false teeth with a cold, deathly pallor. "See? I predicted this, Refael'ke. I told you Refael Leima would fulfill the commandment and honor his father, even though Father has tormented him so much more than me. But I'm ready to go. Honor for the Torah has fallen so low in Zembin that even a zealot like Eli-Leizer Epstein, who can roar like a lion, is too scared of the lowly masses to open his mouth. Out of shame, I'm ready to leave for America."

"But Grandfather demands that you and Draizel go back to Grodno and wait there until the affidavit arrives from America. Grandfather says he'll help you with money, if you have no way to make a living in Grodno. But you have to leave here. If not, he'll be forced to flee Zembin himself. That's how strongly the townspeople are pressing him."

"I dealt with things the way I learned from him as a child. I'm not to blame if Father isn't the same person he was," Shabse-Shepsel answered, sighing, and a twisted smile fluttered again on his lips.

Refael'ke was facing his uncle, his back to the door, and didn't notice that someone had come in. But Shabse-Shepsel saw, and his face lit up. His eyes sharpened and turned moist, as when an old wisecracker chances upon a simpleton he can ridicule. "Draizel'e," he trilled, in the voice of a wedding jester calling the bride to the badeken.

Refael'ke turned to find his aunt at the door. In her scratchy, woolen blouse, with her disheveled hair, her bare feet stuffed into house slippers, she looked shorter and more unattractive than ever. Judging by the way she hurried in, her general demeanor, and the mistrust in her big black eyes, one might have thought she suspected that her last pieces of expensive dinnerware were about to be stolen. "Draizel'e," her husband trilled again. "We deserve a mazel tov! My older brother is taking us to America. But Father, may he live long, is requesting that we live in Grodno until the papers come. What do you say, Draizel'e? Do you want to go back to live in your hometown?"

"What should I say?" Draizel looked at her husband with eyes full of fear, like a little creature chased into a corner by a stronger animal, watching its enemy's every move. "If you move to America and abandon me here in Zembin, I'll be humiliated. And if you leave for America and abandon me in Grodno, I'll be even more humiliated. Everyone knows me there from when I was a child." Draizel burst into tears of self-pity.

Refael'ke couldn't bear to listen. "Auntie, don't cry. My uncle from America is sending papers for both of you. Without you, your husband won't be able to travel."

"Well, you can see for yourself, Refael'ke, that I can't do what Father asks. I can't move to Grodno. Draizel doesn't want it," Shabse-Shepsel said, spreading his hands as if helpless against his wife's will.

"I don't want to because if the two of us are alone in Grodno, he'll torment me even more than here in Zembin. Here he at least has another person to torment—his father. So he forgets about me for a little." And Draizel dropped into a chair, averting her face.

"You hear, Refael'ke, you hear?" Shabse-Shepsel beamed at his wife's words. "Tell your grandfather that his daughter-in-law doesn't want to leave Zembin. No way! Though, of course, I would have *liked* to do his bidding. What difference does it make to me if I wait for the papers in Zembin or in Grodno? And what you say, about me having to leave because of the anger toward Father—who cares if the hoi polloi are throwing tantrums? Father, may he live long, never used to let Zionist freethinkers unsettle him, and now that I'm at his side, he has even less of a reason to be shaken. Who cares!" Shabse-Shepsel shrugged, mimicking his father's former attitude. "But when it's time to go to America, God willing, we'll go. Right, Draizel? There's nothing for me to accomplish in a Zembin or a Grodno. We've got religious functionaries to spare here. But in America, I'll change the world!" And Shabse-Shepsel's thin nose, his soft chin, and the corners of his mouth twitched, already quivering with desire for his future accomplishments.

Refael'ke couldn't tell whether his uncle was truly caught up in these "accomplishment fantasies" or if he was being sarcastic and simply faking it. Something had been bothering Refael'ke, and because he had no one closer in Zembin than his aunt and uncle, he decided to tell them about it. "Grandfather is furious at me, maybe even more than at you. Word got back to him that when you were standing on the bimah, I called Dr. Herzl the first prophet since Malachai. So now Grandfather's claiming that just as your words incited the free-thinkers, mine incited the scholars and Agudah people against him. They'd always been on his side, but now they were full of complaints, upset that he keeps a grandson in his home who compares Dr. Herzl to the Prophets."

"Draizel, out! When the two of us discuss my father, you can't be here. Get out of the room this minute, you hear me?" Shabse-Shepsel stamped his feet, and Draizel jumped off her chair and backed out of the room. "Don't you dare stand behind the door and eavesdrop," he shouted after her, and slammed the door.

"Why did you chase her out? Why can't she be here when we discuss Grandfather? What do you have against her?"

"You don't know her," Shabse-Shepsel replied, distorting his face. "She loves hearing that my father and I are fighting. Relishes it. 'Could it be that an Epstein father and son, cousins of the princely Benvenistes, are at daggers drawn, like sworn enemies?' she jabs. Well, I'm not giving her the pleasure of overhearing our conversation. Just a second." He wrenched the door open. "No, she's not eavesdropping this time. A dog fears a stick," he laughed, and shut the door. "Now you can talk freely. Tell me everything else Grand-father said and how you responded."

"He told me that if I'd studied Torah harder, I'd be remembering

Talmudic passages and not the Herzl anniversary. So I told him that I'd been forcing myself to study Torah only to please him and my parents, and nothing is gained when you force yourself."

"Sinner! If you'd have forced yourself with genuine intentions, you would have gained plenty! But instead you did it perfunctorily, that's why nothing came of it. Ay, you're such a sinner!" His uncle turned his head this way and that and winked cunningly at his nephew, as if they both belonged to the same deceitful gang. "And what else did you say to each other?"

"I told Grandfather that if he was this unhappy with me, I could turn around and go back to Morehdalye. But he yelled at me not to even think of that now. When the right time comes, he told me, he'll send me home himself," Refael'ke said with a boyish face, as if being at his grandfather's home had turned him back into a child.

"And why do you think Grandfather doesn't want to let you go now?" his uncle continued to probe.

"I don't know," the ever-serene Refael'ke replied, impatient now. "Maybe because Grandfather realizes I won't give in to my parents anymore. I'll go to a chalutzim training. I'll get ready . . ."

"You're naïve," his uncle interrupted. "Everyone already knows you won't stick with your Torah studies. No, the reason Grandfather doesn't want you to leave Zembin now is because I'm here. Once I leave for America, he'll chase you home immediately. Me, he suspects of mimicking him, and you—you're always refuting him. So he feels weak. But once he gets rid of both of us, he'll rekindle the fights with his rivals. He's planning to start everything anew." Shabse-Shepsel burst into happy laughter. But then he changed his tone and asked his nephew to sit down. He had an important message for his father that he wanted Refael'ke to relay.

Shabse-Shepsel sat down next to Refael'ke and spoke quietly. As he spoke, he kept glancing at the door, as if this part of the conversation were the real reason he'd chased Draizel out of the room earlier and he suspected her of having returned to eavesdrop. The message Shabse-Shepsel wanted Refael'ke to convey to "Father, may he live long," was a request that he support him and his wife financially until the papers arrived from America. He'd had to shut the dinnerware store down immediately for three reasons: First there was the incident at Dr. Herzl's memorial, which had people threatening not only to boycott his shop but to break his windows and turn his glass-ware into shards. Then there were the antisemitic "Patriots," who wouldn't let the Poles buy from the Jews at all, despite Herzl and his fantasies. And lastly, Draizel was crazy. If she so much as imagined that he wanted to touch her father's remaining dishes and sell them, she hurled herself upon him with her sharp nails, ready to scratch his eyes out. "Father intended to give me money to cover my expenses in Grodno, so why not give it to me here? Will you ask him?"

"Fine, I'll ask." Refael'ke got up to go.

"He probably won't agree at first, but then he'll come around." Shabse-Shepsel gave a little laugh, partly to himself. Refael'ke heard it, but didn't ask his uncle what it meant. He wanted to be out in the summer day as quickly as possible, away from the dusty room stuffed with worm-eaten furniture.

15

SHABSE-SHEPSEL CLOSED his store in such a conspicuous manner, it was impossible to miss. He lowered the shutters over the windows and barred the door with a big padlock. He also stopped using the front entrance to his apartment; instead, he used the back door, to remind everyone that he was cut off from the Zembin marketplace and business in general. At the end of Tammuz, when the market was inundated with fruits, vegetables, meats, and items of every sort, as it bubbled with negotiations and the Poles' harassment of Jewish dealers, Shabse-Shepsel ambled about with a stick in his hand, dressed in a jacket, ankle-high boots, and a stiff hat, as if he were still a young married man supported by his father-in-law. He told everyone that the fight between the Jews and the gentiles, just like the fights among Jews themselves—never mind Dr. Herzl—no longer concerned him. His brother Refael Leima, the rabbi and rosh yeshiva of Chicago, was bringing him to America. And until the papers came, he had a rich father, the Zembin rabbi—may he live to 120!—who would support him.

But through Refael'ke, the Zembin rabbi relayed a message that his financial support was contingent on Shabse-Shepsel leaving Zembin. If he stayed, the rabbi wouldn't give him a penny.

"Well, so be it," Shabse-Shepsel told his nephew, and sent no reply.

A week later, at the beginning of the month of Av, the men in the rabbi's minyan informed him that his son had become a dealer of rags and scrap iron. He'd bought himself a handcart, loaded it up with cheap dishes left over from his dinnerware shop, and pushed it from home to home, exchanging his dishes for tattered clothes and metal scraps. The same Zionist Jews who had wanted to tear him apart like a herring just a short time earlier were now giving him their rags without even taking his dishes in return. Seeing him dressed in tatters rendered them speechless, flabbergasted. That the son of the Zembin rabbi had been reduced to such a sad state! And when asked why his father wasn't helping him, so that he wouldn't be forced to make a living this way, Shabse-Shepsel responded with moody silence, as if unwilling to speak ill of his father. Only when they insisted on an answer did he finally suggest that Vigasia was to blame. She wasn't, after all, the mother of the rabbi's children. He then informed everyone of his plans to go peddling around the villages; collecting rags in Zembin and reselling them to bigger rag collectors was not enough to make a living. In the villages, however, his dishes would be met with more excitement, and he might be able to barter them for a live chicken or a dozen eggs, even an animal hide, a little honey, or fruit and vegetables.

And when people replied, "Are you crazy? Now, at a moment when Jews are practically risking their lives doing business in the marketplace, you're going to peddle to the gentiles? They'll kill you on the spot, and you won't even be buried as a Jew!"—he responded with a sigh, saying, "Well, what can I do?"

Not only the rabbi but the worshippers around him, too, were speechless. They averted their faces, saddened and ashamed to look each other in the eye. Later, when the rabbi was alone with the rebbetzin and Refael'ke, he asked in a low, dejected tone, as if someone gravely ill were lying in the next room, "Is it just an idle threat, or will he really go peddling around the villages?"

Vigasia had a strange habit. Whenever she became angry, she'd suddenly remember that she'd left the oven on. God forbid a piece of wood fell out and caused a fire. Or she'd remember that the pantry door had been left open, and the back door, too, and Lord knows a dog or a cat might cross the backyard, slip through the back door, and turn the pantry upside down. The same thing happened now. "I would not put it past your son to go dragging himself through the villages with a handcart just to humiliate and punish you," she said, and then abruptly slapped her hands on her apron. "Oh dear! I think the pot on the stove is boiling over!"

"I'll send Refael Leima a telegram. I'll tell him to rescue me, to get my rebellious son away from here as soon as possible," the old rabbi said, sobbing.

"Don't do that. It'll scare Refael Leima off and he won't want to bring Shabse-Shepsel over," Vigasia warned, and she left to check on the stove.

"Go and bring him here," the rabbi begged Refael'ke in a shaky voice. "Whether by coaxing or threats, just bring him here."

Refael'ke left for his uncle's. There, he was greeted by Draizel, wringing her hands. Her husband, with his rag collector's cart, had yet to return home. His "shame-cart," Draizel called it, and told Refael'ke that she was afraid to leave the house for even a minute, in case Shabse-Shepsel showed up and snatched the last of her dinner sets to trade them for rags and iron. "He's a demon. He'll do it some-day. I know he'll do it," Draizel cried, and out of great despair, she put her fingers in her mouth like a little girl, gazing up at her nephew with wide, teary eyes.

They both heard the door creak. "He's coming!" she whispered, shuddering, and shuffled out of the room.

Refael'ke looked down at his large, strong hands and instantly lowered them in a strange sort of fear, as if suspecting his fingers might make a grab for his uncle's neck. But when his uncle stepped in, Refael'ke did nothing. Embarrassment coursed through his veins, and it put out his anger the way wet rags choke a fire. Shabse-Shepsel was wearing a crumpled jacket, threadbare trousers, clunky shoes, and a hat with the brim turned sideways. He stood there, crooked and bent, stooping lower and lower until his body was like a wheel on the handcart he pushed.

"Uncle, Grandfather sends for you. He asked that you come right away," Refael'ke said.

"Fine, I'm coming," Shabse-Shepsel replied, with the calm of one who'd made peace with his bitter lot and no longer had any complaints.

"Change your clothes," his nephew requested.

"Why?" Shabse-Shepsel stared at him, shocked. "These clothes match my work and I'm not ashamed of them." He spoke in a cold, hateful tone, as if he were being called to the funeral of a close rela-tive who'd wronged him during his lifetime. Sure, he'd go to the funeral, but that didn't mean he had to think fondly of the dead man.

"Well, *I'm* certainly not bothered by how you're dressed," Refael'ke mumbled, a bit confused. Not in a long time had his uncle spoken to him in such a dry, aloof tone. It was as if his new job as a rag collector had transformed him into a different person.

The old rabbi, too, was baffled by his son's new incarnation—
a Shabse-Shepsel in rags, who spoke without arrogance or false ardor
and awe for his father. With lowered eyes, and in the tired voice of
a man who's lost his fortune, he told his father he was looking for a
buyer for his house and store. But finding a buyer wasn't easy at such
a time, when the bojówkas were forbidding the Poles to buy from the
Jews. And even if he were to find a buyer, he'd be out of luck until
his move to America, because where would he and his wife live? "I'm
not allowed to enter the home where my mother lived, may she rest
in peace," Shabse-Shepsel said, openly insinuating that it was Vigasia
who'd alienated him from his father's house. But Vigasia didn't say a
word in response. She sat across the table from him, on a chair and
footstool near the wall, observing. In her lap lay a skein of yarn, knitting needles, and the beginnings of a project. But she wasn't knitting.
Her hands refused to move, so distracted was she as she gaped at her
husband's son and the transformation he'd undergone.

"How much do you and your wife need so that you won't have to
be a rag collector or go plodding from village to village? Especially
now, at such a dangerous time for Jews," Eli-Leizer said, getting
right to the point.

"Forty zlotys a week. Or thirty-five, at the least," Shabse-Shepsel
said, sighing.

"How can I give you that much if my entire salary now is fifty-four
zlotys and change? You know the community cut my wages."

"I don't know how, either," his son answered in a faint voice,
spreading his hands. "Maybe from the savings Mother, may she rest
in peace, left behind. For so many of those years when Mother was
alive, the rabbi's salary came from selling yeast, candles, and salt.
Mother was in charge of all that, and she saved a lot of money, but
her children see nothing of it." He gave a wan smile. "I don't know
how much my sisters will be left in your will, but I know I certainly
won't be left a thing."

"And what have you done to earn a place in my will?" Eli-Leizer
asked. He stood up slowly, gripping the edge of the table with both
hands. "It's an embarrassment for me to have a son like you."

"True, true." Shabse-Shepsel nodded his head in agreement.
"Even as a boy, I heard this from you: a child who doesn't take the
righteous path is no more dear than a stranger's child. I now realize

myself that I'm a disgrace to you, Father, and if I stay here, you'll be forced to relinquish the Zembin rabbinate in your old age. The best solution, of course, is for me to go to America. But until Refael Leima sends the papers, my wife and I have to eat."

"Refael'ke, where are you?" Vigasia jerked up from her chair. This time she didn't imagine that she'd left a pot cooking on the stove; her fury made her imagine something much worse. "Refael'ke!" she shouted, beside herself.

Her husband's grandson ran into the room.

"Oh, thank God you're home. I was afraid you'd gone to the market and were fighting with the gentiles again." She could barely catch her breath before she began yelling at her husband. "Why are you looking at me with such fear? I'm not the one who's crazy. You are—if you trust your son. He's a con artist! The other day I was telling you he's his own enemy, that in his whole life he's never had a bigger enemy than himself. Well, now I see he's an even bigger con artist than an enemy to himself. He's playacting and you believe him. Support him, give him as much money as you want so that he won't cause you more embarrassment, but don't let him play you for a fool," Vigasia trumpeted. Her hands shook so hard she couldn't lift her knitting materials from the basket. Refael'ke finally handed them to her, and Vigasia stormed out of the room, crying that she couldn't bear to watch it anymore.

"You'll get thirty-five zlotys a week from me. I'll send it with Refael'ke. But never show your face here again," the rabbi said, and shuffled after the rebbetzin. At the door, he turned back to his son with a warning: "If you show up at my doorstep or walk around town in tatters to make yourself into an object of pity, you won't get a penny from me."

For another minute, perhaps, Shabse-Shepsel strained to sit there with an earnest face, in a dignified pose. But he couldn't contain himself, and nor did he want to. His eyes brightened with audacity and with a sort of wonder at himself. "Tell your grandfather I want my weekly wages no later than tomorrow morning," he called out, huffing, leaving Refael'ke amazed at how a person could, in the space of a minute, transform his appearance and behavior to such a degree.

The next morning at nine, Refael'ke went to his uncle with the money. Shabse-Shepsel and Draizel were eating breakfast. They were

sitting together quite amiably, but as soon as Shabse-Shepsel noticed
Refael'ke, he snapped his fingers and reached his hand out for the
money. He accepted the zlotys and paper bills as if he'd been paid a
debt owed, counted them twice, wrapped them up, and stuffed them
in the top pocket of his vest, buttoned snugly over his flat, narrow
chest.

"But half is for me. Why did you give him all the money?" Draizel
wailed.

"You have separate money arrangements?" Refael'ke wondered
aloud.

"Even when he sold *my* father's dishes, he didn't want to give
me a penny. Now that the money's coming from *his* father, there's
no chance he'll give me anything for the household," Draizel tattled
on him.

"I'll give, I'll give," Shabse-Shepsel said, laughing to his nephew.
"Tell your grandfather that no one thinks I'm to be pitied anymore.
I'm back wearing my jacket and a shirt and tie." And he patted the
black satin yarmulke at the nape of his neck as if to send his father
regards from the yarmulke too.

"He's distracting you, Refael'ke." Draizel fluttered her hands.
"Let's see him give me the portion my father-in-law sent me this very
minute. Plus a part of his portion for the food I buy for us."

"Shh, shh, here's your portion, don't shout." Her husband took
the bills out of his vest pocket and counted seventeen zlotys into her
hand. Then he took the pouch out of his pants pocket and gave her
another fifty groschen from there. "Here's your portion of Father's
money, and every day I'll give you more to buy food for breakfast,"
he said, and shoved his change pouch back into his pants pocket. He
told Refael'ke that the only meal he ate together with his wife was
breakfast—the dairy meal. But for lunch and supper—fish, meat, and
the like—he couldn't bear what she cooked and how she cooked it.

"And I can't bear the things you say and how you say them,"
Refael'ke said, and stood up to leave.

"Where're you running to?" Shabse-Shepsel laughed. "Don't be
so naïve. Haven't you figured out yet that the more a husband and
wife fight, the more they love each other? Sit down and have a glass
of tea. Okay, so you don't want tea—fine. But sit down, sit."

In the sunrays slanting over the room, dust motes trembled and twinkled, lighting up the old, faded tables, the crooked rocking chairs, and the cracked credenza—the remains of the antique furniture Draizel had brought along from her father's house in Grodno. The tablecloth, plates, cutlery, and tea glasses weren't looking very fresh, either. Shabse-Shepsel ate his buttered brown bread with gusto, downed a glass of tea, and told them about a dream he'd had the night before.

In it, he stood next to an aquarium filled with goldfish that Draizel had owned back in Grodno. All the fish had morphed into a single fish, with gold scales and a silver belly. He didn't know how, but suddenly he was holding a large wooden ladle in his hand, and inside the ladle was the fish. But the second he wanted to put the fish back into the aquarium, the fish leaped out onto the ground and began to convulse as if it were dying. He was too scared to pick it up with his hands, fearing it would bite him with its powerful teeth. So he decided to plead with it. "You wretch! I just want to save your life!" Eventually, he managed to get the fish back into the ladle, and he dropped it into the aquarium. But it immediately sank to the bottom and lay there like a corpse. "I was overcome with such pity for the fish, I woke sobbing from my sleep. Well, what do you say to that dream, Draizel'e?" Shabse-Shepsel asked, crunching on a hard chunk of sugar.

"What would you have me say?" Draizel said, staring at him with big black eyes, pretending she didn't get that he was comparing her to the fish. Instead of allowing him to provoke her and giving him the joy of watching her explode, she decided she'd tell him about her own dream from that night:

Draizel dreamed she was standing in the kitchen washing dirty dishes. The more she washed, the higher the stack of dirty dishes grew. Never in her home, or in her father's home, had there been such a pile of dirty dishes. Finally, she understood that these dishes were from her husband's entire family: from his father's house in Zembin; his sisters and brothers-in-law in Warsaw and Morehdalye; his brother and sister-in-law in America; his niece and her husband, the Lecheve rosh yeshiva; and from all his other nephews and nieces. For so long Shabse-Shepsel had been bragging of his great Epstein ancestors and their cousins, the Spanish Benvenistes, all the while disparaging his living relatives near and far, from his own father down to a third cousin once removed, but now, all that was left of the whole lot of them was her kitchen full of their dirty dishes. And in her sleep, she collapsed, her strength sapped by the endless chore.

"Oh, but those were your father's dishes, *his* dinner sets, Draizel'e!" Shabse-Shepsel shrieked in delight. "A soul has an easier time separating from a body than you, Draizel'e, from your glassware and dishes, your inheritance from your miserly father. Well, that inheritance turned into a kitchen full of dirty dishes in your dream."

"No, no. Those dirty dishes were from your family, not mine," his wife cried.

"Where are you running off to?" Shabse-Shepsel called giddily to his nephew, who'd stood up and hurried to the door. "Do you see, now, how impossible it is to get along with her?" he said triumphantly. "To share a peaceful home with her?"

But Refael'ke didn't respond. Face flaming, he fled the house.

16

THE SORROW THAT MARKS the "nine days" before Tisha B'Av pervaded Zembin. But the sorrow this year had less to do with the loss of the ancient Temple than with the dismal reality created by the Polish bojówkas. Once the peasants realized that the boycotters would not let them buy from the Jews, who sold their goods at better prices, they stopped coming into the city altogether, not least because there was plenty of work in the fields this time of year. So the Zembin market dealers stood under the scorching sun all day, dust creeping into their eyes and settling on their lips. Lambskin coats, clothes made of burlap, and peasant hats and boots lay piled high on wooden stalls, looking as abandoned and ashamed as their sellers. Fruit and vegetables dried out in baskets, while the dealers paced idly nearby. They stood in their places until evening, when even the sparse crowd dispersed and drove away. Stray dogs and black cats lolled among the brimming stalls. They, too, looked like boycott victims, sunk in depression. Not even the faintest breeze blew through the scattered straw. The silvery-gray, crimson-edged clouds idled on the horizon, and the windows of the houses glimmered in the twilight with a secretive copper-red glow, as if to report that a distant fire was drawing nearer.

Yet the crowd around Shabse-Shepsel in the empty marketplace was roaring with laughter—less out of pleasure, however, than to drown out their troubles with noise.

The wise Rebbetzin Vigasia, who'd advised her husband to give his son an allowance and prevent any further humiliation, had figured wrong this time. Now that Shabse-Shepsel no longer had to work for a living, he didn't know what to do with himself. Studying the Gemara no longer interested him. On top of that, his father had forbidden him from entering his home and Refael'ke wanted nothing to do with him. So Shabse-Shepsel came up with a bright idea. Even as a child he'd had a gift for mimicry, and the older he got the better at it he'd become. And today, performing before a crowd in the marketplace, the subject of ridicule was his wife. He was well aware that news of his actions would spread quickly through town and make its way to the rabbi's house. Indeed, it wasn't long before all of Zembin had something to gossip about.

"So what was it you said you'll do with your wife in America?" the crowd asked him for the umpteenth time that evening in the market square, wanting to hear his answer again.

He feigned innocence, as if they were asking him for the first time. "In America, I'll sell her to a museum . . . What are you all cackling about? She's been collecting moldy old antiques for so long she's become a museum piece herself. I'll make a killing on her!"

"And what you say about her aunts and uncles, is that really true?"

"True as gold. She has this compulsion, God help her!" Shabse-Shepsel let his hands drop to his sides, as if he were talking about a terminally ill person: "Draizel has no relatives, no kin. That's why she's collected little porcelain figurines all these years. They're substitutes for her family. I swear I've never seen her write a letter or get a letter from anyone. But when a neighbor asked her why she looked so despondent, she wrung her hands and replied, 'Oh, my whole world has turned black! I got a letter saying Uncle Shmuel Itza died. Woe is me! I got a letter that Aunt Sarah Baila is no longer.' The neighbors would wring their hands, and Draizel liked that, being the object of their pity."

Shabse-Shepsel began to ape the expressions his wife made when people felt sorry for her, and the crowd in the marketplace burst into a fit of laughter. They guffawed even louder when he mimicked her other tactic, which she started using once she had no aunts or uncles left to kill off for her neighbors. Draizel would faint. "A woman came in. 'Good morning, dear Draizel. I heard from Shabse-Shepsel that it's your father's yahrzeit today. I came to wish you freedom from all suffering and grief.' When Draizel heard this, she jerked her head a few times and fainted. They poured water on her, tried to revive her—to no avail. Suddenly, she opened her eyes like the Angel of Death's and screamed with the voice of a dybbuk: 'I don't have time to lie here fainting today. I have somewhere to be. Come tomorrow.'"

Some women in the crowd were upset that one of their own was being humiliated by her husband, and they went and informed her. "Give it to him with a stick!" they advised. "Rip out his beard and peyes! Go tell his father, the rabbi."

When Shabse-Shepsel stepped into the house, Draizel came running around the table, intending to claw his eyes out. He fled, then stopped, ready to egg her on some more. She ran after him again, and again he sprinted around the table, on and on until Draizel *really* fainted and he had to revive her. Once she came to, Draizel left the room crying. "I'm going to tell the rabbi everything . . . No, I won't tell him. He's your father. I'll tell Vigasia. She's not your mother, and she hates you."

Shabse-Shepsel could barely contain his joy. "Go. Go tell them everything." And so that Draizel wouldn't have second thoughts, he added, "Get our money from Father. The thirty-five zlotys. Refael'ke doesn't want to be the messenger anymore. And if I have to go for it myself, you won't get a fig out of me, never mind your half."

Vigasia sat at the kitchen table listening to Draizel's complaints about the way her husband stained her reputation. Then she got up to cook supper for the rabbi.

"You know what else he says about me?" Draizel wailed.

"What else?" Vigasia turned to her, an onion in one hand and a knife in the other.

"He says I'm as stingy as my father was, and that I buy offcuts of meat and fish and cobble them together to save money. And you know what he's started to do now?"

"What?" Vigasia didn't turn around this time. She put a piece of chicken, along with the peeled onion and a carrot, into a pot.

"He has a new habit of giving charity to anyone who asks, and even when no one asks. He gives to poor people in the street. He also gave to the two trustees of that fund for people who lost their savings. He told me himself that he stopped and gave money to that Jew with the blond beard and fat stick, who walks around with that ledger listing the money he collected for a yeshiva in Jerusalem. And to each of them he says, 'I beg you, don't tell my wife a word—not how much I gave, not even that I gave at all, because she'll eat me alive.' He tells them this, making me out to be a money-grubbing witch."

"So you should give charity to people, too, and tell them not to tell him about it," Vigasia said, speaking into the pot, noticing she'd forgotten to add a potato.

"Where would I get money for charity? From the seventeen and a half zlotys I get from my father-in-law?" Draizel shouted angrily. "You know what else he says about me? He says I fell in love with Refael'ke and that's why Refael'ke stopped coming to our house."

"He's saying that?" Vigasia turned around to face Draizel.

"Yes, yes, that's what he's saying. That I'm in love with Refael'ke and even a blind person can see it. That's what he says about me. I know Refael'ke thinks the same. I know it because he stopped coming," Draizel sobbed in a raspy voice, as if she'd already used up all her tears.

"You idiot! Refael'ke told us he doesn't want to visit you anymore because he can't bear to see how your husband bullies you. Refael'ke doesn't want to *look* at your husband! And you let yourself be convinced that you're the one at fault? Whiner! What a whiner you are!" Vigasia bellowed. But gradually, she quieted and stared at Draizel, stunned, as if she finally understood what Draizel was telling her. "You're in love with Refael'ke—is that what your husband is saying?" And Vigasia burst into hearty laughter. "You know what I'll tell you? Your husband is a demon, sure, but you're no better than him. You're your own worst enemy, just like he is. He gets pleasure out of oppressing you, but you get the same pleasure out of being oppressed. Oy with the both of you!"

Nevertheless, Vigasia later warned her husband that if this situation continued, she'd leave to stay with her sons in Bolekhev. What kind of father, what kind of rabbi, allows his half-insane son to abuse his wife and so desecrate God's name? He should send for his son—the demon!—and warn him that he won't get another groschen, nor the papers from America when they arrive. Why, the rabbi could even have him thrown into prison. The world had laws, after all.

Refael'ke refused to call on his uncle; in fact, he didn't even want to be there when the discussion between his grandfather and uncle took place. Neither did Vigasia. So Eli-Leizer sent one of his followers to summon Shabse-Shepsel. He came right away. He stepped into the rabbi's house with a feigned expression of humility, yet there was no mistaking his little smile, triumphant at having manipulated this turn of events and forced his father to summon him. Indeed, Eli-

Leizer spoke to his son in a pleading tone. "How much more will you shame your mother in her grave? How much longer will you spill the blood of your wife whom you married by the laws of Moses and Israel? You used to study the Gemara! How can a Torah scholar allow himself to treat his wife this way?"

"But she won't even allow me to *look* into the holy books," Shabse-Shepsel said, spreading his hands, as if amazed that his father would be complaining to him and not to the woman who'd kept him from his studies. He spoke with such a stunned expression on his face that his old father became confused. "After closing the store," Shabse-Shepsel told his father, "all I could count on was getting back to my Gemara studies. I figured it would be useful for when I got to America. But my wife began prattling ceaselessly, morning to night, like a ticking clock. 'Have pity,' I begged her, 'let me study.' But my Draizel'e, she talks aloud to herself all day, repeating conversations she might have had with a shopkeeper or a neighbor. She'll say: 'I told her, "But you promised me,"' and then she'll answer herself, 'When did I promise you?' Just like that, on and on without end. It's enough to make you crazy! It must be a habit she's kept from the time she lived alone—I say to her, she says to me . . ."

Eli-Leizer smiled, against his will. He could barely control himself from laughing out loud, so skillfully did Shabse-Shepsel ape his wife's talking to herself. Still, the rabbi knew he couldn't trust his crazy son. Couldn't trust him the length of a hair! He asked, "If you want to study, why do you have to do it at home? Aren't there enough shuls in Zembin?"

"Well, that's the problem. Draizel is afraid to stay home alone," Shabse-Shepsel said, with even more incredulity in his tone, and then, under his breath—as if he didn't want even the walls of his father's home to hear of his wife's madness—he added, "She's deluded. She thinks thieves are hovering over her porcelain dishes and tchotchkes. Every night she imagines the same thing, that thieves are creeping around the attic. Even in her sleep she dreams of thieves."

Eli-Leizer covered his mouth to keep from laughing. But he couldn't help it. Laughter burst from him. "Even during the day she's also afraid to stay alone?"

"Yes! In the day, too," Shabse-Shepsel replied, elated that his father was laughing because he could now laugh along. "Even during the day, Draizel is afraid to be home alone, in case thieves will break in and steal her father's inheritance, those scraps of moldy antiques, and maybe even rape her—the beauty! So I have to sit home all day and watch my 'woman of valor' talk to herself and make bizarre faces: 'I say to her, she says to me . . .'"

Eli-Leizer stopped laughing. He sat with his hands pressed to his knees, head lowered, silent. He knew his son was a liar and a spiteful person, a comedian who liked to shock. But he no longer felt capable of threatening to cut off his son's weekly allowance if he wouldn't stop tormenting his wife. Such is the power of a joke and a jokester.

17

I N EARLY ELUL, Shabse-Shepsel received the affidavit and boat tickets from his brother in America. He became a changed man. Never before had Zembin seen him strut around in such finery, his chin raised high, his words measured, as if he were practicing for how he'd act in America. Or, perhaps, for how he'd act when he came back to visit Zembin as a renowned New York rabbi. Despite all this, he sent Draizel with a message for the rabbi that it was not yet time to rejoice. He still needed to find a buyer for his house and possessions, he and his wife had to get Polish passports, and they then had to travel to Warsaw, to pick up their visas at the American embassy. Much still had to happen before they'd leave. Draizel passed on the message, and the old rabbi got the hint: "Don't get too excited yet," his son was telling him.

Refael'ke, too, was preparing for his return to Morehdalye. His grandfather had blamed him for inciting the Jewish market dealers to compete with the hooligans, creating chaos in town. This, the rabbi felt, along with the older villagers, was what the antisemites had been hoping for: that the Jews would resist with force, inducing all the Poles to join up with the bojówkas. The bojówkas, meanwhile, had grown more aggressive in their tactics to prevent Christians from buying from Jews, provoking more and more fights, which they hadn't done in the past. "Your grandson, Rabbi, is using this as a testing ground for how he'll stir up the Arabs in the land of Israel," the rabbi's followers told him, and the rabbi shared their thoughts with his grandson.

"I fought about you with my rebbetzin, and for nothing. Vigasia's right. We should send you back to your parents; let them take responsibility for you. But what can I do? As long as my crazy son is still here, I feel safer if you're with us."

So Refael'ke stayed on. He had no respect for the older generation of Jews who opposed resistance. And the people who supported resistance didn't appeal to him either. Their interest lay only in the boycott, which they hoped might go away if they demonstrated enough courage and stamina. Yet the fate of Jews in a non-Jewish world did not interest them at all. Of course, Refael'ke could have joined the group of chalutzim, but he didn't. *However hard a rabbi's son may struggle to live in the world among others,* he thought, *he remains the man in the corner—the corner of the beis medrash, where his father and grandfather had studied.* In fact, his sister Bluma Rivtcha had written him something similar from Vilna: It wasn't the curriculum or the studying that was difficult at her nursing school. The difficult part was finding friends and feeling like she fit in. *And will it be any different in the land of Israel?* Refael'ke asked himself. *Will I become a different person there?* The one thing that pleased him was that he'd stayed at his grandfather's since Lag B'Omer—long enough to convince his parents that he'd immersed himself in his Torah studies and found it didn't suit him.

The sun was rising later; dusk fell earlier. But before autumn had begun wrinkling the leaves on the trees, the faces of the elderly Zembin Jews were already wrinkling. Each morning, the blowing of the shofar announced that the Day of Reckoning was drawing near. Jews with heavy hearts awaited the dreary dawns when they would shuffle to Selichos prayers and have a good cry. But the younger generation wanted only to laugh and be merry, precisely because they, too, were weighed down with gloom.

Some of the theater lovers in town had put together an amateur troupe, and they called their small theater "Mockery." And just as with the soccer and firefighter teams, no party lines were drawn in this ensemble. As long as someone proved they could act, recite, sing, or dance, they were welcomed. The troupe had already performed several comedies by known writers, as well as a few twisty, humorous skits. Now the troupe was preparing to perform *The Two Fools* by Abraham Goldfaden. Rumors spread across town that the actors would be putting on a comedy that mocked religious Jews. "Rabbi," the townspeople cried, "at a time like this, when Jews are being oppressed, and with the High Holy Days approaching, will you allow such a thing?"

The rabbi sighed. "What can I do? If the actors' fathers don't listen to me, will their children?"

The town's scholars and the rabbi's loyalists spoke up even more harshly than the rest. "The owners of this theater," they said, "are the very people you placed a ban on. These are the people who drove you out of your house, who forced you and your rebbetzin to sleep in the talmud torah. Yet despite those hardships, you continued to wage a holy war against them. And it worked. In the end, the cinema owners agreed not to perform on Shabbos anymore. And yet now you stand silent?"

"So we'll have to defeat these new rascals, too. We'll have to get them to stop performing on Shabbos, including the eve of Selichos. And for that matter, is it any better to mock religious Jews on a weekday? Ay, it's bad. It's very bad," Eli-Leizer said, spreading his hands apart, gazing imploringly at his friends in the hope that they'd understand: as long as his crazy son was in town, there was nothing he could do.

In order to draw a large crowd, including more traditional Jews, the troupe decided to perform *The Two Fools* on a Saturday night after Shabbos was over, a week before the first day of Selichos. This way, no one could complain that they were desecrating the Shabbos. The large hall was packed with the young, the middle-aged, and even the old and bearded. Electric lights shone on the fresh white walls and ceiling, flooding the stark rectangular theater hall with dazzling brightness, its small stage concealed by a flimsy curtain with no portieres to adorn it. From behind the curtains came the sounds of banging hammers. Ushers ran between rows of chairs, seating attendees, while the idling crowd made a racket.

Squeezed in on one of the back benches was Refael'ke. He'd come to the theater not so much because he was interested in the performance, but to keep his mind off other things. Even once the show started, he had to force himself to watch the spectacle, eking out a smile, while all around him people quaked with laughter. To Refael'ke, it seemed like an old-fashioned maskilic comedy—too crude, silly even. A narrow-minded fanatic from Krakow, a man named Pinkhes'l, wanted to marry off his pretty and enlightened daughter to a fanatically pious young man, a fool who was blind in one eye, limped on one leg, and was a stutterer to boot. The bride, meanwhile, was in love with someone else, a student named Max, who was the fool's first cousin. So Max disguises himself as a fool in order to dupe both the bride's father and the real fool. Refael'ke smiled at the scene where Max and his friends, fellow students, chattered in Germanisms and sang a marching song, imitating the "academics"—as the Polish students roaming the marketplace were called. And why was the bride, Chaya'le, calling herself "Carolina"? This Carolina, Refael'ke thought, looked a lot like his sister Tilza— tall, with big eyes, white hands, a high chest. And like Tilza, this Carolina spoke with a great deal of ardor and melancholy. Refael'ke didn't like the student Max. The actor playing him was a young man with a skinny, unfriendly face, a hard jaw, and an evil sneer on his thin lips. After disguising himself as a fool, he shows up at the bride's father's house, where he meets his cousin, the real fool, the limping stutterer, who gapes at him in deathly terror.

> FOOL: Wh-wh-who are you?
> MAX: And wh-who are you?
> FOOL: I? I am f-fool, the son of Shlomenies, president of the
>   community council of Shakhrayevke.
> MAX: L-liar! How can you pre-pretend you're me? I am f-fool!
>   Can you prove that you are f-fool?

So adroitly and cleverly did Max mimic the expressions of the real fool that the crowd roared with laughter and applause. Only Refael'ke felt pity for the real fool, who had a round, sweet face and pale hands, and who moved about delicately, despite his stutter, his limp, and the patch over his eye. Given how much the audience was enjoying this clash of the two fools, the actors stretched the scene as long as they could. Eventually, though, the moment comes when the real fool allows himself to be persuaded by the fake fool that he is not himself. Suddenly, even Refael'ke burst into laughter. The people around him, who'd been noting his silence, turned to him curiously. Refael'ke himself was even more surprised than they. It was like an invisible being was prodding him to laugh against his will, screaming into his ears, "Be happy! Laugh! Enjoy it like everyone else." And he began to laugh along with everyone at different scenes, until they reached the scene when the disguised student, Max, fools the future father-in-law, the Hasid, Pinkhes'l.

The actor playing the Hasid looked like he was born for the role: average height, slender, with a long, gaunt face and a pointy nose, a fake beard and fake peyes, wearing a black frock coat and a tal-lis katan with its tassels hanging out. Every few minutes he'd fall into a mystical trance, looking as if he were carved of wood. When-ever he mentioned his rabbi, his entire body trembled in awe and his eyes glazed over. He bounced up and down, snapped his fingers, and hummed nonsense sounds to himself—*bim-bom, bim-bam*—perfectly convinced by the stories he'd heard of the rabbi's miraculous deeds. Max confided in the Hasid that he was a lamed-vovnik in disguise. For the moment he was down here on earth, he explained, but soon he'd vanish into the upper spheres. He also told the Hasid that a Divine voice had spoken to him, decreeing that he marry Carolina. To convince the Hasid that he should believe Max and give him his daughter as a wife, a group of masked and shrouded students poured onto the stage. They did a death dance around the Hasid, who cov-ered his face with both hands and trembled like mad, running from one corner to the next. The specters chased him, encircled him, skipped around and sang:

> *What do you want, what do you want, what do you want, dear one?*
> *Why wake us now, why wake us now, from our quiet graves?*

The jam-packed hall seemed to yawn open with laughter, and, in spite of himself, Refael'ke joined in on the guffaws—until, abruptly, the laughter stuck in his throat. A man stepped out from behind the curtain and onto the stage, which was decorated like a poor shtetl home. He was small and slim, wearing a hat and jacket, with a beard and peyes that resembled Pinkhes's. This new actor walked slowly and hesitantly on the stage's planks, as if he were crossing a foot-bridge over a lake. He kept turning his head back and forth, from the hall to the stage, mimicking the Hasid down to the tiniest detail. The audience assumed that the two bearded Pinkheses, one aping the other's expressions, were part of the comedy. But the actors on the stage stopped in their tracks, confused.

Encouraged by the audience's resounding laughter, the stranger on the stage snickered at the other actors. "Well, hey!" he said, and continued to mimic the movements of the actor playing Pinkhes, as if reminding the actor which faces he was supposed to make. But the more he gestured with his hands and feet, the more lost the other actors felt, staring furiously at him. They knew there was no second Pinkhes in Goldfaden's folktale and that the person onstage, with a real beard and peyes, wasn't part of their ensemble. But the players in this operetta—these amateur actors—could think of no solution. Soon enough, the audience caught up with them, realizing that the person who'd crept onstage was not part of this troupe or scene. Refael'ke, eyes still bulging and mouth still agape, heard someone say in a stunned, somewhat fearful tone, "Why, it's Shabse-Shepsel, the rabbi's son!"

A murmur coursed through the rows of people. A shushing. Wild laughter. Refael'ke overheard them.

"It's him, our rabbi's son. Who used to own the dishware store."

"Has he gone insane or did he just want to prove that he can act too?"

"Why are they standing on that stage like sheep? Why aren't they dropping the curtain?"

The cries became louder. But Shabse-Shepsel didn't realize the audience had turned against him; he peered out at the dark hall with a triumphant smile, evidently anticipating thunderous applause. At that moment, someone onstage finally figured out what needed to be done and hastily drew the curtain. There was a tumult in the hall, but the lights were still off. Fear and embarrassment washed over Refael'ke: soon the lights would come on and he'd have to witness what ensued. No! He jumped out of his seat and pushed his way to the exit. Luckily, he'd been sitting in a back row, and he managed to get outside just as the lights flicked on.

His head was pounding. He walked home, taking long strides. Were it not for the pity he felt for his grandfather, who'd begged him to stay in town as long as Shabse-Shepsel was there, he would have fled Zembin that very night. More than once had he felt like grabbing Shabse-Shepsel by his neck and shaking him until the savageness shook from his body. But how could he beat his own uncle? Especially when, lately, Shabse-Shepsel had stopped fighting even with Draizel; he dressed so elegantly and behaved so respectably it seemed he was already playing the role of his new American self in Zembin. But apparently, he hadn't been able to keep it up for long. His lust for scandal and embroilment had propelled him onstage to mimic the Hasid, the way he'd seen the two fools mimicking each other. He knew quite well how much embarrassment this would cause his father. But because he was almost leaving, that's exactly what he wanted.

Part 3

I N SWITZERLAND, far from his parents in Morehdalye, Naftali Hertz Katzenellenbogen felt the depth and the sadness of their silence, a silence like an empty, bottomless well. At the university library, working, at home during meals, Naftali Hertz kept his eyes lowered. Only when he strolled by himself through the narrow, medieval streets of Bern, or afterward, when he sat down on a bench in the park to rest, did he lift his gaze. And he was on that bench now, looking out at the snowy mountains of the Bernese Oberland, his face painted with wonder: Had the Alps so enamored him in his student days that he'd erased his home, his yeshiva, and his rabbinic ancestry from his mind? Had the mere fact that a Christian girl wanted to marry him brought him more happiness than all of that?

Above him, in the twilight glow, the clouds grew redder. And the three giant mountains—the Mönch, the Eiger, and the Jungfrau—drifted to and fro through the lustrous air, their three snowcaps twinkling in the sunset like brilliant crowns. In the distance, the mountain triplets—a massive, three-tined fork encircled by rocks of assorted shapes and sizes—resembled an ancient, vanished city, filled with temples, structures, and inns, stone birds and creatures perched atop their roofs.

Awash in the dusk's colorful Alpine display, Naftali Hertz closed his eyes and thought of the snowy peaks. There were times, in the middle of the day, when he marveled at how clearly you could see in such a large expanse as the glaciers, twisting stone steps, etchings and grooves in the granite. And these very grooves would still be here a hundred years from now, when all that was left of generations upon generations on earth would be dust. How childish and amusing his student fantasies seemed to him now. At the foot of such timeless mountains, conducive to lofty, exalted thoughts, all he'd managed to think was: *If only I can complete my doctorate on the Jewish origins of Spinoza's philosophy . . . if only I can become a professor at a Swiss university, I'll write a major work . . .* Yes, that's how he'd fantasized then.

As always, Katzenellenbogen sat in the park until evening fell, his eyelids swollen from tiredness and contemplation. He heard the quiet footsteps of young couples, their soft words and laughter. Still, he didn't lift his head, didn't open his eyes. He knew from past encounters that, in the darkness, the gleam of the massive mountain would loom like a freshly whitewashed wall, a sky-high barrier that separated him from the entire world. In the end, his doctorate in philosophy and his life at the foot of the Alps had not inspired him to great thoughts, as he'd once hoped. He hadn't become a Hegel, nor written a philosophical mountain poem, a new *Zarathustra*. He hadn't even received a professorship at a university. Instead, he oversaw the Jewish division of the Bern university library, and had a non-Jewish wife and son, an uncircumcised sheigetz.

After all these years, Katzenellenbogen was still wrestling with his boredom and disappointment, still trying to feel at home in Switzerland and to be bewitched anew by its beauty. Tourists, after all, couldn't get enough of Switzerland's historical monuments, the pretty little churches in the peaceful villages, the medieval arches and bridges. They were especially smitten by the Alps, the wooded landscapes and waterfalls. Poets from all over the world came to live and die by the rivers and lakes of the Swiss valleys. And the natives were even more enamored of their country. Whenever the Swiss had a day off, they took to the mountains, backpacks over their shoulders, and came back suntanned, revived and intoxicated by the pure, fresh air. More than once had Katzenellenbogen noticed that when he and his wife walked down the streets of Bern, her mind would wander to the distant mountains and her eyes would light up with the quiet joy of a mother observing her grown-up sons. She became more feminine in those moments, and a sensual smile would flit across her face. She'd open her lips, and he'd see her dazzling, lustful teeth.

Annelyse was thirty-seven, two years his junior, and when she let her mind float to the snowy mountains, or to the jewelry in a shop window, he'd glance sidelong at her face and see all the unfulfilled desires she concealed from him. She no longer spoke to him of the Alps' beauty, as if she'd finally accepted that he'd always be a foreigner, who neither understood her country nor was worthy of understanding it. When she wanted to take strolls around the neighborhood, she'd go with friends from the bank where she worked, or her brothers and their children, or with her son, but never with him. Her "Herr Rabiner," as she called him in good-natured jest—and occasionally with spite—she left at home with his books. And for his part, he was happy not to be in her company. But he, too, had lately felt a desire to take a longer trip to the Alps. Not with his wife, though, nor with his brothers-in-law, the merchants.

In his student years, Naftali Hertz had gone with a group of friends to "Small Crossroads," a station on the Jungfrau mountain ridge. This time, he wanted to take the tram even farther, till the Jungfraujoch station, which stood at an altitude of eleven and a half thousand feet. He wanted to climb the remaining two thousand feet to the peak on foot, along with other mountain climbers. Naftali Hertz knew that even in the summer it was cold at higher altitudes. So he put warm underwear and a sweater in his backpack, along with a mini pharmacy: pills for vertigo; ointments to smear on his face and hands to prevent his skin from cracking under the strong sun; bandages; gauze; and cotton and iodine, in case he scraped himself on the way up. He gathered a pair of heavy hiking boots, a hatchet to chop steps into the ice, and a rope to tie him to the other mountain climbers, smiling to himself as he prepared and packed. If he hadn't managed to climb to the Matterhorn and Jungfrau peaks in his student days, would he do it now that he was almost forty? But he was enjoying the preparations in their own right. And because playing out this fantasy to its end gave him pleasure, he even prepared a long stick with an iron tip for hiking. He kept all the gear, along with his rucksack, in his room at the library, so that Annelyse wouldn't be able to mock her "Herr Rabiner" for attempting such an adventure. At home, Naftali Hertz told the family he was going to the Bern Oberland for a few days and would be staying at a boardinghouse. He knew Annelyse would be pleased; she'd have a few days without his dark silences.

He left his home on a June morning, carrying a suitcase with pajamas, shirts, razors, slippers, and his unfinished manuscript on Spinoza. He needed the vacation to rest and do some work alone, he'd told his family. But before he left, he stopped at the university library, dropped the suitcase off at his office, grabbed his rucksack with his mountain-climbing gear, and went to the railway station. The train twisted and snaked upward, over ravines and chasms, till it reached the Small Crossroads station. A few passengers got off there, scattering to different boardinghouses and the sanatorium. But a group remained, waiting to travel even higher. Naftali Hertz waited, too, apart from the others. He thought about the students with whom he'd visited this very same place, years ago. He couldn't remember what they'd spoken about, nor their faces, but he could still hear their happy, youthful laughter; it seemed to have frozen in the icy air, hovering there, and now rang out anew in honor of his return. All those students—boys and girls—had gone back to their homes. Some had hurled themselves into the chaos of the Russian Revolution, and others had become doctors, engineers, chemists, or teachers in the new Poland. Naftali Hertz himself had cleverly hidden in Switzerland, away from the half-destroyed postwar world. The tram's cogwheels turned, bringing him closer to his stop, and he was glad to be torn from his thoughts.

As the funicular moved upward on its heavy iron chains, an identical tram headed downward on the opposite track. With each passing moment, the enormous, jutting boulders looked bigger and bigger, and Naftali Hertz was overcome by a sense of awe, as if they'd come upon a remarkable temple with extraordinary stone statues. The tram shuddered to a stop at the Jungfraujoch station, interrupting Naftali Hertz's wonder. He entered the hotel, only to discover that the Jungfrau mountain climbers had left early in the morning and already returned. He would have to wait till the next day to find out whether there would be enough climbers for a trek with an experienced guide.

Pleased that his plan to climb to the mountain peak was still uncertain, and through no fault of his own, Katzenellenbogen retired to his rented room and ate some of the food he'd brought along in his rucksack. This put him in mind of his yeshiva years, in Visoki-Dvor, where he'd occasionally nibble on dry foods from a little package he kept in a box on his reading stand.

Later, Katzenellenbogen went down to the hotel lobby. From the buffet came sounds of laughter and clinking glasses. Some hotel guests spilled out of the restaurants and spread out among the sofas and plush chairs. Others stood in cliques, laughing, smoking, and chatting. Among this noisy group, Naftali Hertz noticed, were several tall girls, their hair cut short, wearing dark glasses, sweaters, and narrow trousers pulled tightly over their skimpy rears, their hipbones jutting out. It seemed to him that the girls were bending and twisting their bodies in a way intended to show the men their figures, the lines of their breasts and hips in their tight wool clothes. They spoke English in hoarse, smoky voices. The dark red of the polished furniture, reflecting the glow of the electric lamps, added to the intoxicating atmosphere. The tall, muscular men, wearing checked sportswear, laughed along with the women. But to Naftali Hertz the men's laughter sounded cold, mocking, as if they were doing only what was expected of them. Their minds, Naftali Hertz thought, were occupied with what would happen soon in their bedrooms, when, alone with the men, the women would strip their furry clothing from their dry bodies. He felt a sudden pang, as thoughts of his cold relationship with his wife arose in his mind. Lately, they never even touched. But he didn't want to think about that. Nor did he want to go on observing the couples. He went outside.

The Alps glowed in every shade of red. With her head outstretched on a snowy neck, lying on her mountainous back, the Jungfrau glittered in the copper sunset: a snow-filled river of brilliant sparks. Her breasts—the small and large silver horns, as they were called—shone forth, bathed in the rosy color of young brandy. The lower half of the Jungfrau's body, along with her rocky legs, dangled over the ravine. Resting atop her wooded stomach was the head of the mountain known as "the Black Mönch," as if he were suckling from her bare navel. Around the Jungfrau's head, neck, and hips, chunks of rock—Wildhorn, Nighthorn, Rothorn, and Wetterhorn—had congregated, all with glowing red faces, as if burning with romantic jealousy over the Black Mönch's nearness to the Jungfrau. Naftali Hertz hadn't witnessed such desire for a woman's flesh in a long time. And such an extraordinary conflagration of colors! He hadn't seen that of late, either. The towers and pillars of stone resembled the heads of owls, winged lions, and chimeras. Soon, the rocky camp was transformed into demons from hell surrounding the Lilith of the mountains: the Jungfrau. And in no time, the flaming red grew dim and began to flicker out.

Absorbed by the boulders—which had crystallized into gigantic figures with faces sliced in two, one half still lit by the sunset, the other already shrouded in darkness—Naftali Hertz failed to notice that a storm was brewing. The ravines filled with clouds, wrapping and rolling themselves into balls. Only when a crack of thunder exploded did he wake from his trance. The cracks became stronger and more frequent. Each clap blasted into the low-lying villages and echoed back up into the atmosphere, the echoes multiplying as if the carved, twisting steps in the boulders had broken, scattering a hurricane of rocks. Deafened, Naftali Hertz stood beneath the awning of the hotel entryway, happy as a little boy that the storm was drenching only the valleys beneath him, not the mountains above. He stood at the hotel's entrance for a long while, until the storm gave out and the full moon peeked between the boulders. The icy moon, he fancied, was just as surprised to see his long, bluish shadow as he was: What *was* he doing here? And with the same reverence his father displayed by walking backward out of a beis medrash, in order not to take his eyes off the holy ark, Naftali Hertz walked backward from the gloaming into the hotel.

He lay with eyes closed in his wide, wooden bed, beneath two puffy comforters. As if his mind were a mirror, he saw the room's furniture reflected in it. At one wall: the tall armoire with ornamental carvings on its two doors. At another: a long bench on which sat a water pitcher and a basin. In the center of the room was a heavy, rectangular table surrounded by chairs, and above it hung an electric lamp surrounded by a thick, round lampshade. Naftali Hertz couldn't understand why these furniture pieces, so typical of a hotel room, had become so deeply etched in his mind that he was seeing them through his eyelids, as if they were souls in disguise. He shivered beneath the comforter, from cold and from a strange dread of the silvery, supernatural silence outside. He heard the silence of the mountains and the boulders, all sunken in a rocky trance. They were trying to remember something, trying to remember whether they'd been standing here since forever or had been created in a single day, as it was written: "In the beginning God created . . ." Eyes shut, Naftali Hertz felt the moon still hovering in the window, smirking at him—son of the Morehdalye rabbi, a scholar, climber of the Alps.

His breath caught. Suddenly, he saw his wife and son hiking along a narrow, twisted path on the Jungfrau. Though both were far away, and had their backs to him, he saw them as clearly as daylight. Annelyse was taller than usual, and the farther down the mountain she went, the taller she grew. Her bent back and sluggish pace suggested just how long she'd been plodding down this dangerous path. Their fifteen-year-old, Karl, too—you could tell by his crawl—was exhausted by the hike. His big, hefty rear end, which Naftali Hertz despised because to him it epitomized his son's non-Jewishness, was just as hefty in the dream, and even in his dream Naftali Hertz despised him. The heads of giants, with overgrown faces and long foreheads, drifted from ice-covered caves high in the mountains. Naftali Hertz recognized them: they were his wife's brothers. Why had they fled the city and come up to the mountain caves? Out of shame, most likely, that their sister had married an unfriendly foreigner and a Jew, at that.

The moon hid inside a cloud, and a thick darkness seeped into the hotel room. The electric lamp on the ceiling began to glow through its shade, a dark red flame. And with every blink of Naftali Hertz's eye, it blazed more intensely—but with the sort of austere, melancholy glow of a religious icon burning above an abandoned tomb, somewhere deep inside a cave. Gradually, above the hotel room table, two pale faces shimmered into existence—the Morehdalye rabbi and his wife. Father and Mother turned their heads this way and that, gaping at each other, terrified at where their son had led them. Naftali Hertz wanted to cry out, "It's not like I'm a convert! True, my wife didn't become a Jew and my son isn't circumcised, but I never converted, and I never got married in a church!" He screamed these words in his own head but couldn't say them aloud. It was as if his tongue were stuck to frozen metal. He began to wheeze and wave his hands about, and with each motion a new human shadow appeared in the room, until a mass of figures filled the table.

Naftali Hertz recognized friends from his youth, young men from his yeshiva in Visoki-Dvor. Some of those men had bearded, pious faces now; others were already clean-shaven. A hunger burned in their eyes, and every gesture betrayed their desire for the pleasures of this world. The men didn't notice that the Morehdalye rabbi and rebbetzin were sitting at the same table, and the old couple didn't notice the men either. But Naftali Hertz saw them all, and his heart sank: Had something happened to his parents? He hadn't been back home since his sister Tilza's wedding in 1920. That had been the first and only time he'd visited his parents after the war. Since then, for twelve years, he'd hidden away in the Swiss mountains, until his family eventually stopped sending letters. A cold shudder coursed through Naftali Hertz's spine and spread to his elbows, like a bolt of lightning that forks into leaden clouds and burns out in a flash. His parents and the yeshiva boys vanished, and in a twinkling the room filled with dwarves. Their jaundiced, wrinkled faces smiled cheerfully and innocently. Through glassy eyes, they looked about them like puppets. They were the mountain elves found in the villages of the Alps, Naftali Hertz knew. More and more of them kept popping up, and they drew ever closer to him. Their smiles looked evil to him, cunning and mocking. They were aware of his trembling, both from revulsion and from the fear that they might ensnare him in their webs like a spider, pin him there with their spit before setting upon him, biting, ripping, and gobbling him up. Naftali Hertz awoke in a cold sweat. Through his window, the mass of the Jungfrau shone silver.

At nine the next morning, he was already in the funicular heading down the back of the Jungfraujoch to Kleine Scheidegg. In the car with him were the same English-speaking guests who'd ascended the mountain the day before and whom Naftali Hertz had seen chatting in the hotel in the evening. The long, slim women in wool sweaters and tight pants yawned and stretched with a feline indolence. Against the blinding sunrise, they squinted their eyes still blurred with sleep. And they kept touching the back of their close-cropped hair, as if to assure themselves that, though they were enjoying the same freedoms as men, they were, after all, still women. Their escorts sat silently in their plaid suits, their faces tanned and disappointed. They furrowed their brows for no reason and looked about them with eyes that said nothing, peeved on account of their headaches, their hangovers from last night's drinking. They were exhausted and bored from spending the night with masculine women. Only when they crossed paths with the other funicular heading up the mountain did they break their stupor, dashing over to the windows to gawk at the passengers in the opposite car. Naftali Hertz saw it all through opaque, indifferent eyes. His hotel nightmare had erased even his desire to watch the sun rise over dawn's snowy mountains.

Annelyse greeted her husband lovingly, to mask her displeasure at his early return. "Hertz'ke" pretended not to notice, joking that he must have rented a room where a former guest had left a cloud of unfulfilled fantasies, or rather an unscrewed tank of gas, which had made him sick in the head. He now revealed to his wife that he'd been planning to join a party of mountain climbers to scale the Jungfrau peak, but after a night of shaking with a fever and chills was forced to abandon his plan. Instead, he'd paid for his room after breakfast and told the hotel owner, "I can't stay and wait for another group of mountain climbers because I'm running a temperature. But I'll gladly buy the Jungfrau from you to place on my writing table. I have a large house and a writing table on which I can fit a statuette of a mountain over thirteen thousand feet high. And do you know what the owner answered me?"

"What?" Annelyse asked, looking at him coldly. She could tell by his tone and cruel smile that he was about to make a nasty comment about Switzerland, as he was prone to do of late.

"The hotel owner answered that if the Jungfrau were sold, tourists wouldn't come anymore and the hotels would be empty. He was talking business, when what I expected him to say was 'Switzerland wouldn't part with its scenery for all the money in the world.'"

"Of course Switzerland wouldn't part with its wonderful scenery for all the money in the world. But the owner could tell from your words that you were no friend to our country. He spoke to you exactly the way you spoke to him. And it's true you're not a friend to our country. You haven't even made the effort to become a Swiss citizen."

"All that proves is the attitude the Swiss have toward foreigners. Even though I went to university here, even though I have a wife and son born here, and I work in a library here, I still can't become a citizen unless I make loads of money for this country; that means clout, connections, and wealth. That's the main requirement: put a heap of money in the local banks, and only then can I attain the privilege of becoming a Swiss citizen," Katzenellenbogen mocked, and his malicious smile, more so than his words, expressed the hatred that had grown between husband and wife.

2

W HEN KATZENELLENBOGEN ENROLLED in Bern's philosophy
department, there was a group of Russians there studying—
or rather, creating a racket. To them, Switzerland was a hotel; they
had no connection with its citizens. And if they mentioned them at
all, their comments were derogatory. For example, "The Swiss have
narrow horizons because the Alps block the sky—narrow-minded,
narrow-hearted, and money-hungry." This was before the war, and
the Russian-Jewish students' group was seething with debates, like
a stovetop filled with simmering pots. They debated whether Jews
in tsarist Russia should enter the current of the coming Russian
Revolution and submerge themselves, or whether they should fight
against it.

In the meantime, these students went boating on the lakes in
Zurich, Geneva, and Lucerne, singing the nostalgic "Volga, Volga,
the Ballad of Stenka Razin" and the even more heartfelt "Down the
Mother-Volga River!" They liked to boat on moonlit nights and
dream, romanticize, and sigh in the Russian manner. But Naftali
Hertz couldn't figure out what connection the Jewish students from
Minsk and the female students from Kovno had to the brigand leader
Stenka Razin and why his highwaymen were so beloved in Russian
songs. So he sought out another group, the nationalists. There, the
debates were about whether the Jewish population should live among
other nations or in their own country. Again Naftali Hertz failed to
understand. If you weren't a devout Jew, why not become part of
the international collective of nations and races? There were already
entire communities in western Europe composed of people who
were born Jewish but belonged to the community at large, he argued.
His opponents, however, replied that just as there were no generic
plants or animals, only specific ones, you couldn't have a community

of generic people. In fact, those Jews, the supposed "global citizens" who believed they were welcome guests in every corner, would live to discover they were exiles everywhere, like weeds in a garden. Others replied even more snidely to Naftali Hertz: "You're a former yeshiva boy, so you think the only way to be a good Jew is to sit around in a beis medrash. You think that anyone who's left the yeshiva has left the Jewish nation."

In the clubs and associations that the Jewish student body belonged to, the bony, unfriendly Katzenellenbogen, with his narrow shoulders and high cheekbones, was not a valued member. They considered him too clever, too prickly, like the stubble in the creases of his unshaved face. It wasn't like in the early Haskalah years. Jewish students were no longer enchanted by yeshiva boys who yearned for a secular education. And for his part, Naftali Hertz wasn't drawn to the Jewish students either, especially not the girls, with their thick legs and high breasts, their round faces like fresh buns and shrill, provincial accents in every language. Had he fled his country and yeshiva and come to Switzerland only to attach himself to a hometown girl?

Because he'd abandoned the yeshiva, and because of the manner in which he'd done it, he couldn't expect any help from his father. But ironically, the very things he'd escaped—his rabbinical pedigree and the Talmud—were what helped him sustain his life in Switzerland and pay his university tuition. In honor of his scholarly father, Bern's Jewish community supported him with their fund for religious students. Occasionally, a wealthy Jewish student would also take a Talmud lesson from him, either out of curiosity or out of boredom. But his main income came from a Jewish watch company owner, Emanuel Noifeld, who was originally from Poland. On Friday nights, Naftali Hertz would eat at Noifeld's home, and during the week he was in charge of the factory's Yiddish and Russian correspondence with Russian buyers. When Naftali Hertz made kiddush in Emanuel's home, on Friday nights, reciting it in his father's melody with a yarmulke perched on the edge of his head, Emanuel beamed and his wife's eyes brimmed with tears. Even their two daughters, who were estranged from Judaism, would wear pious expressions for a brief moment. Naftali Hertz, the son of a rabbi and a philosophy student, was pained: What was the point of rejecting the Gemara if he stayed stuck in a Jewish environment anyway? But he earned his living through the Noifields and he couldn't alienate them. Instead, he distanced himself from the religious student body. And the more trips he took to the mountains, the more he questioned himself: *Why should I care more about the Berezina in Belarus and the Dnieper in Ukraine than the blue-green lakes of the Alps?* He felt no love for the Jordan River either. The Rhône River, flowing from glaciers, snaking through and encircling the Swiss lowlands, was incomparably wider and prettier than Palestine's Jordan or his native Narev, whose filthy waters, come springtime, spilled over the shores of Morehdalye.

Whether because he couldn't bear to cut himself off entirely, or because he wanted to justify himself in his own eyes, Naftali Hertz still occasionally attended the Nationalists' gatherings. He sat in a corner, listening in on the discussions. But he had to bite his lip to hide his sneers at the blabbering students and their muddled pronounce-ments. *Who in the world would heed their decision that Palestine must be given to the Jews?* In the evenings, when he went to the beer hall and observed the Jewish university students drowning out the pub with their debates, he felt embarrassed in front of the tranquil Swiss, who sat at their tables calmly sipping their beers, talking warmly with one another, quietly humming folk songs. Even his Jewish colleagues in the history and philosophy departments—instead of organizing sym-posiums about God and the universe, or about whether the cosmos was finite or infinite, about spirit and matter, about whether a per-son had free will or not, or on Hegel's philosophy on history and the history of philosophy—were ever absorbed in the same shouting matches about Jews and non-Jews, and about whether the revolution would free the Jews, too, or whether the Jews would have to lead their own revolution. He felt more affinity for the yeshiva boys who quibbled over the intricacies of the Bible.

At around that time, he'd befriended Annelyse Müller. She worked in a bank and audited lectures on history and philosophy at the university. She'd inherited an interest in these subjects from her late father, a pastor and theologian, though she herself was no longer a practicing Christian. When Katzenellenbogen told her he was a rabbi's son, she burst into laughter. "So, we're 'conversion' relatives!" Whatever Naftali Hertz said, Annelyse responded with a loving glance, a smile. She agreed with him on every topic. They even looked good together: he tall, narrow, bony; she as tall as he, not heavy, with a head of thick chestnut hair, a thin nose, and a wide mouth with chalky lips. She had small, taut breasts; strong, masculine arms; and svelte legs with such rounded knees they aroused all men, even a Katzenellenbogen who was no great connoisseur of women's legs.

Annelyse told her new friend, Naftali Hertz, that she had four brothers. The three older ones were merchants, and the youngest was a pastor. She brought Naftali Hertz—the "Russian"—to her family's home, an old-fashioned, Swiss-style two-story house, wooden, with a carved balcony above its rectangular windows and beams protruding beneath its sloping shingle roof. Inside the house it was always quiet, tidy, and dark, even in the middle of the day. The wide, bowed cupboards and shelves, on which hand-painted dishes were displayed, gave off the scent of pine and nut trees. Big wooden beds, piled high with pillows and comforters, sighed in tired repose. The heavy table and caned chairs bore witness to a life of true comfort and fullness. For a long while, the image of one wall in particular would remain lodged in Katzenellenbogen's mind. This wall was covered entirely in copper flags that sparkled coldly and covertly with the glow of congealed sunsets. And one other detail engraved itself in his memory: the impression of his first meeting with Annelyse's mother—an old, stooped woman with a head of white hair, her face dried out and full of wrinkles, her arms long and veiny. She was like a bent tree, its branches sagging toward the earth. She looked sinister to him, the silent old woman, like the witch of Alpine legend. But so loyally and trustingly did Annelyse smile at him, it was like she'd dreamed of having such a husband since childhood.

He was already twenty-two when he became friends with Annelyse. And though their friendship grew, he didn't dare touch her, growing feverish with lust. The yeshiva he'd fled four years ago had burrowed inside of him. He was terrified of the Jewish student group finding out about his love for a Christian girl, terrified that this information might reach his parents in the shtetl. The more he desired Annelyse, the more clearly and frequently he saw his father in his sleep—and even when awake. His father with lips menacingly sealed, eyes piercing his glasses like the electric beams of a locomotive in the darkness.

Naftali Hertz received letters only from his mother. She kept writing him about his father's heartache and shame, how he couldn't show his face in front of the townspeople. Everyone knew that their son had run away from yeshiva. It was why his father refused to support him. He claimed that supporting a son who had so disgraced God's name was akin to helping him perform idolatry.

But once talk of war started up, and the newspapers kept announcing that war was imminent, Naftali Hertz realized that no matter what his father thought or said, he hadn't yet given up on him, the son who'd run away. They considered it a miracle, his mother and father wrote, that Naftali Hertz happened to be in a peaceful country at this time, one that wasn't engulfed in the fires of war. In fact, however, Naftali Hertz was already thinking about staying forever, even in peacetime, staying far away from the country rife with Cossack whips and pogroms.

War broke out, and in its chaos, which cut neutral Switzerland off from the warring countries like the moon from the earth, Naftali Hertz was relieved of the fear that his father would discover his love. He fell upon Annelyse Müller with the thirst of the desert wanderers upon the daughters of Moab. And when the large, strong Annelyse undulated beneath him, he—intoxicated by lust—remembered the biblical story of Phinehas, the zealous High Priest who drove a single spear through both a Jew and the gentile woman he was sinning with. Remembering this made him even more lustful: the thrill of rebelliousness, the demonic pleasure of the forbidden.

There were many other students, including political immigrants from Russia, who didn't regret the war either. Openly they wished defeat on the Tsarist regime. Others, however, became fervid Russian patriots. Katzenellenbogen couldn't empathize with these Jews; they were shilling for Tsarist Russia with the same ardor with which nations hated each other, and with which all of them together hated the Jews. How placidly and quietly the Germans, French, and Italians lived alongside each other in Switzerland! The longer he lived in Bern, the more he loved the sedate, corpulent, hardworking residents of Switzerland's German district. He adored the peasant who led horse and plow over sloping, sparse fields. He observed with what geniality and affection the residents of a small town assembled on a Sunday at their town hall to vote on a local matter. He envied the serenity of the mountain shepherds blowing into their alphorns as they gathered their flocks of cows, heavy bells hanging from their necks. Why should he live a harried life in a mud-splattered, Russian-Polish-Jewish shtetl when he could be a professor in such a free and beautiful country? First he would wrap up his dissertation on the Jewish roots of Spinoza's philosophy. Then he would write a comprehensive work on the same theme.

Naftali Hertz's acquaintances in the Jewish student group claimed he had no sense of allegiance, nor an eye for a landscape's color, which was why he didn't appreciate the scenery of his native country. In truth, he *did* have a sense and an eye for color, even for the aura of each individual landscape. But he saw no beauty in the weeping willows by his father's ramshackle house nor in his hometown's filthy marketplace. Everything turned filthy there, even the tall green poplars and the white church on the mountain. No comparison at all to Locarno and Ascona in the Italian region of Switzerland! Here, the palm trees grew tall and green around the lakes; a golden sun sparkled above the snow-covered mountains. Where else could you see such regal splendor as in Waldstatt? Where else could you see Mount Pilatus reflected in its waters?

Annelyse would listen with pleasure to his awed tone when he spoke of the towns, castles, and towers on the shores of the Geneva river. She never demanded that he convert to Christianity, nor did she press for a civil wedding ceremony. Naftali Hertz hadn't yet gotten to know her brothers, and her old mother either didn't, or pretended not to, understand what happened when Naftali Hertz was alone with her daughter. At the beginning of their friendship, it made Annelyse upset that he kept her a secret from his Jewish friends. But once they became intimate, she no longer cared, especially because he'd decided to become a lodger at her family's home, paying for room and board.

He'd been living at her house for a few months, and yet her brothers still hadn't made an appearance. In fact, she rarely mentioned them. Naftali Hertz was beginning to think he'd be able to live at Frau Müller's house without anyone, even the Noifelds, finding out. He was thrilled to have Annalyse as a lover. A tall, svelte Swiss girl who gazed romantically into his eyes, and no need to be involved with her family? It was a perfect arrangement.

But one wintry evening, all four brothers showed up at once. The three older ones, the merchants, were shorter than their sister, broad-shouldered, heavyset, with full, rosy faces, their small blue eyes set deeply into their large heads covered in closely shorn bristles. They sat at the table with their sister and "Herr Katzenellenbogen," gabbing idly. But the youngest of the four brothers, the pastor, never even approached the table. He remained standing at the fireplace, near his mother. The old, stooped woman was silent now, as usual. But Naftali Hertz heard her complaints in her youngest son's words. He was taller than his brothers, with a head of thick, silver hair. His face was smooth and rosy, and his long neck was squeezed into a stiff white collar. He spoke little; only for a minute did he remove the short pipe from the corner of his mouth. "Annelyse," he explained to Naftali Hertz, "is the daughter and sister of Swiss ministers. But nevertheless, she's always enjoyed the company of atheists and foreigners. Ordinarily, our family would never have allowed Annelyse to marry a foreigner. But since the neighbors already know and indeed speak openly about it—'Fräulein Müller has taken in a Jew and is intimate with him,' they say—the two of you must become legal husband and wife immediately."

Naftali Hertz was happy that he could get married in a civil ceremony and wouldn't have to convert. He capitulated not only because of his fear of the Müller brothers, but also because he himself felt guilty and embarrassed by his thoughtlessness.

After their wedding, however, Annelyse's readiness to fulfill his every demand lost its appeal. Her submissiveness no longer aroused dark, erotic excitement in him. Annelyse felt the change. She asked, "What were you counting on? A secret love affair our whole life? Or did you plan on sending me away after some time had passed? I never asked my mother or brothers' permission to be intimate with you, but I expected nothing other than to become your wife. After all, you were always going on about a future civilization that didn't segregate by nation or religion. That's why I trusted you. Especially because you come from Russia, where so many nations suffer because of the wild misconceptions and opinions people have about them. Was all of this just talk? Did you mean none of it?"

3

Dᴜʀɪɴɢ ᴛʜᴏsᴇ ᴅᴀʏs when Naftali Hertz was still a believer
in the goodness of the hardworking Swiss, one of his fellow
students—not a Swiss citizen—told him that once, while traveling
through the country, he'd stopped in a village and asked a peasant
woman for a drink of water. In response, the woman pointed to a
lake. "Drink as much as you want," she told him. Naftali Hertz had
accused the student of lying, and the boy let out a burst of scornful
laughter and walked away.

But after he married Annelyse, Naftali Hertz himself began to
notice certain things. Street signs, for example, declaring that begging is prohibited. These warnings pierced his eyes, and he wondered
why he hadn't seen them earlier. Another law held that any unem-
ployed foreigners must have enough of their own money to support
themselves, or else they'd be arrested and deported. What shocked
him was that even Annelyse saw no injustice in these Sodomite laws.
"Otherwise, our country will become flooded with lazybones from
abroad," she argued.

That he could see and hear everything so differently now was a
revelation to him. He recalled that once, right after he'd arrived in
Switzerland, still a mere eighteen years old, gawking at everything,
he'd taken a trip to the mountains of Davos and stayed overnight in
a little hotel. Nothing in particular had happened. But all through
the night a large star shone over the snowy mountains across from
the hotel. *I've never seen such large, green-frosted stars*, he'd thought.
Each mountain was different from the next, and each had its own
star, much like what his father believed about each person having
their own angel in heaven. How happy he had been that night, to
be in such a remarkably beautiful country—where, it seemed, an
eternal Shabbos spirit reigned over the landscape. He realized now

that he'd been deceived. The green twinkling star over the Davos, the red Alps-roses blooming in the snow on the Gotthard mountain pass, the Wilhelm Tell monument in Lucerne, and the monuments to religious reformers in Geneva and Basel—they had misled him, distracted him from seeing the Swiss as they truly were. Just because a country's scenery was wonderful, why should it mean that its people were the same? The Swiss had lost nothing; on the contrary, they'd gained plenty by their country being a safe haven for the committee headquarters of various political emigrants and revolutionaries. The Swiss themselves weren't revolutionaries, nor dreamers, nor idealists. They were good businessmen. Certainly, there were many sincere businessmen and good-natured people among them. But others were dull, brutal, or mercenary, without the slightest empathy for the needy.

And he—had he wanted anything more for himself than to settle down and have a peaceful life? He used to fantasize about starting out as an assistant and then becoming a full professor of philosophy in a Swiss university. But after he'd completed his doctorate, he'd only held lectures on "logic" for a single semester, as a substitute for a professor who'd taken a sabbatical one winter. He was always imagining that his students considered him a joke, partly because of his bad accent, partly because *he* considered himself a joke. He read studies on logic and tried to read the logic of his own life in his listeners' eyes. Had it been worth it? What had he accomplished? He had only one excuse for himself: other foreigners with doctorates were also trying to find a foothold on a university chair in neutral Switzerland, or if not a full chair, at least a single leg of a professorial lectern, the way a group who'd capsized might cling to the overturned boat.

After much effort, he secured a position in the Judaica division of a library in Bern. Aida, the oldest daughter of the Noifeld family, had gotten him the job. Naftali Hertz was no longer working as the firm's Yiddish and Russian communicator, given that orders from Jewish watch merchants in Russia had stopped coming in during the war. The Noifeld factory owner was no longer alive. If he were, he'd never have allowed his daughter to do favors for, and remain friendly with, the rabbi's son—who'd managed his firm's correspondence, made kiddush at his house Friday nights, and then gone off and married a gentile. As it turned out, just as Naftali Hertz couldn't prevent his marriage to Annelyse, he couldn't prevent the Jewish community in Bern from finding out about it.

The year he completed his doctoral dissertation, his wife gave birth to a child. Annelyse didn't demand that the child be baptized, but she also didn't allow him to be circumcised. And she couldn't understand why this brought her husband such torment. He wasn't religious, after all, and he was a worldly man. Why would he want his son to be snipped?

Naftali Hertz was even more tormented by his own narrow-hearted cowardliness. The entire world was yearning for peace, and meanwhile he dreaded the day the war would end and the borders would open up again. Karl's grandfather, the Morehdalye rabbi, and his great-grandfather, the Zembin rabbi, would certainly want to see their grandchild . . .

Annelyse's mother had still been alive then, and when she warmed herself by the coals during the winter, her long, skinny hands gripping the frame of the fireplace, it seemed to her Jewish son-in-law that she resembled a giant spider, the queen of spiders, undaunted by fire. She and her son-in-law still tacitly hated each other. Occasionally, though, Naftali Hertz would think that he himself was the only one to blame. Frau Müller and her sons were decent people, but why should they like him? They knew he'd married Annelyse only at their demand, and never came along with her when she visited them.

And then, to further aggravate things, he and his wife had started fighting over an issue neither had foreseen: home maintenance. A big old wooden house like theirs, with a garden and shed in the yard for wood, food, tools, and utensils, required an owner who was at least a little handy. Annelyse couldn't grasp why her husband didn't know how to trim the trees in the garden. Why couldn't he fix the roof shingles? "Hertz'ke" explained to her that, where he came from, Jewish clergy didn't do this sort of work, and because he hailed from a long line of rabbis, he lacked the innate abilities and experience of working with his hands. But Annelyse argued that her brothers were sons of a clergyman, too, and yet they were able to do all kinds of work around the house. Her youngest brother, the pastor, had added a wing to his home all by himself, and he owned goats, ducks, hens, and a cow. Yet Naftali Hertz wouldn't even *touch* the cat in their house. "I've noticed you have some sort of aversion to live creatures. Was there no dog in your father's house?"

Naftali Hertz burst out laughing. Indeed! A rabbi with a dog!

Annelyse also accused him of having no regard for the Swiss life-style and her parents' inheritance. A chair once broke, a chair with a backrest shaped like a wheel. She was furious that her husband couldn't fix it, but he was even angrier. "You say this chair is pre-cious to you because your grandmother sat on it? Sorry, I did not renounce my father's and grandfather's heritage to idolize a rustic chair in Switzerland."

Annelyse's mother died a month after the war ended, and Naftali Hertz sent his hatred for her along to the next world, too. He could never cast off his half-crazed suspicion that the old witch understood, far more than her daughter did, how scared he was that the war had ended and he could no longer hide from his parents. He felt her schadenfreude at this turn of events.

Gripped by dread, he wrote a long letter home, asked after everyone and everything, and concluded by saying he couldn't come home yet because his co-worker in the Judaica division of the library had quit his job, forcing him to do the work of two people. To his father he wrote in Hebrew, asking him not to harbor old grudges. To his mother he wrote in Yiddish, and sent along two hundred francs he'd borrowed from the bank against his salary, so that Annelyse wouldn't know of it. He'd used his office at the library as a return address.

His parents replied immediately. His father's letter was short, in a rabbinic Hebrew but without stylistic flourishes. He wrote that the family, thank God, was healthy; he was surprised Naftali Hertz hadn't married yet, which he inferred from his not mentioning a wife and children; and he hoped that his oldest son hadn't forgotten Juda-ism and, at the very least, still put on tefillin every day. His mother wrote a long letter in Yiddish, and by what she'd written, Naftali Hertz gathered that his mother had become extremely pious. In the past, she had been the enlightened one in the house; now, she didn't scribble a sentence without a "Praise God." His mother wrote him about herself, his father, his brothers and sisters, his uncles and aunts. Then she thanked him for the two hundred francs he'd sent. A for-tune for them! Morehdalye had become very impoverished during the war and couldn't pay the rabbi even the paltry salary that the community had designated for him, based on the new zloty currency. As for his not marrying yet, his mother hesitated a lot longer than his father, and asked, "In this city where you live, is there no Jewish girl to your liking? She could be educated *and* devout, no?" At the end of the letter, his mother wanted to know when he was returning home. "It's not possible," she wrote, "that you can't get away from your job to come see your family. Here at home, you'll be able to find a suitable match. Plenty of fine, wealthy girls would be eager to have you."

Oh, what he would give to be able to sit in the old Morehdalye house! But could he ever place such a burden on his father and mother as he looked them in the eye? No, he couldn't do it. And once again, Naftali Hertz sent home money.

This time, he borrowed the money from Aida Noifeld. Aida had always thought that, had she shown more interest in this Katzen-ellenbogen while he worked for her father, he wouldn't have fallen into Annelyse Müller's hands and she might not now be husbandless. It was why she was always ready to help him, especially when he confided in her that his parents would drop dead if they found out he'd married a gentile.

Eventually, Naftali Hertz realized he wouldn't be able to hide these secret envelopes from his wife forever. So he told her. And she promptly replied that she was fine with it. "But why don't you invite your parents to visit us, or you and me and Karl can go visit them?"

Naftali Hertz didn't know whether to laugh or cry. He said, "Do you truly have as little sense as your words suggest? What a picture it would make: me and my Christian wife and son arriving as guests to my father, the Orthodox rabbi, and his pious community!"

"Well, do you plan to hide me and Karl from your parents forever?" Annelyse asked calmly.

"Yes, I have to hide it forever, because it could kill them. Before Bern and all of Switzerland, though, you're my wife and Karl is our son."

"You're mistaken," Annelyse continued in the same calm tone. "Not for a single day do my family and friends forget that you're a foreigner and a Jew. Still, had I known this would make our lives so complicated, I would have converted to Judaism before we got married and Karl would have been born a Jew."

"There you are mistaken." Naftali Hertz laughed bitterly. "Even if you'd converted and Karl was circumcised, my parents wouldn't have been happy. Such traditional Jews like my father and mother don't believe you can undo your Jewishness or Christianness with a ceremony. You're worlds apart, even if you sleep in one bed and go to one house of worship. Don't you get it?" But he saw on her face that she didn't and never would.

Naftali Hertz, on the other hand, who *did* know his family, knew how far he could take the lie. His sister Tilza got engaged, and they all expected him to attend the wedding. Two years had already passed since the war's end, and Naftali Hertz had no doubt that if he didn't come, his mother would travel the world by foot, if need be, and track him down. Tilza was the sibling closest to him in age, and Naftali Hertz had spent more time with her than the others. And after he'd set out into the world, he remembered her best and missed her most. When he'd left, she had been fourteen years old, plump, with a clear face, black braids, and big, dreamy eyes. Over her luscious lips grew sparse, moist little hairs, and physically she was so mature she could have passed for an eighteen- or twenty-year-old. At the same time, she radiated a childlike innocence, and his mother's letter hinted that Tilza had retained this innocence. Maybe that was why it had taken so much time to choose her bridegroom. Tilza was already twenty-four. His sweet sister! No way could he skip her wedding.

So Naftali Hertz went . . .

Twelve years had passed since he'd made the journey home, but those few days in Morehdalye still felt like a holiday in a dream, a sort of surreal, joyous occasion filled with movement and song. He still heard the sounds, still saw his family's heads in the distance, their expressions, the flapping of hands. Faces dear to his heart mingled with faces he'd never seen. And it was precisely this impression of vagueness that stayed with him, because he'd deliberately arrived in Morehdalye when it was nearly time to raise the chuppah and left just a few days later, in the middle of the week of festivities.

The wedding had taken place on the eighth day of the month of Adar, Friday evening, before candle-lighting, as was the custom. Even his mother had no time to fuss over him that day. She simply kissed him and shed a few tears, all worked up over seeing him alive after the war, home again at last. His aunts, his younger siblings, the bridegroom's parents, the community's men—all were speaking to him at once and none heard his replies over the racket. All through-out his visit, Naftali Hertz longed to take in his surroundings while others observed *him* as little as possible. But he barely succeeded in watching the bridegroom—a robust, redheaded young man with a friendly face, now looking befuddled and bashful. And Naftali Hertz knew why he looked bashful. His mother had let it be known that Tilza was marrying this boy at her father's behest, and Naftali Hertz could see it on Tilza's sad and troubled face. But this actually worked in his favor. Tilza was too fixated on herself to pepper him with ques-tions about his life in Switzerland. Grandma Elka'le, too, was occu-pied with the bride and groom before and after the chuppah; with the groom's mother, in the women's section of the shul, on Shabbos morning; and then, at the sheva brochos festivities Shabbos evening, she was busy in the kitchen, as well as with the groom's parents at the table. Only once did she flit by him, clutching a challah. "Next year, with God's help, at your wedding!" she told her educated grandson.

But his grandfather, the old rabbi of Zembin, singing and danc-ing more than all the young men, had not spoken a word to Naftali Hertz the entire time. His father, too, spared him only a few words. Which alerted him that the two were preparing for a long, angry dis-cussion, where they'd demand a reckoning of everything he'd done up to now and what he was planning for the future. But he'd already made a plan to avoid such a discussion.

In the meantime, he wanted to take in as many impressions as he could. Later, the image of his younger brother Bentzion would be etched in his memory—the way he wrinkled his forehead and pinched the fuzz on his cheek; the way he stared at Naftali Hertz, amazed that he'd been able to leave home and earn a degree without his father's permission. His younger sister, Bluma Rivtcha, already a thirteen-year-old young woman, squinted her narrow eyes at him and confided that their grandfather was preparing a dowry for her if she'd marry a Torah scholar, as Tilza had. But his youngest brother, ten-year-old Refael'ke, said nothing. He simply searched his oldest brother's eyes quizzically, as if foretelling something. For his part, Naftali Hertz stroked the cheeks of Refael'ke's fresh, round face, mar-veling that he had a brother who was a full eighteen years younger than him.

On Shabbos evening, when the sheva brochos meal was over and the crowd had dispersed, his parents and grandfather pounced, asking him when they'd be able to have a longer discussion. He rattled off the answer he'd prepared, and to this very day he couldn't believe his own audacity. "When I come for a longer visit—very soon, perhaps—I'll have time to discuss everything. But this time around, I'll already be gone by early Monday morning."

His father and grandfather were speechless. His mother began to cry. "After ten years apart, you come for two days?"

He cried, "But I wrote that I wouldn't be able to stay for more than a few days. If you count my travel time back and forth, it comes to ten or twelve days. Did I not tell you in advance about the antique books collection in London that I'm negotiating to buy for the Bern library? And that the asking price is so tremendous that the purchase will be shared by the Swiss government, the university, and the Jewish community? It's the collection of incunabula from an old Sephardic family. A treasure! It's already been shipped from London to Bern. I must return immediately, immediately! I have to be there for the unpacking of this treasure. It was bought through *my* negotiation."

"And why are you still an old bachelor? When will you get married?" His mother wiped her eyes.

"An old bachelor? I just recently turned twenty-eight. Yeah, yeah, I know that's an old bachelor in your world," he said, laughing. Well, how could he tell his parents and grandfather that he already had a goyish wife and a goyish three-year-old son? But then he solved the problem—just as he did with the loan he'd needed to send his parents money—by turning to Aida Noifeld.

"Actually," he said, "I already have a fräulein. I'm all but engaged to the oldest daughter of the factory owner where I work. The late Emanuel Noifeld made a fortune in Switzerland, but he remained a friendly, Polish Jew, and his widow was also a lovely, pious woman who observed Shabbos and kept kosher. The older of his two daughters is in charge of the business now, and she's ready to marry me. But she has a condition. She's insisting that I work in their business after the wedding, and I don't want to be a shopkeeper. I don't want to sit in an office; I'd rather sit over books and be a scholar and researcher."

And amid all his blundering chatter, he managed to distract his mother from her tears, his father and grandfather from their silences, and he left town, bidding goodbye to everyone in a rushed manner and promising he'd be back soon.

For a long time afterward, in every letter to them, he wrote about how busy he was cataloguing and writing abstracts for the newly purchased library collection. When the excuse had grown tiresome, he informed his parents that he'd finally married Aida Noifeld. Now he'd be occupied for quite a while in organizing their life together. Writing this, he well understood how pained his parents would be that they didn't know his bride and hadn't escorted him to the chuppah. Indeed, his mother sent a reply filled with complaints and tears, just as he'd anticipated. His father, however, wrote nothing—not even "mazel tov."

A year later, he wrote his parents announcing that his wife had had a baby boy. This time, his father responded with a short letter, expressing his hope that Naftali Hertz would raise his son "to Torah, to chuppah, and to good deeds." And this time it was his mother who—for the first time in her life!—didn't add a word to the letter.

It's better this way, Naftali Hertz thought. A cold, disloyal son doesn't make parents bury themselves in shame. But the truth could wreak such havoc on his parents' household that he, too, wouldn't be able to go on living. He couldn't turn back the wheel of his destiny. What he had to do, in fact, was stop writing his family.

Time passed, and Naftali Hertz sent no reply to their letter, until finally his parents realized their oldest son wanted nothing to do with them anymore. They, too, stopped writing. So passed one year after another. But the rabbi and rebbetzin had not forgotten their estranged forty-year-old son, nor their grandchild, already fifteen.

4

U PON HIS RETURN from the Bernese Oberland, Naftali Hertz found a letter from Poland waiting for him in his office. He turned deathly pale. It was as if his dream from the hotel had dispatched a note to remind him of the nightmare he'd had there. The letter was from his sister Tilza. Despite his status as the family pariah, she wrote, rarely mentioned in conversation, he was in their thoughts. None of them could understand how a person could alienate himself so thoroughly from his blood relatives. If he'd have spared her a thought when she was unmarried, instead of finding it sufficient to merely dance at her wedding, she would never have had an arranged marriage. Their younger brothers and sister, though, had managed to find a solution. Bentzion was nearly finished with his business courses in Bialystok. Bluma Rivtcha didn't let Father marry her off; she was studying at a nursing school in Vilna. And Refael'ke was in Vilna, too, in a kibbutz for chalutzim. But while the others were all busy with themselves, striving after various goals, they remained dedicated to one another. All except he, their eldest brother, who thought only of himself. "Father says my husband is a Torah whiz," Tilza went on, "and I feel that Yaakov Asher is refined, smart, and kind, but I still haven't gotten used to my role as a rebbetzin. I have a little boy—an angel. And a newborn girl—a doll. I'm not sure exactly when, but my husband is planning to travel to Amsterdam and London to collect money for the Lecheve Yeshiva. I want him to stop by Switzerland and see you, to ask how you're not ashamed that you haven't seen your family in so long. Our parents suffer more for you lately, because none of the children are home anymore. So come and visit them, and when you do, you'll probably want to see me and my children, too. Who knows how long Yaakov Asher will tarry?"

Often, whenever a longing for his parents, brothers, and sisters overwhelmed Naftali Hertz, all he had to do was glance at his son and his feelings of homesickness would halt. Even as a child, Karl's voice, the gleam in his eyes, his every twist and turn, his cry, his laugh, his mischief, seemed to Naftali Hertz those of a sheigetz, a goy who's the son of a goy. And the older Karl got, the more his father looked upon him as a malevolent marvel. The years went by, and his son grew up, developing broad shoulders, a large, fat face, and a happy demeanor. After he turned nine, his mother dressed him in little suits with shirts and ties. But Karl liked to run around with his shirt unbuttoned, his reddish hair astray on his sweaty forehead, laughing freely with big, strong teeth. He spoke a deep Swiss German, a Schweizerdeutsch that even his father found difficult to understand. Naftali Hertz would often observe his own tall figure in the mirror: the stooped, narrow shoulders of a man who devotes his time to religious studies in the synagogue; a bony, sharp-jawed face; and dark, prickly eyebrows over a gold pince-nez. He'd observe his gloomy face in the mirror and ask himself: *What connection do I have to the sheigetz growing up in my house?* With each year, Karl became more and more like his maternal uncles, and the alienation between Naftali Hertz and his son grew. Karl was fifteen already now, and just looking at him made Tilza's letter even more terrifying. He would respond to her immediately, he decided, and tell her in a few short lines that he didn't want to see her husband or anyone else from the family.

But because he couldn't think of a gentler way of saying it, he put the letter off. He couldn't be so heartless. And after all, Tilza hadn't written that her husband had agreed to come to Switzerland, only warned that she'd try to get him to do so. Her husband was going to slog around Amsterdam and London for a while, after which either he would come to Switzerland or he wouldn't.

From the day Naftali Hertz had received his sister's letter, he grew even more fond of solitude. He preferred nothing more than sitting and grumbling in the library's Judaica division, buried alive beneath books and holy texts about Jews and Judaism. Before the war, when Bern was still rife with international students and long-haired Hebrew poets, the reading hall rustled with the furtive sound of turning pages: books, periodicals, old newspapers, new publications. But since the war, Jewish students had stopped coming from Russia, which meant no more young men immersed in thick volumes, and the shelves of books lingered like partially effaced tombstones in a cemetery.

Still, every once in a while, the global director of a Jewish organization with headquarters in Geneva would come to the capital city to meet with a minister. After a short, productive discussion with a Swiss government official, this Jewish activist would have a little time left before his train back to Geneva. Gazing at the Mönch, Eiger, and Jungfrau had already become as boring as a bitter onion, so he'd stop in for a visit at the "empty tavern," as Naftali Hertz called the Judaica division, and amble around, hands folded behind him. He made such a visit now, and studied the Jewish encyclopedias in multiple languages behind the bowed glass cupboards, the Yiddish dictionaries and indexes, bound in black and brown leather with gold-leafed lettering. Afterward, the guest observed the large photographs on the walls, depicting the great rabbis of Switzerland, Germany, England, and France—long dead and forgotten, dressed in ceremonial garb. Some of them wore high, stiff collars; others had snow-white frills or bow ties, and all were dressed in long, black coats. They sported a variety of tall, wide yarmulkes—four-, six-, or eight-cornered—and various forms of trimmed beards—pointy, rounded, and orb-like.

The global director of the Jewish world's headquarters in Geneva (For Work and Health, for Jewish Politics Inside and Outside, National and International) had a pair of small whiskers, and when he smiled with his wide orator's mouth, they'd wander toward his ears and seem to hang themselves there like earrings. The global director paused in front of each photograph and painting, and then paused longest at the pictures of Zunz and Geiger, the towering scholars of the "Science of Judaism." He gazed at them with a scornful expression. "Why do these two have such long locks, like women and poets?" he wanted to ask. But there was no one to ask. The only person in the hall was a Dr. Katzenellenbogen—a grump, a werewolf, a sinister soul sitting behind his enclosure, not even lifting his eyes. Only when the curious guest had left did Naftali Hertz raise his head and breathe more lightly. Lately, he had begun to imagine that every person who walked in was bringing him regards from his parents or sister.

But time passed, and soon it was Naftali Hertz who wanted to escape his wife and son with a visit to his family in Poland. His morose silences permeated the entire house. Annelyse didn't laugh, Karl didn't play. Naftali Hertz felt that even when he went to work, he left a thick silence in his wake, for which his wife and son resented him. His menacing muteness lingered like shadows in the dark corners of the house, where no light could drive them away. In the end, he grew to hate himself. What did he actually want from his wife and son? Was it their fault he was so terrified that his father and mother would find out about his goyish family? Still, his dark mood continued to infect Annelyse. He felt she was suffocating, as if her throat were clogged with dry sand.

Until, unexpectedly, their home began to resound with Annelyse's laughter. As he left for work in the morning, her tittering trailed him; when he came back home, more chuckles. And it wasn't the kind of laughter that follows a joke. It was clear she was laughing out of sheer happiness; she was overjoyed. About what? Naftali Hertz wondered. He pressed Annelyse to tell him, but she pivoted away from him nimbly and coquettishly with her round, full behind and went on laughing, pleased with her secret. Then, she turned back to him, thirty-seven years old already but her face fresh and rosy, her puffy lips spread over her still-young teeth. Even when she wasn't laughing, her eyes smiled with a hidden glow of triumph and muted revenge.

Accustomed to a husband who couldn't fix anything around the house—unlike the other Swiss men—Annelyse had hired someone to rip off their faded wallpaper and replace it. The wallpaper installer— a tall, slim man, dark-haired and flighty, with twinkling eyes and a sweet, chatty mouth—was named Luigi Martini. He hailed from a village in the Ticino valley, in Switzerland's Italian region, and was an expert at his craft. He was also a storyteller, fond of cheerful tales of the heroic acts Sicilian gangs performed for the needy. Wearing a blue apron, perched on a small ladder, he whistled skillfully and sang arias from Italian operas under his breath as he worked. Annelyse helped him. She dawdled around the ladder and handed him rolls of wallpaper.

The man measured the walls, cut the wallpaper, and while he pasted it up, he mocked the tasteless décor in Switzerland's German region. Every house in the German cantons, he claimed, had black-checkered wallpaper on a brown or red background, like fresh-baked bricks just out of the factory. Or else they had wide, vertical stripes over a gray background, like a barred prison. "In a home with living people, the walls must call you to life. Gardens and golden peacocks amid green foliage, that's pretty wallpaper. In a kitchen, there should be aquariums filled with fish. The atmosphere in a guest room should feel very different, with a design of red roses, or blue and white lilies, or tulips and chrysanthemums."

Naftali Hertz tried to chase the bizarre thought away, but he couldn't help feeling that when the wallpaper man spoke, Annelyse stared at him with the same glazed, God-fearing expression with which Maria stared at Jesus on the cross. She would burst into sudden fits of laughter. You could tell it was out of joy that she was standing next to the wallpaper man, who prattled, whistled, and sang without pause. Even after he left, her laughter persisted. A coarse, robust laugh, sly and provocative, with outbursts of joy, as if her youth had returned and she were triumphantly reclaiming all her lost years with "Herr Rabiner."

Naftali Hertz left for work earlier in the morning so as to avoid bumping into the wallpaper man. On his way to the library, he'd think about Karl, who, like Annelyse, seemed to be eager for him— the grumpy outsider Jew—to leave already. He probably couldn't wait for the wallpaper man to come, to make their house brighter and happier. *He must be there by now,* Naftali Hertz thought, *and Karl must be looking at him as a man who could have been a good father. That Swiss Italian is probably having a bite, now, before he starts working.* Luigi Martini liked smoked fried fish. When he ate, he wielded his fork with such agility that the fish's white spine remained intact; not a single broken bone. Annelyse was enamored of his table manners. They were so much better than those of her husband, the doctor of philosophy.

To avoid having to greet anyone, Naftali Hertz hurried through the corridors with his head lowered. He reached his division and was glad to find the reading hall empty. No curious browsers had wandered in, so he wouldn't have to speak. He pushed away thoughts of his wife and the wallpaper man, and a new thought popped into his head: *Now would be the right time for me to return to my research on the Jewish sources of Spinoza's philosophy.* When he'd defended his doctoral dissertation on this very theme, he'd been convinced that it would develop into a great work one day. But instead of studying and writing more, he'd become grease-stained by the pig's lard of the gentile world he'd joined. Katzenellenbogen took his Spinoza manuscript out of his desk drawer and began to riffle through it. But he could barely understand what he was reading. He raised his head to the thick volumes of Jewish encyclopedias and the Pentateuch indexes lined up in the glass display cases, and they looked to him like turtles made of stone.

Naftali Hertz squeezed his eyes shut, straining to imagine what was happening in his house now: Karl must certainly have left for school. He was already a grown-up, already spending time with girls himself, so he presumably realized that his mother and Luigi wouldn't be content with just chatting. Karl had become so infected with his uncles' hatred of his father that he'd be glad his mother was spending time with another man.

Annelyse was alone with the Italian now; now she was laughing; now he'd pushed her toward the sofa and set her down on it. Her strong, long legs were still rooted to the floor, but her dress was tucked up above her knees. She wouldn't yet allow him to come too close, but neither did she shove him away. She wouldn't yet allow him to lift her dress up, but she let him observe, let him be enraptured by her hips and legs in hiked-up stockings. He was panting and she was laughing. No, he wouldn't be able to undress her by force. She was strong like a lioness and still wanted to tease him. Luigi Martini could marry her, of course; he had no wife. But to have a wallpaper man as a husband instead of a doctor of philosophy would bring her no honor. Nevertheless, she was willing to pass the time with him. But let him not think he could take her so easily. He buries his head in her bosom. Just look at how she lets him take out one of her big, round, cool breasts and hold it in his wide worker's palm. He buries his swinish mouth in it. She wants him to see that her breasts are still as firm as a young girl's. Soon, very soon, she'll brag about her strong ab muscles.

Naftali Hertz felt the veins in his temples swell up. Sweat dripped from his forehead onto his face. He removed his pince-nez to wipe off the perspiration, put it back on, and looked at the wall paintings of the scholars. Would they have been capable of writing great works if they'd fancied their wife was enjoying a lover? But no, they'd married their own kind and hadn't brought disaster upon themselves.

Katzenellenbogen turned to the window, hoping to gaze at the peaks of the Bernese Alps. He'd often look in that direction until the frozen mountainside penetrated his brain and froze his thoughts. But now the mountain peaks hovered there cloudily, like angered gods.

And where were things at, now, with his wife and Luigi? Was he still up on the ladder working, or was he already in bed with her? Naftali Hertz jerked toward the door, and in his mind, he was already sprinting through the roads back home. Faster! Faster! He could still make it before the two creatures coupled. He'd crack the wallpaper man's head!

But as soon as he reached the library exit, he began to back up, back through the reading hall. No, he hadn't inherited his father's strength and vigor, wasn't made for such scenes of passion. He couldn't do it. *And now she was discussing her husband with that libertine. Her husband, the Herr Rabiner. They were both laughing.*

Katzenellenbogen returned home late enough to avoid running into the worker. Annelyse's expression was serious, severe, instantly driving Naftali Hertz's suspicions away. The wallpaper man must surely have tried to get fresh with her, and she'd shown him his place. He felt a jolt of joy course through him, and his head felt lighter, his heart, his legs. But he tried hard not to show any change in his behavior, and during the meal he and his wife conversed as usual, like the regular ticking of two clocks. When a flushed Karl returned from the street, though, and said something to his mother that made her burst out laughing, Naftali Hertz felt his veins swell. In her laughter he detected sated desire, a contented woman laughing at her cuckold husband. It's odd, he thought. He felt no desire for Annelyse any-more; in the depths of his heart, he actually hated her. So why was he so insanely jealous? Also, he had to admit she had reason to betray him. Still, his mind reeled at the notion that she may have already done it or was planning to. Sitting in his armchair, perusing a news-paper, he asked, as if in passing, how much wallpapering the Italian had left to do.

"Well, he's a carpenter too," his wife replied, "so he'll have plenty of work to do for us. Don't forget, you can't fix any of the cupboards or doors, or the steps to the porch. Everything in this house has been neglected."

Naftali Hertz went on idly turning the pages of the newspaper.

He hid behind the large spreads, so that Annelyse wouldn't see his trembling face. *Is this what I'll be doing? Sitting in my library cave, day after day, shuddering at what's transpiring in my home?* An old, forgotten Hebrew verse sprang up in his consciousness: "God is right, for I have rebelled against Him." His father's congregants in Morehdalye must surely suspect his father of being a secret sinner; why else would his son run away and want nothing to do with him anymore? As for Annelyse, if she saw how he acted toward his parents, she'd be justified in betraying him and bringing a lover into their home. I'll write to Tilza immediately, he decided. Her husband doesn't have to come looking for me in Switzerland. I'll come see Father and Mother on my summer vacation, and I'll visit her, too.

Annelyse didn't seem surprised at her husband's unexpected decision to travel to Poland. She merely asked whether he had someone to step in for him at the library. "Anyone can replace me," he replied. "Lately, so few visitors have been coming to the Judaic division that there's nothing to worry about. Anyone can replace me," he repeated with a dark, meaningful smile. But Annelyse read nothing into his words, and she let him stare into the tranquil, green-blue depths of her eyes as into a deep, cool, bottomless lake.

5

FROM THE OUTSIDE, the Morehdalye rabbi's house had not changed. The Chanukah menorah, adorned with two lions, still stood in the window of the beis din room, facing out onto the street. Thick, leafy branches still dangled from the old willows. And the mossy, sloping roof had drooped lower over the windows, like an old man who's fallen asleep over his reading stand in the beis medrash, his yarmulke sinking over his eyes.

In the old days, when all the children were still living at home, there were times when the windows would stay shuttered until noon, signifying that the children were still asleep or that the family didn't want any visitors—so tiresome had living in a small town been for them. But since the children had dispersed, the windows remained unshuttered. In the daytime, the pale blue glimmer of the distant sky hovered on the windowpanes. At dusk, there twinkled the twilight gold, mixed with the greenish patina of a bronze candelabrum. And late in the evening, blackness lingered on the panes. Only a solitary strip of yellow light punctured the darkness, indicating that in a far back room the rabbi and rebbetzin were not yet asleep.

On this summer's morning, the rabbi hadn't yet returned from davening, and Henna'le was having a conversation with her son. Naftali Hertz sat on the sofa near the wall, his mother in an armchair beside him. Henna'le was wearing a navy dress, velvet and pleated, along with the big Shabbos sheitel she'd donned every day since her son had arrived. Not wanting to hurt his father, Naftali Hertz hadn't shaved in seven days, and in the mirror across from him he could see that a gray, prickly beard had formed on his skinny face. He observed the silver bunch of hair poking out beneath his hat and cracked the knuckles on his long fingers. "It's the middle of the day in Tammuz, but here in the room it's like sunset," he murmured, and then said loudly to his mother, "You used to have red radishes and green onions in your vegetable garden, and beets with wine-colored leaves, and young, red-skinned potatoes. Now the garden is overgrown with cabbage, thorns, and weeds. You used to have a stable with a cow. You churned your own butter and sour cream. Now you're not even raising chickens."

His mother shook her small head beneath her big, heavy sheitel. She smoothed the pleats of her dress with her thin fingers and bent forward in her seat to answer her son. "It's not on my mind anymore. These last few years, Father's been going around depressed about his children. Should I plant garden vegetables or keep a cow and churn butter? Have you considered what we've lived through at all? How much we thought about you? I still can't understand why you sent no word for such a long time, and Father doesn't understand it either." For a minute, the rebbetzin was gloomily silent, but then her wrinkled face lit up with a smile. "Son, when you talk to me, you yell like you're talking to a deaf person, an old woman." And for the thousandth time, she asked the same question: "Is she that busy, your wife, that she couldn't find a way to come with you?"

"Yes, Aida is that busy." And Naftali Hertz, for the thousandth time, repeated that his wife managed the entire office and the bookkeeping. She ordered parts for the watches from different factories and oversaw her own factory where the parts were assembled. She also dealt with companies overseas and with the tradesmen who came to Switzerland from other countries to buy materials. The more Naftali Hertz repeated the lie, the more sweat broke out on his forehead. He hadn't even gone to the Noifeld family to say goodbye before he'd left Bern. Now he had to shake them loose from his memory, like mothballs from winter clothes, and spout lies about a life with this woman when neither of the two had ever given serious thought to getting married.

"If your wife is so busy with such a big business, you must be a wealthy man. So why do you give off this air of sadness?" his mother asked.

Naftali Hertz strained to make his voice cheerful. "I'm not sad at all. I'm just lost in thought . . . Well, the truth is, I *am* sad. I always dreamed of finding Morehdalye the way I left it. Of course, I knew that in the war the Russians, Germans, Bolsheviks, and Poles were cavorting all over this place. But I hadn't imagined that so many townspeople would be gone. Entire streets of Jews! And, Mother, you might as well know the truth. I'm not as rich as you think. The watch factory also belongs to my mother-in-law and her younger daughter, Janet. Janet has been doing nothing for years, but she takes like it's all been handed to her."

"And why is your son named Karl?" Henna'le asked, not allowing him to change the subject with bogus stories about his mother-in-law and sister-in-law. "Is Karl a Jewish name?"

"Karl comes from Kalmen, my late father-in-law's name. Jews in other countries Christianize their names."

There were no children in the Noifeld family, so Naftali Hertz hadn't been able to think of another name fast enough. On further thought, he didn't want to betray his son's real name anyway, so he'd told his parents that the boy's name was Karl. But when he told the lie about his uncircumcised Karl being named after a grandfather Kalmen, he again felt sweat break out on his brow. The spots of light in the shadowy curtains jumped about as if they, too, were sneering, mocking him in a strange mute language for being such a miserable liar.

"And does she maintain a Jewish home, your wife? Does she keep kosher, Shabbos, family purity?" Henna'le continued to probe.

"I didn't say my wife observes kosher and Shabbos," he answered slowly, and patted the brown cover of the sofa he was sitting on. In fact, why hadn't his father asked him whether his wife was observant? Obviously, he suspected something . . . Naftali Hertz jerked up from the sofa. "I never said my wife was devout; I only said she was Jewish."

"Shh, shh, don't shout. Why are you shouting?" His mother cast him a confused look and pulled him by the sleeve till he sat back down on the sofa. "I'm not even asking if your wife is Jewish. Ha! What else would she be? A goy, God forbid?" Henna'le smiled, wrinkling her cheeks. "You, your father doesn't ask anything, but me, he keeps badgering to find out what kind of home you run. Don't you realize this?"

Good. His father wasn't suspicious, Naftali Hertz thought, and breathed easy. He took his hat off and wiped his forehead. "You know, Mother? I'm thinking about heading over to see Tilza tomorrow."

He wanted to say something else, but at that moment his mother stood up and put his hat back on his head.

"Father's coming. Don't sit with a bare head."

Sholem Shachne still walked with a straight back, his figure slim, but his beard had turned completely white. He was wearing his Shabbos jacket, a fresh, soft-collared shirt without a tie, a wide, bendable hat, and polished boots. He'd gone to a ceremony right after davening, for a man who'd betrothed his daughter to a Torah scholar from Radin. But instead of coming home in a good mood, cheered by the groom's words on the Torah and the whiskey and refreshments, he felt depressed that he hadn't garnered such nachas from his own family. He entered the house and paused, stopping beneath the photograph of his parents that hung between the two front windows. From there, he spoke to his wife and son. "People keep inviting me to events, these days. Next Shabbos I have a bar mitzvah for the beadle's grandchild. And you, what was your son's bar mitzvah like?"

"My son's bar mitzvah?" Naftali Hertz asked in a deathly voice. "My son's bar mitzvah, you ask?" he repeated, trying to find the strength to reply. "If you mean to ask if my son puts on tefillin each day, I'll tell you the truth that he doesn't." Naftali Hertz was certain—even knowing such certainty was pure idiocy—that his father would stride over and spit into his face. "Sinner," his father would yell. "You say your son doesn't put on tefillin every day? But he isn't even circumcised!"

But his father only stood there, head lowered, and said nothing. "You know," he eventually said to Henna'le, "the dayan, Reb Tzadok, doesn't answer me when I greet him 'Good morning.' Instead of *me* bearing a grudge against him, *he's* angry at me. He's so ashamed of his grandson's behavior, he has to convince himself we're to blame."

Naftali Hertz had already heard about the unsuccessful shidduch between Bluma Rivtcha and Zindel, the dayan's grandson. He was glad to be talking about something else, and reminded his parents that just as Tilza had kept sighing at her chuppah, upset about the arranged marriage, Bluma Rivtcha had kept laughing. Her cheeks had been flushed like a child's, then, and he longed to see how she'd grown in these twelve years. He'd assumed that Bluma Rivtcha and Refael'ke would come from Vilna, and Bentzion from Bialystok, to see him. He was disappointed they hadn't.

"Well, they're all convinced they wasted their years in my home," his father said, "so now they're trying to make up for those lost years and don't have time to come." His father smiled crookedly, and Naftali Hertz understood the jab. He, the oldest son, was to blame for all of it. He had started it, and the younger ones had all followed suit.

"Don't you understand, Father?" Naftali Hertz replied, his face looking fatigued. "Generation after generation of Katzenellenbogens have been detached from the material world, from life. So this generation of Katzenellenbogens inherently lacks any knowledge of what's good for them and what isn't, what's real and what's merely fantasy. That's why they fall into more traps than others and have to struggle harder to succeed."

"Well, and your Karl? I assume he wasn't raised detached from the material world, like the Katzenellenbogens. So is he not missing that innate sense of what's good or bad for him?" the rabbi asked, looking at Henna'le. By the way she was stroking the pleats of her dress with her small fingers, he understood how anxious she was that he'd start up a fight. But Sholem Shachne didn't want to yield. He asked, "Your Karl's maternal grandparents probably weren't detached from the material world, either, were they?"

"Karl's maternal grandparents, you ask?" He stared at his father blankly, like a person in a foreign land who's suddenly lost his memory and all sense of where he is, of his own name, even. For a long minute, Naftali Hertz stared straight ahead. Finally, he said, "But I already told you that my wife's father, my late father-in-law, was Emanuel Noifeld . . . I mean, Kalmen Emanuel Noifeld. And Karl is named after him."

"Was he from those German Jews? The ones who go to temple?" the rabbi asked.

"No, no. It's true that the leaders of the Bern Jewish community are Temple Jews, but our sort of Jews exist there, too. They're scattered throughout Switzerland: business partners, expeditors, factory owners. These Jews in Bern, Basel, Zurich, Geneva, and in the villages of the Italian districts, they don't like the Reform temples with their preachers; they daven in our kind of shuls," Naftali Hertz jabbered, enlivened, as if refreshed by the mere recollection of these facts. "My father-in-law, Kalmen Emanuel Noifeld, was such a Jew. True, he didn't have a beard or peyes, but in his entire demeanor he remained an Aleksander Hasid. He was always rushing somewhere, key ring clanging and a wallet full of change. His fingers were perpetually twisting screwdrivers and screws, springs and clock hands. And in the same way, he was constantly talking and laughing. His cheeks were a toasted, brownish blue, like someone who likes hard liquor, though he didn't drink at all. Even in remote Switzerland, this Aleksander Hasid wished for a Hasidic rebbe, but had to make do with a Misnagid, a son of a rabbi, a student of philosophy." Naftali Hertz laughed, staring tensely at his father, who stood partially turned away, listening. "Besides writing his business letters, I also ate at his house on Shabbos and Yom Tov and offered Gemara interpretations at the table. One day, just like that, while he was rushing off somewhere, he collapsed from a heart attack. He lay on the ground, the same happy smile on his face that he wore when he sat listening to me recite a bit of Gemara at his table."

"And your mother-in-law? Is your wife's mother as Jewish as her husband was?" Henna'le asked.

"My mother-in-law, Chana Rochel, is even more Jewish than her late husband, because he tried to make a good impression on Christians, too," Naftali Hertz said, and everything he said about this woman was indeed true, except she wasn't his mother-in-law.

Old Chana Rochel Noifeld shuffled about the bright, tidy rooms of her home, plagued by stabbing pains like pins from a tight corset. She kept her eyes peeled for people on whom she might unload the heartache of a life lived in a country that felt like a borrowed shirt on her body. True, her husband had made a fortune in Switzerland, and they didn't live in fear of pogroms here. But she and her husband suffered the constant terror that their two daughters might marry non-Jews. There weren't many young Swiss-born Jewish men in the area, and the Jewish students from Russia were always jabbering about revolutions and bomb-throwing. So Chana Rochel had been pleased when a rabbi's son, a former yeshiva boy who didn't drone on about revolutions, started handling the correspondence at their factory. Naftali Hertz noticed that once she'd brought the tasty, nourishing dishes she'd prepared to the table, Chana Rochel sat down and gazed bleakly at the mahogany armoires stuffed with Swiss antiques: glassware and carved wooden pieces. She felt no attachment to these carvings, she confided in him, nor did her husband. He merely fussed

over the figurines to show his Swiss business associates how dear
their country was to him. Her husband would have much preferred
to impress Jewish guests with the menorahs and silver kiddush goblets tucked away at the back of the same armoire. At the time when
Chana Rochel Noifeld had told him these things, he hadn't empa-
thized with her. But later, living in the house of his Christian mother-
in-law, whose hateful silence suffocated him, he felt warmer toward
Chana Rochel. Which is why he now spoke so reverently about his
supposed mother-in-law.

But his mother interrupted him. "You keep speaking about your
mother-in-law as if she's the reason you married her daughter. But
what about your wife? You have nothing to say about her? Is she
pretty? Tall?"

"She's lame."

His father swung around, astonished. His mother raised herself
off her chair and quickly sat down again, speechless. It had sprung
from him, as if someone had pushed it up out of his throat. But he
didn't regret it. Now his parents would no longer ask him why he'd
alienated himself for years and why he'd come without his wife. They
would believe he was ashamed of his wife's lameness, and that now,
under pressure, he'd revealed the truth. "Aida is short and she limps.
But she moves very agilely and skillfully. She's practical, energetic,
and even when her father was alive, she managed the factory. When
we got to know each other, I, of course, didn't like that she was dis-
abled. I also didn't like her dry voice and dry lips, and that a web
of blue veins crept through the thin skin of her hooked and bony
nose. Besides her not being very pretty or young, she was much too
immersed in the business. An ordinary girl, I thought. But once I
became better friends with her and observed her more closely, I saw
that when she wasn't at work, Aida overflowed with laughter. And
when she laughed, her plainness disappeared, her forehead lit up.
Her pale blue eyes glowed with kindness. My German was still bad
then, and Aida smiled at me from her desk and asked me to speak
in Yiddish. She said it softly, not implying that I wasn't good at the
language, but simply that she spoke Yiddish anyway, so why strain to
speak German?"

Naftali Hertz spoke with increasing haste and density, as if worried his parents might interrupt him and the entire fantastical story

would implode. His face reddened, his eyes glinted. He became happier, giggling here and there, charging forward with his story. "Even though Aida has a limp, many men had their eyes on her. But she didn't want to tie herself to any of them. Her father took issue with every suitor, and soon enough Aida would come to agree with her father—that's the kind of influence he had on her. One candidate her father found lazy; another wasn't mature and serious enough; a third was neither a Jew nor a gentile. Because her father favored me, she favored me too." Naftali Hertz, face flushed, burst into another spate of laughter. "So that's how we got married. But I was just a yeshiva boy, so I was ashamed to write you about Aida's limp. None of her other admirers considered this a deficiency, and gradually I, too, stopped noticing it. But to write you about it—I was ashamed. I didn't want you wringing your hands that your son took a wife with a deformity."

His father spread his arms, ready to say something, but his mother beat him to it. "If it's fine by you, it's fine by us."

Naftali Hertz again began to speak rapidly. "I understand now that it was foolish on my part. But at the time, I thought that to write with the truth would bring you tremendous grief. And to write about everything else except my wife, who knows what you'd think of that. So I didn't write at all. The main problem in my married life is Aida's sister, Janet. In every way—her character, behavior, appearance—she's my wife's polar opposite. Even in the house, Janet tiptoes around and makes calculated hand gestures, like an actress playing a part. And when she reads a book, even her reading is a theater act. She sits in an armchair, her long, white hands in her lap, her bare knees crossed, and her head turned as if she were reading a letter from a beloved who's on the verge of committing suicide over his unrequited love for her . . ." Naftali Hertz let his words trail off. His mother's stare made him realize he'd misspoken. His father, too, furrowed his brow distastefully, as if he were smelling an impure odor, though he hardly comprehended his son's cryptic language.

Naftali Hertz remembered how he'd felt about Janet when he was frequenting the Noifelds. Her gray-green eyes, her cold face, her tight lips and bored smile made it clear she wasn't modest. She'd shown no interest in spending time with the young Katzenellenbogen, which both insulted and attracted him. Once, when he didn't see her around the house and asked Aida where her younger sister was, Aida cried angrily, "She's not for you. She's had more suitors than you have francs in your pockets." And she burst into laughter. "I know you find my sister more attractive than me, if only because she does nothing and I work from morning to night."

Now that Naftali Hertz had cast himself in the role of Aida's husband, he remembered how he'd felt about her sister, Janet, and told his parents: "My sister-in-law is a constant problem. She lives with us in Bern, even though her husband is in Paris. She'll travel there now and then to make peace with him, but barely has she left than she's back already, determined to get a divorce. This has been going on for years."

"And my father, your grandfather in Zembin, don't you want to see him at all?" his mother asked, insulted that her son was droning on about his wanton sister-in-law in Switzerland and had forgotten his own family.

"Of course I want to see Grandfather. But I won't have enough time. I'd promised Tilza, back when I was still in Switzerland, that I'd visit only you and her. She wrote that her husband was traveling abroad for his yeshiva and she was staying alone with the children."

"Instead of giving lectures to his students, a genius like our son-in-law must plod around the world to collect money," Sholem Shachne said, shaking his head. "It's a miracle that Reb Zalia Ziskind Luria offered to sub in for him in the meantime."

"Reb Zalia Ziskind is in Tilza's town now?" Naftali Hertz cried out, his tone half-pleased, half-anxious. He took off his pince-nez, as if to see the naked truth.

"Yes, your former rosh yeshiva is in Lecheve now with his son, a strange boy. He's attracted to the secular world, like you, but his father is watching over him to keep him from forsaking Judaism." Sholem Shachne paused, despondent, and then glanced pointedly at his son. "When Zalia Ziskind sees you, he might worry that you'll corrupt the Lecheve students like you did the young men in Visoki-Dvor."

"Oh, he'll see right away he has nothing to fear. I didn't come here to corrupt anyone." Naftali Hertz smiled sadly. The old couple and their son were silent for a long while, as if listening to the cacti grow in the cool room and to the stillness of the bare dirt road outside, stretched for miles in its sleep.

6

ZALIA ZISKIND LURIA—the short, hunchbacked genius from Dünaburg, with a big head, big, melancholy eyes, pale hands, and a pointed nose—had such a melodious voice that when he sang, the Volozhin Yeshiva students would set their Gemaras aside and listen to his trilling as to the birds in the woods. When young men from other yeshivas passed through Volozhin, rather than ask them for new Torah commentaries, Zalia Ziskind asked whether they'd picked up any new tunes. Because he was surrounded by Torah scholars, his hunchback wasn't a major defect, certainly not enough to sour his life. The three greatest rosh yeshivas—the Netziv; his son-in-law, Refael Shapiro; and *his* son-in-law, Chaim Brisker—enveloped the short genius with love. And when "Zelme'le," as his friends affectionately called him, recited his Torah interpretations, everyone looked at him as if he were the wondrous Yanuka of the Zohar. He wasn't one for intricate pilpul, but for interpretations that were logical in their simplicity, as if the Torah of Sinai had again been given, this time, into his hands.

His father, Ovadye, a minor merchant, though one with a great pedigree—he was a grandson of the Maharshal of Lublin—had a reputation as a pious Jew with common sense. When his businesses went bad, he was appointed a dayan in his native Dünaburg. Ovadye's mind was neither great nor lacking. In the Luria lineage, the "genius brain" had skipped a generation, only to spring up again in his son Zelme'le—a light in the darkness of Jewish exile.

Contrary to his father's naïveté and gentleness, his mother, Rebbetzin Devorah Itka, had clever, spiteful eyes and sneering lips. Skinny, bent over, with long, veiny, work-worn hands and bulging elbows, she tittered at her husband, a sheep of a man who despite being in business for years had not yet managed to strike it rich. He'd done favors for everyone in town, but no one remembered it. And once he became a dayan, he considered himself an underling compared to the other rabbinical judges. As for herself, she didn't claim to be much of a doer either. Instead of a houseful of children, God had given her one little hunchbacked son who took after his father. But one mustn't sin by complaining. He'd inherited his mind from his brilliant grandfathers, and everyone wanted him as a groom: a Warsaw tycoon, a Minsk rosh yeshiva, a Vilna dayan. Thank God for that, at least.

To his parents' distress, however, he was still unmarried at thirty years old. Each time he met a potential bride, he said, "A fine girl like this can do better than me. She can find someone more resourceful, someone whose spine is straight. What does she want with me?" And he'd dive back into his learning, humming his pleasant tunes.

In the end, he got married in the small town of Visoki-Dvor, into the family of a no-name rabbi with no reputation, a joyless home, and a moneyless girl. It happened like this. The rabbi of Visoki-Dvor had died suddenly, leaving a widow with a house of grown girls. At the funeral, the heartrending cries of the widow and her children convinced the town they needed to find a groom for the eldest daughter and make him rabbi, on the condition that he support the widow and her daughters until they were married. For such a match, they found no interested parties in Volozhin. But Zalia Ziskind Luria could not forget the story he'd heard of this Jewish home, sinking in gloom like a cellar flooded with water. The rabbi's daughters were wasting away at home without grooms, shamed, while in Volozhin hundreds of young men sat waiting for rich brides. Well, why shouldn't he make the match himself and simultaneously set an example for other scholars—that a student of Torah should weigh empathy over dowry?

His reputation as a young man with a rare mind preceded him. The widow had heard that the potential groom was a hunchback, and she'd assumed that was why he was willing to take a poor bride. But her daughter, too, was ready to marry any scholar, hunchbacked or lame, as long as the town would take him as rabbi. It never dawned on the widow that this boy could make a lofty match despite his hunched back, yet for some reason, he was drawn to their bereaved house like a duck to a desolate pond hidden amid thick foliage.

In Visoki-Dvor, Zalia Ziskind found four orphans with ashen faces like deathly moons, their gray eyes shining with the sorrow of an austere Shabbos on a winter's evening. All four girls—with bloodless lips and teased chestnut hair—were dressed modestly in white blouses, ringlets of hair framing their collars, long sleeves down to their wrists. Zisse'le, the eldest, looked no different from her sisters. Only by the way she sat at the table, eyes lowered, could you tell she was the bride.

The rebbetzin, the widow, was wide and heavy. In her long black dress, and in the way she punctuated every sentence with muffled groans, it seemed as if the seven days of shiva had dressed themselves up as a woman and were still roving about the house, though a year had passed since the rabbi's death. Zalia Ziskind realized that, until a man moved into the home, the mourning would not move out. He saw the women around the table observing him with worried smiles: *Could such a small, pale man support an entire family? People claimed he was a peerless scholar. But the townspeople here were no experts when it came to Torah scholars. Who knew if they'd want him as a rabbi at all?* Perhaps the women around the table weren't thinking exactly in those terms. But these were the thoughts Zalia Ziskind read on their faces, and they intensified his desire to become this grieving family's provider.

Zalia Ziskind got married in 5660 on the threshold of the twentieth century. The Volozhin Yeshiva had already been closed by decree of Saint Petersburg, because the rosh yeshivas didn't allow secular education. But there was no lack of places to study Torah. Young unmarried men flocked to Telz and Slobodka, Mir, and Radin. Nevertheless, Zalia Ziskind was such a sensation that before he'd even properly settled in Visoki-Dvor, a large group of scholars had already followed him there. Zalia Ziskind's brilliant interpretations shook their minds. Young married men stood shoulder to shoulder, like pines, around this hunchbacked Jew with short peyes, bare cheeks, and a sparse little beard on the tip of his chin; and they marveled at how he flung thoughts like lightning, how he blazed with razor-sharpness. The townspeople, too, blessed their rabbi and rosh yeshiva—he had revived Visoki-Dvor. The students paid for lodgings and for meals at their stations. The widowed rebbetzin also blessed her son-in-law. He married off two of her daughters and gave their husbands work as assistants in the yeshiva. Only the youngest daughter was left to marry. Everything was looking up, if only Zalia Ziskind didn't occasionally fall into depression.

This depression would come upon him whenever he got news of a tragedy, even one that had occurred to a stranger. For example, on the outskirts of Visoki-Dvor, while crossing the train tracks in a horse-drawn wagon, a driver had not noticed the light had turned red nor heard the huffing approach of the locomotive. Along with the driver, a woman and her two children who were traveling to a village on vacation died. In the beis medrash the people clucked, "May this never happen to a single Jew!" and then scattered to their work in the market, in the shops. Others opened holy texts and sat down to study. But Zalia Ziskind couldn't open a holy book that day. He kept murmuring to himself, "A mother and two little girls? Oy, Lord of the universe! I can picture the girls: blond braids with blue ribbons woven through them. Oy, Father in heaven!" He felt his brain disintegrating from all the misfortunes befalling mankind.

"Died of a cold?" he murmured another time. A Jew had caught a cold that turned into pneumonia and, three days later, was dead. Zalia Ziskind didn't know this man, and from that he deduced that the dead man had been one of those meek paupers who didn't dare go over to the rabbi to say "Good Shabbos." This knowledge exacerbated Zalia Ziskind's suffering. When a student came to him to ask a question on the topic he was studying, Zalia Ziskind merely stared out the window, as if awaiting an answer from heaven on why the world was filled with so many misfortunes. And when he finally noticed the student, Zalia Ziskind sighed. "Forgive me, Krynker, but to answer your question, I first have to review another discussion on the matter. I'll do it another time; I can't now. Now I'm thinking. I'm thinking that so much misfortune plagues this world because of man's cruelty to man or one nation's cruelty to another. Considering that, we might console ourselves by thinking that when cruel people cease to exist, cruelty will have no sway. As we pray on the High Holy Days: 'All cruelty should dissolve like smoke; evil reign shall pass from this earth.' But when misfortunes come *not* through our fellow man, what can we console ourselves with? Unless you have such faith in Divine supervision that you thank God even for misfortune?" Zalia Ziskind chanted in a sort of mystical ecstasy, his somewhat childish hands pressed into fists, and then his eyes widened as he glanced anxiously at the young man, worried that he was corrupting him.

Gradually, Zalia Ziskind rid himself of the depression. His eyes brightened, the furrows on his forehead smoothed. He again asked questions that the Babylonian Talmud had raised about the Jerusalem Talmud, or that the Rif had of the Rambam, and then he answered those questions. After his lectures the students gathered in cliques and discussed his innovative responses. Zalia Ziskind remembered that he hadn't yet answered the question the boy from Krynki had asked. He took a Gemara from the bookcase that lay against the western wall, placed it on the table, leafed through it, and reflected on the matter. Unconsciously, he began to hum a tune. He immediately forgot that he was looking for the answer to a question, but continued singing that sweet, sad tune like the whisper of a cold river, roving among the rocks in confinement and darkness, not knowing where it's leading. The students ceased debating the points of Zalia Ziskind's lecture and listened to the melodious sobs rising from his depths.

Zalia Ziskind looked out the window and pondered: According to the Rambam, Divine supervision corresponded to the level of one's knowledge of Godliness. The greater a person's understanding of Godliness, the more heaven watches over him. It followed, then, that over this beis medrash, filled with yeshiva students, there hung a heaven of the purest light; while above the homes in the back streets, where no one was learned, a much darker heaven loomed; and over the peasants' villages hung a completely dark and empty sky. First, why should it be this way? Second, is it, indeed, so? And third, the non-Jewish woman with the two children whom the train had run over, and the poor village Jew whom a fever had burned through in mere days—under which sky did they live?

So, it was back to depression. Which increased even more when his father, Ovadye, the dayan of Dünaburg, died. During the year of mourning, Zalia Ziskind led the prayers each day, and each day he rushed through them tunelessly, garbling the words. If he weren't the rabbi and rosh yeshiva, the men would have raised a fuss against such a ba'al tefilah, complaining that they couldn't hear a word. Occasionally, though, Zalia Ziskind would burst into song, with a fervor that the congregation could not soon forget.

It was Monday morning. The Torah reader in the beis medrash had just finished reading the weekly chapter, and Zalia Ziskind took over the scroll to finish the davening. His face was pale, his voice battered. Wrapped in his tallis, he stood, a small man at the lectern. With both hands clutching the Torah, and with his head craned toward the ceiling, he sang the prayer hoarsely: "*Acheinu bnei yisroel, Our brothers, Jews, who've been given misfortunes, who've been captured . . . Have pity on them, Father in heaven . . .*" The hearts of his listeners melted from bliss. His eyes darkened, emanating such infinite sadness that, while he was uttering the prayer, it seemed his imagination had voyaged to every place Jews found themselves in difficulty. When he finished the prayer, he continued standing for a long time, silent, lost in thought, with the Torah scroll in both hands and confusion in his eyes—as if his thoughts hadn't yet returned from their ramble around the world with exiled Jews. Eventually, the strained silence and everyone's gaze directed toward him roused him from his thoughts, and he walked slowly behind the lectern with the Torah in his hands.

"Good friends," he called out, smiling at the students surrounding him worriedly. "You know, of course, that young birds chirp a certain way in the woods at dawn and shriek in a different way deep in the middle of autumn. So too does the heart pray differently during joyous holidays than on Tisha B'Av or on Selichos and Yom Kippur. But however the songs may differ, they have one thing in common: without song, man could not endure his suffering, nor express joy in those brief moments of happiness he's been allotted."

7

ZISSE'LE, ZALIA ZISKIND'S WIFE, grew paler each year, though they never lived in poverty. People had already assumed she was barren when, five years after her marriage, she at last gave birth to a boy. The infant's grandmother, Devorah Itka, came down from Dünaburg. She looked just as she had when her husband was alive. She still strode around with alacrity, elbows pointed. Skinny, bent over, irritable, she continued to mock (even more than she used to) all those who bragged about themselves or fanatics who rattled on about how one must be meek. As soon as she stepped into her son's home, her mind reeled with mocking thoughts of her son's mother-in-law, the old, high-chested rebbetzin who still walked around in mourning so many years after her husband had departed to the World of Truth. Devorah Itka also tittered at her daughter-in-law and two younger, married sisters, women with pale faces. "Just look at how they wobble. It's like their legs have no bones or they've just come from a sickbed. Or from the moon!" About her daughter-in-law's youngest sister, Sirka, who didn't yet look as if "all the ships had sunk her," Devorah Itka told her son, "Hopefully, she won't end up with a husband as depressed as you."

His mother finally understood why her Zelme'le had married into this family. He was attracted to this sort of house the way an owl is to dark corners.

She gazed with pride at her grandchild and pleaded with God that he take after a pious, happy Jew, even a woodcutter, as long as it wasn't his depressed father or his mother, the fragile consumptive.

Little Mottel had milky skin, like his mother, and big black questioning eyes, like his father. His furrowed brow foretold his future as a philosophical thinker and a hardhead. He was a quiet baby who gazed about himself belligerently, as if it were beneath his dignity to cry or babble. Devorah Itka didn't want to stay long with her son. She hurried back to Dünaburg, as if other children and grandchildren were awaiting her there. On her way home, she suddenly burst out laughing. *So, this?* she thought. And what she meant was: *Is this the nachas God has allotted me?*

Since everyone knew that Zalia Ziskind fell into depression whenever he heard of someone's misfortune, they kept all bad news from him. But they couldn't keep from him the very worst of it, plain as day on his wife's face: she was dying of tuberculosis, coughing up her lungs. Zisse'le's skin became ever more transparent, the whites of her eyes turned yellow, her lips dry. Her pale cheeks flushed with sickness. But her smile grew ever lighter and purer. Even when she'd lost the strength to get out of bed, she kept smiling, and asked her husband: "Sing something, Zelme'le. Your singing makes me sad, but it also brings sweetness to my heart, like when I was a child and fell asleep to my father's Gemara humming. It does me no good for you to stare at me in silence. Your pitying glances choke me, make me cough."

Zisse'le died in the ninth year of her marriage, when her only son was nearing his fourth birthday. Zalia Ziskind was forty-one when he became a widower, and for a long while he felt as if he were living in a half dream, half reality. His mother-in-law's lamenting to God that He didn't take her instead of her daughter, his sisters-in-law's sobs and screams, the townspeople's words of consolation, the Tehillim his students recited—all this he saw through a fog of yahrzeit candles melting and dissolving. Out of the clamor, however, rose one little voice, pure as a spring, bringing laughter and tears to the mourner's heart: the giggling and crying of his little boy.

"My rebbetzin was named *Zi*sse'le, which means sweet, and my name is Zalia *Zi*skind, but 'God made our fate bitter,'" the widower said to friends, parroting the words of the widow Naomi from the book of Ruth. His back hunched further, his head sunk deeper into his shoulders, his little beard went from gray to white, his gaping eyes filled with a rigid blackness, his singing voice departed. Months passed this way. Finally, he could no longer postpone his teaching duties.

Surrounded by students, Zalia Ziskind stood at his lectern and piled on question after question on the Gemara by both the earlier and the later commentaries. The crowd waited, anticipating an innovative interpretation that would, in a single stroke, clarify every point he'd raised and lead them out of their quagmire, into the light. But Zalia Ziskind merely stood there for a while, looking as if he'd forgotten what he'd just said. Before long, he started repeating the same questions, like a broken record on a gramophone, hoarsely singing the same tune. At last, he offered a trite response, barely drawing a conclusion, with no hint of his former erudition—as if along with his singing voice his brilliant mind had fled.

He stared at his students guiltily, terrified. That they'd never once interrupted with questions of their own made it clear to him that he'd offered nothing new. He stood there, head dropping, and his sad silence resounded like the emptiness in a leafless autumn forest.

At the encouragement of his closest students, he made a second effort; perhaps his former powers would return. As he struggled to ponder the holy texts, he forced himself to sing under his breath, so that the melody would warm him. This time when he stood to give his lecture, the students jumped in right away, lively and cheerful. They urged him along, debating among themselves, each student interpreting the rabbi's words differently, as was customary. But the rabbi himself again stood there in despair, gazing down at the floor like a poor boy who'd lost the few groschen his mother had given him to buy cookies for his younger brothers and sisters. "The lecture has gone over; it's time for Mincha, it's late," an older student said, offering the rest of the group a chance to disperse and relieve their rosh yeshiva.

"I can't get anywhere in my Torah studies anymore; my mind is failing me. Take over the lecture," he later told his brothers-in-law.

Both brothers-in-law were stout, with wide shoulders and bushy beards. When they'd married his sisters-in-law, and Zalia Ziskind had hired them to work at the yeshiva, he'd appointed one as a mashgiach, in charge of the students' behavior, and the other as the dean of practical matters, ensuring that the students had meals and lodging. But rather than feel gratitude for their appointments, the brothers-in-law bore a grudge against Zalia Ziskind for not allowing them to teach. Still, they knew they couldn't compare to the Dünaburg genius, and they knew that the students knew it, too. But now that Zalia Ziskind had lost the drive or was no longer capable of giving the lecture, the students wouldn't rebel against a substitute.

"And what will you do?" the mashgiach brother-in-law asked.

"I'll travel around for a bit, to see my Volozhin friends who are now rabbis in different cities," Zalia Ziskind replied, and turned to his other brother-in-law, the dean of finances. "You'll stand in for me in town, too, giving lectures to the residents. You're a much better speaker than I am."

"And who'll watch over your Mottel while you're away?" the better speaker asked, fingers combing his thick beard.

"The same person who's watching over him while I'm here. His aunt Sirka."

Since he'd become a widower, Zalia Ziskind kept hearing a voiceless conversation inside his head, insisting that Sirka was no longer interested in any old husband, but was raising her sister's orphan and waiting for her brother-in-law to marry her. But Zalia Ziskind remembered the words of his mother at Mottel's bris. She'd liked Sirka precisely because she didn't sound lifeless and wasn't a whiner like her sisters. "She just shouldn't end up with a downer like you," his mother had said. But now Sirka's voice was already starting to sound lifeless. "I don't want to darken her life like her sisters'," the widower said to the family, and this was another reason he wanted to leave Visoki-Dvor. Once he was out of Sirka's sight, she'd find a more suitable husband.

In vain, however, had the widower hoped to relax in the homes of his Volozhin friends. True, they all welcomed him with respect. But when he lamented his inability to accomplish anything in his Torah studies, they smiled as one does to a man who's convinced himself he has a disease. "So the Dünaburg genius's head clogged up overnight?" they said. And when he added that he couldn't sing anymore, they actually laughed out loud. "In Volozhin they used to say that when you sing, the angels in heaven stop to listen. Lead the Mussaf service this Shabbos, and follow up afternoon prayers with a lecture to the town's scholars, so both the learned and the hoi polloi will have a Shabbos to remember."

Such confident words at his expense! He felt acutely sick. Besides, after staying with one of his old friends for a while, he couldn't help but notice the friend's problems. Yet again he was suffering another's pain, depressed by another's misfortunes. And he marveled that his friend, despite his problems, had managed to fatten his cheeks, with a beard like a hay wagon, a thick neck, and puffy white hands. He carried himself with the bearing and bulk of a rich man at the wedding of his youngest child, while in truth he lived off loans. His was a hidden sigh, unheard by others. "What does it do for him, all this posturing? And for me, why slog around this world looking for someone who's happy?" Zalia Ziskind asked himself. "Wouldn't it be more worthwhile to go home and marry my sister-in-law?"

When he bid farewell to his host, Zalia Ziskind exhaled with difficulty, like an ailing bird on a branch in late autumn, doubled over itself, wings soaking wet, eyes half-closed, beak parted.

"Where are you traveling to now?" his host asked.

"I don't know where I'm going. I'm looking for living proof, someone about whom I can say: 'This man is the exception to what the Gemara claims: It would be better for man to not be born.' So far, though, I haven't found him."

"Well, who knows if you'll find such a special person," the host replied. "Go in peace, Reb Zalia Ziskind," he nevertheless wished his guest, "and don't punish yourself so harshly; don't go thinking you've lost your singing voice or your ability to lecture on the Torah."

Only at the Morehdalye rabbi's home did Zalia Ziskind finally feel like he was getting a little rest. His friend from Volozhin, Sholem Shachne Katzenellenbogen, didn't believe it was necessary to deliver novel Torah interpretations. And he had no taste for music. He even joked, "All melodies, I think, are one single melody that everyone twists a different way. But if the Dünaburg genius tells me there's a variety of tunes, I have 'faith in the wise' and believe you." Furthermore, in the Morehdalye rabbi's home, Zalia Ziskind bore witness to no suffering, so he did not have to suffer along himself. In those days, Sholem Shachne's family seemed to be headed on the right path. His oldest, Naftali Hertz, then seventeen, was studying in the town's beis medrash; and his youngest, Refael'ke, hadn't yet been born. So Zalia Ziskind clung to Sholem Shachne's children, especially the older daughter, Tilza. He patted her curly-haired head and her round, pink cheeks. She gazed at him with wonder, as if to ask whether in his own house he had no one to pat or caress.

Just as Sholem Shachne made no demands on his friend to forge any new paths in Torah scholarship, he likewise never reproached him for abandoning his yeshiva. All he asked was that, for as long as Zalia Ziskind stayed in Morehdalye, he study with his oldest son, Naftali Hertz. Zalia Ziskind complied, and with each passing day he became more impressed by the young man's talents. Naftali Hertz awoke in him the yearning to lecture his students, and he began to think of returning home. It was time to come out of mourning. He even imagined he was getting his vocal cords back. All he had to do was cough away his hoarseness, and his singing voice would return along with his Torah interpretations.

"Sholem Shachne," he said. "I'm going back to Visoki-Dvor, to my little son and my rabbinate and yeshiva. If you want, you can send along your son. He has an exceptional head on him, and there's no doubt he'll grow up to be a Torah giant."

The Morehdalye rabbi immediately gave his consent. He didn't yet imagine that things could be different from what he decided. In fact, he didn't even ask his son if he wanted to go. And Naftali Hertz obeyed his father.

But Zalia Ziskind's hope for a change in spirit came to naught. His face grew paler, his body more crooked, and because his beard couldn't turn any whiter, it began to fall out. He again gave lectures to students and led the city's beis din, but you could tell he was wrestling a sadness that was stronger than him. When he had time away from his students and the villagers, he liked to take strolls by himself at the edge of town, over the mown autumn fields. His small cotton coat, billowing in the wind, hung on him like a cloud.

Though he was the leader of a large group of students, he didn't know how to deal with his own son. And for his part, the little orphan was frightened of his father's hunchback and clung to his aunt Sirka. Whenever she spoke to Zalia Ziskind, Sirka was careful to stand a little off to the side of him. She had too many grudges against him to look with kindness into his eyes. His excuse for not marrying her, that he didn't want to poison her life with depression, she neither understood nor believed. Was it better for her to be alone, without a husband? But even once Zalia Ziskind came around and realized his sister-in-law was right, Sirka declined his marriage offer. She didn't want him to marry her as a favor to her dead sister or because she was raising his orphan. Better to remain an aunt to "Marcus," as Sirka called him, than to become his stepmother.

Naftali Hertz spent a term studying in Visoki-Dvor, and his reputation grew. But he'd never been the type to remain a Torah scholar forever. Even while studying Gemara in Morehdalye, he'd already been thirsting for a secular education and for the pleasures of the material world. In Morehdalye he had to be on guard because of his father, but at the yeshiva in Visoki-Dvor the students were free to pick up newspapers and books. Students of Torah studied Russian and grammar too. So during the first half of each day, Naftali Hertz sat in the beis medrash with the Gemara, and during the second, he studied Russian, German, and mathematics with a hired tutor. Later, in his room, he read history and philosophy until the wee hours of the night. Since he didn't have to hide this from anyone, the school board was well aware. But Zalia Ziskind couldn't bring himself to trouble his friend Sholem Shachne by writing the truth about his son. And when Naftali Hertz went home for the holiday, he made sure not to let on that he was gradually abandoning Judaism.

When he returned to the yeshiva for the second term, Naftali Hertz told his friends that he'd merely come to bid them goodbye. His father had consented wholeheartedly to his wish to study at the great yeshiva of Mir. The other students were upset that the leader of their group of maskilim was leaving. But Zalia Ziskind interpreted this turn of events differently—as indication that his friend Sholem Shachne had caught on that his son was drawn to secular education and the modern world, and was therefore sending him to a yeshiva brimming with Torah study and moral introspection, a place where the evil spirit of secular education hadn't yet found a foothold. Zalia Ziskind's brothers-in-law, on the other hand, were simply thrilled to be getting rid of this pedigreed young man, who'd already begun to corrupt himself with impure reading material and was infecting others with this leprosy—yet they couldn't say a thing to him, because his father was the rosh yeshiva's friend from back in Volozhin. To be rid of him now was a miracle! But neither Zalia Ziskind nor his brothers-in-law had any suspicion of what was really going on. They all escorted him out respectfully—and only months later did they discover that they'd been duped. Naftali Hertz had lacked the courage to defy his powerful father. To avoid causing a commotion, he allowed his parents to walk him out as he left for Visoki-Dvor, and allowed the students to escort him as he left for Mir—and somewhere along the way, he fled to Switzerland to study.

8

V ISOKI-DVOR'S YESHIVA BEGAN to fall apart. Some students
followed after Naftali Hertz, leaving to study at universities.
Others placed secular books on top of their Gemaras and read them
in plain view. Both deans blamed their brother-in-law: it was he
who'd brought the freethinker Katzenellenbogen into the yeshiva
and allowed him to corrupt the others. Zalia Ziskind was aware that
his brothers-in-law had an even greater complaint against him. Why
wasn't he tending to the raising of his only son, Mottel? But the widower, who didn't know how to start a new life, didn't know how to
handle a child either.

Soon, war broke out. The big yeshivas of Slobodka, Mir, Radin,
and Novardok, with their hundreds of students, moved deeper into
Russia. But many students didn't want to be so far from home. They
came to Visoki-Dvor, and gradually enrollment grew, until all the
benches were filled with boys thirsting to hear novel Torah interpretations. But Zalia Ziskind stared at them through the black cellars of
his eyes, and muttered, " *'Maasei yuda tovin b'yam v'atem omrim shira?'*
The world is being destroyed and I'm supposed to show off my erudition? It's a wonder I haven't yet forgotten how to daven."

Those around him shrugged their shoulders. It was precisely
at a time like this, they argued, that one must uplift the hearts of
the yeshiva boys with innovative interpretations. But Zalia Ziskind
replied that no Torah innovations were needed, just as no new prayers
were needed. The same old tractates of Talmud and the same old
chapters of Tehillim, in the same old mournful tune, were sufficient.

With his new students, Zalia Ziskind's words provoked astonishment; with his brothers-in-law, a fight. The old rebbetzin wasn't
alive anymore, but her daughters remembered well that when the
Dünaburg genius had come to them she'd believed he was their per-

sonal Messiah. As it turned out, however, his depression brought even greater sadness into the family.

Zalia Ziskind knew that Sirka, who had declined to marry him, was raising his little son to resent him. "Your father pities the entire world, but he loves no one, not even his blood relatives." And to Zalia Ziskind, Sirka said, "You didn't love my sister, either. You married her out of pity. You don't need a wife at all."

Zalia Ziskind could never grasp why marrying out of pity wasn't just as acceptable as marrying a woman out of desire for her beautiful body, or for pedigree or a dowry. And what did his sister-in-law want, anyway? For him to declare his love for her, like a twenty-year-old suitor? Since war had broken out, he couldn't comprehend how people could laugh, fret over money, or bicker over their honor. Everywhere you turned, the world was burning; every day, every hour, people were dying on the fronts. Fathers were dying beside their sons. How could anyone think about anything else?

It occurred to Zalia Ziskind's brothers-in-law that they should move their overflowing yeshiva as far away from the front in East Preisen as possible, just as the Mir group had moved to Poltava and Knesset Beis Yitzchok of Slobodka had settled in Kremenchug. But Zalia Ziskind rejected the suggestion. "At a time like this, you want me to leave my community and flee?" The brothers-in-law tried to show him how the other rabbis had done exactly that. It was impossible to accomplish anything in their cities these days, but in Jewish communities deeper in Russia, where they were greeted with honor, they were spreading religion. There were Jews living in Kharkiv, Kiev, and Rostov-on-Don, too, and they also wanted to learn Torah. But Zalia Ziskind stood firm. He would not emulate the other religious functionaries. If only he'd studied to be a pharmacist or a doctor in his youth, he could be of use to people now. Just as when there's a fire, everyone helps to extinguish it, in a war it was everyone's duty to help the wounded, the impoverished, the newly homeless. So no, he would not run away.

Both deans knew that without Zalia Ziskind they'd be unable to attract students. Left with no choice, they remained in Visoki-Dvor, pinching their beards and mustaches in anger, mocking their hunchbacked brother-in-law, whose sense was even more crooked than his back. Whining that he hadn't studied to become a pharmacist or doctor! What, was there a lack of them? Each person had to do what he was called upon to do and go where he was indispensable. And they not only slandered their brother-in-law to each other, but they denounced him to their wives, too, insisting that, at his core, Zalia Ziskind was neither pious nor even kind. He didn't believe that yeshiva boys stood above the crude, common masses, nor that the merit of Torah study saves people from calamities. "He keeps carrying on that this is a time for consoling Jews. But he—the depressive!—is incapable of consoling anyone. The only thing he's capable of is groaning and grumbling with pity for others."

When Zalia Ziskind had married off his wife's younger sisters, he'd not only given their husbands positions in the yeshiva, he'd brought them in to live in the rabbi's house, *his* home. Even later, as their families grew, they all stayed on in the same squat house, with its off-kilter annexed rooms, its sagging roof covered in tin shingles or, in some spots, in straw. The wooden structure was painted black, now faded from the sun, snow, and rain. In the entryway it smelled of rotten hay, and in the halls, main rooms, and smaller side rooms, there permeated the odor of unwashed diapers, hardened stews, fermented foods, and sweat and steam. Paper, yellowed with age, had been pasted into the cracks around the windows, whose views were obstructed by half-dead indoor plants. Wooden hangers lay everywhere. And on them hung clothes from every family, just as books belonging to all three brothers-in-law intermingled in the bookcase. The cracked wooden beams groaned under the weight of the attic, loaded down by rags and old shingles. The chipped walls ached for a coat of fresh-colored paint. Everything in the house yearned for renovation and reorganization. But Zalia Ziskind treated his Rabbi's House as if it were an inn. And since he was the owner, his brothers-in-law had no incentive to treat it any differently.

Because of the family's coldness toward him, the widower chose a small side room and banished himself there. He preferred eating bread and onion in a corner to having lunch and supper at the table with his bitter family. Not only his siblings-in-law but even his son wouldn't speak to him at the table. Like his father, alienated in his own home, the son, too, was growing into a loner, immersed in his own emotions and thoughts. He came and went from the yeshiva as he wished. There were still some students, remnants from before the

war, who were interested in a secular education. So Marcus learned
Russian, math, and geography with this group. And when the Germans were occupying Visoki-Dvor, he studied German with a religious Austrian soldier who'd come to daven in the beis medrash.
Soon, Marcus was making his way through German books. People
whispered that he sometimes forgot to put on tefillin. Yet his uncles
never rebuked him. Let his father worry! But even his son's behavior
caused Zalia Ziskind no concern, absorbed as he was by news of the
war and the general state of disaster.

The yeshiva boys gave up hope of learning Torah from the Dünaburg genius and gradually embraced his brothers-in-law. As for the
brothers-in-law, their beards and stomachs grew, along with their
desire to give lectures. They took charge of communal matters, too,
giving talks to the townspeople and issuing judgments on halachic
questions. Quietly, the two brothers-in-law started squabbling over
who would become the rosh yeshiva and who the town rabbi. Zalia
Ziskind kept ceding more and more: Enough of being rabbi! Enough
of being rosh yeshiva! And as soon as the war was over, he set out
across the world, so that his brothers-in-law could inherit his roles
even while he was alive.

Word spread through Visoki-Dvor that, just as he'd done during
the year of mourning after his wife's death, Zalia Ziskind was now
hopping through the towns where his Volozhin friends were rabbis. There, in these foreign cities and villages, he would still give
the occasional Torah lecture to scholars and townspeople. Then he'd
move on to a different friend in a different city.

From time to time, he'd return to Visoki-Dvor, looking like a
bowed, scraggly bush in late autumn, enmeshed in white spiderwebs
and covered in icicles. At home he led no Torah discussions and, in
general, was silent more than he spoke, so as not to compete with
his brothers-in-law. They'd greeted him coldly on his returns—both
because of the family's lingering resentment and because of the continued love and respect shown to him by the students and townspeople. To avoid the family's piercing glares, Zalia Ziskind emerged
from his little room less and less often. But his grown son stepped
in to see him ever more frequently, as if to spite his uncles and aunts
who were constantly slandering his father.

Zalia Ziskind was of two minds: happy that his son was becoming closer to him, but increasingly anxious about the parental responsibility that entailed. Marcus told him he didn't want to live with his uncles and aunts anymore. He wanted to be with his father. This meant that Zalia Ziskind could no longer roam from city to city. And where would they live? Zalia Ziskind recalled that, on a recent visit to the Morehdalye rabbi, the latter had told him that his son-in-law was abroad, collecting money for the Lecheve Yeshiva, and that he was looking for a substitute.

Zalia Ziskind temporarily left Marcus in Visoki-Dvor and headed to Lecheve to offer himself as a candidate. "We can see if I'm still capable of delivering lectures," Zalia Ziskind said to Yaakov Asher, pretending to be joking. "But my son comes with me."

The rabbis in the area were well aware that the Dünaburg genius wasn't getting much nachas from his son. On one hand, his grown boy was a loner and a loafer who still made childish demands; on the other, he was a rebel and a contrarian. He'd abandoned the beis medrash, but he hadn't gone out into the world. All of this left Yaakov Asher with a look of worry and hesitation on his face. But Zalia Ziskind rushed to reassure him. "Be certain, my Marcus will do nothing to disrupt the studies of the other Torah students. I'm hoping for the opposite, that your students will influence him to the good. I've already managed to speak with your students and I see they are sincere."

"Righteous and sincere! But nowadays, even a quorum of such young men can't always succeed in leading a lost soul to the righteous path," Yaakov Asher said, sighing. He told Zalia Ziskind about how hard he and his best students had worked on his youngest brother-in-law, Refael'ke, all to no avail. "For a year now he's been living with a group of chalutzim on the outskirts of Vilna, preparing to leave for the land of Israel and live on a kibbutz."

But Yaakov Asher had no other candidates to fill in for him, and either way he would not have been able to decline an offer from the Dünaburg genius.

The month of Tammuz arrived, along with its hot, humid days. On one of those days, Yaakov Asher came home from yeshiva, his face dotted with perspiration, feeling bloated in his tight jacket. His heavy hands, dense with red hair and freckles, poked out of his too-short sleeves. Panting as he walked, he bent his stiff neck to peer down at his thick legs, as if worried that, were he to lift his head, he'd behold the great distance he'd soon have to travel by train and boat. When he entered his house, Tilza greeted him joyfully, holding a letter in her hand. It was from her brother Naftali Hertz, writing to say that he was coming to visit their parents in Morehdalye and then to visit her in Lecheve. "Now you won't have to worry anymore that I'll be here alone with the children. My older brother will be with me."

This worried her husband even more. His brother-in-law, who'd deserted the Torah and mitzvahs, who was off living somewhere in Switzerland, shrouded by mountains and secrets, would be in contact with Zalia Ziskind's son. These two wolves, one older, one younger, would be face-to-face with the lambs and sheep—the sincere and righteous men of Lecheve, a town of Torah scholars.

Zalia Ziskind had the same thought, and he tried to calm the dejected rosh yeshiva, who'd already packed his suitcases for the trip. "I know your brother-in-law, the doctor of philosophy. After all, it was my beis medrash he fled from to go and study . . . I mean, he was supposedly going off to a bigger yeshiva, but in fact, he went abroad. I didn't truly know him well then, and no one expected it of him. But now I know what he's about and will watch him as I watch my son. I'll see everything, I'm certain. I'm one who's already been tested greatly; I won't miss a thing," Zalia Ziskind said, and again assured Yaakov Asher that he had nothing to worry about. But despite all these reassurances, Yaakov Asher left in a state of anxiety, and his substitute, too, was anxious, about how to arrange bringing his son over.

In Visoki-Dvor, Marcus Luria didn't know what to do with himself. The yeshiva no longer interested him, and the town's youth laughed at his expense. On summer evenings, the boys would gather on a wooden bridge. Some of them wore polished boots and hats with stiff brims; the braver ones went hatless, with tousled hair, wearing white shirts with turned-down collars. The Visoki-Dvor youth believed that all people were equal. Regarding God, they were agnostic. Marcus, on the other hand, believed that people weren't equal and God was dead. "Morals," he claimed, had been invented by slaves.

As he said these things, the sunset sky blazed with rigid tongues of fire, and Marcus's eyes glowed red, as if reflecting the fire. "That which you can take yourself, don't allow to be given to you."

"Are you so strong that you don't ask for things, you only take?" one of the boys asked. He was a strapping young man with a tanned face, and he stared at Marcus, the colorless yeshiva boy.

The group knew that Marcus was repeating the words of a crazy German philosopher who had ended up in an insane asylum. "Is this from your fat book,* too, Zarathustra, as you call him?" asked another.

"If one takes without permission, he shall be slapped on the hands. One must earn. He who does not work shall not eat," a third said.

The young men thought it a waste that a fellow with such a good mind should hitch himself to a mad philosopher—a Kraut!—instead of embracing Karl Marx and the universal proletariat. And the young women were even more distressed. They knew the rabbi's Marcus was well-read and they thought him handsome. He was tall, with pale, delicate skin and black curly hair. They also noticed how his eyes devoured them when he thought no one was looking. His full lips would turn dry, as if parched. And when he stood near a woman, he averted his gaze, his pale face blushed, his forehead perspired, and a smile trembled at the corners of his mouth, trapped, like a little fly that can't crawl out from beneath a bright hot lampshade.

The girls of Visoki-Dvor had mature bodies, high bosoms, and jutting hips. They still wore old-fashioned lace-up shoes with heels, their hair still in long braids that dangled over their shoulders. On strolls, they wore wide dresses with big brooches. Some draped a colorful shawl over their shoulders and others clutched a white silk lace kerchief in their hands. Others sported long earrings, twisting their braids around their heads or tying them up at the napes of their necks. This is how they took to the streets, swaying their hips and rears. These were the Visoki-Dvor girls, and they could crush men stronger than Marcus under their heels. But because of his curly hair, his childish bashfulness, and his pedigree, they found him charming. And yet, he dared to gripe: "When you go to a woman, take along a whip."†

The Visoki-Dvor girls were flabbergasted, speechless. "Really?" they finally said, turning to him with their wide faces and breasts like pumpkins. "When you go to a woman, take along a whip? Is that how refined you are? That's the dream you dream?"

* The word used is *pralnik*, literally meaning "thick book for beating on the bimah in shul to restore quiet."
† Nietzsche.

This discussion, too, took place on the bridge where everyone out for a stroll congregated. On both sides of the river, little houses painted yellow, red, or white winked happily to each other. Marcus fancied that the lush, leafy trees along the shore were watching him with envy—he, standing amid a female Eden, as if a garden of sun-flowers had suddenly sprouted around him. Not knowing how to respond to the girls' rebukes, he smiled bemusedly and stupidly and added another wise adage: "'Man in his innermost soul is evil, but woman in her innermost soul is vulgar.' It's not me who says this, but Zarathustra."

The women were again speechless, but among them was a skinny, short-haired girl with the raspy voice of a chain-smoker. She wore flat shoes and a masculine jacket. She shoved her hands into her jacket pockets and, without so much as glancing at the "pretty boy," told her friends, "Just ignore him, the onanist."

The other young men, meanwhile, nicknamed him "the epilep-tic," and laughed about him in the marketplace, the streets, their homes, until the townsmen came complaining to Marcus's uncles: "Does it not bother you that your nephew, with his crazy, enlight-ened philosophies, has become a laughingstock? Even the immoral ones ridicule him."

"Well, what can we do? His father travels around the world suf-fering everyone else's pain, when he can't spare an ounce of empathy for his only son," the uncles defended themselves. And to their wives, they grumbled, "The one to blame is your sister Sirka! It's the way she raised him that made him like this."

Unlike the jaundiced rebbetzins, who shuffled about the house in loose, scruffy clothing, their younger, still-unmarried sister Sirka was always dressed in a long black fitted dress, with white flowers embroidered on her flat chest and on the sleeves that hung down to her wrists. Her high, stiff white collar and her smoothly combed hair, parted down the middle, framed her round face sharply—a face that shone with the cold, pale glint of a winter's day. She was always rubbing her hands' slim fingers, as if she were outdoors and freezing in her long, narrow sleeves. And when she was silent, she wore a bit-ter expression on her face, as if she were chewing dry autumn leaves. Marcus felt that his aunt wanted him to remain a boy—*her* boy—as if in consolation for his father's refusal to marry her. And though it felt good and warm under her protection, at the same time he wanted to escape. Finally, Sirka realized that she'd sacrificed her life for her sister's son in vain, and she married Meir Moshe Baruchovits of Maryampol—another former genius and widower, like her brother-in-law Zalia Ziskind.

In addition to his two black-bearded uncles, Marcus now acquired a red-bearded one—a calm, peaceable man, content with himself and with the world. Though his voice could not compare to Zalia Ziskind's, Meir Moshe, too, liked to sing under his breath, and he greeted each person with a kind face, as if he had a well of cool, clear water in the yard and anyone who wished could draw a pail. Dressed in a clean jacket and fresh shirt, Meir Moshe paced around slowly, hands folded behind his back, a mischievous boy's twinkle in his pale blue eyes. He had the look of someone who'd woken from his nap on Shabbos afternoon, gone to the beis medrash, and started looking for a pious little boy whose downy cheeks he could lovingly pinch and whose head he could pat, before declaring: "Ay, what a boy this is! Tell me, what did you learn this week in Chumash?"

Despite having married such a loving man, however, Sirka only turned paler after her marriage and her silence was laced with even more bitterness. She couldn't simply forget her brother-in-law, the hunchback melancholic, and her suffering over Marcus's new bond with his father intensified after her wedding. Marcus, too, underwent an unexpected transformation. Before his aunt married, he'd chafed at being her clingy little orphan, but after her wedding he went into a wild fury over her marriage to a stranger. He was livid with his aunt, and he hated his new uncle. And his hatred increased each day, no matter how friendly and at ease his uncle was with him. As unexpectedly as his aunt had gotten married, so abruptly did he sever himself from her. Three weeks earlier than planned, he left to join his father in Lecheve.

"I couldn't stay at that house any longer. Aunt Sirka got married."

Zalia Ziskind was silent for a long while, huffing through clogged nostrils. "Who did she marry?" he finally asked.

Marcus told him that his aunt had taken the widower who'd been hanging around, the Maryampoler genius, and that the uncles were saying his genius would attract more students. The son looked curiously at his father, to see whether he was distressed by the news.

But Zalia Ziskind thought of his sister-in-law with grief and empathy: Poor woman, she was so embittered she'd specifically sought out another widower with a reputation as a genius, for revenge. Was she at least certain that the Maryampoler wouldn't poison her life with his grief for his first wife? On the other hand, not everyone had so much trouble finding their footing again. Maybe Meir Moshe Baruchovits was the sort who could start anew, just as the dead would live anew when the time came for them to rise. "Though even there, I can't be certain," the hunchbacked rosh yeshiva muttered to himself in a piddling monotone, like big cold raindrops striking the damp roof of a cave. "I am anything but certain that the dead will rise and start anew."

9

Lᴇᴄʜᴇᴠᴇ'ꜱ ᴍᴀʀᴋᴇᴛ, ꜱʜᴏᴘꜱ, and fancier homes all stood in the valley; the poorer, dilapidated houses hugged the mountain slopes; and the houses of prayer and communal buildings were higher up. The cold, brick shul stood on a mountain that ended in a steep cliff. To prevent any falling accidents, the area was blocked off with a wooden fence. It was a hard climb up to the cold shul, which was why people only davened there in the summer, giving it a detached and sadly pensive look. The daily orbit of the sun around the shul engulfed it in an even deeper, more mysterious silence. And when its tall, narrow, barred windows glowed red at dusk, they trembled and twinkled like nets full of golden fish.

On the mountain directly across from it stood the rabbi's home; on another mountain was the beis medrash; and behind all the crests and dips, still another mountain protruded—a great-grandfather, a giant!—home to the town's cemetery, with its haphazard graves. On Friday evenings in the summer, when weddings were held at the cold shul and the klezmer band played, the windows of the valley's affluent houses glimmered happily, sensually. But on the cemetery mountain, the buried righteous peeked out from beneath their "homes" to look down upon the luminous chuppah, reminding the bride and groom that this world was "vanity of vanities" and nothing more.

Uphill was a well-trodden path; one walked between reeds and past vegetable gardens a family had planted for their own use. Where the path became too steep, steps had been carved into the rocks, or wooden treads had been strategically placed. At the foot of the hills, the Narev spiraled around itself. In certain spots it flowed rapidly; in others, it only trickled, as if piously whispering the verse from Ecclesiastes: "All the rivers flow into the sea, yet the sea is never full."

The wooden beis medrash, which housed the yeshiva, too, was a wide, square building. Age had blackened it in part, in part turned it green from moss. It did, however, have a new shingled roof and large windows, which held the sky's blue by day and the glow of oil lamps at night. So diligent were the Lecheve Yeshiva boys that they studied until late even in summer. The beis medrash's new roof and large windows gave the old, mossy building the look of a gloomy old man, his beard covered in spiderwebs, but wearing a new kashket with a high brim, his happy eyes peeking out giddily from among the many wrinkles on his face.

The beis medrash was permeated by the smell of dusty, unaired books, the sourness of damp towels on the washstand, of tattered clothes, dirty underwear, and sweat-stained wool tallis katans with yellowed fringes, which the students kissed as ecstatically as a boy kisses a girl. Only one unaccustomed to a beis medrash could fail to understand the pleasure felt by a Torah student as he dons his tefillin and pats its leather straps. Only the stranger who's happened by chance on the beis medrash could fail to feel the magic of the yahrzeit candles' gleam. The sun's rays played on the folds of the ark's faded curtain and on the gold peeling from the leather spines of the holy books, the way skin peels from an old man's grooved forehead. But for a man who felt at home on a yeshiva bench—his bones warmed as he took in the scent of holy books or heard an innovative piece of Torah interpretation. Which is why the conscientious Lecheve students were thrilled that the Dünaburg genius would be giving them Torah lectures while their rosh yeshiva was abroad.

But when the students gathered around Zalia Ziskind's lectern, awaiting his erudition, they were surprised to hear him opening with a bizarre preamble: "When I was a boy, I once asked an ascetic, one of those recluses who devote their life to Torah study, a baffling question. Gentlemen, I remember how the ascetic struggled to come up with an answer. No matter what he said, I refuted it. I was young and had a good head, so I kept refuting and outmatching him. In the end, the old man, poor fellow, stood there bewildered, his strength sapped. But when I grew older and began to struggle over this same difficult question myself, I could no longer find the answer. And I finally realized I was being punished by God, for having caused this old man pain in my youth. This story was the first inkling that led me gradually toward a conclusion: that a man does not need to turn the world upside down with his wisdom, but rather he must learn simply. And gentlemen, that's the way I plan to act."

Even when their own rosh yeshiva, Yaakov Asher Kahane, gave a talk filled with brilliant insights, the Lecheve students didn't interrupt with questions and comments, as was the custom in most yeshivas. (And when they did make the occasional comment, their voices rang softly, ethereally, as if echoing from the cemetery mountain.) Certainly, when Zalia Ziskind gave his preamble, claiming there was no need for novel interpretations, they listened without a word. The younger students patted the silken fuzz on their cheeks, the older students pinched their soft beards, and the lot of them stared down at their fingernails as if they were at Havdalah. But though the students remained politely quiet, their astonishment was palpable. What did the Dünaburg genius's greatness consist of if not his innovative Torah interpretations?

Someone was missing among the yeshiva men around Zalia Ziskind's lectern: his son. Marcus had remained in the Lecheve rabbi's home, where he and his father had moved in, and while his father was talking to the students, Marcus was having a discussion with the young rebbetzin, Tilza. On the table between the two of them, on bowed and pudgy legs, stood Baila'ke, Tilza's one-year-old daughter, wearing a tiny shirt. Tilza held her under her arm, so that Baila'ke's fat little hands hung from her mother's thick shoulders like two heavy pails of water dangling from the sturdy shoulders of a peasant woman. Baila'ke snorted through her nose and blew air through her lips. No way could she stand on her own. It was as if she were drunk. She stared curiously at the strange man's face, just as her mother listened with great wonderment to the young man's words.

"When a weak person is on the verge of falling, you must kick him so he falls more quickly. Does anyone bend over to pick up fallen leaves? No, you rake them into a pile and let them rot in the rain and snow. That's what you have to do with defective people, with the leftovers, the riffraff."

"How can you compare people to fallen leaves? And where does it say that when a person's about to fall you should give him a kick so that he falls faster?" Tilza asked, holding her little girl and looking at him with alarm, as if his comment about allowing people to fall were about her child.

"The person who forces us to pity him is our enemy. He's a great danger to us." Marcus moved over to Tilza with hesitant, coal-black eyes. "Take, for example, my father. His pity for people was his downfall. Everyone who knows him knows this. He started out a phenom, a child prodigy, a genius, with a rare singing voice despite never having taken any lessons. But he felt such empathy for everyone that it extinguished his fiery talents and he lost his musical skill. After Mother died, her sister raised me, and she and my other aunts and uncles tried to convince me that, beneath my father's supposed goodness, he was a cold, bad man. But as I grew up, started reading books, and began to think with my own brain, I realized Father was truly good, so good that his empathy for people sapped his life. Maybe he'll recover a bit now. Sometimes, I even hear him humming to himself. I know it's because he's so happy that I'm here with him. The will to live is one of our tremendous strengths. And an even greater strength is our desire to attain a position in life—which is to say, the desire for power. But if we permit ourselves to be affected by misfortunes—our own as well as strangers'—they can break us. That's why I believe in the philosopher who said that compassion is our greatest enemy, and when we see someone falling, we should kick him to fall more quickly."

"Is he a Jew or not?" Tilza asked harshly, and her high breasts heaved higher from great anger. "Which nation is he from, this philosopher?"

"He's not a Jew, he's German. But what difference does it make which nation he's from?" Marcus smiled scornfully.

"Of course there's a difference! A Jew would never say such a thing!" Tilza said. But after a beat she decided that even a goy, if he were an educated person, would never say such a thing. "What's his name, this philosopher?"

"What difference does it make what his name is? Your husband and the young men here have never heard of him," Marcus replied with boyish arrogance and impatience. "His name is Nietzsche. I read other philosophers and moralists, too. But I'm a fan of the ones who hold that a person must think only of himself, only of his own happiness, and not allow himself to be ruined by his pity for others.

I won't allow myself to fall prey, like my father, to empathy for others, and I won't allow others to empathize with me!" Marcus said to Tilza, who was in fact looking at him empathetically, and with curiosity, too.

After all, their fathers were friends from the Volozhin Yeshiva. Tilza still remembered Zalia Ziskind's kind, sad eyes from when she was a child. She had been pleased he would substitute for her husband, and even happier that he, her father's friend from youth, and his son would move in with her. But she noticed that this young man was shy and it took him a while to adapt. A week had passed since he'd arrived and he'd yet to come in and eat without his father. At the table he sat with his head bent. But today, once his father left to give his talk, he came in, uttering all these strange things.

Tilza hugged her Baila'ke to her breasts and smiled maternally at the young man. Marcus couldn't grasp why seeing the mother press her baby to her breast made him so uneasy that he had to avert his gaze. Soon, Tilza left to put Baila'ke to bed, and when she returned, Marcus noticed her wide palms, which looked double their previous size, as if they'd grown from caressing her child.

"Why didn't you go to your father's talk in the yeshiva?" Tilza asked, sitting down on a chair on the other side of the table.

"I came here to be together with my father, but I don't have to sit in the beis medrash and listen to his talks. And when is your husband coming back?"

"Well, it's been only ten days since he left. But soon my brother Naftali Hertz, who lives in Switzerland, will be here. He's visiting my parents now and then he'll come to see me."

"And where will he live, your brother? See to it that he lodges somewhere else, not here with you," he mumbled.

"Well, we haven't seen each other since my wedding and he's coming here to keep me from feeling sad, so why should he live somewhere else?" Tilza smiled at the young man who was talking like a child. "You'll be happy, too, if he stays here. You'll have someone to debate with. My brother is educated, a doctor of philosophy."

"Yeshiva boys like having debates. I don't," Marcus said petulantly, and gave Tilza a sudden glance, his pale cheeks flushing as if a spark from the stove had escaped and landed there. "Here in Lecheve I haven't yet spoken to anyone the way I'm speaking to you."

"And with your father, do you speak? To him, do you say what you think?" Tilza fixed her hair beneath her head-covering.

"Yes, I tell him what I think, but he tells me that everything I say, I say only to spite him and myself."

"Your father's right," Tilza laughed. "You don't seem as bad a person as your words would suggest. The truly bad ones speak with a flattering tongue. Tell the truth. Would you really be able to push a person who's falling to make him fall faster?"

"Probably not," Marcus said. He was panting, and his forehead perspired. "I'm certain I wouldn't be able to! Which is why I don't believe I'll accomplish anything in life." And he told her briefly about how his aunt Sirka, who had raised him, had slandered his father, and was now disappointed in him for not rejecting his father.

Despite her visitor's warning against empathy, Tilza's eyes filled with bright tears. The longer Marcus spoke, the sadder his voice became. At the same time, he scalded Tilza with his eyes and the hot breath from his nostrils. Tilza sensed, rather than understood, that this lonely boy wanted her to become for him what Sirka had been, as well as something Sirka had never been. Confused by his glances and her suspicions, Tilza suddenly noticed that her Heshe'le wasn't around. The six-year-old boy had run out of the house—who knew where he could have gone? She poked her head out the window and called, "Heshe'le! Heshe'le!" But he wasn't outside the house either.

The deep blue sky shone so purely and quietly it seemed that, if one were to utter a word, he'd be answered by all seven heavens, one after the other. But the stillness filled Tilza with even more fear. "Heshe'le! Heshe'le!" Finally, she spotted him, and she felt her heart in her chest again. Dressed in a yarmulke, long tzitzis, short pants, and little shoes, Heshe'le stood on the hill where the old shul was. *He's already drawn to holy places*, his mother thought, and marveled at how her little boy had been able to climb to such a height on his little legs.

"I'm always afraid that my little boy might tumble off a hill into prickly plants," Tilza said, still looking out the window. She was both eager and scared to meet Marcus's eyes. She continued to look out at the rippling greenery. From the foot of the hill up, there was an abundance of crooked trees with full crowns, squat bushes filled with wild burs and thorns, leafy plants with serrated edges, arrow grass, nettles, clover, chamomile, and yellow-white flowers. Without understanding why, Tilza found herself more pleased than usual with the variety of bushes, flowers, and wild aromatic herbs that grew so lushly on her hill, nearly hiding the well-trodden trail up to her house.

10

BROTHER AND SISTER SAT on the glassed-in veranda that jutted
out over the Narev's shore. It was on this veranda that Yaakov
Asher often gave his summertime lectures to the older students. But
since he'd gone abroad, Tilza was making use of it, either spending time with the children or having discussions with Marcus Luria.
Now she sat across from her brother Naftali Hertz. She wore a green
house-robe decorated with colorful blossoms and summer birds. Her
full breasts swelled out of her loose, partially unbuttoned robe. In
front of her brother, after all, she didn't have to be as buttoned and
belted as with Marcus Luria. In a crib off to the side slept Baila'ke.
And at the tail end of the bench, at the long table, sat Heshe'le,
wearing a flat yarmulke and playing lotto by himself. When he grew
bored of it, he began to thumb through a children's book with illustrations of people, animals, houses, and gardens. A serene boy by
nature, Heshe'le was absorbed in his activities and didn't disturb the
adults' discussion.

On his way to Lecheve, Naftali Hertz had worried that, just as
with his parents, he'd now have to spin lies about his family to his
sister, guarding himself, as if from flames, from being engulfed by
his own falsehoods. But after being in Lecheve for only a day, he
realized his fear had been unwarranted. Tilza, who hadn't seen her
brother in years, wanted to tell him all kinds of things about herself,
her husband and children. And she was perpetually busy wiping her
tears. Since the birth of her second child, her nerves had frayed, and
just about anything could bring tears to her eyes. But she smiled just
as quickly, and her smile parted her still-fresh lips, the upper one
covered by black, pearly hairs.

The Narev whirled beneath the mountain, and Tilza told her
brother that somehow, at their parents' home in Morehdalye, the

Narev stirred more peacefully, more genially, more silently. The river there wasn't as wide or as fierce. At her parents' in Morehdalye, the low shores were covered in green grass or white sand. And along their length were fruit orchards, vegetable gardens, fishermen's huts, and peasants' homes. But here in Lecheve, the shores were high, rocky, wild. Eddies swirled at the river's center, so the boys and girls couldn't go out sailing at sunset or on full moon nights. You might see rafts with straw tents perched on a bundle of logs floating along the water; you might see barges with tall black funnels; but never little sailboats, looking like oversized waterbirds.

Tilza told her brother that she liked looking out the window and watching the waves tumble tumultuously, as if angered they couldn't flow beyond the shore. As a girl in Morehdalye, her head still filled with fantasies, she'd never taken notice. But now she listened. She understood more clearly the plaints and whispers of the waves. She understood that even the unfettered waters must stream from one river to the next, until swallowed by the sea. "It's the same for people, they can't prevail; they can't just achieve whatever they want," Tilza said, sighing. But her eyes shone with joy as she watched her boy. Heshe'le had golden-red hair, like his father, and a broad forehead with deep-set temples that were already creasing prematurely, like those of a rosh yeshiva preparing a lecture. The little boy also had his father's short, wide nose. It was clear he'd grow up to be a serious Torah scholar and a man without malice. To pretend her son was already older, Tilza called him "Heshe," dropping the diminutive, and told her brother that her husband, too, had been a kind and happy person as a teenager. But since he'd married her, his spirits had sunk, because he didn't know how to make her any happier with him.

This was why she felt so guilty. And her Baila'ke made her feel guiltier still. Baila'ke with her velvety-black eyes, her soft head and plump lips. When she fell asleep in Tilza's lap or lay in her crib with her eyes closed, as she did now, a smile like a clever old woman's shone on her face, and her translucent ears shone rosily like saplings. Tilza could barely suppress her craving to take Baila'ke's ears between her lips and suck on them . . . And this was the sweet lamb she'd wanted to turn away because she didn't love her husband enough? Now she thanked God she hadn't had the courage and ability to go through with the abortion.

"But as soon as I'm alone with my husband, I feel a gnawing, a grieving. There's no having fun with him, or chatting for pleasure, as husbands and wives do. Why are you laughing?" Tilza cried out, and tensed at the sound of her voice, worried she might wake Baila'ke. Heshe'le, too, raised his eyes from his book and stared at his mother in wonder. Tilza lowered her voice. "You never asked Father permission to go study in another country, and you never asked him whom to marry. So you're laughing at me because I didn't do a thing without Father's permission."

"You already have two children, but you still talk like a child yourself." Naftali Hertz laughed again. His sister's regret that she'd accepted an arranged marriage put him into a scornful, bitter mood. He wanted to scratch his own wounds, and so began to repeat the made-up story about his wife, Aida Noifeld, and her sister. When he'd told the story to his parents in Morehdalye, he'd choked on the lie, but now he drooled with pleasure.

"My wife's sister, Janet, got married without the consent, or even the knowledge, of her parents. But she herself hasn't yet consented to her marriage. She lives with us in Switzerland, her husband lives in Paris, and every so often she visits to let him know that any minute now she'll divorce him. And while she's doing that, she asks him—him!—for his advice. She wants his opinion on which of her admirers she should marry after their divorce. What a deadbeat! What a faker! She can't act onstage, so she acts in life. She speaks and writes German, French, and English, but it's beneath her dignity to manage the business correspondence with our domestic and international clientele. She prattles in all these languages only out of love," Naftali Hertz mocked, then suddenly paused, sitting there mutely, defeated. He remembered how he'd told his wife about Janet Noifeld. The love between him and Annelyse had already started cooling off by then, but they were still on friendly terms, and she'd laughed heartily at the story about Janet. At that time, her laughter didn't yet seem to him naked and vulgar. But thinking back to it now, it struck him as sneering, wanton. Well, there was certainly something to laugh about. She must have thought Janet a weak, silly hen, asking her husband whom to love.

"And how does your wife get along with her sister?" Tilza asked, probing the way their mother had.

"My wife isn't like her sister. My wife is kind, so she gets along even with her sister." He thought about how his life would have been had he married Aida Noifeld instead of Annelyse. "There's one thing Aida and her mother can't understand. They don't understand how I, a rabbi's son, don't go to temple. So I tell them that it's precisely because I'm a rabbi's son that I can't belong to their temple community and observe Shabbos in a perfunctory way. I don't want to sit in temple wearing a top hat and a tiny tallis around my neck. If I'm going to wear a tallis, it's going to be a big one, a wool one, one I'll pull over my head as Father does when he davens. I don't like the way temples put the Prophet's verse above their entryway—that we all have one father. If we really believe that, that we all have one father and all people are brothers, then we certainly shouldn't be isolating ourselves and praying to our own God. Don't you see, Tilza? You can teach an alcoholic to renounce liquor entirely, but you can't teach a drunk to have only one little glass and leave the rest of the liquor in its flask. I'd sooner live without a beis medrash entirely than put up with this sterile temple Judaism. You see?" her brother asked, and with an intense, fevered look, he said abruptly, "My wife is lame."

He expected his sister, like his parents, to at first be confused, and then try hard to show him that if he was okay with it so was she. But Tilza didn't realize she was supposed to conceal the compassion she felt for her brother. "I get it. Her sister Janet walks straight and is much prettier." She shook her head regretfully.

"What do you mean by that? Why do you think my sister-in-law is prettier than my wife?" Naftali Hertz asked, and then caught on. "Aha! You think I'm in love with my sister-in-law and that's why I'm speaking against her."

He looked out at the Narev, and the room filled with a thick silence. It didn't dawn on Tilza, Naftali Hertz thought, that his story was made up; but in truth, if he had indeed married Aida, it was certainly possible he'd have fallen in love with Janet. Naftali Hertz marveled at Tilza's perceptiveness.

She began to speak in a low, sad tone again. "Look at my little boy sitting there, engrossed in his book. Even on a summer day, he's not interested in playing outside. He's already a homebody like his father. Naftali Hertz," Tilza said, rousing her brother from his reflections, "you haven't spoken to Marcus Luria yet. Zalia Ziskind's son. He's a very interesting young man. Talk to him." And her face flushed all the way to the hair follicles on her forehead.

"Fine, I'll talk to him," Naftali Hertz replied, indifferent about the young man, but not about the young man's father. He anxiously awaited his meeting with Zalia Ziskind, who would no doubt reproach him for what he had done all those years ago, fooling him and running away from his yeshiva.

But when they actually met, that very same evening, in the same glassed-in veranda, Naftali Hertz realized his concern had been in vain, just as he'd had no reason to worry about his sister. Zalia Ziskind brightened as he recalled his former student's exceptional mind. "When I gave a lecture and you were standing in the front row of students, I used to tremble in fear that you might negate my entire interpretation with a single question. Do you still have your incredible skills?" And before Naftali Hertz could reply, his old rabbi asked him another question: "You're not upset that I'm addressing you as 'du,' are you?" His eyes shone with tender love mixed with anxiety and humility. "By my reckoning, you're already about forty, you have a family, you're a doctor of philosophy. So you're not upset that I'm addressing you familiarly?"

"No, I'm not." And Naftali Hertz smiled bitterly at the list of his attainments. "I remember you, after all, from my youth, when you used to come to visit us, and you and my father would both reminisce about your youth and your Volozhin days."

"Yes, yes, the Volozhin years were the best of my life. Those memories are precious to me," Zalia Ziskind murmured, more to himself than to Naftali Hertz. "A person who doesn't want to remember his past is even lonelier than someone without relatives, without kin . . . What's with you, Naftali Hertz? Why did you shudder so?"

"Who, me? You're imagining it. And maybe I did shudder from what you just said. I read somewhere, or heard it, or maybe I thought it myself—that a person who runs away from his memories is the loneliest person of all, because he can't be alone with himself. Are you still singing? You used to sing beautifully. And your lectures? They were lightning!"

"Oh, I've detached myself entirely from the music world. I don't inquire about new tunes, nor do I want to remember old compositions. As far as Torah learning, I still give talks to the students, but no pilpul. Would it be appropriate for an old, long-suffering Jew to parade his feats of wisdom?" Zalia Ziskind laughed a feeble little laugh, rolling his upper lip over his front teeth, his weak, sparse front teeth.

He became silent, appearing even paler, sadder, more stooped. Naftali Hertz, too, was silent and stared outside. Throughout the entire long Tammuz day, the sun had hung high over the Narev in the deep blue sky, shining a golden yellow. But now it had moved northwest, to the edge of town, and transformed into a large, round, hellish fire, squatting down ever so slowly onto vegetable gardens and cornfields, as if hesitant to get too close to earth and ignite the treetops and the straw roofs of the village homes. The opalescent clouds, edged in purple, floated from the west to the east side of town, and on the Narev's surface the day's light had already paled, cooled. The current moved more slowly, the river's breadth looked vaster. On the shore opposite the town, it was just as stony and hilly. And the farther from the water, the more thickly grew the trees. The hills turned woodier the higher up he looked, till they reached the horizon and their full, leafy crowns blocked his view.

Naftali Hertz thought again of his student days in Switzerland, when he'd come up with pretexts for not returning home, persuading himself that the natural beauty of the Alps existed nowhere else, as if he couldn't live without green fields of ice or snow mountains or vast forests of pines, high waterfalls and deep cool lakes. The Narev wasn't deep or wide enough for the Morehdalye rabbi's son.

He turned toward Zalia Ziskind and saw that he, too, was gazing agog at the cold shul on the mountain across from them. In the barred windows of the northern wall of the beis medrash, and in the rosettes over the main entry in the western wall, the sunset glowed like coals in a blacksmith's furnace. Zalia Ziskind couldn't tear himself away from the view. He said hoarsely, "Rabbi Nachman of Breslov composed a specific prayer for his followers, beseeching God to protect them from heartbreaking songs. I never considered myself such a saint that I could redeem the world from pain through the power of my singing. But I hoped to lighten my own heart, to be a joyful man, and through my singing to redeem myself, to sing myself out of pain. But since I've realized that's not possible, I don't sing anymore."

"And why are others capable of being happy?" Naftali Hertz asked, his voice and appearance despondent, as though the rosh yeshiva's reply would explain his own failure in life, too.

"I'm not at all sure that a person with a refined soul can be truly happy," Zalia Ziskind said, casting him a rigid stare. "I think that's exactly why the spiritually noble speak of depression so much. Because they themselves are depressed, very depressed. I, too, in my own way, fought to steel myself against my own pain. But the more effort I exerted, the more I realized that the moaning, the sorrows of this world—and within me—do not allow themselves to be suppressed. I cannot under any circumstances convince myself that it was worth it for the world to be created. If a person is a murderer, you can at least console yourself that after his death he'll straighten out, become an angel. But I have grievances with God even greater than Job's. Job took God to task for people who'd been wronged; he questioned why a righteous man's life was bad and an evil man's good.

"But I have more to ask of God. What about bloodthirsty animals, with their nails and teeth? Half the animal kingdom has been surviving since creation by spilling the blood of other animals. Have you ever observed a hare or a rabbit? I've looked at them. They have such big, frightened, innocent, surprised eyes, as if they're always questioning why God created them. They have big ears only to be alert to danger and fast legs so they can flee. But any shabby dog or sly fox can outrun and devour them. And that's the way it goes and will continue to go, forever and ever. The prophecy of Isaiah, 'And the wolf will lie with the lamb,' applies only to a later time when people stop devouring each other. As for now, a true wolf will always devour the sheep in the field, and the rabbits will always have cause to ask God why He made them."

He laughed quietly again, revealing his weak, sparse teeth. For a while he looked at Naftali Hertz, half-smiling, half-frightened, as if he realized that it was inappropriate for him, a rosh yeshiva, to say such things. But then he spoke up again, looking like a bent, sad willow tree, its leaves rustling in the breeze. "Music, they say, comes from another world. And it's true that music proves that an alternate universe exists, since we never hear the sounds in our daily lives that we hear in music. And music's language is entirely different from all spoken languages; it's the language of the soul. The old Lubavitch rabbi told his students that whatever he can't make them understand with words, he would make them understand with song. But I haven't found in music a single answer to my doubts; on the contrary, singing only makes my depression worse. So I renounced it, renounced singing entirely. The only tune I still sing is the Selichos prayer." And Zalia Ziskind tested his gravelly throat, coughed several times, and started singing quietly, under his breath, with a soft, sweet sadness and a well of tears in his voice and eyes. "*Shema koleinu* . . . Hear my voice, Lord, our Lord, have pity on me and accept our prayer with compassion."

Zalia Ziskind interrupted his singing. "Do you still put on tefillin? I mean, are you still following Jewish law?" His teary eyes flickered with a crafty smile, as if to let Naftali Hertz know that people were on to him.

Naftali Hertz winced, anticipating questions about his wife and son. He better not mess it up and tell him something different from what he'd told his parents and sister. "Of course I'm observing Jewish law. I'm much nearer to Judaism now than I was when in yeshiva."

"I didn't mean to demand that you give me an accounting. I'm asking because of my son. My Marcus became an orphan at a young age and wasn't raised under my supervision. There's a lot to discuss, but in short—he's searching and doesn't know what he's searching for. So since you're a man of the world, I thought you might enlighten him, show him there's nothing waiting for him out in the world; it won't be happier for him there."

"It certainly won't be happier for him there, and you can be sure I'll tell him so," Naftali Hertz said, and recalled that his sister, too, had asked him to have a conversation with Marcus.

Head drawn between his pointy shoulders, and large, hornlike nose protruding from his narrow face, Zalia Ziskind sat with closed eyes, brow furrowed, ears alert, as if despite his insistence that he no longer had the heart or ears for song, he was now straining to hear, in the quiet summer night, the soft, melodic lapping of the Narev's waves. Naftali Hertz watched him. He couldn't escape the thought that his old rosh yeshiva might well be the only person who wouldn't reject him for having a goyish wife and son.

11

I N THE STIFLING SUMMER HEAT, a cloud of dust kicked up by a
peasant's wagon hung over the street and valley. The dust crept
into the nostrils and throats of the tired Lecheve shopkeepers sitting outside their shops. Boys and girls loitered around in the empty
marketplace, chewing on straw and joking idly, bored. Suddenly, the
group burst into a roar of laughter, a sound like a gunshot's echo. But
for the exhausted shopkeepers, the cause of the idlers' laughter held
no interest.

A man in a tall hat and heavy boots, wearing his sleeves rolled up
and no jacket, stood on a porch looking out at the sandy country
road reddened by the sun. So intensely did he stare, it seemed he was
determined to finally discover whether sand could truly transform
into gold or it was just a myth from children's books. Another Jew,
round-bellied, in a stiff black dusty hat, a long coat buttoned to his
neck, and with an itinerant shadchan's stick in his hand, stared up at
the beis medrash on the hill. He turned his ear to the students' voices
with the expression of an expert, as if by their chanting he could dis-
tinguish their levels of scholarliness and whether they were worthy
of a quality bride. He stood still, listening, and the voices, too, waft-
ing from the beis medrash windows, hung there unmoving in the
vacuum of the glittering sun's whiteness.

Climbing the hill toward the town cemetery were two men, Naftali Hertz Katzenellenbogen and Marcus Luria. Half their bodies were sunken in the tall weeds. From the earth rose a wealth of
plants, white grains and dandelions with downy heads, yellow teeth,
blue and violet goblets. Colorful butterflies rubbed their little feet
against the stamens and drank like drunkards from the flower-cups.
On broad leaves sat spiders, perforating the fuzzy green. The vegeta-
tion, scorched by the sun, exhaled pungent fragrances. Naftali Hertz

stopped several times, panting. "In the Alps there are paths every-where, foot trails carved into the mountains. But here everything is neglected and wild."

At last, they reached the back of the mountain, where the cem-etery lay. On the other side, they noticed, the trail was even more twisted. Beneath, the Narev reached its widest point in the region. And far off, in the middle of the river, was a sizable island, overgrown with a thicket of trees and hollowed-out sticks. The moist, grayish air blurred the view, but through the fog they could see two fishermen idling in their boats, waiting for their nets to fill with fish. Part of the stream had a yellowish hue; another part shimmered with varying colors, sky blue mingled with the reflected green of the shore. From time to time, great winged birds appeared over the water, flying as quietly as their shadows glided over the river.

"I don't understand why you wanted to climb to the cemetery, of all places," Naftali Hertz said, irritated.

Marcus didn't reply right away. An anxious, somewhat mocking smile quivered on his lips. "The pious have always come to cem-eteries to learn that life isn't worth living. I mean it!" he said, notic-ing that Naftali Hertz was eyeing him impatiently, as if he thought Marcus was posturing. "I really do like to stroll around cemeteries and read the tombstone inscriptions. It makes you realize that the dead are neither all that terrible nor all that saintly." Marcus then stretched his hand out, unexpectedly, to Katzenellenbogen's straw hat, giving its brim a curious pinch. "Is this from abroad?"

"Yes," Naftali Hertz said, and allowed the young man to finger his black tie and brown suit as well. He looked at Marcus and had the thought that he'd already seen a tall, pale young man just like him somewhere else. The handsomely carved profile and well-wrought nose, the black curly hair and long, fluttering fingers all looked famil-iar. He had seen the other young man, a pianist, at a concert in Bern. Under different circumstances, perhaps this Marcus Luria, son of a singer, might have grown up to be a musician. Still, he was better off. Much better that he hadn't studied abroad and fallen in love with a shiksa . . .

"Are you so afraid of death that you have to go to the cemetery to realize that the dead aren't terrifying?"

"It's not so much to realize that the dead don't have to be feared,"

Marcus replied, "as to realize that the dead aren't that holy and we needn't have qualms about tossing the inheritance of dead generations off our shoulders. That's why I go to the cemetery." He stood near the graves of the "greats" and read their praises on the stone tablets, knowing that the reason for listing these praises was so that people would learn from them and emulate them. Just as Samson had ripped the door out of the citadel surrounding the city and dragged it and its frame on his back up the mountain, so must he, Marcus Luria, drag the tombstones of all the past generations on his shoulders. They called this ideology by various pretty names—"our holy inheritance," "the tradition of our patriarchs," "the miracle of the Jewish people's eternity," "the eternity of the law of Moses," "the clairvoyance of the Prophets," "Messiah's times"—and other such terms. But the gist of them all was the same: bearing the weight of gravestones etched with pedigrees of the dead.

"But I don't want to haul this load." Marcus bit his fingernails. "I read in a holy book that you're not allowed to read inscriptions on gravestones because it damages your memory. So I make sure to read the inscriptions even more diligently, because I want my memory damaged, I want to lose my historical awareness. In whatever I feel and think and do, I don't want to repeat past generations. I don't want to be an imitator, even of today's generation, the ones who are alive. I alone should exist in what I feel, think, and do."

"Just yesterday I heard the opposite from your father—that the loneliest person in the world is the one who refuses to remember his past. That must certainly include a person who doesn't want to remember his lineage and origins. And your father's right! But you're too young to understand how right he is." From beneath his furrowed brow, Naftali Hertz stared at the young man, who reminded him of his own rebellious years.

"Well, that's the thing. I don't want to be like my father!" Marcus cried, and his eyes gleamed like two dark nights in the middle of the bright day. "I believe the exact opposite of my father. If a person can take up his life alone, that's happiness right there, already. Whatever Father may tell himself, I believe that his depression and all the failures in his life stem from his inability—as so many others were unable—to carry the onus of inheritance."

They sat down to rest on the mountain slope, their faces toward the

Narev. The humid gray air had cleared. In the transparent blue, they had a clear view of the river island, thickly covered in grass, shrubs, and a forest of tall, thin birches, their fresh bark glinting silver. The air had cleared so completely they could make out the curls of smoke rising from the pipes of the two fishermen on boats in the middle of the river. Somewhere, a stork flapped its large wings, cold and dry. From the river shore echoed the clangs of the peasant women beating their washboards. Opalescent clouds swam to the wooded hills on the Narev's opposite shore. There, all sorts of trees mingled, their branches entangled, their needled crowns swaying up to the edge of the horizon.

Semi-prone, Naftali Hertz sat on the mountain, his eyes closed. He felt the Lecheve cemetery creeping through his neck and deep into his brain. At his side lay Marcus, going on and on about the burden of inheritance. "Anytime a Jew came up with a new creed, a new school of thought, he instantly had to prove that everything he was saying had already been said by the Prophets, the Sages, the pious philosophers, or the Kabbalah teachers. No one was ever able to say anything new or take a single step on an untrodden path. Our heads had to be turned backward, always looking to the past. *That* was considered moving forward, climbing higher. A Jew's feelings and thoughts must be tied to a dead world; he must keep his head buried in the grave of past generations, as the verse says: '*Zekhor yemos olam*, Remember the early days.' Jews must believe that the people of the past were giants atop a mountain, and we of the present are dwarves in an abyss. Without the crutch and support of the older generations, we dwarves and cripples can't stand on our own feet. We can't even move a limb, for fear that some hallowed, moldy artifact might crumble into dust. Is this the meaning of 'Thou shalt have no idols'? No, this is a room full of wood and clay idols, just like the shop of Terah, Abraham's father! But now we're no longer allowed to touch them; they've been consecrated by the fallen dust of Jewish history. But in order to be happy, we *must* be ahistorical. A tree has no history . . . Why are you laughing?" Marcus said with wide, trembling eyes.

"Nietzsche! I'm laughing because you're taking Friedrich Nietzsche's argument against history and directing it against Judaism. Did you read it in German or in Hebrew? I knew you were a Nietzschean before I even saw you. Right after I arrived, Tilza told me about you, claiming you say odd things. For example, when a man is about to fall, kick him to make him fall faster. That's when I knew you'd swallowed up *Thus Spake Zarathustra*."

"And your sister laughed at me?" Marcus asked suspiciously, holding his breath.

"Tilza didn't laugh at you, but she wondered why a young Jewish man, particularly the son of a rabbi, would say such things. And would you really want a hard bed, not a soft one, as Zarathustra says? I think you're much happier that my sister gave you and your father two beds with soft mattresses, not hard planks. How old are you, now?"

"Twenty-seven."

"Twenty-seven!" Naftali Hertz stared at Marcus for a long while, silent. Marcus struck him as childish, not at all adult in his feelings. "My sister Tilza is nine years older than you," he said, as if warning against something they hadn't yet spoken of.

"Nine years older?" Marcus cried, and now it was his turn to be quiet. Eventually, he said, "And I thought . . . I thought you didn't want to remember the past, either, and that's why you ran away from yeshiva and out into the world."

"Obviously, not everything a person hears or reads or even experiences should be remembered. Just as a good memory is a blessing for a person, it can also become his misfortune. A good memory is a blessing, for example, when a person doesn't do the exact same thing a third time after he's failed at it the first two times. But we sometimes become so enslaved to remembering that we can't help but repeat the very things that have brought suffering, embarrassment, and failure upon us again and again." Naftali Hertz's voice turned suddenly hoarse, as if one of his vocal cords had snapped. "But the blessing and curse of memory relates only to the individual, not to the historical memory of an entire nation. The burden of inheritance is not a weight we lug on our shoulders, the way Nietzsche's Zarathustra lugs the tightrope walker who fell and died, or the way, as you described it, we lug tombstones along with us. The weight of generations is carried within oneself. Unless you're a bastard, and there's no father or father's inheritance to reject."

They'd descended the mountain by then and had reached the

town's main street. Naftali Hertz wanted to continue his stroll alone, as he was used to doing in Switzerland. It wasn't in his nature to have long and confiding discussions with strangers. But he forced himself to speak boldly to his former rosh yeshiva's only son. He stopped and put his hand on Marcus's shoulder in a brotherly manner. "Judging by your awe of Nietzsche's rationalization, I'd have assumed you're younger than you are. The world was younger and more inexperienced when it became enamored of Nietzsche's aphorisms. You're a belated Nietzschean, an entire generation late, maybe two. Yes, there was a time when Hebrew writers parroted the babbling of Friedrich Nietzsche, railing against what he calls 'slave morality' and supporting 'master morality,' the freedom of the strong alpha personality who makes his own laws. A Hebrew-writing Jew and Nietzsche— could there be an odder pairing? Yet this very philosopher, with his made-up Übermensch, himself alienated from the world and from life, his eyes sick and his mind even sicker, was very much in fashion in his time—so he attracted our people, who were just as alienated from the world and life, the naïve young men who studied in the synagogues, wasting time studying Torah even after they'd become Hebrew writers. In their confused minds, the Baal Shem Tov and Nietzsche, or the revolution and Nietzsche, made sense together. Stuffy yeshiva boys! Bookworms!" Naftali Hertz worked himself into a frenzy. Though he spoke of Hebrew writers, he was in fact ridiculing himself, for his life of exile in a little room at the library, where he read and read but could never write a word, not even to finish what he'd started years ago, for fear of taking full account of his reflections and achievements—if you could call them that. "You're repeating the same bombastic Nietzschean aphorisms now, decades too late. Well, isn't it all laughable? You have even less experience of the world than those Hebrew idlers, less experience of goyim and goyish Jews. You think all you have to do is run away from your father and your little town and you'll be done with your heritage. You'll lose your memory, turn into a tree . . . Well, goodbye! Tell my sister I'll be coming later."

"And you?" Marcus blocked his path. "You *do* have experience of the world. So answer me this: Are the Swiss cannibals?"

"Of course they aren't," Naftali Hertz replied slowly, shocked at the question, his rage cooling. "There are fine people among the Swiss, just as in other nations. What I meant was that, because you haven't yet cut yourself off from your environment and haven't lived away from home, you don't yet realize how hard it is to excise yourself from your origins. You don't yet realize that it's easier to deny the existence of God than to stop believing a grandfather's superstition. Do you understand that?"

"No, I don't." Marcus's nostrils twitched. "Your sister, she believes in God, in her father, her grandfather, her husband. It's only in the local yeshiva boys that she doesn't believe. She dislikes them for their poor sense of style and their rocking. She holds small grudges against her husband, too, very small . . ."

"Yes, even though my sister is older than you, nine years older, she's not very mature for her age," Naftali Hertz said, and he set off on his stroll down the town's main street. Marcus headed up the hill to the rabbi's house.

On the lawns and bushes near the wooden houses, on their balconies, the shadows of twilight had already spread. Clouds accumulated, drifting low, and the wind whizzed by like the town lunatic, barefoot and in tattered clothes. On both sides of the street, the dusty, thick-leaved branches of maples and acacias rustled and murmured of the coming rain. A corner of sky, still free of clouds, shone with the green clarity of a lake filled with aquatic plants. For a while Naftali Hertz stood at a telegraph pole, listening to its drone. Then he went on walking. He remembered his recent bout of nostalgia, back in Bern, over the crooked willows near his father's house in Morehdalye. But once he'd arrived in his hometown, he felt doubly uprooted. The Swiss landscape wasn't part of his body and soul, but neither could he weave himself back into the rustling old willows by his father's house. Even if burned by ten fires, he could never again have gotten used to the hundreds of Jewish laws and customs. Yet to erase them from his psyche, no, that he could not do either.

A few heavy drops splashed his face, but the expected downpour never came. A gust scattered the clouds, sweeping the sky clean. Naftali Hertz wondered how he'd missed the sunset; neither had he noticed the fall of dusk. A full moon, still reflecting the red sun, seemed to have materialized all at once. Flames glowed in the windows of the houses in the valley, and off the brick buildings on the surrounding hills. He was pleased that the rain hadn't come, that he could linger outside with his thoughts a while longer.

Regardless of how much Naftali Hertz lied and concealed, his family seemed to discern that he was carrying within him a heavy, painful burden, the way one can smell staleness and mold in a cellar without being able to see what's there in the darkness. Which is why he wanted to be alone as much as possible; he didn't want them to notice how troubled he was. And what, in the end, was achieved by so much struggling? It wasn't like he had a choice. He couldn't *not* go back. If he refused to go back, he'd be forced to reveal the truth to his family. Then again, why shouldn't he go back? As much as he disliked Karl's red, gentile face and his big, heavy bottom, he already missed him painfully. More than he'd missed his younger siblings after twelve years away. Naftali Hertz looked up at the sky as if the full moon were the glowing window of his bedroom in Bern. Was Annelyse alone, or had she stopped being ashamed even in front of her son and brought her lover into their bedroom? There was a chance he'd arrive home to find Luigi Martini living in his home. Katzenellenbogen was surprised at how calmly he was able to summon the image. In Bern, at work in the library, when he'd imagined Annelyse with the wallpaper man, he'd felt as if his skin were being peeled from his body. Maybe the distance had helped him understand that the only one to blame was himself? If he weren't so gloomy, spreading his melancholy everywhere, perhaps Annelyse wouldn't have taken a lover.

He stood idly on a street corner, looking around. The curtains had been left open at some of the houses, as if their residents wanted everyone to see their impoverished, yet pious, lives. In one home, a little black-bearded Jew, wearing the hat of a Polish Hasid, sat at a table with a large holy book—a Gemara, it seemed—his head sinking lower and lower toward the book, as if he'd dozed off. Behind him a bewigged woman moved about, and a fluffy white cat lay curled up on the blanket of a double bed. Through the curtainless window of another house, he saw a working-class family seated around a table, sharing a meal. It looked as if the men's work entailed pulling tar from its source, so black were their faces. In the twisted fingers of their large hands, they held wooden spoons, ladling food out of clay bowls. Among them sat a woman in a headdress like a cast-iron pot, wearing a large apron and a shawl over her shoulders, in the middle of summer. There was a bowl of food next to her, too, but she wasn't eating. Her coarse, overworked hands lay still on the table, and she stared outside with big eyes set in her wrinkled face. Naftali Hertz couldn't see anything through the window of the next house, because it had a curtain. A pale light filtered through the sheer fabric, and the inside resounded with the happy laughter of boys and girls.

Naftali Hertz remained standing there, still thinking about himself, his family, and the townspeople. Though his father had become much more restrained than in the past, he was still the same old zealot at his core. His fanatical Zembin grandfather, too, must surely have retained his parochial, rigid mindset. A stagnant pond. And the town's Jews—they hadn't changed either. No matter how many people had died in the war, no matter how many young men never returned from the front, no matter how much they suffered under each new ruler, no matter how much the conditions of life continued to change—the Jews, their character, opinions, and behavior, remained the same. He felt lonesome. And yet, he was no less lonesome in his other home, Switzerland, where for the chance to talk to himself he had to hide in a back room of the Judaic division, like the taharah room of a Jewish cemetery.

12

THE WALLPAPER IN Tilza's bedroom was green, and the doors, two beds, and large armoire were a dark brown wood. Next to the armoire stood a low dresser for underwear, like a short woman beside her tall, broad-shouldered husband. The dresser was covered with a crocheted runner on which stood a pair of copper candlesticks and a photograph of Tilza's parents. And in the wall mirror over the dresser was a patch of blue sky reflected from the summer day. Tilza was ironing a white blouse in the middle of the room, on a table protected by a duvet cover and a sheet, which, in turn, were covered with a damp towel. She wore a long, rose-colored housedress with a belt and a collar that buttoned beneath the neck. The housedress was pleated above her full bosom, which gave off a special kind of warmth, like a wave in a milky fog. Although she was a rebbetzin, she didn't wear a headscarf. Her straight, cropped hair, parted down the middle, fell to below her ears. Slowly she swung the iron back and forth, listening to Marcus Luria.

He stood close to her, speaking impassionedly, as was his way. "Everything in woman is a riddle and everything in woman has one answer: give birth to children. So said Zarathustra. And it's true! If Aunt Sirka had gotten married in time and had children, she wouldn't have wanted me to remain a little boy forever, my whole life—*her* little boy! And she wouldn't be so unhappy now. She's still unhappy, despite getting a husband in the end. That's why you're calm and content with your life. Because you got married and had children in time." Marcus lowered his voice, becoming more secretive. "Besides calm and content, you're also pretty. So pretty and fresh, I can't sleep at night because of you." He murmured these words with a lowered head and suddenly jerked his hands out toward her, as if he'd prepared for this on those sleepless nights.

Tilza stepped back, but his lips were already on hers. She felt a sweet intoxication in her temples and a sense of pity for the pale, handsome, somewhat childish boy who was embracing her, his entire body trembling. With her left hand she lightly pushed him away, placing the iron on the bottom of an upturned copper pan that sat on the table. "Are you crazy! I could have accidentally dropped the heavy iron on your feet!" she cried. But Marcus glowed with joy. She wasn't furious and she hadn't shoved him away forcefully! Tilza opened the door of the little heater in the iron and blew into it. The cooling coals reignited, casting a rosy glow on her face, like a flower in a field that had ripened overnight and bloomed with the sunrise. "Again and again you've said I'm content with my life. But how do you know?" she asked irritably, and started ironing the blouse again.

"I don't understand why you'd be insulted when I say you're content with your husband and children," Marcus grumbled with mocking, spiteful eyes. "It's obvious that you're happy with your life. I can see it the same way I can tell how miserable Sirka is with her blond husband. Meir Moshe Baruchovits isn't even a redhead, he's a blond imposter. And your husband, they say, is a blond, too."

"That's a lie! My husband is dark red; his beard and hair are the color of copper," Tilza cried out against her will. "My husband is a great man. He's a genius in Torah and extremely kind, a refined man . . . It's not nice of you to speak against him, you don't even know him, you've never even seen him." Abruptly, she burst out laughing at Marcus's jealousy of her husband. Then she took in a mouthful of water and sprayed some on the towel that was spread out on the table.

"You see! You're just pretending you're unhappy with your life. If I dare utter a word against your husband, even about his hair color, you start seething and boiling. 'My husband! My husband!'" Marcus mimicked her faces. "'I'm not instructing you about the love of what's near; I'm teaching you the love of what's far.' So said Zarathustra. Yet you keep saying: 'My husband! My husband!'"

Again he hugged her. His hands inched down her back toward her waist. Whether because she found it comical that she herself was constantly bringing up her husband or because Marcus couldn't stop talking about Zarathustra, even while hugging a woman—or perhaps because she couldn't think of a better way to extricate herself from his arms—Tilza sprayed Marcus in the face with the rest of the water in her mouth and laughed out loud. The bewildered boy didn't know whether to laugh along or get angry, and his stunned, confused expression made her laugh even harder. She fought to repress it for a moment and murmured "Someone's coming!" so that he'd move away from her.

The next day, Friday afternoon, Tilza was in the kitchen in her apron preparing the cholent for Shabbos. She placed chunks of beef and peeled potatoes into the pot, poured in some kasha, salted and peppered the dish, and then covered everything with garlic and cloves. Just as the day before, she was again listening with interest to Marcus's mishmash of Zarathustra's aphorisms and complaints about his aunt Sirka. Tilza liked hearing him talk. She also liked knowing that he wouldn't move from her side. She was paring a red onion with a large kitchen knife, and Marcus chose just that moment to embrace her, covering her cheeks and eyes with hot kisses. Tilza didn't resist, fearing that if she tried to push him away, she might slice him with the knife in her hand. "What are you doing?! Here, in the kitchen, at the cholent pot?" She laughed, frightened and embarrassed, as if she were standing there naked. Marcus kissed her again, with even more passion, and she became even more helpless.

Suddenly, he let go and stepped backward. "You won't tell your brother?"

"Tell my brother?" Tilza echoed, astonished. She placed the knife and onion on the table and wiped her hands on her apron. *A mere boy,* she thought, and smiled to herself. "You're not afraid of me, only of my brother? What makes you sure I won't tell your father?"

"You'd be embarrassed to tell my father. Anyway, even if you do, I'm not worried about my father. But I don't want your brother to know. Your brother, the philosopher doctor, has become a penitent. Of course, it's not hard to be a penitent on someone else's account. He wants to convince me that there's nothing for me out in the world, that he regrets his life choice."

"Yes, my brother is unhappy in his marriage. I don't know what's bothering him, but I see that he suffers," Tilza replied, looking worried, and glancing around as if Naftali Hertz might be in the other room.

"I won't let your brother keep me from living in the world! When he ran away from yeshiva, he never asked anyone if it was worth it or not. But now he expects me to take his word that there's no use leaving town, the yeshiva, the Torah," Marcus groused, an unhealthy flush burning his cheeks. The gleam in his hot black eyes and the helpless smile on his moist lips both aroused and repulsed Tilza. The image that came to mind was of a grown boy who still wet his pants. She looked away and listened as he railed against her brother.

"Yesterday evening we were talking and I was telling him the same things I told you during the day. That Zarathustra teaches us to care for the distant, not the near, not the neighbor who stumbles at your feet. And your brother told me I'm just parroting old, tired thoughts and books instead of thinking for myself. 'You regurgitate, you're an imitator!' he yelled at me. 'If you'd think for yourself,' he said, 'you wouldn't come up with such shallow sayings like "Love the distant." To love the distant, to concoct fantasies about strangers—an abstraction, loving humanity in general—isn't difficult at all; what's difficult is to love the individual, especially when he's your neighbor and you see him with all his sorry flaws. Some accomplishment!—to love the stranger you don't know and who doesn't need your help. Try the feat of loving the person you know with all his failings, the one who needs your help. Love thy friend as thyself. Love your friend, your neighbor, not a stranger. The distant, the stranger!' your brother yelled at me, as if he were my uncle, the dean of the Visoki-Dvor Yeshiva, admonishing his students. 'Your Zarathustra claims that of all that's been written, he likes only what's been written in blood, meaning from one's own body and life. So tell me a thought you came up with yourself!' your brother yelled at me, as if I was his assistant in a cheder class. Now do you understand why I don't want your brother to know what we talk about?'"

"Naftali Hertz isn't completely wrong," Tilza said softly, her eyes tender and maternal, as if to redeem her brother's severity. "The result of your talk about loving the distant, the stranger, is that, besides me and to some extent my brother, you end up speaking to no one; not to the yeshiva, not to the townspeople, not even to your father."

"And your brother, does he love those near to him?" Marcus said, stepping closer to her, passion burning in his eyes. "If your brother had loved those near to him, as he demands of me, he wouldn't be off in Switzerland for so many years, without ever visiting his family."

"My brother?" Tilza said, stumped, not knowing what to say.

"Yes, your brother. I'm not yet entirely convinced that your brother even loves the people near to him in Switzerland. He came here without his wife and son, and yet he gives advice to me about whom to love. So I don't want you to tell him about me. I don't want him to give me another philosophical lecture about morality."

"Okay, I won't tell my brother anything, if you promise you'll behave properly from today on," Tilza replied with feigned severity. "If you don't behave, I'll have to find an excuse for your father to explain why you both can't stay at my house anymore. Do you promise to behave in a way that's appropriate for the son of Zalia Ziskind Luria?"

Marcus didn't reply. He merely gazed at her suspiciously with his big, restless eyes, like a captive deer being handed food through its cage for the first time.

13

Friday evening, after a bright, clear day, on the eve of Shabbos Chazon, a drowned man was pulled from the river—a Jew with a gray beard, big frozen eyes, and thick black eyebrows. Nobody knew the man. He had arrived at the town's inn that Friday morning, left his luggage there, and gone immediately to the river. Around noon, a group of Christian women came to the shore to do laundry and found a bundle of men's clothes lying there. An hour passed, then two, until finally the laundresses decided that whoever owned the clothes must have vanished in the water. Jews came running, gathering round, and they noticed a tallis katan among the items. They set out in boats, searching the water for the man. Eventually, one of the boats' rudders bumped into a body lying on the riverbed, among the flora, not far from the shore. They pulled the dead man onto the sand and covered him with his clothes, except for his head, which they left uncovered in case someone recognized him. He lay like that, his big glazed eyes toward the sky, as if he were asking God, "Are You happy now?" Jews crowded around the victim, eyeing him with pain and fear. It was already too late to bury him, with Shabbos approaching. So they took him instead to the Lecheve poorhouse and left him lying in a vestibule through the holiday.

The poorhouse never lacked visitors, especially in the summer. A man who'd gone broke might stop there for a while, as he traveled from town to town collecting money for his daughter's dowry. Itinerant preachers would sleep there overnight, as would alms collectors from Israel or local beggars, vagabonds. But it just so happened that, on this particular Shabbos, no one was staying in the house, which led to the idea of leaving the dead man there. In the meantime, the sun had set, and the men rushed home to change their clothes in honor of Shabbos. The golden flames of Shabbos candles punctured the dark blue sky. In the wooden beis medrash, all the fixtures were already lit. And the cold brick shul on the mountain lit up the twilight, too, its copper trays on the walls twinkling from the reflections of the many lamps. It looked, this old shul where people davened only in the summer, like the legendary cave of Eden, alluded to in the tales of tzaddikim—the hidden palace and garden that may be revealed in honor of Shabbos to a Jew lost in the woods. Now, however, a poor Jewish stranger was lying in the vestibule of the empty poorhouse, and the Lecheve Jews felt the thick darkness gathering around him.

Zalia Ziskind heard news of this event when he arrived at the beis medrash for davening. He turned as mute as a mound of clay, and deathly pale. In Visoki-Dvor, the townspeople knew how easily bad news could sink their rabbi into depression, even when the news didn't concern him or anyone close to him. But people of Lecheve were unaware, and didn't take notice of his altered expression.

"There's not even a beadle or beadle's wife in the poorhouse to make sure that the man doesn't decompose," one person said, sighing.

"To live and die like this . . . a humiliation for a living creature," another groaned.

A third person wondered aloud: "Who is he, this drowned man? Why did he come to Lecheve? Does he have a wife and children somewhere? The inn owner says he didn't get a good look at him. As soon as the man arrived, he left to bathe in the river. They found no passport on him, not a single paper with any information."

The longer the discussion dragged on, the lower Zalia Ziskind's head sunk. He gripped the lectern with his small, pale, trembling hands so that he wouldn't collapse. People stood up to daven, to greet the Shabbos, but the hunchbacked rosh yeshiva stood, unmoving. Because it was Shabbos Chazon, and because of that day's tragedy, the ba'al tefilah leading the prayers refrained from singing too much. But even the Skarbov tune pricked Zalia Ziskind like needles. The burning lamps appeared to him as the eyes of oxen prior to slaughter, full of bloody rage and fear of death. Animals cry out to the Creator, asking why He created a world of so much cruelty and suffering, but bewildered man does everything in order to forget, until Job's misfortunes befall him and he's forced to remember.

Only after davening did people notice that Zalia Ziskind was shaken. They wished him "Good Shabbos," to which he replied, "So does no one really know the drowned man's name and where he came from?" He said this with such fear and pleading, as though word had come from heaven that if he didn't find out who the corpse was, he'd face a similar end, perhaps even worse: he wouldn't be buried as a Jew. His brokenness spread to the other Jews. Later, the men told their families of how Zalia Ziskind had taken the news. And so, on this Shabbos Chazon, all of Lecheve was pervaded by a sinister horror. They thought of the abandoned corpse in the poorhouse's dim, rancid vestibule; and all day the clear blue sky and the dazzling golden sun tormented the Jews. Before their eyes lay the image of the drowned Jew, with his big, frozen eyes, and they couldn't daven or eat or nap.

The funeral took place on Sunday before noon. Young and old escorted the dead man to the cemetery on the hill. After the burial, people consoled one another: It's over! Maybe one day we'll discover the identity of this victim of the river. After all, the Gemara says that a man's feet act as his witness—they lead him to where he's meant to go.

And a fanatical Jew added, "Apparently Lecheve isn't mourning the destruction of the Temple enough in these 'nine days,' so heaven has sent us something else to mourn."

The shopkeepers went back to their businesses, the artisans to their workshops. Old men went back to the beis medrash to study Midrash Eicha, as was the custom before Tisha B'Av, and the yeshiva men sat down to peruse the Talmud's allegorical passages relating to the Temple's destruction. It's not that they forgot the drowned man, but they did their best to push all thoughts of him aside and store him in their memories, so that he wouldn't obstruct them from continuing with their lives. Only Zalia Ziskind couldn't return to himself.

The residents of Lecheve saw the drowning as one of Satan's pranks. They'd believed that by discussing Torah passages with the Dünaburg genius, they'd be able to pull him from the black river of depression in which he was drowning. So when the evil inclination, Satan, the Angel of Death—for all three are one and the same, as the Gemara attests—bore witness to this, he ensured that a Jew who was destined to drown be sent to Lecheve to plunge Zalia Ziskind back into depression. "But with the power of Torah, we'll pull him out again," the students convinced one another, and right after

Tisha B'Av they began discussing the Torah with him again. But they couldn't cheer him up. He gazed at them with no light in his eyes, his lips quivering like wilted leaves.

"No Jew with a beard and a tallis katan would forget that it's Shabbos Chazon and go bathing. Bathing during the 'nine days' isn't strictly prohibited, of course, but a bearded Jew in a tallis katan would never do it. It's obvious he wanted to kill himself, because he could no longer bear his troubles, and when a person's on the verge of suicide he pays no mind to what's allowed and what isn't." Zalia Ziskind raised his head and, for a long while, stared with the wide eyes of a blind man at the stunned, silent students surrounding him. "That he stopped at the inn and then immediately ran off to the river makes it clear that his plan was to commit suicide in a place where no one knows him, so that his family wouldn't have to suffer the humiliation of his unnatural death. I have no doubt about that!" Zalia Ziskind said, but then he appeared uncertain and shook his head sadly. "Would a person who's about to kill himself remember to take his clothes off before jumping into the water? Oh, it's too funny in its way. No, it's plain and simple. The Jew arrived in town all dirty and sweaty, ran to the river to bathe, to refresh . . . Oh, what difference does it make?" Zalia Ziskind groaned like a chopped tree on its way down and turned silent, pained by his vacillating thoughts.

A few days later, his words caused the students even greater surprise. Tugging at his sparse beard and rocking like a mourner on his shiva chair, he said, "The drowned man was no ordinary Jew; he was a messenger from the World of Truth. He came from heaven to teach us, to make us understand the fate of people on earth. But we miss the hidden signs in these kinds of encounters: A man comes and goes—dies!—in barely half a day. We take from it only what we wish—we have no problem understanding Elijah the Prophet coming to earth in different forms, bringing us a bundle of luck, prosperity, blessings for the children, salvation and peace. But we can't bring ourselves to believe that heaven would send a specially chosen messenger in the form of a poor man, who dies in a poorhouse or drowns in a river, in order to force us to think about the things we don't want to think about."

Zalia Ziskind went silent for a moment. Then he burst into such soft, bitter sobbing that tears welled in the students' eyes. "Gentlemen, I invented this version—that the dead man was a special messenger from heaven—to console myself. I wanted to believe that this living being hadn't died for no reason. But the truth is that I myself don't believe what I'm saying, gentlemen. He was surely a human being; woe unto him. Surely he hoped to attain something more in life and was awaiting better days. He didn't even have the privilege of relatives escorting him to his burial, or family members saying Kaddish for him."

Zalia Ziskind's eulogy for the stranger tore a piece out of the hearts of his young students who hadn't yet become jaded by life's misfortunes. Some took it upon themselves to say Kaddish for the drowned man and to study a chapter of Mishnayos for his soul. But they no longer went over to the rosh yeshiva to discuss Torah with him. They realized that doing so only increased his pain and despair.

14

N AFTALI HERTZ HAD NEVER encountered such Torah scholars as those in Lecheve. In his own yeshiva years, the young men had all pulled toward education. They tried fighting their evil inclinations, but in the end, they secretly met up with girls. In Lecheve, though, the students were pious and bearded, with deep, thoughtful eyes like lakes with leaves. They wore the same hats and boots as the town Jews did, unlike the yeshiva boys in Mir and Kletsk, who dressed up in fancy caps and step-in shoes. The diligent Lecheve students were uninterested in Haskalah books and exhibited no curiosity toward Naftali Hertz, a well-educated man from abroad. They wanted to talk about Torah learning, not worldly topics, and as soon as they discovered that the doctor of philosophy had forgotten the Torah he'd once studied, they barely stopped to talk to him on the street or in the beis medrash. They greeted him kindly and continued on their way.

They acted the same toward Marcus Luria. At first when he'd arrived, the students had thought: *Well, this is no small matter—the only son of the Dünaburg genius! He must be a great scholar, pious, assiduous!* But when Marcus stepped into the yeshiva and the boys tried to befriend him, he turned his back on them, answered their questions reluctantly, and bit his long, pale fingers. The boys realized he wasn't, nor did he want to be, one of them—and they let him be. But they watched from afar how he chased the Swiss doctor through the streets and in the yeshiva with such ardor and enthusiasm.

The more entangled Marcus became in his feelings for Tilza, the more embarrassed and scared he was of her brother. Indeed, it was the reason he kept running after Naftali Hertz: to dodge his own guilt. He also hoped to avoid suspicion by engaging in passionate debates. But Naftali Hertz had no interest in discussions. What he wanted most was to sit at a lectern in the beis medrash, studying from a holy book and humming the Gemara tune under his breath. He knew he hadn't become genuinely devout, nor was he now interested in engaging in the Gemara's back-and-forth. Even a believer who spends his time studying, he knew, was not exempt from suffering or failure. Yet true believers didn't wear masks, and his face was a piece of plaster, of clay. He wished he were one of the truly devout, of whom it could be said: "*Achas she'alti m'eis Hashem . . .* One thing I ask of God: Let me sit in the house of God all the days of my life." True, the beis medrash reeked of dust, of books that begged for an airing out, of disheveled, overgrown yeshiva boys in need of a wash; true, the sour odor of the public towel above the ritual washstand filled the room—yet the people here had souls. In their every twist and turn, spiritual light beamed from them.

But why had they been looking at him lately with an expression of surprise and disappointment? Some of them stared at him in silent reproof. Perhaps a rumor had reached Lecheve and any day now it would reach his parents in Morehdalye? Naftali Hertz's mind reeled; the beis medrash swirled dizzily in front of his eyes. Hard as it might be, he must enter into a discussion with someone, perhaps that young man with the gold-rimmed glasses.

"Sholem aleichem! Where are you from?" Naftali Hertz forced a smile.

"From Grajewo," the young man answered calmly, gazing at his long fingers as if he were contemplating which would bear his wedding ring. "I was actually going to ask you; forgive me, but why wouldn't you study with Marcus Luria a few hours a day? His father would be grateful."

"And why wouldn't *you*?" Naftali Hertz retorted.

"Marcus would have more respect for you than for me," the Grajewoer replied with a wide smile. "Besides, you see him more often. He and your father live at your sister's. You should be watching over him, making sure his time isn't wasted on nonsense." He bent toward his Gemara, hinting that he no longer wanted to take time away from his studies.

Naftali Hertz shrugged his shoulders. He didn't understand what the boy wanted, and he walked away toward another student. This one had a big head with coarse and closely cropped fire-red hair, a face full of pimples, fleshy lips, and strong, dazzling white teeth. When he davened and studied, he rocked wildly, moved up and down, clenching his fists as if in the throes of a life-and-death battle with his evil inclinations. His every movement exhibited masculine strength, but his face lacked the luster of refinement or wisdom. He was the kind of boy whose wife, once he married, would pop out baby after baby; and were she to die in childbirth, he'd remarry just after the traditional thirty days of mourning. Then he'd start producing children again.

Naftali Hertz asked him where he was from, and he replied combatively, "I'm from the same town as you—Morehdalye. My father is Yechiel Mechel Buxbaum." Seeing Naftali Hertz furrow his brow, unable to recall who Buxbaum was, the boy said, with even more hostility, "You don't remember? The iron store owner in the old marketplace, Yechiel Mechel Buxbaum? No wonder you don't recall or notice other things!" The redhead launched into a diatribe, becoming more and more incensed: "I can understand why Zalia Ziskind is silent. Marcus is his son, after all, and some say that Zalia Ziskind is completely unaware altogether. But you, Katzenellenbogen, are a man of the world. You have the title of doctor of philosophy, one who contemplates 'the things at the heights of this world, *beromo shel olam*,' lofty thoughts. Don't you see, don't you realize, what everyone sees and knows? Don't you care at all for the honor of your family? And what would your father, the Morehdalye rabbi, say about this?"

"What are you talking about?" Naftali Hertz asked, and felt his lips turning tight and dry.

"About the prohibition of yichud! A man isn't allowed to be alone with a woman even in a cemetery, even in the mourning period. I'm sure you remember the Tosafos commentary, about the widow at her husband's grave and the soldier guarding the hanged man. You remember what came of that? I see you've forgotten this Tosafos just as you forgot the owner of the iron shop. Now I get why you haven't noticed—or just aren't concerned—that your sister spends time with Marcus Luria," the boy said, twirling his thumb and humming the Gemara chant, as yeshiva boys do when they study. "Even if, in this case, it's not an outright violation of yichud—after all it's an 'open door in a public place' and her children are with her—still, by all accounts, it's a desecration of God's name for the Lecheve rebbetzin to be chitchatting day and night with another man. It's only the students whispering about it now. But pretty soon it'll be the talk among neighbors, and then everyone in the marketplace. Is that okay?" he cried, staring with stupid eyes at Naftali Hertz.

Some of the students who wrote letters home used the Lecheve rosh yeshiva's house as a return address. Lately, whenever the boys stopped by to see if they'd received letters from home, they found Rebbetzin Tilza in conversation with Marcus. Each day, Marcus glowed with more lust for her. He laughed nervously and spoke with too much haste. Beads of sweat covered his forehead, and his big black eyes were constantly squinting.

Ever since Zalia Ziskind had fallen back into depression, Marcus held it over Tilza. "See? You and your brother didn't like it when I said that Father's empathy for others had ruined his life. Now you can see it for yourself! A stranger, a poor Jew, went bathing on Friday and drowned, and Father can't lecture the students anymore. He's distraught, in general. I can hear him sighing all through the night. He can barely breathe."

It was about ten in the morning. Zalia Ziskind and Naftali Hertz weren't home. Heshe'le was in cheder and Baila'ke was asleep, swaddled, in her crib in the other room. Tilza was still roaming around the house in her belted cerise robe. Her ripe, voluptuous body and full breasts lay beneath folds of thin fabric; her warm skin emitted a smell of fresh milk. Marcus knew from experience that when he hugged her and buried his face in her swollen breasts, she would stand there helplessly for a while, half-unconscious. She'd once even kissed his brow and told him how heartsick she felt at his being raised without a mother. That's what he'd been missing and still was, she believed. But regardless of what she uttered in those initial moments, and however much she might caress him, she always pushed him away after a bit, determinedly away. Annoyed and frustrated, he reminded himself that she, too, was part of the frightened, confused hoi polloi, as Zarathustra called these folk, a small-town, provincial woman.

Tilza said, "Your father's depression isn't just bad for himself. My husband designated your father as his replacement to give talks in yeshiva and to rule on Jewish law."

"True, true." Marcus nodded his head, not bothering to hide his mocking expression. "If Father won't be able to substitute for your husband, Lecheve will have to look for a new rabbi, and you'll lose your rebbetzin position."

Hatred for him rose up in Tilza. But her anger soon subsided. She clasped his curly head to her brow, yet distanced her body, so that he couldn't press up against her. "Lay your forehead on mine. Yes, just like that. Don't be upset that I'm concerned about the yeshiva. My husband does for the yeshiva what he wouldn't do even for me and my children. He'd never travel abroad to collect money for me and the children; in fact, I wouldn't allow it."

"Again with your husband! My husband! My husband!" Marcus grumbled, rubbing his temples against Tilza's. He felt a velvety smoothness at the touch, a coolness, a tiredness so sweet he closed his eyes from pleasure. "You say you don't want to be a rebbetzin, yet you fret over the fate of the yeshiva. If I'm to take you at your word, you were never in love with your husband and your true feelings are for me. Yet you don't allow yourself to be touched out of fear of your husband."

"I'm not afraid of my husband wanting to divorce me, I'm afraid I won't be able to look him in the eye. I've wanted to leave him several times. But to dupe him? No, that I don't want to do," Tilza said, each word measured, as if she were pleading her case before a judge. "It's not just the yeshiva and my husband; I'm thinking of your father, too. He's already suffered enough, wandered enough. He was hoping to settle here in Lecheve with you. But if . . ."

She stopped. Into the room came Naftali Hertz, his face so enraged that his sister could only stare at him with a mixture of fear and curiosity. Tilza had already prepared his breakfast—cold rice, eggs, and hard white cheese. She asked him whether he wanted to eat, and he grumbled something surly and slumped into his chair. She left the room to retrieve the food and felt her brother watching her harshly from beneath his straw hat.

Marcus, too, was confused, but he forced himself to speak cheerfully. "I'm telling your sister about the origin of morals, how when man no longer had the power to torture others, he began to torture himself. Out of this grew the religion of self-renunciation. Which means that torturing oneself plays a part in every religion," Marcus said heatedly, and abruptly stopped.

Naftali Hertz made a resentful face and impatiently turned away as if to cry, "I've had more than enough of your philosophy already."

Marcus dropped his booming tone and muttered, "I'm talking to your sister about this because of my father. If a stranger drowns, he falls into despair."

Naftali Hertz maintained his silence and kept his face turned away. Marcus grew even more confused. Confused and offended. Only when Tilza came in with a tray of food did he say, "Your brother understands as well as I do that sometimes what's good for the whole isn't good for each of us individually. But he keeps the truth to himself, he doesn't share it with others. Even his sister isn't allowed to know the entire truth. You have to live in darkness, you're not allowed to be enlightened. But I believe that you, too, are entitled to the truth. That's why he's angry and won't speak to me," Marcus cried, and left the room.

Naftali Hertz, silent and sneering, watched him leave. Then he removed the items from the tray and placed them on the table. He took a few spoonfuls of cold rice and spoke mockingly of Marcus: "What a prattler! The other day he was reciting from Zarathustra: 'Guard yourself from good people; they never speak the truth. Everything they consider bad is good.' Such an immature person! Only he, and he alone, has the courage to deny the small, comfortable truth and face a big, hard future truth. Out of his chaos, a new star will be born! That's all he keeps rehashing—strangers' phrases. What a Nietzschean regurgitator! What a lamebrain! To woo you with quotes from Zarathustra!"

The longer her brother spoke with such bile and anger, the gloomier Tilza became. She understood that this anger at Marcus didn't necessarily owe itself to his philosophy of might equals right. Indeed, he confirmed this soon enough. As Naftali Hertz peeled an egg, he unpeeled the real reason behind his anger. "The yeshiva boys spoke frankly to me today, about how you've been spending entire days with Marcus Luria. Even if no one were to suspect anything, it brings you no honor to prattle endlessly with this effeminate, half-insane man. But people *are* talking. And soon they won't assume your innocence anymore. You haven't faced any trouble yet; you don't realize how easily your marriage, your family, can be broken over nonsense." Fuming, Naftali Hertz placed the peeled egg back onto the tray, as if his fingernails had discerned a drop of blood in the yolk.

Tilza replied, with tears in her voice, "I won't deny that it's interesting to talk to Marcus. Am I not allowed? And I pity him, too. He can't make a friend and can't even get close to his father. So I'm friendly with him. But I don't let him get too close to me."

"It wouldn't bother me if you *did* let him get close to you, as long as people don't know about it and don't talk about it." Naftali Hertz jumped up. But he quickly sat back down again and resumed speaking in a calmer tone. "Even if Marcus suddenly left your house and went somewhere else to stay, it wouldn't stop the chatter. People would say you got scared and are meeting in secret. We must see to it that he leaves Lecheve, the sooner the better."

"I need to check on Baila'ke, she's been sleeping a long time. And Heshe'le's coming home from cheder soon, he'll be hungry." She gave her brother a sudden look of alarm. "How will you arrange for Marcus to leave this house? Or leave Lecheve entirely? Will you talk to him?"

"Talking to him won't help. I'll speak to his father, tell him they both have to leave. Zalia Ziskind has been moping around ever since that man drowned and is no use to the yeshiva anyway. And once his father leaves, our Nietzschean Übermensch won't stay here alone even for a day." Her brother laughed, but quickly hushed when he noticed Tilza sulking. His sister, he realized, was already calculating what problems Marcus could cause her, which was why she was no longer protesting. Naftali Hertz sat, head on his fist, and reflected on how, if it weren't for his own troubled marriage, it would never have dawned on him to worry that Tilza could ruin her home.

Naftali Hertz left the kitchen and retreated to the room his sister had set him up in: her husband's library. The sofa and armchair were upholstered in coarse leather. There was a big, low table in the room, along with a wooden bench and a tall oaken lectern. Even in his room at home, it seemed, Yaakov Asher Kahane wanted to feel like he was in a holy place. For Naftali Hertz, though, he sometimes had the impression he was in his library room in Bern, where he sat behind stacks of books, not wanting the day to end, so he wouldn't have to go back to his goyish home. The gold lettering on the spines of books shimmered, just as they did in the Bern library, and just as in the Bern library, here, too, he was beset by doubts. Here his doubts revolved around the unexpected appreciation he'd developed for sitting in the beis medrash. Could it be that the bumbling Nietzsche parrot, Marcus Luria, was right after all? The modern rabbis, in their priestly cassocks, preached that Jewry never went under because of the Prophets and their ideals. But wasn't it equally possible that the Jews' blind stubbornness, their fear-inducing graveyard stories, and their unchanging traditions had played a greater part in the Jews' endurance than the Prophets' ideals?

15

For the rest of the afternoon, Tilza didn't knock on her brother's door. Nor did she send in her children. Naftali Hertz knew that, even though his sister recognized that his plan to send Marcus Luria away was for her own good, she was still furious at him.

In the evening, Naftali Hertz left his room and, avoiding the family, went to the beis medrash. The summer's day had been long, hot, and dusty, so most of the yeshiva men were now out taking a stroll by the river's shore. Only a few students remained in the vast beis medrash, sitting at their lecterns studying holy books or simply daydreaming. Through the row of windows on one wall, you could still see light outside, but through the windows of the opposite wall it was already nearly dark. Zalia Ziskind stood at a table strewn with holy books, gazing blankly at them. *From where will I draw the strength*, Naftali Hertz wondered, *to tell this exhausted old man he must leave Lecheve?* But as soon as Zalia Ziskind noticed him, he said, "I can't carry the responsibility for the yeshiva and the town anymore. Typically, at the end of Av, a yeshiva becomes enlivened; the boys want to study not just during the day but in the evenings, too. And yet, Lecheve is dead. The yeshiva boys are glum, because I'm not giving any lectures. I'm not tending to the townspeople either. Oh, I can't wait for your brother-in-law to get back. When is he coming?"

"I don't know," Naftali Hertz said, breathing more lightly now. It seemed he'd be able to avoid telling the old man about his son's behavior.

But Zalia Ziskind had other thoughts on the matter. "It's too bad. I'll have to carry the responsibility until Yaakov Asher returns. Even afterward, in fact, I hope I can be of some help; being completely in charge, though—that I can't do anymore. What do you think, will he be back for the High Holy Days?"

"Perhaps. But that's still a month away," Naftali Hertz replied, his face clouding over. "I think, given your difficulty leading the yeshiva and taking care of the town, you should probably go. Forgive me for telling you this, I don't want to hurt you, but you must know the truth. Your Marcus doesn't understand what might come of his behavior, spending days on end schmoozing with my sister."

The old rosh yeshiva stood stock-still for so long it seemed he'd fallen asleep standing. Then, in small, stiff steps, he walked hastily out of the beis medrash. Naftali Hertz followed him. Outside, Zalia Ziskind continued to walk quickly, not turning to look back. At last, he reached the cold brick shul and sat down on a stone bench near one of the walls. His breathing was labored, and he kept sucking on his parched lips. Evening had fallen, casting his face in darkness. Only his hunchback was visible. Naftali Hertz hovered over him, straining to hear him, but he could barely make out what Zalia Ziskind was mumbling. "It's true, the tanna says 'Thou shalt not speak at length with a woman,' but I thought Marcus would benefit from his time with your sister. It would help him realize that one could have feminine charms *and* be a devout Jewish woman. It would lead him to follow in your brother-in-law's footsteps: to learn Torah, while he dreamed of finding a bride like your sister. But I understand that outsiders see it differently. They're not his father, after all."

"That outsiders view their schmoozing negatively isn't the worst of it. What's worse is that your son is truly smitten and he's pulling my sister in, too. Soon they'll both imagine they can't live without each other. Imagine the results!"

In the gathering darkness, the trees on the hillside huddled together, their branches entangling, as if they'd turned into a mysterious forest overnight. The dark blue velvety sky twinkled with green stars. From the valley there rose a gray-white fog, punctured by glowing, golden flames. At the foot of the slope, the waves of the Narev slapped against the shores. A wind blew, tousling the leafy treetops. In the daytime, when the shul was drenched in sunshine and shadows filled its nooks and crannies, Naftali Hertz would gaze at it from across the distance of his sister's home and imagine that the dancing lights and shadows were the brick shul's thoughts, or the thoughts of the Torah scrolls inside the ark. But standing near the shul, in the dark of night, Naftali Hertz saw this sacred place as the unchanging truth of a bygone era. It was like spotting the footprint of a prehistoric creature on a cracked rock.

Zalia Ziskind spoke again. "No matter how many times Marcus repeats his philosophy, that we must kick the weak so they'll fall more quickly, I know better than anyone that he empathizes with every cripple and pauper. But he's young and wants to live, so he proclaims the opposite. You know what he told me after that man drowned? He said, 'Don't cry, Father, for this Jew who drowned unwittingly while he was bathing. I've wanted more than once to *deliberately* jump into the water and be done with my fear of life and people.'"

Zalia Ziskind's long, crooked nose and gaunt face blanched in the darkness. His lips wriggled like a fish on land until he finally managed to eke out, hoarsely, "Even before he shared his envy of the drowned man, I was afraid, always so afraid, that, God forbid, he might commit suicide. Time and again, when I heard Marcus repeat his philosophical blabber about how the strong have a right to all the enjoyments in life that the weak are not permitted, I feared that after pronouncing these inflated words he'd run to the water and leap in." For a full minute, Zalia Ziskind was silent. Then he rose from the bench and waved his hands, as if he himself were drowning. "Why dillydally? We must send a telegram this very moment to Yaakov Asher, telling him to come back home. If we don't know exactly where he is, we'll send telegrams to five cities. Or rather, five countries. Come! Come! You'll help with the wording for the telegram." He hurried down the mountain, mumbling to himself all the while to confirm that he was handling this correctly. "Yaakov Asher labored and struggled to establish a cohort of students. Now he's roaming around foreign countries for funds, so that his students should be able to study in comfort. I won't allow God's name to be desecrated; no way will this place of Torah fall to pieces. I won't stay here for a single day more than necessary! My son and I will leave here as soon as possible, long before Yaakov Asher returns."

TILZA HADN'T EXPECTED the old rosh yeshiva to make such a swift decision. From all that Marcus had said about him and all that she'd seen for herself—the mild, gentle, somber person he was—she'd never imagined he could also be strict and fanatical. True, he hadn't once rebuked her. But his lack of blame only made her feel more ashamed, blushing straight to the roots of her hair. She was prepared to find another apartment for herself, as long as the old rosh yeshiva wouldn't have to wander again. But she realized Zalia Ziskind didn't want to stay in Lecheve anymore, under any circumstances. She asked him, "And where will you go now?"

The old man shrugged. "I actually don't know where to go. Marcus doesn't want to go back to Visoki-Dvor, and I can't blame him. His aunt, who'd been a mother to him, has gotten married. The students there keep their distance from him, and he hasn't cultivated friendships with the local boys either. What would he do with himself in Visoki-Dvor? And for me there's even less room there. My brothers-in-law will worry I'm coming back to reclaim my yeshiva and rabbinate," Zalia Ziskind said, laughing, showing his sparse and fragile teeth.

"Maybe you should go to my father in Morehdalye? You're long-time friends. You used to come visit when we were still young children. I don't mean anything by that," Tilza said, seeing Zalia Ziskind had turned his head to cast her a sharp stare. "I didn't mean anything bad," she repeated, hands on her chest, ready to swear that she never intended for Marcus to get close to her. "I just wanted to say that you could be my father's guest, like in the past, until you find a place to settle down."

"Of course. I can go to your father. In fact, that's what I'll do. I'll go to Morehdalye," Zalia Ziskind said, happy and surprised that he hadn't thought of it himself. But then the wavering began. *Will Marcus even agree to go there? And what about me, there's nothing for me there. What will I do?* Tilza listened, each of his sighs piercing her heart, though he hadn't yet hinted—not by a single word—that if she'd behaved a tiny bit more cautiously and wisely with his childish son, he wouldn't have to find a new place to lay his head.

Later on, Tilza felt even worse. Zalia Ziskind, her brother informed her, was telling the students and townspeople that he couldn't stay in Lecheve any longer because of his depression. And when everyone protested, he kept repeating that he, and only he, was at fault. He was determined that no trace of suspicion should fall on "Rebbetzin Kahane," God forbid. Tilza felt her cheeks flare up. Her temples pulsed, and she had a knot of tears in her throat. Agitated, she stopped talking to her brother and set the food on the table without making eye contact. The rosh yeshiva and his son were by now eating alone in their room instead of with the family. They'd been busy packing up their belongings for days, though they didn't have much. It appeared they still hadn't decided where they wanted to go.

Out of great distress, Naftali Hertz had stopped shaving. He sat at the table with a coarse, prickly chin that made him look even surlier than before. All this went on for a while. Finally, Zalia Ziskind realized his only option was to follow Tilza's suggestion and go to Morehdalye.

On the morning Marcus and Zalia Ziskind were supposed to leave, Naftali Hertz waited outside their room to bid them farewell. To apologize for the pain he'd caused his long-suffering rosh yeshiva, Naftali Hertz began by speaking about himself: "Because of what I've gone through, I know well how a person must guard himself against falling into a thorny situation. With many couples it starts innocently, some chattering, and then—"

But the old man interrupted him. "I'll send regards to your parents in Morehdalye. And when you go back to Switzerland, give my regards to your family." Zalia Ziskind extended a limp hand for a shake and quickly pulled it back.

So as to avoid seeing Zalia Ziskind again, or bumping into his son, Naftali Hertz left the house and didn't return until half the day had passed and the rosh yeshiva and his son had already left. He found Tilza at the table, dressed in a navy skirt and tight white blouse that made her look younger and heavier. She was smearing butter on a piece of bread for Heshe'le. Six years old, in a yarmulke, he sat calmly on a chair like an adult, smiling across the table at his little sister. Baila'ke stood in a wooden playpen and smiled at her older brother with her pudgy face, her soft, parted mouth. Tilza, it seemed, was hoping to find some consolation in her peaceful family, a change from the exciting, chaotic days and weeks when Marcus Luria had swirled around her. But she couldn't suppress the crude, tired smile at the corner of her mouth. Nastily, as if to spite her brother, she told him that the most respected townspeople and all the students had come to bid farewell to the rosh yeshiva. Though he'd only been in Lecheve for a short while, the crowd escorted him with so much heartache and love, it appeared as if he'd spent his entire life here.

Men sighed, and the students, tears in their eyes, begged him to come and give them one more lecture. Everyone had been surprised that Naftali Hertz wasn't there to say goodbye.

"You should have told them I left the house to avoid a confrontation with your admirer, Marcus," Naftali Hertz replied venomously. "And how did he say goodbye to you, your lazy Nietzschean bum?"

"He barely gave me his hand and mumbled something with his eyes averted. He's probably angry at me for not pushing back against you. Or he's ashamed to be so reliant on his father. And when are *you* leaving?" she said, casting her brother a look so cold he leaped up.

"I would have left even before Zalia Ziskind and his prize did. I see how much you appreciate what I've done to protect you. But I couldn't care less what you think of me. I did it for Father and Mother, and one day you, too, will thank me. You don't yet understand that a person can't grab everything they want and not have to pay for it. I'll stay until your husband returns. You said he sent a letter that he's coming back for the holidays. Well, when he gets here, I'll leave." He went to his room and sat by himself looking out the window, as he did at the library in Bern.

The trees, just as when they'd been lush with foliage, now, too, stood inert, outstretched, astonished, as if they'd lost their memory and were no longer sure when to turn red and yellow for fall's arrival. But the wind came right on time, already rustling through the thick, leafy crowns with the gloom of the coming autumn. Each day since the beginning of Elul, the blowing of the shofar in the beis medrash reminded the Lecheve Jews that the tear-filled nights and dawns of Selichos were drawing near. But Naftali Hertz didn't want to stay in town for that. He didn't relish the idea of shouting along with all of them, "Hashiveinu!" He was no such hypocrite! Time for him to go back home and return to work. Even long vacations must end.

There'd be no long line of readers awaiting him at the Judaica library, he knew. It was why he was able to leave for an extended period in the first place. Nor was he necessary to his wife and son. Even after his return, they probably wouldn't allow him back into the home. No, they definitely wouldn't let him in! He hadn't received a single letter from them the entire time he was away. They no longer needed him and no longer awaited his presence. And suddenly Naftali Hertz clutched his head in horror. "I'm crazy!" He remem-

bered that, before leaving Bern, he and Annelyse had made an agreement that he would write occasionally but that she wouldn't, because
he'd be traveling around. Surely she'd realized that he didn't want to
receive letters from her, lest the Jewish town discover all he was trying to hide. And here he was imagining that he wouldn't be allowed
back into his home!

Naftali Hertz had to ask himself: *Is my life in Switzerland dear
enough to me that I'm afraid of losing it? Or do I, deep down, want to lose
it, leave it all behind?*

16

O N HIS WAY HOME, Yaakov Asher stopped off at his in-laws
in Morehdalye. Zalia Ziskind was already there. He told
Yaakov Asher the story of the drowned man and his subsequent
depression, which made it impossible for him to remain in Lecheve.
Marcus, too, whom Yaakov Asher didn't know at all, was staying in
the Morehdalye rabbi's home, as well as another young man whom
Yaakov Asher knew very well: his youngest brother-in-law, Refael'ke.
Refael'ke had, of course, studied with Yaakov Asher in Lecheve, only
to then abandon observant Judaism. For the past year he'd been at a
training camp on the outskirts of Vilna, where they prepared people
to emigrate to the land of Israel, and now he'd come home to say
goodbye to his parents before leaving for Israel to live on a kibbutz.

Yaakov Asher had plenty to say about his travels. But as was his
nature, he stayed mostly silent. He even put off reflecting on matters,
as he was in a rush to get home to his family, town, and yeshiva.

When Refael'ke heard his brother-in-law talking about leaving,
he said, "I'll go with you, so I can say goodbye to Tilza. I also want to
see Naftali Hertz. I barely know him."

At the table sat the Morehdalye rabbi and rebbetzin, both very
aged, and Zalia Ziskind and his son, both with a veiled sorrow in their
coal-black eyes. Nearby stood the tall, slim Refael'ke, face freshly
tanned, while Yaakov Asher paced around the room impatiently, red-
bearded and brawny, wearing a tight jacket that he'd commissioned
from a tailor before his trip abroad.

"You're not going to Bialystok to say goodbye to Bentzion?"
Henna'le asked, and Refael'ke replied with his typical serenity that
he'd go to Bialystok, too. "And what about Grandfather in Zembin?" his mother asked, chuckling to hide her distress. She must
have understood that her youngest child had no interest in seeing

his grandfather, hearing the old man rehash his diatribe, fuming and bemoaning Refael'ke's move to an impure kibbutz in the holy land. In the end, Henna'le couldn't control herself and complained to Zalia Ziskind, "Our Bentzion, who's taking business courses in Bialystok, I haven't seen for two years now. And our youngest daughter, I haven't seen for nearly a year. Bluma Rivtcha is studying in Vilna at a school for nurses."

Sholem Shachne, who had gradually made peace with the idea that he had no influence over his children anymore, interjected, "Your son and daughter don't have time for you now. They want to get their diplomas first, like their older brother in Switzerland. What makes it acceptable for Naftali Hertz to avoid us for years and years and unacceptable for them to skip just a year or two?" he asked with mock innocence, yet again repeating this bitter question.

But Henna'le unburdened her heavy heart by lashing out at her son-in-law, asking resentfully, "Don't you have anything to tell us about your trip abroad?"

"That's what I first had in mind, when I came here," Yaakov Asher replied, casting an accusative glance at Zalia Ziskind. "But now, with an unsupervised yeshiva and a town of Jews with no dayan, how can I tarry any longer? I'll tell you about my trip another time. Now I must rush home. Home."

In the train on the way to Lecheve, the rosh yeshiva and the chalutz were silent. His face aglow in quiet happiness, filled with awe at the view, Refael'ke looked out the window at the landscape rushing past. Yaakov Asher barely raised his eyes. He sat beside Refael'ke with clasped hands resting on his knees, the two of them the only passengers in the train car. His head kept sinking lower, as if his gloomy thoughts were weighing down his already overloaded brain: *Did the Dünaburg genius tell me the truth? Had he really been unable to remain in Lecheve because of his depression, or was the story about a drowned man an excuse? Perhaps his impious son had sniffed out my Swiss brother-in-law and the two of them had begun leading my students astray. Perhaps Zalia Ziskind had realized it, become alarmed, and fled town together with his son. He was probably embarrassed to tell me the truth, because I'd warned him this might happen and he'd assured me my fears were unwarranted.* Eventually, Yaakov Asher could no longer bear to exert himself in such non-scholarly deliberations, and he turned to Refael'ke: "Zalia

Ziskind's son looks like he's come out of a mental hospital. To me he looks even more depressed than his father. Is he always like this, do you know? Have you had any conversations with him? He's one of your kind, after all."

"He's not one of my kind, and he's avoided talking to me. So I don't know what type of person he is," Refael'ke replied, gazing through the window at a wooden bridge above a narrow river, where white ducks were swimming. From the haze there emerged a group of little houses, cheerily swirling around a small factory with a red chimney. They danced around the chimney as if it were their pride and honor in this world. A forest of birches whizzed by, birches with long, thin, dazzling white trunks, with crowns of greenish, silvery leaves that rustled constantly, vibrating and twinkling with flecks of light.

"REFAEL'KE!" TILZA CRIED OUT when she saw him enter with her husband. She was beside herself with joy. She clutched his head, pressed him to her, kissed and caressed him, cried and laughed. "Look at how tall he's grown, may no evil eye do him wrong. Taller than Father, even. Naftali Hertz! Naftali Hertz! Refael'ke's come!" she screamed at the top of her lungs toward her brother's room, and only then remembered her husband. "How are you, Yaakov Asher?" She snuggled up to him, but nowhere with as much happiness, as much rapture, as to her brother. Yaakov Asher stood there feeling lost and humiliated. Rather than fall upon him out of great longing, she'd grown even colder to him.

Once Yaakov Asher and Naftali Hertz had greeted each other and schmoozed a bit, the house turned quiet. Yaakov Asher and his wife and children stayed in the bedroom, while the two brothers were in the living room, standing amid scattered chairs and Yaakov Asher's suitcases. They both intended to sit down on the soft, high-backed divan, but for no conceivable reason they remained standing, observing each other. Refael'ke was a head taller than his older brother, with a young, smooth face, a soft blond beard, a wide mouth with luscious, rounded lips, and gentle eyes behind his glasses—a clone of his father in his youth. As for himself, Naftali Hertz didn't have to look into a mirror; he knew what he looked like—his thin, angular face covered in prickly sprigs of hair.

"Bluma Rivtcha always talks about you," Refael'ke said. "She remembered you better than I did, from the time you came to Tilza's wedding,"

"And Tilza talks about you," Naftali Hertz replied, lower and calmer than his usual tone. "She told me about you leaving to a kibbutz near Vilna, and about Bluma Rivtcha leaving home to learn a profession. Yes, leaving came easier to all of you, but I had to run away. I was the first, and Father would have never let me be. See the difference?"

"I get it," Refael'ke said, then was silent for a moment, as if pondering whether he would have done as his brother did and duped everyone, or told the truth. "Bluma Rivtcha is working near Vilna, in a summer camp for children, so she can't come home now. Plus, she doesn't want to come home before she finishes nursing school, so Father shouldn't start up with his old complaints again. But she very much wants to see you. Will you visit her in Vilna?"

"I have to get back to my job in Switzerland." Naftali Hertz sat down heavily on the sofa, as if his legs had given out. *Troubles never cease!* he thought. Now he'd have to go to his sister in Vilna and his brother in Bialystok, would he? And repeat the same hokey story about his lame wife and her watchmaker family! Though they'd rebelled against their father just as he did, and wanted to break their link in the golden chain of rabbis and rebbetzins, even they would view marrying a Christian as no less than treason.

"I wasn't planning on going to Zembin to say goodbye to Grandfather, so that he wouldn't have to relive my decision to move to a non-religious kibbutz in Israel. But now I'm thinking, if you'd come with me, I'll go," Refael'ke said. "Grandfather is in his eighties already and Zembin isn't far. We should go. I spent time with him a year ago; he's not the same zealot he once was."

Naftali Hertz eyed his younger brother with surprise and curiosity. Tilza had already told him about Refael'ke's maturity, how it gave him influence over their father and even their grandfather. Indeed, it seemed Refael'ke was a sensible person, calm and sincere.

"Why don't you sit down? You're standing near that couch as if you're guarding something. But of course, if you want to stand, by all means." Naftali Hertz moaned, and felt an anxious twitch in his jaw. "Tell me. You're going to a kibbutz that doesn't keep Shabbos or kosher, and the men and women live among themselves as they please. Do you know what that means to our father? And yet, you want to do your duty by everyone, even saying goodbye to Grandfather. Is this honest of you?" Naftali Hertz threw his hands across the back of his neck and drummed his foot nervously on the floor. He felt a stirring of affection for his youngest brother and understood why his parents and siblings loved him so. But he begrudged himself the warmth of family intimacy. For some reason, he kept fighting it. He said, "Did you get to know Marcus Luria? He's disturbed, an immature yeshiva boy. But he does have one excellent quality: he doesn't compromise. He loudly and openly rejects the Jewish God and His Torah, and a universal God and morality. He also rejects the ethics of atheists. He has his own god: Nietzsche. Have you spoken to him? Did he spew any Nietzschean aphorisms?"

"I didn't know he could speak. The entire time I was there he was silent and morose. I thought that's how he always was. But you're making a mistake about me. I'm no denier," Refael'ke said, and with the smile of someone much older, he enlightened his brother: "Father and Grandfather think that because I became a chalutz I automatically renounced everything that's holy to them. But I don't feel that way. I believe that some things people think are like fire and water can actually live peacefully together. I know without a doubt that even when I become a farmworker in the land of Israel, or a bricklayer or gardener, I'll still think fondly of Morehdalye, Zembin, and Lecheve, and all their storekeepers and workers. Why do I have to hate everything Jews have attained in the diaspora just because I love the land of Israel? If I didn't consider moving to Israel and building the country my primary obligation, I would have gone to study at a university. I would have lived on bread and water, as long as I could learn languages and study the sciences. Nevertheless, I have no regrets about poring over the Gemara for so many years. Why can't these things coexist?"

"And can Jew and goy coexist too?" Naftali Hertz asked unexpectedly. He gave a sudden burst of laughter at the thought that, even if Refael'ke had ten heads, he could never have imagined what his brother meant by this question.

But it just so happened that Refael'ke and his sister Bluma Rivtcha had thought through such a scenario a year before. They'd imagined more than they wanted to know, and would speak about it in hushed tones and with meaningful glances. Eyes lowered, Refael'ke said, "Certainly there's no shortage of areas and topics where Jews and non-Jews don't see eye to eye. But not on everything. If it were possible for Jews and non-Jews to be united on every matter, the Jewish nation would have disappeared years ago."

"And maybe that would have been for the best!" Naftali Hertz said, laughing in a tone that sounded almost like crying. But Refael'ke didn't laugh. He looked defiantly at his brother, who had suddenly seized up, as if suffering from a chronic intestinal illness. Semi-prone on the sofa, his face in a grimace, Naftali Hertz resembled a dry, uprooted tree stump in a field.

17

T HE GUESTS CAUSED their portion of chaos, and then all went
their separate ways, taking their unanswered questions with
them. At mealtimes, they conversed sparingly and cautiously, with
little interest and curiosity. Refael'ke noticed that, just like his older
brother, his sister and her husband were pained by something. But
unless one of them confided in him, it wasn't in Refael'ke's nature to
interrogate or split hairs trying to figure it out.

His farewell trip before leaving for Israel reminded Tilza of her
girlhood years, when she'd taken strolls with the Hebrew tutor Ezra
Morgenstern, who hated the diaspora and its Jews. He was, however,
very respectful with her. Unlike Marcus Luria, who'd kept jabbing
her with insults. She was provincial, a petit bourgeois, small! Small!
Small! He wanted only to know whether she'd be ready to leave her
husband and children for him, though he himself was ready for nothing, and was in fact afraid to live apart from his father. "And how do
you like Marcus Luria, Zalia Ziskind's son?" Tilza asked, interrupting her frenzied thoughts. "When he was here, he kept talking about
how the strong need show no compassion for the weak."

"He said such a thing? But he himself is a helpless weakling!"
Refael'ke shrugged. "Naftali Hertz told me the same thing. It seems
Marcus Luria was a very different person here. In Morehdalye he
didn't speak at all. He looked pale and depressed."

"Pale? Depressed?" Tilza asked with a guilty expression. But she
was then overcome by the desire to talk about the Hebrew tutor she'd
just been thinking about. "If you see him, tell him I haven't forgotten
him. And that I always regret that I didn't follow him. I know that life
with him would have been more interesting and honest."

Tall and fresh-skinned—like a young pine, its needles glowing golden in the sunrise—Refael'ke stood there staring at his sis-

ter. Then, he asked carefully, "Who are you talking about? Marcus Luria?"

"No. Ezra Morgenstern, the Hebrew tutor who came to Morehdalye." Tilza's face reddened. "You were still a child when he came, but remember when you were studying here in Lecheve, when you confided in me that you wanted to become a chalutz? I told you about him then." And Tilza repeated what she'd said back then. That Ezra's face was like a bronze sculpture. How they'd sat in the field, the two of them together, and how he'd weighed her long, heavy braid in his palm. He'd stroked her head, because he knew that if he hugged her and pulled her toward him, she would burst into tears—she, the rabbi's daughter, with a long braid but short on sense. Pity he hadn't hugged her. "Ezra used to say that when I braided my hair in front of my face and peeked through the long strands, my eyes looked like stars on a dark night in the Wilderness of Judah. He'd never been to the land of Israel, so how could he have known what the nights there looked like? Probably from books and songs. He used to sing a song called 'How Beautiful the Nights of Canaan.' He spoke so much about the land of Israel, and defended it so fiercely. He must have surely gone there. So if you meet him, introduce yourself and send him my regards."

"I'll do that," Refael'ke replied, his expression innocent. But his sister felt that he understood more than he let on.

Though Tilza had been concerned for her husband when he was abroad, her concern vanished as soon as he stepped through the door. She didn't even ask him for details on how it had gone, where he'd eaten and slept. He'd gotten used to his wife not showing him much affection, but still, after three months away, he was unprepared for such disinterest. And here he'd rushed home for the holidays, without even fully establishing a regular committee to collect money for his yeshiva. The fact that he still couldn't get to the bottom of why Zalia Ziskind had so abruptly departed from Lecheve also pressed on him. He'd asked his students, but whatever their personal thoughts were, their only response was what he'd already heard from Zalia Ziskind himself—that his depression over the drowned man had driven him out of Lecheve. But no one, Yaakov Asher noticed, spoke of Marcus Luria, and when he asked about him, they replied with only an incoherent mumbling.

Yaakov Asher brought all of this up to his family at the Shabbos meal Friday evening, and he drew this conclusion: "Now I'm sure that Zalia Ziskind left here so his son wouldn't corrupt the yeshiva boys. No doubt that's what his son had in mind. I can tell by the way the yeshiva boys refuse to talk about him." And Yaakov Asher glanced suggestively at his brother-in-law, trying to infer whether he, too, had had a part in inciting heresy.

Tilza gave her husband a look of astonishment. Her furious eyes did the talking: What a fool! What a sap! Does it not dawn on him that Marcus tried to lead *someone else* astray? And Marcus? He was a good-for-nothing, too! A synagogue idler. The truth was, he wanted nothing. All he did was talk. Tilza turned her head, her neck and lips swollen, as if she could barely control herself from bursting into laughter at her courageous admirer who'd run off and her smart husband who'd come back. But her gaze met her older brother's, his angry eyes filled with a warning: *Don't you dare laugh or say an unnecessary word, or you'll make yourself, your husband, your children, and the entire family miserable.* He looked ready to use his fists on her or break dishes if she so much as opened her mouth. She watched him fearfully and bowed her head as a sign of obedience.

The Friday night dinner passed in silence. Heshe'le, too, was quiet. Wearing a yarmulke that slipped down his shorn head, he sat, absorbed in pinching a chicken wing with his sticky fingers. His little sister, Baila'ke, was already asleep. It was nearly his own bedtime, which is why he got his portion of poultry earlier than the adults at the table. In the window was a velvety, navy sky, seeded with stars, a crooked silver sword—the moon—in the middle. The lamp and candlesticks cast a vermilion glow on Refael'ke's boyish face. Sparks of light trembled teasingly on his glasses, as if they were laughing at his earnestness, out of tune with his youth. Tilza watched him with happiness, with pride, already missing him before he'd left. Oh, what a boy he was, this Refael'ke! And the more enamored she was of her younger brother, the more she disliked her older brother for directing her behavior. Her aversion to her husband grew, too. If Yaakov Asher was a fine man, why did he have such rough, prickly hair on his head and a beard like a piece of copper? How horrifying his red-flecked face was! And how his brow perspired! His belly kept growing bigger, the freckles on his short, fat fingers ever thicker. When he ate, he slurped, chewed, and crunched with such haste it seemed he'd come from a land of famine and would soon be heading back.

Having finished slurping up his plate of noodles, Yaakov Asher cleared the table of challah crumbs, tossed them into his mouth, chewed, and mumbled something about Marcus Luria and his ilk. Though he didn't call the others by name, it was evident that by "Marcus's ilk" he meant his wife's brothers. "After all my travels out in the world, I've proved my belief that those who sit and study Torah have nothing to be ashamed of, compared to worldly sophisticates. Not when it comes to wisdom, nor kindness, nor fine manners. The only area where students of Torah can't compete with the worldly is in the art of smooth talk. Oh-ho! How the worldly can talk! They mask impurity in pure words. And I'm now even more convinced than before—that all the supposedly new opinions and creeds stem from the same old lusts. Anytime a hedonist and libertine desires something, he instantly persuades himself and everyone else that his intention is to save the Jewish nation or the entire world. But the truth is, all he really has in mind are his own lusts."

"And what's wrong if you listen to your heart? If you can attain your heart's desire, there's nothing wrong with that at all," Tilza replied, agitated. There rose up in her mind all she hadn't dared to do in her girlhood years with Ezra Morgenstern and, more recently, what she hadn't dared to do with Marcus Luria, and she wanted to express her feelings, at least in rebellious chatter. But she didn't know how to give these feelings proper expression. Instead, she looked at her husband with such triumphant spite he was stunned.

No less baffled was he by the audacity of his youngest brother-in-law and former student. Refael'ke smiled right in his face and said, "It's not true that all new opinions stem from the same old lusts. The chalutzim, for example, deny themselves many basic needs, like eating to satiation, sleeping on a clean bed, protecting their health and life—things that yeshiva students don't deny themselves. They do this all so they can build their own country. And other movements, too, sacrifice themselves for their ideals, not simply for their own lusts."

Naftali Hertz knew that Yaakov Asher had mainly meant him, not Refael'ke, so he felt compelled to respond. He kept his face averted, as if to conceal the disdain expressed on it for the rabbi and rosh yeshiva, the Torah genius who'd traveled out into the world and had come back as lacking in worldly sophistication and as narrow and dull as when he'd left. "Nobody puts as much impurity into purity as the pious do. We know this from our long history, from our Sages' quarrels, and I remember this from my childhood. Every time rabbis wage battles with each other—they practically devour each other alive—each side claims it's doing it *entirely* for the sake of heaven. They don't mean their own honor, heaven forbid, only the Torah's honor." Naftali Hertz turned his flaming eyes to Yaakov Asher, and his voice went hoarse from indignation. "When I ran away from yeshiva, I didn't do it so I could switch to the Reform Judaism that the Swiss Jewish community adheres to. But both the Reform rabbis and the ones here have all outlived their times. They're irrelevant. They aren't the leaders of the new generation anymore. They're like wooden stumps who think they're still blossoming trees."

Tilza and Refael'ke weren't the only ones who stared at their brother in astonishment; the Shabbos flames, too, twitched and trembled, as if rebuking Dr. Katzenellenbogen in their fire tongue for saying such words in the home of a rabbi. But more than all of them, Naftali Hertz reproached himself. In a flash, the image of his wife's mother passed before his eyes—his stooped, gentile mother-in-law with long flaxen hair, who for years had silently exhibited her hatred of him. And how silent he'd been in his own right—at home with his wife and son, in the library with the occasional visitors. Even inside himself he was silent! He'd kicked out Zalia Ziskind and his son, then warned his sister to be silent. Yet look at how he'd gone blurting things out . . .

During Naftali Hertz's entire diatribe, Yaakov Asher remained silent, stroking Heshe'le's yarmulke as if he finally understood that, other than his little boy, nobody here had missed him. He didn't utter another word. Contrary to the enthusiasm with which he'd slurped his noodles earlier, he now barely touched his portion of poultry. The conversation had cost him his appetite. He mumbled Shir Hamaalos, rinsed his fingers, and waited for his brothers-in-law to finish eating, so that they could say the end-of-meal benediction with a mezumen. But at the last moment, when he sang out, "Rabosai, let us say the benediction!" he regretted having waited. It would have been better to say the blessing on his own than with a mezumen like this! Let his brothers-in-law know what he thought of them! And he began to murmur the blessing in the sorrowful voice of a widower who sits alone in an empty house on Friday night, with only the half-burnt candles to empathize with his pain.

18

A T HER HUSBAND'S REQUEST, Tilza kept the lamps unlit in
her and her brothers' bedrooms Friday night, so that Naftali
Hertz wouldn't put the flame out before going to bed and thus desecrate the Shabbos. As he walked into his room after dinner, Naftali
Hertz was glad to find darkness; it matched his mood. He undressed
in the dark, watching the moonlit knife with the silver blade that
hung above the window. The moon gazed at him as if she were the
only one in town who knew of his secret life. She'd followed him all
the way from the Swiss Alps. There, she'd stood in the window of
his little hotel across from the Jungfrau and listened to his thoughts
about traveling home to Poland; now she was witness to his struggles
over going back to Switzerland.

The worn springs of the shabby sofa jabbed into his sides, like the
thoughts poking his mind. He recalled a letter Spinoza had written
to a friend whose child had died. Spinoza had consoled the friend,
telling him he needn't worry about punishment in the afterlife,
because there was no afterlife, and therefore no punishment. Did
this make the grieving father feel better, Naftali Hertz wondered,
not having to believe in an afterlife, or did it only get harder? "This
Dutch philosopher and heretic, he stole the Jewish God from me
too, and left me naked," Naftali Hertz said out loud to himself, as he
was used to doing in his lonesome room in the Bern library. "As hard
as it would be to come back, I'd still do it, if only I knew where to
come back to, if I could persuade myself that I believe in the things
my father does. Refael'ke's lucky. Quiet and sincere, he sleeps calmly
in every bed." He turned from one side to the other. "As for me, I'm
oppressed by my Jewish family, by my non-Jewish family, and by my
own self—my own broken life. Annelyse and Karl know full well that
it's not just my parents, that I, too, have yet to make peace with their

not being Jewish." He was killing himself, yet he felt a certain bizarre pleasure at being unable to fall asleep. He knew from experience that whenever he struggled like this, he had strange dreams. And though the strange dreams frightened him, they gave him a sense of sweet horror, an erotic suspense and fever. He always marveled that, after a night of such nightmares, he'd wake feeling calmer than when he'd gone to sleep. So he hoped to tire himself out now too. Perhaps he'd see strange visions in his dreams and wake up the next morning with a clear head, unburdened. And so it was: the dreams appeared. Barely had he dozed off when he saw himself in Bern, on the street full of shops, with vaulted passageways, with the big round clock on the bell tower, and atop a pillar the statue of a middle-aged knight, sword and shield in one hand and the flag of the Swiss Confederacy in the other.

The season, now, was the same in Bern and Lecheve: the end of summer. It was dusk, the hour of sunset and glowing Alps. Naftali Hertz couldn't see the three snowy mountains of the Bern Ober-land, because he was walking in the opposite direction. But he was aware that all three—the Eiger, the Mönch, and the Jungfrau—were crouching behind him in the distance. They'd been there since crea-tion, and now they were glimmering under twilight's crimson clouds. For a moment they peeked out from their hazy curtain, only to drift right back into the fog. They looked like tremendous ships huddled together on great, rusted anchors; they looked like gigantic farm ani-mals carved of stone, their necks welded in long chains. Naftali Hertz noticed that he was caught up in a group of people who were rushing somewhere and dragging him along. Outside, it was neither cold nor raining. Still, all of them—the men and the women—had their coat collars up and wore their hats pulled low over their foreheads. None of them wanted their fellow travelers—to both their right and their left—to know who they were.

Naftali Hertz was surprised to find that the shop-lined street now extended so far. It was endless. And what surprised him even more was that not a word was uttered by the people around him. No one gave a laugh or a cough; they all strode in silence. *With such earnest-ness,* thought Naftali Hertz, *do God-fearing village Jews scurry to the funeral of a tzaddik, or to the Kol Nidrei prayer on Yom Kippur.* But he remembered that he was now among gentiles in Bern. In the narrow little streets of this medieval city, master craftsmen and their wives once scurried in just such a God-fearing manner to the auto-da-fé, where they burned Jews accused of poisoning the wells. But by their clothes, faces, and behavior, Naftali Hertz was able to tell that his fellow strollers were not old-time pious Christians. They all had the wide-open, hungry eyes of the insane; their eyes burned with mania, with lust, with a hostile green veneer. As the air grew darker, the crowd became thicker, the congestion greater, the eyes greener. The gas lamps, too, dripped with the green tint of bile and venom. And so did the glowing windows of stores and homes. Naftali Hertz saw fat, lustful lips. Chewing mouths. A furtive hand held them like horses by their reins—the wanton, traitorous smiles on the fat lips—and led them to brothels.

"Me too! I'm going where they're going!" Naftali Hertz cried voicelessly, afraid to look to his right lest he see his adult son—now old enough—on his way to a brothel, perhaps to the very same one he was approaching. He was just as afraid to look to his left, lest he see his wife. Annelyse was hurrying now, hurrying to meet her wallpaper man. No one in the group said where they were going, they weren't speaking at all, nor even glancing at each other. Nevertheless, everyone knew exactly where they and everyone else were going, striding forward. The men and women were pervaded by a cheery, shameless, capricious mood, by the happy anticipation of getting undressed, stripping down. Naftali Hertz felt his face burn in shame at being amid this group of lechers. What bothered and offended him deep in his bones was not simply that he, his wife, and his son were being dragged along on this current of wantonness, but that it was being done with so much idolatrous joy. Ach, how repulsed he was by the swinish pleasure they took in sinning and boozing—shamelessly. This was what tormented him most deeply—the shamelessness. He wanted to lag behind. Let the crowd pass him, pass him. But with the constant kicking at his sides, he knew that to pause would mean to be trampled, trampled to death. With tremendous effort, he shot forward and outpaced everyone, breaking away from the group.

Around him it was dark; no gas lamps burned. By the paltry light filtering through the gray clouds, he saw he was standing amid rows of tall, leafy trees. Though he could barely see an arm's length in front of him, the rustling and swaying of branches made him realize he was in a large, old park. A cold wind blew clouds of leaves at him.

They swallowed him, up to his knees, and more kept falling and falling. Just moments before, he'd been in a city at the tail end of summer; now, he was in an old park in the middle of fall. If he didn't scale the mountain of leaves, he'd be buried beneath them. He started crawling his way through, battling against them as if they were waves swelling in a river, until they subsided, until he emerged onto hard, dry soil and not a single leaf rustled beneath his feet.

He continued down a tree-lined path in the old park, but the rows of trees on both sides were bare, naked. The same gray, clouded sky, dewy-white rays filtering through them, was visible through the scrawny branches. And the trunks were tall, and thin. The farther he walked, the taller and thinner the trunks became, with their long, protruding, naked, motionless branches. He stepped into a land where no wind blew and time stood still at an eternal November. The path was neither uphill nor downhill; it was straight and smooth, hard and clean like a mirror. It was a path with no aim, no end.

He felt his knees cracking from exhaustion; his head shook like a lamppost in the wind. He was aching to collapse to the ground and fall asleep, lie there coiled on the path like a worm. But someone was prodding his back with bony, crooked fingers, speaking to him from behind in a hoarse, raspy voice. "Go, go, and perhaps you'll still make it. If you stop for a minute, you'll live forever under the regime of an everlasting depression, just as I did. Go! Go!" Naftali Hertz recognized the voice. It was Zalia Ziskind, the former Dünaburg genius, the former Visoki-Dvor rabbi and rosh yeshiva, the former wonderful singer—former in everything.

Though Zalia Ziskind was at his back, and it was dark, Naftali Hertz could see what the former rosh yeshiva looked like. He'd become even more emaciated and shrunken—a dwarf on a pair of bent, skinny legs. Only the hunch of his back had enlarged. His face was stretched even thinner, and his coal-black eyes peered out of two open cellars. Naftali Hertz now hated this hunchbacked Jew who was on his heels. The cripple had pretended he'd fallen into depression because of his compassion. A lie! He wasn't compassionate. He was depressed because of cruelty. He was a bad person, just as his brothers-in-law and sisters-in-law had said. His only son thought so, too, despite his claims to the contrary. If it were otherwise, he would not have repeated with such schadenfreude that his uncles and aunts considered his father a wicked person. Had the hunchback not been such a snoop, he wouldn't be trailing him now, shouting, "Go already! Go already!" No, he would not go another step! Naftali Hertz dropped down on the soil of the tree-lined path between the sky-high naked trees.

The hunchback stood over him, scraping off pieces of his skin with long, pointy nails, yelling into his ear, "A doctor of philosophy, are you? You're a deceiver! Now I have to wander from town to town again, eat beggars' bread at strangers' tables, because you imagined my son was talking to your sister too much and who knew what might come of that. But *you* have a gentile wife and son. In the entire world there's not a hypocrite and Ahitophel like you. Get up! Get up!" the hunchback yelled, scraping off pieces of skin like the angel Dumah, who beats fresh corpses in graves with a stick, waking them to come to the beis din in heaven. But Naftali Hertz no longer heard the screams, no longer felt the pain of pointy fingers scratching at his skin. The nightmare released him, sunk him into the deepest of sleeps, the way the dry, parched earth and all its plants and creatures breathe more lightly after a raging thunderstorm.

Part 4

1

M OREHDALYE, SUBMERGED in deep snow, looked as feeble and
pale as its rabbi, Sholem Shachne Katzenellenbogen, who lay
weak and ill, submerged in his white bedsheets.

Sholem Shachne had become sick more than a year before, when
his youngest son, the chalutz Refael'ke, had moved to the land of
Israel, and his oldest son, Naftali Hertz, had gone back home to
Switzerland. He couldn't accept that he held no sway over his children anymore, couldn't make peace with the thought. He kept tormenting himself over it, or as his wife, Henna'le, put it, "He's eating
himself alive." She could tell by the shadows on her husband's face
what he was feeling inside, and knew there was no hope in changing
it. He was as stubborn as his children.

Truth be told, Sholem Shachne had been trying to distract himself
from his own problems by getting involved in the community's. The
antisemitic bojówkas were growing in number and strength by the
day. They forbade Poles from entering Jewish shops, and on market
days kept the peasants from the wagons of Jewish craftsmen. The
Jews in Morehdalye had become destitute. They couldn't pay their
wholesalers or buy provisions for Shabbos. The once well-off were
forced to take out loans and even charity from the larger, wealthier
communities in Warsaw and Bialystok. Left with no choice, they
reached out to the American Jewish institutions that administered
financial aid to the needy in Poland, and they wrote endless letters
to their compatriots overseas, pleading with them not to allow their
own blood and flesh to die. They begged them to prevent the town's
charity funds, poorhouses, and talmud torah from going under. The
elderly Zembin rabbi had long been laboring at this cause, but the
Morehdalye rabbi had not. Now, though, he immersed himself in
these tasks fully and fervently.

Right around this time, he received a letter from his son-in-law, the rabbi and rosh yeshiva of Lecheve, who wrote that he was receiving less and less financial support from abroad and that his students were practically starving. And so, Sholem Shachne now had to beg for funds for the yeshiva boys, too. He traveled around the neighboring towns, holding lectures, reminding his audiences that regardless of how bad their own situation was, it was incumbent upon Jews to demonstrate self-sacrifice and help support their fellow Torah scholars.

But abruptly, in the middle of this whirlwind, he dropped everything and decided to return home. "*Karmi sheli lo notsorti*," he said sadly to himself. "My own vineyard I haven't protected! How am I allowed to beg from others when I haven't safeguarded my own garden?"

That summer, Bluma Rivtcha, who was close to graduating from the nursing school in Vilna, had come home for her vacation. But her father had been quiet during the entire visit, barely speaking a word to her. To his old resentments, a new one was added: *Why, during the entire time she'd spent in Vilna, hadn't she glanced in her parents' direction? But when it came to writing letters asking for money—yes, that she'd done!* Indeed, he had sent her the money she'd requested, though he'd neither written back nor forgiven her for never having shown her face. For her part, Bluma Rivtcha barely spoke to her father, either, though she kept throwing him wounded looks. It seemed to her he'd become even lankier and skinnier.

During his daughter's visit, Sholem Shachne kept shambling around the room, hands folded behind his back, a bitter smile on his face, mumbling under his breath, as if to say, "So this is the pride and joy I've lived to see!"

After Bluma Rivtcha went back to Vilna, Tilza arrived from Lecheve to stay for a few weeks, her children in tow. With her, too, her father showed little warmth, annoyed that she was still bothered by her husband being a rabbi and she, poor thing, a rebbetzin.

The son from Bialystok, Bentzion, hadn't deigned to come at all. He merely sent a letter. His father skimmed the writing and immediately let the sheet of paper drop to the table's edge. Impatient, Henna'le asked what Bentzion had written and why Sholem Shachne hadn't finished reading the letter.

"What's there to read? How he's grown from a colt into a horse? Bentzion writes that he graduated his business courses and is looking for a manager's position in a store or factory. I have no interest in reading on. You want to read? Read it yourself. He wrote it in Yiddish."

But when a letter arrived from Refael'ke, Sholem Shachne's response was different. He touched the sides of the envelope carefully and, without opening it, laid it down at the edge of the table. He circled the table a few times, his face and his eyes reddened with anger, pain, and longing. Henna'le knew her husband loved his youngest son best, making the pain over this son greater than over the others. Eventually, Sholem Shachne peeled open the envelope and delved into the letter.

"Well? What's he saying?" Henna'le asked after a while.

"Nothing." Again, Sholem Shachne circled the table. "If my sons had stuck to the Torah," he said, "they'd be writing me innovative interpretations in Hebrew and asking me to send regards to their mother. But, well, they became whatever they became, so all of them write in Yiddish. Even the chalutz. So you can read it yourself. He's asking how we both are, how all his sisters and brothers are, and about his Zembin grandfather and Vigasia. About himself he writes almost nothing. That he works in a kibbutz, that's all. And really, what should he write? How he desecrates Shabbos? I don't know. Maybe our Swiss son does the smarter thing by not writing at all."

Once Tilza, too, had left, Sholem Shachne immersed himself for a long stretch in Torah study. But Henna'le could tell her husband's studiousness wasn't genuine; he was doing it to escape his brooding thoughts. As he read noiselessly, or hummed the Gemara tune, his eyes wandered around the page the way a man wanders around unfamiliar paths, or a sinner around purgatory. His most painful thoughts, Henna'le knew, were tied to their oldest son. She herself worried about him constantly. For years and years Naftali Hertz had shut them out, and when he'd finally come to see them, he didn't bother to bring his wife and son. Now, a year and a half had passed since the visit, and in all that time he'd written only one letter, to say he'd arrived home safely and was extremely busy. Henna'le and her husband had each written back, but he hadn't responded. Of course, then, his father thought about him constantly, day and night.

But about the exact nature of Sholem Shachne's thoughts, Henna'le was afraid to ask. In fact, she and Sholem Shachne avoided looking directly into each other's eyes, lest they discover the same suspicion lurking there, the same fear that what they suspected was true, true . . .

Henna'le was guarding another fear. She was afraid her husband was sick and refusing to admit it. Every so often he was beset by a pressure in his chest, pain in his left shoulder and up his back, aches and cracking in the fingertips of his left hand. Once, it hurt so badly he'd let out a groan. Henna'le's lips turned pale as dry sand. She was about to cause a scene, but her husband stopped her. He gestured to her not to shout: his pain had lifted.

Henna'le begged him to see a doctor. Though Morehdalye wasn't a big city, it had a hospital with doctors and specialists serving all the surrounding areas. But Sholem Shachne refused to go, even when he was plagued by the pressure again, this time with even more pain, a headache, a severe cough, a cold sweat on his forehead, and a choking sensation in his throat. Henna'le rallied the town's men, telling them to remind her husband that the Torah commands us to protect our health. But instead of taking the men seriously, Sholem Shachne joked that it's unhealthy for a person to know too much about himself: "Knowing one's body too well and all its weaknesses is what really makes a person sick."

For the first time since she'd married him, Henna'le complained about her husband in a letter to her father. Eli-Leizer Epstein, already more than eighty years old, didn't procrastinate for even a day. He wrote a letter to his son-in-law immediately, this time without any flowery, rabbinical embellishments. "I regret giving you my daughter as a wife more than forty years ago," he wrote. "Never would I have imagined that abandoning Henna'le to widowhood wouldn't bother you. I know very well that because your children aren't devout, you've fallen into a depression and aren't minding your health. I, too, am extremely pained that I derive so little joy from my children and grandchildren. But, on the other hand, I know that every person comes into this world to redress something. Therefore, not guarding one's health is a great sin, because though you can atone for something you've brought upon another person, you cannot atone for something you've brought upon yourself. Truly, woe to the generation whose leaders let their arms drop to their sides and ignore their responsibilities to their communities."

So Sholem Shachne went to see the cardiologist in Morehdalye's hospital. Dr. Bennett was short, a mere crumb, with a white, evenly shorn head of hair, stiff white whiskers, small hands and feet, but with a big nose and even bigger ears, as if meant to be placed against the hearts and backs of patients. He also had big, mild, smiling eyes, which calmed frightened patients. The Morehdalye rabbi, however, didn't need to be calmed. He showed no fear, nor even much interest in his illness.

Dr. Bennett, who wasn't a native of Morehdalye and, in general, wasn't close to the town's Jewish community, was highly impressed by Sholem Shachne. Here was a rabbi, and what a man he was—entirely unworried, cleanly dressed, and one who gave succinct answers to all the questions posed to him.

Still, Sholem Shachne couldn't hide his surprise at the questions. Since he had never before been seriously ill, he couldn't understand why the doctor needed to know his precise age, how many children he had, what they did, where they lived, whether he got along well with them, which foods he ate, what he did in the mornings, during the day, in the evenings, when he went to sleep, how well he slept, whether he argued frequently with his wife or with the townspeople, and whether he had undergone any sort of particular stress recently. The doctor spoke a fluent, succulent Yiddish, with a bit of a singsong even, in a Polish diction. He looked into his patient's eyes and throat with a specially made lens and then told him to get partially undressed. He checked Sholem Shachne's blood pressure, tapped on various tight spots and on his ankles, to see if they were swollen. Quickly, agilely, finger following finger, the doctor tapped along the patient's spine, then told him to turn on his back and pressed down on the stomach's corners till they hurt, told him to take long, deep breaths, listened both with a stethoscope and with bare ears that he placed on the rabbi's gray-haired chest.

When it was all over, Dr. Bennett sat down to write a prescription, speaking to Sholem Shachne as he wrote. "Rabbi, you have a weakened and slightly enlarged heart. Your pulse beats too quickly and skips some beats. Your blood pressure is also too high. But even with angina pectoris, which is what this condition is called, you can live to a ripe old age as long as you take good care of yourself."

Dr. Bennett then listed the foods the rabbi was allowed to eat and how much of them he could have. "You can study your Talmudic books, but within limit. When you give talks in the synagogue to the Jews of your community, don't speak too loud or too long. Avoid walking up hills and high steps, definitely don't walk too quickly or carry heavy packages, protect yourself from heat and from cold, and be very careful to avoid stress. Then again, what's there to be stressed about? You told me yourself that the community pays you a salary as long as times aren't too bad. Your children have all moved away, you said, and they're all trying to accomplish their goals, make careers for themselves. With your wife and friends you undoubtedly get along. I can tell just by seeing your refined behavior. So what could cause you distress or worry?"

But when Sholem Shachne arrived home, he again began to brood over his oldest son's behavior, as he pinched and twirled his whitened beard. *How could Naftali Hertz not have brought his wife and son with him, after more than a decade and a half away? He had replied mechanically to all their questions, as if he'd guessed in advance what kinds of things they might ask and had prepared his answers. Not for nothing had he sharpened his brain first with the Gemara and later with philosophy. And whenever he mentioned his family in Switzerland, it was with pride or with anger, at times with reluctance, but never with the love of a husband or a father. Who'd ever heard of a daughter-in-law and grown grandchild never writing a letter to their in-laws and grandparents?*

Sholem Shachne sat down to study, pushed his glasses up on his forehead, and peered into his Gemara. "That our daughter-in-law and grandchild don't write is no surprise. They're alienated Swiss Jews and have never met us, so they don't write," Sholem Shachne sang in a Gemara chant, as if he were settling a quibble between Rashi and the Tosafos. But soon new questions sprang up in his mind, and he sought new answers for them.

Days and weeks passed in this way. It was already the end of autumn; the few remaining leaves trembled on the tree tips. Sholem Shachne looked out at the quorum of naked willows near his old house and tormented himself further: *Naftali Hertz's excuse for not bringing his wife around all these years was that he didn't want to pain his parents by bringing them a lame daughter-in-law. And that's why he'd come without her this time, too. Some excuse! First of all, a little limp is not so terrible a deformity. Second, if he married her and he lives with her, would his parents be against such a thing? Clearly, he was omitting something or lying outright. Could she be irreligious? Well, he himself is irreligious and doesn't deny it. Is she uneducated, and he's ashamed? May she have no worse fault than that! But of course, Naftali Hertz would have never married an uneducated woman. His belief in the Haskalah has never wavered. He'd abandoned the yeshiva because of his maskilic convictions, and that had never changed. He would have rather married a Christian convert than an uneducated woman. Even an actual goy . . . Yes, yes, an actual goy!*

Sholem Shachne was afraid to continue this line of thought, but he couldn't control his brain. The pain in his chest, back, and left arm worsened. He couldn't get his breath, like a wind rushing through a chimney that pushes the smoke from the oven back into the room. He choked, tossed his head, and barely managed to croak: "Henna'le, open a window and let some fresh air in."

Henna'le raised the window but instantly banged it shut again. Such a raw, dismal wind tore into the room, bringing with it an eddy of withered leaves, blowing with such fury it seemed to want to rip the sheitel right off Henna'le's head. It occurred to her that the wind was laughing rudely, poking fun at her: "Where are your kaddishlech?" it was asking. "A mother of three sons and two daughters, and not a single one has come home when their father needs help—a mother like that should have given birth to stones, not children!"

Running out to the stoop, Henna'le raised a commotion: Sholem Shachne Katzenellenbogen had suffered a heart attack.

He came home from the hospital a month later, when the double windows were already frozen over with tiles of ice, and snow had whitened the fields, roads, and paths leading to the town's hovels. The low houses with snow piled high on their roofs, looking lost amid the deep snow on the ground, peered out enviously at the houses along the synagogue street, huddled around the large, square structure, able to hear from up close the sweet sounds of Jews praying and studying. Each day, the Jewish homes sank deeper into the snowdrifts, and the Morehdalye Jews sank deeper into gloom. Even in the frost and blizzards, the Polish bojówkas hovered near the Jewish shops, forbidding Polish peasants from going in and buying from the *zhids*.

But on the hill, where the white church stood, was a cheerful hustle and bustle. Tall, slender poplar trees, their branches covered in snow, peeked out across the parking lot, past the iron railing. They resembled white-veiled, aristocratic brides taking vows before a priest. Outside the church, the market was being set up. Bundled peasant men and kerchiefed peasant women swarmed around it. They brought wagons laden with chickens, dairy, eggs, fruits, animal hides, and live calves and pigs. With their earnings, they bought kerosene, salt, sugar, linen, and iron. They sold their products to Poles and Jews, but when it came to buying, they remembered to stick to their own, "*Swoj do swego!*" and patronized only the new stores owned by faithful Christians and Poles.

In the window of the rabbi's house burned the first Chanukah light, a pale blue elongated flame, dancing breathlessly this way and that. It seemed to be fighting off strangulation, burning lonely in an eight-pronged menorah, winking at the great white vastness. Sholem Shachne, who'd left his bed to light the Chanukah candles, lay down on the divan in the room. He sighed. "I can't bear this lonesomeness anymore," he told his wife. "I must see the children."

Henna'le had already informed the doctor about Sholem Shachne's pain over his children, and the doctor had told her that this might have been the cause of her husband's heart attack.

"The children know you're sick, and they would have come to visit," Henna'le said, "but the doctor says you're too upset over their behavior, that it's better they don't come. For now, at least. Once you're healthy again, and calm, they'll come see you. Once you're completely calm."

"I'm calm, completely calm," the rabbi said in a weakened voice. "I don't worry about my daughters, because I know what they're doing. Bentzion and Refael'ke, too. Bluma Rivtcha will be a nurse, I see, Bentzion a merchant, and Refael'ke a chalutz. So I'm not that anxious to see them now. The one I'm worried about is our eldest. We've barely heard from him since he left. Actually, even when he was here, we hardly heard anything about his life. I mean, he spoke plenty, but somehow about nothing of substance. I want to see him. Have you written him?"

"Naftali Hertz knows about everything that's happening with you. In fact, he sent a telegram to say he's coming soon," Henna'le said, then admitted that she hadn't wanted to inform Sholem Shachne when the telegram arrived, fearing it would upset him. Instead, she'd taken it over to the community bookkeeper, who read German. "Naftali Hertz writes that he'll be here by Chanukah. That means this week. But don't get upset, Sholem Shachne, don't get upset."

From his spot on the divan, the rabbi gazed at the little blue flame, the first Chanukah light, and thought back to the time when Naftali Hertz was still their only child. *Perhaps*, he thought now, *it is better that Naftali Hertz didn't tell us anything substantial.*

"I'm calm," Sholem Shachne again reassured his wife, as if to guard her from hearing his thoughts. "I'm completely calm."

2

I N THE WINDOW sat the menorah, five flames already burning. But even though they were a group now, like the fingers on a hand, the flames didn't look any happier. They burned impassively, rigidly. Only from time to time did one quiver or snap, as though hiccupping forth a complaint: *In other homes they fry latkes in honor of the fifth light; they play dreidel and lotto. But here, everyone looks at us miserably, like we're yahrzeit flames.*

There they stood, a trio—father, mother, and oldest son—in the beis din room, silently gazing at the menorah near the doorpost by the window. In honor of Naftali Hertz, who'd arrived that morning, Sholem Shachne had put on a fresh shirt with a detachable collar, accompanied by his Shabbos frock coat and soft Shabbos hat with the wide brim. But he couldn't summon such enthusiasm as he blessed the Chanukah lights. His voice came out in a ghostly timbre, as from an ailing porush who lives in the cold anteroom of a synagogue, nourishing himself on bread crusts.

The rabbi's long, skinny body and emaciated face held as much life as his elongated shadow on the wall. His hands were stuffed into their opposite sleeves. And the short Henna'le stood there just as gloomily, shaking her head and musing to herself: *Not that long ago, our children, one smaller than the next, stood round their father while he lit the Chanukah flames, all of them singing in harmony. Maoz tzur . . . O mighty stronghold of my salvation. . . . Now the only one here is our "guest," Naftali Hertz, staring at the flames with a stranger's eyes, as if this Chanukah ritual were unfamiliar to him, and has been for years.* Even non-practicing Jews, Henna'le knew, placed a Chanukah lamp in their windows. Could it be that Naftali Hertz didn't light a menorah in his home in Switzerland?

Her husband had been awaiting Naftali Hertz's visit with so

much longing. But ever since he'd arrived—this morning, covered in snow—his father had barely exchanged a word with him. This so bewildered Henna'le that she unthinkingly copied her husband, barely speaking to her son. But the absence of chatter stressed her, and she let her pent-up anger spill onto her husband.

"What are you standing and staring at the flames for, Sholem Shachne, as if they're orphans, heaven forbid?" It was rare that she spoke to her husband with such ire.

The rabbi shuddered. "Like orphans, you say? Why like orphans? Oh, how a woman thinks!" he said, and stomped out of the beis din room and into the kitchen. He took a chair at the table and touched his forehead, as though to remind himself of what he'd been thinking about.

Henna'le followed him. "And what are you going to eat?" she asked through the open door of the beis din room.

But it was Naftali Hertz who replied. "I'll eat whatever you give me," he said, still gazing at the menorah.

In his mind's eye, Naftali Hertz could see the Christmas fir hung with colorful lights that his wife and son had put up in his home. Their eyes, too, would be illuminated by light and joy, the wish to be companionable and kind to all. An ecclesiastical piety of one sort or another would wash over them during Christmas, despite Annelyse never going to church and Karl's religion-less upbringing. Only he, Naftali Hertz, used to stand there, feeling alienated. He'd have thought the Chanukah flames, at least, would feel dear to his heart. But no. They felt no more precious to him than the decked and glowing tree.

And if I considered myself an "international Jew," he mused, *these flames would have felt even more distant. These skinny candles—a half hour's worth of fire—and the frozen windows of the darkened town: What connection did they have to the Hasmoneans and the Israel of yore? The memory of the Maccabees had been paved over with prayers and greased with a penny's worth of flames for so many years that their strength against the Greeks had been transformed into the swaying and murmuring of the Shimoneh Esrei prayer: "God has given the evil into the hands of the righteous . . . vezeydim beyad oyskei torahsecha . . . and the wicked into the hands of those who study the Torah." So play, Morehdalye children, with your Chanukah dreidels, and sing "Al Hanisim," thanking God for His*

*miracles. And you, Chanukah flames, keep peering out, gloomy and fright-
ened, through the crooked windows in the dense, snow-swirled darkness.
Refael'ke has gone to Israel so that he can experience a true Chanukah, just
as I ran away from the Jewish diaspora years ago. But all I did was fall
right back into an exile, an exile among Swiss gentiles.*

So went Naftali Hertz's thoughts.

"Naftali Hertz, go and wash up. The food is ready. It's on the
table," his mother called out to him.

Henna'le had set only a third of the large dining table, beneath
the dim electric chandelier, as though the fixture lacked the strength
to light up the entire room. She was in no mood to be particularly
festive, and she herself ate nothing. But she watched to make sure
her husband ate the liquid kasha and warm milk. Because of her husband's dietary restrictions, her son, too, received a dairy supper: hard
white cheese, soft-boiled eggs on a saucer, fresh butter, rye bread,
and a glass of tea, translucent and red as berries. "Really, I should
have cooked a better dish for Father today for Chanukah. A raisin
and plum pie, maybe," Henna'le told Naftali Hertz. "And for a guest
like you, I should have fried some latkes. But Father has to be careful
not to eat too much or too heavy foods, especially in the evening. But
I'll fry some latkes for you on Shabbos night, for the seventh light
of Chanukah. And what do the Swiss Jewish women do? What kind
of foods do they make for Chanukah? Same as here? Does your wife
fry latkes?"

"Latkes?" Against his will, Naftali Hertz felt a crooked smile
forming on his face. "Sure, my wife fries latkes. Every so often, not
just for Chanukah. And such big ones, they fill the entire frying pan."

"But filling an entire pan is for pork lard. That's what goyim fry,"
Henna'le burst out, and went speechless with shock. Scared that her
husband would join the conversation and start probing, she quickly
began chattering—the wise little woman!—about the different ways
people prepare latkes: "Some women fry latkes with duck fat. Some
use only hens' fat, mixed with eggs and butter. There are these gluttons who like latkes filled with cheese or made from soaked bread
and doused with sour cream. There are even a few crazies who like it
filled with liver, like Russian pie. But the best are made from grated
potatoes." Abruptly, she asked Naftali Hertz, "How long do you plan

to stay?" and her shrunken face, with her small, protruding chin, glistened as if she had, indeed, eaten fatty latkes.

"I didn't take a vacation the last two summers, so I can stay as long as I'd like. Besides, I now have a new, educated colleague who can stand in for me." And just as he'd done two years ago, talking with sudden swiftness, he told a long-winded story about why he hadn't written all this time. "When I returned home after my last visit here, I found out that my assistant at the library had left for a better position. And finding someone to replace him, someone versed in Jewish bibliography, isn't easy in Bern. All the work fell to me, and I had no time for anything else. Right around that time, it happened that a Sephardic family in London was selling a Judaic library they'd been amassing for generations. So I first had to travel to London, to inspect the treasure trove, and I spent weeks there. I never saw such a set of books in my life! But the heirs wanted a fortune, an unbelievable sum. So I went back to Bern and spent an exorbitant amount of time and effort until I finally convinced my superiors at the library to make the purchase. This issue went so high up, it reached the minister of education. The president of the Swiss League-Republic, too, came to look at the first editions and rare manuscripts. But the real work for me began after the acquisition, when I had to catalogue the rare books and manuscripts. Myself, with no help. Only after everything was finished did we finally find a suitable candidate to be second librarian. My assistant, Dr. Zev Tsikendorf is his name, is Hungarian. Besides his doctorate in the pre-Tanach dead languages, he also graduated from a rabbinical seminary. This man's nose looks like a bird of prey's, and his lips look like a child's. Who knows, with these Hungarians, what kind of people they are? He already seems a bit too eager to take over my position as chief librarian of the Judaic division. But when it comes to rabbinical questions and answers, he doesn't know the first thing, this Dr. Tsikendorf." Naftali Hertz then listed examples of rabbinical books that were nowhere to be found except in the newly purchased trove from London.

He spoke with zest and enthusiasm, as though to ensure that his father would be fascinated enough to not ask him the simple question: "Were you so busy rewriting the title pages of books onto index cards that you didn't have a moment to jot a letter to your parents?"

But Sholem Shachne listened to everything, his face bent, and in the end asked something entirely different: "When you were here on your last visit, you told us that the Jews in your city aren't great intellectuals, not real scholars. Then why do they need such a library of rare books and manuscripts? For whom? Who will delve into them? Who will study them?"

Naftali Hertz laughed at his father's naïveté. "A university library is for the select, for learned people who study ancient books and write their own books about them, not for Jews who go to the prayer house to daven and study a page of Gemara."

But later, when he lay down in his room to rest from his long trip, he was no longer laughing. He had the feeling that his father and mother were deliberately asking him easy questions. The trickier ones they avoided. Naftali Hertz looked around the bedroom in which he'd slept as a boy and later as a teen, when he'd come home from yeshiva. But he refused to let the shabby furniture and other tokens in the room tug him back to his youth. The hump of memories he'd brought from Switzerland was enough of a drag, weighing down his back. No need for the memories of his cozy youth to weigh him down in the front. One hump was enough! There would be time, soon enough, for those memories to confront him.

He put out his lamp and from his low bed stared through the window at the darkness outside. Across the street, a row of unlit windows from the other houses on the synagogue street. In the pale light of the high-swirling snow, a black chimney was visible, and the bark of a tree with bare, gnarled branches, a doorway, a park, and a sloping roof from which the wind had cleared all the snow. *How many times*, Naftali Hertz thought, *have I sat like this, in darkened rooms, the lights out so that no one disturbs me, scratching at the rash on my body and on my life?*

Two years before, when he'd stepped onto the train back to Switzerland, his first thought was that he should never have come to visit his parents and should never do it again. Never reply to their letters, even, until they left him alone. How had he not realized that unless he severed his relationship with his family, his parents and even the not-so-bright Tilza would try to figure out why he hadn't brought his wife and son along? In truth, even if he were to alienate himself from them completely, they'd still try to figure out what had happened to him. They had means at their disposal. They could write letters to the Swiss rabbis, ask friends traveling abroad for medical treatment or alms collectors out raising funds. In fact, his Lecheve brother-in-law, or even Father himself, might come. In the end, they'd uncover the truth. But then, at least, they would understand why he'd run away. He wouldn't come across as so conniving. The abominable act that he was putting up with his wife and her beloved was bad enough.

Later, on that same train ride, his thoughts returned to harass him. *Should I continue to play the cuckold, pretend I don't know what everyone around me knows, or should I tell my wife bluntly that I'm not the blind bookworm she thinks I am, and refuse to take part in this comedy?* Back in Bern he'd gotten the impression that Annelyse would be neither shocked nor ashamed to learn that he knew everything. More than once she'd laughed right in his face, standing proudly on her strong legs, hands on her hips. He'd felt, then, that her laughter wasn't about being rude or provocative, or even to show him that he no longer figured in her equations. No, she was laughing because she was happy. She'd finally gotten what he'd never been able to give her: gratification. Healthy, romantic love from a man. Still, he'd never revealed he was aware of her infidelity. By all rights, he should have left her, and as long as he didn't, she was entitled to disdain him.

He had escaped his gloomy situation by traveling to his parents in Morehdalye. But the time spent with his parents and the townspeople, the routines he'd observed, the situation of the Jews among the Poles—all of that had proved to him that he could no longer return to the old ways. And he was even further removed from the nationalist Jews—from the type like his brother, the chalutz.

He had returned to Switzerland, therefore, determined to continue the charade with Annelyse, pretending he knew nothing. It was true, he thought, that Luigi Martini had the passions of a common lout, a gangster, but he *was* handsome and young, with the figure of an Italian opera singer. After enduring her doctor of philosophy husband all these years, a "Herr Rabiner" with a bitter face and cold personality, no wonder Annelyse found solace in this crude, healthy young man from the Ticino valley. And yet, she'd chosen to mostly conceal the relationship from him. Perhaps she'd done so because of Karl. *In that case,* he thought on his way home to Bern, *I, too, for my son's sake, should officially keep our crumbling family together. After all,* he tried to console himself, *this kind of thing happened all the time: a duped husband, a cuckold. Worldly people took it with much more grace than the children of rabbis, former yeshiva boys, who had absorbed the "synagogue rot." Still, to so deceive a father and mother, a rabbi and rebbetzin, while you were living with a Christian woman and had an uncircumcised son—such a vile, sinister act would horrify even a cynic who was rotten to the core.*

But when he'd arrived back home, those years ago, he'd discovered that his wife was now even more entangled in her relationship. Which left him with two choices: go on swallowing bile or run back to where he'd just come from.

$$\rightarrow\ 3\ \leftarrow$$

FOR THE THOUSANDTH TIME, Naftali Hertz found himself mulling over the same idea, unable to recall whether he'd read it somewhere or had come up with it himself. The idea was this: A man with pleasant memories is never lonesome; the man who's lonesome is the man who's afraid to remember his past. Indeed, he was just such a lonely person. He couldn't even count those first good years with Annelyse as happy, because all the while he'd been trying to block out memories of his home and family. Now, here at his parents' home, he was trying to block out the memory of his Swiss family. But he couldn't push the thought of them aside, not for a single hour, just as when he'd visited his parents two years before. Naftali Hertz looked out the window of his room at the solid sheet of snow, at the darkness, and thought of the long wintry night ahead. A night of twisting and turning, waiting for the dark to give birth to a cold and dreary dawn.

In time, Luigi Martini, the wallpaper man, had ceased coming to the house, and Annelyse herself had stopped finding excuses to leave their home in the evenings. Naftali Hertz felt like a freed man: no longer would he have to play the revolting game of pretending to know nothing. True, the intimacy he once shared with his wife had lapsed. She was too crass for his taste, and he too unfriendly and emasculated for hers. Still, when she brought food to the table, he felt a tenderness in his limbs. Her hands were so deft, she did everything with such dexterity, with such confidence and skill, that just observing her movements brought him a measure of satisfaction. Sometimes, at work in the library, he'd catch a wisp of the scent of her dry, freshly washed body and his nostrils would flare, as though he were in a forest of pine trees fragrant in the sunshine, breathing in the green needles, the moss and tar.

He and Annelyse must continue their life together, he realized. If not out of love for each other, then for the sake of their son, who was already eighteen years old. Naftali Hertz didn't deny that he, too, was disappointed in his perfunctory life, the doctorate title and position as head librarian of the Judaic division. On the other hand, his visit to his parents had shown him just how estranged he'd become from Jewish life in a Polish shtetl. And so he was ready to give the doting family life another shot.

But Annelyse wasn't. After she'd ended things with her lover, her strained face would sometimes swell with hostility toward her husband. At the table, now, he began talking about the peculiar behavior of the Jews in Polish shtetls. But Annelyse impatiently turned away and asked her son a question, cutting her husband off. Naftali Hertz hadn't forgotten the way she once burned with curiosity and empathy whenever he regaled her with tales of the pious Jews from home. He turned silent now, humbly lowering his head. Atop a tray on the table lay a chunk of browned pork, filling the kitchen with its sharp, spicy odor. His wife and son, stirring restlessly in their chairs, were waiting for him to slice it. The pork's sharp odor incited and tickled their nostrils. But the head of the family, their husband and father, was still occupied with his own food. He sat, dejected, his spoon submerged in a half-empty plate, and chewed on a crust of bread. Sitting at the table with his Christian wife and son, he felt like a yeshiva boy during essen teg, when they'd eat at a different person's home each day. It occurred to him that as long as Annelyse's "friend" was around, she could afford to be patient with her husband, even allowing him to mope around the house in misery. But now she could no longer hide her revulsion.

His son didn't resemble him at all. Karl took after his mother's brothers—tall and broad, with a short neck that looked like a hill had sprouted from his nape. When he spread his wide palms and invited a friend to wrestle him, even the tall, strong Swiss boys backed away. He had blondish-red hair and intense blue eyes. He would debate powerfully, with shouts and laughter bursting past his large teeth, wide lips, and puffy cheeks. Though he was constantly involved in sports—running and swimming, soccer and skiing—he never neglected his studies. At seventeen and a half years old he'd already finished high school, and at eighteen he was studying at the

Mountain Institute, completing his degree in engineering, to build wells on the Alps.

Though he was now a university student, he still enjoyed the boyish pleasure of carrying a tall stack of books in his hands rather than in a backpack. They often toppled over, and when he bent to pick them up, still more would drop, and he'd keep laughing and bending over to retrieve each fallen book, as if he were playing with dogs.

His status as a half Jew didn't cause Karl any grief. No one brought it up. Though he himself felt bewildered and anxious about having a father who was different from everyone around him. It was especially obvious during the holidays. All their guests drank, sang, and laughed, but the owner of the house—Papa—barely cracked a smile. Though he tried to fit in, he couldn't. Annelyse never turned her son against his father. But Karl noticed how, day after day, she grew more and more distant from him and treated him with more disdain. In those moments when Naftali Hertz spoke to his wife and son, they felt a connection to him, but when he turned silent—and his silences were becoming longer and more frequent—Annelyse and Karl felt as if they were lost on an unfamiliar mountain, among dark, unfriendly woods and overgrown lakes.

Two decades had passed since their wedding, and Annelyse still had an upright figure, slim legs, and firm knees. She'd only recently become a bit chubby, her breasts no longer stiff as apples, and her chestnut hair had begun to look faded and rumpled. Her gray-blue eyes, once clever and vibrant, now regarded her husband angrily, coldly. At times, her gloomy gaze would linger over him like a cloudy autumn day. *She is lonelier than I am*, he thought.

Naftali Hertz's own appearance hadn't changed much over the years. Only his thick black hair now shone with ribbons of silver-gray, and his narrow, pointed shoulders slouched from constantly hunching over old volumes at the library. His thoughts, however, had undergone a much bigger transformation. He'd come to a conclusion he hadn't anticipated.

Back when he'd been a philosophy student, enamored of Spinoza, he'd told himself that the Jewish God was not merely the historical God of Judah Halevi. The Jewish God was also the metaphysical God of Maimonides, washed of all corporeal features, including positive attributes. Yes, that God, too, was the God of the Jewish religion and the Jewish nation. But Naftali Hertz had abandoned the yeshiva and run to university in Switzerland precisely because he believed that if God existed, it was a universal God. Individual nations could have their fake Gods; but the one God could be only the substance that is its own reason and the reason of the entire cosmos. Such were his ideas in the past, when he was thinking rationally. But the older he became, the more clearly he understood that, in those times when he *was* a believer, the only God he believed in was the Jewish God, not a universal one, nor a metaphysical one. Though he didn't observe God's Torah, he was able to believe only in the God of Abraham, Isaac, and Jacob. Either he believed in the God of Abraham or he did not believe in a God at all.

Not only had he never learned to accept a universal God, he hadn't even learned to like his neighbors, the Swiss. The fact that he had never been granted Swiss citizenship, because he earned too little and offered no particular assets to the country, gave him tremendous pleasure. His wife and son were Swiss-born citizens, but he didn't have enough money to buy their national pride and pedigree! Had a poet ever passed through Switzerland and not waxed poetic about the Alps? But the Swiss themselves had turned the Alps into a business. And they'd made a business, too, of selling freedom. Once, Switzerland had been a safe haven for the central committees of Russian revolutionaries. These days, they rented their halls at a fee for the assemblies of dreamers who wanted to change the world. But the Swiss themselves were neither idealists nor fantasists. Everyone was welcome in Switzerland—if they had money! The sick in sanatoriums, the students at universities, the tourists in hotels—all bearing money, all welcome.

True, not all of the Swiss were evil and money-hungry; some were sincere and good-natured. But none of them were overly kind, and they lacked empathy for strangers. Naftali Hertz knew he was being ungrateful to the country that had furnished him with a home, a job, and a title. But his repugnance for his ruined life overrode his common sense. He laughed, and the laughter felt like stones in his belly. More than twenty years he'd been living in western Europe, and still each night his heart and mind went to sleep in Morehdalye.

Even worse than the Swiss Christians, for Naftali Hertz, were the "Temple Jews" of Bern's Jewish community. He hated them for the holiday attire they wore to temple, their top hats, frock coats, white vests, and slip-on shoes; hated them for their small silk prayer shawls and truncated prayers, for their thin whiskers and close-cropped beards. Everything was halved and shortened with them, except for their slavish loyalty to Switzerland. That was measureless and infinite. What luck had befallen them—they were Swiss citizens! And how they squirmed with shame and hurt if he spoke a single word against a canton president or their federal government.

Soon, Naftali Hertz had become so bitter that Fräulein Aida Noifeld, at whose home he'd once been a welcome guest, no longer found him charming. Her mother, the old, kind Chana Rochel, who had always been so nostalgic for her little shtetl in Poland, wasn't around anymore. With her passing, the pleasant aroma of homey Jewish dishes disappeared from the Noifeld home. The younger of the two heiresses, Janet, had finally decided to move to Paris and live with her husband. She'd come back to Bern to collect her share of earnings from the clock factory. And each time she returned, she astonished her older sister with a new hairdo dyed a new color. Janet was no longer sitting around in the decorated hall with a book, her expression that of a woman reading the final letter of a husband who's shot himself over her or one who's died young from consumption. If Katzenellenbogen visited Aida when Janet happened to be there, she didn't even pause her crass haggling over how much money she was owed—so little did Naftali Hertz's presence count. Aida, too, no longer felt as warmly toward him as in the past.

One evening he came in and found Aida sitting in the dining room, at the big square table, with several empty chairs around it and a crystal chandelier above. Across from the table was an old-fashioned credenza crammed with porcelain and silver dishes. But on the table was only a single dish, prepared for Aida. She didn't invite Katzenellenbogen to eat with her, because she hadn't been expecting him. Not only had he arrived uninvited, but adding insult to injury, he sat down and proceeded to mock the local "Temple Jews."

Fräulein Noifeld replied sharply, angrily. "I don't understand you. You have a Christian wife and son, but you're making fun of Temple Jews because they pray in German? Because they pray from abbreviated prayer books, because men and women sit together in the synagogue, because they have an organ? You say the Rabiner's preaching is comical, completely different from that of your father, the Orthodox rabbi. But how can *you* criticize us? Other than not being baptized, you live entirely like a non-Jew. Does your father, the Orthodox rabbi, know about this? Why are you laughing?"

He laughed because he suddenly had a vision of the scene at his parents' house, saw himself lying to his parents that Aida Noifeld was his wife. He realized, though, that if he told her how he'd used her name to fool his parents, she'd be more offended than by his ridicule of Temple Jews. "True, Fräulein Noifeld," he said, "I don't live like a Jew at all, but I like whole Jews, not half-Israelites."

After that, he never came by to see Aida again, fearful that he'd spill the story of how he'd duped his parents, calling Aida his wife and the mother of his grown son.

$$\rightarrowtail \quad 4 \quad \leftarrowtail$$

I'm like an evergreen tree high up in the mountains, Naftali Hertz thought, *where it's too cold for the branches to grow upward toward the sky. Instead, its prickly green branches stretch horizontally over the earth, growing outward. I, too, crawl on my stomach, bending myself to the needs of my despicable life.*

His situation at home had become even more painful after the letters he'd received from Poland. First, his father had written him in Hebrew, in rabbinic, ornamental handwriting, asking why they hadn't heard from him since he'd gone home. Then, his mother wrote in Yiddish, in a round, sparse, childlike alphabet, about how empty and lonely the house felt since all their children had dispersed. But at least their other children wrote them letters, she noted, while from him they'd heard absolutely nothing.

Not long after, two more letters arrived. These were from his sisters. Tilza wrote that his visit had brought her much less joy than she'd expected, and she wasn't very surprised that she hadn't heard from him since. But what she couldn't understand was how he could live with himself, not writing to his parents. Bluma Rivtcha, besides also admonishing him for not writing their parents, added—with haughtiness and anger—that she was not at all certain he was her brother (and perhaps she wasn't allowed to address him with the familiar "du"), since he hadn't even bothered to come to Vilna to see her. He knew, after all, that she was working at the hospital and couldn't travel home.

Naftali Hertz received these letters at the library. Each time he reread one of them, he gazed out the window at the snow-tipped mountains of the Bernese Oberland. He sat there, staring for hours, until twilight bathed the peaks of the Jungfrau, Mönch, and Eiger in a red glow. He gazed at the crimson and violet clouds veiling the mountaintops and wished he were a speck of sunlit dust, or an icicle, one particle among the many millions that hung quivering in the Alpine dusk and then sank behind the mountain range, forever buried. He couldn't grasp why he'd never demanded that Annelyse convert to Judaism before they married. And later, why he'd never demanded they circumcise Karl. Had he assumed the war would never end, that neutral Switzerland's mountains would cut him off from the rest of the world forever? Had he figured his father and mother would die before the war was over and he'd never have to account for his actions, to anyone ever? His visit home had only magnified the thoughtlessness of his youth. Well, what could he do now? He would not reply to the letters! That was the only way out. He would silence himself, and eventually the entire family would give up on him.

At home, Annelyse and Karl knew nothing of the letters he'd received at the library's address. To excuse his constant irascibility, and because he couldn't refrain from talking about his old home, his conversation at mealtimes centered around the news of antisemitic excesses in Poland that he'd read about in the papers. Hatred ran rampant in the cities, and in the villages there were pogroms. At the universities, Jewish students were confined to a ghetto, forbidden to share benches with Polish students. From his one visit home, Naftali Hertz had gleaned enough to talk about the antisemitic National Radical Camp and its splinter group, the Falanga, with its even more stubborn Jew-haters and hooligans.

"Worse than the political confrontations," Naftali Hertz explained, "is the economic boycott. The Polish Jews call it the 'quiet war,' because by not letting the Poles do business with Jews, they're starving out entire cities and towns. And the Polish government is helping them choke the Jews through supposedly legal means: high taxes, barring Jews from the government monopolies and tobacco and liquor factories, and forcing Jews to keep their shops closed on Sundays. On Saturdays, of course, Jews keep their shops closed for religious purposes. But the government's now forcing them to close on Sunday, too."

Possibly because Annelyse didn't understand that beneath her husband's worry for all Jews lay the real source of his suffering—his fear for his own family in the shtetl—or because this wasn't the first time he'd launched into this topic just as they were sitting down to eat, making both her and Karl lose their appetite, she replied, her face cold and surprised, "The Jews in Bern keep their shops closed on Sunday and open on their Sabbath. Let the Jews in Poland do the same."

"I've already explained to you many times that our local Jewish community can't be compared to the Polish Jews. It's like comparing a stick figure to a real live person," her husband replied impatiently. "Even the Orthodox Jews here, who do keep their warehouses closed on Shabbos, have no national consciousness."

"They have the national consciousness of Swiss Jews." Annelyse calmly worked her fork and knife into the chicken on her plate.

"A man might be Swiss on his passport, but a national consciousness he carries inside his heart and mind, not on a piece of paper," her husband replied, even more agitated than before.

Karl ate his piece of chicken in the way of ill-bred American children: with his hands. He gnawed at the soft, sweet little bones, pulled his large head back from his short neck and broad shoulders, and generally drowned out the room with his noise. "Papa, Mama, why are you bickering over this? According to what I read, Poland is home to different ethnic groups who all hate each other and fight each other. Here, in the twentieth century, why can't the Polish join forces and establish a community, the way people in the cantons of Uri, Schwyz, and Unterwalden were wise enough and civil enough to do in the 1300s? In Switzerland, everyone lives together peacefully: Protestants, Catholics, Germans, French, and Italians. Everyone speaks their own language. In some neighborhoods, they still speak Romansh and Ladin, a kind of leftover of Latin."

"You don't know what you're talking about," his papa accused him, enraged. "Even if the other Slavic groups were willing to join with the Poles and establish a confederation, like they did here in Switzerland, the Jews would never be granted equal rights, not even lesser rights. To non-Jews, the Jews aren't only another religion, another nation, another race: they're something even more alien—they're Jews. You see?"

But Karl didn't understand, and his father stormed away from the table, trailed by his son's astonished glances and his wife's exhausted expression, as though her husband's Jewishly slumped shoulders reminded her of a clumsy turtle's armor.

That year, Yom Kippur fell in late autumn, when the trees were busiest shedding their leaves. The library's Judaic division was closed, and Naftali Hertz found himself at home, pleased to be alone, without wife and son. The mild autumn sunrays illuminated the Swiss ornaments carved into the oak and walnut furniture, bringing them into relief. A sunny tranquility coated everything, as if brushed into the skins on the floor. The cupboard shelves lined with dishes, the accent tables with flowerpots, the embroidered curtains on the windows, the mirror and chairs—everything glimmered cleanly, tidily, with German precision and monotony, like the chime of the wooden clock on the wall and the wooden cuckoo that jumped out each time the minute hand reached twelve.

Naftali Hertz looked out at the homes across the street, at the two- and three-story Swiss houses with sloping, shingled roofs and balconies with carvings beneath the windows. Between the two rows of houses on their street, along the length of the sidewalks, stretched a line of trees. Piles of their leaves swished around them. Naftali Hertz gazed through the window at an overgrown tree, which in autumn looked dirty and disheveled, its brown, oblong leaves spilling from it. From an aspen with silver bark, round, crimson leaves fell quietly and sparsely. On the highest branches of a tall and skimpy birch, leaves of greenish gold and sheer yellow still trembled and flickered. Most of the trees on the street were thick-trunked, long-branched maples of different varieties. From them stretched threads of leaves in all shades of gold, wine red, copper, flaming fire. Naftali Hertz recalled the Yom Kippurs of his home and yeshiva. Back then, too, it sometimes happened that Yom Kippur came in late autumn, when the leaves fell thickly. He began to hum the tune of the Yom Kippur prayers, and gradually his timbre rose; he sang with a sob in his throat, with tears gathered in his eyes. *Lord, God of our forefathers, forgive us our sins on this day of Yom Kippur, erase our past sins from in front of you . . .*

He felt someone standing behind him. He turned, and there stood Annelyse, laughing lovingly. She said, "I see what's going on. You're singing songs from the Jewish prayer book. All the Jewish shops are closed today, and the Jews are in their synagogues. It's their holiest day. So why don't you go to temple? All my old friends wonder about this. They ask if my husband has become a Christian or is still a

Jew. He doesn't attend synagogue or church, they say. Some of them think you're still a Russian atheist, one of the ones who became Russian Bolshevists." She drew closer to him.

He had already wiped his teary eyes. "Either I act like a non-Jew or like a Jew from an Orthodox home. On a day like today, on the holiest day of the year, I would have found it especially hard to be with the 'Israelite Jews.' But since when have you become interested in my religious habits?"

"No, it doesn't interest me." She laughed voicelessly, and only then did Naftali Hertz become aware that, though he hadn't heard Annelyse come in from the street before, she had at some point already changed into a short, tight housedress, buttoned down the front. Her breasts appeared rounder and firmer, as though she'd pulled the bodice tighter. Her smooth knees shone, as did her bare feet tucked into slippers. From the pleats of her dress's thin fabric and the skin glistening between the buttons, Naftali Hertz realized that his wife was stark naked beneath her housedress. She was smiling like a she-devil, ambiguously, intoxicatingly, demandingly.

She squinted her eyes, and her large body rocked back and forth. It occurred to him that she was waiting for him to draw nearer, that she would then keep moving backward, hit the bed, and fall onto it. Naftali Hertz couldn't believe that, after all this time of estrangement and indifference, she was suddenly aflame with desire. No, there was something else she wanted. She knew that even though he wasn't fasting or going to temple, this day was nevertheless holy to him. What she wanted was to see which held greater power over him: her body or his Jewish God. Or perhaps she simply wanted to test how much power her body still held over a man. Whatever the reason, Naftali Hertz felt no desire for her now. He stood there with the detached expression of one who's already too tired or too wise for such tricks and games.

UNLIKE HER HUSBAND, the "Herr Rabiner," Annelyse did not yet feel too old for a new love. Just as with the wallpaper man two years before, she again brought a friend into her home. Hans Taauba was the vice-director of the bank where Annelyse worked, a forty-five-year-old unmarried reprobate with soft, graying hair, a fleshy jaw, and the fat lips of a man with a sweet tooth. Cold-blooded, prudent, fond of a bargain, he was the sort who, when talking with buddies, would wink first with one eye and then with the other, as if to say, "I'd rather be an old bachelor spending time with other men's wives; let other men deal with prickly wives, not me."

The first time Annelyse brought him into their home was for her birthday. The guests included her brothers, their wives, and their grown children. After eating and drinking, everyone dispersed. The noisy young ones went into Karl's room, and the older ones went into the parlor. Katzenellenbogen schmoozed with his brothers-in-law, and his wife laid her arm on Hans Taauba's high shoulder. Annelyse laughed merrily at the vice-director, who was acting boyish, trying to show her a new dance. Naftali Hertz continued to schmooze with his guests, as he obliquely observed his wife clinging to the old-fashioned playboy. Taauba led her carefully across the room, and with a lewd smile on his fat lips, looked over her shoulder and down at her wide, full rear end.

But Annelyse had bigger dreams. She wanted more than to merely spend time with another man and be his toy. And so, she pitted her vice-director against another friend. Dr. Rauschenbach was a psychiatrist, divorced and estranged from his children, a muscled man of medium height, bowlegged, with wide-set feet, a large and bald triangular skull, and severe black eyes—an unusual combination of degenerate and government officer. He didn't appear to be a man who wastes time on talk or one who was out to find a lover. Nor did he seem a romantic who makes a fuss over a woman when he's alone with her.

Rauschenbach acted respectfully toward Katzenellenbogen, the doctor of philosophy, and made angry eyes at Annelyse: What was this all about, bringing him together with her husband and that tall imbecile, her vice-director? What cards was she shuffling here, and whom was she trying to pit against whom? If she was scheming to divorce her husband and marry him, her efforts were in vain. Rauschenbach and Katzenellenbogen understood each other and avoided each other's eyes. Naftali Hertz knew he was still too weak to sever himself from his life. But his desire to disappear for a while was even stronger than it had been two years earlier.

Right around this time, he received a letter from his mother informing him that his father had suffered a heart attack. "The doctor claims," wrote his mother, "that by all indications, the heart attack resulted from all of his stress. No wonder! More than two years he's suffered without a word from you, our eldest son. If you don't want your father's heartache to strike him again, a more devastating blow, come home immediately. If you refuse, your brother-in-law, Tilza's husband, will travel to Switzerland to find out what's become of you."

His enlightened worldview, and all his knowledge of philosophy, couldn't keep Naftali Hertz from seeing God's finger in all this. Two years ago, his wife's horrible behavior had driven him to visit his parents. Now, the exact same thing was happening again. Was this not Divine Providence? Still, he was a dratted rationalist and too conceited to admit it. He refused to become a ba'al tshuvah and return to religion. He was a Job without faith. If he didn't believe in a personal God, how could he have complaints against Him? Oh, better for a man like him to have never been born.

5

Vayehi miketz shenasayim yamim upharaoh kholem v'hinei omed al ha'yeohr: "And it came to pass at the end of two full years, that Pharaoh dreamed: and, behold, he stood by the river." The Sages say that, because Joseph had asked the Saar HaMashkim, the pharaoh's butler, to remember him to the pharaoh, he was punished with another two years in the dungeon, in addition to the ten years of imprisonment that had been decreed for him. As the verse says, "Happy is the man who places his faith in God."

Behind a pillar of the bimah in the large Morehdalye beis medrash stood Naftali Hertz, listening to a rabbi as he studied the weekly parsha with his students around a table. The rabbi was Zalia Ziskind Luria, Naftali Hertz's former rosh yeshiva, and the students were elderly Morehdalye Jews: shop owners with gloomy faces, craftsmen with stooped shoulders and soiled fingers. In the frosty winter evening, the students with tangled beards sat, wearing coats and boots, sheepskin hats and cloth caps with earflaps. Crowded close around the table, they warmed each other's icy shoulders, shook their heads sadly, and mumbled: "Yes, of course! Woe to those who rely on people, as we say in our prayers: 'Do not rely on noblemen or humans, for in them does not lie hope.'"

Naftali Hertz perceived a certain happiness in their gloomy faces, a quiet, innocent joy. How lucky they were, in their old age, for the chance to go back, at least for an hour, to the cheder from which they'd run when they were boys. They regarded the rabbi explaining the weekly parsha with both respect and regret. These Jews knew what a tremendous scholar Zalia Ziskind was, the former Dünaburg genius. The townspeople of Visoki-Dvor had once prided themselves on having him as their rabbi and rosh yeshiva. Now here he was in this little room in Morehdalye, collecting a pittance from the com-

munity for assisting the Morehdalye rabbi, his friend from the
Volozhin Yeshiva. The Morehdalye dayan, Reb Tzadok Kadish, had
also taken ill of late, and was even sicker than the rabbi, so Zalia Ziskind was substituting for the dayan, too, just as he'd substituted for
Kahane in Lecheve when he'd traveled abroad to collect funds for his
yeshiva. Apparently, the former Dünaburg genius was now content
to be a substitute, to stand in for another, and just as content to be
the kind of small-town preacher who studies a bit of Chumash with
Jews around a table.

Naftali Hertz saw that Zalia Ziskind's back had become even more
hunched in the last two years, his gray beard sparser, his big black
eyes sunken deeper. His beautiful, melodious voice was completely
gone; it had probably grown hard and dry, like that of an exhausted
mourner who's finally accepted he cannot wake the dead.

Naftali Hertz continued observing him from behind the pillar.
Zalia Ziskind spoke of how Jacob and his children were dragged into
exile in Egypt. The electric lamp above the table cast a circle of light
in the dark beis medrash, shining golden yellow on the bearded faces
of the huddled Jews. *If only I weren't so bound by reason, what solace it
would be if I, too, went back to cheder,* Naftali Hertz thought. *The fate of
these simple, overworked Jews, my fate as a failed doctor of philosophy, and
the fate of my former rabbi have all converged in the end and balanced out.
No longer does the genius Zalia Ziskind have any interest in shaking up
the world with his novel interpretations on the Torah; a bit of Chumash is
enough for him. And no longer am I interested in metaphysical philosophical
speculations, nor in the history of philosophy. Seriously, do I really care about
the connection between the Gnostics and the first Christians, or how much
of Albertus Magnus and Thomas Aquinas is derived from Maimonides?
And if these two scholastics have, indeed, adopted their theories from Maimonides, will the hooligans and brawlers of the Polish Falanga stop inciting
a boycott against the Morehdalye Jews? At least Zalia Ziskind has stuck
with a bit of Chumash, but what have I stuck with?* And so, Naftali Hertz
went on gazing at the Jews around the table, as if peeking over at the
Garden of Eden, at the righteous men sitting with crowns on their
heads, delighting in Godly pleasures.

But when the Jews around the table closed their books of Chumashim and stood for evening prayers, they didn't look at all like
the saints in the Garden of Eden, not even like cheder boys awed

by Chumash stories. They looked like plain old worn-out fathers and grandfathers. Each person in the minyan crawled to a vacant bench in a different corner, and you could hear their sighs—sighs that revealed their depressing thoughts: *If we've accomplished nothing after all our toil in this material world, what can we common folk hope for in the World of Truth?*

When prayers were over, the men slowly dispersed across the snowy village; and in the circle of light at the table, piled with closed Chumashim, only Zalia Ziskind and Naftali Hertz remained sitting. They spoke quietly, almost whispering, as though careful not to wake the shadows of the pillars and chandeliers floating on the walls and ceiling from their silent inertia. Shadows fell from the steps of the aron kodesh, too, and from the bimah and the benches with their shtenders, shadows that looked like the thick, large roots of an ancient tree on a hill. The darkness in the beis medrash grew denser. In this dense darkness, the wine-red flame of the ner tamid sputtered and choked as in its death throes, and Naftali Hertz spoke into his former rabbi's ears like a quiet stream murmuring into an overgrown ditch.

"It's strange how the stories of the Chumash have the power to captivate a child and an elder, an ignoramus and a scholar, even a freethinker, as though the histories of the patriarchs and the Jewish spirit itself have, indeed, hailed from the same source. A religious book, I've always thought, is never dated. But when someone writes a book about Immanuel Kant, for example—or, like me, who's always meaning to but still haven't gotten myself together to write a book about the Jewish sources of Baruch Spinoza's philosophy . . . Well, say this book shakes up the scholarly world. I still know that a generation later, a different professor will write another book about Spinoza or Immanuel Kant, and the book that just a generation before had stunned the world will now be buried. But the commentaries on the Torah, whether from the *Ohr HaChaim* or the *Alshich*, are never tossed aside, no matter what new commentary or publication follows it. You see what I'm saying? When a world-renowned French writer died—his name was Anatole France—his young rivals wrote that he was dead even when he was alive. Can you imagine such a thing, after the death of an old rabbi or rosh yeshiva? Young students talking about him in such a way?" Naftali Hertz said, openly envious of the devout and old-fashioned world, where so much respect existed between older and younger generations.

Zalia Ziskind listened to him reluctantly, his head turned partly away, as he pinched his beard impatiently and waited for Naftali Hertz's diatribe to end. Naftali Hertz, too, was tense. Soon his rabbi would stab him, he thought, stab him with words. "You're such a saint, aren't you?" his rabbi would say. "*Lo hamedrash ha-ikar . . .* It's not studying that's most important, but deeds. Do you put on tefillin? Does your wife go to the ritual bath? In fact, who *is* your wife?"

But when Zalia Ziskind spoke, it was obvious he'd been thinking about something else entirely. "You know," he said, with a tremor in his voice, "my Marcus is here in town. He's a different person now. He has to hide from the police. I'm telling you this so that you don't give any hint to any of the Jews here that he's irreligious. It's a matter of life and death."

Naftali Hertz's parents had already told him in secret that Marcus had become a communist and that Zalia Ziskind lived in constant fear of his only child being arrested. Every so often, Marcus would come to stay with his father in Morehdalye for support and to elude his captors. To avoid any further suspicion, he acted Jewish and religious when in Morehdalye. In fact, one of the main reasons Zalia Ziskind remained in Morehdalye was so that his son would have a safe haven.

"But Marcus was the opposite of a socialist or communist," Naftali Hertz had remarked to his parents when they'd told him about the situation. "When did he change?"

They had no answer for him, but simply reiterated several times that he shouldn't divulge this to any of the townspeople. Now, when Zalia Ziskind himself confided in him, Naftali Hertz asked him the same question. "Two years ago, when I was in Lecheve, your son was a Nietzschean, constantly quoting Zarathustra. 'A person's greatest danger is his pity, his empathy for others.' Since when did Marcus come to believe the exact opposite, that a person should sacrifice himself for the weak and the poor?"

"I don't know," Zalia Ziskind replied, displeased that Naftali Hertz was more interested in Marcus's new principles than in Zalia Ziskind's new problems.

For Naftali Hertz, however, his doctoral studies in philosophy were suddenly rekindled; he spoke vivaciously of Friedrich Nietzsche, who'd been dead now for decades. "Many years before his death, he lost his sanity. He went crazy. But he continued to hold great influence, especially over the educated young men in western Europe, who didn't worry about earning a livelihood and hadn't yet found their path in life. Poets or pseudo-poets who lived in spiritual contemplation, like Nietzsche himself. You know that Nietzsche, the great philosopher-poet, the great thinker, lived only in places where the masses roiled with discontent and revolutionaries, wanted to upend the world of rich and poor. He was insane. That's why no one pays attention anymore to Zarathustra's aphorisms. And that's why I was so surprised," Naftali Hertz said, "that in a Jewish Polish village, mired in poverty and alienation, a village burning with the hatred of Jews—that in such a village there should be a young man, the son of a rabbi, wandering around quoting Zarathustra's tired belief that the greatest danger for the elite is empathy for the weak."

"You've forgotten what you yourself convinced me of then: that Marcus was saying these things to spite himself, because he was the exact opposite of a cruel person. In truth, I knew this before you did." Zalia Ziskind smiled sadly. "From what Marcus had told me, I understood that his teacher, too, this Nietzsche, said these things to spite himself."

"True!" Naftali Hertz burst out, astonished and pleased that Zalia Ziskind had retained his brilliance, even on an unfamiliar topic. "Friedrich Nietzsche criticized philosophies and philosophers he'd practically idolized before. In this way, he hoped to free himself from their influence, from being enslaved by them."

"We see this in daily life, too, even among Torah scholars. There are people who can't, under any circumstances, make peace with the thought that they're in debt to someone who's done them a favor, and they become their benefactor's blood enemy." Zalia Ziskind again smiled sadly and was quiet for a moment—thinking, probably, of his brothers-in-law, for whom he'd relinquished his position as rabbi and rosh yeshiva in Visoki-Dvor, and of how they'd repaid him.

"What you said earlier," Zalia Ziskind continued, "isn't true either. You claimed that among secular, learned men, the young insult the old, but that with Torah scholars there's tremendous respect between the young and the old. Sadly, this isn't the case. But with respect to my son, yes, he should have found himself a better teacher than this Nietzsche." Zalia Ziskind gave a short laugh and looked around the dark holy room at the cases of holy books, as if he were speaking to them, too. "By any account, this Nietzsche was no kindhearted person. No kind person would propose a philosophy that if someone is falling, let him fall. Modern-day people believe that ancient men were feral and cruel. But from our Torah we see that it isn't so. Even though our Torah is thousands of years old, the verse *verakhmav al kol maasev*, that we should take pity on all of God's creatures—it's already written there. You say that my Marcus now feels exactly the opposite, and you wonder when he underwent such change. As far as I know, Marcus's beliefs aren't very different from what they used to be. From what I've seen and heard about the Bolshevist revolt— and even more, from the kinds of things you hear about them doing now, the way they behave toward Jews and their own peasants in Russia, toward anyone who opposes them, really, you can see that they have even less empathy for human creatures than during the times of Nikolai. But in the past, Marcus couldn't say for certain who the 'great man' of his generation was. But now, he knows, without a shadow of doubt, that the great man is Lenin, along with his present-day Bolshevist heirs. Get it?" And Zalia Ziskind turned quiet, letting his mind wander around the austere darkness of the beis medrash.

An odd thought occurred to Naftali Hertz: *Could Marcus have become a communist out of desperation, because I disrupted his romance with my sister and he had nowhere to go back to?* His interest in meeting Marcus grew. He anticipated a great debate, the way they used to debate in Lecheve when Marcus kept drawing him into conversations.

As it turned out, though, Naftali Hertz was in for a different sort of experience. The next morning, when he arrived at the beis medrash for davening, Marcus Luria was already there. But as soon as he noticed Naftali Hertz, Marcus turned away from him toward the wall. Throughout the davening, all Naftali Hertz saw of Marcus was his swaying back. Even afterward, when Marcus was taking off his tefillin and rolling it up, he remained facing the wall. Then, he hastily left the beis medrash, face cast down like a pious Torah scholar who's careful with his speech, avoids looking at women, and regrets every moment that isn't spent studying Torah. *He disguises himself better than I do*, Naftali Hertz thought. *But he has a reason to hide, while I'm a mere hypocrite.*

The next morning, in the beis medrash, their eyes met and Naftali Hertz began walking toward him. But when they were close, Marcus hissed, his face twisted in anger and scorn, "Whaddya want?"

Two years before, he'd never addressed Dr. Katzenellenbogen with the familiar "du," nor had he ever spoken to him this rudely. Marcus looked ashen, exhausted already at this early hour. He panted heavily, as if he'd been out running before he got here and would soon be running again. An air of bitterness and depression wafted off him, the bitterness of a man who's being pursued, who sleeps in one place and spends his days in another. On the other hand, he seemed a lot stronger than in the past. His crafty eyes flashed with audacity, with suspicion, and in his tightly sealed mouth was an energy and decisiveness.

Naftali Hertz, without a word, backed quietly away, despite how annoyed he was with himself at suddenly having developed such respect for and fear of the young man. Though he well knew the source of his confusion and defeat in front of Marcus: Marcus was disguising himself as a devout Jew to protect himself from the Polish political police while he was being a hypocrite in order to fool his parents.

Throughout the entire davening, Naftali Hertz didn't take his eyes off Marcus's father. Zalia Ziskind, he noticed, was stricken with fear. Marcus prayed in one corner of the beis medrash and his father in the other, but Zalia Ziskind kept turning his head to watch the door, as if terrified that police would appear.

After prayers, once Marcus had left the beis medrash, his father tailed after him—at a distance, as though to protect him. Through his parents, Naftali Hertz had heard that whenever Marcus showed up, his father flew into a frenzy, terrified not only of the Polish spies, but fearful that his son would find kindred spirits here in Moreh-dalye, would start inciting the peasants in the surrounding villages, the young workers in town. But then, even after Marcus left town, his father found himself trembling yet again, pleading with God for his son's return, because as long as Marcus was around, his father could make sure he wasn't leading an insurrection against the government. The closer he was to his father, the less danger he was in.

Marcus Luria vanished as unexpectedly as he'd appeared, and Naftali Hertz, too, breathed easier, freed from the unexpected bewilderment the rebellious young man had brought upon him.

6

In years past, Sholem Shachne Katzenellenbogen would take the occasional trip to Bialystok and Warsaw for rabbinical gatherings, or to Vilna to buy religious books. During his travels, he would pass through neighboring towns and give talks to raise funds for the Council of Yeshivas. And on occasion he'd stop for a visit with his father-in-law, the elderly rabbi of Zembin, or with his son-in-law and daughter in Lecheve. The Morehdalye residents didn't mind their rabbi's little vacations from their town. They knew he wasn't on the hunt for a bigger rabbinate. And neither was Rebbetzin Henna'le opposed to these trips. She understood that her husband needed to get away from the confinement of their small town and from all the festering resentments he felt toward his children. But since Sholem Shachne had become ill, he could no longer consider such trips. Henna'le knew how much this confinement would crush her husband, so she'd written not only to her children but to other family members, too, asking them to come and visit.

On a Wednesday evening, two weeks after Chanukah, into the rabbi's house stepped his older brother, the dayan of Bialystok. At sixty-seven, Avraham Alter Katzenellenbogen was even portlier than he'd been in years past, but he'd become less vivacious. Old age had come upon him suddenly, extinguishing the fire in his restless eyes. His long, rounded beard, like a porcelain seder plate, no longer stood out stiffly from his face; its crocheted, knotty curls had grown shaggy and tangled. Like his beard, his partnership in the textile factory and the rentals in the courtyard compound had unraveled, too. He no longer dealt with lottery tickets either, because his customers complained that they never won. Nor was he called as often for business arbitrations, because when he did arbitrate, both sides would leave unhappy with his decisions. There was no reason for anyone to envy him anymore, but the other Bialystok dayanim continued to gossip about his ruthless business practices. Despite all this, Avraham Alter had not become a depressed and temperamental old man. He was still the kind of person who got along with everyone, a warm Jew with an imposing figure. He was also the first of all the relatives to hurry over to his sick brother in Morehdalye.

Avraham Alter arrived at the rabbi's house at nightfall, while a snowstorm was raging outside. He removed his tall galoshes, his coat, and his shtreimel, and he put on his yarmulke. His rabbinic frock coat looked illustrious, festive on this ordinary weekday. He stuck his hand out to his brother. "Sholem aleichem, Sholem Shachne, how are you?" and they kissed each other. "And how are you doing, Henna'le?" he said, using the familiar "du" with warmth and heart. "Sholem aleichem, Naftali Hertz! If I hadn't known you were here visiting your parents, I probably wouldn't have recognized you." He spoke in an affectionate tone and kissed his nephew. But as he leaned in for the kiss, he shot him solemn, searching glances, which Naftali Hertz picked up on. He felt disconcerted, as he did whenever he met a new family member.

The first time Sholem Shachne's children rebelled against their father was in their hatred of his brother, Avraham Alter, the business-man dayan of Bialystok. Avraham Alter was aware of their hatred, but he told himself it didn't bother him. Lately, his own children hadn't been bringing him very much nachas, either, though he consoled himself that they were still a long way from Sholem Shachne's sinning rebels. Look at Naftali Hertz, for example. Until his father fell ill, he'd never bothered coming at all.

Avraham Alter's thoughts burned with the zeal of a bundle of straw in the wind. And with that same ardor, he said to his nephew, "I've heard there are religious and secular Jewish communities in Switzerland. Which type do you belong to? One with our type of rabbi or one with a Rabiner? I'm told you're a librarian in a very big library. So why did you have to study for a doctorate in philosophy? Here I was thinking that once you'd earned a doctorate, you'd become a professor at a university there. I could use someone like you to organize my personal library; it's groaning under the weight of my overloaded shelves. I have entire rooms of shelves, floor to ceiling, which I've prepared for the time when I'll be able to spend my days studying. So far, though, I haven't found that sort of time."

"You're staying for Shabbos?" Henna'le interrupted her brother-in-law, whom she liked as much as her children did.

"It's only Wednesday evening. How can I stay till after Shabbos? No, I'm heading back tomorrow night." Avraham Alter played with the hairballs in his beard, their knots and curls, and once again shifted his attention to his nephew, who was sitting across from him, silent and distant. "Don't you have a grown son? Why didn't you bring him along to see his grandfather? And why didn't you drive down to visit me in Bialystok when you were here two years ago? You could have met my entire family."

"Did your son secure a rabbinate position yet?" Henna'le again interrupted. "And what about your son-in-law? What does he do?"

"My son and son-in-law are shaking up the world!" Avraham Alter replied, in a tone that made it impossible to tell whether he was bragging about his successful children or making a cutting remark. "My son manages my rabbinical house, and my son-in-law gives Torah lectures to the town's scholars. All week, following his talk, Bialystok is busy arguing the subtleties of my son-in-law's novel interpretations."

Naftali Hertz excused himself, saying he had urgent letters to write, and left for his room. Remaining at the table were the rabbi, the rebbetzin, and their guest. For a while Avraham Alter continued to fiddle with the curls in his beard, lost in a cloud of thought. Suddenly, his big, heavy beard shuddered, like a lion's mane, and the hairs he'd twirled untwisted. He began to speak again, his words now very different from before, when Naftali Hertz had been sitting there. "You're asking about my son and son-in-law? I'll tell you. My son smokes the most expensive cigars. His stomach is growing and so are his ambitions. If he's going to become a rabbi, he says, then it should at the very least be in Grodno. In the meantime, no one wants him, not even towns as tiny as a verse in a siddur. With my son-in-law, it's even worse. Sure, his scholarly talks create a stir, but at the same time, he's instigating my daughter to run away with him. Somewhere on the other side of the ocean, that's where he wants to go. Where people don't keep Shabbos or kosher or family purity. 'But they rake gold in the streets there,' he says."

Exasperated, Avraham Alter stroked his whiskers and scratched his neck beneath his beard, wearing such a twisted expression on his face it seemed the hairs had transformed into electrical wires. He shot up and paced the room in long strides, his hands behind his back. Henna'le watched him curiously. She'd always wondered how two brothers could be so different in character and appearance. Her brother-in-law had sprouted a forest of beard and peyes, and his movements were sprightly despite being the older of the two. Sholem Shachne was taller, slimmer, with a modest beard, yet with the substantial whiskers of a baron, tranquil in demeanor even when he might be eating himself alive inside.

Now, too, he spoke to his older brother calmly, with a smile. "Two years ago, when I visited you in Bialystok, you told me, I remember, that your children hadn't abandoned the Torah and Yiddishkeit because you'd never made material pleasures off-limits to them. Since that day, I've thought many a time that perhaps you were right. You live with compromises, and I'm an extremist. But, it turns out, you haven't been successful either. Well, what do you say now?"

"I say nothing." Avraham Alter shrugged, and halted across the table from his brother. "Smarter people than me have failed to resolve the difficult relationship between parents and children. Let's talk about happier things. Actually, I owe you a mazel tov. How do you like Bentzion's bride? He's brought her by, right? Not that he ever comes by my house. I had to find out about his engagement from the clothes dealer he works for. He saw me in the street and wished me mazel tov."

Only then did Avraham Alter notice his brother's and sister-in-law's perplexed faces and realize they hadn't heard a word of this. Astonished, he stood there mutely. But soon he recovered and said, "The entire story is probably a lie. I shouldn't pay any mind to that old clothes dealer, Tzalia Gutmacher, and his blabber. Maybe your Bentzion took a stroll with a girl, and now his boss thinks—oh, a bride! If the situation had really progressed that far, your son would have surely written you."

"All he wrote was that he graduated his business courses," Henna'le said, looking with alarm at her husband.

"It's very like Bentzion not to let us know he's chosen a bride." Sholem Shachne smiled painfully. His anger reddened his ashen face and weakened his voice. "Even as a boy, Bentzion couldn't bear anyone giving him advice on how to behave. And the older he became, the more he suffered from the delusion that people were meddling in his life. That's why he left yeshiva. That's why he left home. He wants to be 'his own man,' as he calls it. In Bialystok, he even tries to live only around people who don't know he's the son of a rabbi. If people treat him more respectfully because they know he's a rabbi's son, he calls that 'meddling in my life.'"

"Don't get angry, Sholem Shachne. You've already gotten sick from heartache once. Please, have pity on both of us," Henna'le pleaded with her husband, then turned to her brother-in-law. "Maybe you can convince him not to get himself so riled up."

"I'm not getting angry; I'm just saying we'll have to give thanks to our son if he deigns to invite us to the wedding," Sholem Shachne said, giving a quiet, resigned laugh and waving his hand toward the room down the hall where Naftali Hertz slept. "Our oldest son didn't invite us to his wedding, either."

The rabbi and rebbetzin sat in silent despondence. Avraham Alter again started twisting the curls in his beard. He was troubled by a question: Sholem Shachne was a greater scholar and more devout than he was; why did he deserve so much suffering from his children? And he gazed around the old house, as though searching the walls for leprosy, for the hidden sins of his younger brother whose children caused him so much grief.

7

As soon as Avraham Alter returned to Bialystok, he sent a special messenger to Tzalia Gutmacher, the ready-made clothes merchant, bidding him to come immediately. Tzalia pondered the implications of this summons. He didn't, after all, own a butcher shop that sold treyf. What, then, might the rabbinical judge want of him? Perhaps he wanted to censure him for keeping his shop open late Friday nights, running over into Shabbos? Or could it be that the town's fanatics wanted to ban him from selling clothes made from shatnez? Well, his customers were about as worried about wearing shatnez as they were about eating a fatty piece of treyf Polish sausage. Still, when a rabbi summons you, you have to go.

What Tzalia did not expect was for the rabbi to greet him with a shout: "Are you a Jew or not?"

Avraham Alter strode back and forth across his beis din room, incensed. "If you're a Jew," he bellowed, "you should take that clerk of yours, my nephew, and kick him out of your shop like a dog until he goes to visit his sick father. Not only did he not come here to tell *me* that he's engaged—I had to hear it from you!—but the ben sorer u'moreh, that rogue, didn't write his parents with the news either. They found out from me. Can you believe it?"

"Of course I believe you, Rabbi. Your nephew gets a case of stomach cramps if anyone so much as mentions his father, the rabbi." Tzalia Gutmacher's breath came more easily now. So long as the tempest wasn't about him! Just as he'd offer a customer a sample of fabric, he now presented Avraham Alter with a sample of the words he planned to say to Bentzion. "I'm going to ask him," he said. "I'll say, 'If your rabbi father and uncle are no honor to you, what kind of honor do you hold for me? And if you don't bring your bride to your father and get his blessing, you won't set a foot in this store again.'

That's what I'll tell him. 'And before you go, you better visit your uncle, our Bialystok moreh hora'ah, and apologize to him. You hear me, you deadbeat?' That's what I'll tell him."

BENTZION CAME TO his uncle sporting an angry little smile beneath his short whiskers, planning to ask him what right he had to meddle in his business. But his uncle didn't give him a chance to open his mouth. "It's the hour of the Messiah! He actually came?" Avraham Alter called out mockingly, and dashed into a room where he found his son, then to another wing where he found his son-in-law, and then, leaving the two loafers—albatrosses around his neck—he returned to his nephew with increased fury. "Your education and sense of decency are worth an onion peel to me! Same for your brothers and sister. And that's exactly how much I care—an onion peel!—that you didn't come to tell me you're engaged and I had to find out from your boss. But that you should keep this secret from your parents—well, either you have a screw loose," his uncle poked his forehead with his finger, "or your bride is a gentile."

"A gentile?" Bentzion said, looking hatefully at his uncle, and at his uncle's son and son-in-law, who had both, through separate doors, trundled into the beis din room and were standing there, listening— the son with his belly, round beard, and bloated face, a cigar stuffed between his fat lips; the son-in-law with his smooth, feminine face, his long peyes coiled up behind his ears, and the cold, perceptive look of a man who knows both the roads of Nehardea, in the Gemara, and the suspicious back alleys of Bialystok. Oh, how Bentzion detested his uncle's parish! He had taken business courses on making an honest living, but they were conducting business with God and His Torah. "Would I take a gentile?" he cried.

"Yes. If you're hiding your bride from your parents, that's a sign she's either a gentile or comes from a family of thieves," his uncle replied. His son and son-in-law, standing in the doorways, smiled disdainfully. They considered their cousin Bentzion a naïve, unworldly man rather than a freethinker, just as Bentzion thought of them as playboys, swindlers, and hypocrites.

"My bride isn't a gentile and doesn't hail from thieves," he said. Despite his fury, he restrained himself from saying that to be God's thieves was perhaps even uglier than hailing from thieves. "Tzalia Gutmacher's threat to fire me doesn't scare me in the least. Now that I've finished my courses, I can get a better job somewhere else. And I have my own reasons for not introducing my bride to my parents yet and not writing to them. But since they know about it anyhow, we'll go."

But Bentzion refused to bring his bride to meet his uncle, and he took pleasure in the knowledge that despite his uncle's pretending it didn't bother him, it did.

Bentzion and his bride arrived in Morehdalye on a morning when a quiet, watery snow fell from the sky. The town's men and women poked their heads from their doorways to see tiny star-shaped snow-flakes twirling, dropping, dipping, then landing on the hat and fur collar of an unfamiliar girl in a white peacoat. Soon, they all learned who the couple was, and were pleased that their sickly rabbi's son was finally coming to introduce his bride.

The girl flashed her pale blue eyes as she entered the house. She removed her hat to reveal a blond head, dazzling with the golden brilliance of ripe wheat in the middle of winter. She wore her hair combed back concealing the top half of her ears, culminating in a bun at the nape of her neck. Then, she took off her boots and peacoat, under which she wore a teal-colored suit of thick, rustling fabric. The dress had a narrow cut, but was long enough to cover her knees, and the jacket's narrow sleeves were long, too, reaching down to her wrists. Her pale, elegant face and nose were reddened by cold. And for a moment, her striking forehead wrinkled up like an old woman's, only to smooth out a moment later, sleek and polished as a mirror.

The tall rabbi and his short wife stood side by side in the middle of the room, greeting their son and his bride with a tender, melancholy look in their eyes, as though they were a portrait on a dresser or a pair of extinguished candles in the candelabrum on the table. The girl stuck out a dainty, slim-fingered hand to Henna'le.

"Good morning, good year," Henna'le said cheerfully, and ex-changed kisses with her future daughter-in-law.

The girl had not expected this, and her face brightened. Feeling more confident now, she stuck her hand out to the rabbi and moved in closer, to kiss him, too. But in that very moment, she caught sight of her bridegroom pinching his whiskers anxiously, his face twisted in vexation. He had never imagined that his mother would kiss a girl she didn't know, triggering the girl to bend in to kiss his father. So he hadn't thought to warn her that a rabbi would never kiss his daughter-in-law, let alone a girl who wasn't his daughter-in-law yet. To make matters worse, Bentzion wasn't sure if he'd marry this girl at all. Which was why he hadn't yet brought her to meet his parents and hadn't written that he was soon to be engaged.

The girl discerned that she'd made some kind of misstep, but she didn't know what it was. She looked at the rabbi quizzically, but he smiled at her with such tenderness that she again felt the urge to approach him, and indeed would have done so, had it not been for Bentzion's frantic gesturing.

After this scenario, Bentzion and his parents kissed, and so did Bentzion and Naftali Hertz, who had come in from his room. "Mazel tov, you!" he wished his younger brother, whom he'd last seen as a little boy. But Bentzion, instead of being excited to see his older brother, grimaced unhappily. He couldn't, after all, blurt out the moment he arrived that he wasn't yet due a mazel tov.

But his girl acted differently. Though she was aware of her boy-friend's doubts, and had fought with him over it more than once, she wasn't thinking about all of that now and happily replied to Naftali Hertz's question. "My name is Suzannah. Suzannah Zakheim."

"Suzannah probably comes from Shoshana," said the rabbi affably, still standing stiffly by his wife and observing the bride. It appeared that both he and Henna'le liked the girl.

"Suzannah is Shoshana, and Shoshana is Raizel. Raizel'e!" Henna'le announced with great joy, as if this girl were already her daughter-in-law, her own child. "Well, why don't you sit down, Raizel'e?" Henna'le said, to the dismay of Bentzion, who again grimaced unhappily. *No*, he thought, *I'm not certain, not at all certain, that I'll marry Suzannah.*

In the meantime, his mother went on with her chatter. "I know everyone will laugh at me, but I've always imagined that a Raizel'e must be a pretty brunette; now I see a blondie can be a Raizel'e, too."

What followed just after her words, no one expected. Even Bentzion himself would never have imagined he'd so thoroughly lose his temper. If only his uncle and boss hadn't meddled, he later thought, compelling him to introduce his bride to his parents, he would never have exploded this way.

He began to quiver and shout. "Her name isn't Raizel, Raizel'e, or Shoshana. Shoshana is a lily. A rose is *khavtzeles* in Hebrew. And her name is Suzannah. Suzannah Zakheim."

Henna'le stared guiltily and with alarm at the men in the room. She couldn't understand why Bentzion was fuming, even if she *had* made a mistake. But the rabbi turned to calm her, reassuring her that her error wasn't so grave. "In cheder, the teachers would interpret the verse in Song of Songs, '*Ani khavtzeles hasharon shoshana ha'amkim,*' by explaining that *khavtzeles* and *shoshana* are both types of flowers."

Naftali Hertz watched it all unfold. Bentzion's outburst reminded him of his early days in Switzerland, when he'd started dating Annelyse Müller. Before all else, he was enchanted by the magic of her goyish name. His younger brother, too, it seemed, wanted his Jewish bride to at least not have a Jewish name. "Are you still in school or are you working in a shop?" Naftali Hertz asked, just to make conversation.

"I studied chemistry and work in a laboratory now," Suzannah answered with an offended smile, lowering her blond head with its wheaten gleam. It hurt her that her boyfriend hadn't written home explaining who she was and what she did, which was proof that he was still wavering over his decision to marry her.

Henna'le covered the table with a white tablecloth, in honor of the guests, and laid out refreshments: a small decanter of wine, black sponge cake and strudel, and a few kinds of fruits. As she moved back and forth from pantry to table, her mind jumped from thought to thought. *Since there are three men in the house,* she mused, *plus me, the mother, it wouldn't be unseemly for the bride to sleep in Bluma Rivtcha's bedroom. Bluma Rivtcha was finishing up her classes at the Sisters of Mercy; if only she'd learn how to be a merciful daughter and come visit her sick father. Then again, she can't be blamed. She didn't want to cut her studies short just when she's about to finish. And they wouldn't allow her to skip her rounds in the Vilna Hospital. Even Sholem Shachne didn't want that. He didn't want that, he said, because Bluma Rivtcha was already complaining that he was the reason she'd started classes so late; he didn't want her to now have reason to blame him for not finishing those classes. Sholem*

Shachne wasn't showing any coldness or severity to Bentzion and his bride, not the way he used to with his children in the past. His illness had changed him . . .

And abruptly Henna'le sat down at the table, joining everyone else. She'd realized, apparently, that continuing to bustle back and forth would lead her thoughts toward this riddle: Why had Bentzion, having abandoned his father's devout ways, nevertheless brought his bride to see them, when Naftali Hertz had never once brought his wife and son, though nearly eighteen years had passed since his wedding?

"So you're saying your father is a pharmacist and his name is Solomon Zakheim? For some reason, the name sounds familiar. In any case, Zakheim is a kosher Jewish surname," the rabbi said from the other side of the table to Suzannah, who was looking at him with ever more sympathy and trust.

Naftali Hertz couldn't believe his ears. His own father, unperturbed by the idea of a Jew named Solomon?! Bentzion, in the meantime, was happily nipping at his whiskers. Though he hadn't yet decided if he and Suzannah were a match, he was still pleased that his parents liked her. It meant he wasn't the loser his boss Gutmacher had made him out to be, just because his uncle had spoken nastily about him.

"You know what Uncle Avraham Alter told me?" Bentzion gave an angry, triumphant laugh. "He told me that if I don't bring my bride over here to see you, it means she either comes from a family of thieves or she's a gentile."

Suzannah gave him a look of dread and astonishment. Henna'le, who had been listening with pricked ears beneath her heavy sheitel, kneaded the tablecloth with her hands. She thought: *Oh, woe is me! This bride is smarter than her groom.*

But Sholem Shachne smiled and spoke serenely, his elbows against the table's edge. "Neither I nor your uncle would suspect you of such a thing. How could anyone even imagine that a son of mine would take a Christian wife? Your uncle just said it because he's angry that you never visit him."

"I don't visit him because I don't like him and I don't like his family," Bentzion said, with a hostile guffaw. "Uncle's not as smart as people say he is. He told me that not bringing Suzannah to see him meant she's not a Jew. By that reckoning, Naftali Hertz's wife and son aren't Jewish, either, because he never brings them around. Well, is that what you'd call smart?"

Naftali Hertz felt as though his lips had turned to sand. His heart sank like a crumbling pail into the rank water of an abandoned well. Through a haze, he watched his mother sitting there, her head pressed to the table, her face with the stiff expression of a porcelain doll, the kind she always wore when she wanted to avoid seeing or hearing something. His father, too, sat in silence for a long while with a lax smile on his ashen face. "You're wrong," he said at last. "Your uncle, Avraham Alter, is very smart. Merchants, you see, have long chosen him as an arbiter in their disputes. But it's true, even the smartest person can sometimes say or do something stupid."

From the quiet confusion at the table, Bentzion realized he'd said something he wasn't supposed to. Naftali Hertz felt like he had to say something, or perhaps start laughing, but he was afraid to do either, lest the family notice his charade.

Abruptly, Suzannah began to chatter, and everyone at the table breathed easier. "In Bialystok," she said, "whenever it snows, it's all stepped on and muddy in an instant, but here, in this town, the roads are as dazzlingly white as the roofs. When I look at the houses, their roofs piled high with snow, I imagine I'm seeing dwarves wearing oversized fur hats. And who in Bialystok greets each other good morning? Only acquaintances. But here, on the way from the train, strangers kept saying good morning to me!"

8

THE NEXT AFTERNOON, at his parents' silent urging, Naftali Hertz went for a stroll with his brother's bride. His parents wanted to talk with Bentzion alone. Naftali Hertz and Suzannah walked the well-trodden path that led from the rabbi's house to the bridge over the Narev River. The snow-covered fields surrounding them gleamed with billions of diamonds. The trees on the roadside, with their heavy branches and braids of ice, resembled giant menorahs with twisted branches, or chandeliers with crystal lamps. "So, where are you planning to live after your wedding?" Naftali Hertz asked.

"I don't know yet," Suzannah replied, with such reluctance it seemed she wasn't at all excited—not by her bridegroom, nor by the clear blue sky, nor by the clean fields of snow, nor by the glittering windows of the poor hovels on the shores of the frozen Narev.

"Why don't you know yet?" Naftali Hertz asked.

"I don't know if this relationship between me and your brother will come to anything." Suzannah raised her timid eyes, flashing blue and green, to Naftali Hertz. She gave him a hesitant glance and suddenly flushed. "Your brother told me you were a doctor of philosophy, and it shows. Anyone can tell you're an educated, worldly man. Your brother isn't at all like that. Maybe you can explain to me why, on one hand, Bentzion isn't devout at all, and on the other, he's so old-fashioned?"

"In what way is he old-fashioned?"

Rather than reply, Suzannah turned her head with a pained smile on her thin, fresh lips. She strolled along mutely, listening to the squeaking of her boots on the snow.

"Well then, how is Bentzion old-fashioned?" Naftali Hertz insisted.

"He'll tell you himself." The girl burst into loud, scornful laughter. "Bentzion told me that your father is an old-fashioned rabbi, and all of you children left to get educated against his will. But I really like your father, and he seems less old-fashioned than Bentzion." Again, she gave a short laugh. But all through the stroll, no matter how much Naftali Hertz probed, she refused to say how her bridegroom was old-fashioned.

Bentzion, sitting alone with his parents, told them that he didn't yet know if he and Suzannah would marry. When his parents sat there speechless, he grew angry. "You're meddling in my life!" he yelled. "Even though Suzannah and I have been together for a year, I'm still not sure we're a good match. That's why I've kept this secret. I didn't want to bring Suzannah to Morehdalye until I was sure we were really engaged. But once my boss Gutmacher found out, and told Uncle Avraham Alter, this whole mess ensued."

"You've been with her for a year?" his father and mother burst out, dumbfounded. The bright snowy day, equally astonished, peeked in through the window: to be with a Jewish girl for a year and not yet know if you were engaged to each other?!

Bentzion, growing angrier by the minute at their interference in his life, shouted, "Before Suzannah, I dated another girl, who was even less of a match."

"Why aren't these girls a match for you?" his mother asked, heartache in her voice.

Face distorted, as if already repulsed by life before it had rightfully begun, her son replied, "In the Torah it is written '*V'hu umoshel buh*, the husband must rule over his wife.' But I haven't had the luck of finding the sort of woman who obeys. Whatever I say, Suzannah says the opposite. And the girl before was the same; she didn't agree with me on anything."

"A girl like that, the kind of girl who agrees with you on everything and lets you rule over the home, as the Torah says, you might have been able to find that kind of girl in a pious family. But girls today, who come from irreligious homes, they have their own opinions about everything," Henna'le said, glancing anxiously toward her husband. Sholem Shachne's lips, she noticed, were already trembling with rage and frustration. He wanted to say something but couldn't.

Furious, Bentzion replied, "Why should I pretend? I can't take a pious girl because I'm not pious, so we'd make each other's lives miserable. Besides, I'm not attracted to the pious girls of the Bais Yaakov schools. They're narrow-minded. But the worldly girls are even worse."

His father now joined the conversation. He spoke quietly, but with fire in his eyes. You could tell he was straining not to shout. "One girl, you say, you've already rejected. That means you've already humiliated one Jewish daughter. Now you want to humiliate another? Suzannah is a very fine girl."

Bentzion burst out laughing, and Henna'le, too, gaped at her husband. She'd have understood had he agreed with Bentzion that his behavior contradicted the Torah or that he was bringing dishonor to his parents. But now his main concern was a girl he'd only met the day before?!

"Suzannah isn't as fine as you think," Bentzion said.

"Meaning?" his father said, drawing his eyebrows together, as he did at a din Torah when one party tried to present himself as though he were a saint and his opponent entirely wicked.

Bentzion said, "It's true, I don't want to live off my pedigree, but I haven't forgotten where I come from, and I don't allow myself certain behaviors. But Suzannah refuses to accept that. She says, 'If you're not devout like your father, you shouldn't be bothered by a woman smoking in the streets.'"

"On Shabbos?" his father cried out. And his mother wrung her hands.

"We're not talking about Shabbos, not Shabbos," Bentzion said. "Suzannah doesn't smoke at all, in reality, not even on weekdays. But if we go for a stroll and I don't like it when a woman passes me smoking in the street, Suzannah tells me I'm an old-fashioned grouch who's always thinking about what's seemly and unseemly. Plus, she fights with me, she fights with me nonstop." Bentzion groaned like an old man suffering from multiple illnesses.

"Well, if Suzannah never smokes, not even on weekdays, does that mean the match has to fall apart just because she has a different opinion on the matter? Just because she thinks a woman is allowed to smoke?" Sholem Shachne scrunched his shoulders.

"Not just over that, not over that alone." His son grimaced and twisted around in his chair, as though plagued by a rash in an indis-

creet area. He again became incensed. "Father, you were always tormenting us kids if we davened too fast, if we didn't roll the leather
straps on our tefillin the way we were supposed to, if we didn't shake
the esrog and lulav properly on Sukkos. Every mitzvah, you used to
say, is the only mitzvah and the biggest mitzvah in the world in the
moment it's being carried out. But what it means when one woman
thinks it's fine for another woman to smoke in the streets—that you
don't understand, Father. Even if she herself doesn't smoke, her feelings on the matter are very telling of how she's behaved and will
behave in the future, when married to her husband." You could tell
from Bentzion's exasperation and rage that something else, something he refused to admit, was at the root of his vexation.

The next morning, Suzannah stayed in the house with Bentzion's
parents, while both brothers left for morning prayers in the Morehdalye beis medrash. Now, in the winter, on the days when there was
no Torah reading, the sickly Sholem Shachne didn't go to daven in
the beis medrash. This was at the behest of his wife and the warning
from his doctor. But both sons, despite their father's silence on the
matter, understood on their own that for them not to go would bring
him heartache and shame. They also hadn't had the chance to have
a real conversation between the two of them, and they knew they'd
find no better place to speak in private than a corner of the house of
prayer.

In truth, they weren't all that eager to converse. Bentzion both
envied his older brother for having moved so far from home and
berated him in his heart for having abandoned his parents and siblings for so many years. And he was scornful of his brother for having
become a simple servant in a library after all his studies in philosophy. He'd have been better off remaining a yeshiva boy and becoming a rabbi like their father! Naftali Hertz, for his part, held Bentzion
in low regard, for his shopkeeper ambitions and the business courses
he'd taken. Naftali Hertz had left behind a young boy and returned
to find a swaggering champ: a qualified business manager! But for the
sake of appearances, at least, they both felt they had to make an effort
to be close and spend time together.

The group davening in the first minyan, the older townspeople,
sat at the table learning Mishnayos together. Their heavy, snow-
white beards pulled their elderly heads down toward the holy books

lying open on the table. Middle-aged scholars with dark beards, also part of the first minyan, sat separately at their lecterns with Gemaras, looking vexed and out of sorts. All of them, whether studying quietly, murmuring hoarsely, or swaying silently, seemed unhappy. They scratched their necks beneath their beards and wrinkled their foreheads. Of course they were unhappy, these first minyaners. Instead of holding a rabbi's position in a large city, these men—once celebrated for their erudition—would soon be closing their Gemaras and running off to manage their small shops.

In the second minyan were the lower-tier merchants, shopkeepers, and craftsmen, Jews in boots and misshapen hats. The first minyan, the respectable men, were constantly groaning that the second minyan was made up of "shorteners": they shortened the davening, shortened their beards and peyes, and even shortened their clothing, wearing jackets, wraps, and half-sized coats. They never wore overcoats or frock coats, not even on Shabbos and holidays.

The beis medrash itself looked no less common. Snow, dragged in by shoes and boots, piled up on the floor, trampled and muddy. The floor around the sink was wet from spilled water. And hanging beside the sink, a sopping towel emitted a repulsive, sour odor. The curtain on the aron kodesh was wrinkled, without a trace of gold or silver ornamentation. Outdoors, in the winter air, the daylight dazzled, but the moment it sifted through the large, unwashed double windows, its crystal shine turned as gray as a rain cloud, crawling over the tables strewn with tattered holy books, over the uncovered bimah, over the scattered benches and lecterns. Worshippers chatted with each other, even during the prayer sessions when talking was forbidden. Then, they'd abruptly start swaying, with tefillin on their heads, with frayed and yellowed prayer shawls on their shoulders.

The only one in that second minyan wearing a fresh new Shabbos tallis was the rabbi's eldest son, Naftali Hertz Katzenellenbogen. He'd already donned his tallis and head tefillin while Bentzion was still toying with the straps of his arm tefillin. He then placed his head tefillin on his forehead, glanced at Naftali Hertz, and laughed. "It looks like you were married last week, with a tallis that new. Perhaps you wore your other tallis out, from all the davening you do in Switzerland, and you had to buy a new one," Bentzion said, laughing even harder. But then he abruptly tugged at his whiskers and went silent. He didn't want the Morehdalye Jews to overhear him teasing his brother about not wearing a tallis.

The brothers took a spot at the northern corner of the mizrach wall and stood with their backs to the crowd, to discourage people from coming over to greet them. As they swayed along with the minyan, they each prepared topics to discuss with one another. Bentzion wanted to know about the commerce system in Switzerland. His brother's wife and son held no interest for him at all, though Naftali Hertz didn't know this. He was sure Bentzion would again go rambling on about how he hadn't brought his wife and son to Morehdalye. It had been different with Refael'ke, when they'd met two years ago at their sister Tilza's house. Refael'ke was smarter. He hadn't asked Naftali Hertz why he hadn't brought his wife and son. Perhaps he'd discerned the reason. Yes, yes, he must certainly have figured it out. A gush of pride for his brother washed over Naftali Hertz. He didn't have such feelings for Karl, his only child; none of this pride, joy, and yearning. Certainly, he'd be scared to death if anything bad happened to Karl, heaven forbid. But what could bring him pride and joy about Karl? His fat behind and hearty peasant face? His plans to become a surveyor of mountains? Big deal!

Bentzion still dreams of becoming a businessman, Naftali Hertz thought. *At least Refael'ke is turning his dream of working the land in Israel into a reality*. "Ay, Refael'ke, Refael'ke. Would that your oldest brother had the strength to emulate you," Naftali Hertz murmured instead of the davening, even as he laughed at his own ridiculousness. *Empty dreams! I don't have the strength to change my life—and then what, start somewhere fresh?*

At the cantor's pulpit, the ba'al tefilah had finished the davening; the mourners had already said Kaddish. Naftali Hertz took off his tefillin and turned to his brother. "When I went strolling with your bride yesterday, she kept saying you're old-fashioned and that she wasn't sure yet if you two will get married. Though exactly how you're old-fashioned, and why she's not sure you'll marry, she wouldn't say. Maybe you can tell me?"

Though Bentzion despised being interrogated, couldn't stand when others pried into his life, he still longed to confide in someone. As much as he didn't want to share a thing with his parents the day before, that's how much he now felt at ease about confiding in his brother.

"Suzannah considers me old-fashioned because I asked her if she's still a virgin. She refuses to tell me under any circumstances."

"Why do you have to know?" Naftali Hertz stared at him, wide-eyed. "If you two love each other, what difference does it make whether she's a virgin or not?"

"Now you sound just like Suzannah," Bentzion said. "She, too, says that if I love her, it should make no difference to me. The girl I went out with before Suzannah argued the same. But of course there's a difference! It makes a real difference! It's the reason I left the first girl. And honestly, I don't know what's going to come of this relationship. Do you really believe it shouldn't make a difference, or are you toying with me?"

"I mean it. I can't fathom that a worldly, modern man would require his wife to have never been touched by another man." Naftali Hertz shrugged his shoulders, looking exactly like his father as he did so.

"Look who's saying such things!" Bentzion jabbed his finger into Naftali Hertz's face. "You're the Morehdalye rabbi's son, you're a Katzenellenbogen, and you studied in a yeshiva! Before you got married, did it make no difference to you if your bride was promiscuous or not? A girl who has relationships with men before she's married will have them after her marriage, too. Of this I'm certain. If I'm to believe you, then what you're saying is that it makes no difference to you what your wife did as a girl and that it's no big deal what she's doing now. Only I don't believe you're serious."

Naftali Hertz turned pale. He felt the veins in his temples swelling. This blabbermouth had unknowingly hit the nail on its head. *Am I*, he thought, *really such a cynic that Annelyse taking a lover two years ago and a new lover now hasn't bothered me at all, or am I simply a weakling, a rag?* And Naftali Hertz gave a laugh.

"Why are you laughing?" Bentzion asked impetuously.

Naftali Hertz had been laughing at himself, but what he replied was: "You're still a young man, that's why you speak this way. But I have to admit, I didn't expect this. You quarreled with Father for the right to educate yourself and go out and find work—I wouldn't expect such a person to pester his bride about being a virgin."

By nature more combative than his older brother, Bentzion gnashed his teeth like an aggravated animal in a cage. "Educating myself and finding work has nothing to do with forgetting where I come from. I want to attain things on my own merit. That's why I can't stand when anyone mentions our father, the Morehdalye rabbi. But I never forget that I'm a Katzenellenbogen and not one of those half-corrupt clerks in the clothing shop where I work. Of course, I know that a modern man wouldn't ask a girl if she's a virgin. He'd be afraid she'd laugh in his face, tell him he's rotten with prejudice. And the truth is, it's not important to me either that my wife has never been touched or that I'm her first. I'd have even married a divorcée. But I don't trust the type of girl who gives herself to a man without the benefit of marriage. And now, she doesn't want to talk about it. Only a thief likes to make everything a secret." Bentzion, in the mood now to speak bluntly, suddenly burst out, "I live in Bialystok because I want to attain a position in life. But I love Father and Mother and would have never been able to live for years in Switzerland without seeing them. I would have died from missing them."

"True, true." Naftali Hertz nodded and finished folding up his tallis and tefillin, his eyes cast down to show Bentzion he had no intention of excusing himself, and he wanted to end the discussion. He kept his eyes lowered as he walked out of the beis medrash, to prevent the other men from starting up a conversation. In his heart, he was pleased that he and his brother hadn't grown any closer. A provincial with a business diploma, that's what he was!

Bentzion, for his part, was seething. Why had he revealed to his brother what he hadn't told his parents? It was Suzannah's fault! If she hadn't complained that he was old-fashioned, Naftali Hertz wouldn't have asked him about it, and he wouldn't have confided in Naftali Hertz. Whose business was it if he and Suzannah wanted to marry or not?

As soon as Bentzion made it home, he found Suzannah and took her to task. "Not only your father," she cried, "but even your brother is smarter and more likable than you." All Thursday afternoon they fought like this, in one of the bedrooms of the rabbi's house.

Friday morning, the rabbi, rebbetzin, and their oldest son were already at breakfast when the young couple appeared, faces glum, and Bentzion informed his parents that he and Suzannah were leaving. His parents and Naftali Hertz were speechless.

"Did you put on tefillin already?" his father eventually asked.

"Yes, in my bedroom," Bentzion said.

"But Suzannah hasn't eaten. And you haven't put a morsel in your mouth either," his mother said.

"If we sit down to eat now, we'll miss our train. It leaves at exactly ten o'clock," Bentzion said.

Suzannah didn't utter a word.

Again, silence descended. Bentzion felt he needed to explain what had happened. Shamefacedly, he grumbled, "When I went to Suzannah earlier, to call her to breakfast, she told me she was leaving immediately. So what should I do? Let her go and stay here by myself?"

The rabbi glanced at Suzannah in surprise, as though he'd have sooner believed this of his son than of her.

"Why don't you both stay?" Henna'le said, letting her eyes linger on Suzannah.

"I can't stay. I must go back," Suzannah replied in a whisper. She was trembling, and the rabbi decided not to press the matter. The rebbetzin thought: *Hmm, nice of my degenerate son to not let her go back on her own.*

But Naftali Hertz didn't raise his eyes. Since he'd left the beis medrash the day before, he hadn't looked at his brother once. Even now, as they bid each other goodbye, the brothers barely shook each other's hands, simply muttering, "Be well."

But when Bentzion kissed his parents, the pain he felt at causing them heartache was visible on his face. Visible, too, was the cost of his fight with Suzannah, which he was nonetheless ready to resume at any moment—because look, he was in the right, he alone, and he would not cede, not a chance. Suzannah, on the other hand, kept herself under control and said goodbye lovingly. She kissed Henna'le, pressed Naftali Hertz's hand with warmth, and gazed with respect and love at the old rabbi who didn't shake hands with women. She regarded him with a rapt expression, to show the family how much more impressed she was with the rabbi than with his angry son.

"Don't worry, they'll forgive each other," Naftali Hertz consoled his parents, after the couple left. A gloom had gathered in the corners of the room, as in a dried-out riverbed, empty but for bare black rocks.

"And here I'd baked and cooked up a lavish meal for Shabbos. Who's going to eat it all?" Henna'le fretted.

"May you never have greater troubles than this," Sholem Shachne said with forced gaiety. He didn't want to show how distressed he was. In a nonchalant tone, he asked Naftali Hertz why he'd been so cold to Bentzion, despite their not having seen each other for so many years.

"Maybe that's the reason. Because it's been so many years, we felt like strangers," Naftali Hertz said, inventing the reason on the spot. He didn't want his parents to know that Bentzion couldn't find himself a bride because he was out there asking each girl if she was a virgin. The news would pain his parents, without question. He looked at their saddened faces with great pity, wondering, *Why do they get so little joy from their children?* He remembered what Tilza had told him, when he'd spent time with her in Lecheve. That when they were kids, Father and Mother had been so busy with each other, in love like two little doves, that they didn't notice their children were growing up and abandoning them. Naftali Hertz remembered his sister's words precisely, because they'd rung so bizarre and false to him. But perhaps Tilza hadn't been all that wrong? He sat at the table now, rubbing his smooth, hard chin. He'd shaved his bristly gray beard at dawn to impress Fräulein Suzannah Zakheim. And here she'd gone and fled.

Henna'le needn't have worried about the pots of food she'd cooked for the couple. Nor had Naftali Hertz shaved his beard in vain. At ten in the morning, Bentzion and Suzannah left for Bialystok, and at noon, four hours before Shabbos was to start on that short winter's Friday, an entire group of unexpected guests arrived from Warsaw: Henna'le's three sisters—Kona, Sarah Raizel, and Chavtche—Kona's husband, Banet Michelson, and their two daughters, Tubya and Bania.

9

EVEN A STUPID PERSON could figure out that the only one who'd come up with a plan to travel on a short winter Friday would be Chavtche. Her older sisters, brother-in-law, and nieces were still puttering about in the front room, removing their snow-covered coats, hats, shawls, and boots, but Chavtche was already pacing the innermost rooms in mid-heel slippers. She kept her small hands folded beneath her beige jacket and wore a white blouse with a black collar, the same style she'd worn the past year, two years, three years. Chavtche's taste in clothes hadn't changed at all, nor had her behavior or her placid gait, which resembled a red-footed bird strolling across a straw roof. The only thing that changed was the color of her hair. Once, it had gleamed blond, now it burned copper-red. Her cheeks, too, were covered in more rouge than in the past. Since she'd become engaged to Leopold Silberstein, Chavtche had been trying hard to look younger. Silberstein was a Polish native and had studied in a German university, but never graduated because of the horrific antisemitism there.

Everyone in the family had been desperately wishing for Chavtche to get married, thinking it would lead Sarah Raizel to get engaged, too. And even if Sarah Raizel couldn't find a husband, at least she wouldn't have to work so hard anymore to pay for food, clothes, and entertainment for Chavtche the exploiter. But Sarah Raizel felt differently than her family. Mutely, her terrified eyes asked Chavtche: *Will I now have to support your husband, too?*

But instead of responding to the question in Sarah Raizel's eyes, Chavtche informed her they were going to visit their father in Zembin. "Now that I'm getting married, Father must give me my share of the inheritance. He's already misled me long enough."

Sarah Raizel, with her high bosom and big eyes, stared at her sister, astonished. "What kind of share does Father owe you? In what way has he misled you? And for that matter, how do you even know if Father has any money for you to inherit?"

But Chavtche insisted that their mother had left some money. "Even when I was still a child, Father used to tell me he was preparing my dowry. If Vigasia hasn't duped him into giving her sons his savings, Father must now give me the dowry he promised."

Chavtche then persuaded her sister Kona to join them on the trip. "We'll stop at Henna'le's house in Morehdalye on the way," she said. "Her husband had a heart attack, and their son from Switzerland, the one who's been absent for years, is there visiting them. Never mind that, once again, he's failed to stop off in Warsaw to see us, his aunts, and his nieces. Well, let's go get a look at him now. Let's see what he's so proud of, the little braggart."

Once Kona decided to go, her husband joined. Without his wife at his side, his shipping agency held as much appeal for him as playing chess alone. After that, Chavtche started working on her nieces. "Come. You'll get to see your aunt and uncle, and your cousin, the doctor from Switzerland. Afterward, you'll visit your grandfather, and then, just because, let's travel across the province. The snow is as clean and fresh as in Tatarstan. What can you lose?" Indeed, Tubya and Bania realized they had nothing to lose, and they, too, joined.

"You never wrote to say you were coming," Henna'le said with a distant little laugh.

"I did write," Chavtche said. "I wrote that we were getting ready to go see Father in Zembin and might stop in on the way. Besides, what difference does it make if I wrote or not? You could still broil an entire ox before it's time to light the candles for Shabbos. Kona and Sarah Raizel will help you."

Chavtche gave a light nod to her brother-in-law, Sholem Shachne—who never shook a woman's hand, not even a sister-in-law's—and skipped over to her nephew. She stuck out her hand for him to kiss, as the Polish do. But either Naftali Hertz had no manners or he didn't want to or understand how to kiss a woman's hand. Chavtche smiled at him with fake graciousness, with a visibly sarcastic smile. She asked, "Is your wife educated like you? Did you visit your sister in Lecheve? Are you planning to visit Grandfather in Zembin? Tell me, when you come from Switzerland to Morehdalye, do you never stop in Warsaw?" She tossed these questions out one after the other. Chavtche was his aunt, though she was the same age as Naftali Hertz. As she questioned Naftali Hertz, she couldn't help thinking that her fiancé, Leopold, was incomparably more educated than her nephew, and looked both younger and more worldly than this highly schooled good-for-nothing.

"And here you were, worried about what to do with all the food you'd cooked for Shabbos," Sholem Shachne said to Henna'le. "You see? God sent you more welcome guests." Though the unexpected arrival had surprised Sholem Shachne and Henna'le, they were pleased to have the company. It would help them forget that Bentzion and his bride had left in a quarrel.

All were still in the middle of exchanging greetings, and already Tubya's booming laughter could be heard. And like a ballerina when she hears the orchestra, Bania started twirling to the rhythm of Tubya's laughter. Twenty-five-year-old Tubya was still unmarried. Though she was tall, broad, and fair-skinned, and had a dazzling long white neck and thick, clean chestnut-colored hair, in personality she was dull, a bit too good-natured, yet not at all stupid. Boys wanted her as a friend or girlfriend, but not as a wife. This didn't seem to bother Tubya. She waited patiently for someone with good judgment to choose her, and in the meantime, she embraced laughter. She laughed like a foolish woman, sometimes at comical situations and often for no reason at all, just for the pure pleasure of laughing. Then she'd choke on her laughter and start laughing again, as though her laughter were its own echo in the mountains, resounding everywhere.

Her parents, at times, felt her laughter might drive them insane. Kona, thick-legged and with large, warm hands—Kona who constantly worried over the welfare of her sisters, brothers, brothers-in-law, nephews, and nieces—was pained by Tubya's constant giggling. And her husband, the shipping agent Banet Michelson, the miserable maskil with a bald head and long, wooden face like the carved handle of a cane, was even more annoyed by his daughter's endless laughter. And it wasn't only her laughter. He couldn't bear the way she dressed, either, always in masculine wool suits with a checked pattern and sewn-on pockets. *All she's missing is red boots*, Banet thought, scowling.

And his younger daughter was no better. Bania, five years younger than Tubya, liked to go around in colorful silk rags with numerous pleats and creases, which resembled nightgowns rather than dresses. She liked pulling the fabric as tightly as possible around her figure, to bring out her curves, then she'd twist her soft, lithe body and shimmy like a belly dancer. Her face, however, wasn't much to behold: scant teeth and scant hair, with a tuft of bangs over her forehead. And her eye color was some sort of vague, watery blue. Which was why she liked to emphasize the gracious movements of her long arms—her white hands and rosy fingers like the wings of a flamingo—and the verve of her agile figure, making the boys around her feel like their veins were about to burst.

As soon as the two girls walked into the rabbi's house and were introduced to their cousin, the doctor from Switzerland, they began their routine. Bania twisted her body like a screw and Tubya rolled with laughter, though keeping her body ramrod straight, as though she were a laughing tree.

Kona and her husband exchanged distressed looks. "What's all this merriment for?" their mother muttered to herself, distressed. "Because it's icy outside and it's a short Friday? Because Chavtche achieved the impossible and convinced everyone to set out in the middle of winter? Are they not at all bothered that their uncle Sholem Shachne is ill? Tubya's constant laughter has driven away all potential grooms, and now she's an old maid. Bania, even with her constant shimmying, turning every boy's head, has yet to snag a bridegroom." Her mother sighed.

Their father was even more upset. Tubya had abandoned her schooling because, at university, one had to actually study, not neigh like a horse. And Bania had never bothered to enroll. Shaking her behind, after all, was knowledge she'd possessed since the fourth form.

Banet turned away from his daughters and his sisters-in-law. Such geese! Not even with his brother-in-law, the rabbi, did he have any-thing to discuss. What could he talk about with a fanatic? Craning his long wooden face forward, and with a mocking smile turning up the corners of his mouth, Banet went over to look at the book-filled shelves. Mostly, there were Talmuds and halachic texts, a few Torah explanations and glosses, but not a single Haskalah book among them. Folding his arms behind him to make his detachment clear, Banet moved closer to his nephew. In a bit of a nasal twang, meant to prove his ease among philosophers and philosophy, he said, "Do you have even one person in Morehdalye to talk with about Immanuel Kant?"

Naftali Hertz barely heard what his uncle was saying, so nonplussed was he by this mob of relatives. Soon they'd start interrogating him about his wife and son, and he'd again have to start singing his opera of lies. Meanwhile, Banet Michelson was buzzing in his ears: "Well, admittedly, Immanuel Kant wrote in a difficult German. I myself can barely make sense of it. So how would someone from Morehdalye know about him? But Hebrew, the Morehdalye scholars supposedly do know Hebrew. Well, do any one of them ever consult the *Sefer Ha-Ikkarim*? And what about *Akeidat Yitzchak* or the *Abarbanel*—do they look into those? What do they know about philosophical theories?"

His nephew's mind was apparently elsewhere at the moment. He replied, unthinkingly, "The authors you mention write commentary on the Torah. They're not real philosophers, not at all."

Banet Michelson stood there open-mouthed, as when he lost a game of chess, or as when one of the women in the house chided him for writing down the wrong instructions: instead of shipping flour and grains to the merchant in Zshelekhov, he'd sent him crates of metal bars and locks that were supposed to be shipped to the merchant in Vengrov. The tall, skinny shipping agent, Banet, who liked drinking clear glasses of tea and humming to himself, would stand speechlessly during such times in his slippers and long floral silk robe, his hands tucked inside the belt of his dressing gown, pressed against the flat sides of his skinny stomach. Which was just how he was standing now, facing his nephew from abroad, trying to salvage his pride.

"But what do you have to say about the *Bekhines ha-Olam*? You know that its author was on the side of Maimonides—fabulous! And what a master of language he is! I pore over his books every Shabbos after eating cholent. Well, what do you say about him?"

"What should I say about him?" Naftali Hertz said, wondering why he felt not an inkling of joy or interest in these newly arrived family members. All he felt was pity for his mother, who would now have to prepare a Shabbos meal for so many people. "About *Bekhines ha-Olam*, you ask? It's a book of fragmented verses, bits of flowery language. Only unworldly men and yeshiva boys delight in him."

Banet shifted away from Naftali Hertz, murmuring, "So he's a doctor of philosophy, is he? A rude man, that's what he is."

In the beis medrash that evening, Banet Michelson grew tired of stashing his sneer in one corner of his mouth, so he pushed it to the other. The Morehdalye residents were well aware of the Warsaw guest's disdain. At the davening, Banet glanced around for a while before his eyes fell on a full-cheeked Jew with a cropped gray beard, wearing a short jacket, a wide, soft hat, and a shirt and tie. *A provincial maskil*, Banet thought, and edged closer to him in a nonchalant, cosmopolitan way, as when he ambled around his house in his dressing gown and slippers.

"I see bookcases and tables filled with holy books," Banet said to the man. "Is there a Chumash with a biur somewhere around here, too?"

The Morehdalye resident, a merchant who'd just returned from a business trip late in the afternoon on this short winter's Friday, had hurriedly changed into Shabbos clothes and rushed to the beis medrash for davening. Even now, as he recited the Song of Songs, he was still huffing and puffing, exhausted. "A Chumash with a biur?" He raised his eyes from the siddur on his lectern and looked politely at the Warsaw guest.

"Yes, a Chumash with the biur on the Ramban," Banet replied, with great pomp and erudition.

"But the blessing of biur chametz* is made before Passover, not in the middle of winter," the man said, as confused as a cheder boy who's expecting the teacher to slap his cheek.

The maskil Banet recoiled from the small-town ignoramus as from a slimy reptile, a frog speaking in a human voice. "Are these the kind of dolts for whom my brother-in-law is rabbi?" Banet muttered. "Well, let him have them. Fanatic! Let him have them." Banet gave a laugh, and for the rest of the davening he spoke to no one else.

Even later, when the whole family was around the Shabbos table,

* The merchant, apparently unfamiliar with Mendelssohn's biur, assumes the word *biur* must refer to this ritual.

he didn't utter a word. But he kept a fierce eye on his daughters, making sure Tubya didn't laugh and Bania didn't shimmy.

Banet's eyes wandered from his daughters to his wife, gazing at her as though he were noticing her appearance for the first time. *Just look at that high bosom she has, this woman of mine, this whiner who takes the problems of her entire rabbinical parish to heart. Just look at that pair of bloated udders she has—this wife of mine, mother of my two lasses, one neighing like a horse all the time, the other always chasing her tail like a cat. Kona, my cow, doesn't realize that it's her whom the Song of Songs speaks of in the verse, "Ani khomeh v'shaday kemigdalot, I am a wall, and my breasts like towers." And of her sister Chavtche, the dear little bride, in the verse, "We have a little sister, and she hath no breasts: What shall we do for our sister in the day when she shall be spoken for?" Indeed, what could be done with a woman who had a washboard where her breasts should be? Nothing could be done with a woman like that. But then you talk to her and she thinks everyone's falling head over heels for her. Oh, how she walks with such light feet, the little bride Chavtche, as if she were wearing the very first head on her shoulders.*

Shabbos morning, when the men left for the beis medrash, Chavtche and her two nieces set out for a stroll around town. Back at the house were the three older sisters, who'd been anxiously waiting for the chance to discuss family matters alone. Outside, the snow whooshed and whirled. It brought the deep, eerie silence of distant worlds. Kona and Sarah Raizel sat at the dining room table with uncombed hair, wool shawls over their shoulders, drinking tea, which came from a pitcher that Henna'le had taken out of the oven and wrapped in rags to keep warm. Some pieces of challah and cookies, remnants of Friday night's meal, were scattered on the white tablecloth, along with a jar of preserves, a few plates of cold fish, and a porcelain bowl filled with sugar cubes. While the Warsaw sisters sipped their tea and nibbled on refreshments, their oldest sister was davening. Henna'le wore a long red satin dress, with mother-of-pearl buttons, and her gold pendant earrings, the same way she dressed when she went to daven in the beis medrash on Shabbos Rosh Chodesh, sitting at the little window in the women's section, across from her husband's seat at the holy ark in the men's section. The only difference was that she didn't wear a hat over her sheitel, as she did in shul. Despite that, she davened well, as thoroughly as always. With her small finger, she nimbly turned the pages of her thick Korben Mincha siddur, and her tight lips burbled the words rapidly, rapidly. Her younger sisters watched her, thinking, *Well, if you're married to a rabbi and have countless troubles with your children, of course you'd become more pious in old age.*

Finally, Henna'le closed her siddur and, without pausing, asked her sisters, "Who is this Leopold Silberstein that Chavtche is marrying?"

The tall, portly Sarah Raizel, who was adept in the workplace but tongue-tied when faced with Chavtche, spoke candidly now that Chavtche wasn't there. Kona, dangling her thick, clumsy legs, kept tossing in words as well, so that in the end Henna'le got a general picture of Chavtche's groom. Leopold Silberstein: As a young man, he'd left his Polish town for London, and meandered about there for years. After the war, he'd come back to his hometown to see his parents. But then he couldn't return to England, because he hadn't bothered to become a British citizen during the time he'd lived there. And with no way back to England, he went to Germany instead. But there, too, he couldn't work his way up to anything, because of the tremendous antisemitism permeating Germany since they'd lost the war. Once again, he returned to Poland, but he was now dreaming of moving to Ethiopia. In Ethiopia, he claimed, they were raking gold in the streets. He spoke often of gold, in general. In South Africa, he said, new gold mines kept popping up. But the truth was, they were "salted." What did that mean—"salted" gold mines? Swindlers, he replied to this question, would pour bits of gold into the mine and then spread a rumor that a new vein of gold had been discovered. Then, they'd create a corporation, and people would buy fake shares in the company. Of course, once the digging started, nothing would be found. A government committee would come down and determine that gold dust had been mixed into the sand. By that time, the swindlers had vanished with the money, and the customers were left with worthless scraps of paper. Those were the kinds of stories Leopold Silberstein told, and with just such stories did he captivate the clever Chavtche. He didn't, however, appear to be a swindler himself, but rather a bachelor, a dreamer, a loser. In the middle of his talking and scheming, he'd often turn silent and blush profusely, as if he suddenly realized he sounded like a child, building castles in the air.

"Never would I have believed that the shrewd Chavtche, who used to turn her nose up at every suitor, would saddle herself with such a dreamer and a loser," Kona said, sighing deeply as was her manner.

"On the contrary, she likes him *because* he's so helpless. You know Chavtche likes bossing people around, especially people who don't challenge her," Sarah Raizel burst out. Her striking, pale blue eyes bulged, swollen with the bitter knowledge that, though she was the earner, Chavtche the idler had always been her boss.

"Okay, so we know what Chavtche saw in him. But what did he see in Chavtche?" Henna'le chanted in a Gemara-like melody, the way her husband did when he studied a difficult topic. "The dowry she's offering him?"

"What he liked about Chavtche was her pedigree," Sarah Raizel said, and Kona nodded in agreement.

"Yes, yes, he likes the family name," the sisters told Henna'le. "Leopold Silberstein can already list every single member of the Epstein, Katzenellenbogen, and even the Michelson family by heart, down to the most distant cousin. Of course, he got all his information from Chavtche. You know, she pretends that all people are equal in her eyes. But day and night she barraged the gold-digger Silberstein with family facts: Her father is the Zembin rabbi; her brother-in-law is the Morehdalye rabbi; her brother-in-law's son-in-law is the Lecheve rabbi and rosh yeshiva; her brother-in-law's oldest son is a professor of philosophy in Switzerland; and his youngest son in Israel is leading the chalutzim in a war against the British, the Arabs, and even the Jewish exploiters, the vineyard owners. Chavtche, who'd always thought of herself as a free agent, a rebel practically, spoke so often of her pedigree that her fiancé could hardly believe he'd be joining such a remarkable family. He became so involved, he even began inquiring about his two brothers-in-law in America, Refael Leima and Shabse-Shepsel. Though Chavtche didn't tell him much. She didn't want him to find out about Father's quarrel with his sons."

"But he's keeping his distance from Tubya and Bania," Kona said. "And he isn't coming with us to Zembin, either."

"He's avoiding your daughters on Chavtche's orders. Because your girls don't show him respect. And Chavtche was the one who wouldn't let him come to Zembin. She's worried Father will dislike him and deny her her inheritance," Sarah Raizel said, becoming more upset the more she spoke, her large, arresting eyes quivering as though blinded by sunlight.

Outside, the snow was relentless, evoking the strange quiet of a winter Shabbos from the beyond. In the house, the only sound was the ticking clock. Its round dial looked like an outlandish water creature, with just a head, twelve slits for eyes, and two spindly legs for crawling, one longer than the other. Sarah Reizel seemed not to hear her own loud, yearning sigh: "Ay!"

The sisters eyed her quizzically. "Oh," she said, "I was just thinking about how good it used to be when we were girls in Mother's house, quarreling about whose turn it was to wash the dishes."

She became silent, and her sisters, too, were silent. They understood what Sarah Raizel was implying: that a person like this Silberstein wouldn't look out for her either. She was used to working hard and taking care of others. Once Chavtche stopped needing her, she'd start working to find grooms for Kona's daughters. But she herself would likely remain an old maid, forever neglected.

Shabbos passed, and it was soon time for Henna'le's sisters to leave. But even when she said her goodbyes, she still hadn't shared her thoughts on Chavtche's match. Chavtche was a schemer, she thought, and in Silberstein she'd found her equal.

But weeks later, when her sisters had already left Zembin and returned to Warsaw, Henna'le realized that this time Chavtche the schemer had indeed schemed well. Henna'le received a letter from her father telling her what a saint Vigasia is. "Chavtche dropped into Zembin, as from the sky," he wrote, "and demanded a dowry from me, her inheritance, her share of her mother's fortune. I informed her and Sarah Raizel, Kona, and her two daughters that I have nothing to dole out. Everything I've saved during better times, including the money from the lottery ticket, has been spent on renovating the talmud torah, on traveling expenses for Shabse-Shepsel and his wife to America, and on supporting myself and my wife. The Zembin community is now so impoverished it can't even pay me a reduced salary anymore. So Vigasia took her own hard-earned money, saved from the time she was a widow, and gave Chavtche enough to set herself up after her marriage. She also gave Kona's daughters money for clothes. Chavtche wanted to have the wedding in Zembin, but

Vigasia advised her that, because her groom was not observant, it wouldn't be a good idea to bring him here. People in town would gossip that the rabbi's youngest child was marrying a Shabbos desecrator. 'You probably want to have the wedding here to save on wedding expenses,' Vigasia told her. 'I'll send money to Warsaw for the wedding costs.' That's what Vigasia said to Chavtche, and Chavtche listened. Well, isn't Vigasia a brilliant, pious woman?" the old rabbi asked in his letter to his daughter.

This led Henna'le to ask her husband, and not without resentment, "Well, Sholem Shachne, do you see why Tubya and Bania let Chavtche persuade them to go along to Zembin? They went to extract gifts from their grandfather and step-grandmother. But our children have cut themselves off entirely from their grandfather. Bluma Rivtcha was his most beloved grandchild, and she'd have received the nicest gifts from him. But it's been years since she's visited, just so she doesn't have to listen to his scolding."

"Bluma Rivtcha would never have asked for gifts, and even if they were offered, she probably wouldn't have taken them," Sholem Shachne said slowly, as though thinking out loud. "But imagine your father's joy if Naftali Hertz had gone to visit him and brought along his boy, all grown up—a great-grandchild." He cast his wife a meaningful look, one that revealed his thoughts about his son's family in Switzerland.

But Henna'le returned his look with mute fear, lest he bring to his lips what they both were thinking, or, heaven forbid, blurt something out when Naftali Hertz came into the room.

$$\rightarrow 10 \leftarrow$$

Shir Hamaalos . . . A song of ascent: In my distress I cried unto the Lord, and he heard me.

It was the end of the Shabbos day, the beis medrash illuminated by the dark blue snow shining in, secretive and cold, from beyond the windows. Inside, it was dim, crammed with worshippers and their interwoven shadows. According to the clock, it was already late enough to recite Maariv and light a fire. But the worshippers were stretching the holy day out, sitting in the dark and reciting the Shabbos Tehillim.

The recitation, accompanied by heartrending cries, had begun at the "poor" table behind the bimah, around which sat the simple Tehillim-reading folk. The prayer leader's face was invisible, shrouded in darkness, but his hoarse, feeble voice made clear who he was and what kind of mood he was in. Almost certainly he was that Jew who ran a small-time business selling farm produce—a man of medium height, with a little white beard he had a tendency to pluck, who wore a jacket over his skinny frame. That man—if indeed it was him—owned a wood hovel he'd inherited. He had a house full of grown daughters, a sickly, exhausted wife, and a boy of cheder age. The boy happened to be a quick learner, but there was no money to pay tuition. This Jew was also a member of the burial society—the man everyone in town remembered whenever a poor person died, leaving behind no money or family. The burden of the poor man's burial fell upon him and the community. But as he read the words of Tehillim, instead of lamenting his own difficulties his voice broke tearfully for the suffering of the Jewish community and for the banishment of God's glory.

Oyeh li ki garti . . . Woe is me, that I sojourn in Mesech, that I dwell in the tents of Kedar!

The first ones to finish these sobbing verses were the overworked craftsmen, with their bent shoulders, darkened faces, and twisted fingers, and the market dealers who stood at their wagons even through snowstorms, ice in their bones, dressed in lamb's wool coats and hats with ear flaps. Hands stuffed into opposite sleeves, these Jews idle by the town's entryway, straining to catch sight of a village wagon with a live calf. They wait for a miracle, for Elijah the Prophet to appear in the figure of a peasant with a few chickens, a crate of eggs, some potatoes, cabbage, and apples in sacks.

Shir Hamaalot esah eynei el ha'horim . . . I will lift up mine eyes unto the hills, from whence cometh my help, they shout, and then answer themselves, rasping: *Ezri ma'im Hashem . . . My help cometh from the LORD, which made heaven and earth*. The well-to-do and more scholarly Jews, those who sat on the benches closer to the honorable mizrach wall, were enkindled by the despair and faith of the Tehillim readers, and all the congregants sighed along, sang along, swayed along, as when the wind rocks the thick branches of trees all the way up to their crowns, till the entire forest is roiling and its array of leaves murmur with the muteness of the twisted bark and the buried, centuries-old roots.

Hidden in a corner among the crowd sat Naftali Hertz. For a while, he tried to convince himself that this was good for him now, that he belonged to the collective, the community. He was a leaf on a tree, a droplet in a river, a sheep in a flock. But then he asked himself: "Will the diaspora be easier for the Jews if I, Naftali Hertz Katzenellenbogen, freeze along with the other sheep in the wintertime? What difference does it make if I join them or not?" He knew he couldn't become an illegal revolutionary who wanted to transform the world, like Marcus Luria. And it was already too late for him to become a chalutz and build a new life in the land of Israel, as his brother Refael'ke had. But could he become a pious sheep, bleating in terror with all the others when a wild animal attacked the pen? No, he could not become a naïve innocent, a Tehillim reader. Nor did he want to. The fact that he was reciting Tehillim along with the others didn't prove a thing. Even goyim did it. They called it "Psalms," but it was Tehillim: same text, same content, same spirit, albeit with different interpretations of verses. And from the time pagans became Christians, both the stranglers and the strangled, the burners and the burned, outdid one another in ecstasy as they chanted the Psalms. Ah, the way the Catholic Inquisition, while its members were torturing and burning, were also parading with crosses and singing religious hymns! And each time Cromwell sliced his enemies into slivers, never did he forget to open his Protestant eyes wide and sing a song of praise to the Lord. Not that the victims were lesser hypocrites. Like that Scotsman who, just before he was hung, mumbled Psalms and kissed the hangman on his cheek, so people would see that, like a true Christian, he'd forgiven the hangman who would soon hang him. What repulsive, revolting pious cruelty! And who knows what the Jews would have done with the Tehillim over these last two thousand years, had they had more power.

Shir Hamaalos habotkhim b'Hashem khar Zion . . . A song of ascents: They that trust in the Lord shall be as Mount Zion, which cannot be removed, but abideth for ever.

Behind his pulpit, at the corner of the holy ark, sat the rabbi, singing along with the crowd. *Yerushalayim harim saviv lah . . . As the mountains are round about Jerusalem, so the Lord is round about his people from henceforth even for ever.* Lingering in Sholem Shachne's mind was the knowledge that, amid the crowd there in the darkness of the beis medrash, sat his eldest son, Naftali Hertz, and in the darkness of his beis medrash, among the holy books on the table, lay a letter from his youngest son, the letter that had arrived that morning and which was now awaiting Havdalah, after which he would open and read it. What Refael'ke had to say in this new letter, his father did not yet know. But he remembered the previous letter and thought of it now. According to Refael'ke, there was no great difference between him and Sholem Shachne. "I, too," Refael'ke had written, "wanted to be a perfect Jew, and that's why I left for the land of Israel."

This both angered Sholem Shachne and made him smile. *So I put on tefillin every day and he doesn't—and he sees no difference between the two of us? What a sheigetz! Still, I must thank the Creator that my children have begun to treat me gently, at least since I've become sick. Well, Refael'ke has always been delicate, careful not to cause me or his mother pain. But even Naftali Hertz, now, is trying to repair what he'd once wrecked with his bold rebellion. Though in truth, Naftali Hertz was already so ensnared that only God could help him crawl out of his trap and make amends.*

Shir Hamaalos beshiv Hashem es Zion khayinu k'kholmim . . . When the Lord turned again the captivity of Zion, we were like them that dream.

Perhaps, Sholem Shachne thought, *my youngest son should serve as an example for me and I, too, should go and settle in the land of Israel. Perhaps, if I were to do so, I would serve as an example to him in return, inspiring him to observe the Torah and mitzvahs. But my fading strength . . . the constant pressure in my heart . . . Who knows if I'll ever get to live in the land of Israel?*

The stiff, snow-covered world outside listened in silent astonishment to the singing from the crammed beis medrash. The farther the song drifted from the shul, the more it shed its bodily sounds and transformed into a quiet, trembling plea, a frozen exaltation, a cold and concentrated thought. Soon, the holy spirit of the book of Tehillim had mutated into an invisible figure, standing behind the darkened windows of the rabbi's house. There, in the dark, sat Henna'le, waiting for the beis medrash to light up, so that she could light a candle herself. She was impatient for Havdalah, even more impatient than her husband, who was eager to read Refael'ke's letter, which lay on the table among the holy books in the beis din room, like a grandchild who'd fallen asleep between his grandfathers.

At last, Sholem Shachne arrived, and immediately after Havdalah he opened the letter and became absorbed. When her husband didn't read the letter aloud, Henna'le understood that Refael'ke had written in Hebrew, likely about something philosophical. Usually Refael'ke wrote in Yiddish, so that his mother, too, would be able to read and understand the words. Still, Henna'le couldn't bear to leave the room while her husband was reading a letter from their youngest child. She found ways to keep busy. She took the candelabrum off the table, removed the Shabbos tablecloth, replaced it with the checked oil-cloth she used on weekdays, and set out a wicker bread basket, salt shakers, and a sugar bowl. Then she asked her husband and son if they wanted to wash up and eat something.

Sholem Shachne, still absorbed by the letter, shook his head no, and Naftali Hertz silently turned the pages of one of the holy books from his father's shelves. Henna'le looked around for more to do. She remembered she needed to move the plants out of the chilly hall so they wouldn't freeze, and from there her thoughts skittered: *Even cacti have to be watered from time to time. Now where did I put the metal can with the twisted spout? Refael'ke was interested in gardening even before he'd thought of moving to Israel. He was always our most well-mannered child and still is. Since he found out that his father is ill, he writes home every week.*

Henna'le continued waiting for Sholem Shachne to comment on the letter, and finally he did. Half to himself, half to his wife and son, he said, "Apparently, Refael'ke is learning the new *Ivrit*, modern Hebrew. I don't understand every word here, but I certainly get the gist of it. Our Refael'ke has become a disciple of someone named Aaron David Gordon. Plain old Aaron David Gordon, without the title of 'moreinu.' Refael'ke had already mentioned him in a few of his earlier letters, but in this one he quotes Gordon at length, as though he's quoting from the *Messilas Yesharim* or the *Choves Halvoves*." He snickered, and by his smile, Henna'le could tell how dearly Sholem Shachne held his youngest.

Sholem Shachne then repeated Refael'ke's new teacher's chalutz-like theory: "'When a person feels the smallness of himself in relation to the *eyn-sof*, the infinity, what he's also feeling is his religious sensibility. And no matter how many questions a man asks, what he's actually asking is a version of the single eternal question: 'Who created the world, and what is its main reason for being?'

"Not that I see anything very novel about this," Sholem Shachne continued, "but to this point, at least, this Gordon's words concur with those of our Sages and their holy writings. It's what he says after that, this holy rabbi of the chalutzim, that's at odds with our Sages, may their memory be a blessing. What he says is that religious sensibility depends on each person's individual character; it's the mystery of individuality. But the shape of belief, its face, comes from the nation." Sholem Shachne laughed. "And here I thought the Torah and its six hundred and thirteen mitzvahs were thrust upon us at Mount Sinai. But no. Turns out Jews chose a Torah themselves, one that suits them, just like the Turks chose red fezzes for their heads. And it gets worse. According to the theory of this master and rabbi of chalutzim, 'Sometimes it seems to man that God is dead. In truth, it isn't the God inside the people that has died, but rather, that the religion has become fossilized; its old forms have outlived their time. One's religious sensibility must be in the category of a spring that continuously pumps fresh, clean water. Faith must constantly be renewed. The only true believer might be the independent believer who isn't welded to old beliefs and influences, to rules that have been accepted and passed from generation to generation . . .'"

Sholem Shachne stopped reading the letter, stopped reviewing its contents. He let the few densely filled papers drop and slammed his fingers on the table. "Now I get why it isn't necessary to put on tefillin, to observe Shabbos and other such rules that were given to us thousands of years ago. The religious sensibility of the genius Gordon doesn't believe in this ancient, fossilized Torah and mitzvahs. I get it, I get it," he said, knocking the table with increasing agitation.

"Is this Gordon person, whom your brother seems to swear by on his beard and peyes," Sholem Shachne asked Naftali Hertz, "is he considered one of the big thinkers?"

"In my philosophy classes, he was unknown. Personally, I've heard of him and seen some pictures of him. He has a beard and peyes, but not a Jewish beard. He doesn't wear a hat. His hair is disheveled, and he gives the appearance of a peasant, something like the Russian writer Leo Tolstoy. In my eyes, he's no great thinker," Naftali Hertz said heatedly, imagining what he'd say to Refael'ke were he there now: "Idiot! Even if *you* had a few original thoughts to offer, it wouldn't have been worth it to cause Father pain."

"You understand, Father? This Gordon influences others not so much with original ideas but with the example of how he lives his own life."

"Then he's reached a high level indeed," Sholem Shachne said, with no small degree of sarcasm. "He's not just a good talker, but also practices what he preaches."

Sholem Shachne picked up the papers again and skimmed them to see if Refael'ke had perhaps included some more substantial news. "My children have a problem," he said. "They can't lie, even if they want to make their father happy. And when they do try to lie, it's so obvious, it literally screams: 'I am a lie!'"

Does he mean it's Refael'ke who can't lie, or does he mean me, too? Naftali Hertz thought, holding his breath, his eyes bouncing from his father to his mother. But his mother stood rooted to the floor in the middle of the room, staring speechlessly at the door. She looked at Naftali Hertz as if he were a cat sculpture or a stuffed deer, the kind that wealthy Swiss set out on their lawns to confuse passersby, who couldn't tell whether they were seeing a live animal or art.

Noticing his wife staring at the door, Sholem Shachne turned his gaze there, too, and like her, he went speechless. At the door stood Henna'le's younger brother, the one who'd left for America two years ago—Shabse-Shepsel Epstein!

A short while before, Sholem Shachne and Henna'le had received a letter from the Zembin rabbi. A dark cloud was drawing toward him, he wrote: His older son, Refael Leima, had written him that Shabse-Shepsel was headed for Israel and stopping in Poland on the way. In the letter, Refael Leima told his father about how much suffering his brother had caused him, and that he'd given Shabse-Shepsel the money for the trip on the condition that he take his wife along. If it were up to Shabse-Shepsel, he'd have been fine leaving Draizel in America. The old Zembin rabbi had wept over his letter to Sholem Shachne, saying that he and Vigasia were already quaking in anticipation of the disgrace their half-insane son would again bring upon them. Refael Leima, too, in his letter, had mentioned that his brother didn't seem entirely sane. Oh, what to do? What to do?

Sholem Shachne didn't know how to console his father-in-law, and replied simply, "*Dey letzoreh beshateh*, there'll be time enough to suffer when the difficulty arrives. No point in suffering in advance. Perhaps Shabse-Shepsel would regret his decision midway and not stop in Poland at all. What a crooked mind like his might come up with was unpredictable."

In the meantime, Refael'ke had also written to his parents: "Mazel tov! Uncle Shabse-Shepsel writes me from America that he's coming to the land of Israel to wait for the Messiah."

As a result, Sholem Shachne and Henna'le had been awaiting word from Zembin of Shabse-Shepsel's arrival. They had absolutely not expected him to turn up in Morehdalye!

"Good week! How're you doing, huh?" Shabse-Shepsel called out cheerfully, and he stuck his long hand out toward his brother-in-law. "How're you doing, Sholem Shachne?" he said informally, with a certain chutzpah, not even deigning to remove the cane hanging from his arm. "We've just come from Bialystok, could barely find a coachman at the train station. Sholem Shachne, I tell you, you've planted yourself in a doomed town, a godforsaken place, the backwoods. You couldn't become rabbi in Grodno?" And he paced around the room as though he lived there.

Enraged, Sholem Shachne burst out, "On Shabbos? You traveled from Bialystok to Morehdalye on Shabbos?"

"God forbid!" The guest gave a mock shudder. "We stayed in a small hotel in Bialystok, right across the train station, and left right after Havdalah." He swiveled round to his wife, who was just then shuffling in from the front hall with their suitcases. "Right, Draizel'e? We left right after Havdalah, right?" He winked and sneered at the others in the room, as if to encourage them to laugh along with him at his wife's appearance: her short stature, her clothing, and the way she panted like a goose as she dragged in the suitcases.

"True, true, we left right after Havdalah," Draizel said, nodding, and glanced fearfully at the people in the house, worried they'd throw them back out.

It seemed that Shabse-Shepsel, too, was afraid they'd send him packing, which was why he was behaving defensively, acting with provocative chutzpah. His appearance had hardly changed. The same skinny body, sparse beard, and twisted, laughing face. His step was now even lighter, with more of a hop in it. And his pale blue eyes burned with even more madness and cold cruelty. The smile on his face flitted about like a hungry, predatory animal in a cage. Anyone observing how he spoke to Draizel instantly felt he was releasing his entire evil and craziness upon his exhausted wife.

Draizel's physical appearance hadn't changed much in the past two years either, nor had her clothing. Her big black wildcat eyes had become a bit smaller, and her high, striking forehead had a few more wrinkles. When she took off her oversized coat, one's eyes went right to her long, old-fashioned dress, full of pleats, and its long, mud-died train. On her head she wore a round fur hat with worn fringes. Some of the buttons were missing from her knitted jacket. She wore black stockings with high-laced shoes on warped heels, as though she'd walked the length and breadth of all New York's cobblestoned streets.

Shabse-Shepsel, meanwhile, was wearing a brand-new jacket, which his brother Refael Leima had bought him right before he left America. He also wore a new hat and checked pants. But despite his fine clothes, his every move suggested the forlorn distress of a vagabond. But he was trying hard not to look like a broken man, and he addressed Naftali Hertz with an uncle's gracious smirk. "Sholem aleichem to you, Naftali Hertz." Then, to Sholem Shachne and Henna'le, "Welcome to your guest!" He paced around his nephew, first in one direction, then the other, as though he were sniffing out whether the person before him were a tiger or a chicken. "You're a graduate of philosophy, I know," he said, "so prove to me that there's a God. I spoke to a lot of professors in America, and I saw that whatever I don't know, they don't know either. They just use fancier words to say it. Well, and what about the Messiah? Do you believe in him? I'm on my way to the land of Israel now, to await him there, to spite all of Herzl's Zionists who don't believe in the Messiah." For a moment, he became mute, and gave his head a shake, as though from dizziness. "I see some dishes on the table. Is there anything to eat? Draizel and I haven't put a morsel in our mouths since this morning," he suddenly admitted with a faint, jaundiced smile. And both his sister and his brother-in-law felt a stab of pity in their hearts for him and his suffering wife.

11

Since the children's bedrooms in the rabbi's house were empty, Shabse-Shepsel got settled in one of the rooms and told his wife to take another. Draizel raised a fuss about the separate rooms, not ashamed to do so in front of the rabbi, his wife, and their son. They were husband and wife, after all. Husbands and wives slept in one bedroom. But the more bitterly Draizel quarreled with him, the more puffed up with joy Shabse-Shepsel became, just as things had gone in Zembin before they'd left for America. Henna'le and her husband were horrified. They realized Shabse-Shepsel operated in one of two ways: either he crumpled like a wimp or he issued orders to anyone who let themselves be manipulated. Even when he spoke to his brother-in-law, he acted like a rabbi giving orders to his beadle.

"Write a letter to Zembin," he barked to Sholem Shachne. "Tell my father I need a thousand zlotys for travel expenses and another thousand to get by once we arrive, until we get settled."

"Why didn't you and your wife go directly to Zembin?" Sholem Shachne asked.

"Huh! Do you hear what you're saying? If we'd have gone straight to my father, he'd have died of fright," Shabse-Shepsel said, laughing.

"So why don't you write to your father yourself to tell him how much money you need?"

Shabse-Shepsel laughed even harder. "I never write to anyone, besides a few words here and there, to this one or that one. Like to your Refael'ke, for example, to tell him I'm coming to Israel. Or to my father, to say I'm coming to Poland. Did you get many letters from me from America? In fact, that's precisely why I left America. Because I hate to write anything down."

Shabse-Shepsel paced around the room with an airy gait. With great enthusiasm, he began regaling them with his failures in America. "In Grodno, Bialystok, and Zembin, I used to keep the calculations of all my businesses in my head. I never wrote anything down. But in America, everything has to be written down. Well, I arrive in New York with my fortune of zlotys exchanged for dollars, and I open a business together with a partner on a street called Delancey. Not far from this street is a garden with no trees, synagogues with no worshippers, a train overhead, a train underground, and a train on a bridge over a filthy river. Anyone looking for an easy death has merely to jump from that high bridge into the water—a pleasure! In my store, we sold Chanukah menorahs, candelabra, mezuzahs, prayer shawls, and rom'l books, siddurim, and machzorim. And if anyone wanted to buy an umbrella or a walking stick, I'd sell those, too. But I couldn't get along with my partner. What a pedant. He used to daven only with a siddur—even Ashrei that ignoramus didn't recite by heart—and in the same pedantic way he demanded that all our earnings and expenses be put into writing. All day my partner stood in front of a metal cash register, and every time he took out a few cents or put a few cents back in, he pressed the buttons on the register, and it clanged—it could drive you crazy! I thought my veins and temples would burst from all the clanging. So I left the business and went to Refael Leima, to the yeshiva. Ach! A yeshiva? A cheder for rascals! That's what it was. Better to convert to Christianity than to give a shiur on the Gemara for such good-for-nothings.

"What did I tell you before, Sholem Shachne—that I need two thousand zlotys for travel to Israel?" Shabse-Shepsel interrupted his own parade of American stories and pinched his beard as he recalculated. "Wait! Five zlotys equals one dollar. So two thousand zlotys would be only four hundred dollars. Some money, that is! Sholem Shachne, write Father that I need at the very least a thousand dollars. And if he won't send it to me here right away, I'll come to Zembin and sit on his neck, and my wife will sit on his neck, too. You'll come, Draizel'e?" Shabse-Shepsel turned his head to her seductively, as though mimicking the snake that convinced Eve to eat from the Tree of Knowledge.

When her husband wasn't ordering her around, Draizel usually sat stony-faced, hands in her lap, like a pauper before an oven's extinguished fire. But when her husband baited her a bit too much, she'd break her inertia and leap up, her wide eyes gleaming with the hatred of an alley cat that either flees from all people or attacks them. Now, too, Draizel's eyes widened with hatred and schadenfreude. She spoke in a raspy voice, licking her lips with the pleasure of revenge. "Shabse-Shepsel can't sleep in peace if he doesn't wreck everything in his wake. But his partner in New York didn't let him squander the money and inventory the way he'd squandered my father's inheritance—both the money and the fine china. Shabse-Shepsel had to quit the business in disgrace. He went to his brother Refael Leima, to the yeshiva, humiliated. But instead of acting kindly to the American students, the way Refael Leima did, he chased them with a stick. Well, his students misbehaved even more, and they beat him up till he had to quit the yeshiva, too. Refael Leima then hired him to be the Torah reader in his shul, to lead the services; to be a beadle, in short. But during the reading and davening, Shabse-Shepsel made such wild gestures that everyone instantly realized what he was— a meshuggener. To make matters worse, instead of catering to the men of the shul, he shouted at them and treated them like cheder boys. He had his brother Refael Leima tearing his hair out of his head. Shabse-Shepsel was making him miserable. Refael Leima begged his brother to take pity on him and leave the shul."

"Draizel'e, why don't you tell them about my ironing gig?" Shabse-Shepsel said, delighted that his wife was dragging him through the mud.

"Yes, he ironed, too, until they threw him out of the shop like a stinking herring because he deliberately burned all the pants he was pressing."

Shabse-Shepsel's gaunt, jaundiced face glowed. He laughed merrily, as though being reminded of his boyish pranks. No longer did his sister and brother-in-law have any doubt that Shabse-Shepsel had lost even more marbles in America and would now stoop to even lower lows. They'd have to write to Zembin immediately, as he'd demanded.

But after Sholem Shachne sent the letter to his father-in-law, Shabse-Shepsel announced that he was in fact still mulling over his decision to leave Poland. Perhaps he shouldn't leave at all? "Father is old already, very old. So why can't I become his assistant in the meantime, and when he goes the way of all people on earth, I can be his successor and become the new Zembin rabbi." When he saw his sister and brother-in-law gawking speechlessly at him, he burst into scornful, demonic laughter. "Don't be so alarmed. By the time the letter reaches Zembin and we get a reply, I may well change my mind again. Maybe I *will* go to Israel."

From the moment he'd set eyes on Shabse-Shepsel, Naftali Hertz despised him. Day after day he kept away from the house for as long as possible, to avoid having to witness Shabse-Shepsel's machinations. His nephew's unconcealed hatred left Shabse-Shepsel a little perplexed, but it hardly scared him. He even took a bit of pleasure in the knowledge that the doctor of philosophy had to flee the house while he himself frolicked about freely.

Though Naftali Hertz steered clear of the home, his parents kept him informed, and he listened in on the whispers from their bedroom. Henna'le was worried for Refael'ke. If his uncle moved to Israel, he might cause untold difficulties for Refael'ke. Maybe it would be better if Shabse-Shepsel *did* regret his original decision and chose not to go to Israel. But Sholem Shachne felt there was no need to worry. Even if Shabse-Shepsel were to stand on his head, Refael'ke wouldn't lose his calm. What they really needed to worry about was this lunatic staying any longer in their home. Who knew what kind of a chillul Hashem he'd bring about? Sholem Shachne sounded anguished, and Henna'le feared for his health.

But Naftali Hertz calmed his parents. "True, Shabse-Shepsel is a lunatic, but he's a coldly calculating lunatic. He's made a life out of scaring people with the threat of scandals. He came here," Naftali Hertz insisted, "for two chances to squeeze out money, once from you for the price of his leaving here, and once from his father for the price of his not traveling there. Now he's threatening not to leave Poland at all, so he can extort even more. He's a blackmailer, a thieving swindler!" Naftali Hertz gritted his teeth and clenched his fists. Abruptly, words he hadn't intended to say shot out of his mouth: "Now do you see why I found a wife in Switzerland and decided to stay there? I wanted to keep as far away as possible from relatives like Shabse-Shepsel."

"And with your wife's family, there are no such nuisances, or even worse?" Sholem Shachne stared down at a patch of afternoon light by his feet, which had slipped in from the snowy outdoors.

"Whatever my wife's family members are, there's none as mixed-up or exploitative as the ones we have here," Naftali Hertz burst out, with more viciousness.

Father and son stared at each other with glittering eyes, on the verge of letting out what they'd both been suppressing. But Henna'le had already placed herself between them, extinguishing their rage with her mock-innocent loquacity: "If only I had some money saved, I'd give my brother and sister-in-law as much as they needed to leave. But in all my years in Morehdalye, I haven't saved a single groschen." Abruptly, she thought of something and clapped her hands. "You know what I say? In tough times, when someone needs their head on their shoulders, you can't rely on a man. Write another letter to my father right away. Tell him Shabse-Shepsel wants even more money, and that he's still vacillating about his move to Israel. Have Father send Vigasia here immediately. She's the only one who can cope with Shabse-Shepsel. And why not! She's more man than all of you."

Sholem Shachne turned toward his wife, so amazed by her cleverness that even Naftali Hertz had to smile. "I hadn't thought of that," Sholem Shachne murmured. "Vigasia helped with your sister Chavtche. Now Chavtche is able to get married. And Vigasia gave Kona's girls wedding gifts. It stands to reason that she'll help your brother and his wife, especially because she'll be saving her husband from the horror of his son at the same time."

"But Shabse-Shepsel cannot know about this second letter, or he might start thinking up some new plan," Henna'le whispered, and she stood hovering over her husband's shoulders as he wrote the letter. Then she herself added a few lines, urging Vigasia to come to their rescue as quickly as possible.

While the rabbi and rebbetzin whispered secretively in their closed bedroom, Shabse-Shepsel ambled about the rabbi's house, a bemused smile on his dry, crooked lips, as if he were testing himself to see how long he could hold this confident pose. For the most part, he felt pretty certain that his father would send him the requested sum. *So long as he leaves Poland; just let him go, go!* he imagined his father thinking. But now and again Shabse-Shepsel would turn his head worriedly, wink, and smile, as though sensing that some intrigue was stirring behind his back. But even in his fearful suspicion lurked a strange expectation, a craving, almost, for failure, the way an escaped psychiatric patient, bored of his freedom and of feigning sanity, waits for someone to finally catch on and lock him up again.

The rabbi and rebbetzin, and especially Naftali Hertz, avoided conversation with Shabse-Shepsel. Only from time to time, when passing by her brother, would Henna'le remark on the snowstorms that were probably holding up the reply from Zembin. To project confidence, Shabse-Shepsel assured them all that, to the contrary, he was pleased his father had not yet sent a reply. In fact, he wasn't at all certain that he'd be going to the land of Israel.

"The choice is yours," both his sister and his brother-in-law told him, feigning indifference. In their hearts, they prayed to God for Vigasia to arrive and rescue them all.

At times, Shabse-Shepsel grew bored of meandering around the rabbi's house and went to the beis medrash for a change of scenery. Those days everyone in the house could breathe more freely. Except for Draizel. While her husband was around, she watched him with the fear and hatred of a trapped animal who's not yet accustomed to being in a cage. But then, if he so much as hinted he might go out somewhere, Draizel stood rooted to her spot, broken and terrified, as if certain he'd be leaving her forever. "Where are you going? When are you coming back?" she tormented him, and he deliberately gave no answer to frighten her even more. He merely warned her not to dare follow him. And he left the house with a grave expression on his face, as though he were the head of a giant beis din, prepared to cast judgment over the world, or as though he himself were going before a giant beis din, preparing to be judged.

The moment he left, Draizel would start pestering her sister-in-law. "How far is it to the beis medrash? Do you think he might have gone somewhere else?"

Henna'le scratched her head incredulously, unable to believe her eyes and ears.

One time, after Shabse-Shepsel had left the house, Henna'le took Draizel into a private room and spoke to her angrily, disgustedly, deeply offended for the honor of women. "Are you not ashamed to be such a dishrag? He's my brother, and I'll still say openly that I don't understand how a woman could put up with him. You don't stop whining that he squandered your father's fortune and ruined your life. So why did you run after him to America? And what makes you so terrified every time he steps out of the house? Explain it to me!"

"Well, what can I do now? Get divorced and start a new life? I'm not even sure he would give me a divorce. He's liable to leave me an agunah." Draizel shook her head sadly. She sat at the edge of her chair, hands in her lap, her frozen glance fixed on the snowy desert outside the window. The snow had been falling without pause, and still, across the road, she could see the warped, blackened wooden fence of the public park.

Gradually, Draizel's frozen face came to life. "I'm actually quite surprised, my sister-in-law," she said, "that you can't understand why I wouldn't want to separate from my husband. No matter how much pain he causes me, and how many problems, I can never forget that he's a 'Benvensti.' After all, the name Epstein is just a front. And for a husband who's a 'Benvensti,' it's worth the suffering."

"I don't understand. What are you saying?" Henna'le muttered, worried that Draizel had gone insane. "The name Benveniste sounds familiar, but I don't remember when and where I heard it."

"Familiar? And you don't remember where you heard it?" Draizel cried, astounded, and told the story of how Shabse-Shepsel had courted her. "I was still in Grodno then. I still had my trove of fine china and lived in the big house Father had left me, so I wasn't all that impressed by a rabbi's son—some small-town Epstein. But then Shabse-Shepsel explained how his family hails from the late Jewish count of Spain, the Benvensti family, and that your ancestors later changed their name to Epstein. When he told me this, I was very impressed. As a girl, I read untold books, and I knew that what was known as a count and countess in Russia, in the Kaiser's times, was called a Don and Doña in Spain. Shabse-Shepsel explained that if he were to go by his real Spanish name, he'd be called Don Shabse Benvensti—the way the former Jewish minister in Spain was called Don Yitzchak Abarbanel—and that I would be Doña Draizel Benvensti. That's why I'm so surprised at you, Sister-in-law," Draizel said, "that you don't remember you, too, are a Doña Benvensti, on your father's side. Have you really forgotten?"

"It flew out of my head. I completely forgot," Henna'le said, thinking, *Woe is me. She's even more meshuggah than he is!* "And what do you gain from the fact that your husband comes from Jewish counts in

Spain? In America he had to be a beadle and a presser of trousers. He couldn't even work as a full-fledged tailor there, because he doesn't have the skills. What do you gain from his title and pedigree?"

"A lot! Even if Shabse-Shepsel was a beadle and a presser, you could tell in his every movement that he's a Don Benvensti. Just look how he carries himself." Draizel jumped up and started strolling across the room, mimicking her husband's airy gait, her arms spread wide, her head turned arrogantly backward. But because she was short and wearing a long, shabby dress, high-laced shoes with crooked heels, and a loose black blouse with wide sleeves up to her pointy, wrinkled, reddened elbows—from which gaunt arms protruded like matchsticks—her imitation of her husband, the Benveniste, made such a pathetic impression that Henna'le, not one to mock by nature, had to look down to keep from laughing. Draizel noticed her lowered eyes and said, "Look at me, Sister-in-law. Watch how your brother walks and moves, and you'll recognize instantly that he's a born count, a 'Benvensti.' Then you'll understand why he holds such power over me. It's true, in America he was no more than a beadle. But he used to hand out talleisim and siddurim to the worshippers—those boors!—with such airs they felt he was doing them a favor or giving them charity." And Draizel mimicked her husband sneering and smiling at everyone and everything. "And his Shabbos hymns, today!" she said, even more enraptured. "When he starts singing at the Shabbos meals, or sometimes when he davens at home with his tallis over his head, I can hear the angels singing in his voice! For such a pleasure, even if only fifteen minutes in a week, my struggle is worth it."

"Well, if you value him so highly, why do you fight with him?" Henna'le asked.

"Because he wrenches my veins from me, one by one," Draizel cried, with such fury and bitterness, as if she'd just hurled herself into a shul's aron kodesh to plead on behalf of a dying man. "You can tell by his poor treatment of me that he's a Benvensti, a Spanish murderer. Our sort of Jews don't have such murderous hearts." She burst into sobs with childlike abandon, wiping her tears like a stray orphan.

Henna'le shuddered, shocked. From whom had her brother caught or inherited such cruelty? Certainly not from their mother, may she rest in peace. And not from their father either, because when her father wasn't waging war on behalf of Judaism, he was a kind-hearted man. Though Henna'le did feel she had to admit one thing: Her father had never given her mother much regard. He believed a woman was capable only of cooking and bearing children. Perhaps that was why his children hadn't followed in their father's footsteps, and only Shabse-Shepsel, in his crazy way, was emulating him. *This is why,* Henna'le continued her train of thought, *when I chose a husband for myself, I chose a man I felt wouldn't look down on me.*

Indeed, she and Sholem Shachne had lived their lives together like two doves. Even if their daughter Tilza saw this as a flaw. More than once had Tilza assailed her with the same argument: "Although your marriage was arranged, you and Father overflow with love for each other, and you barely looked your children's way. It never dawned on either of you that I belong to a different generation, that forcing me to have an arranged marriage would mean a lifetime of unhappiness." Even now Tilza kept on with this argument, though her husband was good as gold to her and she had two little children—treasures! In fact, the older and heavier and more wrinkled Tilza became, the more upset she was that her father hadn't given in to her girlish fantasies. Lately, she'd become especially neglectful and sloppy, and she hadn't even rushed over to visit her sick father.

"Listen, Draizel," Henna'le said, finally emerging from her thoughts to resume the conversation with her sister-in-law, who was again sitting stiffly and sadly, like a squirming bird on a bare tree, naked of branches. "The world says that God sits up there and tinkers about down here. But sometimes I think that up there in heaven, God is moaning and groaning that no matter how much he does for the people down here, they're never satisfied."

12

T HREE WEEKS INTO the month of Shevat, unexpectedly, a dazzling golden sun emerged, melting the snow. From nowhere
came mild, gentle winds; the ice thawed. The Morehdalye residents
pulled on their tall galoshes, so they could plod through the sodden
snow, but unwound their woolen shawls from around their necks.
Faces glowed with smiles and eyes squinted against the sparkling sun.
People raised their heads heavenward and sighed, relieved that the
frost was letting up earlier than usual this year. But they soon realized
that their confidence had been premature.

Just a few days later, the clear sky was again covered by smoky
clouds. Again a frost gusted in and blanketed everything in frigid,
silvery breath. The damp transformed into glittery ice, glazing the
branches of trees, telegraph poles, and the edges of roofs and windows. The ground became slippery, mortally dangerous. The townspeople stood by their front doors, on stairs and stoops, banging iron
crowbars against the ice, which cracked and crumbled beneath them.

Across from the rabbi's house, a man stood in front of his home,
pushed up the tall fur cap that had fallen over his ears, and with the
sleeve of his hooded fur cape wiped the sweat from his forehead. He
searched the sky for a bit of sun, to no avail. Bloated clouds crawled,
low and quiet, like barefoot thieves stealing laundry from attics. Suddenly, the man noticed, along the slippery hill that descended toward
the rabbi's house, a sleigh driven by a coachman, the kind that sits
by the train station and waits for passengers. The horse slogged as if
encumbered by weights. Finally, the sleigh stopped before the rabbi's
house, and with the help of the coachman, a bundled-up woman proceeded slowly up the stoop. This was the Zembin rebbetzin, Vigasia.

Sholem Shachne and Henna'le hadn't yet given up hope that
Vigasia would show up, but they hadn't expected her in such weather.

Even the coachman was surprised when he saw Vigasia step off the train. "Auntie," he'd said to her, in his casual coachman's manner, "why the devil did you set out in such a snowstorm?"

"Take me to the rabbi's house and don't ask pointless questions like a woman," she ordered him. During the ride, she again instructed the coachman not to speak too much. The driver was sufficiently intimidated. When they arrived, he took her arm in his big hand as if it were made of porcelain and guided her into the rabbi's house, keeping silent all the while.

Reluctant to let the coachman hear even a single word of her exchange with the rabbi's family, Vigasia barked the moment the door was opened, "Give the coachman two zlotys. That's half a zloty more than the trip would have cost if it weren't so treacherous. And send him off."

Bound and bundled as she was, with shawl wrapped over shawl, Vigasia resembled a bowed, overgrown fruit tree wrapped in burlap to prevent freeze. She groaned and grumbled at her layers of clothes, like a coachman to his horses: "Don't you want to crawl out from under here?" As she tugged her tall boots off her feet, she panted especially long and hard. Draizel untied the knotted shawl draped over Vigasia's back. She hadn't forgotten her Zembin days, when Vigasia had been her only protector. Which is why she now bustled about the old lady cheerily, as though she were a tiny, sprightly ladybug bustling about its mama and Vigasia the large black beetle that, in moments of danger, puts her children on her back and carries them forward.

But the moment Draizel caught sight of her husband, she shrank from Vigasia, trembling in fright. With fury and hatred, Shabse-Shepsel eyed his father's wife.

Shabsel-Shepsel realized that, with his father's wife, the "Cossack Vigasia," around, he would not have it easy. Whose bright idea had it been to bring that witch down here? Shabse-Shepsel's glance skipped from person to person, and when he heard Henna'le's cheery, mock-innocent laughter, he knew in a flash that it had been her idea. It was Henna'le who had written—or had someone write—their father to send his villainous wife. And now they would use her, like a broom, to sweep him out of the house. *Well, let's just see about that*, Shabse-

Shepsel thought, and his pale blue eyes hissed and sizzled with even more derision and evil than usual.

"Rebbetzin, did you come down here to block the road to Zembin, so I can't go? Sure, let's see you stop up the Narev with a toothpick! Believe me, I still have more spirit and vigor in me than any river, thank God. I'm just waiting for the weather to turn milder. I don't want my Draizel'e, heaven forbid, to catch cold on the trip. Soon as the weather turns, we leave for Zembin."

"Sure, go to Zembin, go," Vigasia replied. By now she was standing, hands folded over her protruding stomach, wearing only her outfit and a peasant's headscarf, the kind worn by village women who argue with their children's melamed or by a seasoned itinerant beggar. "And what will you do in Zembin, if I may ask?"

"Hear that? What a question! What will I do in Zembin!" Shabse-Shepsel laughed with confidence. "I'll start by giving a shiur to the Zembin scholars. They've never heard such novel interpretations from my father like the ones I've come up with. They couldn't have! Father is a rabbi with a businesslike slant. His teaching style is as old-fashioned as the rest of his behavior, while I've adopted the new teaching style of my rosh yeshivas, Reb Chaim Brisker's disciples. Though I must say, even they don't impress me much. I run circles around them, like the *Ketzos HaChoshen* and the *Minchas Chinuch*— the world trembles at my skills! I'll give lectures to the regular Zembin townspeople, too. My clever quips, my melodious chanting whenever I give a talk, even my gesturing will practically raise them from the dead. Father never had a way with the simple Jews. He liked them the way he likes an ache in the eye, and they liked him exactly the same. I can even give talks to the educated Zembin population if necessary. With them, I'll discuss the wisdom of nature, medicine, and geography. Don't forget, we've come from America! And when Father goes the way of all men, I'll become his successor and call myself 'Rabbi and Genius Reb Shabse-Shepsel Epstein, Head of the Rabbinic Court of the holy community of Zembin, son of Rabbi and Genius, Rashkebehag Reb Eli-Leizer Epstein, may his memory be a blessing forever and ever . . .' Why do you look so alarmed? It's not like I'm wishing death upon Father, heaven forbid, but a man can't live forever, especially a man as old as him. Well past eighty already,"

Shabse-Shepsel said, and his eyelashes, nostrils, and lips twitched in scornful pleasure at his success in vexing and frightening everyone.

Only Vigasia kept calm. She continued to stand with both hands folded over her stomach, leaning back slightly to get a better view of everything. When she spoke, it was in the singsong tone of a fir-zugerke.

"Don't be surprised, and don't take his words the wrong way. What'd you think, if a person goes to America half-insane he comes back whole? You should know it's not like that. No, if you travel to America half-insane, you come back *entirely* insane."

"Ha! Your skin is quaking with fear that I might come to Zembin," Shabse-Shepsel said, still laughing, though with less heart now. His eyes held the wounded sadness of a vagabond. "But I'm coming, I'm coming." He smacked his lips loosely, like an old, toothless man.

"Come. Of course, be sure to come," Vigasia said, in a hard, masculine voice. "But before you come, listen well, and remember my words. When you settled in Zembin and first opened your china shop, for a while people still thought you were normal. But this time you'll end up straight in a psychiatric ward or a prison. You are witness," Vigasia pointed at Draizel, "that I warned him in advance."

Draizel started to whimper.

To keep from crying herself out of sympathy for this tormented woman, Vigasia shouted, "What's there to cry over? You silly thing! When you and your little man were still living in Zembin, and I watched how the two of you behaved, you know what I said? I said to my husband, may he live long, I said, 'This son of yours, your Shabse-Shepsel, is his own worst enemy. And your daughter-in-law enjoys her suffering.' It's true. If you didn't enjoy it, you'd run to the ends of the earth to escape this bloodsucker."

Draizel sobbed even harder, and Shabse-Shepsel, with the wan, pathetic smile of an anemic pauper, began to plead with her, "Don't cry, don't cry. We won't go to Zembin and become a laughingstock there. I thought Father wanted to see us, to bid us farewell before we leave for Israel. But if he doesn't, that's fine. And even if he won't help us pay for the travel, that's fine, too. You've convinced me: I'll set out across the neighboring towns to collect alms. Poverty is nothing to be ashamed of. 'The most honest earning is a donation,' a brilliant saint once said, especially if a Jew is collecting money for travel to the land of Israel."

It was hard to say whether Shabse-Shepsel was making another one of his demonic calculations, trying to scare and embarrass everyone by threatening that he, the Zembin rabbi's son, would travel around like a beggar, or if he truly meant it.

Perhaps his tactics worked on Vigasia, or perhaps she simply took pity on him, but the old woman suddenly changed her tone and demeanor. She spoke warmly and good-heartedly, assuring Shabse-Shepsel and his wife that they'd be getting money for travel expenses, and perhaps a bit more to tide them over until they got settled in Israel. "Shabse-Shepsel, it's not your father who'll give you the money," Vigasia said. "The rabbi, may he live long, has already spent his last penny. Week after week, he's had to supplement his measly rabbi's salary with his savings, and he gave some of his money to community charities. We have to do good deeds, after all, and prepare for the next world, too. It's my own money that I'm giving you, the money I saved up from when I was a widow. And if that isn't enough, I'll have my sons, the Bolekhev watchmakers, contribute. If I tell them to, they'll give. But Shabse-Shepsel, don't start with your threats again. Threats don't scare me. And you, Sholem Shachne, how are you doing? How's your health?" She addressed Sholem Shachne with the respectful "ir." Then, she made excuses for her old husband: "Your father-in-law, the rabbi, may he live long, hasn't been able to visit you lately because of the bad weather. He's more than eighty, you know—may he live till a hundred and twenty." And Vigasia went to wash up for dinner.

Henna'le filled the table with plates of cold food: pickled herring, chopped liver, a veal cutlet, sour pickles, and a basket of fresh white bread. But Vigasia didn't touch the food. Instead, she chewed on a hard crust of bread that she'd dug out of her own basket. She asked for a glass of tea, but with just a pinch of sugar. It was clear Vigasia took a certain pleasure in suppressing her bodily desires, the devouring of the material world, though she never spoke with glazed eyes in a fanatical, self-righteous tone; no, she spoke simply and plainly about the winter weather, the inflated food prices, and all that her husband had to endure from his congregants. Her chatter cracked the ice around the table, and the mood began to lighten. Then Naftali Hertz stepped into the house, and yet again, a scene ensued.

Naftali Hertz had taken to leaving the house for most of the day, to avoid all sight of "the charlatan," as he called Shabse-Shepsel, and only in the evenings, when he was hungry, did he return. Upon entering the house now, he noticed, among his family at the table, an unfamiliar, poorly dressed old woman, to whom everyone was listening with reverence. When Shabse-Shepsel saw his nephew come in, he leaped from his chair and began pacing around the room with a pained smile planted on his face. He grimaced as though being stabbed by a handful of needles, though he was able, with great effort, to maintain his gentle gait, back stiff, as if nothing were the matter. And though Shabse-Shepsel scoffed at his nephew—and revealed his scorn with a sardonic smile—deep down, it pained him that the doctor of philosophy held him in low regard and didn't even try to hide it. Now Vigasia would see as much and know it, too. Naftali Hertz and Vigasia would team up to laugh at him in front of the entire family and all of Morehdalye.

"This is our son who lives in Switzerland," Henna'le introduced him to the guest. "Naftali Hertz, this is your grandfather's wife, the Zembin rebbetzin, Vigasia."

Naftali Hertz was delighted. He knew how eagerly his parents had been waiting for her arrival, to rescue them from Shabse-Shepsel. But the feeling of delight went unreturned by Vigasia. The woman in the rumpled dress and patched-up blouse was not impressed one bit by the doctor of philosophy. Sneering and not at all politely, she said, "So, Morehdalye rebbetzin, this is your son from abroad? Well. That he has no beard or peyes is his business, not mine. But he's your son, which means he's my husband's grandchild. And yet he doesn't respect his grandfather enough to visit him. Well then, I have no respect for him."

"He's still planning to visit his grandfather," Henna'le stammered, taken aback. "But he came here to visit his father . . ."

"To visit the sick, yes." Vigasia seized the opportunity and trumpeted in her masculine voice, which echoed across the room, "If his father hadn't fallen ill, he wouldn't have come to visit him either. I understand." She nodded. Then, she shouted over to Shabse-Shepsel, "Why are you twisting this way and that? You're making me dizzy. Stop and tell us why, out of nowhere, you decided to move to the land of Israel? Refael'ke moved to Israel, too. Oh, that Refael'ke is something! Light of my life. I'd do anything for him. Your grandfather loves him with all his soul. And I love him like a biological child," Vigasia said to Henna'le, as though to say, *If only your eldest, the doctor, had even a third of the personality of your youngest.* "Well, Refael'ke I understand. He took his time and prepared for the move. But how did you so suddenly decide to throw away the golden land of America and move to the land of Israel?"

"We're living in the age of Messiah, so I'm rushing to Israel to greet the Messiah when he comes. And I'm rushing now, too, to beis medrash for Mincha and Maariv," Shabse-Shepsel said impetuously, and hurried out.

Through the window you could see his unbuttoned coat—the one he wore between seasons—flapping in the wind. You could see him rowing his elbows and swaying from side to side to steady his heft on the slippery hill up to the beis medrash. The farther he moved from the house, the thinner, the slighter, his figure appeared; pitiful to look at—a lonesome black dot, like a little bird in a world of snow under the low gray sky. The silence of the winter's air and the last flecks of light of the expired day penetrated the rabbi's house and dimmed the faces of the family around the table.

Naftali Hertz didn't join them. To the Zembin rebbetzin's rude greeting, he'd responded with silence, a wordless jab. *True, I'm not Refael'ke,* the silence said. *And I don't visit Grandfather because I'm not interested in hearing his admonishments, and I'm even less interested in hearing his third wife's shrill peddler's voice.* Smiling, Naftali Hertz said that he had to write an important letter—an excuse he'd already used several times when he wanted to avoid spending time with guests. He left the room, hunched over like a stubborn mule. It was because of such types, the thought occurred to him again, people like Shabse-Shepsel or Rebbetzin Vigasia or even her husband, his grandfather, that even in his student days he knew he needed to find a home in a non-Jewish environment.

Crushed by Vigasia's anger at their son and, even worse, ashamed of their son's lack of politeness toward his grandfather's wife, Sholem Shachne and Henna'le didn't urge Naftali Hertz to stay or try to detain him at all. Vigasia herself seemed to have all but forgotten him, and with her strong housewife's voice she blared to Draizel, "Tell me the truth. That husband of yours, that shlimazel, that nasty man—does he put on tefillin every day or does he sometimes skip? Does he always wash before eating and say the blessings afterward, or does he sometimes forget?"

"Sometimes he does forget to say the after-meal blessing, and once in a while he doesn't put on tefillin in the morning," Draizel replied, unruffled, as though she'd long been accustomed to this. "When Shabse-Shepsel was ironing trousers in America, I used to scold him. 'How can you bring yourself to skip davening?' I used to ask him. But he laughed at me. 'In America people only daven and say the after-meal blessing on Shabbos and on holidays, when they have more time,' he said. So then I needled him a little. I said, 'How long is it since you were your rabbi brother's assistant in his beis medrash and yeshiva?' He got angry and yelled that I should hold my tongue. He said that other sons of rabbis hadn't been persecuted by their fathers over a watch and a yarmulke the way he was. That's why those others were more devout than him. And then he told me a story. When he was a boy, he owned a pocket watch, a big, bulging pocket watch, that he loved very much. One day his father saw him winding the watch on Shabbos and he took it away. No matter how much Shabse-Shepsel cried and swore that he'd forgotten that it was forbidden to wind a watch on Shabbos, and no matter how much he promised never to do it again, his father refused to give him the watch back. He'd forget again, his father claimed. And the yarmulke story was this: One day his father couldn't find his velvet yarmulke. He accused Shabse-Shepsel of hiding it and he berated him like a goy, a drunk. He pinched pieces of skin off him, even though Shabse-Shepsel cried and swore up and down that he hadn't seen the yarmulke. In the end, his father found the yarmulke mixed up in his own pile of underpants, and only then did he stop persecuting Shabse-Shepsel."

"Well, judging by Shabse-Shepsel's character," Vigasia said, "even if he didn't steal the yarmulke that time, he was bound to have done it eventually. I've heard from the rabbi many times about the hardships Shabse-Shepsel caused him as a child, with his dirty tricks." Vigasia excused her "old man," as she always did when the Zembin townspeople came to complain about her husband. "From this one story," she continued, "you can understand Shabse-Shepsel's nature. That he clings to this grudge from childhood and doesn't put on tefillin or say the blessings because of it. These are the kinds of people about whom you say: 'He's angry at the cantor, so he doesn't say Amen.'"

"But sometimes, when he does say the after-meal blessing, he sings the words so sweetly that everything I endure from him is worth it," Draizel said, her face brightening. "And even though he sometimes skips a davening, at other times he stands with his tallis over his head for hours on end and davens with such sobs and emotion you'd think it was Yom Kippur."

"And why didn't he want to stay in America?" Vigasia asked.

Draizel glanced around furtively, to make sure no one outside was listening. In a frightened whisper, she said, "We had to leave America because Shabse-Shepsel couldn't bear the tall brick buildings of New York. They made him sick. On the streets and at home, awake or asleep, he was in constant suffering. He suffered from the delusion that a man stood on the roofs of the buildings, a strung-out man with bulging eyes who stood there as though possessed, in a dark depression, so dark—Shabse-Shepsel would say—like water in a flooded cellar. And this man was about to jump. The taller the building, like the ones that seemed to reach the clouds, and the thicker the forest of long chimneys swirling with smoke, the clearer Shabse-Shepsel saw the man standing high up there, his sinister eyes staring out like the extinguished windows of a ruin. Those were the poetic words Shabse-Shepsel used. He'd say, 'That man up there has such sinister eyes, they're like the punched-out windows of a ruin. The man is about to jump, but before he does, he wants to ponder something, discover something.' Shabse-Shepsel tormented himself with questions: Who is that up there? What does he want to ponder and what does he want to discover? Once, Shabse-Shepsel said that the person up there is a murderer. He'd killed someone and escaped to the roofs, because the entire city was chasing him with rods and sticks. Another time he claimed the fugitive up there had run away from his wife. Now he wanted to go back to her, but he'd forgotten where she lives, what her name was, and even what she looks like. And then, another time, Shabse-Shepsel said that that person was standing up there just because—because he wanted to contemplate the reason for man's existence on this earth. Shabse-Shepsel used to shout in his sleep: 'Hold him back. He'll jump!' And even afterward, when he awoke and realized it was a dream, he still writhed and groaned in bed. 'Who is that up there?' he said. Until finally, one day, he said, 'The man up there is me, Shabse-Shepsel. And I feel that sooner or later I'll climb that roof and I'll jump, to put an end to the delusions that torment me. Let's leave America, instead.' And so we left."

Sholem Shachne and Henna'le exchanged looks of alarm. *Is that how far it went?* Shabse-Shepsel, harboring such an obsession—they had not expected that. Instead of laughing, they felt like crying.

Vigasia, too, was rattled. She sighed. "I wouldn't wish this on anyone." She realized it wasn't right to have spoken as harshly as she had to such a befuddled person.

But Draizel, triumphant, said proudly, "Well, what do you say now, Mother-in-law? And you, Sister-in-law? You understand why I'm willing to endure so much from my husband? Plenty of people suffer from mad dreams and delusions, but when they try to talk about it afterward, there's nothing interesting to hear. But Shabse-Shepsel has such fascinating fantasies, it takes your breath away. And when he tells you about these fantasies, he paints such a pretty picture with his words, like the colorful paintings on my father's fine china—the ones my insane husband squandered. Living with him, my thief and oppressor, is very interesting for me," Draizel said, and the tears in her eyes sparkled like streaks of gold, like the eyes of the expensive porcelain dolls from her squandered collection of china.

13

M ARCUS LURIA WAS ARRESTED and thrown into prison in Bialystok. Zalia Ziskind found out about his son's imprisonment
in a letter that began with these words: "This letter is written to you
by your son Marcus's girlfriend . . ."

The girl, whom Zalia Ziskind had never heard of, described how
Marcus had been working among the Polish villagers and had protested against Poland's capitalist, imperialist power. Marcus enlightened the masses, arguing that Poland should return lost sections of
western Ukraine and western Belarus to the Soviet Union, and that
Poland must declare itself a workers' and peasants' government.
"Marcus," the girl wrote, "fought for this belief and will remain a
hero through the trial, together with his comrades, his fellow political prisoners. For this reason, he's requested that his father, the rabbi,
not appeal to communal functionaries or religious businessmen to
intercede for his release before the trial, and especially not to revoke
the charges against him. Marcus spurns the Jewish mindset and hates
Jewish capitalists as much as non-Jewish ones. And he doesn't want
to be more privileged than his comrades. The movement will be taking care of food and book deliveries in prison, as well as a lawyer for
the trial. But Marcus wants you, his father, to know what has happened to him, so that you won't find out about it from others and try
to rescue your son in a manner that would insult his proletariat pride
and consciousness," the letter writer concluded. She didn't sign her
name or give her address.

Though Zalia Ziskind had understood everything the first time he
read the letter, he reread it so many times that each word burrowed
into his brain and hardened there, as if he'd been standing for hours
beneath a sluggish autumn rain, and his tattered woolen coat had
become saturated with raindrops looking like dead eyes.

Afterward, Zalia Ziskind went to the Morehdalye rabbi's house, and sitting at the table with Sholem Shachne, Henna'le, and Naftali Hertz, he passed the letter around for each of them to read. Despite its awkward, unfamiliar language, the rabbi and rebbetzin got the gist. A sad hush fell over the table. Zalia Ziskind's pale, shriveled face matched the gray, dreary day peeking in from outside—the sky low and cloudy, snow blanketing a vast, motionless world.

"What does she mean when she says she's my son's girlfriend?" Zalia Ziskind murmured.

"Who knows?" Sholem Shachne shrugged. "I understand as much as you do."

And Zalia Ziskind nodded his head. Yes, he understood. Well, why did he ask, then? Apparently, he either hoped someone would deny it or he liked to torture himself.

Sholem Shachne didn't want to add to his suffering friend's pain, but the young generation's debauchery so angered him that he couldn't bear it. "With today's youth, a girlfriend means, plain and simple, a mistress, a wife without the benefit of a chuppah. Indeed, what use is a chuppah when you can do it without one?"

Naftali Hertz smiled sarcastically. Even angrier than his father, he said, "So Marcus belongs to a faction in the battle between the Poles and the Russians over who really has a claim to West Ukraine and West Belarus? He's fighting for a workers' and peasants' government? Well! He has a deep connection to the proletariat and peasants, does he? One day he'll be ashamed of his communism the way he's now ashamed of his Nietzschean past."

"Well, his future regret and shame won't help him now. Now, he's sitting in prison awaiting trial," Zalia Ziskind muttered, so low you could barely make out what he was saying. His hunchback appeared more prominent than usual, his nose stretched, cheeks hollow, and his big black eyes looked cold and glassy, like a fish tossed onto dry land. His sparse gray beard hung down like the twigs of a ragged broom. "Marcus says I shouldn't try to intercede for him. But even if he'd asked for the opposite—that I do use my clout—I wouldn't know which door to knock on."

Their old family friend's misfortune made Sholem Shachne and his wife even more depressed. Both were still exhausted, rattled, dazed by the mayhem Shabse-Shepsel had wrought. After he and Vigasia had finally come to terms on the amount he and Draizel would get for their move to the land of Israel, he again regretted his decision and declared he wouldn't go. Shabse-Shepsel raged and threatened. Vigasia laughed in his face and told him she had zero fear of his threats; Naftali Hertz called him a charlatan and started pelting him with his fists; and Henna'le was terrified that the agitation would cause Sholem Shachne to have a second heart attack. Still, Henna'le continued to act kindly toward her brother. She pressed some coins into his hand to contribute to the trip. She did this with her husband's knowledge, but kept it secret from Naftali Hertz and Vigasia, to prevent them from fighting even more with Shabse-Shepsel.

Finally, Shabse-Shepsel and Draizel left for Warsaw. When he bid his farewell, Shabse-Shepsel shouted at Vigasia, "What luck that you haven't forbidden me from going to say goodbye to my sisters and their families in Warsaw."

The squabble hung like a cloud over the rabbi's house, even after Vigasia went back to Zembin. Henna'le felt dismayed for her brother, who couldn't even say goodbye to his father, and worse, she cried for her old father, who'd been so afraid to meet with his mad son. For Vigasia, too, Henna'le felt an ache in her heart: What a kind, smart woman! And yet here she was, forced to act as hard as stone, to protect her husband from his own son. "Everyone has their burden; God spares no one," Henna'le muttered, wiping her eyes.

But others' misfortunes were no consolation to Zalia Ziskind. He sighed, weak and helpless, continually wiping his dry, sore mouth with a folded handkerchief. He thought: *I'm like the man in Proverbs who "runs from a lion and comes face-to-face with a bear." He walks into his home and presses his hand on the wall—lo, a snake comes and bites him.*

"A girlfriend?" he repeated to himself in wonderment. "And I'd completely forgotten that it's already time for Marcus to marry. Well then, he's chosen a girlfriend by himself . . ."

Soon enough, all of Morehdalye got word of Zalia Ziskind's misfortune, and the people felt terribly sorry for him. Everyone already knew that this hunchbacked Jew, standing in for their sick rabbi—studying Gemara with the homeowners and sweetly explaining the Chumash to the workingmen—this man was no amateur rabbi. No, he was a great scholar, once a world-renowned rosh yeshiva. But he'd become a widower very young, and could never rid himself of his depression. This new misfortune with his son garnered him even more empathy and respect: that such a tormented Jew, such a genius, a tzaddik, and a humble man should have a communist prisoner for a son! People's eyes began to follow him in the streets, but he didn't notice: he didn't notice because, without even realizing it, his own eyes had begun to follow—girls!

As he walked down the synagogue street, approaching him was an unmarried girl wearing a belted coat, thick and rumpled, but a fresh, rosy, full-cheeked face shone beneath her headscarf. Zalia Ziskind stood rooted to his spot, his eyes trailing her, lost in thought: *Is Marcus's bride this tall, too, and with such a friendly face?* Since his girlfriend—as she called herself—had written the letter in Yiddish, he knew she must be Jewish. What's more, she longed for a world that was good for everyone, including Polish workers and peasants. *Why, then, doesn't she want to get to know her fiancé's father?*

Zalia Ziskind jerked away from his spot and hurried to the beis medrash. He still owned his old rabbinical coat, with the brown fur collar, from his better days. But it was now too big for his emaciated body, and heavy as lead. He again had to pause along the way, barely able to catch his breath. *There's no question about it,* he thought. *For years and years, I took almost no interest in raising Marcus, so it's only natural that he remembers our time with bitterness and wants me to go on ignoring his affairs, even while he's in jail. And perhaps it's the jail that's intensifying his anger toward me? But what I can't help wondering is how my son, so timid among people, showed no fear in speaking and acting out against the government. Could it be his girlfriend emboldened him? If that's the case, it might be said that he's aspiring to carry out my principles of empathy for people, the principles I've spoken about my entire life. Though all I did was talk.*

Zalia Ziskind lived in a sort of cellar, six steps below ground. His landlord, a milliner, and his wife, who worked as his assistant, were a childless couple, both short with large heads. They never conversed while at work in their shop, nor did they exchange words with Zalia Ziskind. In the market, when they stood by their wagon selling hats, they'd respond to bargaining peasants with only a silent nod or a shake of the head. The Morehdalye residents wondered why the former rosh yeshiva had taken up lodgings with such an ordinary couple, eventually concluding he'd accepted the hardship as a form of atonement. Indeed, Zalia Ziskind had no desire to live in a bright or happy home; he was loath to disturb others with his heavy mood, and didn't want others to disturb him either. In this home, a permanent dimness pervaded the rooms, a furtive silence. Even when the lady of the house brought in food for him, she never uttered an unnecessary word.

Once inside the door, there were yet another few steps to descend. His room resembled the anteroom of an old synagogue, with its tall ceiling and one narrow window, high up from the floor. The decrepit table, the pair of chairs, and the wooden bed looked as if they'd been pulled from storage, where they'd been sitting because their owner didn't have the heart to burn them. Hanging on hooks, on the bare walls, were some threadbare clothes, a black hat, and an umbrella. What few holy books he owned were stacked on the sill of the one high window, rather than on proper shelves. To grab a book or look outside, Zalia Ziskind had to climb up on a chair. But these days he felt less and less inclined to stretch for a book, and less and less curious to peek outside. He either sat with head bowed, sunk in thought, or head raised, thoughtless, gazing up at his tefillin pouch, which hung on the wall so that mice wouldn't gnaw through it.

In just this pose did Naftali Hertz find Zalia Ziskind, when he came down to visit. It was sometime around noon, a day after Zalia Ziskind had shown them the letter from Marcus's girlfriend at the rabbi's house.

As Naftali Hertz walked down the crooked cellar stairs, Zalia Ziskind watched him with bleak, veiled eyes and did not utter a word. He simply waved him toward a chair across the room and continued to sway over the barren table, as over an open book.

In a confidential, somewhat secretive tone, Naftali Hertz said, "I was up all night. The thought that I, too, might be to blame for Marcus kept me awake. I'm afraid that, because of me, because I demanded you and Marcus leave Lecheve, he was so disappointed he decided to drift to the Left. On the other hand, imagine how much everyone—my sister, her husband, my parents, even you—how much you'd all have suffered if anyone discovered that Marcus was going after a married woman. And that my sister, a mother, a rebbetzin, the Lecheve rebbetzin, was slowly being drawn into a love affair. Can you imagine what would have happened?"

"Of course, of course, you don't have to mention it," Zalia Ziskind replied hastily, and gave a sad smile. "I don't argue with God about His actions, just as I don't argue with His Ten Commandments. Certainly not with 'Thou shalt not covet the wife of your friend.'"

The old rosh yeshiva went silent for a while, and his former student gazed up at the high, narrow window. Through it he saw the faded winter's day, reminding Naftali Hertz of the dazzling snow outside his windows in Bern. *The hole they've got Marcus locked up in probably isn't much worse than this cellar where his father lives,* Naftali Hertz thought. *And I'm sitting in a prison, too. Sitting at my parents' in snow-muddied Morehdalye. And it's worse, I'm sitting in a voluntary prison, imprisoned by my own prejudice against my wife and son because they aren't Jewish. Then again, I'm also a stranger in the place I've made my home, in the Swiss community with its carved balconies, cornices, and pillars. In fact, I feel more imprisoned there than here, even less free. But the distance has made me forget.*

"Listen to me, Rabbi. Another of my teachers, a philosopher, a great philosopher—the world calls him Benedictus de Spinoza but I call him by his Jewish name, Baruch, from the family of Spinoza—he once wrote that a person is aware of the things he does but not the reasons for doing them. And the reason, the 'why,' is what's most important. Actually, I'm not even sure why I'm telling you this. But I came here . . . Yes! Why did I come here? Aha, I remember now. I came here to tell you that I'm ready to go to Bialystok with you, to try everything we can to get Marcus out of jail. For someone like him, jail must be especially hard; by nature, he doesn't belong to the criminal Left at all. I'm ready to do whatever it takes. That I live in another country is actually an advantage in this situation. In Poland, office doors open more quickly for foreigners than they do for native Polish Jews. And we needn't pay any mind to what the girlfriend wrote, supposedly in Marcus's name. I'm not even sure he told her to write that, so let's—"

"Heaven forbid!" Reaching his long, skinny arm across the table, Zalia Ziskind grabbed Naftali Hertz by the shoulder. "On the contrary, I don't have the slightest doubt that Marcus told her to write that letter, so it would be wrong for me to do anything against his will, even if I knew I could change things." Zalia Ziskind drew his arm back slowly. He spoke more calmly now, with a full, knowing smile.

"His girlfriend wrote that Marcus doesn't want people to mediate for him because he hates religious functionaries and religious business-men. She also wrote he doesn't want any privilege over his friends in prison. But besides all that, I think, Marcus is ashamed of me. He doesn't want his girlfriend and his friends to know that his father is a cripple, a little Jew with a patchy beard and a giant hunchback. That's what I've been thinking since this morning. Though what I thought last night is no less true—he doesn't want me to concern myself with him now because I didn't concern myself with him for so many years. At the same time, Marcus isn't lying when he says he loathes inter-vention and doesn't want to feel any more privileged than his friends. At any rate, that's what he thinks he believes. Like your philosopher Baruch Spinoza says, 'Man knows what he does, but not why he does it.' He's certainly right about that. As for whether I'm right about Marcus, I'm not sure at all. Hmm, maybe I really shouldn't heed what my Marcus says, maybe I *should* do whatever I can to save him. What do you think, Naftali Hertz?"

"If Marcus doesn't want you to get involved for deeper reasons, as you say, I don't know if you should," Naftali Hertz replied, as though he, too, had become infected by his rosh yeshiva's probing and hesi-tations. "Especially since it's far from certain that we can accomplish anything."

"Is that so? Far from certain?" Zalia Ziskind suddenly paused his swaying, like the pendulum of a broken clock. "You're not sure?" he repeated anxiously, buried in his bleak thoughts the way his head was buried between his pointy shoulders.

Naftali Hertz hadn't come to talk to Zalia Ziskind only about his jailed son. He had selfish reasons, too. Over time, he'd concluded that the only person he could entrust with the secret of his life was his former rosh yeshiva. Certainly, even he would be shocked at first. But he wouldn't tear his clothes in mourning, nor jerk away from him as from a leper. The "appalling situation" would gradually settle in his mind. His own son had gone all the way over to communism and yet he hadn't disowned him, so he'd be just as understanding of his student who'd lost his way. Naftali Hertz was counting on it. But more than that, he was counting on the fact that Zalia Ziskind was in a perpetual argument with God. An arguer like that could never be a fanatic, and maybe not even that big of a believer. *And I must confide in someone*, Naftali Hertz thought. *If I continue to smother the secret of my wife and son, the veins in my temples will swell and burst. I won't make it; I'll explode like a barrel of gunpowder.* He could also find out from Zalia Ziskind if his parents had any suspicions, if they'd realized that domestic harmony wasn't the only thing lacking in his family life, as he'd told them—that an inner abscess was dripping pus and rot there, that a wild growth was growing, a growth he could no longer sever from his body and life. His father and Zalia Ziskind had been friends since their days in Volozhin, so in whom, if not Zalia Ziskind, would his father confide? All of this is what Naftali Hertz had been thinking earlier. But he saw, now, that his former rosh yeshiva's feeble character made him the wrong person for dispensing any sort of consolation or advice.

"Why aren't you answering me, Naftali Hertz? I already asked you twice. Who should be the first person I talk to about Marcus? Where do I start? Who should I talk to?"

"With a lawyer. First thing we have to do is go down to Bialystok and hire a lawyer who specializes in political prisoners. He has to find out what the charges are. He'll go see Marcus in jail and meet with his friends and relatives. This will cost us a hefty sum, I imagine. But if you reach out to your former students from the Visoki-Dvor Yeshiva and your old friends from the Volozhin Yeshiva, you'll be able to raise the money. Father already told me he's ready to write to the rabbis of communities large and small to explain your situation. He's sure people will respond from all over, for your honor and because of the mitzvah of pidyon shvuyim."

"Heaven forbid!" Zalia Ziskind shuddered. He was about to say something when a coughing spell came over him, and it was a while before he could croak out the words: "It's all my fault. All my life," he explained, "I've been asking God terrible Job-like questions about His management of this world, and I never got an answer. But there was one question I never asked, I couldn't ask—why my only son had brought me no nachas. I couldn't ask this question, because I had abandoned my son for years, left him in the care of his aunts and uncles. So how can I now go to my students and friends asking them to help, when this situation was all my own doing? I allowed Marcus to raise himself and choose his own path in life. And what will Marcus say when he finds out I collected money from rabbis? No, no, no!"

"If we can't reach out to your friends for help, we're in trouble. Without money, we can't do a thing," Naftali Hertz said.

"Is that so? It's a dead end without money?" Zalia Ziskind looked even more worried. "Hm, you may be right. If I decide to travel around collecting money for pidyon shvuyim, I can only do it with the help of rabbis."

"And to get Marcus released until the trial, we'll also need rabbis. The only way it can be done is if a delegation of rabbis guarantees that the accused man won't flee. Rabbis are the only ones the Polish government still trusts a little."

Zalia Ziskind grew even more alarmed. "And what if Marcus does flee before the trial? His girlfriend might persuade him to run away with her, somewhere overseas, or to Russia. That will mean I dragged these Torah scholars into trouble. Is that right?"

"No, it isn't right," Naftali Hertz said, surprised at himself now for his earlier desire to confide in Zalia Ziskind. *How could I have wanted to confide the secret of my life to such a weak man? And if Father had any suspicions about me, he would never have confided in him either.*

Naftali Hertz's pity for his old teacher grew, and he lingered there in the cellar, exchanging old memories with Zalia Ziskind. "When I was studying under you in Visoki-Dvor, you were quite the singer. They used to call you King David's fiddle, which hangs on the wall and plays on its own. Because often you didn't even realize you'd started singing. I myself sometimes saw how, in the middle of preparing your talk, you'd launch into a song that meshed into another song, as if you were going up a spiral staircase, higher and higher. You'd completely forget that you were in the middle of preparing a shiur. You lost sight of the open books around you. And the students, too, would stop studying their Gemaras and listen to your singing. But I haven't heard you sing at all of late, not even to hum a tune."

"Forgotten." Zalia Ziskind smiled the way an old man does when someone reminds him of his childhood games or adolescent dreams. "I forgot the songs first, even before I forgot my Torah interpretations. And I don't mourn their loss. I don't cry over it: 'Pity for those who have been lost and aren't forgotten.' And it doesn't impress me anymore when I hear others singing; it's as if I'd been born deaf, practically."

"A real pity that you're not interested in music anymore," Naftali

Hertz said. "I myself am not a singer, nor is my father or any of my brothers and sisters. But a philosopher, one of those who think that the whole world is meaningless, he wrote, 'The language of music is proof of an alternate existence, a secret, supernatural existence.' We don't have the sounds of music in nature. Music lovers say that it's the greatest pleasure and the greatest consolation in life, so it's really a shame that you've abandoned such a source of consolation."

Zalia Ziskind stopped smiling. His temper—rarely seen—cut through his next words: "That's the very reason I abandoned music! Why exactly should I seek consolation in such an inconsolable world?" A darkness glowed in his eyes, as when one opens a door to a late autumn rain in the middle of the night.

"Remember what you used to say," Naftali Hertz reminded him, "when the Visoki-Dvor students would marvel at your brilliant interpretations? You used to sigh and say, 'It's possible to live a full, peaceful life without having ever answered the difficult questions on the Rambam's *Mishneh Torah*. But it's hard, extremely hard, to live with the unanswered questions one has about God's actions.'" Naftali Hertz turned silent. He saw a shudder pass through his old rosh yeshiva's entire body.

"Talk, talk, don't mind me." Zalia Ziskind smiled.

Naftali Hertz couldn't extricate himself; he had to keep talking. "I wanted to say, what I've heard people saying is that your questions on Divine Providence have become even harsher since you've become a widower. But really, the question about why the righteous man has it bad and the evil man has it good has already been asked by so many: the Prophets, the author of Tehillim, Job, they've all already asked this. Still, everyone in the world continues to live with this unanswered question. Only you have taken this question so much to heart that your entire world has, quite literally, come to a halt."

"I can't really say why I've taken the 'tears of the robbed,' as Kohelet calls the injustices of the world, more to heart than other people. Maybe my hunched back is at fault." Zalia Ziskind gave a short laugh. He was silent for a long while, a bleak gaze filtering through his lowered eyelashes. Eventually, he said, "The truth is, I never really suffered much because of my hump. Growing up in an environment of Torah scholars, my sharp mind and clear understanding of Torah made up for my crooked back. And my hump didn't prevent me from finding a shidduch. But some people didn't realize. They looked at me with pity, and I'd look back at them with even more pity—I pitied them and their entire being. But if you set out on the path of questioning Divine Providence, and if you aren't cowardly in your thinking, your agitating, you must go further than the Prophets. Habakkuk lamented, '*V'saaseh adam k'dgi hayam*, Why should man be like the fish in the sea?' Meaning, why should people be as vulnerable as fish in the sea. But for the actual fish, who swallow each other up, the prophet shows no concern at all."

The old rosh yeshiva pressed his elbows down into the table and set his large head—on which a yarmulke perched, falling back toward the nape of his neck—into his pale hands. He spoke in a murmur, as if talking to himself. "Have you ever watched a stork catching a sizable fish, one of those fish with a white stomach and silver back? Just a moment before, that fish was freely swimming and diving. Now he flounders in silence between the tongs of the stork's beak, trembling violently, shuddering, and then he's swallowed. Have you ever seen this? Or try to imagine a little sheep covered in soft wool, a sheep with a moist little nose inside the teeth and nails of a scrawny, hungry wolf. And imagine a snow-white hare with frightened, innocent, squinty eyes, with its big, sheer, rosy ears perked up, imagine such a gentle creature in the nails of a fox or other predator. How could a person not ask this dreadful question: Is this what God's mercy looks like? Moses said, 'Hashem, Hashem, God of mercy!' And the Gemara tells us that the trait of mercy must be learned from God—'Just as He is full of mercy, so should you be full of mercy.' But rather than create a peaceful world, where everyone eats grass, He created a world of bloodthirsty animals who gobble up not only their equals but creatures who can do nothing more than tremble and succumb."

Zalia Ziskind rose from the divan on which he slept and strode to the other side of the table, near Naftali Hertz. In the high-ceilinged cellar, where the winter's gray, stingy light flickered in the narrow window, he looked even shorter, his hunchback even bigger. To Naftali Hertz, he resembled a large, strange spider that hung from the ceiling on a single thread and would soon start asking an endless series of riddles; or else a dwarf that had crawled up from beneath the earth to tell of primordial times. He made odd gestures with his small, pale hands and spoke with the depth of pain and depression. "For sins of man against man or nation against nation, there's an answer and defense: God is not to blame when a person chooses evil. Everyone has free will and can choose to be righteous. Besides, there's always the hope that the evildoer will mend his ways. But what about the animal world? It may well be that these questions come to me not because I'm so good-hearted but because of my rattled nerves. In any case, it's not a matter of showing-off on my part, and it's not philosophical, nothing I'm trying to explain through logic. It's intrinsic; I feel it in all my limbs, with all my life. Even though I'm not one to stroll through the woods, and certainly not in the winter, I lie in my bed at night and hear howling, grating teeth, and such screams from devoured creatures that I shudder. Isaiah's prophecy of the wolf and the sheep, the tiger and the goat, the cow and the bear, the lion and the bull, how all of these creatures will feed together, will eat straw together, and a small boy will be their shepherd—this prophecy is nothing more than an analogy. It's meant to imply that peace will reign among all kinds of people in the Messiah's time. But as far as animals are concerned, even in the distant future, the wild beast will belch and lick the blood of its victim from its mouth. Now, I know you're asking yourself, 'Doesn't he have better things to do than grieve over a fox slaughtering chickens?' Well, listen. You can see I'm crazy. With such thoughts and emotions—I'm clearly not in my right mind."

Zalia Ziskind circled back around the table, sat down on his spot on the divan, clasped his little gray beard in his hands, and mumbled as if through frozen lips—though Naftali Hertz could hear him— "There are still people in the world who pity animals, and even some who don't eat meat at all. But sometimes there's a person on whom no one takes pity. Even his mother is ashamed that she gave birth to him. A traitor, let's say. Because how can you empathize with someone who betrayed his nation and country? But I," Zalia Ziskind said, "when I used to read in the daily papers, during the war, how they caught such people, people sentenced to hangings, and even now when I read in the Warsaw papers, how this one or that one has been sentenced to execution because he divulged Poland's military secrets to another government for money, I'm anguished by their fates. God in heaven! Across the land and in all the seas there's not a lonelier person than this one. He'll go to his death knowing that no one will feel sympathy for him, his relatives will deny their connection to him, his name will be wiped out forever and ever. Isn't it dreadful that God created a world with so much distress?" Zalia Ziskind raised his head to the ceiling and froze that way, head tilted back, as though awaiting an answer from heaven.

"But see, even after all your pondering about how God runs the world, even after all your suffering for these wretched creatures, you still never once proposed that there's no Divine Providence at all? That maybe the world functions on its own, according to its own eternal laws? You never dared to go that far, did you?" his former student asked with a hard, mocking tone.

"If there's no Divine Providence, that means there's no Creator of this world, heaven forbid, and the entire creation is nothing more than a death machine that brings forth each creation and then grinds it to shreds. Then why would I suffer or sympathize?" Zalia Ziskind stared at his former student in wonder, as if Naftali Hertz had asked a child's question during a shiur for older students. "Precisely because I believe in God and in His supervision, I suffer for animals, humans, and even for God Himself, who created such an unkind, unwise world."

"No true believer would have such a bizarre complaint against God: why didn't He create a world full of grass-eaters," Naftali Hertz said.

"No, it's precisely the believers who have grievances. Like the Prophets. But everyone does it in their own manner." Zalia Ziskind sighed.

"It's all talk with you, Rabbi. That's where you stop. You've never once dared to not put your tefillin on or skip a single Shabbos." Naftali Hertz said this with a strange sort of fury, and he noticed Zalia Ziskind gaping at him, astonished.

"What do you mean, not put tefillin on or observe Shabbos? Are you laughing at me?"

And indeed, Naftali Hertz burst out laughing. "You see," he said, "when I started having doubts, and then heretical thoughts, the first decision I took was to travel abroad and educate myself, to not stay to live in the shtetl. I admit, my decision might have been too extreme, a bit too excessive. But you've never gone any further than to bemoan the miserable world. That's why you fell into a depression. That's why, even today, you can't pull yourself out of your diabolical condition. You didn't have the courage or the will to let your rebelliousness against God move you to action. You're like a person who sets fire to a house and can't save himself, because he's boarded up all the doors and shuttered the windows beforehand. You're like an old crumbling well where droplets drip down its shiny black stones, all the way to its rotten depth. Forgive me for saying this to you. You were my rabbi, and in many respects, you still are. But your failures pain me as if they were my own, and that's why I'm telling you the truth."

"True, true." Zalia Ziskind nodded in agreement. "By now I've come to realize that something's not quite right with me. You see that pile of newspapers there? Those are Warsaw papers." He pointed toward a corner of the cellar, where a stack of dusty, yellowed papers lay on the floor. "I collect these papers because of the tragedies they contain. I look at other pages, too. They publish news about disputes between different governments and government officers. I read articles, memories of the past, and current events. I even look at the silly bits of news on the bottom of the pages. But out of everything I read, what sticks in my memory are mostly the articles on all sorts of tragedies. The greater the tragedy, the crueler, the more absurd, the more there's no rhyme or reason to it, a tragedy that makes no sense, no why, no when—the deeper it drives into my heart and into my memory. It bores through me, drills through me, and I can't bring myself to throw these old newspapers away. I keep imagining that if I throw them away or turn my thoughts away from the tragedy that befell this man or that woman, I'll be adding to that person's suffering and shame. It would be as if that person had never lived or isn't worth being remembered, like a stone slipped under the water and forgotten. These are the kinds of tragedies that pile up in my mind: A mother burned to death in a fire, along with her five children. In her sleep! Maybe she even choked on the smoke as she tried to save her little innocents. Then there's the story of a young girl who knew there was no cure for her illness, so before her death she wrote a letter to the government. She told them that if scientists would work on discovering new treatments to save people with her illness instead of working on discovering new poisonous gases, she would die in peace. 'Even if they don't end up finding the cure,' she wrote, 'I would die easier, knowing that the world I'd lived in wasn't such a cruel one.'

The other day I was reading about this artist, a woman, still very young and a great beauty. The most revered singer and performer in the world, an Italian, I think, or maybe French. In any case, just as long as she'd shone on stages all over the world, that's how long she later struggled in agony on her deathbed. *Vey al hey shifra divlei b'afra.** The old rosh yeshiva said these Aramaic words in a broken voice, the same Talmudic verse usually recited in eulogies for Torah scholars, now used for this stranger, this goyish artist. "I saw written somewhere—it was attributed to the Roman sages—that while a person is still alive, you can't say they've lived a happy life, because no one knows how that person's life will end. I see I've tired you out with my talking. You're leaving already?" Zalia Ziskind cried out, surprised, seeing that his guest had stood up.

Naftali Hertz was standing, looking down at the chair where he'd been sitting the way someone with too little sleep looks at the hard bench on which he'd tossed and turned through a long night, waking with broken bones. No longer was Naftali Hertz concerned that his words would hurt his former rosh yeshiva. "Two years ago," he said, "when I met you in Lecheve and heard your son quoting Nietzsche, about how a man's greatest enemy is his compassion, I asked myself: How does it come to be that the son of a rabbi identifies with the philosophy of a German, an artillery officer from Bismarck's times? Even more interesting, *when* was he identifying with him? After a bloody world war. True, years ago, some ex-religious Hebrew writers were still falling into reverential awe over Nietzsche's thoughts. They each regurgitated Nietzsche's words in their own way. But today, no one regards him highly, and only your Marcus was still hunting around in such broken wells: 'broken wells incapable of holding water.' I'd thought then that Marcus liked bold thoughts pulled from books because he lacked courage in real life. But now I understand better. I realize that you played a great part in his confusion. You're so oppressed by your compassion for strangers, and even for fish in

---

* "Woe that such beauty will rot in the earth." The quote is based on a story about Rav Eliezer and Rav Yochanan. When Rabbi Eliezer lay dying, Rav Yochanan came to visit him. Rav Yochanan was a beautiful person, and his beauty literally lit up the room. In the light, Rav Yochanan saw that Rav Eliezer was crying, and he asked him why.

"I am crying that such beauty will eventually rot in the earth," Rav Eliezer said (Talmud Bavli, Berachos 5b).

the sea, that for Marcus even Nietzsche's teachings were more agree-able. Things like, if you see a weak man falling, give him a shove so that he falls even harder. Still, your Marcus knows that Nietzsche ended up in an insane asylum, because he tried to save himself with a doctrine that people must be hard as stone while he himself was a knot of raw nerves. Besides, we're living in a different time, and the tablets Zarathustra engraved about the supposed 'Übermensch' are now broken tablets. That's why Marcus switched over to Karl Marx. Today's youth rally around his *Communist Manifesto*."

"Yes, yes." Zalia Ziskind nodded again, pleased that he, not his son, was to blame for everything. He followed Naftali Hertz up the cellar steps. "So, what do you think? Will we be able to get him out of prison? On one hand, you're right to disregard what his girlfriend pens in his name. I'm his father. I have at least as much right in this case as this girlfriend of his. On the other hand, if I ignore Marcus's request, then not only will the Poles have taken Marcus's freedom away by locking him up in prison, but they'll also have taken away his right to decide what should be done about him. How can I accept the thought of seeking help from people of my standing and my environ-ment, if Marcus explicitly told me he doesn't want it? What do you think, huh?"

To avoid being rude to his old rosh yeshiva—he wanted to shout into his face that he couldn't endure his dithering anymore—Naftali Hertz grunted and hurried out of the cellar.

Slowly, Zalia Ziskind walked back down the stairs. He stood at the bottom, head and beard raised in the air. His dry lips stirred, as though he were standing in the depths of a cold, empty synagogue, murmur-ing: "*From the depths I call to you, Lord!*" But instead of a prayer, he mumbled ordinary words, same as before. "Well, what should I do? Should I put aside my embarrassment and go from place to place to collect donations? Should I free my son from prison against his will?"

14

MARCUS LURIA'S UNCLES and aunts had not heard from him since he'd left Visoki-Dvor. But when he was jailed, the same girlfriend who'd written to his father had also written to them. She made the same request: Marcus did not want their help because he hates religious functionaries and doesn't want to be any more privileged than the other political prisoners.

The brothers-in-law hadn't yet forgiven Zalia Ziskind for abandoning Visoki-Dvor. His departure had caused a decline in the yeshiva, with the sharpest boys running to the yeshivas in Mir or Radin. As a result, Visoki-Dvor was reduced to a yeshiva ketana, with classes for younger teens only. The sisters-in-law hadn't forgiven Zalia Ziskind either, upset that, in the wake of his wife's death, he'd abandoned his orphaned son to the care of his sister-in-law Sirka. Upset, too, that he'd let Sirka wait, parched, pining for him to marry her—until she couldn't wait any longer and married someone else. Marcus then left to join his father, and, other than Sirka, who missed the child she'd raised, the aunts and uncles were glad to be rid of their reprobate nephew.

When the letter arrived announcing that he was in jail, the entire family was of one mind: "It's his father's fault!" they cried. "The supposedly compassionate Zalia Ziskind was busy pitying the entire world, except his own flesh and blood. While his 'good heart' drove him from place to place, his son, without a father's supervision, rolled downhill all the way to the communists."

At first, furious at their nephew, the aunts and uncles said, "Let him rot in prison!" But Sirka still held him close to her heart, and her mind roiled at the thought of her sister's son in prison. Gradually, the other family members came to understand that they needed to get their nephew out of jail and then spread a rumor that he'd been mistakenly imprisoned. Or that someone had lied and defamed him. Because how would it look for their family, for their yeshiva and rabbinate, if word were to get around that all three uncles, Torah giants, and their wives hadn't been able to keep their nephew from becoming a communist? How could they be trusted to lead a town and a yeshiva and even dare to rebuke others?, people would say.

No, the family would have to intercede. It never occurred to any of them that they should consult with Marcus's father before doing anything. First of all, the problem was entirely his fault, for having neglected to raise his son. Second, what could they expect from this hunchback, this dunce, this wimp who was now helping the sickly Morehdalye rabbi instead of leading Jews himself? Could they now expect his help in getting his son released from prison? They'd sooner expect him to ruin the whole operation.

By all appearances, the three brothers-in-law lived in harmony. But quietly, each of them harbored resentments against the others. The brother-in-law who served as rabbi felt aggrieved that he wasn't allowed to give a shiur in the yeshiva. And the two brothers-in-law who served as rosh yeshivas were upset at the rabbi brother-in-law for not allowing them to be involved in communal matters. Between the pair of rosh yeshivas, too, resentments simmered. They couldn't evenly divide their salaries, nor their prestige among the students. And now, when something had to be done for their imprisoned nephew, Sirka's husband, who had become the second rosh yeshiva after his marriage, quickly extricated himself from traveling to Bialystok. Instead, only the rabbi and the first rosh yeshiva went.

As they made their way by train, the two refrained from discussing their mutual resentment or the anger they felt toward Sirka's husband—who seemed unbothered by it all—or their anger toward Sirka—sitting across from them—for being *too* worked up over her nephew. For her part, Sirka was silent, too, worried over her sister's son and nauseated by her brothers-in-law's sour faces.

It never crossed the uncles' minds that they should take the letter from Marcus's girlfriend into account. But it didn't matter anyway. After spending days running around to Bialystok lawyers, rabbis, religious businessmen, and city councilmen, the family, as well as their intercessors, were led to understand by both the Polish police and the prosecution that the accused man's guilt had been absolutely proven. Without being coerced by anyone, he'd admitted that he was an independent, conscious communist activist. If, however, the family could prove—as they claimed—that the accused was insane and had demonstrated symptoms of mental illness before this arrest, there was a chance he could avoid the long-term prison sentence he was likely to get. A man who's not in his right mind would not be kept in jail.

The police wanted to know something else. "Marcus Luria has a father, a rabbi, with whom he's lived for the past few years. Where is this father? Why doesn't he come and bear witness that his son is mentally ill?"

And so the family left Bialystok and hurriedly traveled to Morehdalye.

The unexpected guests from Visoki-Dvor caused a minor scandal when they arrived in Morehdalye—staring, whispering. The townspeople suspected that Zalia Ziskind's family had come to him to brainstorm ideas on how to save his son from prison. The guests stood out for their garb: rabbinic shtreimels and furs with brown beaver collars, knitted wool gloves, and tall boots. But more than for their clothes, they stood out for their height and posture.

The Visoki-Dvor rabbi had a square beard, interwoven with gray strands. Coarse, thick, coal-black whiskers hung down over his beard, and heavy, coal-black eyebrows protected his eyes. The pores of his fleshy face, too, were filled with coarse, prickly hairs. Contrary to the rabbi's squareness, his brother-in-law, the rosh yeshiva, was tall and slim, a bit stooped, with a narrow back, a milky-white face, pale blue watery eyes, and a flaming red beard like a long, fallen branch still covered with leaves that rustle in autumn's breeze. In another contrast to the robust rabbi: the rosh yeshiva was sickly, with no sharpness to his speech or a very sharp mind, as became immediately apparent after discussing some Torah with him.

Nevertheless, the two religious functionaries made a distinct impression on Morehdalye, especially when compared to their brother-in-law, the short, hunched Zalia Ziskind. But it didn't take long before the townspeople realized that these two were brusque and impatient. When the people in the beis medrash pushed toward them to shake their hands, they returned the greeting with two limp fingers, standing in hostile silence, with arrogant, bloated whiskers and lips. They spoke sparingly and quite aloofly even with the town's rabbi, Sholem Shachne, and with other of the town's respectable men. It became clear to the townspeople that these two must have been at odds with their brother-in-law for quite some time, and that their resentment toward him had now worsened over the shame that his son, the communist, had brought upon their rabbinical family.

The two guests stopped at the town's inn, where people very rarely spent the night. This led to even more gossip among the Morehdalyens. "Well, where else could they stay?" the people said. "With their brother-in-law, in the hatmaker's storage cellar?"

But Zalia Ziskind took care of his sister-in-law Sirka, arranging for her to stay in the Morehdalye rabbi's house. And though Henna'le hadn't known Sirka before this visit, they quickly became friends. Henna'le could see that Sirka was a quiet, kind, and long-suffering soul. She had only one vice: she thanked too profusely for every tiny thing.

Sirka had never looked very young when she was a girl, but then again, she hadn't aged much over the years either: a pale face with bloodless lips, a straight, longish nose, and soft gray eyes. Only the hair beneath her head-covering had turned gray. She still dressed the way she had as a girl: in a long, black skirt and white silk blouse, with embroidered frills around the collar and along the edges of the narrow sleeves that reached her wrists. In her girlhood, she had moved about with an expression of odd wonderment, lost in thought, as though she woke up in a field one summer morning, already an adult, not knowing who she was, where she came from, or who her parents were. Only after she'd spent years raising her nephew, and could no longer wait for her brother-in-law, the widower, to marry her, did the bitterness seep in. She tried infecting her nephew, the child she'd raised, with hatred for his father. But as soon as she married Meir Moshe Baruchovits, all the rancor she'd felt toward her brother-in-law burst and oozed out of her like pus from a wound.

Sirka remembered then how Zalia Ziskind had married off her two older sisters, and how after his wife's death, when he'd fallen into a depression, he gave the rabbinate away to one brother-in-law and the yeshiva to another, though they'd already forgotten this. For years, it had grieved Sirka that her brother-in-law wouldn't accept her as a substitute for her sister, Zisse'le, but later she liked this about him:

he hadn't taken her for a wife because he could not forget her sister. And she hated him even less when she compared him to her husband.

Perhaps it was mere coincidence, though it did appear odd, that Sirka had found as a husband a widower who was similar to Zalia Ziskind in so many ways. Meir Moshe Baruchovits, too, had been a renowned scholar as a teen. People called him the "Maryampoler genius," and he even had a reputation as a good singer. Despite these details, however, there was such a tremendous difference between her husband and her brother-in-law that Sirka had no choice but to think about it. She thought about it no matter how much she reproached herself for doing so, no matter how many times she told herself that Meir Moshe was her husband before God and man, and that Zalia Ziskind was nothing to her.

Baruchovits was somewhat shorter than average, broad-shouldered, a manly man with a squat neck and a large head, calm and mild-mannered by nature. In his younger years, he'd had a head of dark, curly hair, curious, cheerful eyes, thick lips, and the mouth of someone with a sweet tooth. Indeed, he was just as he appeared: a man who enjoyed life's pleasures. Still, that hadn't kept him from being a diligent, distinguished scholar. It was his ardor, in fact, this restlessness, that brought him to realize in time that the best path in life is the "golden path," the middle way. He gained control over himself, and his nose was the evidence of that control—his short, firm, meaty nose ruled over the middle of his broad face like an iron handle in the middle of a wrought-iron door.

Over the years he grew heftier and more sedate, defying the common belief that a genius must be wild, or a barbarian, even. His black curly hair thinned out. The beard on his full face grew sparser, too, and from between his sparse hairs protruded a satisfied jaw and rounded chin, as though stuffed with wheat buns. He always wore a clean jacket and velvet yarmulke. His ruddy face and high scholarly forehead were always a bit sweaty. And his lips tightened every so often, as though he were sucking on a sweet-and-sour candy. He moved about with hands behind his back, giving off the tranquil astuteness and pleasure of a respectable relative at a wedding: far enough, yet simultaneously close enough, to the wedding party that he could enjoy everything, but without the obligations of the father of the bride or groom who can't partake of the pleasures, busy as they are doling out honors and refreshments to their guests. Meir Moshe never took upon himself the role of serving others, nor did he work too hard or get overly upset—no matter what happened. When his wife died, he was in mourning for a year before he got engaged, though by Jewish law he could have married after thirty days.

Nobody could ever accuse him of pushing himself to the head of the table. In general, it was impossible to find a stain on his behavior, just as no stain could be found on his clothing, as befit a Torah scholar. His two daughters had gotten married while their mother was still alive, and these daughters were the ones who'd in fact pushed him to remarry and end his widowerhood. He settled on an old maid—the youngest daughter of the Visoki-Dvor rabbinical house. And when it was suggested to him that he become the second rosh yeshiva in the local yeshiva, he agreed. His reputation and scholarliness would have allowed him to attain a position in a larger yeshiva, with more students and a higher salary. But even during his first marriage, he'd lived on a recluse's miserly salary, because he'd been unmotivated, or simply too lazy, to push for a rabbinate. Certainly now, in his later years and a second marriage, he had no interest in climbing any ladders.

Meir Moshe made careful preparations for his talks, offering Torah readings to his students that were built on robust hypotheses. But each time he returned home after his shiur and paced about the few little rooms, his hands folded behind him, feeling pleased with himself, humming a tune under his breath, his wife became sad, downright gloomy.

Sirka would watch him and, against her will, compare him to her brother-in-law. It was true her husband hadn't gone to great lengths to become a rabbi or rosh yeshiva, but he would have never stepped away from his position, as Zalia Ziskind had done. Her husband would also never have fallen into a depression because of a tragedy that had struck a complete stranger. And whoever his wife may have been, he would never have remained a widower his entire life on her account. True, Meir Moshe could warble like a cantor, but not with such beauty and melancholy that could melt hearts, as could her brother-in-law, with his big hump on his slight body, skinny as a stalk. Her brother-in-law was a man of heart through and through— though no one could compare to his brilliant mind, either—while her husband was the kind of man who took hardly anything to heart and swallowed all his hardships.

To Sirka's dismay, her opinion of her husband proved true—and worse than she'd thought—during the family's deliberations on how to get Marcus out of prison. Meir Moshe gave a vigorous excuse, as though answering a difficult Rambam, that it made no sense for him to travel to Bialystok because he didn't know Marcus at all. When he argued with his brothers-in-law, Sirka remained silent; but when they were alone, she accused him of selfishness. He knew, didn't he, that Marcus held a dear place in her heart, like her own child? She'd raised him, after all. Meir Moshe shouldn't be digging for reasons to excuse himself from the trip.

But her husband's reply shocked her. It revealed that, though he never spoke about it, he knew and understood her secret thoughts and feelings. "You raised his son like a biological mother, and now, even now you can't get Zalia Ziskind out of your mind. That's it, isn't it? I don't want to and I don't have to get involved with your nephew's problem. You and your brothers-in-law, go. You're the ones who raised him."

So Sirka tagged along, first to Bialystok and then to Morehdalye.

15

ZALIA ZISKIND HURRIED INTO the rabbi's house, head and pointy beard bent forward. "Where's my sister-in-law Sirka?" he panted through thin nostrils, scanning the room. He looked fatigued, like a man who'd drowned in a river and crawled up onto an island and would soon have to start swimming again.

"She's still in her bedroom," Henna'le told him. "She'll probably be out for breakfast soon. We're waiting for her. Maybe you should join us and go wash up to eat?" But instead of thanking Henna'le for the invitation, he strode to his sister-in-law's room and impatiently knocked on her door with his bony fingers.

It was warm in the room. Outside, too, no ice crackled underfoot. Yet Sirka was freezing. Wearing a gray wool shawl over her shoulders, she sat at a table and leaned on her elbows, smoothing her hair down with her pale fingers. She covered her eyes with her hands and sat there for a long time, though she knew her hosts were waiting for her for breakfast. For a little while longer, she wanted to indulge her habit of thinking about her brother-in-law. No, it wasn't just a habit, it was an illness, a craze, because hundreds of times, maybe even thousands, she'd had the same thought: Had Zalia Ziskind married her, her life would have seemed tragic to other people. Those years when she'd waited for him, even her sisters had yelled at her: "What do you see in that depressive, that hunchback?" But not for a minute did she doubt that life with him would have been warm, interesting, even happy. And she would have been a blessing to him, too. With her he would not have become as prematurely old and broken as he had. Sirka took her hands off her eyes and looked out the window, as though to refresh herself with the sight of the clean, snowy day. But the winter's day stared back with the ashen face of a dying man, whose tormented life has already grown tiresome. This late in the month of Adar, the sun still hid behind clouds at the edge of the world, and who knew how long it would be before it returned to Morehdalye to melt away the snow?

There was a knock on the door. Sirka turned to see her brother-in-law stepping in. The first thought that popped into her mind was to pull her shawl over her head. And that's what she did, though in her own home she wasn't that pious, never alarmed if a man saw her with her hair exposed. A faint flush spilled over her cheeks. She stood up, a quizzical expression on her face.

"Where are you going? Stay seated," Zalia Ziskind said quickly.

"It's not appropriate, maybe?" she murmured, not knowing what she meant by that.

"Why wouldn't it be appropriate?" her brother-in-law asked impatiently, his tone ordinary, businesslike. "During the day, and with an open door, it isn't yichud. We're allowed. Sit down, I have to talk to you about something." And he sat down on a chair opposite her.

His hurried, prosaic manner of speaking subdued Sirka. She was annoyed at herself for still being as self-conscious as a bride in front of her former brother-in-law. All those years he'd avoided giving serious thought, even for a day, to marrying her. That's why he was unruffled when he was with her. Sirka sat with downcast eyes but listened keenly to his words.

Zalia Ziskind told her that the brothers-in-law had already informed him of their plan: He should travel with them to Bialystok and explain to the investigator, meaning to the Polish interrogator, that his son was not in his right mind, not a sane person. That way there'd be hope for his release. "Well, what do you think? You think Marcus wants us, plain and simple, to declare him insane so we can get him out of jail?"

"No, he doesn't want that," Sirka said, still not raising her head.

"How do you know? Did you talk to him?" Zalia Ziskind asked, and instantly answered himself. "You couldn't have spoken with Marcus, because no one's allowed to see him. You probably spoke to his wife, or, as she calls herself, 'Marcus's girlfriend.' And she must have told you that Marcus doesn't want to be declared insane in order to be freed. Did he at least take a fine wife, our Marcus?" Zalia Ziskind asked in a broken voice.

Sirka felt heat coursing through her body at the way her brother-in-law again addressed her with the familiar "du," as he had when his wife, her sister, was still alive, and she, the baby in the family, had still been a young girl.

She raised her head, and her quiet eyes grew bright. "In her letter to us, too, she signed off as 'Marcus's girlfriend,' and I was put off by it. But when I met her, I found her to be a nice girl from a respectable home, dark-haired and charming. And she isn't his wife, she's his fiancée. Her parents also want her to have a Jewish wedding. Her name is Chayenkeh. Chayenkeh Zilberberg. She told me that if we get Marcus released by declaring him insane, he might be so embarrassed before his friends that he'll commit suicide."

Zalia Ziskind shuddered. His hands trembled, and he said quickly, "I, too, realized that what my brothers-in-law were suggesting was slaughter, bloodshed. Marcus's fiancée specifically said, in his name, that no one should intercede on his behalf. Of course, it's possible he told her to write this out of anger at me and his uncles. But to destroy the reputation of a person by saying he's insane—that itself could make him go insane. It appears as if his uncles don't care what happens to their nephew, as long as he's not seen as a traitor and doesn't mar their reputations. They don't have a crumb of empathy in their hearts! Well, what do you think, Sirka?" All at once, Zalia Ziskind became alarmed at his loss of temper and started speaking more softly, a plea in his voice. "You were like a mother to him. You raised him. So, what do you think?"

"Yes, I stood in for his mother, and I love him like my own child, as if he's my only son, too, not just yours." Sirka's eyes turned moist. "But because he's so dear to me, I don't know what to tell you. I don't know if he'll be more miserable in jail or out of it, free but ashamed and abandoned by his friends."

"I don't know either," Zalia Ziskind murmured, hands at his sides. He looked wretched, as if he were already standing at the prison entrance, waiting to be let in. "Anyway, you were saying she's a fine girl, Marcus's fiancée?" He smiled pathetically and sighed, like someone who knows it's not his lot to be happy even when he's given a bit of nachas. "And what is your husband doing?" he asked suddenly, with the same pathetic smile. "I heard you did well. And I know he's a great scholar and has a good head." Then, as though he deliberately wanted to absolve his sister-in-law from the need to respond, Zalia Ziskind left the room as abruptly as he'd entered.

An open quarrel broke out among the three brothers-in-law in the Morehdalye rabbi's home. Sholem Shachne, Henna'le, and their son were all present, but they didn't get involved, not with a single word. The Visoki-Dvor rabbi, with his big, meaty face and square, prickly, salt-and-pepper beard, and his brother-in-law, the rosh yeshiva, with his milky face and long, narrow, flaming red beard—both addressed their eldest brother-in-law, Zalia Ziskind, with fury and arrogance. "Are you serious? You want us to care whether Marcus will feel worse, in prison or free without his gang of degenerates? No, the problem is the tremendous desecration of God's name and the shame he brings to our entire family."

"But I am a father, and I am concerned for him," Zalia Ziskind replied, not as soft and hesitant as usual.

"If you'd have really been concerned for him after he was orphaned, we'd never be in this situation in the first place," the Visoki-Dvor rabbi said angrily, and looked at Sirka, waiting for her to back him up.

But not only did she not come to his defense, he saw her staring at her hunchback brother-in-law with reverence, as if he were an angel from heaven.

"I don't understand you at all, Zalia Ziskind," said the poorly spoken rosh yeshiva. "You should be pleased if the girl and their gang of Leftists abandon Marcus once we get him out of prison. By all means! Let them go, then he can come back to being Jewish."

"If he comes back to Judaism just because he lost his friends, it won't be worth anything. He'll never do it, anyway," Zalia Ziskind croaked.

Sirka's big, kind eyes lit up with anger. "All of Marcus's problems stem from his lack of friends. He didn't have friends as a child, and he didn't later when he was in yeshiva. Which makes it worse for him than others if he's left without friends again. You're not thinking about what's better for your nephew; you're thinking only about what's better for you."

The two brothers-in-law with bushy whiskers stared wide-eyed at her, as at an enemy from the inside, a traitor. Before, she'd still been in the category of a sotah who's given bitter water to drink, and it is uncertain whether she has or hasn't betrayed her husband. But now she was an open traitor of the family—she'd thrown off her mask. No wonder she'd been so adamant about coming along. She wanted to protect the child she'd raised, to make sure he wouldn't, heaven forbid, be wronged.

And if that weren't enough, Zalia Ziskind, with his crooked back and even more crooked mind, added commentary to her matronly plea. "In jail, Marcus will dream of his release and how he'll be able to accomplish what he wants in life. But if they free him now because he's supposedly insane, the whole world will become his prison. He'll never forgive me for testifying that he's insane."

"Yes, you say that! Just admit openly that having a communist and a prisoner for a son doesn't bother you, just as it didn't bother you to abandon the yeshiva and let it go to ruin," the rabbi brother-in-law exploded, storming toward the door.

"And Sirka, we'll talk to you separately. Your husband isn't a full rosh yeshiva yet, and he's never going to be," the rosh yeshiva brother-in-law threatened Sirka, and he, too, strode toward the door.

But at the last minute, they both remembered that good manners dictated they bid farewell to their hosts. So they called out, "Good day to you, Morehdalye Rabbi," furious with him, too, for keeping Zalia Ziskind as his assistant. That was why the world had a saying: "Show me your friends, and I'll show you who you are."

An oppressiveness hung in the air after the quarrel, like low clouds on a sultry day. Sirka was embarrassed that the Morehdalye rabbi and his family had witnessed the fight between her relatives. But Zalia Ziskind, the victim of their attack, remained humbly calm, as though he believed he'd rightfully earned these humiliations.

Later, when Sirka was alone with him for a little while in the beis din room, she tenderly tried to persuade him to travel to Bialystok and get to know his son's fiancée. "Chayenke Zilberberg comes from a respectable family and isn't an ardent revolutionary at all. When Marcus gets out of jail, she'll want a quiet, peaceful life with him."

Zalia Ziskind's face brightened; his eyes opened wide. Such pleasure coursed through him at hearing his sister-in-law's opinion of his son's fiancée. But simultaneously, he shook his head no, he would not go to Bialystok. "I sense that Marcus doesn't want me to meet his fiancée. Maybe because of old grievances, which could be exacerbated in his current situation, and maybe because he's ashamed of his hunchback father." He said these words without a shred of resentment.

Sirka turned even paler, looking like the last glimmer of an autumn dusk. By now she longed to be back in Visoki-Dvor with her husband, who, it was true, never took anything to heart, but also didn't tear her heart in two with his words. Zalia Ziskind had always suffered and was always bringing suffering to others. All his genius was applied in the service of suffering. Only because she was in another person's home and would soon be leaving did Sirka force herself not to burst into sobs or tear the hair from her head, as she'd done when her sister Zisse'le died so young, leaving an orphaned child. Already then, it seemed, her heart had foretold that her brother-in-law would remain a widower, plagued by depression, and Marcus would be unhappy all through his youth. And then—he'd land in prison for wanting to change the world, so that others wouldn't suffer as he did.

16

T HE DAYAN, TZADOK KADISH,* had never made peace with
the fact that the Morehdalyens had appointed him dayan and
made Sholem Shachne rabbi. For a short while, when it appeared as
though his grandson, Zindel, would become Sholem Shachne's son-
in-law and inherit his rabbinate, Tzadok's long-simmering resentment waned. But once that shidduch came to naught and Zindel left
for the other side of the ocean, Tzadok's grievances against the rabbi
grew. Worse, when Sholem Shachne brought over his old friend
from the Volozhin Yeshiva, Zalia Ziskind Luria, to be his assistant,
the dayan became a mortal enemy of both.

After Zalia Ziskind arrived, Tzadok had initially appealed for justice to the leaders and respectable townspeople of the community.
But he quickly realized that no one was on his side. They admonished him right to his face. "The rabbi, may he live long," they said,
"is sick, and you, Reb Tzadok, are not so young yourself and no
longer at your best. The town must have someone who can make
judgments when halacha questions come up. They must have someone to officiate at an arbitration, lecture on a page of Gemara, and
study a chapter of Chumash with the workingmen. It's a miracle from
heaven that we found ourselves someone like Zalia Ziskind, a man
the world regards as a genius and who considers himself a nothing; a
man willing to do everything for pennies or even for free; a man who
lives on breadcrumbs in a hole, while the rabbi and you, Reb Tzadok,

---

* In the Yiddish version, Grade refers to the dayan here as "Yakov Yosef Kadish,
or Reb Yekele, as he was called." From here until the end of the book, the dayan is
always called "Yekele." This is an obvious error, as the dayan was called "Tzadok"
in the first half of the book. Since the first half of this book in Yiddish had already
been prepared for publication, it's clear that Grade intended to keep the name
Tzadok. To prevent confusion, I changed the name Yekele, wherever it appears,
to Tzadok.—Translator's note

continue to take your full salaries. How can you stand against him?"
The dayan had nothing to say to that. And because everyone considered him in the wrong, his situation vexed him even more.

Everything Tzadok ate, he threw up. God could not have sent him
a worse punishment—he, a man with a reputation for being fanatical
about cleanliness. It was said of him that he'd stayed a widower for
fear that he might get a slob for a wife. Tzadok had always had stomach trouble, so his breakfast had always been stale challah dunked in
milk. Not a crumb ever stuck to his beard. He wore a clean frock coat
even on weekdays, a pristine white shirt with a white collar, and atop
his buttoned vest was the gleaming silver chain of a pocket watch.
The rooms in his home, too, sparkled from cleanliness. Not a single
book leaned in his bookcase, and there wasn't one dirty dish in the
kitchen. After much pleading by the townspeople, he'd finally hired
a maid, on the condition that if he didn't approve of her cleaning
methods, he would fire her immediately. But the maid didn't have
much to do. Even Tzadok's bed was unwrinkled in the mornings,
as though he had no body. Which was why, when he grew sick and
began to vomit his food onto the white napkin around his neck or
onto his clean beard, it was the greatest punishment anyone could
have thought up for him. And this was in addition to the pain from
his intestines.

As careful and neat as the dayan had been with his appearance and
clothing in his younger, healthy years, so careful was he not to say an
unnecessary word. Even during the quarrel over who should be rabbi
in Morehdalye—he or Sholem Shachne—he raised no objections to
his rival. Those who knew Tzadok knew that he never forgot any
slight done to him. And that when happy wrinkles gather at his eyes,
it is a sign that he's fuming, like water that ripples when it seethes.
But when he was young, these feelings didn't show on Tzadok's face,
unlike Sholem Shachne, on whose face all feelings and thoughts
could be easily read.

But since the dayan had become sick, he was no longer able to
hide his resentments. Townspeople came to visit and said, worriedly,
"Reb Tzadok, you must go see a doctor and spend some time in a
hospital, so they can figure out what's wrong with you. The rabbi,
may he live long, obeyed the doctor and stayed in the hospital until
he got better."

"I've been to the doctor," Tzadok said angrily. "I already went. And I'm not going to the hospital. It's as dirty as a public toilet. And don't compare me to the rabbi. You hear? The rabbi is mortally ill!"

The visitors thought the dayan might be even sicker than the rabbi, and certainly angrier. They stopped coming to visit. And when he realized he had no visitors anymore, he complained to his maid, "For forty years, they came to me every day with all their halachic questions, but now they can't be bothered to step in and ask how I'm doing."

The maid knew she had to pretend to be a deaf-mute, because no matter how she responded, the sick, angry man would only get angrier. Though Tzadok wasn't related to the maid, he felt comfortable enough to complain to her about the townspeople's lack of veneration. "Reb Sholem Shachne they call 'the Rav, may he live long; the Rebbe, may he live long,' but I'm called Reb Tzadok, plain and simple."

When he heard from his maid that Zalia Ziskind's son had been imprisoned, he cried triumphantly, "Of course! The Gemara says, *Bro kareh davueh.** The apple doesn't fall far from the tree. The odor of the father's heresy permeated the son, and he went a tiny bit further and became an open communist. Everyone is probably pitying Zalia Ziskind: Poor father! Poor him! But the object of their pity knows all too well how to come off as small and humble, how to sneak his way in and be a trespasser . . ." The pleasure of gossiping and mocking eased Tzadok's suffering for a while. "This Zalia Ziskind used to be known as a Torah genius. Yeshiva boys were awed by his tremendous Torah innovations. But there's nothing left of it in him anymore! Anyway, even if he'd once turned the heads of young students with his intricate pilpul, it doesn't necessarily follow that he's capable of making halachic judgments on treyf or kosher, or if something is chametz on Pesach."

Even in his younger years, the dayan couldn't stomach those distinguished scholars who spent their days debating controversial topics. Tzadok was not wise, nor very talented; instead, he sat for long hours and studied diligently, until he received rabbinical ordination. Years later, when he tried lecturing on a page of Gemara in the beis

---

* Literally, "A son is the knee of his father."

medrash, even ordinary townspeople turned up their noses, claiming his Torah was dry as pepper. So, along with everything else, Tzadok hated Zalia Ziskind for his former moniker, the "Dünaburg genius."

Old age, loneliness, and illness exacerbated the pain he felt over his only grandson, whom he'd raised and sent to be educated in Hebrew and secular studies. Yet when Zindel graduated from the Warsaw Tachkemoni, instead of returning to his grandfather, he'd moved overseas to Canada. He wasn't able to unite his separated parents there, as he'd dreamed, and he wrote less and less to his grandfather. Out of a sense of duty, perhaps, he occasionally asked his grandfather if he needed money, wrote that he was studying again and was close to becoming a Rabiner, and consoled his grandfather by telling him that when he got married, he and his wife would come and visit. He no longer mentioned his separated parents in his letters.

All the heartache and bitterness he felt toward his grandson the old dayan unleashed on the town. Morehdalye was to blame for everything! One day, Tzadok sent his maid to the rabbi to invite the rabbi's son, Dr. Naftali Hertz Katzenellenbogen, to come see him.

Even as a child, Naftali Hertz hadn't liked the dayan. He considered Tzadok a stickler and a bad-hearted Jew. If a boy was too playful in the beis medrash, Tzadok would reel him in with a smile sweet as honey and then pinch the boy's cheek with such force he'd be left breathless before bursting into sobs. Naftali Hertz remembered all the times a woman had come to his father's house crying that Reb Tzadok had declared the chicken she'd bought for Shabbos treyf. After the woman left, his father would seethe. "A Jew with such a brutal heart should not be allowed to be a dayan!" But now his parents asked him not to tarry but to go immediately to visit the old, sick dayan.

In Tzadok's bare, cold, meticulously cleaned home, the varnish on the walls, windowsills, and doors gleamed yellow-white, and in some spots the paint was peeling from age. But not one stain, not one dot, could be seen on the paint. The table, chairs, and bookcase looked sunken in an angry stupor. The clock on the wall ticked angrily, too, as though it concurred with Tzadok's complaints, old resentments that he'd dredged from his memory, as though they'd been stored away in mothballs and were now shaken out and aired. He grimaced simultaneously from the pain in his intestines and his resentment of Morehdalye. "Morehdalye is to blame for my grandson's move across the ocean," he said to Naftali Hertz, "leaving me here alone, all alone. Zindel saw how the town disrespected me. Me, his grandfather, the old-fashioned scholar. Naturally, he didn't want to be an old-fashioned rabbi himself. He went to study at Tachkemoni and then moved abroad. And even more blame lies with the Morehdalye rabbi."

"Really? My father is at fault?" Naftali Hertz asked.

"Yes, your father." Tzadok's face contorted, and he smiled furiously, the wrinkles beneath his eyes and on his hairy cheeks creasing. "Your younger sister didn't want a yeshiva boy cut from the old-fashioned cloth. That's why your father consented to taking my grandson, the Tachkemoni student. He studied with Zindel for his rabbinical ordination and promised him the rabbinate seat. But your father did it because he felt forced. He kept moaning the entire time that my grandson wasn't devout enough, wasn't enough of a scholar. Of course, this really bothered Zindel, and he started wondering if this was a suitable match for him after all. You're a graduate, too, a doctor, so you tell me: Is it bad if a Torah student has a diploma in foreign languages as well? Without it, a rabbi nowadays has no standing, neither with the government nor with the townspeople. But for your father, my Zindel was damaged goods because he was educated. What do you say to that?"

"The way I took it, Father's complaint was that your grandson hadn't informed him that he planned to move abroad with my sister after the wedding."

"But it's better to live in a country where Jews aren't persecuted and a rabbi's salary is paid in dollars, not Polish pennies. Isn't that right?" Tzadok stuck all the fingers of his hand into his beard. "I think you, too, like living abroad better than here."

Naftali Hertz remembered Tzadok's son, Beinush Kadish, as an unhappy, unfriendly man. He was like an angry animal that growls in its sleep or while it's gobbling its food, to keep anyone from coming close. He ended up leaving town, and later went to Canada, where he and his wife separated because she was too much for him. Zindel had done the same: abandoned his almost-fiancée the way his father had abandoned his mother. And he'd had the same attitude as his grandfather, too: angry at all of Morehdalye. *"A thread continues to weave," as the women liked to say,* Naftali Hertz thought, and laughed at himself. *I'm a Beinush, too, in my own manner, an unhappy, growling animal.* Nevertheless, he restrained himself from saying anything harsh to the old dayan. But he defended his father for not wanting a son-in-law who'd be a rabbi in America. "In America a rabbi isn't allowed to rebuke his congregants, and the people who have the say in the beis medrash are the wealthy ones, even if they're crude men. And the rabbis there try to get rich. Zindel might very well have become a Rabiner in a temple where men and women sit together and daven from a truncated siddur—and this is treyf as pork for an Orthodox rabbi. Besides, Zindel never seemed certain that he wanted my sister as his bride at all."

"Not true! It was your sister who was crumbling. She was unsure if she wanted him as her groom." Tzadok's eyes glowed red and fiery under his thick eyebrows and lashes. "That my grandson wanted to become a rabbi in a half-goyish temple isn't true either. He promised me he'd become a rabbi in our kind of synagogue, and he's keeping his promise. My enemies made up a lie about me, that I'm one of those disguised maskilim. Are you and your brothers better than my grandson? None of you wanted to be religious functionaries at all, not even enlightened Rabiners."

"You're a man of faith, Reb Tzadok. You believe that a person's match is a matter of destiny, so don't be upset that nothing came of the relationship between my sister and your grandson. It's a sign they weren't meant to be a couple." Naftali Hertz was losing his last bit of patience for the fussy old man. But he wanted to accommodate his parents' request that he be gentle and soft with him, console him. "Zindel will no doubt write you soon to say he's found a match, just as my sister Bluma Rivtcha has found one. She's coming here with her fiancé, and they're staying over Pesach."

Naftali Hertz soon regretted these words. Why had he chattered on about his sister and her fiancé? At first, Tzadok sneered and said, "Mazel tov to you! Your sister should have gone under the chuppah a long time ago. I'm curious to know who her groom is!" But suddenly, he burst out crying, and a thick stream of tears soaked through his hairy face and long beard. He hiccupped and whimpered, and Naftali Hertz could barely hear what he was saying. His complaint was to God: "First, my only son, Beinush, deserted me, left me to my grief and anguish. And instead of at least bringing me joy from a distance, I had to hear that Beinush and his wife separated. Then, I was left with my one and only grandchild. But he went away, too, leaving me here alone like a stone in the field."

When he stopped crying, Tzadok looked even sadder. He sat there wordless, motionless, with the silence of a denuded stretch of forest where only a single stump is left rotting, its roots down in the earth and only a bit protruding upward.

What had come as such a surprise to the old dayan hadn't been as surprising for Bluma Rivtcha's parents. All winter, their daughter had written home that she'd be coming to visit as soon as she graduated from the Vilna school of nursing. Later, Bluma Rivtcha had let them know that she'd already passed the most important exams and would be home soon. She added, however, that it was a pity to be leaving Vilna, for she wouldn't be able to have the seder at the same house she'd been at the year before, when she hadn't come home for Pesach. Why this house was so dear to her and why it was a pity not to be there, she would tell her parents when she arrived home.

"I know why!" Henna'le cried out. "She's seeing a boy from that house."

"What ideas the woman has!" the rabbi said, shrugging.

But a few days later, another letter arrived. "I don't want to hide this from you anymore," Bluma Rivtcha wrote. "I've been seeing a boy for over a year already. He is a former yeshiva student, and I'm going to marry him. Indeed, it was his mother's seder that I attended last year. Naturally, I'll be coming to Morehdalye without him."

The rabbi was astounded at his wife's shrewdness. She, meanwhile, was surprised her scholarly husband hadn't thought of it. Sholem Shachne—instead of getting riled up as he had years ago when his older daughter, Tilza, had dared fantasize of picking a husband for herself—smiled, pleased. "At least Bluma Rivtcha has let us know about her fiancé. Her brother Bentzion kept his secret from us. We had to find out from others." The rabbi said this to his wife, but Naftali Hertz heard and understood his father's unsaid words: he, their oldest son, carried even more secrets than Bentzion.

"Bluma Rivtcha writes that her fiancé is a former yeshiva boy, but what he does now she doesn't say," the rabbi added, sounding curious.

"Right—why doesn't she say what he does now?" Henna'le said, even more curious.

Naftali Hertz joined the conversation. "There's no such thing as a *former* yeshiva boy. Once you're a yeshiva boy, you're always a yeshiva boy, even if you convert and eat lard and soups full of pork."

He uttered these words mockingly and with apparent self-hatred. Sholem Shachne listened to his son with an expression of ridicule and bitterness, but he didn't look at Naftali Hertz, nor respond with a single word. Father and son were eating at the table, and Henna'le was puttering around the kitchen. Eventually, Sholem Shachne recited the after-meal blessing, covering his eyes with his hand. All through the recitation, he saw before his covered eyes the image of the naked trees outside his window, as though they were reflected on the nape of his neck. Against the charcoal backdrop of a low, wide sky, the bark and crowns of trees stood out in relief, already free of snow, their stiff, bare black branches mired in mute rigidity. The rabbi felt them on his back and in his brain, as if they were engraved there, as if they knew his secret fear—that the lifeblood in him was growing steadily weaker. Only God knew how long he'd be worthy of seeing the trees outside his windows.

Sholem Shachne removed his hand, and standing from the table, he said, "I'm going to write Bluma Rivtcha immediately and tell her to bring along her groom for Pesach. You should add a few lines to the letter, too. Write that you absolutely demand it."

The rabbi and rebbetzin understood each other instinctively this time. Without having to say a word, they both realized that if they didn't want to lose this daughter, they must make her fiancé feel welcome, even before the marriage.

17

EARLY IN NISSAN, when Bluma Rivtcha and her fiancé arrived in Morehdalye, the sky had already lifted, shining blue and clear. From the nearby Narev wafted a fragrance of fresh water and stale foliage—last year's withered plants, strewn along the length of the riverbank. The sound of chirping birds was not yet audible, but somewhere children were playing, and their happy voices rang out. The town was preparing for Pesach, cleaning their houses, baking matzoh, purifying pots, and buying products for the holiday. But Henna'le lagged behind the other housewives, too busy awaiting the arrival of her younger daughter and her fiancé.

The rabbi, too, had abandoned his regular routine, guarding the town from chametz with less dedication than in years past. Instead, his assistant, Zalia Ziskind, trudged through the mud from purveyor to purveyor and oversaw the matzoh kneaders, rollers, perforators, and bakers, making sure they were careful not to let the dough leaven. No one in town expected their ailing rabbi to attend to such a task. But neither did he have the patience for the women who came in asking which foods were allowed to be used. In his wool tallis katan—ironed at the corners in the shape of a heart—Sholem Shachne meandered around the room, stroking the lapels of his Shabbos kapoteh and staring out the window in hopes of spotting the guests from Vilna. Naftali Hertz was home, too, and he joined his father in staring out the window, thinking about how the two of them had hardly spoken at all of late.

Suddenly, the rabbi called out, "Henna'le! They're here, thank God!" Through the window you could see the coachman who helped passengers off the train drawing nearer to the rabbi's house. Sholem Shachne and Henna'le became so excited they didn't notice Naftali Hertz backing out of the beis din room.

He passed through the corridor, strode into his room, and locked the door behind him. "What am I doing here?" he muttered to himself. "I'm a stranger in my own family. A stranger! My guts are twisting inside me. I'm disgusted at my own falseness. Even Father is getting worse from the stress of having to pretend he doesn't notice. Every day he speaks less to me and grows more distant. Maybe he wouldn't be so suspicious, but he can see I don't send or receive any letters from home. And really, why would Annelyse write me? I left home supposedly for a month, and I've already been here almost three. I'll lose my job, too. And if Annelyse felt I was happy with her, she wouldn't have gone and looked for another boyfriend. At the beginning of our relationship, I'd told her that I wasn't judgmental, that I was indifferent to religious and national origins, only for her to discover that not only was I not indifferent, I was *enslaved* to my origins, to the opinions and customs of my grandparents. And she saw that I was unhappy with her, with our son, with our home. Of course, she started looking for happiness among her own people. How are the Swiss any worse than me?"

He cursed the burden of his inheritance more than ever now. How could he live with it! Everyone who had saved themselves during the war had found a haven in tranquil, magnificent Switzerland, so he, too, had planted himself among the Swiss mountains. *Good riddance to this business!* he'd thought. He did not yet know, then, that Judaism isn't the sort of business you could be rid of. The struggle raging inside him now, he realized, was owed to his fury with himself. Once again, he'd have to put up an act, this time with his younger sister. Still, he had to go out and greet her. When he'd gone abroad, Bluma Rivtcha had still been a child, and he hadn't seen her since. She'd been at school in Vilna during his last visit.

He stepped toward the door of his room just as someone knocked on it. "Naftali Hertz! Naftali Hertz! It's Bluma Rivtcha. Are you sleeping?" a woman's voice sang out.

He opened the door, and his sister grabbed him and kissed him. Behind Bluma Rivtcha stood his mother, who gestured to Naftali Hertz to be pleasant to Bluma Rivtcha and her fiancé.

"This is Khlavneh Yeshurin," his sister said, introducing the young man at her side.

Naftali Hertz scrutinized the boy even before he'd properly looked at his sister. He didn't seem like a former Gemara student at all. Somewhat shorter than average, he had the broad shoulders of a messenger boy. He was portly, with a heavy gait and a pale, broad face like a full moon. Through his large glasses peeked a pair of wistful blue eyes. He had thin blond hair, a high, deeply wrinkled forehead, big ears, and a small mouth with somewhat childlike lips. His face kept turning foggy beneath his vague, confused smile. He wore a new navy suit, though its cut was inelegant. His hat he wore like a businessman, not tilted to the side like a dandy, nor pushed back to his nape, the way yeshiva boys wore them. For a boy with such a robust appearance, his hands seemed too refined, with short, soft fingers, the kind called "ladies' hands," but which can also be pressed into fists. If the conversation interested him, he listened with a partly open mouth and the awed look of a child. He stared with astonishment at the large bookcase in the rabbi's house. And he gazed in wonder at the tall rabbi and stooped rebbetzin, and at the old, bare willows outside the window, as though he'd already seen these same trees somewhere and was wondering: *When had these trees managed to transplant themselves outside the rabbi's window?* But when he noticed the family's eyes on him, appraising him, his expression turned cross and he gave his body a sort of shimmy, shaking off their knowing looks like a prickly fir shaking off raindrops.

"How are you doing, Bluma Rivtcha?" Naftali Hertz asked with a forced smile. He had seen his sister eyeing him, probing him. "You're due a mazel tov," he added. "I think you got your diploma already?"

"Yes, I graduated from the school of nursing," his sister replied, checking her tone to keep from showing too much pride, as well as her happiness that she'd now be able to support herself.

Bluma Rivtcha fluttered about, aflame and confused. She wanted to talk to her brother, whom she hardly knew. And she burned with curiosity, tinged with fear, wondering whether the family liked her fiancé and if he was making a good impression. She didn't want her parents to notice how badly she wanted them to like him, so like a bird polishing its feathers and flapping its wings, she kept tossing her short black hair and walking here and there on her high heels, as though she wanted to make sure nothing had changed in the house, everything had remained the same. Her onyx, Mongolian-slitted eyes narrowed and squinted. Sparks of light trembled on her lashes, like early morning dew on a web of leaves. Though she was round and chubby, her movements were agile, nimble. She kept moving deliberately close to her fiancé, as if to remind her family that she wasn't taller than him, even in her high heels; and without her heels, she was certainly shorter. "Oh, it's so good to be home!" she said, and her face shone with festive excitement. She didn't have to add that the next time she came back, she would already be married. Her parents understood that on their own. Her beige wool jacket and skirt creased around the curves of her body, and her stiff breasts stood out against her snow-white blouse, like a raised, long-legged bird from a leafy hiding place.

In the meantime, Khlavneh continued to scan the bookcase in the beis din room. He thumbed through the spines of the *Shas*, the *Shulchan Aruch*, the Midrashim, the *Sh'aylos U'Tshuvos*, and then pulled out a book with a green linen cover and gold letters on a dark brown case: it was a *Shiteh M'kubetzes*. He expertly opened the heavy volume and began to riffle through it.

Suddenly, he noticed the rabbi near him, looking over his shoulder at the open sefer. Apparently, he wanted to see what interested Khlavneh. Since Khlavneh's hands were occupied, holding the sefer with one, leafing through it with the other, he nodded toward the bookshelves.

"You have a world of seforim. When I was studying in yeshiva, I was dying to have my own *Shiteh M'kubetzes*, but I didn't have the money to buy such an expensive sefer." He spoke casually, without the posturing of conspicuous politeness and graciousness.

"Wasn't there a *Shiteh M'kubetzes* in your yeshiva?" the rabbi asked.

The young man replied instantly: "Of course there was. But I was studying diligently at the time, in yeshiva during the day and in my lodgings at night. Taking a Gemara to my lodgings was permitted, because there were plenty of Gemaras in the beis medrash. But there was only one *Shiteh M'kubetzes*, and the other yeshiva boys used it, too."

Absorbed by his conversation with the rabbi, Khlavneh didn't notice that Bluma Rivtcha, her mother, and her brother were all standing in a corner of the large room, listening.

"Out of all the commentaries, why were you interested in buying the *Shiteh M'Kubetzes* in particular?" the rabbi asked.

Khlavneh replied confidently, loudly, "Because it lists the positions of many Rishonim: Rabeinu Chananal, the Rav'ad, the Ramban, the Rashba, the Ritba. And the sefer also provides commentary on many tractates."

"Well, by now you can probably afford to buy a *Shiteh M'kubetzes.*" The rabbi smiled.

"I don't study Gemara anymore now, so why would I need to know the commentators' positions?" Khlavneh shrugged and returned the sefer to its place.

Sholem Shachne asked nothing further, but held his smile. He felt like adding, pretending to tease: "You're right. If you don't open a Gemara, you don't need a *Shiteh M'kubetzes.* But why, pray tell, do you never open a Gemara, you sheigetz?" Yet not only did he not censure his guest, he went on peering brightly and warmly through his glasses at him, as though he were pleased with the boy's candid, honest reply.

But Naftali Hertz didn't like the boy, right from his first impression. Naftali Hertz never forgot that when he'd fled abroad to study, he didn't have the courage to tell the truth. Instead, he lied to everyone, claiming he was just moving to another yeshiva, the same way he was now lying about his wife and son. Marcus Luria had also been unable to sever himself completely from the beis medrash, until he'd leaped knowingly toward the communists, right into jail. *One's ancestry*, Naftali Hertz mused, *with all its roots and branches, keeps rabbinical children entangled with their source, so that they cannot tear themselves free.* But this Khlavneh Yeshurin, former yeshiva boy from Vilna, whom his sister had brought with her, seemed to be kneaded from a different dough. He didn't lack audacity. Naftali Hertz very much wanted to question his sister about her fiancé, who spoke so loudly and freely, and with such certainty—not at all like the typical fiancé visiting his bride's home for the first time, trying hard to make a good impression. The rabbi and rebbetzin, too, wanted to speak to their daughter alone. Realizing this, Bluma Rivtcha led Khlavneh to the bedroom that had been prepared for him, Bentzion's and Refael'ke's old bedroom. She told him to unpack their suitcase and then have a wash. "The kitchen is on the right side of the corridor, and the sink is there."

The moment she returned to her parents, her father asked, "You wrote that your fiancé used to be a yeshiva boy. And what does he do now?" Since the young man wasn't a ben-torah, it didn't make much of a difference to Sholem Shachne what kind of job he had, but when he saw Bluma Rivtcha hesitate to answer, he repeated his question anxiously. "What does he do now?"

Her mother sounded even more anxious. "Tell us, already. Tell us what he does."

"He's a writer," Bluma Rivtcha said in a forced tone. She had expressly left this bit of information out of her letters to her parents, knowing how distressed it would make them. And she hadn't been mistaken. Her father gave her a look, then turned his gaze to his wife, his son, and back to her. No, she wasn't making a joke. This meant he wasn't a young man who'd left the Gemara and gone into business, or had become a bookkeeper, or was studying to be a doctor. A writer? Was he one of those people who wrote that there was no God and made a mockery of Judaism? Maybe he was even one of those who wrote obscenities in the newspapers? Henna'le looked dejected, too. From what she'd heard, writers were drunks, always swapping wives and creating all kinds of scandals.

"What books has he published?" Henna'le asked. "What are the names?"

"He hasn't published any yet." Bluma Rivtcha flushed scarlet, knowing how confusing her answer would be to her parents. "About a year or two ago, Khlavneh published his first poems. He's a poet."

The rabbi stood there, head bowed, and muttered, "A poet? First poems? In Torah learning he was already up to studying the *Shiteh M'kubetzes*, but now he's publishing little poems, for only a year!" Raising his head, he called out to his rebbetzin, "You hear this, Henna'le?" and in this question lay all he'd left unsaid: "Our daughter didn't want to become a rebbetzin, so we supported her when she went to study nursing in Vilna. She finally graduated, and look what she came back with: a boy who threw away the Torah and publishes little poems . . ."

BLUMA RIVTCHA'S EARS BURNED in anger, and tears hung in her eyes. She wanted to both fight and cry, but she controlled herself. She hadn't seen her parents in a long time, and Father was sick and not allowed to become agitated. Also, Khlavneh might hear them fighting and think her parents were unhappy about him. Bluma Rivtcha, hands on her hips, spoke quietly, a smile twitching on her lips. "Father, Mother, you probably think a poet is someone who only writes songs and rhymes. But a poet is also the kind of person who feels and thinks differently, sees things differently, expresses himself differently. And I trust Khlavneh. I have no doubt that just as he excelled at Torah learning, he'll excel at writing poetry, so much so he'll be able to make a living from it. And until then, we'll live off my earnings. I have a position waiting for me in Vilna, a nurse's job at Mishmeres Cholim."

"How old is he?" her father asked.

"He's twenty-four." Again, Bluma Rivtcha flushed.

"He looks older than you, and he's actually younger," her father murmured, and his face looked even more despondent.

"So what if the bride is three years older than the groom?" Henna'le interjected.

"Your poet writes in Hebrew, surely," Naftali Hertz began, but his sister rushed in to correct him.

"No, in Yiddish. Khlavneh writes only in Yiddish, just like the other young poets in Vilna."

So astounded was her brother that he couldn't remember what he'd intended to say. He stood there with a vacant expression on his face, as if he'd been deafened by a blow to the head. Gradually, he recovered. With no small degree of revulsion, he asked, "He writes in Yiddish? In jargon? You'll have a jargon writer for a husband?"

Bluma Rivtcha looked dumbfounded. "Not a jargon writer. A Yiddish writer. Why do you find this so upsetting?"

Her father agreed. "What difference does it make if he writes in Yiddish or in modern Hebrew? Modern Hebrew is *Ivrit*, not *lashon kodesh*. Makes no difference which language a person writes in; the important thing is *what* he writes. Even the Shema, the *Hashem elokeinu Hashem echad*, is allowed to be said in any language."

But Naftali Hertz could not be persuaded. His astonishment and anger at his sister grew with each passing minute. It seemed to him she was spitting in the face of the entire pedigreed rabbinical Katzenellenbogen family. Spitting in *his* face for all the years he'd spent in the yeshivas of Torah and Haskalah, all the years he'd studied at the University in Bern. At home in Switzerland, he spoke solely in German, and only here at his parents' did he speak in this vulgar tongue, the way everyone in town did. But to have a jargon writer as his brother-in-law? Naftali Hertz burst out laughing in bitterness. A jargon boy for a brother-in-law! He wiped the nonexistent sweat from his shiny, but dry, forehead.

Seeing how he was carrying on, his mother said, "What? It's not as if your sister brought a goy into the house."

"A goy?" Naftali Hertz creased his dry, shiny forehead and blinked. Later, he marveled that he'd had the strength to restrain himself from crying out, "Goyim can be refined, educated people. My wife is a goy, too. But a jargon boy is a common person, an ignoramus, a boor." He refrained from saying this but stared in bewilderment at his parents and sister, who didn't understand the humiliation they were taking upon themselves.

Bluma Rivtcha, too, gaped at her brother, her astonishment growing. *Was this what he'd studied so much for in yeshiva and university? To have such prejudices? What right did he have to offer his opinion at all? He'd never concerned himself with his siblings or parents!* Even greater than Bluma Rivtcha's anger was her heartache. She was so sad that she wouldn't be able to hug and kiss her brother, to talk and talk, enough to make up for all the years she'd thought of him and heard all about him. On her way to Morehdalye, she'd imagined she was bringing her parents their future son-in-law and would meet a recently discovered brother. *Such joy! Such luck*, she'd thought. *Naftali Hertz, the doctor and philosopher, would understand Khlavneh the poet better than other people could.*

As if Naftali Hertz had heard her daydreams and wanted to mock them, he said, with an angry sneer, "You wrote he's a former yeshiva boy, and I said to Mother and Father that there's no such thing as a former yeshiva boy. You stay one forever. But your Khlavneh doesn't look like a real yeshiva boy to me. A yeshiva boy who becomes a writer would write in Hebrew."

"I get it now. Khlavneh simply studied in a yeshiva; he was never a true yeshiva boy. *You* were the real yeshiva boy, and you still are, even with your doctor title and your home abroad!" his sister shouted, laughter on her fresh lips and tears in her voice, as though her voice were a small, pure waterfall, rushing over stones. Bluma Rivtcha whirled around to her parents accusingly—why were they not saying anything?—turned on her high heels, and stalked off toward Khlavneh.

She found him standing at a wall mirror, shaving. When they'd left for Morehdalye, she warned him not to remove his hat at her parents' house. "And what about shaving?" he'd asked. "Shaving is a much bigger sin than standing with a bare head." But Bluma Rivtcha had told him he was allowed to shave, because she couldn't kiss him when his face was prickly. Now, bosom heaving, filled with fury at her brother, she pressed against Khlavneh and threw her arms around him. "I'll cut myself with the razor," he muttered. He washed and dried his face, then asked her how her parents liked him.

"They like you very much." She placed her flaming cheek against his cool, freshly shaven face. "Give me a kiss," she begged, as though she needed a strong drink to recover. Soon their bodies were wrapped round each other, like two roots entangled. Their meshed lips became ever stickier, like tar trickling down the bark of a tree on a hot summer day.

"Have you told them already that I'm a writer?" he said, tearing his lips from hers for a second.

"Told them!" And her squinty eyes clouded over in sweet intoxication.

"And what did your parents say to it? Do they want a Yiddish poet as a son-in-law?"

Instead of replying, Bluma Rivtcha clasped him tighter to her breast, as though her desire for him were the best proof that her parents wanted him as a son-in-law. But he also wanted to know what her brother had said. Bluma Rivtcha was silent, as if her rampant desire had distracted her from his question. But then she changed her mind, realizing she had to prepare Khlavneh for her brother's attitude.

"My brother isn't pleased that you're a Yiddish poet and not a Hebrew one. But don't pay him any mind. My father does like you, right from his first meeting with you. Later, he'll like you even more."

Though this made him uneasy, Khlavneh replied, "I'm not very impressed with your brother, either. Let's go back in with your parents. It's not appropriate for us to be alone, away from them for so long." He pulled Bluma Rivtcha by her hand.

"You're a yeshiva boy, just like my brother," Bluma Rivtcha said petulantly. "Here at home, everything is appropriate." Bluma Rivtcha tugged him back into the small bedroom, her eyes twinkling with bliss, like windows on which the sun rises and sets.

On the bedroom wall hung a picture that Refael'ke had put up when the room was still his: a large photograph of a group of guards in Palestine, from long ago. The guards were young, black-bearded men, wearing striped robes and turbans or astrakhan fur hats, ribbons across their chests, armed with rifles, long swords, and revolvers. It seemed to Khlavneh that they were watching him and his fiancée kiss and were winking at him: *That's good! Don't be stingy!* But on the same wall hung a different picture of a Talmudic scholar, a relative—perhaps distant, perhaps close—of the Katzenellenbogens: an old man with a tender face, a sparse, silver beard, and pious eyes. He looked with pity at the sinning couple, entangled with each other. Khlavneh imagined he heard the old silvery man sighing: "Ay, children, children! Is this permitted? Are you husband and wife yet? Even when you *are* married, this isn't permitted just for pleasure's sake, but to fulfill the commandment of 'Be fruitful and multiply.'"

18

I<small>N A SNOW-WHITE NURSE'S COAT</small> and sailboat-like bonnet, Bluma Rivtcha leaned over the dayan Reb Tzadok and gave him a shot to dull his pain. She covered him with the blanket and assured him he would soon fall asleep. His pain, along with his constant bitterness, abated for a while. Tzadok's gaunt hands, yellow, wrinkled, and thick with white hair, continued to tremble for a minute on the blanket. Then they came to a rest. With one cheek pressed to the pillow, the old man dozed off, his knotted beard drooping down feebly.

The nurse gazed through the window at a young, slender tree, its branches naked, still shaking from cold in these early spring days. The tree, an aspen with a velvety grayish-silver bark, rocked happily in the light breeze, as if letting Bluma Rivtcha know that regardless of what happened to the sick patient, she, the aspen, would soon burst into rosy bloom. "If you look around," the aspen was saying, "you'll see that wherever the snow has been cleared, fresh green grass is peeking out. No need for you to suffer along with your patient so much. You've come here to Father and Mother, after all, and brought your fiancé." But Bluma Rivtcha pretended not to hear what the tree outside the window was babbling. She turned to the woman who stood at her side watching her work. "I'm going home now," Bluma Rivtcha said. "I'll come back at three."

"Go and come in good health. God first, then you, Bluma Rivtcha'le," the dayan's maid, Chaya Sarah, replied.

Chaya Sarah was a bulky woman with a clunky gait, like a big trained animal who's learned to stand on its hind legs and walk like a human. But she had bright, kind eyes. Nobody besides her would have tolerated the fussy Tzadok. She swallowed in silence each time the old dayan tossed himself about, shaking and shouting. He was sick, poor thing, very sick.

The morning after Bluma Rivtcha arrived home, she'd showed up at the sick dayan's house. At first, Tzadok didn't recognize her. Then he became confused and croaked out that he wasn't to blame that the relationship between her and Zindel had come to nothing. Nowadays, grandchildren didn't ask their grandfathers for their opinion.

"I have no complaints against your grandson, and never did. And I certainly have no complaints against you. I'm here simply because I want to help you. My brother Naftali Hertz says you asked about me. So I came. But you must do everything I tell you to do," she said strictly, squinting her narrow eyes.

With each passing day, Tzadok became more emaciated. He suffered from constant stomach pain and had lately seen blood in his stool. He threw up his food, his voice grew raspy, and he developed a cough. He hurled this cough from his intestines with such fury it sounded like a desolate cry from a deep and winding cave, a cry that crumbles when it hits the open air and echoes like a demon's cackle. But no matter how much Tzadok tossed and turned on his bed from pain, he refused to go to the hospital again for a checkup. Into his pillow he moaned that he'd already been to the hospital, and it was as dirty as the communal outhouse. He wanted to return his soul to God in a clean bed.

But when Bluma Rivtcha arrived, she succeeded in convincing him. "Without a doctor," she explained, "I don't know how to help you."

Tzadok let himself be taken to the hospital, his eyes tightly squeezed together as though he were martyring himself for God's sake.

For the one week the dayan lay in the hospital, the rabbi's daughter wasn't allowed to look after him, because the hospital had their own nurses and doctors. As obsessed as the dayan was with cleanliness, he forgot all about it in the hospital, such pain did he suffer there. With large electric lamps they illuminated his gaunt, waxy body, pushed drops into the openings from which he urinated and passed stool, stabbed him with needles, and drew his blood. The two doctors, both Poles, prodded and turned him unceremoniously, the way he had ripped apart the entrails of the chickens that women brought him to make sure they were kosher.

One doctor was of average height, with a fat, shiny face, a wreath of white hair around his bald spot, and oily, mellow, tired eyes. He looked like a big round lobster with multiple claws and tentacles, while the other doctor, a tall goy with short, prickly hair and stiff gray whiskers, resembled a long, thin fish. Both doctors had orderlies milling about them, Christian women in white aprons, with high bosoms and strong working hands. Though they treated the old rabbi more gently than other Jewish patients, they gave off a whiff of antisemitism, like the odor of raw meat at a butcher.

A third doctor worked even more frequently and longer with Tzadok. He was a young man with a long, handsome face, chiseled as if from stone, with a thick tousled head of hair and black Roma eyes. The dayan would have sworn on a Torah scroll that this young doctor was a Jew, but when Tzadok spoke to him in Yiddish, the Roma doctor stared at him with such eyes it seemed he was hearing this language for the first time in his life and the odd sounds made him want to laugh. Apparently, this doctor was a fresh graduate who needed the practice, because he kept turning and poking the old man. The groaning Tzadok let himself be poked, but he mentally took revenge on his torturer by comparing him to King David's rebellious son, Absalom, who was hung from a tree by his long pretty hair. Eventually, the young, handsome doctor called Fräulein Katzenellenbogen into his office and told her to take the patient home. There was nothing they could do. He gave her painkillers, which she could administer to ease his suffering until he passed.

Bluma Rivtcha left the doctor's office with her head bowed, so that no one would see her flushed face. She hadn't yet become accustomed to what she'd seen in the Vilna hospitals. With the patients themselves, some of the doctors were still careful about discussing their illnesses. But behind the patients' backs, the doctors spoke of them with such coldness and indifference, as if they were discussing the chemical elements. Or mechanical constructions. And this young doctor in the Morehdalye district hospital had started even earlier than the others, perhaps because he felt that the old man had already lived enough, or because he was bored of his work at this small hospital. Perhaps, too, he wanted to see what impression he made on Bluma Rivtcha, whether his handsomeness would throw her off. She hadn't yet started her career. She knew she would still have battles to wage. *Let this resident doctor not think I'm one of those night-shift nurses who serves as a doctor's concubine.*

The Morehdalyens didn't have to ask the rabbi's daughter about Tzadok's sickness. They had perceived what was happening to him. Because he was constantly recollecting more and more wrongs the community had done him in the past, they quipped: "Is it any wonder that he's so angry? He has that sickness! As the verse says, '*Rak rah kol hayom,*' Only the bad, all the time." And indeed, the old man's pain had awoken hardened memories in him the way a wind stirs a static body of water, bringing skeins of grass and debris swimming up to its surface.

Tzadok began to recall grievances and resentments that had lain dormant as stones for years beneath his heart, even resentments he'd already forgotten about. Amid his recollections, the memory of his wife swam up, too, his wife who for more than a quarter century had been lying in the Morehdalye cemetery. *Certainly, Sima was a woman of valor,* he thought. *The dishes and every corner of the house used to sparkle. But how could a woman have such large hands and such a wide, heavy body? And her laugh! She laughed too much and too loudly. She befriended everyone as if they were her equal and saved all her complaints for me, for ruling so strictly when people came with halachic questions.* "It's not like you're one of those fanatics," Sima would tell him. "You hate Jews with messy tzitzis or tangled beards and peyes. You like to read newspapers and can't bear preachers who sing the tune of eternal damnation, fire and brimstone. But to the questions brought to you, you almost always answer: *Treyf! Treyf!* Is it any wonder the Morehdalye women would rather go to Sholem Shachne than you?"

Oh, he would never forgive her for this! Her words implied that Morehdalye had chosen well and wisely when they'd picked Sholem Shachne over him as their rabbi. Though Sima had long since gone over to the World of Truth, he would never forgive her, never! And what had been driving her to hilarity all the time? What had she been so happy about? But Beinush, his son, was the opposite of his mother. He avoided others and remained in a state of perpetual disgruntlement. Whenever Sima spoke about their son, her laughter stopped. "The apple doesn't fall far from the tree," she used to tell him. "Beinush takes after you."

"Did you say something, Reb Tzadok? Are you thirsty? Do you want a drink?" Chaya Sarah asked, bending over the patient. She'd been sitting at his bedside, watching over him, until Bluma Rivtcha would return.

"Me?" The sick man raised his head and squinted at the woman as if through a fog. "I don't say anything anymore." And his head fell back onto the pillow.

He didn't like Chaya Sarah. True, she was clean and pious. But when he writhed in agony, she stood there like a dimwit and didn't know how to alleviate his pain. Barely moved, the turtle! But though Tzadok had just said, "I don't say anything anymore," he now wanted to say something, something he couldn't say to the rabbi's daughter. Straining, he lifted his head from the pillow and rasped, "The rabbi, Bluma Rivtcha's father, is sicker than me. Much sicker."

This wasn't the first time Chaya Sarah had heard this refrain, and she couldn't understand what kind of consolation it could be to Tzadok that the rabbi was sicker. But she would not bring this up to him. Again, she praised and blessed the rabbi's daughter, who was easing his pain, and refused even to take money for the injections she purchased. "Bluma Rivtcha hasn't seen her parents for quite some time, but still, she leaves them, her fiancé, and her brother, to come here a few times a day."

The old dayan actually agreed, but he couldn't stand Chaya Sarah's sharp tongue. He replied angrily, "I've heard you say this already. Of course, she's a fine girl and a devoted daughter. That's why she wants to right her father's wrongs against me, for all these years he's the rabbi here and me the dayan."

Again, Tzadok's mind wandered. Now he thought about his only son, Beinush, in Canada. Ah, yet again it was one's own who caused pain! The rabbi's oldest son had studied philosophy and was referred to as "Doctor Katzenellenbogen," but his Beinush had been only a schoolteacher in a talmud torah, first in Morehdalye and then in Bialystok. And in Canada, he'd learned how to fill prescriptions. A pharmacist, that's what he was, nothing more. And really, would a son of a dayan aspire to anything greater?

It had always been a source of wonder to Tzadok that his son had chosen a wife who was similar to his dead mother—tall, broad, always laughing, a woman who liked to make a racket, a woman who wanted to enjoy life. A person with a large appetite for worldly pleasures isn't usually a serious person by nature. Such a person doesn't usually want to think deeply about things. Indeed, it hadn't worked out between Beinush and his wife, Shterke Teitelbaum. But as long as they'd lived in Morehdalye and Bialystok, they stayed married. Only in Canada did they separate, because Shterke couldn't forgive him for not allowing her to bring along their little son. Instead, they'd left Zindel with him, his grandfather.

The old man sunk deeper into a trance, as though his intestines were swampy phlegm and he was drowning inside himself. He did not feel his freckles skipping around his face, nor his once silky, now sticky, beard swirling like a wave. And yet, he clearly heard his thoughts burrowing and clambering around in his brain. Inside him, someone was once again thinking about his deceased wife, about his son and daughter-in-law and their separation. Apparently, Beinush had loved his mother and missed her. Why else would he have chosen a wife so similar to her? But then, why had he separated from this wife? In his letter, Beinush had written that Shterke fought with him and kept accusing him: "Your father doesn't get along with anyone, and you avoid people, too. That's why you moved from Morehdalye to Bialystok and then to Canada, where no one knows you. And that's why you didn't let me bring my little son. Because a child requires attention. A child crawls on your lap, and you hate to have your lap crawled on." Beinush had written this as proof of what a witch Shterke had become, forcing him to divorce her. But perhaps, thought Tzadok, Shterke wasn't entirely wrong.

The old man began to cry in the middle of his nap, and his crying woke him. Though he didn't hold Chaya Sarah, the silly maid, in high regard, he was pleased that she was always willing to listen. And so, he sometimes launched into long speeches about how much he'd endured when his only son, Beinush, had left with his wife for the other side of the ocean and abandoned him here alone with the Sodomites of Morehdalye. He'd been left with only one consolation—his grandson, Zindel. "What more can you do for your own flesh and blood than what I did for Zindel? I clothed him in the nicest clothing, fed him birds' milk, let him study Torah and secular studies at Warsaw's Tachkemoni—and all this out of my meager salary. I didn't demand a groschen from my son in Canada to support his own child. In fact, I was happy in my heart. I thought that if I was my grandson's only provider, he wouldn't abandon me in my old age. But just like his father, Zindel didn't want to stay in Morehdalye. He even rejected the shidduch with Bluma Rivtcha, so long as he could leave here. And how many nice excuses he had! He wants to be in a community where a rabbi can be educated without being accused of heresy. He wants to spread Judaism on the other side of the ocean. He wants to unite his separated parents and bring his grandfather over there, too. Well, look! See how he's bringing me there!" The old man sniveled like a beaten child who has no strength left to cry.

Chaya Sarah tried to console him. "Don't cry, Reb Tzadok, don't cry. Bluma Rivtcha will come soon and give you an injection, and the two of us will change the linen on your bed." While she consoled him, the woman thought, *No wonder! He was always quarreling with the town, calling them Sodomites; no wonder his son and grandson didn't want to live with such wicked people. No wonder they left.*

When the nurse arrived, she found the old man tossing and turning, as if a thirsty animal, a rodent, had wormed its way into his stomach and was sucking on his intestines. The pain couldn't find an opening through which to escape, so it crawled up through his body all the way to his forehead. The nurse and the maid administered an enema and placed a pail beneath him for his bowel movements. Tzadok always thought that every pain he had came from constipation. Afterward, the women washed up his dry, jaundiced, wrinkled body and placed fresh sheets on his bed.

Despite her training in the Vilna hospitals, Bluma Rivtcha was still gripped by embarrassment every time she worked with the robust bodies of young male patients. And when she served elderly patients, it was worse. She felt embarrassed for the person who'd become so depleted and crippled, ravaged by age or illness. As she busied herself about Tzadok, she also remembered that he was the grandfather of her former fiancé. But Zindel had been a healthy, handsome young man. His handsomeness and cultured manners were the qualities that had seduced her, until she realized he wasn't, in fact, all that cultured and was essentially the yeshiva-boy type, not to mention arrogant. You could sense his arrogance even when he was silent, in his raised shoulders and nose pointed in the air, proud that he was a Tachkemoni student preparing to become a Rabiner. Her brother

Naftali Hertz was just as wedded to his yeshiva mindset. Ironically, Khlavneh, whose entire knowledge came from his yeshiva years, was less of a yeshiva boy than Zindel or her brother. But Khlavneh was too rash and confrontational, brazen like the other boys around the Vilna butcher shops where he was raised. She actually liked his fearlessness, liked that he said exactly what he thought. Still, she was determined for him to win the affection of her parents.

As Bluma Rivtcha's thoughts churned, one tumbling over the other, she bustled around the old man and prepared his injection. At the prick of the needle, Tzadok grimaced for a moment, but he soon sighed in relief and started pestering the nurse: "What's the matter with me? Still the same tumor in my stomach?"

"Yes, still the same tumor," Bluma Rivtcha said.

"If I wasn't so old, I'd have allowed a surgeon to cut this tumor out, and with God's help, I would feel better." Tzadok looked at Bluma Rivtcha, his questioning eyes fearful and suspicious.

"Sure. If the tumor were removed, you'd feel better," Bluma Rivtcha lied. She took after her father in her revulsion for doctors who tell patients the truth about their devastating situation. Since she was a child, she'd heard her father saying that it was a mitzvah not to tell a gravely ill person the truth, and whoever did, and took away even a single minute of the person's life or peace, was evil.

But apparently Tzadok didn't believe his own words. In a sudden rush of wild fury, he jerked up and started ranting about Zalia Ziskind Luria. "They say he was a big rabbi and rosh yeshiva. No small thing—the Dünaburg genius! But judging by his behavior in Morehdalye, he shouldn't have been allowed to rule on Jewish law at all. To almost every question the women ask him, they already know what his answer will be: 'Kosher! Kosher! Kosher!' Now, on the eve of Pesach, when pots must be made kosher for the holiday, he hardly pays attention to the coppersmith, to make sure he scorches the frying pans white. He's even worse in the matzoh bakery. He pays almost no mind to the woman doing the kneading, to make sure her pieces of dough aren't too thick and don't sit out too long on the table. He doesn't yell 'Faster! Faster!' at the women rolling out the dough, the way I, Tzadok, used to yell. Zalia Ziskind doesn't shudder over the prohibition of chametz the way I, Tzadok, used to." And the old dayan waved his hands about, kicked his feet.

"So all of them—from the women working at the matzoh bakery to the wealthy townswomen and respectable business owners—they're all waiting for me to die already and for the hunchbacked Zalia Ziskind to become the dayan here. It will be good for them. All will be permitted, and that will be that!"

The maid, Chaya Sarah, wanted desperately to reassure him that no one in Morehdalye was awaiting his death, heaven forbid. But the woman was scared to utter a word of protest. So she remained standing there, mouth open, legs rooted to the ground, and a pair of clumsy, heavy hands hanging by her sides. Only her kind gray eyes turned ever more stunned and astonished at how a Jew, an old man, a dayan at that, could be such a hard, bitter radish. The rabbi's Bluma Rivtcha was also disconcerted. Still, she took a chance and told Tzadok a story about Rabbi Yisroel Salanter. Once, his students wanted to bake shmura matzoh for the rabbi and asked him what they had to watch out for when they were baking. "More than anything," he replied, "watch out that you don't rush the kneader to death. She's a poor widow."

"And who did you hear it from? Your father, the Morehdalye rabbi?" Tzadok's mouth twisted into an angry sneer.

"No, not from my father. From someone else," Bluma Rivtcha stammered. She blushed, and then was angry at herself for stammering and blushing. "I heard it from Khlavneh. That's my fiancé's name." She said this as if it were an announcement and with a bit of singsong in her voice, as she tended to do whenever she was annoyed. Khlavneh had told her that his mother had once been a kneader in a matzoh bakery. One year, before Pesach, his father had been ill in the hospital, and they didn't have money for the holiday. Khlavneh had been a child then, but to this day he couldn't forget how his mother had torn herself apart kneading the dough with her thin, tireless hands. He watched his mother, drenched in sweat, never daring to catch her breath. The supervisor hovered over her, rumbling nasally, "Knead, knead. Don't let the dough leaven." That was why Khlavneh still remembered what he'd heard among the musarniks. "Rabbi Yisroel Salanter said," the musarniks asserted, "that when baking matzohs, one must be careful above all not to rush the women kneaders."

"Is that so? Your fiancé is from the musarniks?" the dayan drawled, incredulous.

Only then did the maid Chaya Sarah dare to insert a word. "Forgive me, Reb Tzadok, for interrupting. But since Bluma Rivtcha is sitting with you, I can leave now and go prepare supper for my husband. He'll be coming home hungry from work soon."

"Go, go," Tzadok groused, and watched as the maid shuffled out of the house. A fog filled his brain, hung suspended in front of his eyes. Still, he remembered where he'd paused. "If your fiancé is from the devout musarniks, your father got what he wanted, even more than if he'd succeeded in getting you my grandson. My Zindel was from Tachkemoni, where they teach Haskalah, too."

"My fiancé isn't devout anymore. He left the musarniks even before I got to know him."

"But your father got his way anyway," Tzadok insisted. "Your father hated me all these years, and then he put his hunchback friend, this Zalia Ziskind Luria, above me. And the hunchback is determined to put himself out there as a maykil, so the town will see how much better he is than me. Soon he'll be allowing peas and beans on Pesach. Someone already repeated to me in his name that the Polish boycott on Jewish merchants is considered a war according to halacha, and everything that's allowed a lenient ruling during a war's famine years should be ruled leniently now. This little saint may well allow peas and beans on this Pesach, too. And even if your father knows just as well as I do how severely our rabbis prohibited eating all kinds of kitniyos, he'll still agree with his hunchback substitute, just to get at me. And he'll prevail! Everything your father dreamed up against me in his life he accomplished. In that alone I can see how much your father had his way against me." Tzadok coughed the words out, and his voice turned hoarser. "Your father is convinced that I'm to blame for how things went with you and my grandson. He actually believes, your father, that because of my anger at the Katzenellenbogen family I deserve to have a grandson who's run off to be a Rabiner somewhere in Canada, leaving me here as lonely as a stone—as long as your family doesn't get their way. That's the kind of enemy your father thinks I am to your family. And he sends me his daughter to cure me, so that the world will see *he's* the kindhearted one, *he's* the forgiving one, not me. Well, has he not succeeded against me, your father?"

But no matter how much the old dayan ranted against the rabbi and his daughter, his gaze held so much sadness and trust there was no need for him to say how much nachas he would have derived were she his grandson's wife. Exhausted from so much talking, he fell onto his back and turned silent. Bluma Rivtcha was silent, too. She understood that, no matter what she said, the old man would cling to the delusions he'd lived with all these years. Tzadok lay with eyes wide open, sunken into their sockets. The early evening light of the empty April day reflected coldly and indifferently on his face. The sick man looked up at the ceiling and uttered his thoughts out loud. His words fell sorrowfully, powerlessly, like droplets from a faucet: "There won't be anyone even to inherit my holy books."

In front of his sister he was careful, but to his parents Naftali Hertz called Khlavneh "the jargon boy" and pushed them to oppose the match. Neither could the rabbi and rebbetzin get used to the thought that, after all the nachas they'd anticipated from their younger daughter, she'd chosen an aspiring Yiddish writer as her fiancé. In the meantime, they didn't even know for sure whether he had the talent to become a writer at all.

Khlavneh, too, was annoyed. He should have never allowed Bluma Rivtcha to convince him to come along. He felt that the rabbi and rebbetzin didn't approve of the match, though they treated him gently. "But anyway, who's asking them?" he muttered to himself; and to his fiancée he said, "Just as your brother, the little doctor, is still a yeshiva boy, you're still a rebbetzin. You desperately need your parents and your brother to be impressed by me."

Instead of retorting that he was more upset than she that her parents hadn't yet offered their approval, Bluma Rivtcha remained silent and sneered, with a spark in her narrow eyes.

In the morning, Khlavneh went to the town's beis medrash and put on tefillin. Once home, he washed for breakfast. This was how he'd behaved on the two days—Thursday and Friday—since their arrival. On Friday night, the rabbi didn't go to the beis medrash for Kabbalas Shabbos and Maariv, so that his breath wouldn't catch in the cold wind that had suddenly swept over the spring day. Khlavneh did go to the davening. But though he was a guest from the big city, and should have been the object of the town's curiosity, it was he who found himself curious, surprised by the sight of the worshippers' gloomy faces.

In honor of Shabbos, all the electric bulbs in the chandeliers were lit, as well as the candles in the branches on the rabbi's pulpit. Shadows crawled beneath the tables and into the corners, but darkness stuck to the people's faces. Some of the men near the mizrach wall stood unmoving behind their lecterns the entire time. Other men, those who davened behind the bimah, strolled continuously back and forth, pacing absentmindedly as if it were a weekday evening in an empty marketplace. The ba'al tefilah sang, the worshippers moved their lips, swayed their bodies, someone quickly and loudly said Kaddish, and people murmured "Good Shabbos" to each other. It appeared as if the Jews themselves didn't know what they were doing, as when a wind whips through a naked tree and the helpless branches just let themselves be shaken. Most of the worshippers didn't notice the stranger davening in their midst, and those who did never bothered to look his way, despite knowing his connection to the rabbi's Bluma Rivtcha.

Khlavneh noticed the same weekday gloom on the faces of the rabbi and rebbetzin at the Shabbos table. In the light of the white tablecloth and the candelabrum's golden flames, their sadness was more noticeable. To Khlavneh the Morehdalyen residents looked as if they were portraying the sinful souls wallowing in the World of Chaos without rest, even on Shabbos. When they sat down to eat, the rabbi gave Khlavneh a yarmulke to put on, so that he could remove his hat, which was making his forehead sweat. After the fish was served and eaten, the rabbi said affably, "Now taste it with a bit of challah." Each time the rabbi addressed him with the respectful "ir," Khlavneh felt that the old man hadn't yet approved of him. That was why he wouldn't address Khlavneh with the more casual "du," as one did with a future son-in-law.

Khlavneh chewed the piece of challah like gum, and in an inquisitive tone he told them about the gloominess he'd felt in the beis medrash.

"And why are you surprised?" Sholem Shachne stared at him. "In Vilna they don't know what's happening in the Jewish shtetls? Polish bojówkas forbid the peasants from stepping into Jewish stores, and Jewish dealers are afraid to set foot in the village. They'd be putting themselves in mortal danger. It's nearly Pesach for the Jews and nearly Easter for the Christians, but business has come to a standstill.

The town hasn't shopped for Pesach yet, so they're deeply depressed. Do you know nothing about this?"

"Sure, I know about the pogrom-bojówkas from all kinds of Endikes, Oneravtzes, and various hooligans," Khlavneh said, "but in other towns, I know they've put up an organized resistance. Here in Morehdalye it's deathly silent, like a cemetery. You must respond with force!" Khlavneh stopped mid-argument. He didn't understand why the rabbi was giving him a furious eye.

"Now I see you've abandoned the Torah entirely. A ben-torah, even a young, rash one, doesn't talk about fighting back. He knows the antisemites are waiting for Jews to fight back, so that they can justify pogroms. My youngest son, the chalutz—I'm sure you've heard of our Refael'ke—he felt the same way you do about fighting back, and that's what he did, he fought. Of course, he, too, had completely abandoned the Torah by that time," the rabbi boomed, elbows on the table. He swung his head this way and that, as though his fury had made him lose his breath.

Khlavneh cast Bluma Rivtcha an angry look. At the beginning of their relationship, and for quite a while after, she'd never mentioned her family. But since they'd become intimate, she couldn't stop talking about them: her parents, her brothers and sisters, aunts and uncles, grandmothers and grandfathers. And here he'd thought she was an independent person! Khlavneh could clearly see that Naftali Hertz was looking at him with a crooked, hateful smile, as he continued to slurp his chicken broth. *The little doctor of philosophy with the skinny, prickly face and Adam's apple hates me. Why does he hate me?* Khlavneh became enveloped by a cold blaze of wrath.

The rebbetzin went into the kitchen to prepare the meat course. Bluma Rivtcha wanted to follow her and help out, but she remained seated, restlessly turning her head back and forth. Khlavneh was speaking heatedly to her father, which made her afraid to leave. "True, I'm not a ben-torah anymore, not at all, if being a ben-torah means bowing one's head and keeping silent about everything. Since the times of Rabbi Yochanan ben Zakai, Torah scholars have almost always, in almost every place, been against retaliation. They believed in going through mediators, giving bribes, submitting to their rulers, singing their praises and crawling on all fours for barons and lords, crying and pleading for pity. And when there was no way out, dying for the sanctification of God's name. But they didn't believe in resisting with hammers and knives, tooth and nail. And why that is I can't understand. Maybe because the fanatics have been beating their chests over their sins for so long, have let themselves be deluded for so long—by the Prophets, the Sages, the musar books and preachers— deluded into believing that *they* are the sinners. They've been saying the Viduy for so long, *Ashamnu, b'gadnu, g'zalnu*, they have no strength left to strike back. But I absolutely support beating up those who beat us, the pogromniks. And even if it doesn't save a single life, it saves the honor of the Jewish people."

"Who do you mean by 'the Jewish people'? Those who speak jargon and read jargon books?" Naftali Hertz asked from the side, his face twisted with unconcealed hatred.

Khlavneh had not expected such a question and such ridicule. For a moment he was thrown off-balance. But then his temper rose within him, and he was glad for his anger, as a person is for a fresh stream of rushing water. But he didn't want to explode; he wanted to hit back with dry, prudent smacks, the way the strong youths from his town did. He noticed Bluma Rivtcha winking at him from across the table, urging him not to answer. But he tossed her an angry, arrogant look: I *will* answer! Even if it means she'll have to break off the engagement! But he drew out his words calmly, slowly, mockingly. "Yes, yes, when I say the Jewish people, I mean the people that speak jargon and read jargon books. And what kind of Jewish population do you have in your Switzerland?"

"There are no jargon men and women in Switzerland, of course. None," Naftali Hertz replied, his face creased in ridicule and so much schadenfreude that even his father gaped at him, astonished. "Maybe, somewhere, a few old immigrants from Poland or Lithuania still speak jargon in secret, but in public the Jews speak German, French, English, or Italian. Our Jews are divided between those who go to temple with Reform rituals and religious Jews who go to the old-fashioned beis medrash and observe the mitzvahs. But real, whole Jews—even our Orthodox Jews aren't that."

"Now I don't understand at all," Khlavneh said. "Up until now you were saying that you don't consider the speaking of Yiddish, or jargon

as you call it, a clear sign of being a Jew. Then again, Reform Jews
are also only part Jewish, Jewish scraps in your estimation, because
they haven't taken the onus of mitzvahs, laws, and conditions upon
themselves. But now I'm hearing you say that even your Orthodox
Jews aren't whole Jews. Why?"

"Because our Orthodox Jews have equal civil rights, and they
demand even more equality with Swiss Christians. That's why I consider even those who belong to the strictly religious group not whole
Jews."

"The food is getting cold," Henna'le interjected.

On each plate lay a piece of chicken and a beef and rice stew. The
rabbi and rebbetzin chewed slowly, while Bluma Rivtcha scarfed her
food down with fury. She was reconsidering her decision to bring
Khlavneh here. She should have waited until after their wedding.

Khlavneh didn't touch his food. He waited on tenterhooks for the
doctor of philosophy to explain why he didn't consider Swiss Orthodox Jews to be whole Jews because they insisted on full civil rights.
But Dr. Katzenellenbogen started from much further back. In a professorial tone, he began holding forth about the power that had kept
Jews united. His manner of speech reminded Khlavneh of a devout
Misnagid scholar and his icy rapport with God, the Misnagid who
recites the Shema with eyes tightly squeezed in utmost concentra-
tion, who's pedantic with every word, every letter, and if he's not
certain that he enunciated the *shin* correctly, he repeats the word
again and again: *u'vkhol naf*-sh-*khe, naf*-sh-*khe, naf*-sh-*khe.** Perhaps
it was because Katzenellenbogen thought his thoughts in the solitude
of the Judaic division in Bern's university library, a forgotten man
in a foreign world, stuck in rooms with books from floor to ceiling,
books by dead Jewish Sages about contrived Jewish studies, perhaps
that was why he spoke with the strange ecstasy of a possessed man,
the recluse ascetic in the attic. But what interested Khlavneh was

* A common stereotype of the devout Misnagid (one who belongs to a subgroup
that opposes Hasidism) is that he lacks the warm connection to God that Hasidim
emphasize but is a stickler for halacha, sometimes to an obsessive degree. The
example here is of this type of Misnagid who's concerned that he hasn't enunciated a letter of a verse correctly—thus rendering the verse invalid—and therefore
repeats it several times.

not why Naftali Hertz spoke this way, but rather what he was saying and the pretense with which he portrayed himself as the "diploma-holding yeshiva boy."

Naftali Hertz had by now moved on to the next chapter of his spiel: the topic of netzach Yisroel, the eternity of the Jewish people and the Jewish faith. "God gave His Jewish nation a Torah, and we all have the free will to follow it. Neither the legends of idol-worshippers nor the fantasies of the enlightened nor even the logic of philosophy has played a role in the Jewish religion. Only later was philosophy dragged into Judaism by outsiders. The Jewish faith began with the first word of the Ten Commandments, *Anochi*, and continued with the words that followed: what is allowed and what is prohibited. It is a Torah of faith and laws, not of metaphysics; a Torah with hundreds of mitzvahs that developed into thousands of laws and customs for all the days of the year, from birth to death; a Torah of deeds and of belief in God, but not philosophical specu-lations about the essence of God and His image. Even after phi-losophy was dragged in from the outside and the greatest of our philosophers* undertook to prove that 'Torah and philosophy are one,' he, too, wrote that the characteristics, the attributes of God, do not determine His essence, but rather are characterizations of His acts. And in this way did the forest of six hundred thirteen mitz-vahs, along with the supplementary rules, laws, customs, and quite simply, the Jewish character, branch out and expand over the last thousand years—a large, dense, tangled forest that on the one hand keeps the people who abandoned it entrapped and on the other protects whoever hides themselves inside it. No matter how many select individuals, heretics and rebels, no matter how many schools of thought and sects of Jews arose and wrangled with the onus of mitzvahs as though their life depended on it, it didn't help. Anyone who wanted to abolish Jewish laws or alter them significantly—the Samaritans, the Karaites, the Shabbatei Zeviniks—all were booted from the Jewish community. The only ones who remained are those who accepted the entire dense forest of the *Shulchan Aruch*. True, those people did argue over whether one is allowed to interpret

* This is a reference to Maimonides, to whom the quote "Torah and philosophy are one" is often attributed. Naftali Hertz would have assumed that Khlavneh would understand the reference without spelling it out for him.

mitzvahs according to philosophy or Kabbalah, in the style of Hasidism and Musar. Since the times of a Jewish Greek philosopher,* in the pre-Temple era, to the times of Rabbi Yisroel Salanter and his disciples in Lithuania, there have been disagreements over the reasons for mitzvahs, our understanding of the Torah's intentions. But this was a heimish quarrel, sometimes tedious and boring, sometimes fiery, but always heimish. One side never pushed the other out of the house because they all accepted the mitzvahs and merely bickered over the reasons behind them. And this is how the Torah overpowered everything, like a sea depositing its salt wherever its water reaches, and the way the Alps can't be moved from their spot, as the verse says, 'Your charity is like the mighty mountains; your judgments are the vast abyss.' Sure, there's a tremendous outpouring of emotions in Tehillim, but non-Jews can recite Tehillim, too. In fact, they do! And wrangling with God, complaining about Him but still believing in Him—goyim can do that, too. In fact, there are even those who claim in the Talmud that Job wasn't a Jew. A man who suffered so terribly and still cried out, 'Though He slay me, yet I will trust in Him,' and still there are those who say he wasn't a Jew. But the one thing a goy doesn't want to take upon himself is the burden of mitzvahs: the laws of treyf and kosher; what is allowed, what is prohibited; of purity and impurity; when one is or isn't permitted to approach even one's own wife. Only as long as we lived in our wooded tangle of laws could we be a nation in exile, and even have moments of redemption and revelation."

"And the Jewish ideologies?" Bluma Rivtcha asked. Getting involved in a debate wasn't in her nature; typically, she just liked to listen in. But this time she blushed and stammered, "And what about the ideologies of the Prophets?"

"The Prophets' ideologies were already adopted by other nations hundreds of years ago, thousands of years ago. For being the first bearer of these prophetic ideologies, we have the merit of great-grandfathers, and nobody wants to take that away from us. But if the only thing we lean on are these merits, we can't continue to exist," Naftali Hertz concluded, triumphing over his befuddled sister.

Khlavneh listened, observing Naftali Hertz, and thought: *His*

---

* A reference to Philo of Alexandria, aka Philo Judaeus.

hands shake like an epileptic's. What's this epileptic's intention? Does he want to show his father, the rabbi, that though he abandoned this lifestyle and became educated, at his core he keeps the six hundred thirteen mitzvahs? But the rabbi, who had finished eating by then, listened to his oldest son with a dismayed expression, seemingly quite unmoved by his son's display of piety. Khlavneh moved the plate of chicken and stew, now cold, closer to him. He figured he might as well finish eating while Naftali Hertz finished his speech.

20

THE IDEOLOGIES?" Naftali Hertz grimaced and tittered, like a madman glimpsed through the barred windows of a hospital. Though he was in his father's home in Morehdalye, sitting at a Shabbos table with candles burned down to their nubs, the vision of a cold, clear, steely day in Bern danced before his eyes—a narrow street with vaulted passageways, lined with shops, and, on the horizon, the snowy mountains of the Bern Oberland, the Jungfrau, the Mönch, and the Eiger, three tremendous snowy giants, eternal witnesses to his life in the library, for they peeked through those windows day after day, watching him struggle amid the walls of shelves filled with thick, dusty volumes. "The ideologies of the Prophets? The religious spirit?" It seemed that though Naftali Hertz was talking to his family in Morehdalye, in his mind he was mimicking a Reform preacher in Switzerland. "Almost all of them start with the idea that the biggest invention of the Jewish religion is the oneness of God, the absolute spirit, the immortal God, whom no one can fathom and whose endless attributes exist only in the negative, meaning they negate their opposite. God isn't even a 'strong, fearsome God' in the positive sense, because such praise in a positive sense would limit Him in His omnipotence. Because in the definition of what He *is* there would have been a determination of what He is *not*. Understand?" Naftali Hertz asked his sister, who was looking increasingly more puzzled, understanding less and less of what he was saying. "But there are also those who say that monotheism, for which Jews pride themselves so, the very notion of oneness of God in the Jewish spirit, is a primitive understanding of God, a sort of idolatry, because giving Him a purely spiritual existence sets our material existence outside of His realm, meaning that God rules over all the worlds but His existence doesn't fill all the worlds. Get it? The truest, highest, purest level of oneness of God, claim the devotees of Spinoza, can be found specifically in Spinoza's doctrine, which insists that God and nature go hand in hand, are one and the same. Bluma Rivtcha, you've heard of Baruch Spinoza? Even the jargon papers have been making a fuss about him lately, because it's the three hundredth anniversary of his birthday now, unfortunately for us. He lived in a time when, to avoid rotting in prison, he had to be very cautious and clever about the words he used. It's clear he wanted to undermine the Jewish Torah. In his heart, he laughed at all of it. And the theologians, the rabbis and the bishops of his time, were never really fooled by him, meaning they knew he was trying to deceive them. Supposedly, Spinoza's words were in compliance with the Bible, with their Protestant church and community. He used such words to avoid torture. But whom he truly fooled was the naïve Basel Zionist Congress of our time. Indeed, Spinoza must be the greatest diplomat in the history of philosophy, if he managed to convince the Basel Zionist Congress, three hundred years later, that he truly meant his words, that Jews were God's chosen nation and God could again confer a kingdom upon them if they deserved it. So, it's to this person, the smartest of the smart and loneliest of the lonely, this excommunicated Jew from Amsterdam, that the gullible Hebrews of Jerusalem universities cry: 'Annulled! Annulled!' They recanted the cherem that was placed on him three hundred years ago, despite his never hinting with a single word that the cherem ever bothered him. What did he care? Somewhere among the hundreds of commentaries written on him are a few from Jews who are, but for a baptism, essentially Christian converts. They claim that Christ and Spinoza are the Jews' two biggest Prophets, and that Spinoza's God is the one and only Jewish God in His highest recognition, freed from senile Aristotle and all his Jewish interpreters, the Rav-ad, the Rambam, the Ralbag, and the rest, as they're called there. You understand?" Naftali Hertz said to his sister, who looked at him—at the froth foaming on his lips—with alarm and empathy. The rabbi and rebbetzin also sat there with mute sorrow in their eyes. They understood that their son was talking about his own struggles.

Dr. Katzenellenbogen continued to mock the Rabiners in stiff white collars, theosophists with fancy beards and fancy language, who were still poring over the old, stale philosophical debate over what defines Orthodox Judaism, its moral creed or the hope for a Messiah who will redeem the entire world. "Is the Jewish God the God of Truth or the God of Mercy or the God of Vengeance? Is the entire Torah embodied in 'Love thy friend as yourself,' or do we side with those who insist that religion stands not on love and mercy but on justice and judgment? Some people say the foundation of Orthodox Judaism is to have no idols. Others cry that Judaism means the joy of life. Believing in life and enjoying its pleasures within limit—that's the main idea. Someone, a German philosopher renowned for his book about life's meaninglessness,* an angry gentile with the prickly beard of an old tomcat, says he hates Jews and Judaism because they believe in life. Another says that Judaism means reason, the law of logic. A third says Judaism means purpose, having a goal, consciousness, actions.

"And what is meant by the Jewish nation, Jewish ethnicity? Ah, here's where the real battles start among these types of big wheels, fellows who speak with lots of Rs, party theorists without brains, without eyes, without heart and soul, but with a tiny dogmatic idea that they expatiate on at the impassioned conferences of idiots. And what's the difference between Judaism and Christianity? Judaism, they say, is law, while Christianity is love. Let's say that's true. Was it worth it, for this, for Jews to let themselves be killed by fire and water, to be burned and roasted at the stake? Because of a difference in definition, was it worth it for so many to die? But what about the universal ideologies of the Prophets? The utopia of a Messianic era, where wolf and lamb will feed together, the dream of a world without wars, no rich or poor, all the slogans of the French Revolution, the Russian Revolution, all other forgotten revolutions. My guts turn in my stomach when I hear that these human ideologies are the basis of Judaism!" Naftali Hertz shouted, throwing his hands about like a sick, feverish man who must escape the doctors and orderlies surrounding his bed, for he sees them as a gang of demons trying to drag him to hell.

His mother and sister felt pained. Naftali Hertz was tearing himself to pieces with his words. But his father pinched his beard resentfully. Sholem Shachne understood his son's seething better than his

---

* Reference to Friedrich Nietzsche.

wife and daughter did, so he had less sympathy for him. Khlavneh, again, mentally mocked Naftali Hertz: *See how he's overwhelmed by his fit of rage! See how he's looking for permission to be an assimilated Jew. He's not speaking to me at all, the epileptic!*

It was true. Naftali Hertz was avoiding Khlavneh and spoke only to his parents and sister. "The more individuals and nations that adopted the Prophets' ideas and ideologies, the more the Jews lost out. Once others adopted the ideas and became accustomed to living with the prophetic vision of a Messianic era, Jews lost their distinguishing characteristic. Though it's also true that the gentiles are all talk; so far, they've done nothing to bring the Messianic era closer. For that matter, what have *we* done to draw the Messiah's times nearer? Well, you'll say, 'We were the first to have the concept of a Messianic era! For that, the world should coddle us.' But listen, even without us, the crowd of other nations is too big and too cramped. Our demand for a share makes us just like that shadchan who demanded his bed be placed in the same room as the young couple, because he'd suggested the match." Naftali Hertz laughed, avenging his own life.

All at once, he swiveled around to Khlavneh. "Not in the Prophets' ideologies, not in the spirit of Judaism—which, anyway, no one knows exactly what it is or how to eat it—not even in the recognition of God's oneness is the secret and miracle of the Jews' perpetuity. No, it's the Torah of laws and rules that has held us together. The *Shulchan Aruch* is what's welded us."

Because Khlavneh was looking sharply at him, with the tightly sealed lips of one who's patiently awaiting his turn to speak, Naftali Hertz lowered his voice and began to speak more calmly, in a tone of compressed ridicule, frozen spite. "And it's not just philosophy. Neither did poetry play a role in the everlastingness of the Jewish people. Jews didn't want the Song of Songs to be a poem about a boy and girl. I understand you don't like that. You're a sort of poet, after all. Not in Hebrew, true, but still, a poet." Naftali Hertz sneered at the jargon boy and then changed his tone. Again, he spoke in the cold, mystical voice of a recluse ascetic in an attic, a superstitious heretic whose only consolation in life is his own toiled-over beliefs.

"Since it's not the ghetto gates the gentiles have erected that keep us united, but rather the fence of laws and customs that Jews themselves put up, the hatred of other nations toward us is actually a good sign. Because it proves we're still whole Jews. We never succeeded in getting equal rights from the gentiles until we showed—and were believed—that we're patriots, ready to die for the nation and country where we lived. Our enemies claim we've always been and still are a nation unto ourselves. So we had to let them know, and our Christian friends vouched for us: 'We're not Jews anymore! We're as German or French or Polish as everyone else, or we'll soon become so. As soon as you give us our conditions, that's what we'll become.' But if we had really intended to remain Jews, and were honest with our non-Jewish neighbors, we'd have told them, 'Let us live, let us exist, but don't give us the same rights you have. Keep the partition between us. We're a foreign nation among you, and that's what we'll remain. By giving us equal rights, you're robbing yourselves and us.'"

And to show his sister Bluma Rivtcha what he thought of her fiancé, Naftali Hertz turned to his parents and spoke about Khlavneh as if he weren't there. "It seems our guest, the poet, doesn't know that the Jewish tenant farmer of old, who kissed his landowner's hand and sang his praises, was secretly laughing at the nobleman and his entire lordly court. That tenant farmer who crawled on all fours and danced with the bear* remembered, while he danced, that he was a prince, and he even pitied the nobleman for his human decadence. Did a Jew really want to have the same rights as his landlord, the drunk gentile? The truly pious individual and truly pious community of today shouldn't want the same as their non-Jewish neighbors. Only a small Jewish minority, the ones who desire to mingle with the non-Jewish majority or have already assimilated, only they have a basis to ask for equal rights. This minority may perhaps be allowed to resist with force against the people in power who refuse to recognize their equal rights. Why are you laughing? What are you neighing about?" Naftali Hertz wheeled around to his sister's fiancé.

"It's taken you too long to get to the point you should have started with," Khlavneh said, pressing his elbows into the table's edge. "What you're saying is that you and your kind deserve equal civil rights in Switzerland and Poland because you've already assimilated or are almost there. But we, meaning such types like me and my kind, we

* Reference to a tale in Jewish folklore, where a nobleman forced a Jewish tenant farmer (or innkeeper, in some versions) to dance with a bear for the amusement of the nobleman's drunken coterie.

don't have the right to demand civil rights in Poland because we're Jews and want to remain Jews. Not for nothing did you compare the Torah to a big, thick, overgrown forest. You said the forest protects its inhabitants, so that they can remain Jews. But what you really meant to say is that whoever wants to continue to belong to the wild Jewish forest-tribe isn't permitted to stick his head out of the woods, out of the ghetto, out of the *Shulchan Aruch*. But *you* can't live according to the laws of the woods anymore, is what you meant to say. You can't lead this stale, old-fashioned lifestyle anymore. You're already one of the enlightened ones and don't avoid your neighbors. You're even more educated than your civilized neighbors, Herr Doctor, which is why you and your kind, the assimilated, the intermarried, deserve all the civil rights that me and my kind, the jargon men and women, don't deserve. Right? You odious, assimilated Jew!" Khlavneh gritted his teeth.

More than the pleasure of taunting the doctor, Khlavneh took pleasure in knowing that he was willing even to break his engagement, as long as he could speak his mind. Bluma Rivtcha, too, belonged to this pedigreed rabbinical clan, so let her see who she was taking as a husband! Khlavneh laughed rudely into Naftali Hertz's face. "Oh, so you're a coward too? You're running away from the table? Just like you ran away from your subversive theory that anyone who wants to be a real Jew isn't allowed to poke his head out of the ghetto, just like you ran away from Poland to Switzerland to escape the Jewish lifestyle. Now you're running away from the table to avoid hearing the truth about yourself and your rotten theory."

Naftali Hertz sat back down. He looked at his father's rigid face. Impossible to tell whose side he was on. Henna'le, not stirring either, watched her husband, and Bluma Rivtcha, too, was silent. Only her cheeks glowed red, furious at Khlavneh for speaking so hotly, so coarsely, for attacking his rival personally, and not caring about the impression it would make on her parents. On the other hand— and for the same reasons—Bluma Rivtcha's eyes burned with pride. Her man had courage, and he didn't lack the words to express his thoughts.

The flames in the candelabrum burned out. Shadows gradually spread from the corners of the dining room. Through the shade of the electric chandelier, hanging a bit too high above the table, a crimson glow fell upon the strained, dismayed faces and drove the holy Shabbos from the room. The wrinkled tablecloth, strewn with leftovers that Henna'le no longer felt like clearing, added even more of a weekday atmosphere. For a minute, Khlavneh regretted the fight he'd started, that he'd hurt the rabbi and rebbetzin, not to mention Bluma Rivtcha. But soon, anger boiled up in him again. What a hypocrite the rabbi's son was, coming up with this cushy theory, to make it soft and comfortable for himself to assimilate. Khlavneh lowered his voice, though his tone was still agitated and furious. "The laws of Shabbos, you say, are what held us together? The *avos melachos* and *toldos*? It's forbidden to hoe, dig, or level a field. Sowing, or watering what's sowed, is also not allowed. Cutting, tearing the grains with the hand, etc., etc. Even things that are similar to this type of work aren't permitted. There are barriers decreed by the rabbis and others by the Torah. We must make eruvei khatzeiros, eruvei techimen, etc., etc. And all these things, what's forbidden and what's allowed, are what have kept us together, the way metal hoops keep the staves of a dried-out cask together. True, yes?"

"True, true." Naftali Hertz nodded his head. "These laws, and only these, nothing else, have kept us together."

"And the laws of Pesach, obviously. The prohibition of eating chametz, the prohibition of having chametz in the home, and the separate prohibition of looking at chametz that happens to be found in the house on Pesach. And all the other prohibitions listed in the Torah, and those that the Mishna and Gemara infer from the Torah, even if they aren't written specifically in the Chumash. But what has kept us Jews together is the law that says that even if there's chametz in the house during Pesach, we're forbidden from deriving any pleasure from it. True? In this lies the power of the remaining Jews and the eternity of the Jewish people, right?" Khlavneh mocked, and Naftali Hertz, as if to mock him back, nodded his head.

"Yes, yes. In this and in eating shmurah matzoh and drinking four cups of wine. So, what of it?"

But Khlavneh hadn't quite finished his questioning. It seemed he wanted to show the rabbi that he hadn't forgotten what he'd studied in yeshiva. "And of course, the laws and customs of grieving, too? The way the corpse must be moved from the deathbed to the floor, the purification, the shrouds, the tallis with the posul tzitzis, the covering of the person, the Kaddish, the kriah, the lining up, the shiva, the thirty-day mourning period, the yahrzeit—all of this is what has kept us together? In these laws lie the secret and basis of the continuance of the Jewish people, right?"

"Yes, yes, in these lie the secret of the Jewish people's continuance." Naftali Hertz nodded his head and raised his deadened eyes. "What are you getting at?"

"What I'm getting at is that everything you've said is a lie!"

Khlavneh again spoke heatedly, fervently, as though he'd caught the stones that had been hurled at him and he instantly hurled them back. He spoke either directly to his opponent or to his fiancée and her parents. "Of course, the laws of mourning and the superstitions about the dead have helped us remain a community. But so, too, has the way people empathize with the pain of the mourners, the forgetting of all resentments in light of the person's tragedy, the sobbing during the recitation of Tehillim, and the pleading at the funeral that the corpse be an intercessor in heaven for the brokenhearted people left behind. Jewish loyalty and goodness when taking part in another's misfortune, the sympathetic tears of those attending the funeral, the kindness of the neighbors who come to console the mourners—all these things have secured Jewish burial rites in the hearts of people, so it's impossible to forget them. But Dr. Katzenellenbogen needs the Jewish ritual to be merely a web of laws and customs, not out of belief but of superstitions and sinister ceremonies. He needs it so that he, the enlightened, educated man, will be permitted to escape the Jewish cemetery. And to escape the Jewish lifestyle, he needs the Pesach holiday to be composed of only prohibitions by the Torah and the rabbis, boundary upon boundary, strictness upon strictness. But his entire invented argument about Pesach is also a lie. If Pesach were only a ceremony of what's permitted and what's forbidden, and not a holiday, would alienated Jews from all corners of the world, Jews who'd rejected religion, be nostalgic for such a dull ceremony? For Dr. Katzenellenbogen, it's not worth it to remember that Pesach is also a holiday of freedom, of spring, of the Song of Songs. Someone like him doesn't see or feel the charm, the magic, that warms and lights up the forest of Jewish laws like sunshine. Dr. Katzenellenbogen needs the woods to be without sunshine, without even any trees, only the iron railings of laws and customs. That's why Shabbos, too, for him, is just a *Shulchan Aruch* of what's allowed and what's forbidden according to the Rambam, the Tor, the Beis Yosef, the *Mishna Brurah*. Poetry, he claims, never played a role in Jewish life. The prayers we say three times a day during the week and on Shabbos and holidays aren't poetry, according to Dr. Katzenellenbogen. He also took the pesukei dezimra, the Lamentations, the *Slikhe*, and the liturgical poems, and he dried them out like pepper and tobacco. All that remained were laws and conditions. The truth is that, more than anything else, it's the songs and the pouring out of the heart that have kept Jews together, and still do. More than all the rules in the *Ohr HaChaim* about forgotten, omitted, or rushed-through prayers and blessings. And the most beautiful poem, the one Jews can't live without, is Shabbos itself. Who hasn't written about it? Even the apostate Heinrich Heine has written about it. But the poetry of Shabbos doesn't lie in the thirty-nine melachos, the laws and prohibitions, but in their symbolism of creation and our exodus from Egypt—that all people have the equal right to rest—and in the mysticism that Kabbalah and Hasidism have brought to the Shabbos, about body and soul, about the Congregation of Israel and the Holy One, blessed be He. In these things lie the power of Shabbos! In the neshama yeseira, in the hymns, the clothing and food, the fish and the cholent, in the afternoon nap and the slow stroll with hands behind one's back to Mincha prayers . . ."

"But in order to be able to enjoy the holiness and beauty of Shabbos, you have to observe the laws," Sholem Shachne interjected unexpectedly. His tone was loving, calm. "For this you must, first of all, be a Shabbos observer."

"Not necessarily," Khlavneh replied in as hostile and hotheaded a tone as he'd used with Naftali Hertz. "For someone to whom Shabbos is a forest of iron railings, a forest of only laws and customs, that person must reject Shabbos once he stops having faith in the Torah. But I, and people like me, we carry the poetry and philosophy of Shabbos inside ourselves even if we don't observe it."

"He's not wrong," Naftali Hertz said amiably, to the surprise of his family. "He and his type carry the poetry and philosophy of Shabbos in their hearts and minds. That's why they don't have to be Shabbos observers. But what about the ordinary masses who don't carry this same poetry and philosophy in *their* hearts and minds?"

Perhaps Naftali Hertz meant his question seriously, in part, but Khlavneh heard only the mocking tone. He replied sarcastically, "There are different kinds of marriages. Some people marry for love, others for money, still others for pedigree. Or, say, a widower with children, he might look for a woman who's willing to raise his orphaned children. In the same way, Dr. Katzenellenbogen needs a Torah with mitzvahs for the ordinary masses, a Shabbos for all Jews. For himself, though, he wants nothing of this outdated lifestyle."

"Are you finished? Can I go now?" Naftali Hertz stood up.

"No, I'm not done. You can't go yet." Khlavneh stayed in his chair, and Naftali Hertz reluctantly sat back down. "Not the mitzvahs and not even the reasons for the mitzvahs have welded us together, soldered us together, held us together. They, too, have played a part—the laws, I mean—but what had the main impact was the aggadah, the stories and allegorical passages of the Talmud that are discussed within the laws. Just as the eyes are the liveliest part of the face, and Shabbos is the crowning day of the week, it's the legends that have captivated the Jewish heart more than the laws themselves. The history of the patriarchs in the Chumash and of the tannaim in the Talmud, the allegorical passages about Elijah the Prophet and the stories of the lamed-vovniks, the stories about Jews who'd martyred themselves for the sanctification of God's name—in these lie the charm and magic, and these are what breathed life into Jewish laws. But the most beautiful are the Prophets' ideologies, and to you those are mere abstractions—the ideologies about a God-and-world unity, about social justice, their belief in a Messianic era. You say you don't know what is meant by the spirit of Orthodox Judaism. But we can't determine what is meant by life either. And yet, we know the difference between life and death."

"But you don't consider the Torah a 'Torah of Life,'" Naftali Hertz interrupted, halting the excitable Khlavneh for a minute. He spoke softly and earnestly, with surprise in his eyes, and without the palest shadow of his earlier ridicule. "You don't believe in tradition, in the Jewish mesorah. You've rejected all that, I think, you and your kind."

"We haven't rejected anything, not me and not others like me! We just understand religion and Jewish folklife differently than our predecessors did. I'm just now getting to my main point: You had said earlier that if we were whole Jews and honest people, we would have said to the other nations, 'Allow us to exist among you, but don't give us the same rights. Keep a partition between us, because we have been strangers among you and want to remain so. That's why we don't deserve the same civil rights as you.' This, you say, is what we must say to the nations we live among, if we are whole, honest Jews. I don't want to start a new debate with you on whether we can remain whole Jews if we enjoy the same rights as gentiles. I want to ask you something else. Answer me this: In your personal life, in your thoughts and actions, are you so pious that you feel morally justified to advise Jewish villages in Poland to give up their demands for full civil rights, because you do the same? Or are you advising us, Polish Jews, because you have full civil rights in Switzerland, so it doesn't play a role in your life anymore?"

"Maybe you should speak on topic, instead of mocking?" Henna'le finally decided to interject, and she gave a sort of wave with her hands like a fettered chicken waving its wings. But then she abruptly turned silent. She noticed her husband listening with interest, even with enjoyment, as though he were *pleased* that someone was mocking his oldest son.

"I'm not mocking, Rebbetzin. I don't mean to insult your son. It's a style of talking, for me, especially because he, too, spoke to me like this," said Khlavneh, stammering a bit.

But he'd been taking the debate too seriously to keep quiet for long or even to modulate his tone. He bit his lower lip. Suddenly, he jumped up and took a step toward Naftali Hertz. "What you said is disgusting! A disgrace! Not because you and Switzerland are bathing in luxury while you suggest that we in Poland give up equal rights; no, your words are shameful and repulsive because you don't really believe what you say. You know no one will listen to you, and maybe you don't even want anyone to listen to you. But you want to be right in theory. You delight in your deductive method. You want the pleasure of drush vekabel skhar, talk and its reward! You're using our bodies and lives to build your supposed rationale, a discourse of cynical rationale with axioms, main sentences, concluding sentences, as if you were a Spinoza and were writing an 'Ethics' on how Polish Jews must act: meaning, they should let themselves be starved. This is the vilest thing about you. You simply want to experience the pleasure of your rational deductions and then ride back in peace to Switzerland and your family . . . Why did you shudder like that? Wait another second!" And Khlavneh blocked the kitchen doorway. "The devout tenant farmer of old, you say, who sang the praises of his landowner, kissed his hand and danced before him draped in a bearskin—that Jew, you say, was secretly laughing at the nobleman and even pitied him for his human decadence. Now answer me: For what price are you willing to go back and stand in that tenant farmer's or innkeeper's place, to be degraded by the nobleman like a dog, while secretly laughing? For no money in the world would you do it— go back to that supposedly proud, happy Jew crawling on all fours. I've already heard this kind of talk from 'paper ba'al tshuvahs.' I call them 'paper ba'al tshuvahs' because just like you they don't really want to go back to their former piety. They only mean it theoretically, philosophically, historically. That's why these paper ba'al tshuvahs can allow themselves to babble with pious lips that the beaten, spit-on innkeeper was a proud, happy Jew. But that's nonsense! Woe to the spit-on man who must console himself with the thought that he's morally superior to the spitter and cannot break his piggish chin to pieces! When that innkeeper recited the Lamentations on Tisha B'Av and the Selichos before Rosh Hashanah, when he read the part 'Servants rule over us; there is none to deliver us from their hand,' he cried bloody tears. But you, a guest from Switzerland, you need that proud, happy Jew of old the same way you need a Torah of only laws and rules, because that way you can pity and console yourself that you alone cannot, alas, live this kind of life anymore. All you can do is be nostalgic for it. That's why you so hate us, the jargon boys and girls."

"Why do I hate you?" Naftali Hertz murmured, bone-weary from listening to Khlavneh's seething rant.

Khlavneh, too, realized he'd been speaking for too long now, and too heatedly, too much like a monster. It wasn't nice or smart of him to behave this way in a rabbi's house, where he'd come as a guest and fiancé. But the words danced on his lips like flashes of lightning. He didn't even try to control himself. "You hate the jargon boys and girls because they have the courage to be different from their fathers and grandfathers, even to wage battles with their fathers and grandfathers, and yet, they don't run away from home. We fight the enemies outside of our community while fighting to change ourselves within. We don't run from either front. That's why you hate us."

Khlavneh finished just at the point that Henna'le couldn't bear another second of it. She said to her daughter, "Is this his nature? He's a matchstick!"

Bluma Rivtcha was silent, burning and confused. She sided with Khlavneh but was angry at him for attacking her brother.

But then something happened that no one expected. The rabbi burst into laughter from great amusement. In a fatherly fashion, he patted Khlavneh's back. "I see now that you do have a writer's talent and that, indeed, you've studied under the musarniks. The way you conduct a debate not by law but by deed, and the way you scold a person for his faults right to his face, shows me you're a true musarnik. You could even have been a preacher. But for that you'd first have to observe mitzvahs."

This was the first time Sholem Shachne addressed Khlavneh with the familial "du," and with this, implicitly gave his daughter permission to marry her fiancé. Naftali Hertz grasped this and was bewildered. He saw clear satisfaction on his father's face, as if the chutzpah-nik with the big mouth had said what his father had been thinking all along and never voiced. *Well, if this is what my father thinks, let him keep this street urchin as a son-in-law, and I'll go back to my quiet little corner in the library*, Naftali Hertz thought, and went silently back to his bedroom, without even bidding his family goodnight.

21

S HABBOS HAGADOL MORNING ROSE upon Morehdalye with a high blue sky and temperate weather. The sunrays were felt more than seen, like a wedding band heard through an entire shtetl, though the musicians are nowhere in sight. But as festive and clean as the sky was, so dirty and trampled was the ground: trod-upon snow, muddy puddles of water, last year's yellowed grass. Only here and there could a clear patch of earth be seen. To Khlavneh, the shtetl's residents looked just like their town. The men wore their Shabbos clothes and talleisim, the beis medrash was full, and the ba'al tefilah at the lectern davened in the Shabbos tune and style. But in the bright light of day, the weekday worries over their livelihoods showed even more harshly on the townspeople's faces. Their voices rang out sullenly, they didn't savor the tune. In fact, they conversed with each other more than they davened. Every so often, an old man would bang on his reading stand to rebuke them for speaking during davening. But no one paid him any attention. Neither did they pay attention to the clear blue sky peeking in from the large window in wonder: *Is this what the chosen Shabbos of the year, Shabbos Hagadol, looks like in Morehdalye?*

Khlavneh knew that the discussions were focused on ways to resist the Polish boycott. Once again, he felt his anger against Naftali Hertz welling up. Last night's debate still brewed inside him like water in a large lake that continues to boil and froth after the storm has passed and the waves have calmed. From behind his reading stand, at one of the center benches in the beis medrash, Khlavneh looked up to the mizrach corner, where the rabbi, Sholem Shachne Katzenellenbogen, stood: tall, slender, with a white beard and a pale, otherworldly face. At the other end of the same mizrach wall stood the rabbi's son, his back to the crowd, his tallis draped over his bowed shoulders. He swayed slowly, as though absorbed in his prayers. But Khlavneh observed him with distrust and thought, *Let him live the way he prays, the deserter, the assimilator, the hypocrite!*

When the Torah was taken out of the ark for the leynen, a short, hunchbacked Jew with coal-black eyes and a sparse gray beard came over to Khlavneh. He wore a round, flat, greasy yarmulke and a frayed, weekday tallis. As soon as the man came over, even before he'd said his name, Khlavneh figured out that it must be Zalia Ziskind Luria. From when Khlavneh and Bluma Rivtcha became intimate, Bluma Rivtcha had spoken not only about her large family but about the Visoki-Dvor's former rabbi and rosh yeshiva, her father's friend from Volozhin, who was now helping with the work of the Morehdalye rabbinate. Khlavneh instantly discerned that this hunchback was, indeed, an extraordinary person. That such an old man, a renowned genius in his youth, should come over and address him without ceremony proved it. "I know who you are," Zalia Ziskind said. "You're Bluma Rivtcha's fiancé. Your bride used to sit on my knee when she was a two-year-old girl. Well, and do you believe in the immortality of the soul?" He sighed, brow furrowed, as though his thoughts bothered him even in his sleep. "I mean, do you believe that after the body goes back to the earth, the soul goes up to heaven?"

Before the Vilna guest could give any thought to how to answer such an unexpected question, Zalia Ziskind shuffled back to his corner somewhere behind the bimah, as though he'd suddenly realized it was unbecoming for him to stand and schmooze while the Torah was being taken out and the entire congregation was singing and reading along with the cantor. Khlavneh stood there, stunned. What had the man meant with his question? *Does he want to know if I'm learned in philosophy? Or if I'm a believer?* Bluma Rivtcha had told him that her brother, the doctor, had once studied in Zalia Ziskind's yeshiva and run away to study abroad—though he'd lied at the time and said he was going to study in a bigger yeshiva. Apparently, the educated traditionalist, the rational cynic, had been a liar since his youth.

What an odd shtetl! A guest arrives, the rabbi's future son-in-law, and no one looks his way. Of course, their minds were on something else, their troubles from the Polish bojówkas with their "*Swoj do swego!*" And the town knew that it was not the rabbi who'd chosen this son-in-law but the daughter who'd found herself a groom.

This is why the townspeople aren't paying attention to me. I'm just a plain young man to them. In typical Khlavneh style, he fumed at himself and Bluma Rivtcha, angry that he'd let himself be convinced to come along to her parents. But he quickly remembered that he'd already drawn this conclusion that morning.

The beadle came over to him and asked for his name, so he could be given an aliya. Indeed, Khlavneh was being called up for a very respectable honor: Shishi!*

When Khlavneh walked up to the bimah, he felt everyone's eyes on him. The man who'd been given an aliya just before him, and who was still standing at the bimah, had peyes curled like a Havdalah candle, a drooping lower lip that kept quivering, and such soft, velvety eyes it looked as though he'd been born a grandfather. On one side of the Torah stood the Torah reader, a skinny man with a straight back, barely leaning his head toward the Torah's parchment, as though singing the tropen at the weekly sedrah each Shabbos had left his back stiff as a stick, not allowing him to bend. On the other side of the Torah stood the gabbai, an old man with a white-twined beard and trepidation in his eyes, as though he felt guilty for still being alive. Everyone on the bimah pressed the Vilna guest's hands warmly, and the gabbai even excused himself for not having given him the greater honor of maftir; they needed to save it for someone who had yahrzeit that day. "We'll rectify it when you get married, may we live to see it with happy hearts." The elderly gabbai sighed.

When Khlavneh walked off the bimah, he again noticed that everyone was looking at him, but the glances were preoccupied, troubled, even a bit harsh, as if the Morehdalyens were letting him know: "Dear groom, you came at the wrong time. Polish bojówkas won't let us earn money for Pesach or partake in the joy of anyone's happy occasion."

After maftir, while the Torah scroll was placed back in the holy ark and the crowd recited the "Mizmor L'Dovid" chapter of Tehillim, Zalia Ziskind again appeared next to Khlavneh and began speaking raspily about the same topic as before—but in a bizarre way, as if he could read Khlavneh's thoughts on his forehead.

"Don't think it's my intention to know if you're knowledgeable in

---

* The sixth aliya.

philosophy or that I'm someone's messenger sent to find out if you believe in the immortality of the soul. No, I simply heard you're a thinker, and even a poet, so I wanted to steal a conversation with you. I myself have drawn the conclusion, in the style of philosophy books, that without faith in the Messiah's coming, in the eternal Shabbos, the afterlife, it's impossible to understand why the Creator created human beings in general, and Jews specifically. What do the Morehdalye Jews have in their lives besides struggle?" The hunchback nodded his head toward the worshippers and gazed sadly at Khlavneh. "Do you understand now why I asked you if you believe in a soul's immortality?"

"Hard to place trust in it," Khlavneh replied. "According to some philosophers and all Kabbalists, I think, three things reside in a person's body: the nefesh, ruach, and neshama, meaning the life force, the spirit, and the soul. I even saw in a book of Kabbalah that the soul doesn't reside in the body, but rather, the body resides in the soul, because the soul takes up a third of the world. Still, if a bullet pierces a man, a tiny metal bullet filled with gunpowder, all three—the nefesh, the ruach, and the neshama—fly out of him like birds from a cage when its door is opened. This means that all the tremendous eternal strengths can't keep life in a physical body when it is pierced by a tiny hole. How, then, can I say I believe in the soul's immortality?"

Zalia Ziskind gaped at the young man, as if he'd never expected an answer backed by such strange reasoning. But he said nothing and returned to his spot, so that he could start the Mussaf Shmone Esreh together with the others in the beis medrash. Khlavneh stood with his head bowed, confused and embarrassed that he'd answered with the common sense of a peasant or child. If his simpleminded answer were to reach the doctor's ears, he'd have something to laugh about. And now Zalia Ziskind probably wouldn't approach him again.

But Khlavneh was wrong. After davening, Zalia Ziskind came over to him for the third time, but he didn't ask any questions. He said "Good Shabbos" and started talking right away. "There's another thing people possess, which is called shar ruach, a greatness of spirit. Even people who don't believe in the soul's immortality don't deny this. Many people who aren't convinced that a person has a soul still believe that some individuals possess a neshama yeseira, a special soul. In the same way, those who deny that the soul is immortal can still believe that people possess a shar ruach. But in one person the shar ruach is manifested in his good, pure heart, and in another, in his exalted thoughts. And those who are worthy are blessed on both levels. The shar ruach in a lofty person serves as a consolation during all his troubles. But for the simple person who doesn't possess this shar ruach and doesn't believe in the soul's immortality, life is bitter, very bitter. Then there's another matter: what a man is at his core. There's the man who lives his entire life with everyone considering him a genteel person, and he thinks of himself that way, too. But then something happens in his life that neither he nor anyone could have foreseen. And that's when his silken façade unravels and it's revealed that, at his core, he's a rough, crass soul. Sometimes it's the opposite. A person might have a reputation as being combative and angry, someone who cuts others down, a savage. But when everyone attacks him, tears him apart limb to limb, instead of returning the blows, he bursts into tears, and all he does is complain: '*Mah pishi* . . . how have I rebelled, what sin have I committed that you hound me so?' "*

Khlavneh was certain that the old man must have heard about his fight with Dr. Katzenellenbogen the night before. That's why he was saying these things. But then it occurred to Khlavneh that the old man was referring to the Morehdalye Jews—even the strong ones among them—who weren't tough enough to hit the Polish bojówkas back.

Zalia Ziskind's thoughts, however, rarely stayed on one track. He plucked a hair from his little gray beard, as though he were plucking out a new thought. "I heard about a Jew who was imprisoned for swindling, and everyone says he *did* commit the crime. But when he was asked what he wanted to take along to prison, he said he wanted nothing except his tallis and tefillin. What I deduced from this is that at his core, he's a tallis-and-tefillin Jew, not the swindling type. A drunk would have asked that they bring him a bottle of whiskey every day." For a few moments, Zalia Ziskind paused and looked Khlavneh in the eye with a sad, trusting gaze. "I'm sure you already heard that my son is in prison for aligning himself with the communists. I would like to know what he's reading in prison, communist books or the Tanach. Then I'd know where he stands now." The old man turned

* Genesis 43:31.

his glance to the mizrach corner and suddenly spoke in a strict, commanding tone, as though he'd reassumed his old rosh yeshiva position and he was lecturing a student who'd been misbehaving, or was timid when he shouldn't be, or arrogant. "Go to the rabbi. He's standing there, waiting for you." And Zalia Ziskind rushed away, back to his spot, removed his tallis in a hurry, and shoved his way out of the beis medrash together with the paupers from the back benches.

At Sholem Shachne's sides walked Naftali Hertz and Khlavneh, not exchanging a word. The rabbi, too, was silent, but not in a hostile way. It seemed he wasn't bothered that his son and future son-in-law had already had a falling-out. But he stopped in his tracks several times and, with a melancholy smile, contemplated the houses on the synagogue street and the trees with their naked branches, already trembling with the arrival of sticky pink flower buds. Increasingly, Sholem Shachne would feel a faintness come over him. At times, he felt his heart sinking down into an abyss, as when you fall in a dream. But he hid this from his wife and instead began observing the nature around his house a bit more, the path that led to the wooden bridge over the Narev, and the sky over his head—things he never used to notice.

When they stepped into the rabbi's house, Khlavneh could tell right away that Bluma Rivtcha and the rebbetzin had had a talk. It was obvious that the mother sided with her son and Bluma Rivtcha with her fiancé. Nevertheless, the rebbetzin acted friendly during the meal, joked with Khlavneh that he was a good guest and she had a sign to prove it: the cholent had turned out well.

Naftali Hertz, on the other hand, was silent through the entire meal, his silence so thick and indignant that Khlavneh could feel it suffocating him. *Just look at how enraged the doctor of philosophy is, gobbling up his cholent! Socrates drank his goblet of poison with more composure.*

The rabbi tried to lighten the atmosphere and kidded with Khlavneh: "It's Shabbos Hagadol today, which means the town's rabbi has to say a pilpul. But Morehdalye has three rabbis and none of them can give a talk today. There's me, warned by my doctor not to give speeches. The dayan, Reb Tzadok, can't even get up from his bed. And then there's Zalia Ziskind. But when he was asked to give a talk, he said, 'You hear that? If I was up for giving speeches and pilpulim, I'd have still been rabbi and rosh yeshiva in Visoki-Dvor.' Khlavneh, maybe you want to give the talk today?" The rabbi smiled. "At last night's debate, I saw that you know how to speak and can eat your adversaries alive."

Khlavneh didn't know if this was the rabbi's way of sneaking in a reproach while acting good-natured. But at any rate, he forced himself to smile, and he, too, remained silent.

Whether she was really in a rush or could no longer bear the tense silence at the table, they couldn't tell, but Bluma Rivtcha suddenly stood and said she had to go to the sickly dayan, Tzadok. "Every day he suffers more, and grows more and more angry, more and more capricious. He's unbearable, but I have to go."

"Go, go," Sholem Shachne murmured sadly, and then lapsed into silence for a long while. Tzadok, it seemed, now suspected that Sholem Shachne had sent his daughter, the nurse, as a way of getting even with him. But not to send Bluma Rivtcha would be even worse. Alleviating the terrible suffering of a mortally sick man was more important than protecting himself from a baseless accusation. To Henna'le, Sholem Shachne said, "God in heaven is my witness, I'd be willing for the dayan to fight with me forever, and not owe me for any favors I may have done him, as long as he didn't have to suffer so much."

22

OR SHALOSH SEUDOS, Naftali Hertz went to his former rosh yeshiva, Zalia Ziskind, to avoid having to share a table with Khlavneh. Bluma Rivtcha sat at the table, incensed at her brother, the grumbling hedgehog; at her mother for siding with her brother; and at Khlavneh for turning the discussion into a fight. Added to that, she was still fuming from her visit to the sick dayan. Her injections that were supposed to mitigate his pains were helping less and less, and his resentment against her growing more and more. Henna'le was preparing the food in the kitchen, the rabbi was drumming his fingers on the table, and Khlavneh was making imaginative comparisons in his head to alleviate his boredom in the tense silence.

The red electric lamp above the table, which had been glowing since Friday night, was transformed in Khlavneh's mind to a spirit from the dead, lurking behind a partition among the living. A minute later, it changed; now he compared the lamp to a tree with last year's yellowed leaves; now to the bloody eye of an owl in the woods, and from there to the hidden eye of Divine Providence. The cold, spent candelabrum on the table he compared to two orphaned children, holding hands, taking an evening stroll through a lush forest with even rows of tall trees. But if one looked more closely, the tall trees turned out to be shadows, long thin shadows between earth and sky, not wooden trunks at all. How the candelabrum had created such an image in his mind Khlavneh did not understand, nor did it bother him much. He was pleased with the comparisons and fantasies that sparked easily from his mind and were known by no one. Bluma Rivtcha did in fact understand the metaphors in his poems. But to read the unwritten poems in his eyes—that she could not do. Now Khlavneh brought into his World of Chaos a large round moon: the wall clock. And he began to weave the furniture into his fantasies. Until the rabbi cut him off with a question: "Why aren't you eating?"

Bluma Rivtcha went into the kitchen to help her mother bring in bowls of cold, red borscht whitened with sour cream, slices of gefilte fish, and small bowls of plum compote. They all ate in silence, with no appetite. Khlavneh imagined he could hear the family thinking about their doctor of philosophy, who was absent from the table.

Sholem Shachne slurped his borscht too loudly, too hastily, not at all with the manners of a refined Jew. What he'd said during the cholent course as a joke now truly vexed him. Out of the three rabbis in town, there wasn't one who could give a talk in honor of Shabbos Hagadol. They were lucky, in a manner of speaking, that the Morehdalye Jews were so worried about the boycott and didn't have any speeches in mind. "A miracle from heaven," the rabbi joked to himself bitterly, not touching his portion of fish. *Last night,* he thought, *Khlavneh really gave it to my oldest son—that comment about how he has a habit of running away. First, he ran from yeshiva, then from the Jewish community in Poland, and today he runs from his father's table. In all these years, Naftali Hertz hasn't changed one iota! Has he worked on himself not to change? The jargon boy, as Naftali Hertz calls Khlavneh, is more devout than my son, much more!*

Nevertheless, Sholem Shachne didn't leave Khlavneh alone, perhaps out of vexation, or because he wanted to get to know him better. The rabbi touched a lock of hair on his left cheek, as though there lay the poisonous root of his gloomy thoughts, and he spoke to Khlavneh across the table. "Because of the tense debate with my son last night, I didn't get to ask you two questions: Why did you abandon Jewishness, and why did you choose to become a writer?"

That morning at davening, Zalia Ziskind had questioned Khlavneh, and now it was the rabbi interrogating him. He found all of this tiresome, so he shrugged his shoulders and replied curtly that he didn't know why he'd left Jewishness or why he became a writer. "I feel like that philosopher who claimed people are conscious of what they do but not why they're doing it." But by the rabbi's smile and Bluma Rivtcha's surprised glance, Khlavneh understood that shirking a reply in such a way was even ruder than giving a sharp answer.

Khlavneh's blue eyes darkened, widened. He bit his lips, and through his nostrils blew out the warm gust of words that burned like sand on his tongue. "And who said I abandoned Jewishness? I left the synagogue and went to the Jews in the street. This is why the rabbis have lost their influence over Jewish life, and continue to lose more each day—because when someone leaves the world of the beis medrash, they take it to mean that the person has left Jewishness or even that they've abandoned the Jews. That's why rabbis are religious functionaries now, but not leaders . . ."

The pleasure of responding, of hitting back, intoxicated Khlavneh. Boiling, feverish with the desire to debate, he didn't care that Henna'le was imploring her daughter with her eyes to restrain Khlavneh, to keep him from frothing and roiling so. In vain did Bluma Rivtcha plead with him, silently, to say what he wanted to say but to say it calmly, courteously, softly. But only about love and poetry was Khlavneh able to speak softly, provided he wasn't embarrassed to admit his dreams and emotions to the person with whom he was talking. But in a debate, particularly when he'd been accused of betraying the Torah, that he'd become a heretic, he completely lost his temper. And though the rabbi hadn't actually used these precise words, they were implicit in his question. And so, his future son-in-law replied with an outburst of harsh words, as though he were at the point of divorce:

"The professors, the speakers for the Reform on one side, and the philosophers for the religious on the other, the clean-shaven Rabiners and the old-fashioned rabbis with thick beards and peyes; both the Orthodox and the Reform, no matter how much they may hate each other and move increasingly farther apart, in their correlation to the Jewish community both types of leaders are in the category of limbs 'hanging by a thread.' The leaders tremble and live their lives separately, and the larger Jewish community trembles and lives separately. The Reform have always been jumping out of their skin trying to prove that Judaism and universal ideologies are one and the same! The same! But to the terrible luck of these philosophical, universal Jews, it is written somewhere in the Talmud, 'Greater is the one who is commanded and fulfills the mitzvah than one who isn't commanded and still fulfills it.'* And from all the holy books that Torah students hang on, the same idea emerges: Whoever observes

* Kiddushin 31 a–b. *"Gadol ha'mitzuveh v'oseh mi'mi she'eyno mitzuveh v'oseh."*

ethical commandments because God gave them to us is on a higher level than those who observe the same commandments by their own determination. Well, that doesn't comply with Immanuel Kant! According to him, ethics is a categorical imperative. A person is the one who gives himself these morals, not a God outside of him—and not to reach a goal, to improve the situation of the poor, say, or because another person's lonesomeness gnaws at his heart. Heaven forbid! Ethics, according to Kant, is autonomous. It takes commands from no one except itself and has no need to satisfy anyone or anything except its own categorical imperative, as though man's morals were a German kaiser, the only one who can give out commands for himself. Well, then it doesn't comply with the ethics of the Prophets—and it must! In the ancient times of the philosopher Philo of Alexandria, the Torah of Moses complied with the Greek Plato; in the times of the Rambam, the Torah of Moses complied with the Greek Aristotle; and during the times of the Ramban—which is how the maskilim ceremoniously refer to Reb Moses Mendelssohn—the Torah of Moses complied with the enlightened Germans. So now, the Torah of Moses must comply with the Ethics of Immanuel Kant! A bridge! A bridge for the universal Jews. Where does one find the invented and contrived bridge to tie together the two paper planets of Moshe Rabbeinu and Immanuel Kant? Till finally, the founder of 'Folk Psychology,' the great erudite man and even greater windbag, Professor Moshe-Moritz Lazarus-Latzarus, with all due respect, for he's a corpse by now . . . till he finally built this bridge and saved the planets of Moses' faith! Not because God gave the commandments are they moral, but because the moral laws within people are their categorical imperative. That's why God gave it to them. It follows that God isn't the lawgiver of ethics but the symbol and embodiment of ethics. Now everything is clear and has been answered in the twinkling of an eye!

"Then, a much bigger professor and a 'sincere' Jew—he was observant even in his old age—proved through his entire philosophical logic that Jewish morals and the morals of Germany, of Protestant Germany, are generally and specifically as similar to each other as two drops of water. Listen, there was a reason he was the professor and sage, Hermann Cohen! So that he could twirl and untwirl philosophical treatises around his thumb! But the Orthodox, who don't have such philosophers and world-renowned windbags as their theorists, do have more than enough pious German Jews, Galician thinkers in yarmulkes, and writers in Polish hats from all kinds of Hasidic courts, who also write their fingers off. But they are out to prove exactly the opposite of what the Reform Jews are claiming: they want to prove that we *are* different. '*Mah bein beni* . . . What is the difference between my sons and my father-in-law?* *Mah bein nevieh Yisroel* . . . What is the difference between the Prophets of Israel and the prophets of other nations? What's the difference between the monotheism of Abraham and the god of Malchei Tzedek, king of Shalem? And why must we say *lehavdil* a million times between the "Thou shalt not murder" that is etched onto Moses' tablets and the "Thou shalt not murder" on the clay tablets of other nations and that now stands as the general belief? And in which way were the Jews at the time of their conquest of Canaan different from other immigrants and conquerors? Why was Jehoshua ben Nun allowed to command his soldiers to ride over the necks of the Canaanite kings; and why was King David allowed to survey, count, and kill a third of the Moabites, while another king, one who practiced idolatry, was permitted to do no such thing? And in which way were the Jews different from their neighbors during the First Temple era, the Second Temple era, and all other eras? And in which way is the ideology of a Jewish Messiah fundamentally different from the ideology of a redeemer and the redemption of all other nations on earth? And in which way are the best of the "righteous of other nations" who want to abolish rich and poor, loneliness and hate, in which way is their dream of a future different from the Jewish dream of a Messianic era? In which way is the Jewish faith different, the Jewish psychology different, and the lamentations and songs different—solidly, definitively different? Indeed, what is the idea behind the belief that even the most sinful of the sinful—as long as he has a Jewish spark, the sort of spark espoused by Hasidism and Kabbalah—is different and stands far, far above a non-Jew? In what does the secret of the Jewish soul lie, and wherein lies the secret and foundation of the Jewish laws? Why are the laws of all nations in the world formed according to their character, but for Jews it's the opposite: their character was

* Genesis 25:33.

formed according to the Divine commandments on Mount Sinai? Yes, and in which way are Jewish excommunications and penalties and lashings so different from just such punishments by other religions, *lehavdil* a thousand times?' These are the things Jewish philosophers kill themselves over: in what ways are Jews different. And the preachers for a universal Judaism struggle to prove in what ways pure Jewry is *not* different. The enlightened are separated from the nation, and the fundamentalists don't take the nation into account. 'The Torah doesn't take the reality of general life into account,' say the men of Torah. But the one who's truly woven into the fabric of the Jewish community, with all his blood and marrow, when he's truly a 'living limb' of the Jewish body, those people know by their own body and soul in what way Jews are different from their neighbors. At the same time, they also know in what ways Jews are worldly and humanistic and *not* different from their neighbors. And they don't want to be different, no matter how much Jews themselves or their neighbors keep them fenced and grated and separated from the entire world."

Toward the end of his tirade, Khlavneh stood and shouted across to the rabbi, as though the rabbi were on the other side of a river's shore. Henna'le looked at her daughter, and her eyes spoke volumes: *I understand now how this man seduced and captivated Bluma Rivtcha.* Just as the evening before, when Khlavneh had debated her brother, Bluma Rivtcha now felt proud of her fiancé. But at the same time, she looked anxiously at her father. Besides his oldest daughter, none of his children had heeded him. Each of them had chosen their own path in life. But they had done it with stubborn silence and cast-down eyes, while Khlavneh spoke boldly and openly straight to his face.

Khlavneh wiped the sweat from his forehead and added, "The racket on the street where I live spilled through the windows of Shaulke's shtiebel, where I studied for years, where my words sang out onto the street. The street and the prayer house are like twins to me, a pair. Even the people from my neighborhood who haven't stepped over the threshold of a beis medrash for years, they carry it inside them, though with a different face. You shouldn't ask me or my kind why we left the beis medrash, because in our own way, we haven't left. Perhaps you should ask someone else this question,"

Khlavneh concluded. He saw quite well how this comment provoked Henna'le. The audacity to stab them so unrestrainedly about their oldest son!

Sholem Shachne sat completely still—pale, mute, his face pained. Khlavneh became quiet and sat down, looking confused. After unloading his torrent of words, he understood that he shouldn't have let himself get so carried away or speak as sharply to the rabbi as he'd spoken to his son.

Apparently, Sholem Shachne sensed Khlavneh's regret, and he smiled warmly. But aggravation still trembled in his voice and eyes. "My son says that Jews can't be real Jews if they don't observe the mitzvahs. But he himself isn't a mitzvah observer. You, on the other hand, speak about the nation, the nation, but forgive me, I don't detect too much love for Jews in you. Never mind that you and my son both forget about the power of love for Torah. Both of you have studied for years, after all. Have you forgotten that Jews give away their own family's food to support those who study Torah? Do you see nothing in the fact that such an impoverished shtetl like Morehdalye is supporting a dayan, a rabbi, and a rabbi's substitute?" Sholem Shachne sighed. He didn't wait for an answer, and Khlavneh had no intention of answering. But Sholem Shachne hadn't forgotten his earlier question, and he repeated it: "So why did you become a writer?"

"I don't know why, exactly, and I don't know yet if I'll remain a writer. I started only a few years ago." Khlavneh was quiet for a while, as though mulling over whether to continue speaking. "But since you ask me, I'll tell you the truth. What I really think is that just as I left the yeshiva to live the life of those on my street, I became a writer to depict that life." Suddenly, he gave the rabbi a furtive look and said in a boyish voice, "If you want, I'll tell you something I've never told anyone, not even Bluma Rivtcha."

23

H ENNA'LE GAVE HER husband and daughter a tense look, as
though to ask them whether it might be best not to know this
thing he'd yet to tell a soul. A young man of his age must understand
that some things shouldn't be said. But it seemed he was one of those
types who, once they start talking, let everything spill. And apparently, her husband and daughter didn't share her feelings, because
they looked somber and curious as they readied themselves to hear
what he had to say.

Khlavneh took a long time formulating the right words. The
shadowed figures at the table—and, it seemed, the blue Shabbos
night in the windows of the rabbi's house—listened as the young
man recounted a childhood experience that was etched in his memory. "My parents and I lived in Vilna then, up Zavalne Street, in
a cellar a few steps down from the street, in Eisenstadt the wine
dealer's courtyard. Father kept a cheder with students there, and
Mother a tearoom. I was seven years old. This was in the war years,
and I used to play 'soldiers' with the other children in the street."
Khlavneh remembered suddenly, as though from a dream, the melody his father sang when he studied the weekly sedrah with the
cheder boys. He remembered, too, the women who'd come down
the cellar steps to buy teakettles of hot water from his mother. "My
mother also cooked dinner for people from the street. And villagers
who came to the city for a few days and didn't have enough money
to stay in an inn used to sleep in our cellar. Three lodgers lived with
us year-round. One was a Jew from Ukraine, who'd been injured in
the war and had a limp. The second, a Vilna shlimazel with a goatee,
carried around a crate of knives and bags of needles, ribbons, and
shoelaces to sell. And it's because of the third lodger that I'm telling you this story. I barely remember how the first two looked. But

I remember very well how the third one looked on a certain day of his life—his last day.

"I don't remember him from before, I didn't know his name or who he was. He and I were alone at home one afternoon. Until this day I don't know how it came to be that there was no one besides us in the cellar. Me, a boy of about seven, and him, eighty-something—as I found out years later. Even though he was very old, he put the fear of God in me with his big, thick, heavy body. He had long hands, a large, full face, pitch-black eyes, thick hair, and a beard that wasn't yet gray. I remember, he was in a semi-prone position on a sofa, completely dressed, and he was dying. That this was the hour of his dying, I later understood. Then, at seven years old, I waited there, I remember, in a corner, and I watched, mute with fear, the way he shuddered violently, how he panted and snored, how he smacked his fat lips and froth bubbled from his mouth. But no less powerful than my fear was my wonder at a set of pencils sticking out from his jacket pocket. I couldn't run away, I was paralyzed by fear and by my desire for those long, sharpened pencils. His dying ebbed and soon rose again, he raised his head, his eyes fixed, and he wheezed. In those early childhood years, I'd heard people crying over war victims many times, the ones who'd died of hunger, the ones who'd died of epidemics, but this was the first time I stood face-to-face with death, and I didn't know what it was. I remember to this day how I shuddered and trembled. I couldn't even scream, so terrified was I. But at the same time, I couldn't tear my eyes away from the pack of pencils in his upper pocket. I didn't think to crawl over and take out a pencil, but the desire I had for those pencils, at least for one of them, I still haven't forgotten. I don't remember if my parents arrived before the man died, or after. But I remember that later, serious, respectable men came down to the cellar and questioned Mother about something for a long time. I remember that the entire Zavalne Street was flooded with people, and they all pushed into our cellar. That was probably the next day already, and the large crowd came to escort the dead man.

"Gradually, that deathbed scene got pushed to the recesses of my memory, and only years later did it get dredged up in my recollection. I was already a bar mitzvah then, and for days on end I'd devour religious storybooks. They used to be called 'white books,' because they didn't have hard covers, only paper backs. One time my mother looked into such a book and cried out, 'Who are you reading? Yehoshua HaLevi Mezach? That's the writer who lived in our cellar for a little while and died here.' Mother didn't know anything else about this man. I didn't ask Father about him either. I wasn't very interested. Soon, I threw away the storybooks, became more and more drawn to Torah study, and left for a yeshiva. Years passed in this way, until I began writing poems and became interested in this Yehoshua HaLevi Mezach. I leafed through his books and looked for information about him in the memoirs of old writers."

"I've never read him," Bluma Rivtcha said, feeling antsy that, in response to her father's question on why he became a writer, Khlavneh was telling a story about a miserable Jew. "I've never even heard his name."

"The other Yiddish writers hadn't read him either, and some of them had never heard of him. But I wanted to find out more about him because he was the first Yiddish writer I'd met and the first person I'd seen die," Khlavneh said, and continued his tale about this forgotten writer. "Yehoshua Mezach wrote in lashon kodesh in all the publications of his day. His language was flowery, interlaced with biblical verses, as was the style of the other maskilim of that time. He wrote against the leaders, calling them imposters, bloodsuckers, leeches, all of it in the language of the enlightened people of that day. But he believed in faith in God, too, not just in the Haskalah. He vagabonded through all of Russia up to Crimea. In one place he was a teacher, in another a merchant, in a third a traveling salesman. From the money he earned he published anthologies with childish, innocent names like *Flower Garden* or *Flowers and Roses*. He published these anthologies or notebook collections in Vilna, Warsaw, and Berditchev, and he paid the writers out of his own pocket until his money ran out. But he continued to write, write, write, and found patrons to publish his writings: some well-to-do maskilim, a Rabiner, and a Jew who worked as a censor in the tsarist government. In this way, year after year, he published his *Mikhtavim M'sar shel yam*,* in which the world is a sea where the bigger fish devour the smaller ones, and he, Yehoshua HaLevi Mezach, dreams of being the lord of the sea

* *Letters from the Minister of the Sea.*

that punishes the predators and robbers. Among real writers he was laughed at for his naïveté, but he believed in himself. No matter how much he wrote, he could never forget the great misfortune that befell him. At an inn in Berditchev, his diary, in which he'd recorded his wanderings and encounters over decades, was burned. There, in that Berditchev inn, his clothing caught fire, his beard was singed, his body left with branding scars, but for years and years all he bemoaned was the loss of his writings, his book of memories, his book of travels."

"What did he write about so much?" Henna'le interjected with feigned curiosity. Like her daughter, she couldn't understand why he was telling this story.

But it didn't occur to Khlavneh that the women were, quite simply, not interested in Mezach's works. Which is why he replied heatedly, "About what *didn't* he write? He wrote in Yiddish more than in Hebrew, about everything that's sad and everything that's joyful. About the misfortunes and calamities that Jews have experienced, all over, from the times of the Temple's destruction to today. And he called his little books *Nidchei Yisroel,** Part One and Part Two, *Shearis Yisroel,*† Parts One, Two, and Three, in the style of old chronicles. He wrote stories about the Patriarchs, about Elijah the Prophet, about lamed-vovniks, about the Baal Shem Tov and his disciples, about Alexander the Great and other kings, stories about Kabbalists, Jewish popes, wildcats, and cursed souls. Besides that, he wrote about nature, about all kinds of different animals and birds, about the stars in the sky and the plants in the seas. And he wrote and published calendars with jokes, collections of anecdotes and sayings, prayers for women, a Haggadah for Pesach, and the five megillahs with his own commentary. But more than that he wrote tales, plays for the theater, and novels with many parts."

"And you remember everything this man wrote? Was he such a great writer?" Henna'le asked, and this time Khlavneh picked up on her ridicule, on her surprise that his mind was crammed not with Torah and education but with storybooks. But he wouldn't let himself be provoked by his future mother-in-law, as he had the evening before by his future brother-in-law.

---

* *The Outcasts of Israel.*
† *The Remnants of Israel.*

He turned his head this way and that and replied agreeably, "As I said before, Rebbetzin, this Yehoshua Mezach is not considered a good writer. And I became interested in his life and works because as a child I witnessed his death and longed for his pencils . . . Well, where was I? Naturally, his storybooks sold better than any of his other writings. It's said that his storybooks used to sell by the hundreds of thousands, and even more, though this seems greatly exaggerated. But what is certain is that Mezach's storybooks made his publishers rich. Each book had thirty-two sheets and the author got a ruble for it. Each week, he prepared such a book, but the ruble he received was not enough for even half a week's living. On occasion, the publishers paid him with a certain number of copies of his book, which he'd carry around and sell, the way itinerant booksellers used to sell storybooks to the housemaids and poor, pious authors toted their books around to wealthy homeowners."

"I don't understand why you're talking about this outdated writer and his storybooks. Are you his heir? Are you comparing yourself to him?" Bluma Rivtcha cried.

Khlavneh had intended to respond even more angrily—"You romantic bride, you probably thought I'd start comparing myself to the English poet Byron!"—but in the jaundiced light of the electric lamp above the table that had been on since Friday evening, Khlavneh saw that the rabbi was listening very seriously, with great interest. So he restrained himself and replied, "I can't explain why, but I feel that the story has a connection to me and is an answer to the question of why I became a writer. I am speaking about human fate."

Seeing that Sholem Shachne was listening with more attentiveness than his rebbetzin or daughter, Khlavneh stopped looking at the women and spoke only to the rabbi. "In my childhood years, and later in yeshiva, I forgot that scene from the cellar. But since I started writing and publishing poems, I saw that image of Yehoshua HaLevi Mezach dying more and more, right before my eyes, and I saw myself, a boy of seven, watching from a corner of the cellar. About the time I became a writer, I got to know an outmoded man of letters from Vilna, one of the only ones who'd known Yehoshua Mezach well and had written respectfully about him. This biographer of Mezach was also a failure, inept, ignored already in his lifetime. But there's a kind of man who's never quite forgotten in his lifetime, only because he gives heartless people the chance to make fun of someone, and that's the sort of victim this Mezach biographer was. He liked to speak with pathos and lots of Rs: *Karrrl Marrrx, rrrevolutionary, prrroletariat.* He wore a coat with threadbare sleeves and missing buttons, a vagrant's wrinkled hat, and misshapen shoes. He walked with mincing steps and kept adjusting the pair of pince-nez that was constantly falling off his nose and hung on a black cord, like a little boy's mittens, strung through his coat sleeves so he wouldn't lose them." Khlavneh, who had just called the mockers "heartless people," laughed loudly.

But he quickly gained his composure and continued his narrative: "It's possible that because this man of letters was a failure himself, he liked to write biographies about unrecognized or ignored writers, and he happily conversed with anyone who wanted to listen to him. And so, I befriended him and questioned him about the object of his writings, Yehoshua HaLevi Mezach. He was extremely happy I was reading his biographies. He said, 'The critics committed a terrible crime against Mezach!' Whatever he talks about, this biographer of Mezach, he uses the most flowery language. For example, if he complains about a young poet who makes fun of him for being old-fashioned, he'll say, 'And I had still edited his first poems! That snake I carried on my neck . . .'"

"Well, what did he tell you about Yehoshua Mezach?" the rabbi prompted him, so that he'd realize his digression.

"The biographer," Khlavneh replied, "told me a bit about Mezach's character and a lot about his poverty, which the biographer hadn't written about so as not to give Jewish literature a bad name. Though Mezach had written an entire library, had traveled the world and met a great number of people, he remained a naïve Jew. Added to that, he had this delusion that he knew things about everyone they didn't know about themselves, and so, he looked at everything with a crooked, untrustworthy smile. He lived out his life quibbling with, and then apologizing to, the other maskilic writers of his generation, who basically belittled him. But he didn't have enough talent to understand that he was allowed to doubt himself a little. Still, his self-confidence gave him the strength to endure his extreme loneliness and poverty. For a quarter of a century, he lived in a little room with a door right to the street. From the filthy outdoors you fell into a filthier apartment, four feet by four feet. For twenty-five years he lived in this storage room with unpainted walls and an unopened little window. No one ever wiped the dust there or swept out the cobwebs that hung from the ceiling and hovered in all the corners. The panes of the only window were black, dirty paper pasted all around them, and the walls were covered in rot. Moss grew from the floor. His room—a trashcan, strewn with foul rags, a wobbly chair, and an equally wobbly table and bed. To keep them from buckling and breaking, their owner placed books beneath their legs. And there were more books on the windowsill, strewn across the floor, beneath the bed, in the corners; books, brochures, journals, bundles of newspapers and stacks of writings—long, yellowed, densely filled sheets of paper. But the shambles was even messier with writing instruments. Everywhere lay pens, pencils, chalk, and inkwells: some filled with ink, some dried out, empty black jars, bowls, saucers, and pails, all black and dirty from ink. And beside these were kerosene lamps, clay candlesticks, pieces of not-yet-burned-down candles. A crowdedness, a darkness, and odors—you could suffocate! And in the midst of this dirt and debris sat Yehoshua HaLevi, writing and writing . . .”

"Stop already! Your description, too, could make a person suffocate, go insane!" Bluma Rivtcha cried, jumping up.

"He came to your house later?" the rabbi asked, as though to show his daughter that he *was* interested in what her fiancé was relating.

"Yes, he came to our cellar later," Khlavneh replied in a low voice, suddenly crestfallen. He realized that Bluma Rivtcha was angry with him for telling this entire story. Actually, he himself didn't really know why he'd told it. But the rabbi was waiting for the conclusion, so Khlavneh had to go on with his saga, now explaining how the writer Mezach couldn't live off his one ruble a week from the publisher and began to deliver newspapers, too. "Yehoshua Mezach, an old man of over seventy, started delivering newspapers. His biographer testified to this. He also said that in the war's famine years, Mezach stood for entire days in the communal kitchen line to get a meager cup of soup for free, or nearly free. By then the once-strong man was complaining that he was old and weak. But still, he was driven by the desire to write. '*Yaser yasrenu yuh*,' he used to say: 'God punished me with a burning passion for writing.' But his punishment was also his blessing. Writing gave him vitality. And though he was already stooped, extinguished, in a line for free soup, he lit up each time he saw another old, starving, and forgotten writer approaching. 'Ach, ach,' he sighed for them, as though he were envious of younger writers. They would outlive the bad years and continue to write, write, write . . ."

"It's obvious that for Yehoshua Mezach writing became a sickness." Sholem Shachne smiled sadly.

Khlavneh agreed. "So it appears. His writing became a sickness, and living in filth became a sickness, too. But what old age transforms into a sickness is a passion in a person's young, vibrant years, and Mezach's burning passion stemmed from this type of healthy source. A writer writes because his nature demands it, the way a tree blossoms in the springtime. But a tree can't have the thought that its purpose is to bring forth fruits, while a person can come up with a goal based on what's actually his nature. Mezach also devised a goal, a maskilic goal for his passion to write: he wanted to educate the nation by telling a story with a moral lesson."

"Did you tell that scribe, that biographer, as you call him, that Yehoshua Mezach died in your parents' home?" the rabbi asked.

"No, I didn't," Khlavneh replied, taken aback. The rabbi had asked the one thing he didn't want to talk about, but by now Khlavneh was trapped. He realized Sholem Shachne was waiting, extremely interested, for some reason, to hear the answer to his question. "In fact, the biographer told me only a little more than what he'd already written in his book. He said that Mezach disappeared for a period of time. Nobody saw him or heard from him. Then, people said that Mezach died and was lying in a deep cellar somewhere, a cellar with a tea shop on Zavalne Street. The biographer said he didn't know if Mezach had died in that cellar or on the street and was taken to the cellar afterward, where he'd been living among coarse people who hadn't even known who their lodger was. I wanted to answer this man of letters, this biographer, to tell him that yes, Mezach had died among poor people, but they were refined—my own parents' cellar. My father was pushed down there with his cheder of students through the misfortunes of war. My father, who was enlightened and well versed in Tanakh, *did* know who Mezach was and treated him with respect, that's what I wanted to tell him, this biographer who wrote about people as outdated and ignored as he was. I also wanted to tell him how I watched Mezach's dying from my corner and stared in awe at the sharpened pencils in his upper pocket. But I didn't utter a word about remembering Yehoshua HaLevi Mezach in the last hour of his life. And I couldn't understand why I'd been so reluctant to tell him, which gnawed at me. I met him again another time, again drew him into a conversation, and again heard the same tale that the folk writer Mezach had died in a deep cellar, or on the sidewalk near the cellar, where he'd lived with coarse people who had no idea who he was. Once again, I said nothing, and to this day I don't understand precisely why. Was I ashamed to admit that it was me and my parents living in that cellar, or did I feel guilty that I'd craved Mezach's pencils while he lay dying? Maybe I was silent because I understood that the failed, embittered biographer needed the consolation that Yehoshua Mezach, too, was not valued and had died forgotten among coarse people. Lately, I haven't seen this biographer around. He avoids me because he probably suspects that I, too, laugh at his writing and at the way he talks with such pathos. I don't laugh at him. But because he avoids me, I follow him around to keep him from thinking that my previous conversations with him were because I wanted to make fun of him."

The entire time that Khlavneh spoke to the rabbi, he sat with his back to his fiancée and her mother, as if he wasn't at all bothered that they thought harshly of him. But the longer he spoke, the more it seemed to Khlavneh that he was saying unnecessary things. Droplets of sweat gathered on his forehead. The rabbi would think he was a chatterbox.

Apparently, though, that's not what the rabbi thought. For a while, he shook his head in quiet sorrow, and then he glanced out the window to the dark outdoors, where lamps were starting to light in Jewish homes. "Time to daven Maariv and say the Havdalah," the rabbi said, standing up.

While Khlavneh spoke with her husband, Henna'le had listened in angry silence. Her thoughts pressed on her mind like lead: *What a hotheaded, loquacious man he is. You can tell that the thoughts in his head boil like potatoes in a pot of hot water. Not an easy life for Bluma Rivtcha, with a man like him. But heaven forbid I say a word! I would be both the fool and the wrongdoer. Anyway, Bluma Rivtcha would listen to me like a hole in the head. All I'd achieve would be to make my daughter sin by not obeying her mother.* Henna'le's leg was numb from sitting in one place for so long. Groaning, she stood up and looked at the door, as though wondering why Naftali Hertz still wasn't back. Was he sitting with Zalia Ziskind for that long? At such times, the saying applied: "The neighbor steps in and the owner is driven out." Bluma Rivtcha brought in a boy, and their biological son was driven out of the house.

After Havdalah and the evening's bread, when the rabbi and rebbetzin had already retired to their bedroom, Khlavneh and Bluma Rivtcha lingered in the dining room. Lit up by the dark red bulb of the electric lamp, the couple stood at the table and argued quietly. Bluma Rivtcha reproached Khlavneh for talking about Yehoshua HaLevi Mezach the entire time. "I bring you to my parents, and you regale them with the happy scene of you as a child watching an old, poor, abandoned Yiddish writer dying."

"Well, your mother didn't, but your father understood very well why I was telling it. You're just ashamed that I told them I come from a poor family," Khlavneh replied.

"Not true. You're the one who was ashamed to tell the biographer that Yehoshua Mezach died in your parents' cellar. So why weren't you ashamed to tell it to my father? And why did you never ever speak about Yehoshua Mezach before?"

"Because you never asked me, like your father did, why I became a writer. So I never told you about this episode from my childhood, when I longed for the pencils in the pocket of a poor dying writer."

Though Bluma Rivtcha had seen people dying in hospitals, she shuddered at the image Khlavneh had depicted. She didn't want to fight. Still, she couldn't make peace with Khlavneh's character and behavior. "You're odd. You hold a debate with my brother, turn the debate into a quarrel, and you don't leave any room for conversation. My father asks you a question, and you tell him everything without leaving anything out." Bluma Rivtcha exhaled, exhausted, and sat down on the sofa near the door.

"It was your brother who started the fight, because he called Yiddish a jargon." Khlavneh, too, sat down on the sofa, but not next to her. "And as far as what you're saying that I don't leave anything out, I'm glad you think so . . . Did you notice how I kept talking about Mezach's biographer but never mentioned his name? And your father didn't ask for it. You know why?"

"No. It didn't occur to me to ask."

"But your father noticed it very well, and he didn't ask," Khlavneh ended triumphantly, and moved farther away from his fiancée. "It's true that you're a rabbi's daughter, but I know better than you how Torah men behave. When you say that someone is a subject of ridicule, you're not permitted to say his name, because it's forbidden to tell others about someone else's failure. That's why I didn't say. If I'd have mentioned a name, I'd be reduced, in your father's estimation. But I knew that telling him about my parents' poor home would raise his opinion of me. Your father knows this verse from the Gemara as well as I do: 'Be careful with the children of paupers, because from them come men of Torah.' So why can't Yiddish poets come from poor homes?"

"What's the name of the biographer?" Bluma Rivtcha moved closer to her fiancé.

"His name is A. I. Goldschmid."

"The teacher Goldschmid?" Bluma Rivtcha cried, astonished. "I know him from the Jewish school where I'm the nurse, and from the summer colony in Verek. It's true, he's a loser. I myself saw how his students rode on each other like Cossacks on horses during his lessons." Bluma Rivtcha laughed, the way everyone did at this teacher and writer.

But Khlavneh didn't laugh. He said, "Just as I stared at the pencils of the dying writer when I was a child, Goldschmid was the first Yiddish writer who came to read my poems, back when I was still sitting over the Gemara in Shaulke's shtiebel. I wondered many times why Goldschmid took the trouble to come to me. Did he still believe in that maskilic ideal, that Torah learners must be rescued out of the beis medrash? Only later did I understand it was just the opposite. It was he who missed the beis medrash. And a beginner poet sitting at the Gemara might still hold him in the kind of prestige that more sophisticated people wouldn't. Through the pince-nez on his nearsighted eyes, Goldschmid used to absorb himself in my verses, which I'd written on the sides of notebook paper. He'd cry out in awe, 'This poem is a two-syllable iamb! And this one is a three-syllable dactyl!'

I admitted that I didn't know the forms. I didn't even know meter. But Goldschmid was even more impressed. 'That's because you're a true poet. You know all the forms and rhythms without even having studied them.'

"But I was confused by Goldschmid's appearance, by his impoverished clothes. He wore an outdated elastic collar, yellowed cuffs, a pince-nez on a black cord, and such a shabby hat it looked as if someone had put it on him to humiliate him. I asked myself: 'Is this what the writer's life looks like?' And I vacillated even more than before, over whether I should leave the Torah or not. Still, even after I left the beis medrash, and the group of young poets took me into their clique, I stayed friends with Goldschmid. It hurt my heart that everyone laughed and sneered at him. The young poets had a low opinion of Goldschmid's nationalistic poems. In the teachers' room, they avoided him because he'd abandoned his revolutionary ideals. In class, the students spun circles around him, and there was such chaos that the other classes couldn't learn either. He had studied history and languages when he was in jail, as a young unmarried man, and in the cellars where he lived. But the people who studied with him in the university said he was a researcher without discipline. He immersed himself completely in biographies of ignored writers, or writers who'd died young, tragically—but people criticize him for having no restraint. He's an enthusiast. The community gave him a position in a museum. His job was to guard the dead world. But he wasn't paid a salary. In the winter he froze, and in the summer, he choked on the dust. But he was the biggest failure of all to his wife and children. Still, his son has begun to write poems. Maybe because, fundamentally, he likes his father and wants to emulate him; or maybe it's just the opposite, he despises his father and wants to show him that he can best him even at poetry."

"And why can't it be that he writes poems not out of love, not out of hate, but simply because he was also born with a talent for poetry? You always like to cast everything in a bad light," Bluma Rivtcha said, infuriated. "And why do you only talk about unlucky writers like Mezach and Goldschmid? Haven't you met any lucky ones? Do you want to scare me into breaking our engagement, or are you testing me?"

"It's not true, what you're saying, that I always like to cast everything in a bad light." Khlavneh was angry, too. "Of course, I know some famous writers, and I'm jealous of their success. But my heart isn't drawn to the successful ones, nor to the ones who are right. It's true I don't observe mitzvahs, but I'm more stringent with the 'between man and man' commandments than many devout people. There's a verse that says God sides with the persecuted. And the Gemara says God sides with the persecuted even when the persecuted is evil and the persecutor is righteous."

"What a kind person you are." Bluma Rivtcha snuggled up to him. She was weary of the long discussions, but worse, of the dark red light from the electric lamp, which had been lit since Friday evening, for more than twenty-four hours. She stretched her arm across the sofa and twisted the socket. Sudden darkness washed over them. Bluma Rivtcha anticipated that her fiancé would press her hard against him after a long day of chatter and more chatter. But she was out of luck. Into the house stepped Naftali Hertz, and he remained standing in the doorway. Though he couldn't see, he instantly sensed who the couple on the sofa was. Silently, he felt his way across the darkness till he passed the room and reached his bedroom. Bluma Rivtcha was dismayed. Had her brother gone to bed hungry because he hadn't wanted to disturb them? Khlavneh was dismayed, too. Had the doctor refused to stop because he didn't want to talk to him?

"You know why your brother hates me? Because he hates himself. And he hates himself because he can't stop being a Jew." A thought occurred to Khlavneh, and he became so astonished by it that he burst into laughter. "You know what? Your brother hates me and he hates himself because, besides other reasons—and in fact, mainly for this reason—his wife hates him!"

"What makes you think his wife hates him?" Bluma Rivtcha stopped snuggling.

"Just look at how despondent and sour your brother is, and you can tell, like you're reading his palm, that his wife hates him. If she's tall and pretty, she for sure hates him. But if she's short, he hates her. That's definitely how it is."

"You're no giant, and without my high-heeled shoes, I'm shorter than you. Do you hate me?" Bluma Rivtcha wanted to know.

But Khlavneh stood his ground. "Besides being short, your brother's wife is also ugly. For sure."

"You're a bit too sure of everything you say. It so happens that my brother's wife is tall and pretty. He told me. See?" Bluma Rivtcha stretched him out, somewhat forcefully, across the sofa.

"Who cares what your brother says? Did you see a picture of her?" Khlavneh let himself be stretched and pulled his fiancée with him.

"He doesn't have a picture of his wife and son. He says he forgot to bring one."

Triumphantly, Khlavneh said, "Some excuse! He didn't bring a photo of his wife because she's short and ugly, a slob. For sure."

Bluma Rivtcha didn't want to hear anything more. She sealed his lips with her mouth, only wanting to feel the taste of his hot, fleshy kisses. But unwillingly, thoughts of her brother and his disturbed life entered her mind. He didn't hide the fact that he and his wife weren't getting along, but he never said why. Her mother had told her that, the whole time Naftali Hertz was here, he hadn't received a single letter from home. Bluma Rivtcha remembered clearly how she and Refael'ke had maintained an implicit silence on the subject of Naftali Hertz. In his letters from Israel, too, Refael'ke said nothing about Naftali Hertz. Now, she had noticed, her father and mother avoided looking Naftali Hertz in the eye. Could it be that her parents, like Refael'ke and her, suspected that his wife might be Christian? For what other reason would he have avoided visiting his parents for so many years? And when he finally did come, he didn't bring his wife and son with him, not even a single photograph.

"Unbutton my blouse in the back," Bluma Rivtcha said, unlocking her lips for a moment from Khlavneh's.

"Your parents or brother might walk in," Khlavneh murmured nervously, but unbuttoned the blouse down her back.

"Nobody will come in." She could barely breathe, choked under his heavy body, intoxicated by the sweet pain of her full, velvety breasts, like plump bunches of grapes.

24

AFTER A SHABBOS of so much talk and debate with the rabbi's son and the rabbi himself, Khlavneh was happy to stay in his bedroom—the room in which Bentzion and Refael'ke had once slept—through the first half of Sunday. Bluma Rivtcha had already gone to the sick dayan in the morning, and Khlavneh had plenty of time to think about the family he was marrying into. In Vilna he'd gotten to know Bluma Rivtcha's youngest brother, the tall, broad-shouldered Refael'ke, with his blond beard and quiet eyes beneath large glasses. While Refael'ke had been in Vilna, completing his agricultural training for the move to Israel, Khlavneh hadn't paid him much attention. He hadn't even noticed that when he'd chatter on and on without interruption, Refael'ke would listen with a smile in his quiet eyes and on his full, beautifully chiseled lips. Only after the chalutz had left for Israel did Khlavneh start bringing him up more to Bluma Rivtcha. "You know, I really miss Refael'ke," he'd say. "I hadn't even realized what a sweet, polite boy he is. Is your brother Bentzion the same way?"

"Bentzion's a different sort," Bluma Rivtcha replied reluctantly. "He wants to be a merchant, or at the very least, manage someone's business." And in response to Khlavneh's question about her old-est brother in Switzerland, Bluma Rivtcha was even more curt: "I barely remember him." But when Khlavneh asked about her older sister, Bluma Rivtcha burst out, "Tilza is a dishrag. She married the man Father chose for her, and now she can't forgive herself for it. But if she had to do it over again, she'd again have obeyed Father, rosh-yeshiva'te that she is. And Bentzion isn't as quiet and kind as Refael'ke; he's busy with himself only."

Afterward, Bluma Rivtcha was clearly upset at herself for bad-mouthing her own siblings, and she cried in a singsong tone, "Why're you asking me? You'll meet them, and you'll see for yourself. Not that you're very perceptive about people. You only got what Refael'ke is about after he left."

Now that Khlavneh had met Naftali Hertz, and had had that debate with him, he marveled at Refael'ke even more. It had never occurred to Refael'ke to say a single unkind word to his sister for choosing a Yiddish poet as a boyfriend. How different he was from his brother, the assimilator, the piece of shatnez! What a nobody! Khlavneh hated Naftali Hertz not only for his words but for his high, striking forehead and prickly hair, for his raised, skinny, pointy right shoulder and his low, drooping left shoulder, like a scale weighted down on one side. *Just look at that trickster with his hands in his pockets, as though he's just gone to the toilet and is searching for tissues to wipe himself. That bookworm! How can a wife love someone like him?* Khlavneh thought, but then a sense of pity for Naftali Hertz suddenly rose up in him. *He walks in this kind of sideways manner, as though he feels peripheral, redundant in this world. Why did I have to lash out against him like that?* Khlavneh felt bothered, and a fear of sorts came over him. In the rabbi's house, they were now awaiting the arrival of their middle son for Pesach, Bentzion, who'd taken business courses in Bialystok. Bluma Rivtcha didn't love him as much as she did Refael'ke. So what would *he* make of his sister's jargon poet fiancé? Wouldn't he, the businessman, jump up the way his brother, the little doctor, had? There was a chance that the sister from Lecheve, too, the rosh yeshiva's wife, would come by on chol hamoed to take a look at her sister's fiancé. And secretly, Bluma Rivtcha was planning for him to accompany her to see her Zembin grandfather. Supposedly, she wasn't asking for anyone's opinion, yet she was dying for him to be liked by her entire rabbinical and enterprising family. *What a provincial woman she is*, Khlavneh laughed, and again felt the sweet intoxication of the night before on the sofa with Bluma Rivtcha. The entire time he was romping and playing with her lush, tight body, a cold breeze blew over him, a sober fear that her parents or brother might come in. But she hadn't even wanted to go to his bedroom, where it was safer. "Silly you!" she'd whispered into his ear. "A pious coachman might go checking on his daughter to see if she's not lollygagging with her fiancé, but a rabbi doesn't do that." Apparently, she wasn't as intimidated and naïve as he'd thought. But still, she was dying for him to impress her family, even her Zembin grandfather, who had a reputation as a fanatic.

Khlavneh was already bored in advance, imagining himself at the seder sitting across from the rabbi's two sons, the sour doctor of philosophy and the business course graduate. He would have to recite the entire Hagaddah and watch his words, mindful of the rebbetzin who had already called him a "matchstick" and was terrified lest his mouth ignite the house, the entire world. Every day of Pesach he would have to go to the shtetl's beis medrash and sway as he davened among the gloomy congregation, depressed by the Polish boycott. And where were the young people of Morehdalye? True, the rabbi hadn't gotten out of bed to keep tabs on his daughter, but he'd no doubt be furious if her fiancé met up with the town's rebellious youth. Compounding his boredom was Bluma Rivtcha's absence, off at the sick dayan's house for days on end. Because the dayan's grandson had nearly been her fiancé and they'd broken it off, she made a point of not missing a day by his grandfather's side. And Khlavneh was already nauseated, as if by a bitter onion, from looking at the two pictures hanging on the wall: a group of guards, long ago, in the orchards of the land of Israel; and the rabbi, the saint, with the sparse white beard and mystical eyes. Out the window to the backyard of the rabbi's house, the scene wasn't much cheerier: black, rain-drenched chicken coops, a decrepit storage hut for firewood, a sunken park around a former garden. In one corner of the yard there was still a patch of snow and in another corner a young, skinny, naked tree was already trembling, its nascent pink blossoms like a young, bony girl with the buds of ripening breasts. Instead of the sky clearing and blueing for Pesach, smoky, spare clouds stretched across it. A dampness hung in the air, a biting cold, as though nature had confused the order of time and was getting ready for gray autumn instead of spring.

Someone knocked. Before Khlavneh could answer, the door opened slightly and through the narrow opening, as though wedging himself in, stepped the rabbi's assistant, Zalia Ziskind Luria. He looked deathly fatigued, barely able to draw a breath. His hat, frock coat, pants, and even his shoes were caked and dusty with flour. He'd come straight from the matzoh bakery. No sign remained of the former Visoki-Dvor rabbi and rosh yeshiva. He looked like what he had, indeed, become—a hunchbacked Jew, an inspector of kosher laws in public kitchens, with a little gray beard and half-closed eyes on the verge of sealing shut as he fell asleep standing from great exhaustion.

Without preamble, he said, "I'm sure you've already heard about my son, that he's stuck in jail and why he's there." Zalia Ziskind sat down on a chair and placed his large, bony hands on the table, fingers spread. "You heard about my Marcus?"

"I heard. Bluma Rivtcha told me."

"So, I had a thought. Since you're from the same sort of stock as him, would you maybe be able to help me, through your people, get my son out of jail?"

"I don't understand." Khlavneh stared at him with astonishment mixed with fright, scared that he wasn't in his right mind. "I'm not a communist like your son. I oppose the communists. But in Poland, even communists don't know their leaders, because the party is illegal. So how can I help get your son out of prison?"

"Is that so? You're an opponent? So why did you abandon Torah learning?" Zalia Ziskind drummed on the table with his large bony fingers and wrinkled his forehead, as though starting the conversation on the topic of his son had merely been a pretext to debating and philosophizing. "From everything I saw and heard about you, I assumed it wasn't a secular education and philosophy that led you to abandon Torah, like my student, Naftali Hertz. Someone like you does it because he doesn't want to wait for the promised Messianic era when the wolf and lamb will eat side by side. No, he wants to change the world immediately, rich and poor should be equal. But if that isn't the reason, then why did you leave the Torah?"

"The rabbi asked me the same question, and we talked about this all Shabbos, so I don't have the patience to discuss it again," Khlavneh murmured, grimacing and twisting around in his chair, bored to death.

"Is that so? You discussed this with the rabbi all Shabbos? Pity, such a pity, that I didn't know. I would have come and sat here and listened." The former rosh yeshiva and Dünaburg genius spoke with the humbleness of a pious yeshiva boy who wants to learn from everyone. "I heard you write poems. Are you a composer, too? Do you make tunes for your lyrics?"

"I sing a little. As a child, I even sang with a cantor, but I don't write music to my poems. I'm not a composer," Khlavneh replied, becoming more and more surprised that this once-great genius and singer spoke as if he didn't know the difference between a writer and a singer, had conflated leaving the Torah and communism, and skipped from subject to subject. "If you really want to know what I told the rabbi, I can give you the very short version. I left the beis medrash in order to become the poet of my street, my destitute street in Vilna, not to write poems just because, but to abolish rich and poor, though not in the way of the communists. Their path is bloodshed. That's the path they're following in Russia, and that's the one, more or less, they'll follow everywhere. Obviously, I'm a socialist. There's no such thing, I think, as a Yiddish poet who isn't a socialist."

"I understand, I understand." Zalia Ziskind nodded in agreement. "You feel that rich and poor must become equal, but through benign ways, not through bloodshed as by the Bolsheviks in Russia. I get it, I get it! And what will happen, say, if the fight is over, and everyone is equal, will they not then shoot a boy who steals a loaf of bread?"

"Since rich and poor will be abolished, there will be bread for everyone. A boy would have no need to steal a loaf of bread, so he wouldn't be shot," Khlavneh replied, again suspecting that the former genius might be a bit confused. "Where did they shoot a boy who stole a loaf of bread?"

"No, no, I made a mistake. It wasn't a loaf of bread, but a box of candy. He escaped into a cellar and locked the door from the inside, because a policeman was chasing him. If he was an adult, or he hadn't been so frightened, he probably wouldn't have locked himself in a cellar. The policeman stuck his head into the cellar's small window and ordered the child to open the door and come out with the box of candy. But the boy didn't obey, either out of fear or out of audacity. In any case, all we're talking about here is a box of candy. And this protector of justice, this policeman, knew that the entire theft was just a box of candy. But since he'd ordered the thief to come out, once, twice, and the boy didn't obey, he went and shot the child through the window and killed him. The boy lay there, bloodied, with the box of candy. Well, you'll ask how I know this story. I'll tell you. I read about it in a Warsaw newspaper. I have a student, a merchant in Warsaw, one of my former Visoki-Dvor students, and he found out I wasn't a rosh yeshiva anymore but a wanderer from place to place. He looked for me until he found me and asked if he could help with anything, maybe I needed money. I need nothing, I told him, absolutely nothing. But I wanted him to send me the Jewish newspapers published in Warsaw. I'm sure he was surprised, but he sent me entire packages of old newspapers. I developed a tremendous passion for reading as many newspapers as I could, to see how the Creator presides over his world. Is it really so bad? Is the world really as sad and terrible as I imagine it, or is it better than that, and it's only in my eyes that everything seems bad and dark? I discussed the things I read in the papers with Naftali Hertz Katzenellenbogen, my former student, many times, and now I'm talking about it with you. And I discussed it with other knowledgeable people, who study esoteric topics, worldly people, and I asked them, 'For stealing a box of candy, is it right for a guardian of justice to shoot a boy?' And this wasn't a case of Jew and non-Jew. According to the writing, it seems the policeman and his victim were both Poles. The child had a Polish father and mother. Those knowledgeable people answered me that the foundation of every bourgeois enterprise is 'mine is mine, and yours is yours.' Now, if mine is mine and yours is yours, if this is at the foundation of a government, a policeman is allowed to shoot and kill a boy who runs away with a stolen box of candy. And now, we come back to the beginning. Are you sure that in the government you'll establish, they won't shoot a boy?" Zalia Ziskind's eyes widened as he spoke, swimming with despair, like a cellar flooded with water.

"In the government we establish, as you call it, such an outrage cannot realistically happen, because capitalism, with its murderous laws of private ownership, won't rule there," Khlavneh said, moved by the story he'd just heard. "In a socialist society, without bloodsuckers who deprive the workers of their labor, it's impossible to imagine such murderous law-protectors who shoot a boy just for stealing a box of candy."

"I'm not yet convinced they won't shoot." Zalia Ziskind sighed and tucked the edge of his gray beard into his mouth, as though siphoning his gloomy mood from its hairs. "Whether the world ends through force, as my Marcus thinks, because otherwise the rich won't step back, or it changes by agreement, as you think, the changed world won't be any better than this one, so long as it's run by the 'rule of law' and not the 'rule of mercy.' When we try criminals with the rule of mercy, we first thoroughly consider the reason for that person's action, and if we dig deep enough and get to the motive of the crime, we usually view the crime as more minor than when we didn't have an excuse for it. But the rule of mercy doesn't always mete out the lesser punishment. In fact, when the rule of mercy is in power, it sometimes leads to a harsher punishment in areas where the rule of law wouldn't punish at all. Rule of law punishes for theft, but it can't punish at all for the worse, uglier crime of geneives daas, deceiving someone. When a person is caught for stealing a money pouch, he gets a certain amount of jail time. The victim of the theft might forget about his loss a week later, never mind a month later, and certainly a year later, while the thief still rots in jail and will go on rotting. But the one who deceives or misleads someone gets nothing in our earthly court, nothing at all, because he hasn't broken any laws. The person who was duped allowed himself to be duped. In fact, the fooled one is considered the idiot and even the criminal, because he's the one making demands and crying and shouting. But rule of mercy, the criterion employed by our merciful Father, knows the difference between a pathetic thief of a money pouch and someone who steals our trust, our heart, our feelings. And it's specifically rule of mercy, not rule of law, that demands our merciful Father to stand up for injustices to the humiliated, the man bent to the ground, who can't collect for his pain and insult in any court in this false world. Because it's not true that rule of mercy forgives the evil man, the scorpion that creeps on short, fat, human legs and cries with supposedly human tears. Rule of mercy in the Jewish conception doesn't ask for forgiveness for such contemptible people. On the contrary, the true man of mercy knows whom he's not allowed to pity. But he also knows that the criterion of human justice can't be involved here. Instead, he waits for the merciful Father to get involved and trample the scorpion, the fleeing snake, and the twisted snake. But waiting for the involvement of Godly powers is the biggest torment in the world. Waiting for revenge for the tears of theft victims—what can be sadder for a mortal man? You used to study Torah, so you know what I mean. Now we come back to where we started. The Torah tells us, 'For the poor shall never cease out of the land.' There will always be poor people, which means you can't abolish poverty no matter how much you change the world, whether by agreement or by force. And the sickness of our world lies not in the fact that there are poor people, but in that we pursue the norm, the law, and we disregard rule of mercy."

Zalia Ziskind spoke in such a broken tone it seemed he was eulogizing his own life. Khlavneh liked the man more and more, this old renowned genius who'd renounced his greatness and had become a beadle, an assistant. He was drawn by the way Zalia Ziskind spoke with such heartbreak, the way Rabbi Yisroel Salanter did in his letters, though unlike Rabbi Yisroel, Zalia Ziskind didn't alarm others with talk of gehinnom. Perhaps he didn't believe in its existence. One thing was certain: the gehinnom of this world scared him more than the gehinnom of the next.

"It seems to me you're saying what I said to Bluma Rivtcha yesterday, but in different words. I said to her that what remains embedded in my heart from my years of learning in yeshiva is the verse from the Gemara that God sides with the persecuted even when the persecutor is a saint and the persecuted is evil." Khlavneh's voice also became sadly quiet, as though Zalia Ziskind's hunchback and long gray beard had suddenly sprouted on him, as had happened to the tanna, Reb Elazar ben Azaria, according to the Sages. "What you call rule of mercy is what the world calls moral law, or the struggles of our conscience."

"I don't know if I mean the same thing." The old rosh yeshiva sighed, and the darkness of his dejected eyes seemed to spill onto Khlavneh. "I don't have high regard for the world's language, because you never know what's hiding behind a term. By the world, a man whose conscience bothers him for a wrong he committed in the past is a good person. But what wicked man doesn't struggle with his conscience? He would have to be Ashmedai himself for his conscience not to bother him. Generally, every evil man's conscience bothers him, and that's actually part of the pleasure of his evil act, knowing his dirty conscience will bother him. I've heard it said that a murderer feels drawn to go back to the place where he committed the murder, and that's how he gets caught. Well, does that make him less of a murderer? And if he isn't caught for his first murder, won't he commit a second? In which way is this evil person, whose dirty conscience aggravates him every time he devours a victim, in which way is he better than the horrid spider who devours the flies caught in his web and has no conscience to aggravate him at all? It's not in the aggravation that the goodness of a person lies, but in just the opposite! A person who truly has a conscience takes care to never arrive at a place where his conscience bothers him. He is as scared of remorse as of an incurable illness. Which is why I hold that a person who follows a rule of mercy is not of the sort whose conscience briefly pricks them after their quiet evil acts. Those people are extremely wicked, because their conscience wakes up only after the fact, and they get over it quickly, until they commit the next evil act. I've heard that barbarians in the past used to eat their old fathers and deliberately choke themselves with their cannibalistic food. You probably call that conscience. What did they call you in yeshiva, Khlavneh Vilner?" Zalia Ziskind said abruptly, smiling in a warm, fatherly way. "So, you're saying, you *do* know how to sing? You were even in the cantor's choir as a boy? The moment I saw you in beis medrash I thought you must know how to sing. Bluma Rivtcha's fiancé must be a singer, too, I thought. I told you already, yes?—that she used to play on my knee as a child."

Zalia Ziskind was trying to speak breezily, cheerfully. He wanted to leave things in a happy state, so that it wouldn't be said that he left depression in his wake. He began to sing in a hoarse, but sweet, voice. "*Od yizkor lanu* . . . May the Lord's love for Abraham be remembered for us." But he paused his singing and again began to speak. "Music is like suffering. Just as there are different sufferings—from a sick body to a sick soul, from fear to thirst for revenge or the pain of love, when the heart can't bear its yearning and love—in the same way, the words of one prayer can be sung in a melody and tone of fear, or anger and hate, or despair, or happiness, or undying love. So, I want to hear the feelings you sing with. Again: *Od yizkor lanu ahavas* . . ."

"*U'vkhein hanekad* . . . And because of his son Isaac who went to be bound and sacrificed, may the judgment of Satan be disrupted, and in the merit of Jacob, may God, the mighty, pull our judgment to fairness, for today's day is holy, our Lord," Khlavneh chimed in, singing in a resonant voice, with all the flourishes of an ancient Rosh Hashanah tune.

"You can tell that you're still young, a man of strength. You sing loudly and robustly, not so much with sweetness and heart as with power." Zalia Ziskind suddenly burst into laughter. Perhaps he had meant what he said, but Khlavneh immediately stopped singing and thought, with some embarrassment: *He's laughing at me for letting myself be persuaded like a child to amuse him, like a little choirboy for a small-town cantor.*

Just then, Sholem Shachne appeared at the partly opened door, wearing a high yarmulke and a clean, fitted frock coat, though his face looked sickly, jaundiced, and swollen. "You're singing the davening of the High Holy Days before Pesach?" he said softly, with a bright smile.

The hunchbacked Zalia Ziskind, in his weekday, flour-dusted clothes, cast him a glance, a sharp gleam in his eyes, as though displeased to have been interrupted by this man with the look of a satisfied father of the bride. Still, he answered, half-jokingly, "When I test a boy on his singing abilities, I test him with the Yom Kippur prayers, not the prayer for rain."

"And did you test him on his Torah knowledge, too?" the rabbi asked in the same light tone.

"No, I didn't. On the whole, he doesn't seem like the kind of young man who lets himself be tested," Zalia Ziskind said, smiling at Khlavneh.

But it seemed to Khlavneh that the old man was smiling to avoid answering: "He probably doesn't have much, as far as Torah learning, because even in yeshiva he was into other things."

Zalia Ziskind was suddenly in a hurry. "I must go back to the matzoh bakery," he excused himself, "and then I have to rush to the cheder sheni in the beis medrash, where the women know I usually sit, to answer their Pesach questions."

As soon as Zalia Ziskind left, Khlavneh became tense and began pacing the room. This was the first time the rabbi had come over for a conversation between just the two of them. Had he come to say he didn't approve of the match? If so, he would tell the rabbi calmly and courteously, "You must say this to your daughter, and I will do whatever she wants."

But in the meantime, Sholem Shachne was quiet and, in fact, was thinking about something else: *Zalia Ziskind, my friend from Volozhin, my helper, isn't saying anything, but in his heart he's upset at us for not getting his son out of jail. But what can I do?* Sholem Shachne sat down on the chair Zalia Ziskind had just vacated. He sat for a long while, eyes closed, forehead in his palms. *Maybe Zalia Ziskind is avoiding conversation with me lately because Naftali Hertz confided in him what he hides from Henna'le and me. Or maybe Zalia Ziskind realized himself that there's something fishy about my oldest son and his wife. Why shouldn't the Dünaburg genius figure out what Henna'le and I already have? Bluma Rivtcha has the same suspicion. I know this because she never talks about Naftali Hertz to me or Henna'le. She used to talk about him nonstop, and with envy for the way he succeeded in making his way in the world. Now she must have realized there was no reason to envy him. But I trust she hasn't said a word to her fiancé. His fight with Naftali Hertz shows that Khlavneh doesn't know. He had no idea how closely he'd hit the target with his harsh words against alienated Jews. "He prophesied without knowing he was prophesying."*

"Reb Zalia Ziskind is still the Dünaburg genius," Sholem Shachne said, just to start the conversation, and he took his hands off his eyes.

"I see he's also a deep thinker and a sensitive person," Khlavneh said, "but despite being a thinker and knowledgeable about the world, he's still provincial and naïve. He decided that if I left the yeshiva, I must be as far left as his son, and he asked me to help get his son out of prison."

There's a saying: You talk to the daughter, but you mean the daughter-in-law, Sholem Shachne thought. *Zalia Ziskind spoke to Khlavneh, but he meant me. He's upset I'm not helping to free his only son, though he knows I can't do anything.* Sholem Shachne raised his dull eyes to Khlavneh. "I came in here to say to you, since you and Bluma Rivtcha have already decided on each other, may it be with luck. I have nothing against you. Honestly, I myself don't understand why I'm telling you this. You and my daughter didn't even ask us if we agree to the match, so why would you need my approval?" The rabbi laughed quietly, his two weak but whole front teeth shining from his mouth.

Khlavneh understood he was meant to jump up joyously and thank the rabbi for his approval: thank him, thank him, and thank him again. Yet he didn't jump, didn't even open his mouth, and even his face expressed no joy. Had he suddenly become scared of the responsibility he was undertaking by getting married? Was he mourning the loss of his freedom as a single man? Did he not love Bluma Rivtcha? But he did love her! Yet she'd come to him without any struggle. Perhaps that was why he was so confused now and wasn't feeling happy. Khlavneh couldn't figure it out, not at that moment, nor later.

"When do you plan to get married?" Sholem Shachne asked.

"When?" Khlavneh grew more confused. "You're asking when? Whenever Bluma Rivtcha wants. You have to talk to her about this."

"Since you're both decided on the marriage, you shouldn't procrastinate. But I came here for another reason. Bluma Rivtcha wanted me and her mother to see you and get to know you. Well, we saw you, spent time with you, and we don't oppose the match. Now you have to go back to Vilna for Pesach. Your mother is a widow, and you are her only child, so I don't understand what you were thinking when you traveled here for the holiday. Who will make kiddush for her and spend the holiday with her?"

The rabbi spoke softly and with surprise; still, Khlavneh couldn't quite believe Sholem Shachne's concern for a woman he'd never met. Khlavneh knew, on the contrary, that his mother was pleased he was traveling with his bride, the rabbinical daughter, to her parents for the holiday. *The rabbi wants me to leave because he knows Bluma Rivtcha and I lay together on the dining room sofa last night. Regardless of Bluma Rivtcha's comment that the rabbi isn't a coachman who comes checking up on his daughter, he must be displeased. Hadn't he just said bluntly that they shouldn't put off the wedding date?*

"Fine. I'll do what you want and go back."

"It's not about what *I* want; you have to do it for your mother." The rabbi stood up to leave, visibly unhappy that he'd been forced to have this conversation. As though to remove all suspicion, he teased Khlavneh, "Bluma Rivtcha got herself a bargain. You're not asking for a dowry or room and board?"

This was Khlavneh's opportunity to settle the score with all the yeshiva men and the rabbi himself, who likely found fault with him for abandoning his learning. "But I'm not a Torah learner, saint, or distinguished scholar. They're the ones who refuse to go to their chuppah before they're assured of their dowry and room and board."

"Well, a Torah learner who's going to spend his days studying must make sure he's provided for," the rabbi began, but he didn't finish his thought. Through the partially open door they heard someone stepping from the stoop into the front room, the beis din room, and they both realized it was Bluma Rivtcha. Khlavneh followed the rabbi through the corridor. From the dining room, Henna'le came to the doorway.

"I can't bear the dayan anymore!" Bluma Rivtcha exploded in tears. "Today he was screaming about how he'd be happy if he dies soon, while we're in the month of Nissan when eulogies aren't allowed. That way his enemies won't be able to pretend they're his good friends, to act like they're mourning him and sing his praises, while in their hearts they'd be happy to be rid of him. 'I mean the Morehdalye rabbi, too,' he shouted into my face. He even regards *me* as his enemy, because the medications don't work to dull his pain as well as they used to."

Henna'le stood silently by the dining room door. Khlavneh and the rabbi, standing by the hall doorway, were silent, too. Bluma Rivtcha sat down at the end of a long bench, near the beis din table, breathing heavily. She unbuttoned her light gray gabardine coat, removed her boots, took off her round, dark gray hat, and gave her short hair a shake, like a thick young evergreen shaking off sparkling droplets of rain. She spoke more calmly now. "Even when the pain ceases, he has complaints about me, but of a different sort. He says, 'So just because you didn't marry my grandson, you don't consider me a friend and I can't get to know your fiancé? You think I'll give him the evil eye? I see I'm not important enough to you to bring your fiancé here for a conversation.' So, I promised him that I'd bring my fiancé over on a day he's feeling better."

"You shouldn't have promised that. You won't be able to keep your promise, and he'll have even more complaints," Khlavneh said from the doorway. "Your father is right that I must go back to Vilna to lead the seder for my mother." He stressed each word, so that Bluma Rivtcha would grasp that she herself had brought this about, by not listening to him last night and sleeping with him on the sofa.

"We have the children here for the holiday," the rebbetzin interjected, and turned to her daughter, speaking very softly, as if apologizing, "You came, Naftali Hertz is here, and Bentzion is coming from Bialystok. His mother, too, deserves to have her only child with her."

For a long minute, Bluma Rivtcha stared mutely at her mother, father, and Khlavneh. Then she smiled, her lips quivered, and a purple gleam of rage inflamed her cheeks. "I get it!" She burst into curt laughter, her eyes filled with tears, and she shouted, "I get it! Because Naftali Hertz has been avoiding Khlavneh since their argument, you're afraid that Khlavneh might get into a fight with Bentzion, too. You're sending him home with the excuse that he should celebrate the seder with his mother. Well, I'm telling you, Khlavneh was in the right in that argument with Naftali Hertz, and he'll be right when he goes up against Bentzion, the business manager. Out of all his goals, Bentzion chose to become a servant of merchants! Ha." Bluma Rivtcha stomped forward.

"If you and your parents know I'm going to have a fight with your other brother, I'm leaving of my own will," Khlavneh said, offended. He didn't say another word, but in his mind he was laughing to himself: *Sure, I'm dying to have a conversation with a business agent! Such an interesting person! No question the little businessman will look down on poets, worse even than his brother, the little doctor, who at least holds Hebrew poets in high regard.*

"Then I'm coming along with you to Vilna," Bluma Rivtcha announced, as though to spite her parents. Before Khlavneh could say he didn't want her to join him, Bluma Rivtcha cried out, "Here he comes!"

Outside, on the stoop of the rabbi's house, Naftali Hertz was walking up the stairs.

Neither the rabbi and rebbetzin nor the engaged couple had figured out the real reason behind Naftali Hertz's behavior, acting so dejected and quiet all Shabbos and not even joining them for meals. The family assumed that the debate, which had turned into a fight between the future brothers-in-law, was to blame. But Naftali Hertz hadn't revealed the true motive even to his parents.

On Friday he was walking past the post office when, on a whim, he went in and asked if he'd received any letters by general delivery—certain there wouldn't be a letter from his wife or son. He'd already concluded in advance that they didn't need him. And not just Annelyse—because now she'd seen how many men were still interested in her, despite being forty—but even his son didn't need him. In Karl's appearance, in his every move, one could sense his non-Jewishness, going back generations. What did he a need a father, a Jew, for? And he wasn't needed in the Jewish division of the library either. Another bookworm was standing in for him. But to his surprise, there was a letter. The return address was Annelyse Müller of Bern, Switzerland. The letter, with wobbly crooked lines on one side, had no date on the top, so he couldn't know when it was sent. Typical of a woman, not to write a date, either because they had no patience to remember which day of the month it was, or because they were doing it coquettishly to show how impractical they were, or perhaps to show that the feelings expressed in the letter were beyond time. But the letter's contents were quite sober and firm, despite opening with "My dear Hertz'che."

Annelyse wrote that things couldn't continue the way they had. Since he couldn't come back home and hadn't even written a letter, she was going to travel to him and his parents. She'd known from when they'd married that he was afraid his Orthodox parents would discover he had a Christian wife and son, but she wanted to put an end to it once and for all. Either his parents would agree to it, or he had to stop being concerned about their old-fashioned opinions, or—she would free him to live however he wished.

About their son and her family, she wrote one short sentence: "Karl is in complete agreement with me, and so are my brothers."

Naftali Hertz understood in a blink that Annelyse was using this tactic to force him to come back, because she knew very well that his parents would never approve the marriage, nor would he allow her to come to the Jewish shtetl. He would have to go back right away. He couldn't yet decide what had happened. Had her admirers become disgusted, or was she going to marry one of them and wanted to divorce him by law? Whichever it was, he was prepared to travel home. He had no more strength for this tormented life at his parents', who anyhow didn't believe a word he said whenever he spoke about his family in Switzerland. He'd noticed, too, that the shtetl Jews were surmising more about his situation every day. It was only because they were living in fear of pogroms, and were constantly worried about earning a livelihood, that they didn't have the time or interest to think it fully through. But he could not show Annelyse's letter to his parents. What should he tell them, then? Why was he suddenly going back on the eve of Pesach? To lead a seder for his Christian wife and son? He might have had the audacity to go on lying if it weren't so clear from their faces that they didn't believe a word he said.

In truth, Naftali Hertz was telling himself the same thing his wife had written: this situation could not continue! Indeed, he would go right home, so that Annelyse wouldn't come and the news about the Morehdalye rabbi's daughter-in-law wouldn't ring all over town, over half a world. But he must tell his parents the truth before he went. They knew it anyway. And since he didn't have the courage to start with them, he would start with his former rosh yeshiva. After all, Zalia Ziskind had a son who was a communist in jail, and he often spoke against Divine Providence the way Job did. He'd be able to handle what Naftali Hertz had done. But when Naftali Hertz arrived at Zalia Ziskind's room, in the back of the shoe repairman's cellar, they again got onto the subject of philosophy and entered an endless debate. He could not bring himself to roll the stone off his heart and tell Zalia Ziskind the whole truth. He saw clearly that Zalia Ziskind had also figured out the secret of his life, because, like his parents, his old rosh yeshiva asked him nothing about his family in Switzerland anymore. It seemed Zalia Ziskind was trying to convince himself he was mistaken, that his suspicion was false, and Naftali Hertz didn't have the heart to force the truth upon him. Oh, to be released from this torment. Better to go to sleep and not wake up than suffer like this. And in such a mood did he step into the house, splattered with springtime mud. By his overgrown hair, wrinkled face, and sloppy clothes, he could have been taken for a pauper, a foot traveler who didn't have the money for a wagon ride from the train into town.

In the beis din room, Naftali Hertz found his parents looking dejected. Bluma Rivtcha's fiancé seemed befuddled. And Bluma Rivtcha turned on him the second he stepped inside. "You ordered Father to send Khlavneh back, because you still can't forget what he said to you?"

"Me?" And then Naftali Hertz fell silent, as if pondering whether it was worth answering at all. "Would I demand that they send back your fiancé?" he said eventually, and began to laugh. He was about to say that if he'd learned how to bear sitting at a table with his wife's lover, he could certainly bear sitting at a table with a jargon boy. "I'm leaving for Warsaw tomorrow, and from there taking the fast train to Switzerland."

He saw that his parents and sister did not yet understand what he was saying to them. Naftali Hertz was in such despair, his life so wearisome, he'd have found it easier to just blurt out his wretched secret. If only Khlavneh hadn't been there. He would not spill his confession in front of a stranger. Not that the Yiddishist's triumph would have bothered him anymore, but he could not shame his parents.

He began to speak feverishly. "I got a letter from home on Friday, saying I should come back as quickly as possible. Yes, yes, I should come back for the holiday. But I didn't want to tell you earlier so as not to disturb the Shabbos. That's why I'm telling you now that I must go back immediately. There are six days left till Pesach. If I leave tomorrow early morning, I'll make it in time. If I don't go, my wife and maybe even my son will come here. But then, they would be traveling on Pesach . . ." He stopped, interrupting his stammering words.

His father, who'd been standing in the hall doorway with Khlavneh, walked slowly into the beis din room, and sat down on the bench at the table. He placed his hands on his knees. Mutely, he sat there, his expression blank. His mother was silent, too, still standing in the doorway to the dining room, her eyes locked on her husband, terrified he might have another heart attack.

The first to recover was Bluma Rivtcha. She said to Khlavneh, "Why should we stand here? If you're traveling home, come, I'll help you pack. Then we'll take a stroll at the edge of the shtetl. I'll show you the Narev. The ice has already melted." And not waiting for an answer, she pushed him into the hall and followed him, leaving her parents alone with her brother.

Bluma Rivtcha and Khlavneh had barely made it into her room before Khlavneh turned on her. "You and your brother, and probably your businessman brother from Bialystok, too, you're a small-minded family. You carry around secrets, you're terrified that an outsider might peek in a window and see your life. Your brother threatens your parents that if he doesn't go there, his wife and child will come here. And why shouldn't they come? And why should he say they might travel on Pesach? Don't they know that you don't come to a father, a rabbi, on the holiday?"

"You could have asked him yourself what he meant." Bluma Rivtcha gazed at the floor as though searching for an earring she'd lost. "I hardly know anything, not just about his wife and son, but even about him. I was a child when he left home, and he's lived abroad all these years. He became very alienated there. But if he's leaving, you can stay here for the seder."

"If I stay, I'd be implying that your father is a liar. I'd be showing that his supposed concern for my mother not to stay alone was only an excuse to get rid of me. Do you want that? He's the most likable of all of you. Besides—"

"You're the one who wants to leave, because it's boring in the shtetl with me," Bluma Rivtcha said, cutting him off with the impatient, capricious tone of a bride who doesn't want to wear the modest dress her parents chose for her.

"True, it is boring here. But the real reason your father wants me gone, I wanted to tell you, is because he knows that you lay with me on the sofa last night. I kept telling you: 'Don't do it!' Your parents didn't come in, but they know."

"Then I'm pleased." She laughed and threw her arm around his neck. "I didn't do it to deliberately spite them, but if they know, it's better. I'll be coming to you tonight, too, but in the meantime, hug me, give me a kiss." Her tone was light and airy, yet she kept turning her head anxiously toward the beis din room.

"Your father told me bluntly that we don't have to put off the wedding," Khlavneh grumbled.

Bluma Rivtcha gaped at him, stunned, and took a step backward. "So, you're saying Father really knows that we're like husband and wife? And he didn't say a word to me? If you had known my father before, you'd realize how much he's changed!"

Unlike Bluma Rivtcha, who didn't want to play pretend, Henna'le deliberately acted oblivious. She did so to protect her husband from a heart attack, to protect her desperate son, and even to protect herself. She saw, as if reading a palm, that Naftali Hertz wished to reveal everything. But God in heaven, spare him from doing that! If he hadn't shared much about his family till now, he must have had a good reason for it. Well, he wasn't obligated to tell them, nor did they want to know. Let him just continue to live where and how he wanted, whatever his common sense, feelings, and idea of fairness dictated. Henna'le didn't say these exact words to her son, but acting innocent, with a smile and a loving tone—as Sholem Shachne sat on the bench, elbows pressed to the table, sinking deeper into silence as into a dark abyss—she said, "If your wife demands that you go home for the holiday, you must go back immediately. I'll tell you the truth, my son. It really is wrong that you've been away from home for so long."

"Yes, Mother, that's true."

"I'm sure your wife already prepared matzoh, fish, and meat for Pesach. And wine for the Four Cups. The six items for the seder plate you'll be able to prepare on that last day, when you arrive home." Henna'le looked her son straight in the eyes.

"There's quite a large Jewish community in Bern. You can get anything you need," Naftali Hertz replied expressionlessly, like a man partially anesthetized for a surgery.

"Your son will ask you the Four Questions, and here Bentzion will ask them." Henna'le spoke calmly. "To tell you the pure truth, I'm a bit upset that you didn't see your grandfather in Zembin, and that Tilza and her husband won't meet you. They're coming on chol hamoed. Well, so be it. With God's help, you'll see them when you come next year, or maybe sooner. Then maybe you'll bring your wife and son, too." And to prevent Naftali Hertz from inserting a word of contradiction, Henna'le spoke even faster. "My sisters, your aunts Kona, Sarah Raizel, and Chavtche, will probably be upset that you didn't stop in to see them when you passed through Warsaw. But I'll bear that sin myself. If you stop to see them, it might be Pesach already by the time you get home."

"Yes, yes," Naftali Hertz nodded, standing in the middle of the room. His mother went on talking, saying Bentzion would feel so foolish that he'd missed seeing his older brother, and Naftali Hertz continued to nod his head. He knew he had to let his mother speak, to nod his head at everything, and to avoid looking at his father. Inexplicably—he himself couldn't grasp it, in this current situation—his thoughts fastened themselves to the image of two old bears who lived in a cavern beneath a bridge, in the cursed city of Bern, where his life was being buried. The printed guides for tourists in Bern all mentioned these black bears in the cavern, claiming they were the children of a couple who'd lived in the cavern before them, and that those bears' parents, too, had been born in this cavern. And so, their black-bear ancestry stretched as far back as Wilhelm Tell. Naftali Hertz despised the black-bear cavern in his city, but when he happened to visit Basel, he liked going to the zoo and standing for a long while at the pen of a tremendous polar bear. All around the gated area lay rocks and icebergs; and on its bottom lay a chasm filled with water. The polar bear would take a step, then another, over the rocky terrain, then a third, until his paw hung over the chasm, after which he would turn back. Then, he'd start again: one step, a second, a third, to the edge of the cliff, his enormous paw with all its claws hanging for an instant in the air—until he pulled it back again. Over and over, nonstop. A shudder, a deathly fear, as well as a wild desire, would course through Naftali Hertz as he watched the animalistic pleasure of the great white bear with his paw dangling over the cliff.

Translator's Note

In 1983, Alfred A. Knopf signed a contract with Inna Hecker Grade, Chaim Grade's widow, for a novel tentatively entitled *The Rabbi's House*. Knopf had already published a memoir by Chaim Grade, *My Mother's Sabbath Days*, in 1982, the year Grade died. And there was another work by Grade in production at the time of his death, a novel entitled *Rabbis and Wives*. Inna worked on that translation with Harold Rabinowitz, and it was eventually published in 1986.

But when work was to have begun on the translation of *The Rabbi's House*, Inna went silent. The novel had been typeset in Yiddish, and the plan was for Inna to send Mel Rosenthal—a copy editor then working at Knopf—a few translated chapters at a time. Knopf had never been given a copy of the Yiddish galley proofs, and when Inna stopped communicating with the book's editor, Ash Green, the project languished until Inna's death in 2010.

In 2013, the YIVO Institute for Jewish Research, along with the National Library of Israel, was named executor of Chaim Grade's estate, and the hunt began in Inna's apartment for Grade's unpublished works-in-progress. Sometime in 2014, the Yiddish galley proofs for *Bais Harav* were unearthed—148 8½" x 14" typeset pages, with Grade's handwritten corrections to typographical errors in the margins.

In 2015, I was hired to translate this text into English. In the agreement I signed, the book was to be called *The Rabbi's House*, it would be about 450 pages long, and it was a completely finished novel. None of those things turned out to be true.

Translators' methodologies differ. Many insist on reading a full manuscript before attempting to translate it, and I admit there are benefits to that approach. Yet I prefer to keep my curiosity piqued, and so I tend to read and translate simultaneously. Because of this, I had invested about a year's work and nearly completed the 450-page translation before I realized that the novel was unfinished.

Right around that time, I received an email from Yehudah Zirkind, then a graduate student at Tel Aviv University, who informed me that he was writing his thesis on Chaim Grade and had collected fascinating archival material, including personal correspondence between Grade and others. Since Zirkind had heard that I was translating *The Rabbi's House*, he thought I'd be interested in seeing the material.

I certainly was!

Among the various correspondence he forwarded to me, I came across a handwritten letter from Chaim Grade to his patron and friend Abraham Bornstein, dated January 14, 1982, four months before Grade's death. Toward the end of the first page, I found this: "After much contemplation and struggle, I decided to do what I told you by phone. I will first publish the first part of *Beis Harav* [The Rabbi's House]; then I will, with the help of God, finish writing and publish the second half of the novel."

And so, one mystery was solved. The 450-page manuscript had felt unfinished because it *was* unfinished. It appeared to be the first part of a two-volume book. The predominant questions then became: Would we find the second volume? And would the novel be complete? But first, there were more of Grade's letters to sift through.

What quickly became apparent was that Grade's central struggle, in his life and in his work, including in *The Rabbi's House*, was the tension between his desire to live and write as a secular human in a modern world and the constant nostalgic pull of his yeshiva past, the traditional Jewish Vilna of his youth.

"From when I started writing *Beis Harav*, many years have passed," Grade says in a letter of January 12, 1979, when he'd already been living in America for thirty years. "And I see myself well as I read the material. Dread befalls me, because I realize that even now, I have *not left the yeshiva*. The problems that interest me, the battles I wage, my loves and hates, my good and bad protagonists, what I praise and what I criticize—all of it is from [the perspective of] a *current* yeshiva boy, not a *former* one . . . And indeed! In my work, I have not, after all, left the beis medrash."

About a year later, in a letter dated May 14, 1980, describing a trip to Toronto where he'd given a talk and received the Marilyn Finkler Memorial Award, he writes, "Already fifty years from when I left the yeshiva and almost forty years from Vilna. I wandered across Russia, all the way to the borders of Afghanistan and Iran. Then, I wandered across two-thirds of the world. Nevertheless, I still live in the yeshiva and cannot cut myself off from the Vilna courtyard."

"The writer inside me," he writes in another letter, dated March 5, 1973, "is a thoroughly ancient Jew, while the man inside me wants to be thoroughly modern. This is my calamity, plain and simple, a struggle I cannot win."

There's a famous line in W. G. Sebald's novel *Austerlitz:* "Just as we have appointments in the future, it may be that we also have appointments to keep in the past." For Grade, writing served as a way to keep appointments in his past, a past that had been wrested from him by the Holocaust. He felt a responsibility to document the life of prewar Jewish Vilna. It became his calling, an appointment he could not refuse to keep. In his final years, when he was still working hard to finish *The Rabbi's House*, he already knew that the audience for his books was dying out, that it would make more sense for him to write about modern life, appeal to a modern American readership. He said as much in many of his letters. And yet, he could not. His heart—and his art—was in Vilna.

"Worse," he writes in a letter to Bornstein, dated August 8, 1977, "is that toiling over *Beis Harav* (more later on this process), I find myself constantly shooing away one thought, like a stubborn fly: For whom are you toiling? . . . But I disregard the words of my evil inclination. I feel that I owe this book, the *Beis Harav*, to the Jewish people, and to you and Rikl [Bornstein's wife]. I've always found it strange that I have so little faith and yet believe, with complete faith, that Providence saved me and allowed me to live, in order to immortalize the *great generation* that I knew."

This sense of faith, of Divine Providence guiding his work and life, was contagious to me as a translator of this book. It provided a glimmer of hope that there would be more to this narrative than the first volume, the 450 pages that had initially been given to me. With the help of the processing archivist of the Grade estate, Beata Kasiarz, I began sifting through the existing material housed at YIVO. To my excitement, I discovered that, indeed, work had gone on beyond the copy already in my possession. That elusive second volume existed, although not in finished or book form. Instead, I had to review the serials in various newspapers to piece together the continuation of the narrative.

Chaim Grade began writing this book at least as early as August 1965. At that time, the first installment of *Dos Alte Hoyz* (*The Old House*) appeared in the *Tog-Morgn Zhurnal*. *The Old House* ran from August 27, 1965, to February 29, 1966. Then Grade became ill and put this story on hold for about two years. In September 1968, he published the first installment of *Zin un Tekhter* (*Sons and Daughters*), which was the new title for the reworked and revised story, again in the *Tog-Morgn Zhurnal*. The chapters of *Sons and Daughters* ran from Friday, September 13, 1968, until Friday, August 6, 1971. Two years later, Grade took the story over to the *Forverts*, where installments appeared weekly from Sunday, November 11, 1973, to Sunday, May 30, 1976.* In the *Forverts*, Grade renamed the novel once again, this time to *Beis Harav* (The Rabbi's House).

What to name the English translation? In the Yiddish iterations of this book, three titles existed: *The Old House*, *The Rabbi's House*, and *Sons and Daughters*. After some deliberation, *Sons and Daughters* was chosen for this book. It is the most fitting of the three, first because the overarching concern of this saga is family, specifically the heartaches and joys that sons and daughters bring to their parents. Novels often chart their own course, with themes evolving and characters undertaking actions that even the writer might never have foreseen. The theme of tzar gidel bonim, the trials of raising children, ultimately turned out to be the principal leitmotif of this novel, much more than, say, the goings-on in a rabbi's house or court.

Second, it is clear from several of Grade's letters and interviews that he wanted *Sons and Daughters* to be the title, certainly at least of the second volume. In the essay "A Writer in Search of an Audience:

---

* In the May 30 issue, there was a note from the editor at the end of the installment: "Our contributor Chaim Grade will return to the last part of this novel when he will be done with the material." But *Beis Harav* never returned to the *Forverts*.

Profile of Chaim Grade," published in 1978,* Morton A. Reichek writes:

> For the past two years he [Chaim Grade] has been reworking the longest of the untranslated works, *The Rabbi's House*, into novel form. The story ran as a serial in the *Forward* for three years during the late 1960s.
>
> "I'm afraid to do it," Grade said. "It's a terrible problem. It's easier to write a new book than to convert a serial work into a regular novel. I see all the mistakes I made. And then I'm so busy writing poems for the newspaper, preparing speeches, and quarreling with my wife and then making peace with her."
>
> He is now trimming the original 2,000-page manuscript by about 50 percent and has changed the title to *Sons and Daughters*. He is also rewriting the ending, which now dissatisfies him.

Grade was clearly worried about the tremendous labor involved in converting this work from newspaper installments to a bona fide book. Indeed—unless we discover otherwise in the future—he did not live to accomplish it. For me as the translator, working off the newspaper clippings caused some issues, too. The second volume, published only in serial, never underwent the extensive editing that a publishing house like Knopf would have provided had the manuscript been readied for book publication. As a result, I encountered several discrepancies in the manuscript. Along with the editors at Knopf, we made the executive decision to fix these issues, believing this to be in line with what Grade would have done had he seen this work through to publication.

For example, in part 4, chapter 16, the character of Tzadok Kaddish is suddenly referred to as Yaakov Yosef Kadish, nicknamed Yekele. Another character, Ezra Morgenstern, is referred to as Stern in part 3, chapter 17. To prevent confusion, I retained the names Tzadok and Morgenstern throughout. Additionally, Sirka's husband is called Rachmiel Rozenau when we are first introduced to him, and later he becomes Meir Moshe Baruchovits. I kept the latter name.

Besides names, other minor discrepancies showed up in the man-

---

* *Present Tense* 5, no. 4 (1978): 40–46.

uscript. For example, in part 4, chapter 6, the character of Tzalia Gutmacher, whom we'd known as the owner of a clothing shop, is referred to as a confectioner. I continued describing him as a clothes dealer.

And the most challenging textual conundrum was in part 4, chapter 18, where a short part of the installment was missing. Instead of imagining what Grade would have written, I left an ellipsis to indicate the missing text. In fact, our early copies of this book were printed with the ellipsis.

But then, in a remarkable twist of scholarly serendipity, Yehudah Zirkind—who had received an early copy of the book—reached out at the eleventh hour with a crucial discovery. Despite our exhaustive searches at YIVO, the missing paragraphs were not found in our primary archives. Instead, Zirkind located them in the National Library of Israel, where a substantial portion of Grade's materials are preserved. This last-minute discovery filled a critical gap in the text.

Throughout this translation process, I, and everyone involved in the publication of this book, held out hope that we would find an ending. We dreamed that somewhere, among the many papers, the conclusion of *Sons and Daughters* lay hidden. But it was not to be. None of our searches turned up the missing final chapter or chapters.

But then, after about eight years had passed since my first look at this manuscript—after Covid had pushed off publication, after a long editing process with the extraordinary editor Todd Portnowitz, and after YIVO had digitized the entire Grade collection—I was riffling through the online archive in search of more background material when I stumbled across two pages typed by Grade. At first I wasn't sure what I was reading; but then, in a flash, I got it: Grade was mapping out an ending! He was telling us how he wanted the book to conclude.

Here, then, is a translation of those pages:

One day and half a night after Naftali Hertz Katzenellenbogen had left for home in Switzerland, his father, the Morehdalye rabbi Sholem Shachne Katzenellenbogen, died of a heart attack. This so shook Morehdalye and its surrounding towns that it seemed the earth had split and its deepest abyss had spilled over, flooding every-thing in waves. But soon the gushing, surging abyss hardened, and the waves congealed into mountains, into a fear staring fixedly from everyone's eyes, welding mouths shut, so that no one could emit a scream or even a moan. As though of its own volition, the thought occurred to everyone at the same time—as surely as it was now the eve of Passover—that the rabbi had died because there was no lon-ger a shred of doubt—not in his mind, nor in his wife's—that their son had a Christian wife and an uncircumcised child in Switzerland. For anyone able to count to ten, there remained not the slightest doubt of it. As many times as he'd come to stay at his parents', Naf-tali Hertz had never brought along any of his family from abroad. He'd also never invited any of his family to come visit him. But what mostly convinced the townspeople that he'd married a gentile woman—even more than if they had seen the woman herself—was the fact that the Morehdalye rabbi had died a night after the son left.

The sensitive Morehdalye rabbi, who'd already had a heart attack once, was no longer able to hide the knowledge from himself that he had a Christian daughter-in-law and an uncircumcised grandchild. All the lies that the son, the doctor of philosophy, may his name be erased, had fabricated during his visit to his parents, disintegrated like an illusion as soon as he left. And his father could not—and probably did not want to—live through that.

It was the month of Nissan, already several days before Passover, and every Morehdalye resident felt that it was practically God's grace, God's pity for the rabbi, that he'd died at a time when it was prohibited to say eulogies. Morehdalye would have drowned in tears, gone insane from the wailing, and everyone's praise of the rabbi would have dishonored him, become strewn with mud, because the more they'd laud him, the deeper it would bore into everyone's heart and mind that the dead man, our rabbi for so many decades, has a gentile daughter-in-law and an uncircumcised gentile as a grandchild.

But not one rabbi from the area skipped the funeral. Nor did the father-in-law of the dead man, the deeply stooped eighty-five-year-old Zembin rabbi.

So, here it is. Not an actual ending, but a glimpse of what we might have gotten had Grade completed *Sons and Daughters*. It will have to suffice.

ACKNOWLEDGMENTS

Translating this book has been an incredible journey, and I wish to acknowledge those who have made it possible:

Todd Portnowitz, an editor par excellence, whose meticulous work truly elevated this translation.

Altie Karper, the first editor of this book, who not only shaped its early stages but also provided advice throughout.

Jonathan Brent for entrusting me with this translation. I am thankful for the opportunity to contribute to the legacy of this important work.

The Yiddish Book Center, whose yearslong fellowship provided me with the resources and time necessary to bring this translation to fruition.

Aviya Kushner for her mentorship on this project during my fellowship year at the YBC.

Nathaniel Deutsch, Yehudah Zirkind, and all who believed in this project and supported me in various ways. Your contributions, both large and small, have made this translation possible. Thank you for your belief in the power of literature to transcend languages and cultures.

Glossary

Adar: The twelfth month in the Jewish calendar, during which the Purim holiday falls, on the fourteenth day. (See also **Purim**.)

Agudah: A shorthand reference to Agudath Israel, an Orthodox Jewish religious/social/political organization formed in early-twentieth-century Poland to support traditional religious practices and beliefs that were being challenged by the Enlightenment and by Reform, political Zionist, socialist, and communist movements that arose during the eighteenth and nineteenth centuries. Now an international organization and a religious political party in Israel.

agunah: Literally, "chained woman." A married woman whose husband refuses to grant her a Jewish divorce and who is therefore unable to marry another man, even after the civil dissolution of their marriage.

aliya: The calling up of a congregant to the bimah to read a section of the Torah. (See also **bimah**.)

Amalek: Canaanite tribe described in the Bible as the original—and perennial—enemy of the Jewish people; they first attacked the Israelites when they were newly liberated from Egyptian slavery. Also the name of the grandson of Esau (brother of Jacob, founder of the Israelite nation), the founder of the Amalekite tribe.

Amalekite: A member of the tribe of Amalek.

amud: Raised platform in the synagogue from which the prayer leader conducts the services.

aron kodesh: Literally, "holy ark." Large cabinet situated along the eastern wall of the synagogue, in which the Torah scrolls are stored.

***Aruch Hashulchan*:** A multivolume work that codifies, sources, and summarizes biblical and Talmudic Jewish law, compiled and edited by Rabbi Yechiel Michel Epstein (Lithuania, 1829–1908).

Asara B'Teves: Literally, the tenth day of the month of Teves (the tenth month in the Jewish calendar). A day of fasting and mourning that commemorates the beginning of the siege of Jerusalem by the army of the Babylonian king Nebuchadnezzar II in 588 BCE, which culminated, seven months later, in the destruction of the First Temple and the exile to Babylon of the Jews of the Kingdom of Judah. (See also **Tisha B'Av**.)

Ashmedai: The mythic "king of the demons" who is featured in Talmudic stories as a malevolent antagonist to King Solomon. Also appears in Muslim and Christian scriptural sources.

Av: Fifth month in the Jewish calendar, during which both the First and Second Temples in Jerusalem were destroyed, on the ninth day of the month. (See also **Tisha B'Av**.)

avos melachos, toldos: The laws of Shabbos consist of thirty-nine *avos* (literally, "fathers"), main tasks, along with their *toldos* (children). These encompass all the tasks that are forbidden to be done on Shabbos. (See also **thirty-nine melachos**.)

Baal Shem Tov: Literally, "master of the good name." Name by which Rabbi Yisroel ben Eliezer (1698–1760) was known. A Ukrainian-born rabbi and mystic, he was the founder of Hasidism, a sect within Judaism that emphasizes the spiritual, mystical, ecstatic, and populistic aspects of Jewish religious philosophy and practices. (See also **Hasid**.)

ba'al tefilah: The leader of the prayer service in the synagogue.

ba'al tshuvah: Non-observant person who has become observant.

badeken: The prenuptial ceremony during which the groom covers the bride's face with a veil.

Basel Zionist Congress: First Zionist Congress, the inaugural congress of the Zionist Organization (later to become the World Zionist Organization in 1960), held in Basel, Switzerland, from August 29 to August 31, 1897.

beis din: Rabbinic tribunal convened for adjudicating matters of religious and, occasionally, civil law. (See also **din Torah**.)

beis medrash: Study hall located within a synagogue or in a religious school building.

ben sorer u'moreh: Biblical term for egregiously disobedient offspring.

Berlintchkes: An uncomplimentary term used by Eastern European Orthodox Jews to describe German Jews who identified with the Reform movement.

besamim: Spice mixture used in the Havdalah service that marks the conclusion of the Sabbath. (See also **Havdalah, Shabbos.**)

bimah: Raised platform in the synagogue on which the Torah scroll is publicly read during the prayer service. (See also **aliya.**)

biur: Moses Mendelssohn's translation of and commentary on the Pentateuch. Because Mendelssohn is the "father of Jewish Enlightenment," religious Jews generally eschew his works. The biur, despite its biblical content, is considered a heretical text by traditional Jewish communities. (See also **Haskalah.**)

biur chametz: The ritual of burning chametz the morning before Passover begins. (See also **chametz.**)

challah: Braided loaf of bread prepared specially for the Sabbath and festivals.

chalutz (pl., **chalutzim**): Pioneering agricultural worker in pre-state Israel.

chametz: Leavened food products that are forbidden to be consumed during Passover.

Chamisha Asar B'Shevat: Literally, the fifteenth day of the month of Shevat (eleventh month in the Jewish calendar). The holiday that marks the beginning of the agricultural cycle in the land of Israel. Described in the Mishna as the "new year of the trees," it is a day during which fruit native to the land of Israel is eaten in celebration and trees are planted. Also known as Tu B'Shevat.

cheder (also, **cheyder**): A privately run religious primary school. In prewar Europe, usually in a single room in the teacher's home and for boys only, who were taught Hebrew, the Bible, the Mishna, and the Talmud.

cherem (also, **cheyrem**): The act of rabbinic excommunication for significant, specific violations of Jewish law.

chevra kadisha: Religious burial society responsible for ritually preparing the body for burial and burying it according to Jewish law.

chillul Hashem: Desecrating the name of God by acting immorally in public, in word or deed, usually in the presence of gentiles.

cholent: Multi-ingredient Sabbath stew whose primary ingredient is, traditionally, meat. It is slow-cooked beginning before the Sabbath to avoid the prohibition of cooking on the Sabbath.

chol hamoed: The intermediate days of the weeklong Sukkos and Passover holidays. Many actions not permitted on the first and last days of these holidays (e.g., writing, traveling, using electricity) are permitted on these days. (See also **Pesach, Sukkos.**)

chremsl (pl., **chremslach**): Deep-fried pancake made with crushed or ground-up matzoh and eggs, to which other savory or sweet ingredients and toppings can be added. A filling main course or side dish, its primary purpose is to use up leftover Passover matzoh.

Chumash: The five books of the Hebrew Bible that comprise the Pentateuch. (See also **Tanach, Torah.**)

chuppah: Wedding canopy.

daven (**davened, davening**): Pray.

dayan: Judge in a Jewish religious court.

din Torah: Arbitration by a Jewish religious court that litigates civil or religious adversarial situations. (See also **beis din.**)

Elul: The sixth month in the Jewish calendar.

Endikes: Members of NDK, a Polish nationalist, antisemitic party.

eruv: Ritual enclosure that establishes, by various physical means, specific boundaries within a public area, within which a limited carrying of items in public is permitted on the Sabbath.

eruv khatzeiros: Usually made with bread or other food, this enables Jews to carry items on Shabbos in a shared courtyard or other shared spaces in a building, such as hallways, lobbies, etc.

eruv techimen: Enables Jews to walk on Shabbos beyond the techum Shabbos (about one kilometer in each direction).

esrog: Citron. Ritually held while reciting a blessing each day during the Sukkos holiday, alongside the lulav. (See also **lulav, Sukkos.**)

essen teg: Literally, "eating day." Community-based arrangement for poor students boarding at a yeshiva that could not afford to feed them; it enabled them to have dinner each evening, on a rotating basis, at the home of a charitable community member.

fir-zugerke: A learned woman who would lead the synagogue prayer service in the women's section—sometimes translating the Hebrew text into vernacular Yiddish—for women who were unable to read the prayers on their own.

gartel: Ritual belt made of either black or white fabric that is worn by men in some Orthodox Jewish sects to create both a physical and a metaphysical distinction between the upper half of the human body, which is governed by the intellect, and the lower half of the body, which is governed by physical impulses. Worn by some only during prayer, by others throughout the day.

gehinnom: The afterlife destination for the souls of the wicked, where they will be divinely punished for the sins they committed during their lifetimes. Often translated as "hell" or "purgatory."

Gemara: One of the two main components of the sixty-three-volume Talmud, which records legal arguments and debates, Midrashic tales, biblical analyses, and commentaries on the Mishna (a six-volume compilation of Jewish oral law) that were made by hundreds of rabbis in both personal and intergenerational dialogue. Compiled and codified in the sixth century CE. (See also **Mishna.**)

gemilas chesed: Altruistic acts of kindness performed without expectation of reward or reciprocity.

haftorah: A relevant selection from the book of Prophets that is publicly read in the synagogue as part of the Sabbath morning service, at the conclusion of the public reading of that week's designated portion from the Bible. (See also **sedrah, Tanach.**)

Haggadah: The compilation of biblical, Talmudic, and Midrashic excerpts; prayers; ritual instructions; and traditional songs that tells the story of the liberation and exodus of the Israelites from Egyptian slavery and sets down the order of the Passover seder. It is read as part of the seder. (See also **Pesach, seder.**)

halacha (adj., **halachic**): Jewish law, initially drawn from both the Bible and from oral transmissions that were eventually written down and compiled into codes of Jewish law. (See also *Aruch Hashulchan*, **Gemara**, **Mishna**, *Shulchan Aruch*.)

hamantaschen (sing., **hamantash**): Triangular, open-faced pastry filled with any type of sweet or savory filling. One of the traditional foods consumed in celebration of the Purim holiday, it is named for Haman, the vanquished villain of the Purim story; its etymology and origins are the subject of lively cultural and culinary speculation. (See also **Purim.**)

Hasid (pl., **Hasidim**): Member of one of many subsects that comprise Hasidism, a religious movement founded in eighteenth-century Ukraine by the Baal Shem Tov (Rabbi Yisroel ben Eliezer, 1698–1760), which emphasizes the mystical, ecstatic, and populistic aspects of Jewish religious philosophy and practices, and includes a belief in the primacy of the rabbinic sect leaders who function as both personal advisors and mystical intermediaries between humanity and God.

Haskalah: Derived from the Hebrew word for "intelligence," an intellectual movement and worldview that flourished in Europe in the eighteenth and nineteenth centuries, advocating for enlightened Jewish engagement with secular knowledge, culture, and politics, and arguing against exclusive religious authority and isolationism.

Havdalah: The prayer that marks the conclusion of the Sabbath day, which includes blessings made over wine, spices, and a lit, braided candle. (See also **besamim, Shabbos**.)

heimish: Literally, "homestyle." Used to describe certain types of European Jewish home cooking; can also be used to describe a specifically Jewish in-group approach or situation, for good or ill.

Iyar: Second month in the Jewish calendar.

Kaddish: Aramaic call-and-response prayer exalting and glorifying God's omnipotence and benevolence that is recited at specific points during all three daily prayer services by mourners during their mourning period.

kapoteh: A type of long woolen and/or silk frock coat of medieval origin worn by Hasidic men and by some non-Hasidic Orthodox men.

kapparos: A pre–Yom Kippur ceremony of personal atonement that involves passing a chicken over one's head while reciting a prayer of supplication. The chicken is then ritually slaughtered and its carcass donated for charitable purposes. (See also **Yom Kippur**.)

kashket: A cap with a high crown, usually made of wool felt, worn outdoors by Orthodox Jewish boys in nineteenth- and early-twentieth-century Europe, when wearing a yarmulke (skullcap) in public was forbidden by Russian authorities. Nowadays worn mostly by Hasidic boys. (See also **yarmulke**.)

kibbutz: A planned community based on the philosophy of communal living, originally agricultural in nature but now also with industrial and high-tech versions. First established in the early twentieth century in many locations in pre-state Israel, it is run in accordance with a combination of socialist and Zionist principles.

kitniyos: A category of food that includes legumes, rice, corn, and seeds, which are not consumed during Passover by Ashkenazic Jews due to their similarity, in their ground state, to flour made from the five species of grain (barley, rye, oats, wheat, and spelt) that cannot be eaten in leavened form during Passover. (See also **Pesach**.)

Kol Nidrei: The declaratory prayer that is recited in the synagogue at the beginning of the evening Yom Kippur service that proactively annuls all personal and religious vows that will be made to God during the year that has just begun, so as to preemptively avoid the sin of making vows to God that are not fulfilled. (See also **Yom Kippur**.)

Korben Mincha: The name given to a prayer book to which Yiddish commentary was added, it was created in the eighteenth century and intended specifically for women.

kriah: The ritual of making, as an expression of grief, a small tear in the garment of a mourner at the funeral of a parent, spouse, child, or sibling, accompanied by the recitation of a blessing.

kugel: A baked pudding, traditionally made with noodles or potatoes, prepared before sundown on Friday and eaten on the Sabbath.

Lag B'Omer: Holiday celebrating the thirty-third day in the forty-nine-day countdown beginning on the second day of Passover and concluding with Shavuos, the holiday that commemorates the giving of the Ten Commandments to the Israelites on Mount Sinai. It marks the conclusion of the quasi–mourning period of the first thirty-three days of the countdown. (See also **Pesach, Shavuos.**)

lamed-vovnik: One of thirty-six unknown, hidden-in-plain-sight righteous and saintly people inhabiting the world at any given time, whose Godly presence sustains the world. A concept mentioned in the Talmud and expounded upon in Jewish mystical writings.

lashon kodesh: Literally, "holy language." Synonym for Hebrew.

l'chaim: Literally, "to life." A celebratory toast over wine or spirits.

lehavdil: Literally, "to separate." A parenthetical aside uttered when making a comparison between a concept or occurrence within the Jewish world and a similar concept or occurrence outside of this world, which asserts the essential incompatibility between the two worlds.

leynen: Literally, "reading." The public reading of the Torah and haftorah in the synagogue, using the proper cantillation. (See also **haftorah, trope.**)

lulav: A date-palm frond specially bound together with willow and myrtle branches. Held with an esrog, it is ritually waved while reciting a blessing during the morning prayer service every day (excluding the Sabbath) of the Sukkos holiday, which also celebrates the autumn harvest. (See also **esrog, Sukkos.**)

Maariv: The daily evening prayer service.

machzor (pl., **machzorim**): Prayer book used for holiday services, in place of the siddur, which is used for weekday and Sabbath services. (See also **siddur.**)

maftir: The concluding section, on any Sabbath or festival, of that day's public reading of the Torah in the synagogue. The congregant called to the bimah to make the blessings preceding and following this reading will then chant the related haftorah reading. (See also **aliya, bimah, haftorah, parsha, sedrah, Torah.**)

Maharam: Acronym for Rabbi Meir of Rothenburg (1215–1293), a notable German-born rabbi, poet, and Talmudic commentator.

Maharam Schiff: Acronym for Rabbi Meir Schiff (1608–1644), a notable German-born rabbi, kabbalist, and Talmudic commentator.

mameh: Yiddish for "mother."

mashgiach: 1. Rabbinic executive in a yeshiva who serves as the spiritual counselor for the students. 2. The kashrus supervisor/monitor in a food-processing factory or anywhere that food is publicly served.

maskil (pl. **maskilim**): One who has abandoned religious faith to pursue a path of secular enlightenment.

maykil: A lenient rabbinic interpretation of or ruling on Jewish law.

mechuten (pl., **machatonim**; f., **machatainesteh**). Father-in-law of one's son or daughter (who, perforce, becomes a member of one's extended family).

melamed (pl., **melamdim**): Teacher (in prewar Europe, exclusively male) of Hebrew, the Bible, the Mishna, and the Talmud to young children.

Mendelssohn, Moses: German-born Jewish philosopher and theologian (1729–1786) who was one of the founding theorists of the Haskalah, or Jewish Enlightenment, a movement that challenged traditional Orthodox beliefs about the place of Jews in the modern, secular world. (See also **Haskalah.**)

menorah: 1. Seven-branched golden candelabrum used in religious rituals, initially in the portable Tabernacle and eventually in the Temple in Jerusalem. 2. Nine-branched candelabrum lit in the home in accordance with a specific ritual on each of the eight nights of Chanukah.

mesorah: The generational transmission of religious knowledge, belief, and practice.

Mezach, Yehoshua HaLevi: A writer, journalist, columnist, and editor (1834–1917).

mezumen: A quorum of at least three post-bar-mitzvah males at a meal that included bread, which allows for the call-and-response recitation of a brief prologue to the Grace After Meals. (A quorum of at least three post-bat-mitzvah females is called a **mezumenet.**) (See also **rabosai.**)

mezuzah (pl., **mezuzos**): Small rectangular piece of parchment onto which a scribe has written, in Hebrew, specific passages from the book of Deuteronomy. It is rolled into a case which is then affixed onto the right doorpost of the front door and of every room in a home, to supply spiritual protection to the home.

Midrash: Umbrella term for hundreds of years of rabbinic exegesis on the Bible. Midrashic texts appear throughout the Talmud, as well as in many compilations of later rabbinic interpretations of and commentary on the Bible.

mikveh: Small indoor pool made to rabbinically mandated specifications that contains naturally sourced rainwater and/or spring water; used by women and men for ritual immersion. For women, used for re-sanctification following menstrual periods and childbirth. For men and women, used for sanctification before marriage and other life-cycle events, as part of the conversion process, and, by some, before Jewish holidays and the Sabbath.

Mincha: The daily afternoon prayer service.

minyan: Quorum of ten post-bar-mitzvah males that must be present at a prayer service so that all rituals of public prayer can be performed, including the recitation of Kaddish by mourners and the day's designated Torah reading. (Non-Orthodox congregations include women in the minyan.) (See also **Kaddish.**)

mishmar: Evening Bible and Talmud study, usually in a study hall, above and beyond regular classroom study during the day.

Mishna (pl., **Mishnayos**): Six-volume compilation of Jewish personal, ritual, communal, and civil laws that is believed to have been originally orally transmitted, beginning with Moses at the time of the revelation on Mount Sinai. Assembled and codified by Rabbi Yehuda HaNasi (Judah the Prince) in Roman Palestine sometime during the second century CE from a multiplicity of rabbinic discussions, opinions, and rulings. (See also **tanna.**)

Misnagid (pl., **Misnagdim**): Opponent of the Hasidic approach to religious philosophy and observance, as well as to certain specific Hasidic practices and beliefs. (See also **Hasid.**)

mitzvah: A precept to be performed as a religious obligation, as outlined in the Bible and in codes of Jewish law. Also, colloquially, a good deed or an act of kindness.

mizrach: Literally, "east," the direction diaspora Jews face when praying, which is toward Jerusalem.

Mizrachi: Organization of Orthodox Jewish Zionists founded in Europe in 1902 that was also an Orthodox Zionist political party in Israel. Also used to describe Jews from the Middle East, North Africa, Central Asia, and the Caucasus.

mizrach wall: In the synagogue, the eastward-facing wall, against which rabbis and other communal dignitaries are traditionally seated.

mohel: Ritual circumciser.

moreh hora'ah: Literally, "teacher of rulings." In prewar Europe, the chief rabbinical decisor in any given town.

motzei: Literally, "departure." The hours immediately following the conclusion of the Sabbath or any festival, which serve as a transitional period between the sacred and the everyday.

musar: Ancient Jewish study and practice of self-improvement that was systematized and popularized in nineteenth-century Lithuania as the Musar Movement. It involves methodical religious instruction in the areas of moral conduct, ethical behavior, and spiritual practices.

musarnik: An adherent of the self-improvement practices that form the basis of the Musar Movement.

Mussaf: Additional prayer service on the Sabbath and certain holidays, immediately after the morning Shacharis prayer service.

nachas: Joy and gratification specifically derived from properly functioning, successful offspring.

ner tamid: Literally, "eternal light." Perpetual lamp (oil, candle, electric, or solar) that hangs over the aron kodesh in a synagogue. (See also **aron kodesh**.)

neshama: The human soul.

neshama yeseira: Literally, "additional soul." A spiritual boost of joy and serenity that is brought about through Sabbath observance.

niggun: A type of religious song that can consist of biblical verses, classical Jewish poetry, and/or wordless melodic improvisation. Can be sung either as a lament or in joyous celebration.

Nissan: The first month in the Jewish calendar, during which Passover falls.

Oneravtzes: Members of ONR, Obóz Narodowo-Radykalny (National Radical Camp), a group that envisaged Poland as a Catholic state.

parsha: Literally, "section." Popularly used interchangeably with sedrah to describe one of the fifty-four portions into which the Torah is divided. (More accurately, it is actually a subsection within a sedrah.) (See also **aliya, Chumash, sedrah, Torah**.)

Pesach: The Passover holiday, which commemorates the liberation of the Israelites from centuries of slavery in Egypt sometime in the middle of the second millennium BCE. (See also **Haggadah, seder**.)

pesukei dezimra: Literally, "verses of praise." The first section of the daily morning prayer service that consists of blessings and excerpts from the Bible that are in praise of God. It is considered a form of preparation for the prayers of supplication that follow.

peyes: Sidelocks on Orthodox Jewish males belonging to sects that prohibit the cutting of hair in the sideburn area, based on a Talmudic injunction against shaving the hair adjacent to the ear.

pidyon shvuyim: The religious obligation to redeem or otherwise work toward the release of fellow Jews who have been kidnapped or unjustly imprisoned.

pilpul (pl., **pilpulim**): In-depth Talmud study through intense textual analysis and rabbinic disputation.

porush: A scholarly recluse who is exclusively devoted to the study of sacred books.

posul: A sacred parchment text that is unfit for ritual or ceremonial use because it has become in some way damaged or defective. Can also refer to a person who for some halachic reason is disqualified from participation in a Jewish ritual. (See also **halacha.**)

Purim: Jewish holiday, falling on the fourteenth day of the month of Adar, that commemorates the victory, in the fifth century BCE, of the Jews of the Persian Empire over Haman, the antisemitic vizier of King Ahasuerus, who was the architect of a genocidal governmental decree against the Jews. Purim is celebrated by giving charity to the poor, exchanging gifts of food, a festive afternoon meal, and evening and morning readings of the book of Esther, in which the story of Purim is recounted. (See also **Adar, hamantashen, hushan Purim.**)

Rabiner: German for "rabbi." Can also refer more specifically to a rabbi who was ordained by a Reform rabbinical seminary in Germany.

rabosai: Literally, "gentlemen!" The declarative opening statement to get the attention of meal participants for the recitation of the brief prologue to the Grace After Meals. (See also **mezumen.**)

Rambam: Acronym for Rabbi Moshe ben Maimon (1138–1204), also known as Maimonides, a towering figure in medieval Jewish philosophy, science, law, and Talmudic scholarship. Born in Spain, he fled persecution there and eventually settled in Egypt, where, in addition to writing seminal, groundbreaking works of Jewish scholarship, he served as head of the Jewish community, was a practicing physician, and was one of the court physicians to the Levantine Muslim sultan Saladin.

Ramban: Acronym for Rabbi Moshe ben Nachman (1194–1270), also known as Nachmanides, a notable Spanish-born rabbi, kabbalist, teacher, and biblical commentator. The success of his forced religious disputation with the Christian convert Pablo Christiani resulted in his banishment from Spain and eventual settlement, in 1267, in Jerusalem, which was then under Muslim rule.

Rashkebehag: Acronym for Rosh kol bnei hagola, meaning "the leader of the Diaspora."

Rif: Acronym for Rabbi Yitzchak Alfasi (1013–1103), a notable Algerian-born rabbi, decisor of Jewish law, teacher, and Talmudic scholar. Moved to Morocco in 1045 and then to Andalusia in 1088.

Rishonim: Leading rabbis, biblical and Talmudic commentators, philosophers, and decisors of Jewish law who lived from the eleventh through fifteenth centuries.

rom'l books: Rom'l is an acronym for rabbonim u'melamdim (rabbis and children's Hebrew teachers).

Rosh Chodesh: The first day of any Jewish month, during which additional prayers are said. Sometimes celebrated for two days, due to the complexities of establishing the beginning and ending of months in a lunar-based calendar system.

rosh yeshiva (pl., **roshei yeshiva**): The headmaster—i.e., the head rabbinic figure and teacher—in a yeshiva. (See also **yeshiva.**)

ruach hakodesh: Literally, "holy spirit." Prophetic capabilities bestowed upon an individual by God.

Salanter, Yisroel: Lithuanian-born rabbi, scholar, and rosh yeshiva (1809–1883), who is regarded as the father of the modern Mussar Movement, which considers the formal study of moral conduct and ethical behavior to be as important for spiritual and religious growth as the study of sacred texts. (See also **musar, musarnik.**)

Sambatyon River: Described in rabbinic literature as the mystical river that the ten northern tribes that constituted the biblical Kingdom of Israel crossed as they were forcibly exiled from their lands by Sennacherib, the Assyrian conqueror of northern Israel, circa 722 BCE. The whereabouts of the "Ten Lost Tribes" remains unknown to this day; some Indo-European and African peoples claim to be their descendants.

seder: The Passover celebratory meal, which includes reading from the Haggadah, drinking four cups of wine, and consuming ritual foods, including matzoh. (See also **Haggadah, Pesach.**)

sedrah: One of the fifty-four portions of the Bible that are read aloud, in weekly rotation, during the Sabbath and festival morning services. A part of this portion is also read at the Monday and Thursday morning services and at the Sabbath afternoon service.

sefer (pl., **seforim**): Literally, "book." Commonly used to refer to specifically religious works such as the Bible, the Talmud, and books of commentaries, law, and philosophy.

Selichos: Penitential prayers recited on the days leading up to and during the High Holy Days, and on some other fast days during the year. (See also **Yom Kippur**.)

Shabbos: The Jewish Sabbath, the biblical seventh day of the week, a day of religious reflection and rest from the labors of the previous six days.

Shabbos Chazon: The Sabbath before Tisha B'Av, named after the opening word of that day's haftorah reading, from the book of Isaiah. (See also **haftorah, Tisha B'Av**.)

Shabbos Hagadol: Literally, "the great Sabbath." The Sabbath immediately before the start of Passover, during which it is customary for the synagogue's rabbi to deliver a sermon relating to the observance of Passover.

shadchan: Matchmaker—professional or informal.

Shalosh Seudos: Literally, "three meals." Refers specifically to the third of the three required meals of the Sabbath day, which is eaten either immediately before or after the Mincha service. (See also **Mincha**.)

shammes (pl., **shammosim**): The synagogue sexton.

Shas: Another name for the sixty-three volumes of the Talmud, which references its six-volume Mishnaic component. (See also **Gemara, Mishna**.)

shatnez: A garment containing both linen and wool. Passages in Leviticus and Deuteronomy state that such a garment is forbidden to be worn. Various reasons for this prohibition have been suggested by rabbinic commentators throughout the centuries.

Shavuos: Literally, "weeks." Holiday that, as described in the Bible, celebrates the giving of the Ten Commandments by God, via Moses, to the Israelites on Mount Sinai. It falls forty-nine days (i.e., seven weeks) after the second day of Passover. It also celebrates the beginning of the wheat harvest in Israel.

Sh'aylos U'Tshuvos: General title given to volumes of halachic responses to contemporary questions of Jewish law, compiled by rabbinic scholars and legal authorities. (See also **halacha**.)

Shehecheyanu: Literally, "who has kept us alive." Shorthand reference to the blessing of gratitude recited when performing any one of several holiday- or lifecycle-related rituals, or upon eating a fruit that has not been eaten during the preceding twelve months.

sheigetz: Uncomplimentary term for a non-Jewish male.

sheitel: Wig worn by women after marriage, to fulfill the religious requirement that the hair of a married woman be fully covered in public.

Shema: Literally, "hear!" Shorthand reference to the foundational six-word declaration, from the book of Deuteronomy, recited every day as part of morning, evening, and bedtime prayer, which affirms one's belief in covenantal Judaism and in a single God. Also recited at the deathbed and in times of religious persecution.

sheva brochos: Literally, "seven blessings." Seven blessings over a cup of wine that are recited as part of the wedding ceremony and at the end of the wedding dinner, as well as at the conclusion of meals celebrating the bride and groom that take place during the week after the wedding.

Shevat: Eleventh month of the Jewish calendar, during which the Chamisha Asar B'Shevat holiday falls. (See also **Chamisha Asar B'Shevat.**)

shidduch (pl., **shidduchim**): A matrimonial match made via a matchmaker. (See also **shadchan.**)

shiksa: Uncomplimentary term for a non-Jewish female.

Shimoneh Esrei: Literally, "eighteen." Prayer containing elements of praise, supplication, and gratitude that is said in an undertone and while standing; a central component of the morning, afternoon, and evening prayer services.

shin: Twenty-first letter of the Hebrew alphabet.

***Shiteh M'kubetzes*:** A well-known sefer; commentary on the Talmud. (See also **sefer.**)

shiur: Lecture or class on a religious text or subject matter.

shiva: Literally, "seven." Seven-day mourning period that begins immediately after a funeral. Mourners remain at home, sitting on low chairs, and receive visitors who offer food, consolation, and support.

shmurah matzoh: Matzoh whose production has been supervised by observant Jews from the harvesting of the wheat that will be ground into flour to the eighteen-minute baking cycle of the dough, to ensure that no leavening occurs at any stage in the process and that the matzoh therefore meets the requirements for consumption on Passover. (See also **seder.**)

shochet: Ritual slaughterer of animals and fowl.

shofar: Ram's horn that is sounded with a specific pattern of blasts at designated times during the Rosh Hashanah (New Year) service and at the conclusion of the Yom Kippur service. Also sounded at the conclusion of the morning service during the thirty days of the month of Elul, leading up to Rosh Hashanah. (See also **Elul, Yom Kippur.**)

shtender: Lectern on which religious books are propped up during individual study or during a class or public lecture.

shtetl: Small village or town in pre–World War II Eastern Europe, populated primarily by Jews.

shtiebel: Small, one- or two-room synagogue.

shtreimel: Round fur hat worn by Hasidic men on the Sabbath, holidays, and festive occasions. Of uncertain origin, it may have been inspired by fur hats worn by gentile European nobility.

Shulchan Aruch: Literally, "set table." Authoritative four-volume code of religious, personal, and commercial Jewish law compiled by Rabbi Joseph Caro in 1563 in Ottoman Palestine.

Shushan Purim: The day after Purim, which is celebrated as an extension of the Purim holiday in Levantine cities that have been surrounded by walls since approximately 1250 BCE. This includes Susa ("Shushan" in Hebrew), which was the capital of the Persian Empire when the events recounted in the book of Esther took place. (See also **Adar, Purim.**)

siddur (pl., **siddurim**): The daily and Sabbath prayer book.

Simchas Torah: A holiday that occurs in the month of Tishrei, immediately following the seven-day Sukkos holiday. It celebrates the conclusion of the yearlong, weekly Sabbath cycle of public Bible readings and the beginning of the new cycle, with readings from the end of Deuteronomy and the beginning of Genesis. It is also celebrated by carrying the Torah scrolls throughout the synagogue, in song and dance. (See also **Sukkos, Torah.**)

sotah: As described in the Bible, a woman who is suspected of adultery and subjected to a public trial that will prove either her guilt or her innocence.

Sukkos: Literally, "huts." Seven-day festival that begins on the fifteenth day of the month of Tishrei and commemorates the forty-year sojourn of the Israelites, newly freed from Egyptian slavery, in the Sinai desert, during which time they lived in portable huts (sukkos; sing., sukkah). Also celebrates the fall harvest season in the land of Israel.

taharah: Ritual washing and dressing of a dead body, in preparation for burial.

tallis (pl., **talleisim**): Large, fringed prayer shawl worn during morning prayer, customarily made from wool. Through a hole in each of the four corners are threaded tzitzis, ritually knotted woolen fringes. (See also **tzitzis.**)

tallis katan: Small rectangular under- or outer-garment worn daily, customarily made from cotton or wool. Through a hole in each of the four corners are threaded tzitzis, ritually knotted woolen fringes. (See also **tzitzis**.)

talmud torah: 1. In prewar Europe, a primary school for boys only that taught Hebrew, the Bible, the Mishna, the Talmud, and Jewish law, and was partly supported by communal funds. 2. In America, a religious after-school for boys and girls attending public school.

Tammuz: Fourth month in the Jewish calendar.

Tanach: Acronym for the three parts of the Hebrew Bible: "Torah" (the Pentateuch), "Nevi'im" (the books of the Prophets, including Joshua, Samuel, Isaiah, Jeremiah, and Ezekiel), and "Kesuvim" (literally, "writings," including the books of Psalms, Proverbs, Job, Song of Songs, Esther, and Ruth). There are twenty-four books in all. (See also **Torah**.)

tanna (pl., **tannaim**): One of a group of rabbinic sages from the first two centuries of the Common Era, whose legal and ethical discussions and rulings are recorded in the Mishna. (See also **Mishna**.)

taygelach: Holiday dessert that consists of small crunchy balls of dough that have been boiled in a honey syrup and then garnished with nuts and cherries.

techinos: Prayers of supplication recited by women in the synagogue and at specific ritual events.

tefillin: Phylacteries. A set of two small square black leather boxes into which have been placed parchment scrolls onto which have been hand-written specific verses from the Bible. One box is affixed to the forehead and the other to the upper arm; both are then secured with black leather straps. Worn by post-bar-mitzvah-age males during weekday morning prayer. Also worn by women among the non-Orthodox.

Tehillim: The biblical book of Psalms, which appears in the Kesuvim section of the Hebrew Bible and consists of 150 chapters that take the form of hymns. Individual psalms also appear as prayers throughout the siddur, the Haggadah, and other books of Jewish liturgy. Traditionally believed to have been composed mainly by King David (with certain chapters ascribed to others), chapters of Tehillim are also recited personally and/or communally for purposes of supplication, thanksgiving, and celebration. (See also **Haggadah, siddur, Tanach**.)

Teves: The tenth month in the Jewish calendar.

thirty-nine melachos: Thirty-nine categories of labor biblically prohibited on the Sabbath and certain holidays. They form the basis for many other types of rabbinically prohibited labors that are derived from these thirty-nine. (See also **avos melachos, toldos**.)

Tisha B'Av: Literally, the ninth day of the month of Av, the fifth month in the Jewish calendar. The date on which both the First and Second Temples were destroyed in Jerusalem—the former by the army of the Babylonian king Nebuchadnezzar II in the sixth century BCE, and the latter by the army of the Roman general Titus in 70 CE. On both occasions, the city itself was also destroyed and its inhabitants sent into exile. The day is commemorated with a twenty-five-hour fast and relevant prayers and scriptural readings.

Torah: The five books that comprise the Pentateuch, i.e., the Hebrew Bible: Genesis, Exodus, Leviticus, Numbers, and Deuteronomy. (See also **Tanach**.)

Tosafos: A compilation of commentaries on Rashi's (Rabbi Shlomo Yitzchaki, France, 1040–1104) commentary on the Talmud, by more than fifty rabbis from France and Germany, spanning the twelfth through the fourteenth centuries.

treyf: Specific types of animals, fish, and sea creatures whose consumption is biblically prohibited. Also, meat and dairy products that have come into contact with one another, and whose consumption is therefore also prohibited.

trope (pl., **tropen**): The cantillations used in the weekly public reading of the Bible and haftorah, and the five special holiday readings from the Kesuvim. (See also **haftorah, Tanach**.)

tzaddik (pl., **tzaddikim**): An extremely pious and saintly person.

tzimmes: Stew customarily made from some combination of sweet potatoes, carrots, prunes, raisins, honey, and/or sugar. A feature of the Rosh Hashanah meal that symbolizes the hope for a "sweet" new year.

tzitzis: Four strands of ritually knotted woolen fringes that are threaded through holes in each of the four corners of the tallis and the tallis katan. (See also **tallis, tallis katan**.)

Vaad HaYeshivos: Lithuanian-based organization founded in 1924 that raised funds to support yeshivos in Lithuania, Poland, and Belarus; worked to get students out of Europe during World War II.

Viduy: Prayer of confession of sin, alphabetically arranged. Part of the Yom Kippur service and also to be recited privately by someone approaching death. (See also **Yom Kippur**.)

yahrzeit: Annual anniversary of a death that is commemorated with the recitation of Kaddish in the synagogue and the lighting of a memorial candle in the home. (See also **Kaddish**.)

Yanuka: A child prodigy mentioned in the Zohar. (See also **Zohar**.)

yarmulke: Brimless skullcap originally intended to be worn indoors in place of a hat, to fulfill the rabbinic requirement of covering one's head to signify God's constant presence, particularly while praying and eating. In modern times worn outdoors as well, if a hat is not being worn.

Yavneh school: Part of a network of Orthodox Jewish day schools for boys and girls founded in Europe in the 1920s.

yeshiva: Religious school that extends from primary grades through high school and beyond. May also include the study of secular subjects. May be male-only, female-only, or coeducational.

yichud: Literally, "seclusion." Shorthand reference to the biblical prohibition of a man and woman who are not married to each other or first-degree relatives being alone together in a non-public indoor or outdoor space.

Yizkor: The memorial prayer for the dead, recited during the prayer service on certain festivals and on Yom Kippur.

Yom Kippur: Solemn day of prayer, repentence, and fasting, to atone for the sins of the previous year. Begins at sundown on the tenth day of the month of Tishrei and concludes twenty-five hours later.

Yoreh De'ah: One of the four volumes of the *Shulchan Aruch* code of Jewish law. (See also ***Shulchan Aruch***.)

Zohar: The foundational work of Jewish mysticism. It is believed to have been compiled by Rabbi Shimon bar Yochai (Roman Palestine, second century CE) from mystical, orally transmitted doctrines and practices of Judaism and biblical interpretations that are known collectively as the Kabbalah. Additional teachings were promulgated by Kabbalists in medieval Europe, and in sixteenth-century Ottoman Palestine by Rabbi Isaac Luria (Safed, c. 1534–1572).

A NOTE ON THE TYPE

This book was set in Janson, a typeface long thought to have been made by the Dutchman Anton Janson, who was a practicing typefounder in Leipzig during the years 1668–1687. However, it has been conclusively demonstrated that these types are actually the work of Nicholas Kis (1650–1702), a Hungarian, who most probably learned his trade from the master Dutch typefounder Dirk Voskens. The type is an excellent example of the influential and sturdy Dutch types that prevailed in England up to the time William Caslon (1692–1766) developed his own incomparable designs from them.

Typeset by Scribe,
Philadelphia, Pennsylvania

Designed by Cassandra J. Pappas